KEE
LOST
OF
THE
CITIES

THE GRAPHIC NOVEL
PART 1

WITHDRAWN

ALSO BY
SHANNON MESSENGER

THE KEEPER OF THE LOST CITIES SERIES

BOOK 1: *KEEPER OF THE LOST CITIES*

BOOK 2: *EXILE*

BOOK 3: *EVERBLAZE*

BOOK 4: *NEVERSEEN*

BOOK 5: *LODESTAR*

BOOK 6: *NIGHTFALL*

BOOK 7: *FLASHBACK*

BOOK 8: *LEGACY*

BOOK 8.5: *UNLOCKED*

BOOK 9: *STELLARLUNE*

THE SKY FALL SERIES

LET THE SKY FALL

LET THE STORM BREAK

LET THE WIND RISE

KEEPER OF THE LOST CITIES

THE GRAPHIC NOVEL
PART 1

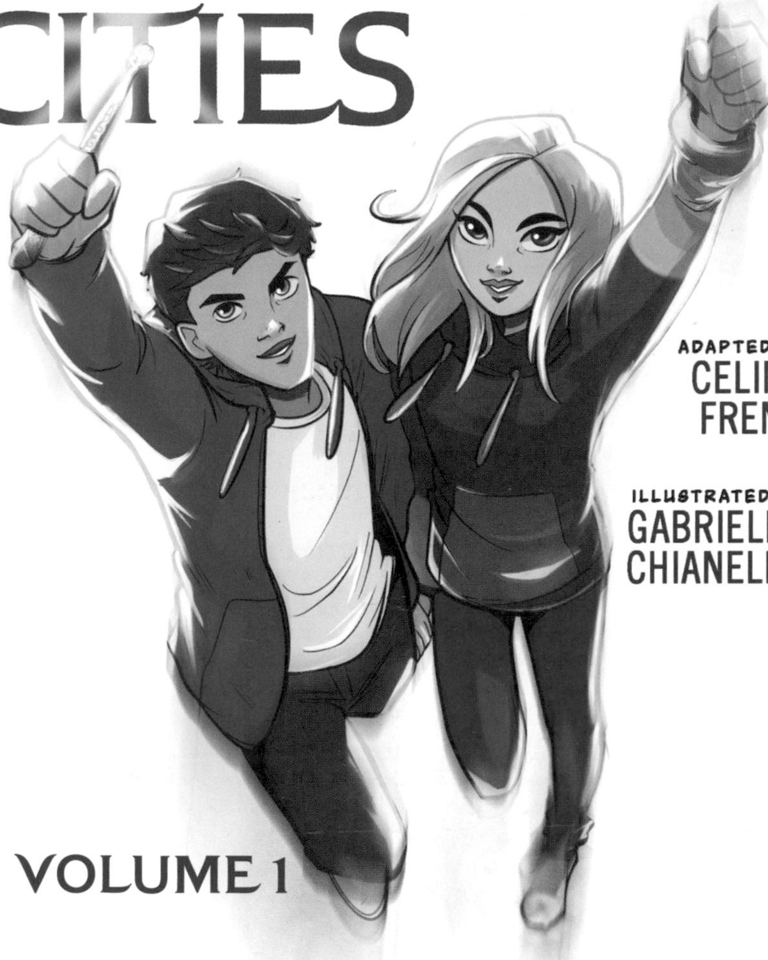

ADAPTED BY
CELINA FRENN

ILLUSTRATED BY
GABRIELLA CHIANELLO

VOLUME 1

SHANNON MESSENGER

ALADDIN / NEW YORK LONDON TORONTO SYDNEY NEW DELHI

This book is a work of fiction. Any references to historical events, real people, or real places are used fictitiously. Other names, characters, places, and events are products of the author's imagination, and any resemblance to actual events or places or persons, living or dead, is entirely coincidental.

ALADDIN / An imprint of Simon & Schuster Children's Publishing Division / 1230 Avenue of the Americas, New York, New York 10020 / First Aladdin edition November 2023 / Adapted from *Keeper of the Lost Cities*, published in 2012 / Cover illustration and interior pencils and inks by Gabriella Chianello/Glass House Graphics / Assistance on inks and backgrounds by Onofrio Orlando/Glass House Graphics / Colors by Nataliya Torretta, Francesca Ingrassia, Francesco Boccadutri, Gaetano Gabriele D'Aprile, Gaetano Ingaliso, Giuseppe Romeo, Martina Yuki Ritano, and Michelangelo Stassi/Glass House Graphics / Art consulting by Manuel Preitano / Lettering by Giuseppe Naselli/Grafimated Cartoon / Supervision by Salvatore Di Marco/Grafimated Cartoon / For information about special discounts for bulk purchases, please contact Simon & Schuster Special Sales at 1-866-506-1949 or business@simonandschuster.com. / The Simon & Schuster Speakers Bureau can bring authors to your live event. For more information or to book an event contact the Simon & Schuster Speakers Bureau at 1-866-248-3049 or visit our website at www.simonspeakers.com. / Cover designed and interior art directed by Karin Paprocki / The illustrations for this book were rendered digitally. / The text of this book was set in CCFaceFront. / Manufactured in the United States of America 0923 LAK / 10 9 8 7 6 5 4 3 2 1 / Library of Congress Control Number 2023935247 / ISBN 9781534463370 (hc) / ISBN 9781534463363 (pbk) / ISBN 9781534463387 (ebook)

Dear Keeper readers,

I am ***so ridiculously*** excited you're here!

It's always been an enormous dream of mine to see one of my books come to life as a graphic novel, so I can't wait for you to dive into this version of the story. Whether you're brand-new to the world of the Lost Cities or you've read every Keeper book cover-to-cover and are impatiently waiting for me to finish the next (writing as fast as I can, I promise!), there are so many fun surprises ahead!

This is not a line-by-line, word-for-word adaptation of *Keeper of the Lost Cities*—but don't worry! That's actually what makes this version even more exciting. Graphic novels and prose novels are two very different things, and I've been lucky enough to have a brilliant team of people who have all worked tirelessly to ensure that everything we love about Sophie's story is captured within these pages exactly as it should be.

Even better, when you get to the end (which, by the way, is only the end of part 1 of the story), you'll find awesome bonus pages filled with a special behind-the-scenes look at how this book came together, plus a section teaching you how to draw some of your favorite characters.

So I'll stop distracting you from all the awesomeness. Settle into a comfy chair (if you haven't already), and get ready for an adventure. The fun begins as soon as you turn the page!

Happy reading!

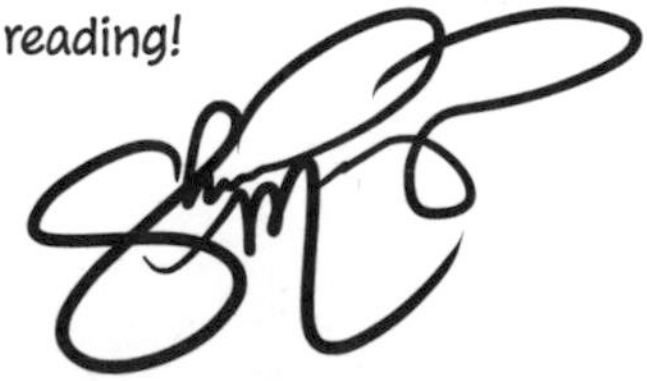

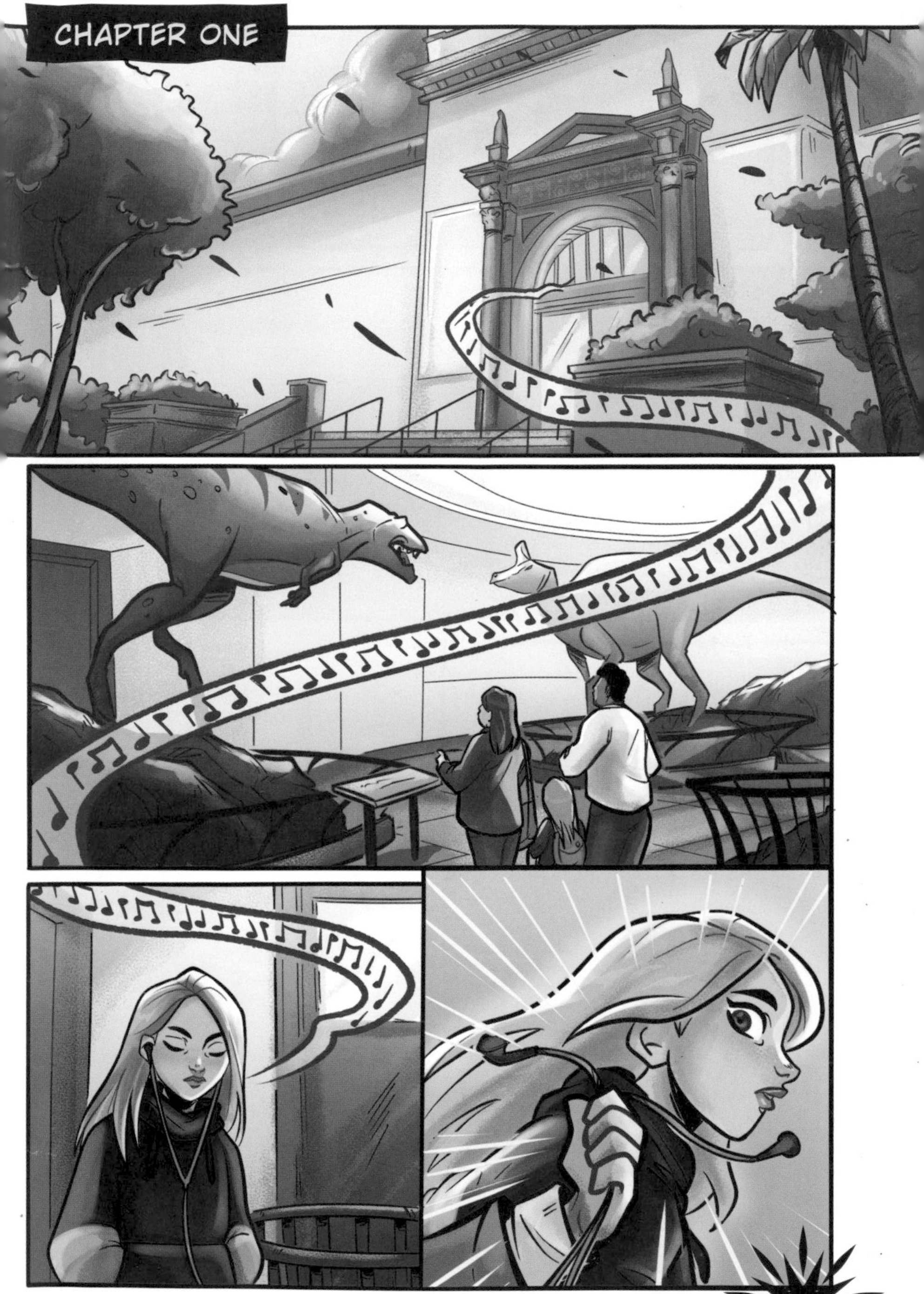
CHAPTER ONE

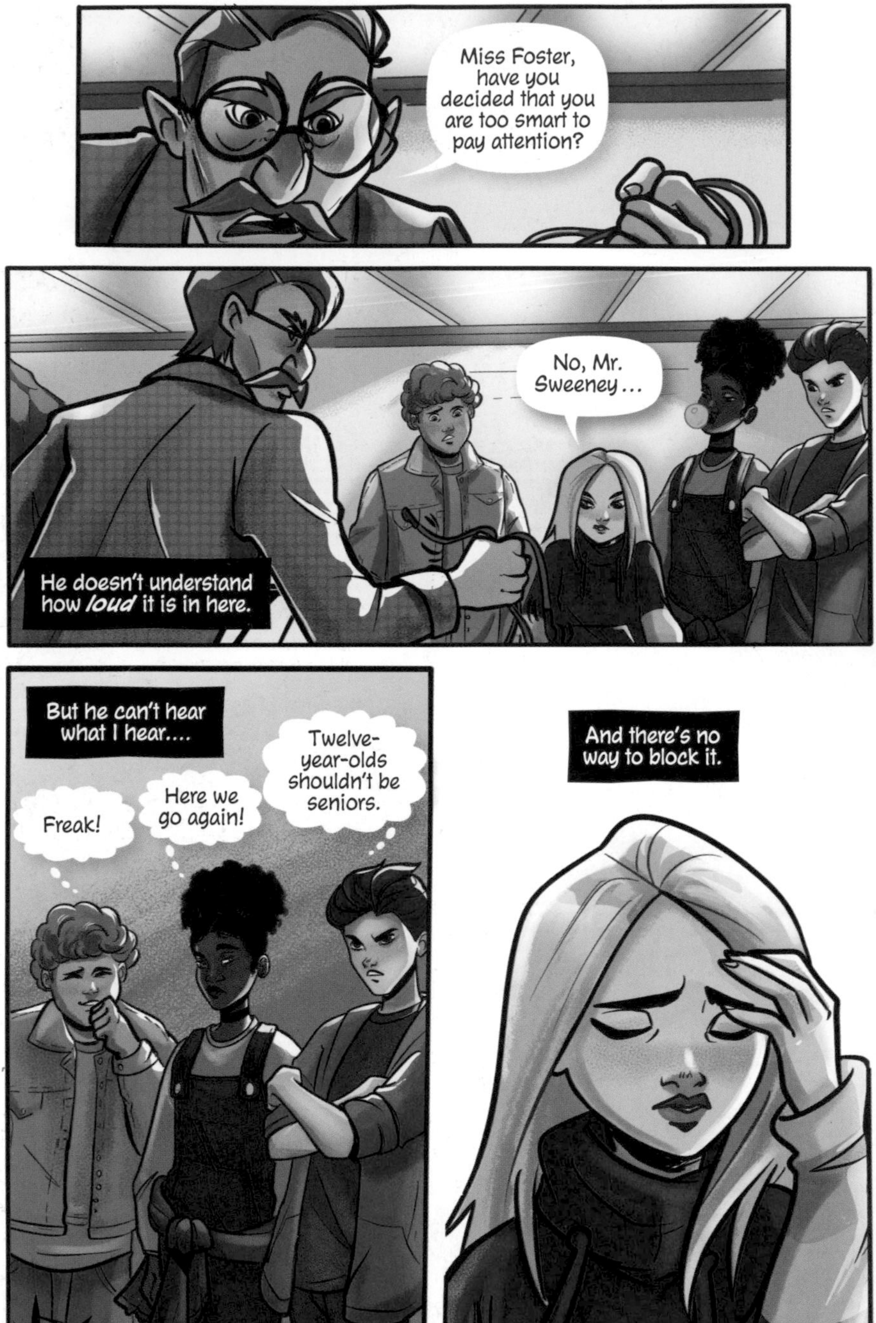
Miss Foster, have you decided that you are too smart to pay attention?
No, Mr. Sweeney...
He doesn't understand how *loud* it is in here.
But he can't hear what I hear....
Freak!
Here we go again!
Twelve-year-olds shouldn't be seniors.
And there's no way to block it.

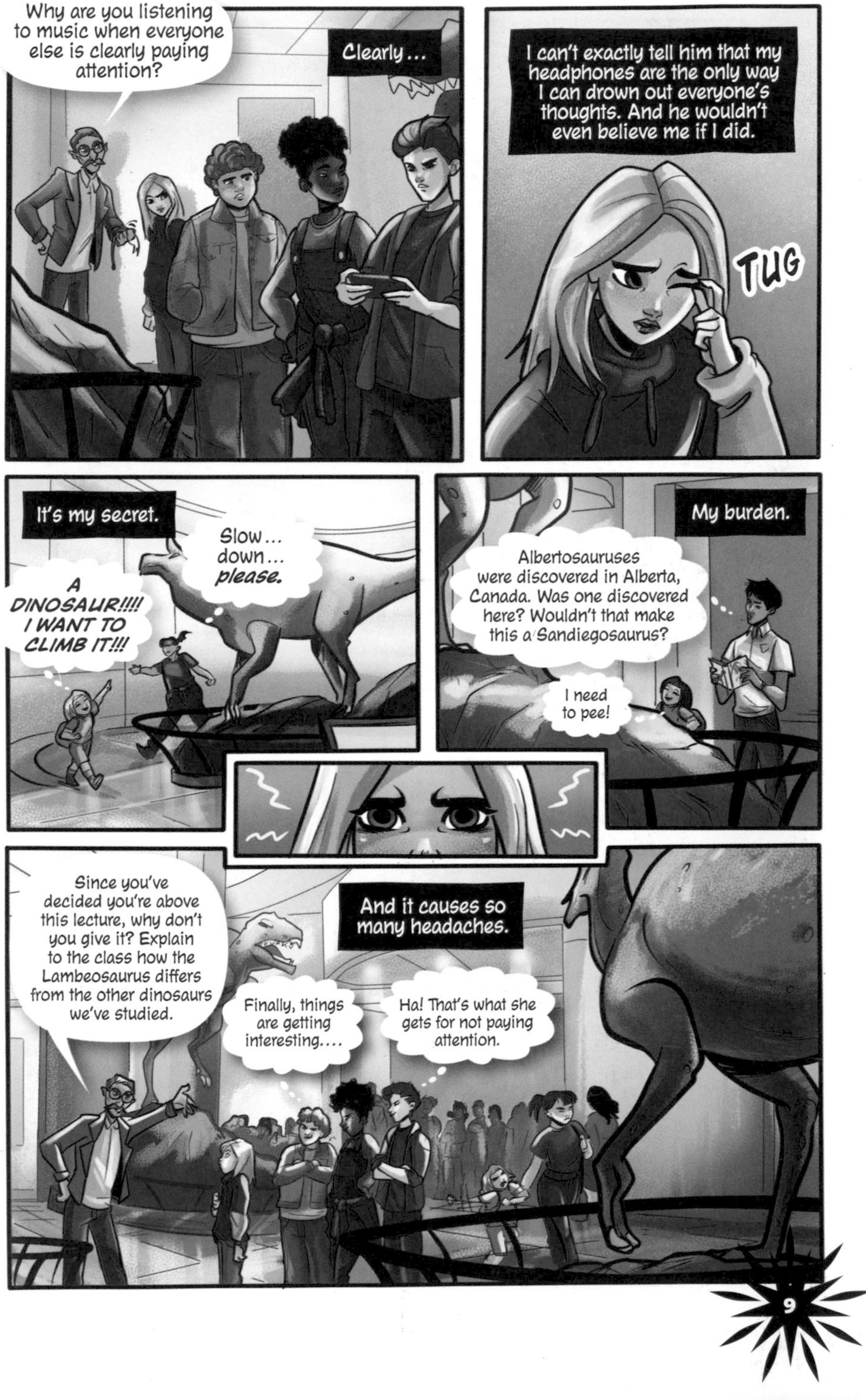

Why are you listening to music when everyone else is clearly paying attention?
Clearly...
I can't exactly tell him that my headphones are the only way I can drown out everyone's thoughts. And he wouldn't even believe me if I did.
TUG
It's my secret.
A DINOSAUR!!!! I WANT TO CLIMB IT!!!
Slow... down... *please.*
My burden.
Albertosauruses were discovered in Alberta, Canada. Was one discovered here? Wouldn't that make this a Sandiegosaurus?
I need to pee!
Since you've decided you're above this lecture, why don't you give it? Explain to the class how the Lambeosaurus differs from the other dinosaurs we've studied.
And it causes so many headaches.
Finally, things are getting interesting....
Ha! That's what she gets for not paying attention.

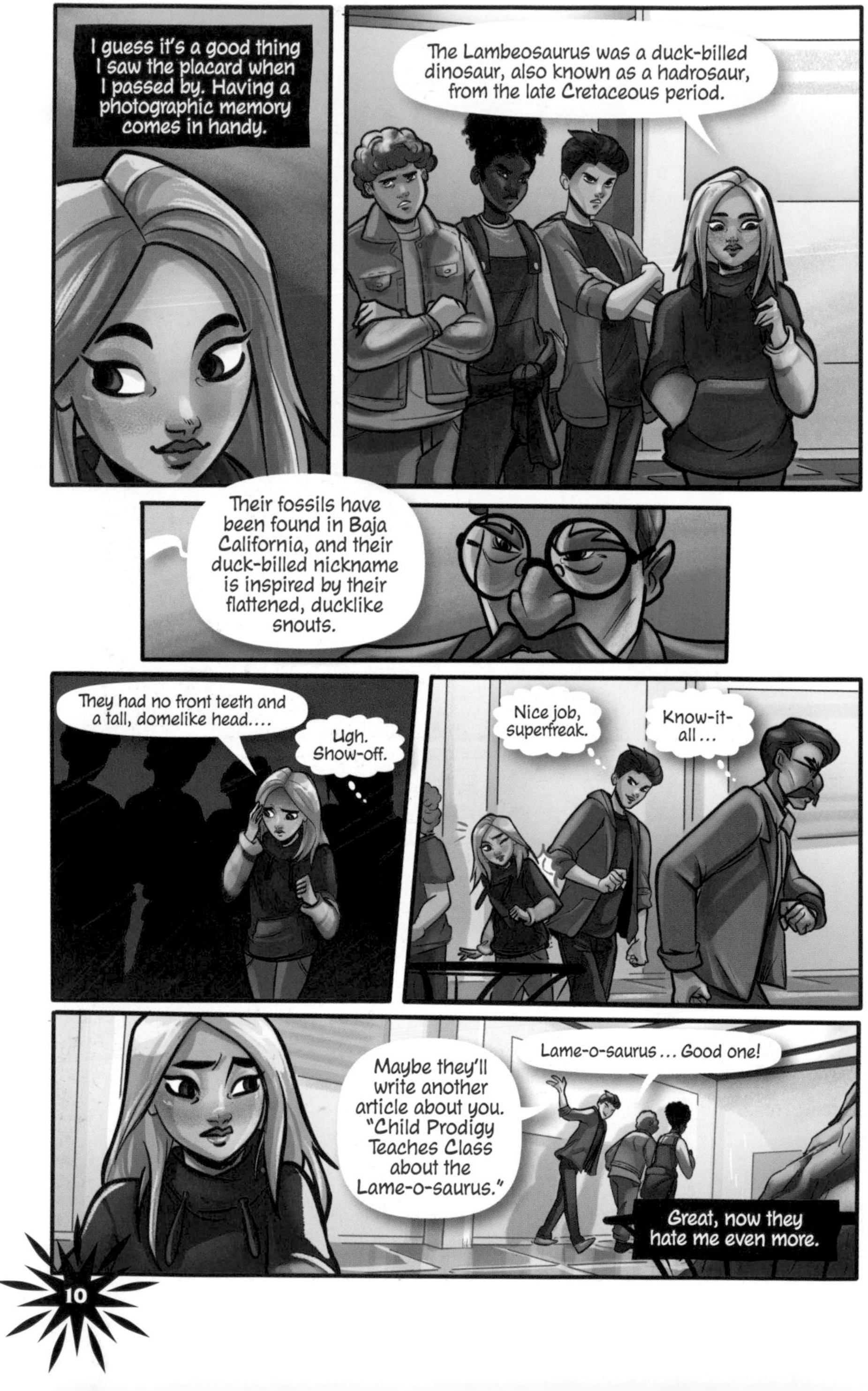
I guess it's a good thing I saw the placard when I passed by. Having a photographic memory comes in handy.
The Lambeosaurus was a duck-billed dinosaur, also known as a hadrosaur, from the late Cretaceous period.
Their fossils have been found in Baja California, and their duck-billed nickname is inspired by their flattened, ducklike snouts.
They had no front teeth and a tall, domelike head....
Ugh. Show-off.
Nice job, superfreak.
Know-it-all...
Maybe they'll write another article about you. "Child Prodigy Teaches Class about the Lame-o-saurus."
Lame-o-saurus... Good one!
Great, now they hate me even more.

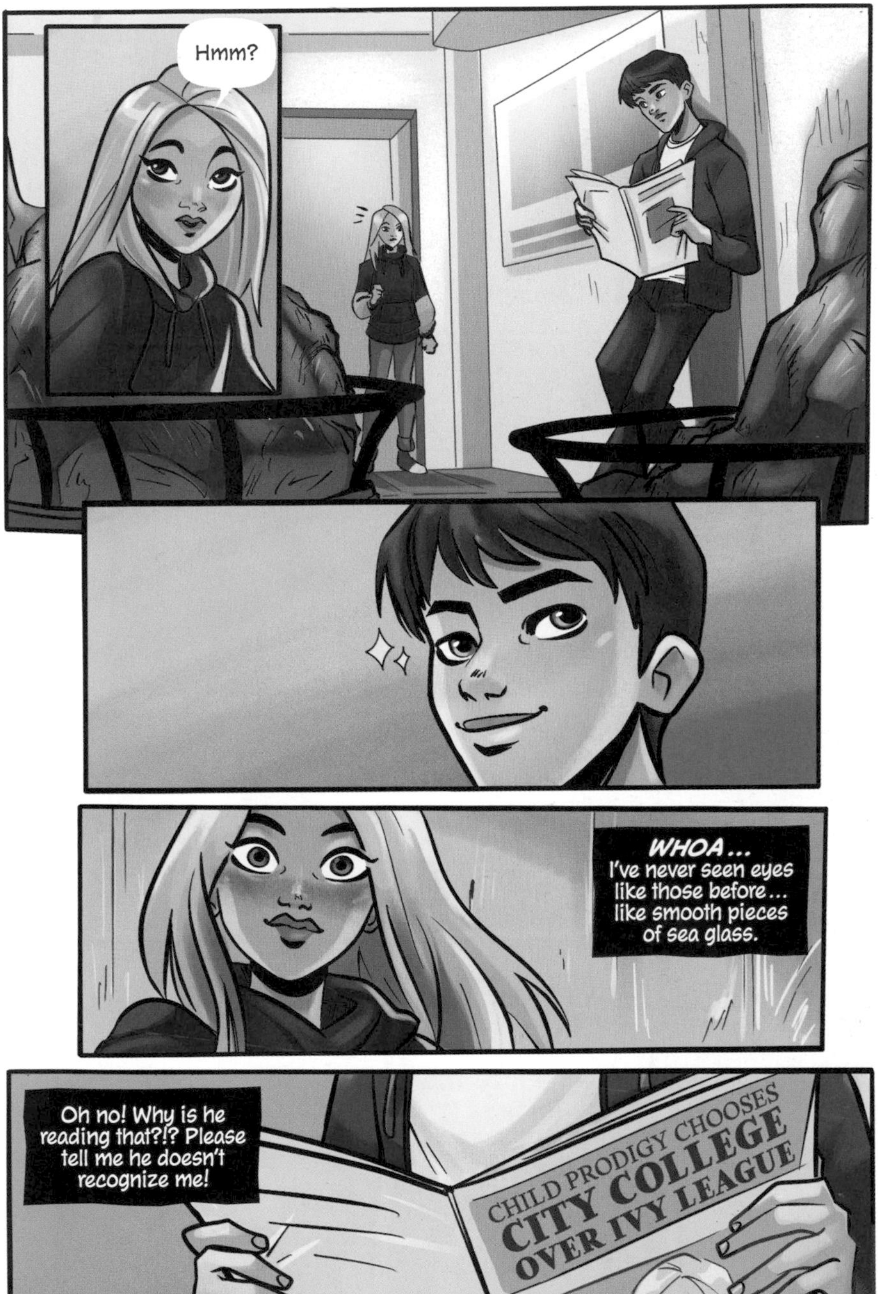
Hmm?
WHOA... I've never seen eyes like those before... like smooth pieces of sea glass.
Oh no! Why is he reading that?!? Please tell me he doesn't recognize me!
CHILD PRODIGY CHOOSES CITY COLLEGE OVER IVY LEAGUE

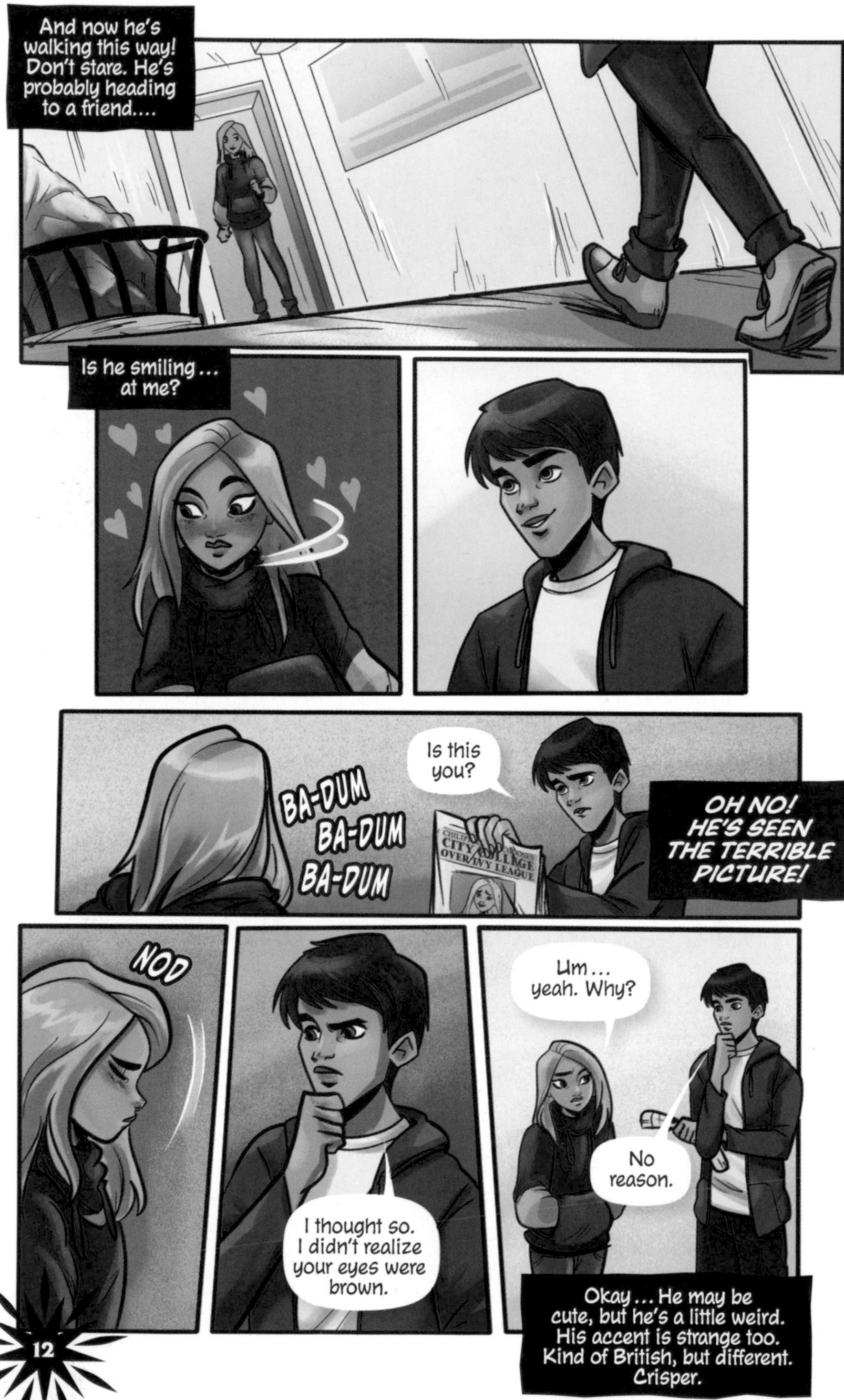
And now he's walking this way! Don't stare. He's probably heading to a friend....
Is he smiling... at me?
BA-DUM
BA-DUM
BA-DUM
Is this you?
OH NO! HE'S SEEN THE TERRIBLE PICTURE!
NOD
I thought so. I didn't realize your eyes were brown.
Um... yeah. Why?
No reason.
Okay... He may be cute, but he's a little weird. His accent is strange too. Kind of British, but different. Crisper.

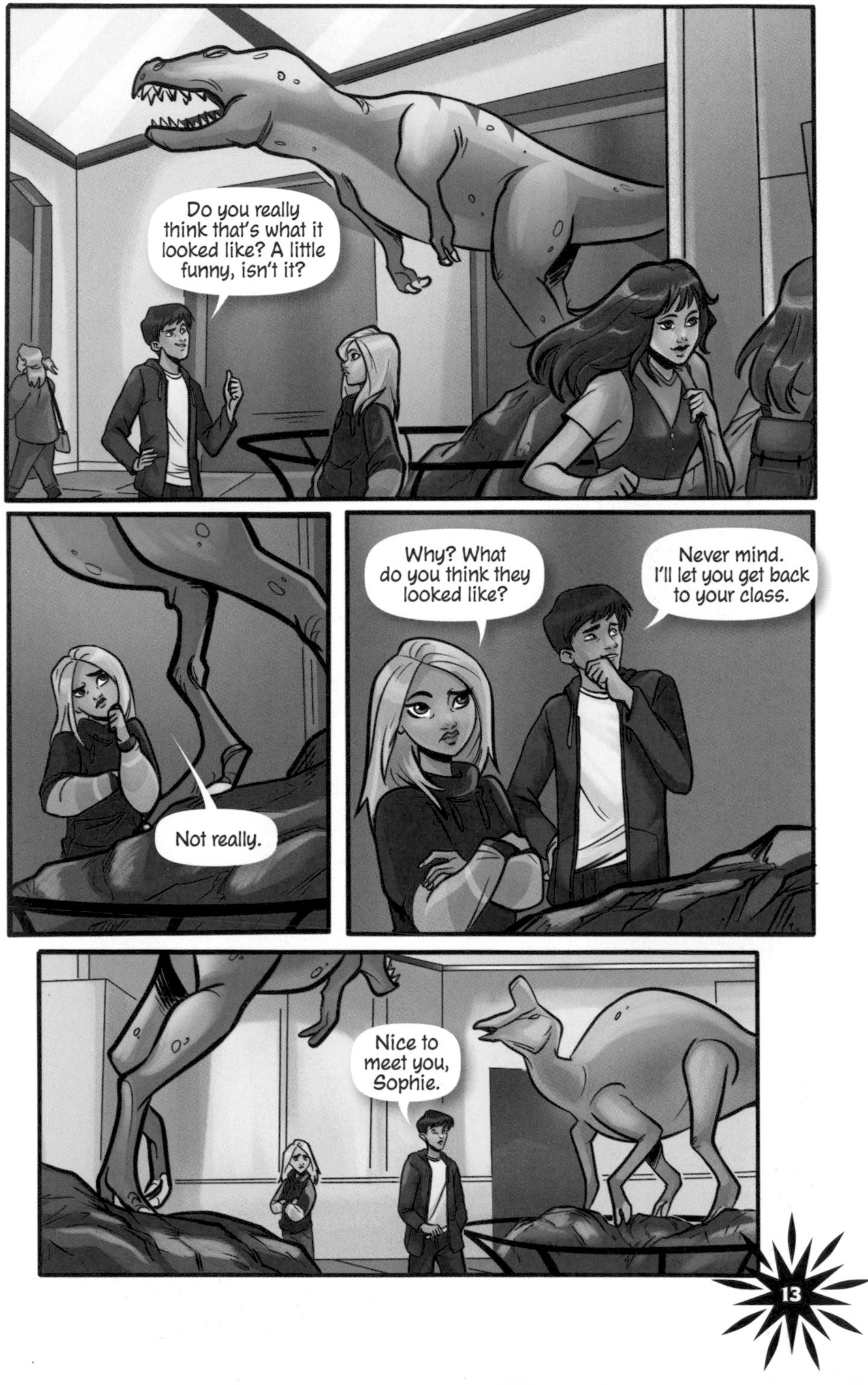
Do you really think that's what it looked like? A little funny, isn't it?
Not really.
Why? What do you think they looked like?
Never mind. I'll let you get back to your class.
Nice to meet you, Sophie.

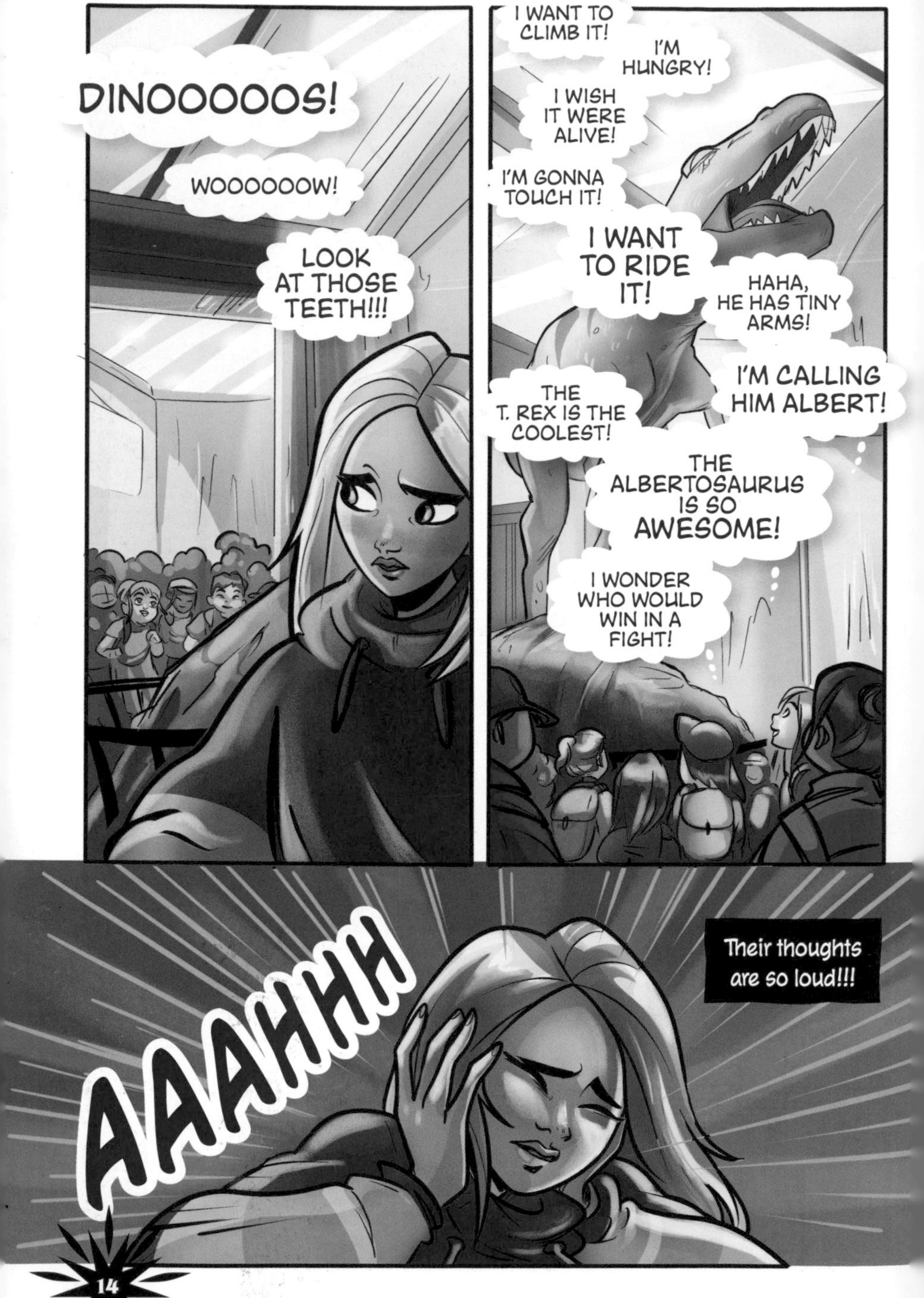
DINOOOOOS!
WOOOOOOW!
LOOK AT THOSE TEETH!!!
I WANT TO CLIMB IT!
I'M HUNGRY!
I WISH IT WERE ALIVE!
I'M GONNA TOUCH IT!
I WANT TO RIDE IT!
HAHA, HE HAS TINY ARMS!
I'M CALLING HIM ALBERT!
THE T. REX IS THE COOLEST!
THE ALBERTOSAURUS IS SO AWESOME!
I WONDER WHO WOULD WIN IN A FIGHT!
AAAHHH
Their thoughts are so loud!!!

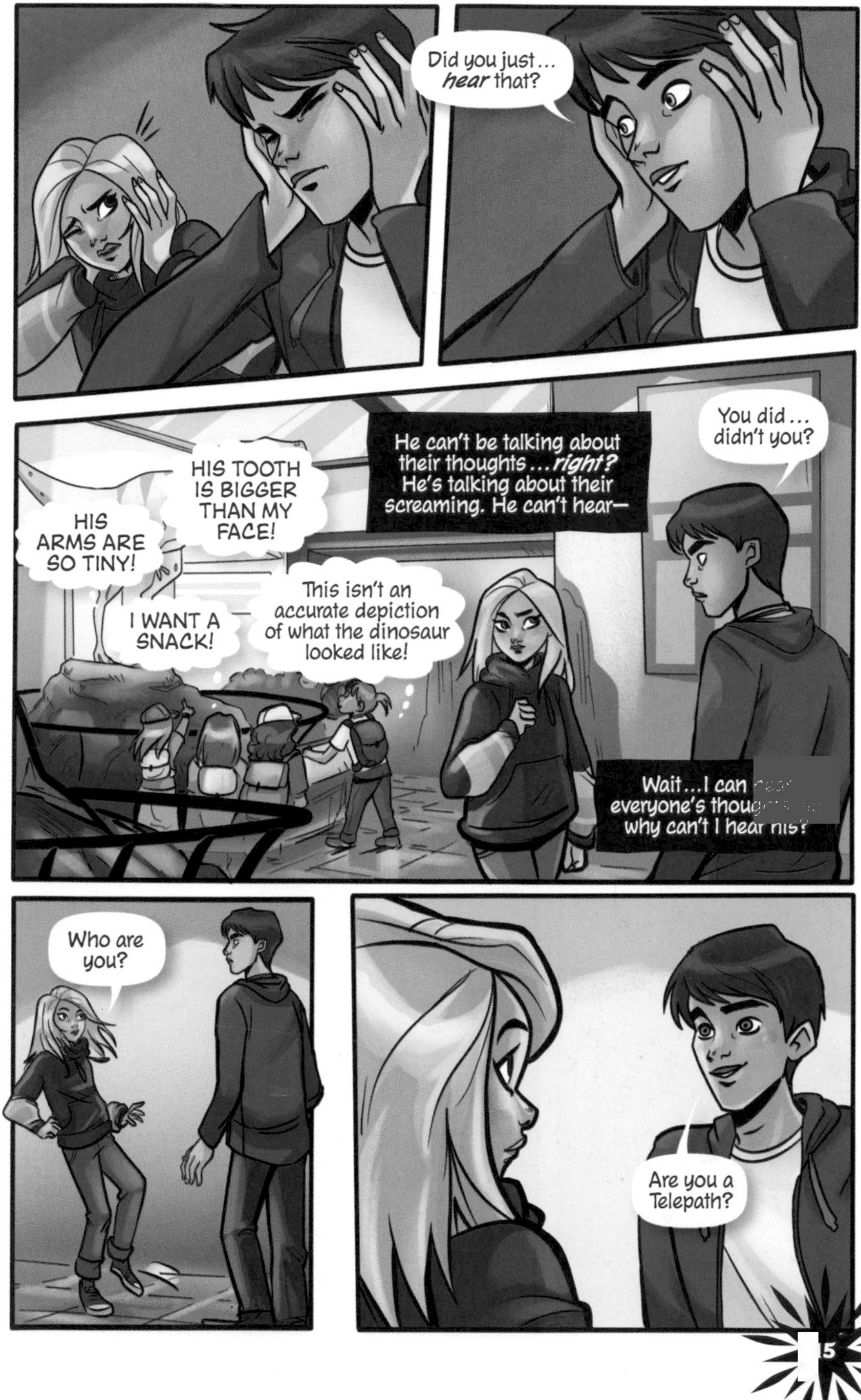

Did you just... *hear* that?
HIS ARMS ARE SO TINY!
HIS TOOTH IS BIGGER THAN MY FACE!
I WANT A SNACK!
This isn't an accurate depiction of what the dinosaur looked like!
He can't be talking about their thoughts... *right?* He's talking about their screaming. He can't hear—
You did... didn't you?
Wait...I can
everyone's thoug
why can't I hear his?
Who are you?
Are you a Telepath?

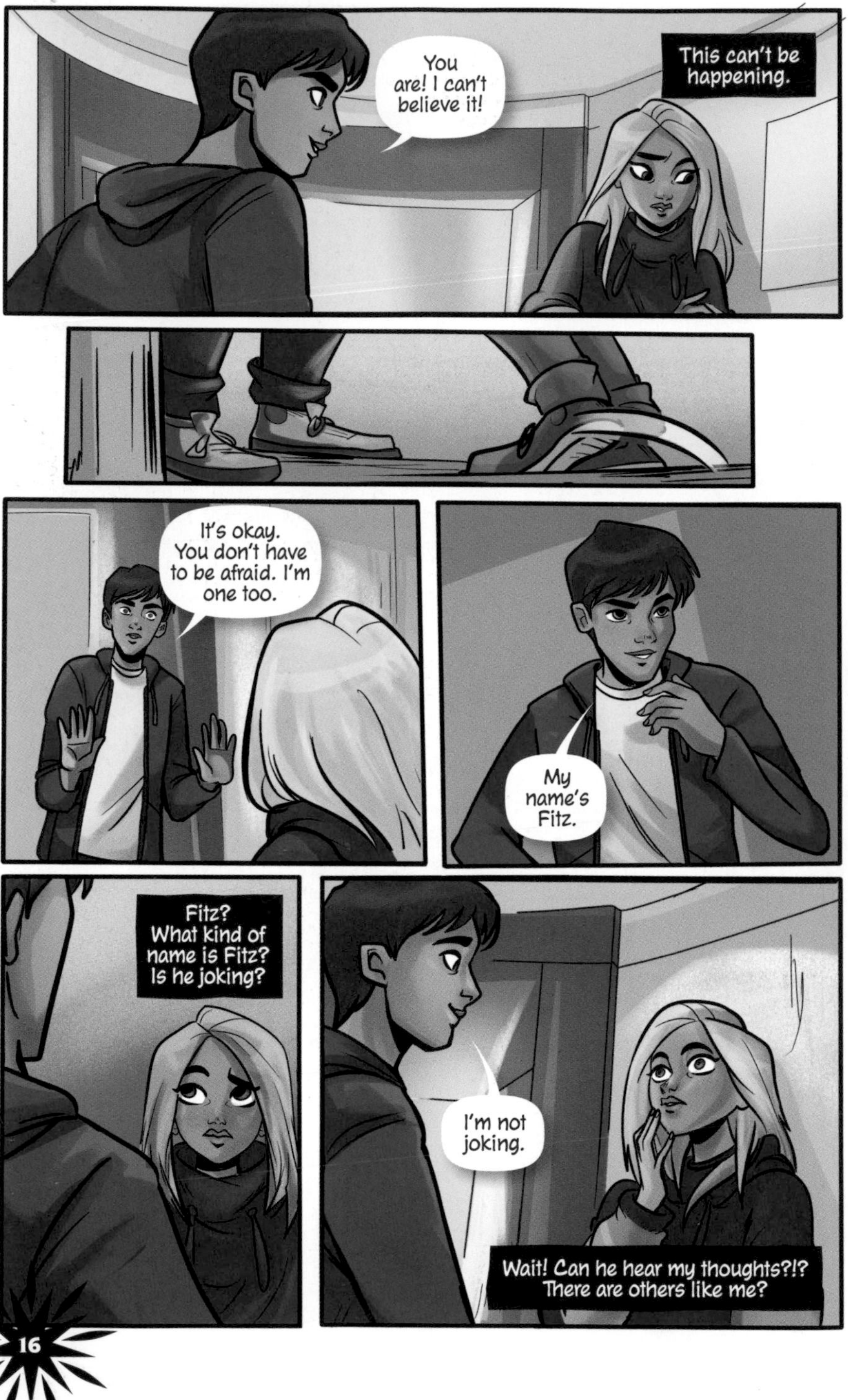
You are! I can't believe it!
This can't be happening.
It's okay. You don't have to be afraid. I'm one too.
My name's Fitz.
Fitz? What kind of name is Fitz? Is he joking?
I'm not joking.
Wait! Can he hear my thoughts?!? There are others like me?

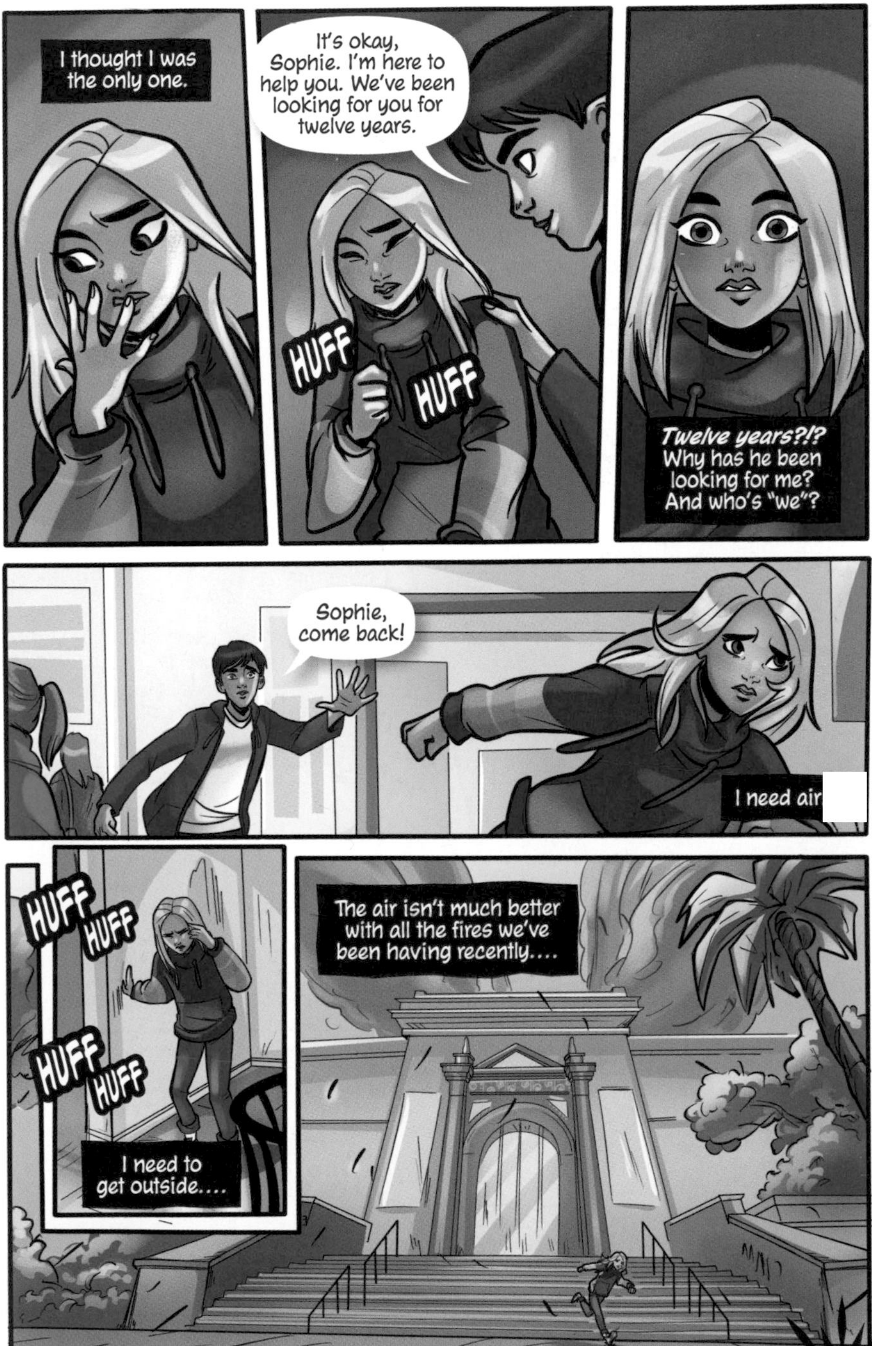

I thought I was the only one.
It's okay, Sophie. I'm here to help you. We've been looking for you for twelve years.
HUFF
HUFF
Twelve years?!? Why has he been looking for me? And who's "we"?
Sophie, come back!
I need air
HUFF
HUFF
HUFF
HUFF
I need to get outside....
The air isn't much better with all the fires we've been having recently....

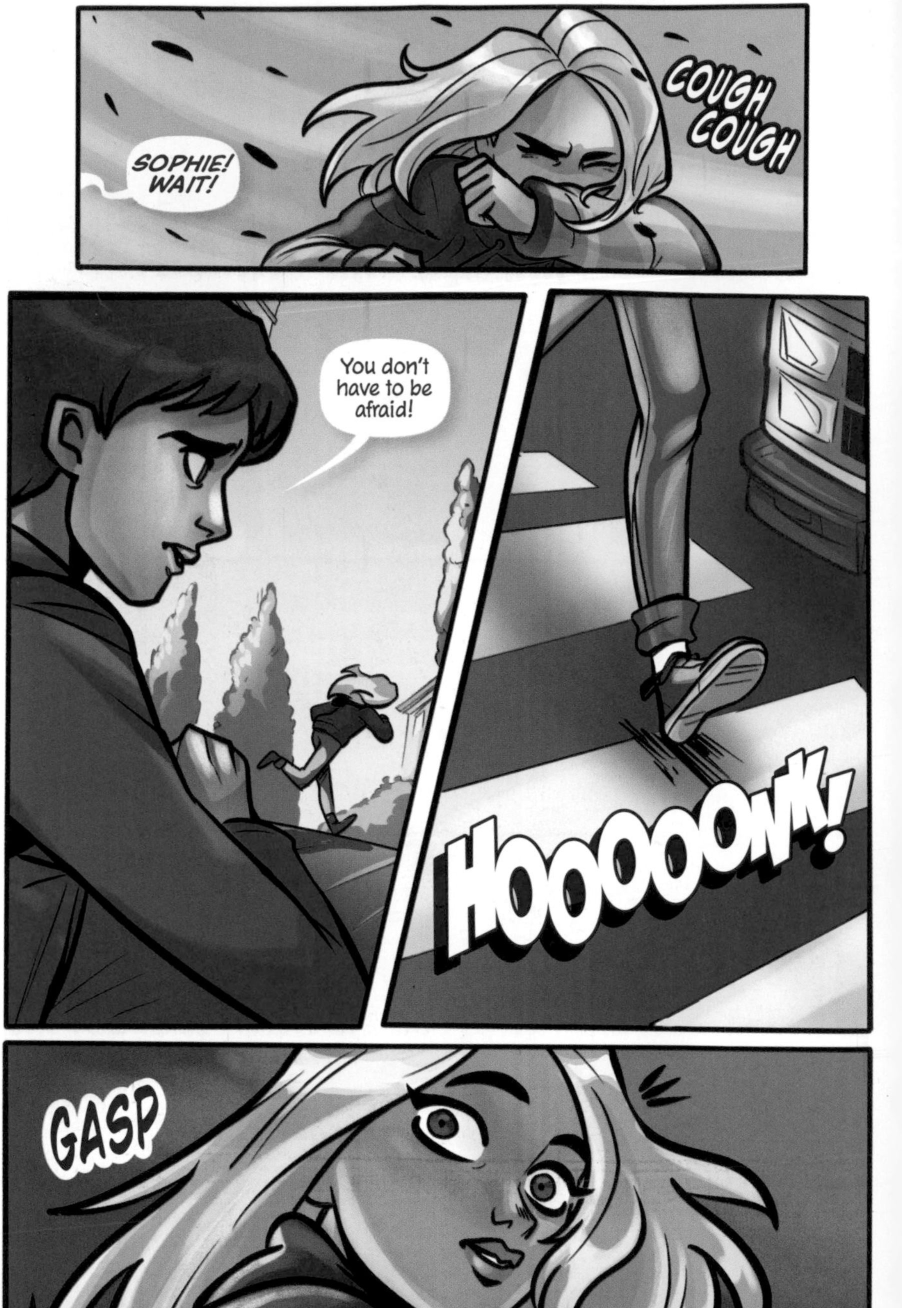
SOPHIE! WAIT!
COUGH COUGH
You don't have to be afraid!
HOOOOONK!
GASP

CHAPTER TWO

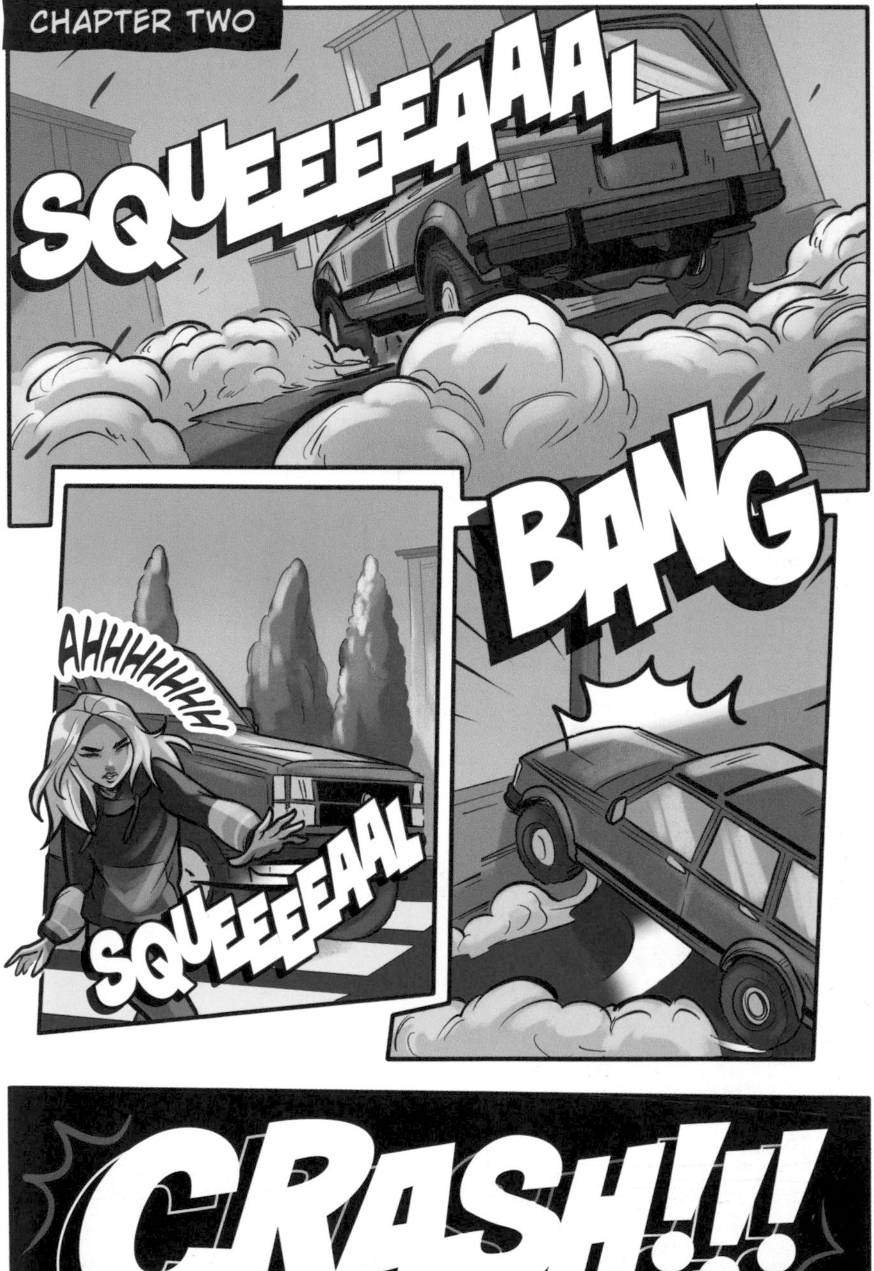
SQUEEEEAAAL
AHHHHHHHH
SQUEEEEAAL
BANG
CRASH!!!

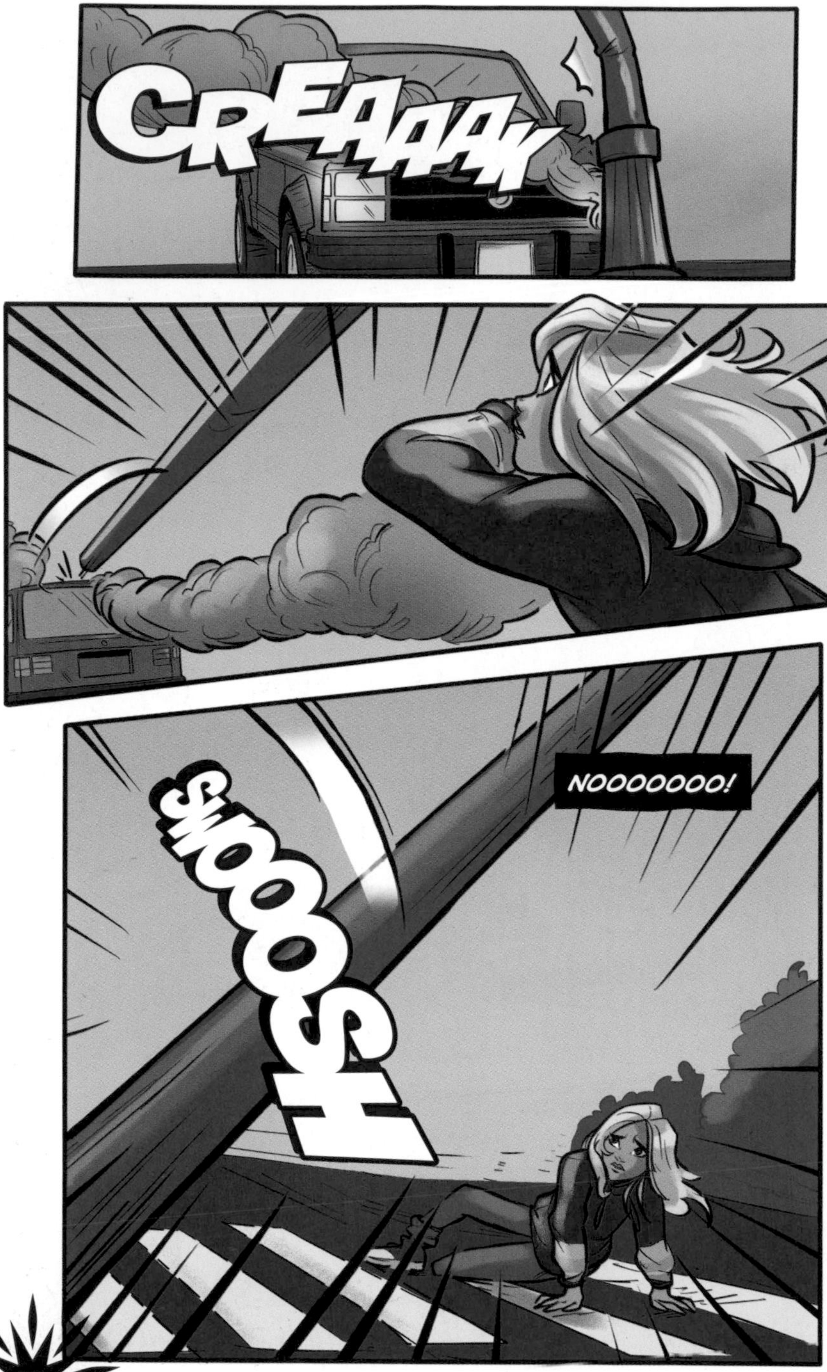
CREAAAAK
SWOOOOSH
NOOOOOOO!

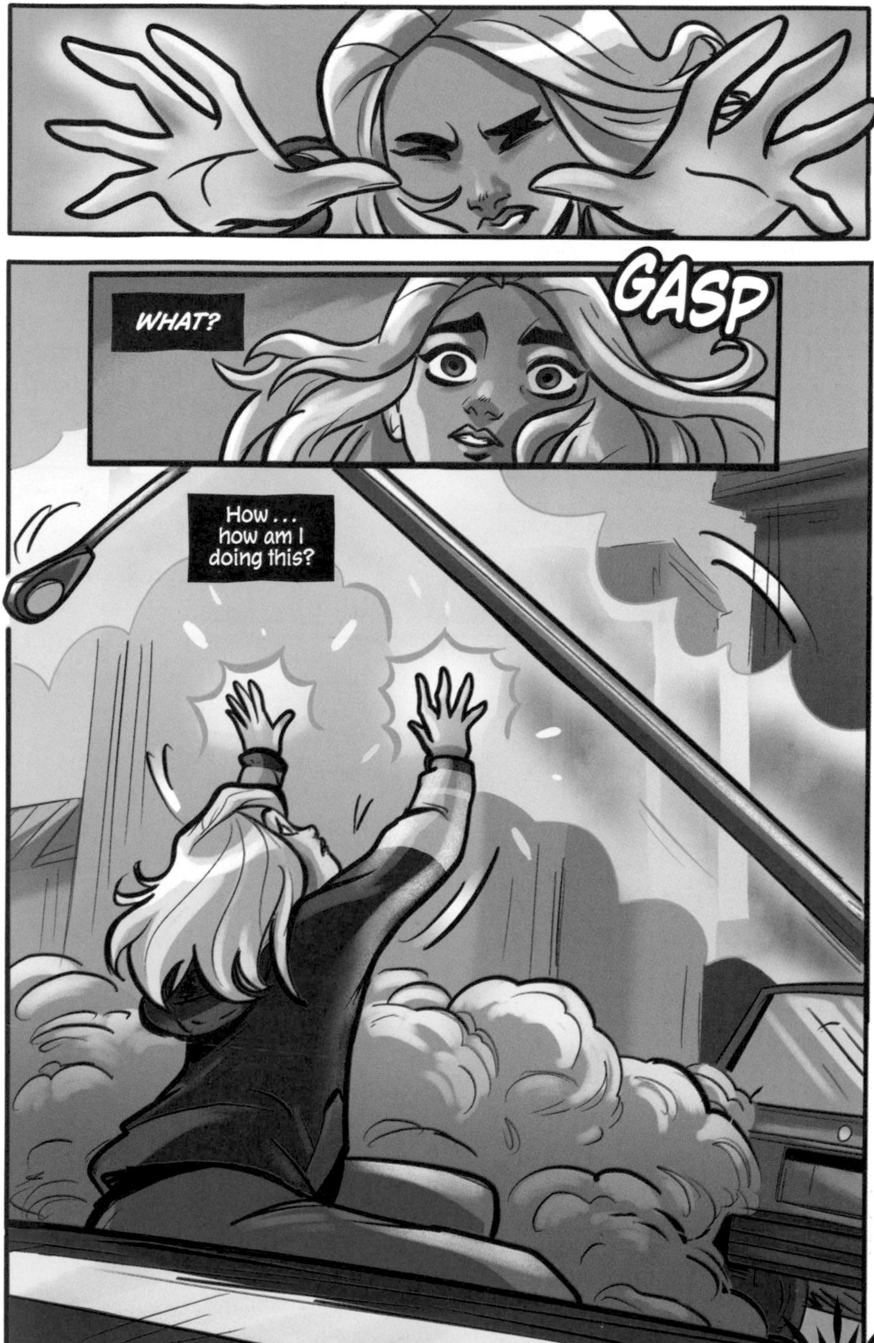
WHAT?
GASP
How . . . how am I doing this?

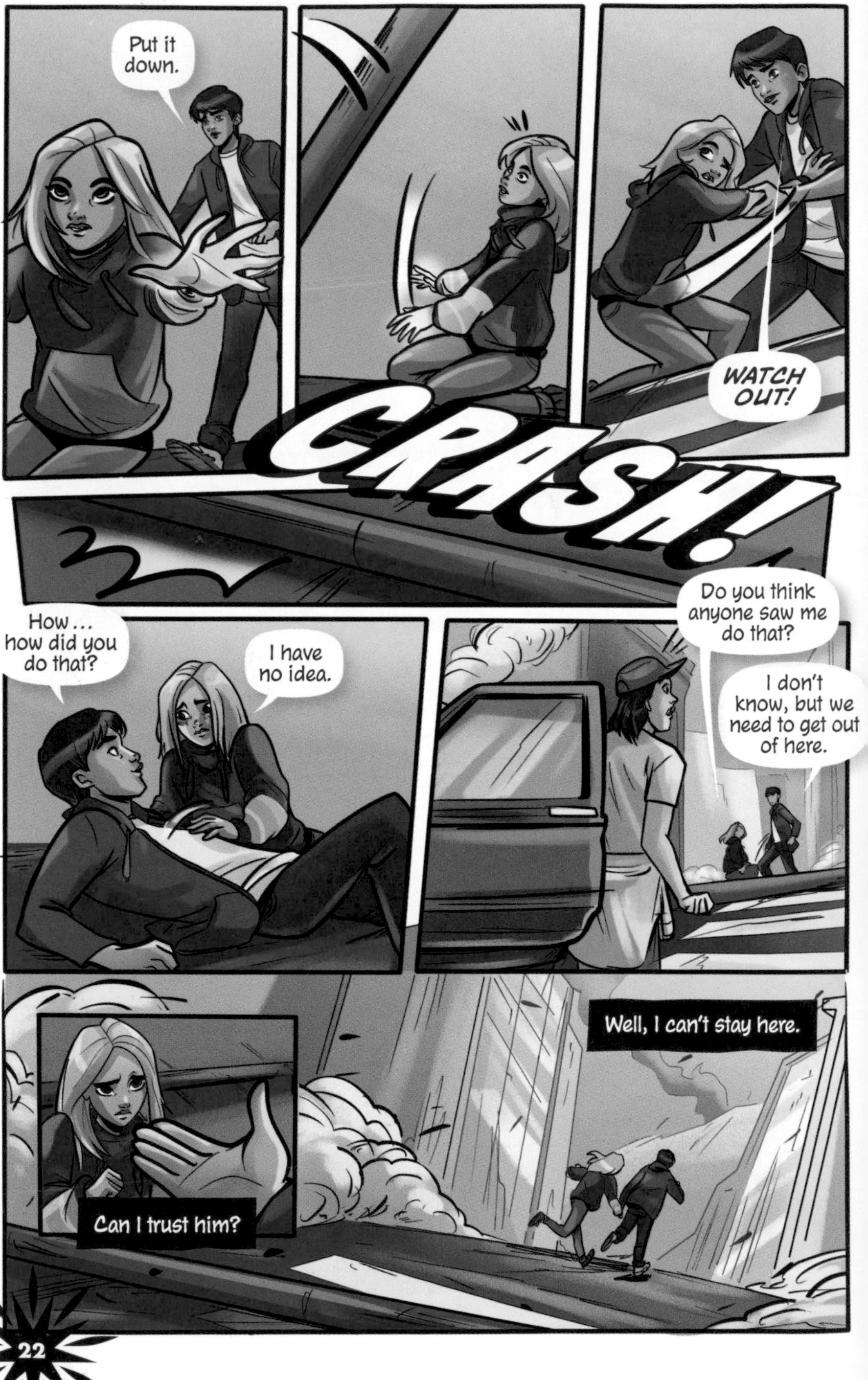
Put it down.
WATCH OUT!
CRASH!
How... how did you do that?
I have no idea.
Do you think anyone saw me do that?
I don't know, but we need to get out of here.
Can I trust him?
Well, I can't stay here.

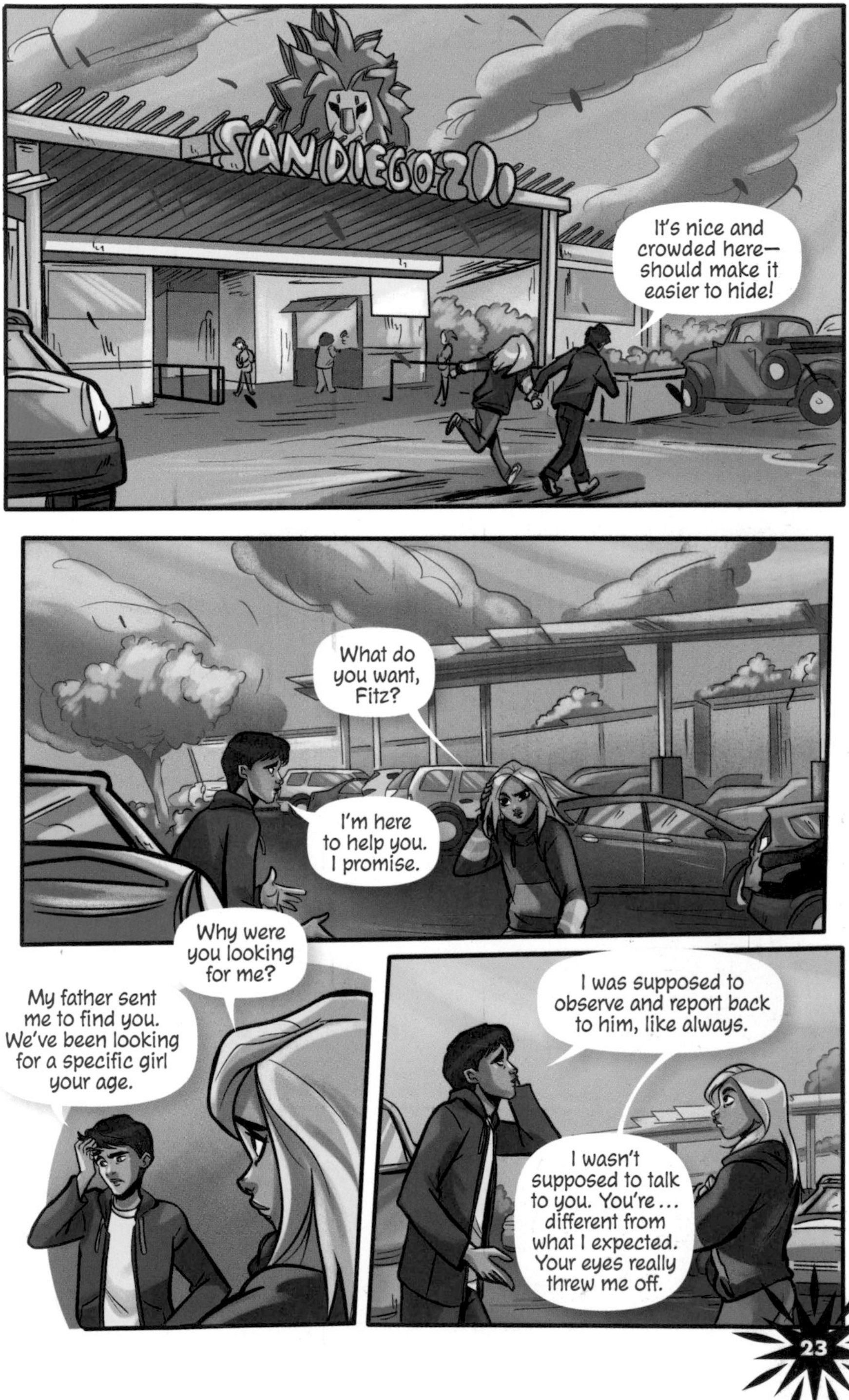
SAN DIEGO ZOO
It's nice and crowded here— should make it easier to hide!
What do you want, Fitz?
I'm here to help you. I promise.
Why were you looking for me?
My father sent me to find you. We've been looking for a specific girl your age.
I was supposed to observe and report back to him, like always.
I wasn't supposed to talk to you. You're... different from what I expected. Your eyes really threw me off.

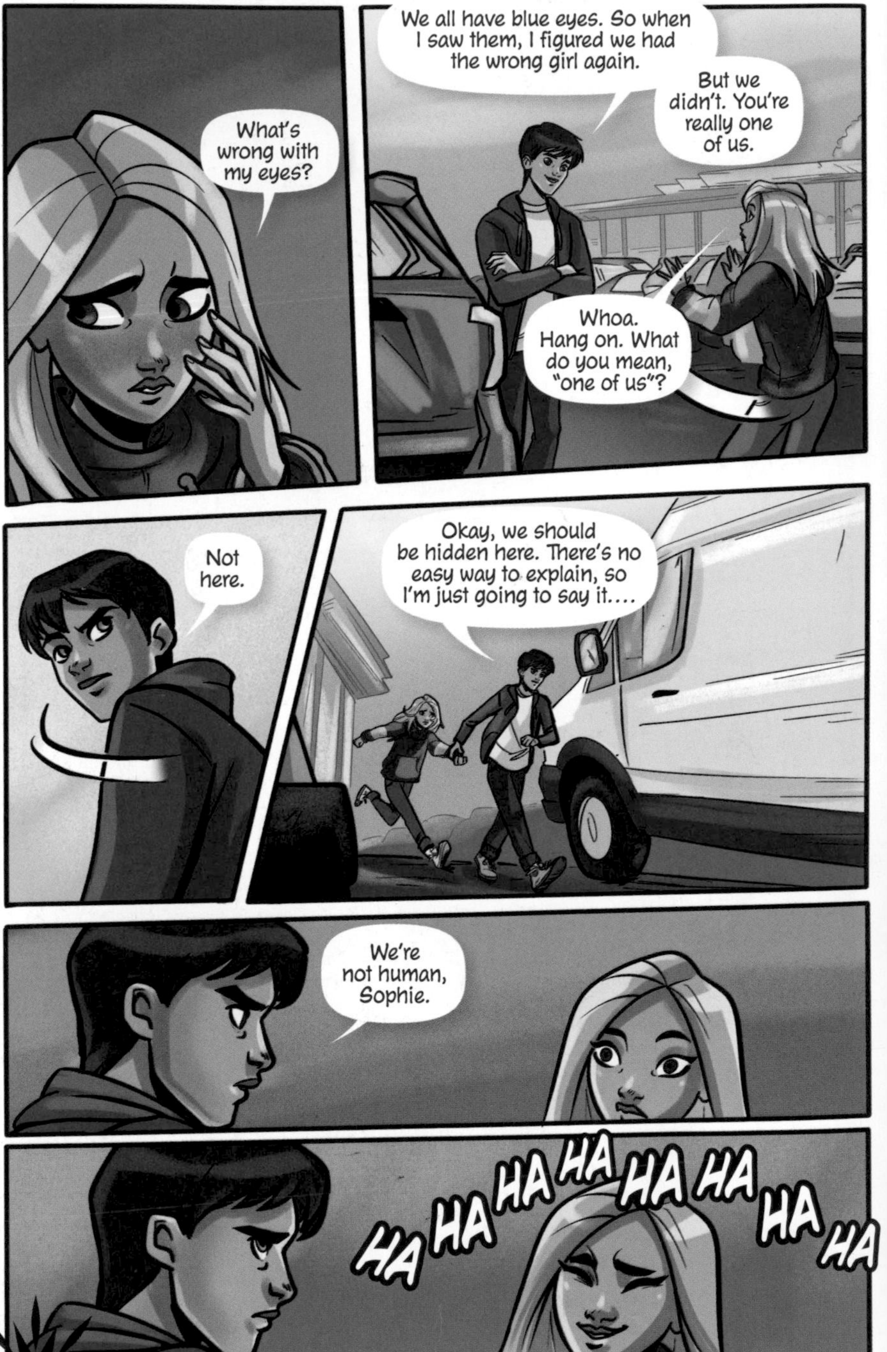
What's wrong with my eyes?
We all have blue eyes. So when I saw them, I figured we had the wrong girl again.
But we didn't. You're really one of us.
Whoa. Hang on. What do you mean, "one of us"?
Not here.
Okay, we should be hidden here. There's no easy way to explain, so I'm just going to say it....
We're not human, Sophie.
HA HA HA HA HA HA HA HA

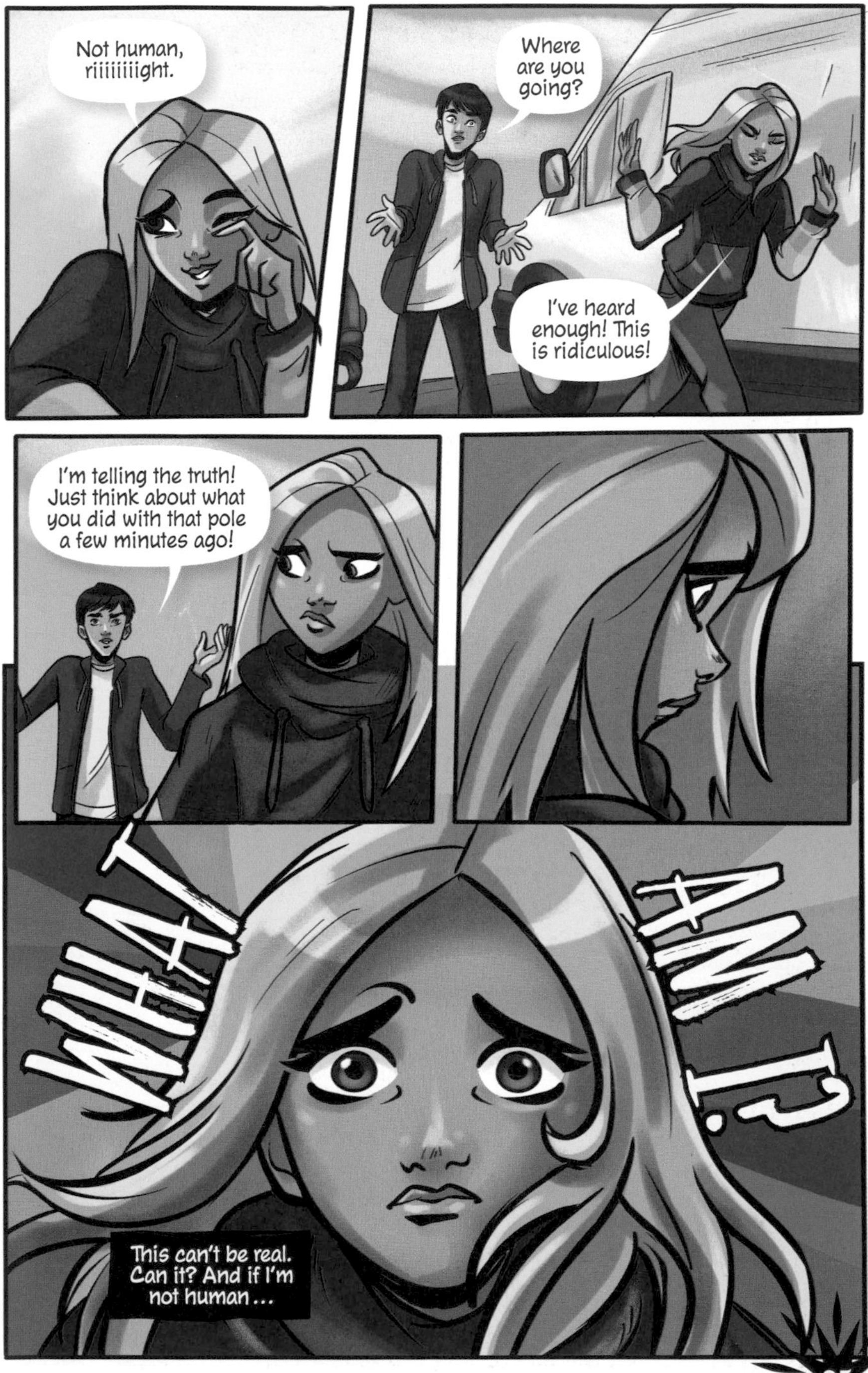
Not human, riiiiiiiight.
Where are you going?
I've heard enough! This is ridiculous!
I'm telling the truth! Just think about what you did with that pole a few minutes ago!
WHAT AM I?
This can't be real. Can it? And if I'm not human...

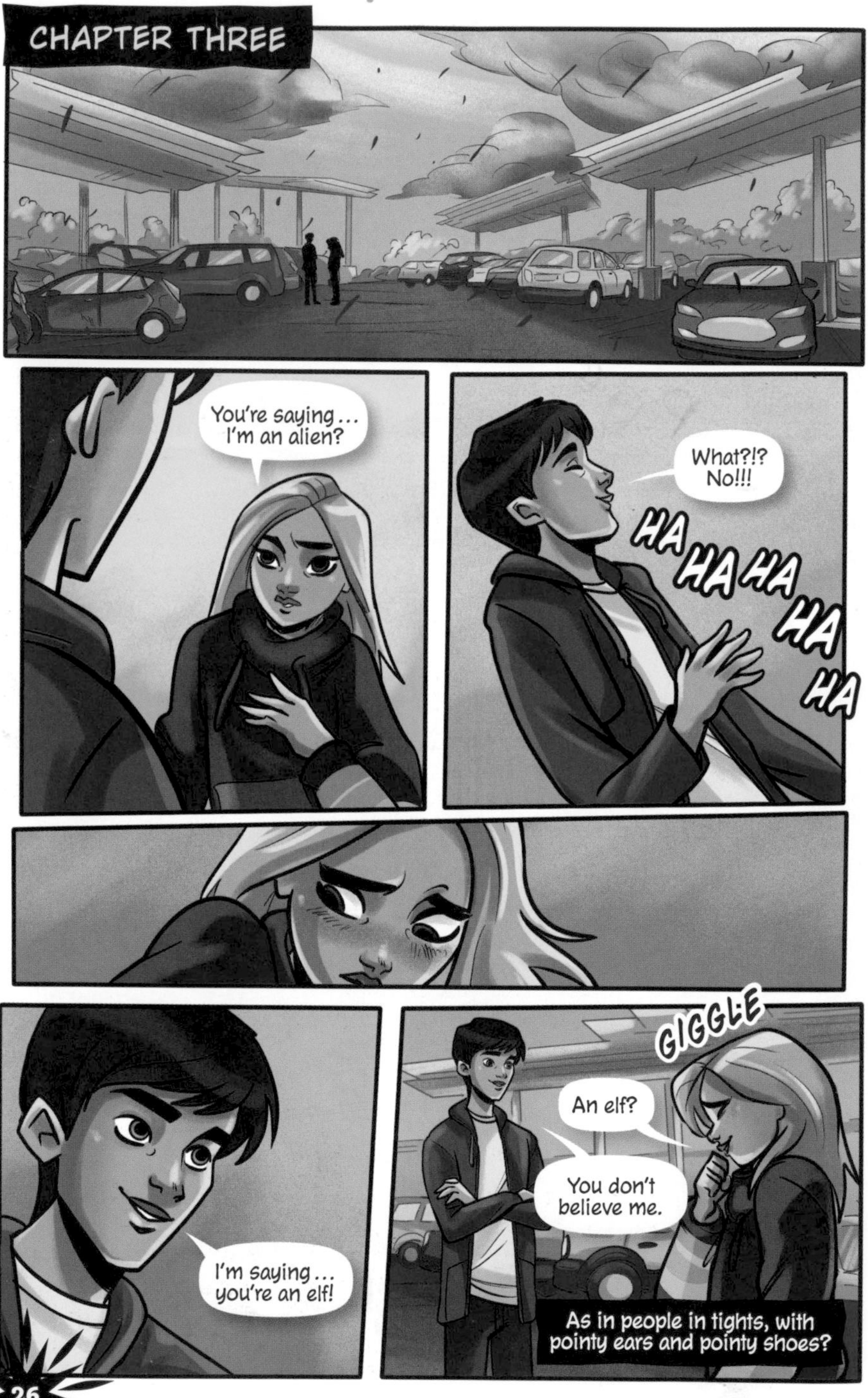

CHAPTER THREE
You're saying... I'm an alien?
What?!? No!!!
HA HA HA HA HA HA
I'm saying... you're an elf!
GIGGLE
An elf?
You don't believe me.
As in people in tights, with pointy ears and pointy shoes?

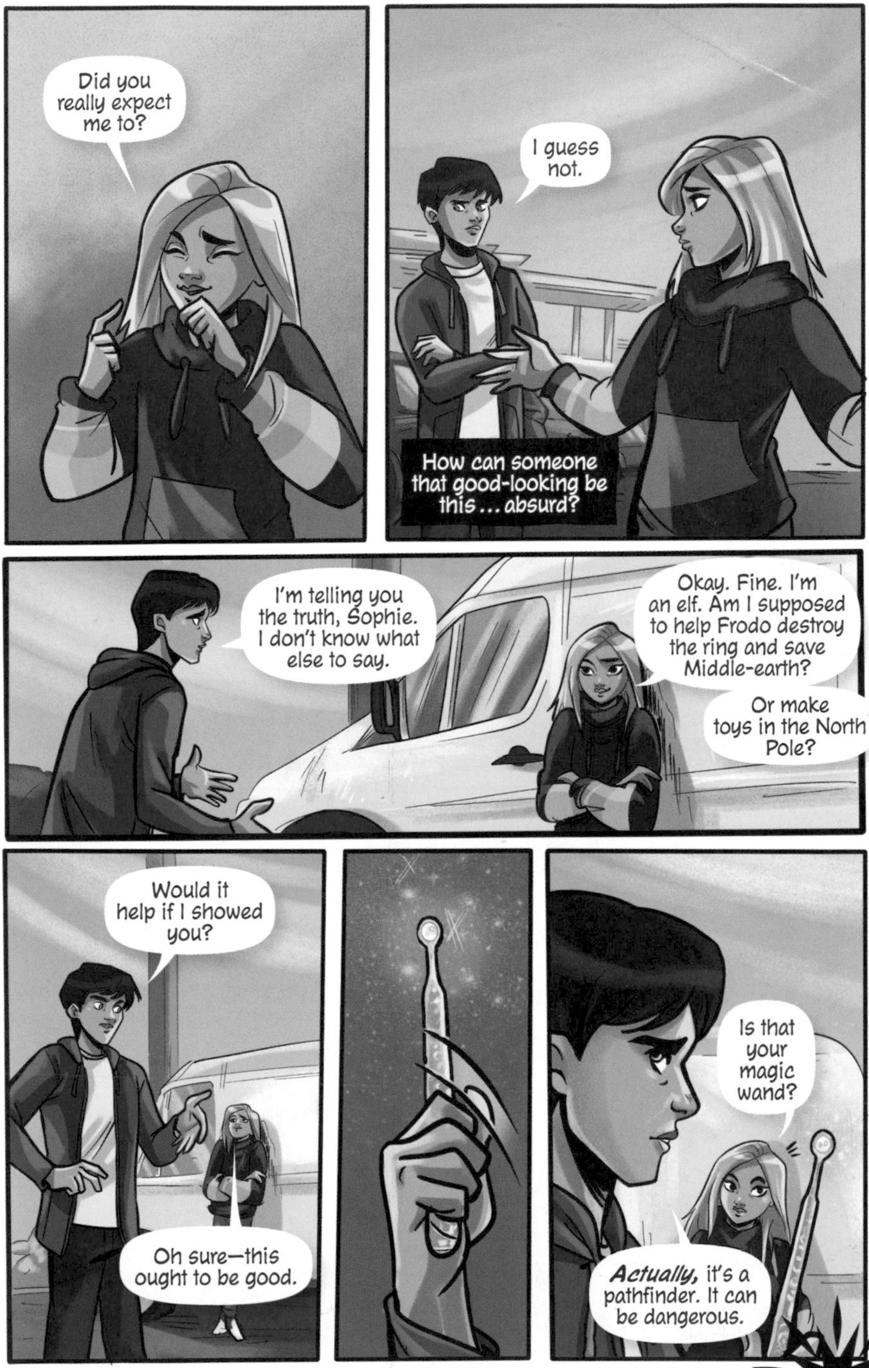
Did you really expect me to?
I guess not.
How can someone that good-looking be this... absurd?
I'm telling you the truth, Sophie. I don't know what else to say.
Okay. Fine. I'm an elf. Am I supposed to help Frodo destroy the ring and save Middle-earth?
Or make toys in the North Pole?
Would it help if I showed you?
Oh sure—this ought to be good.
Is that your magic wand?
Actually, it's a pathfinder. It can be dangerous.

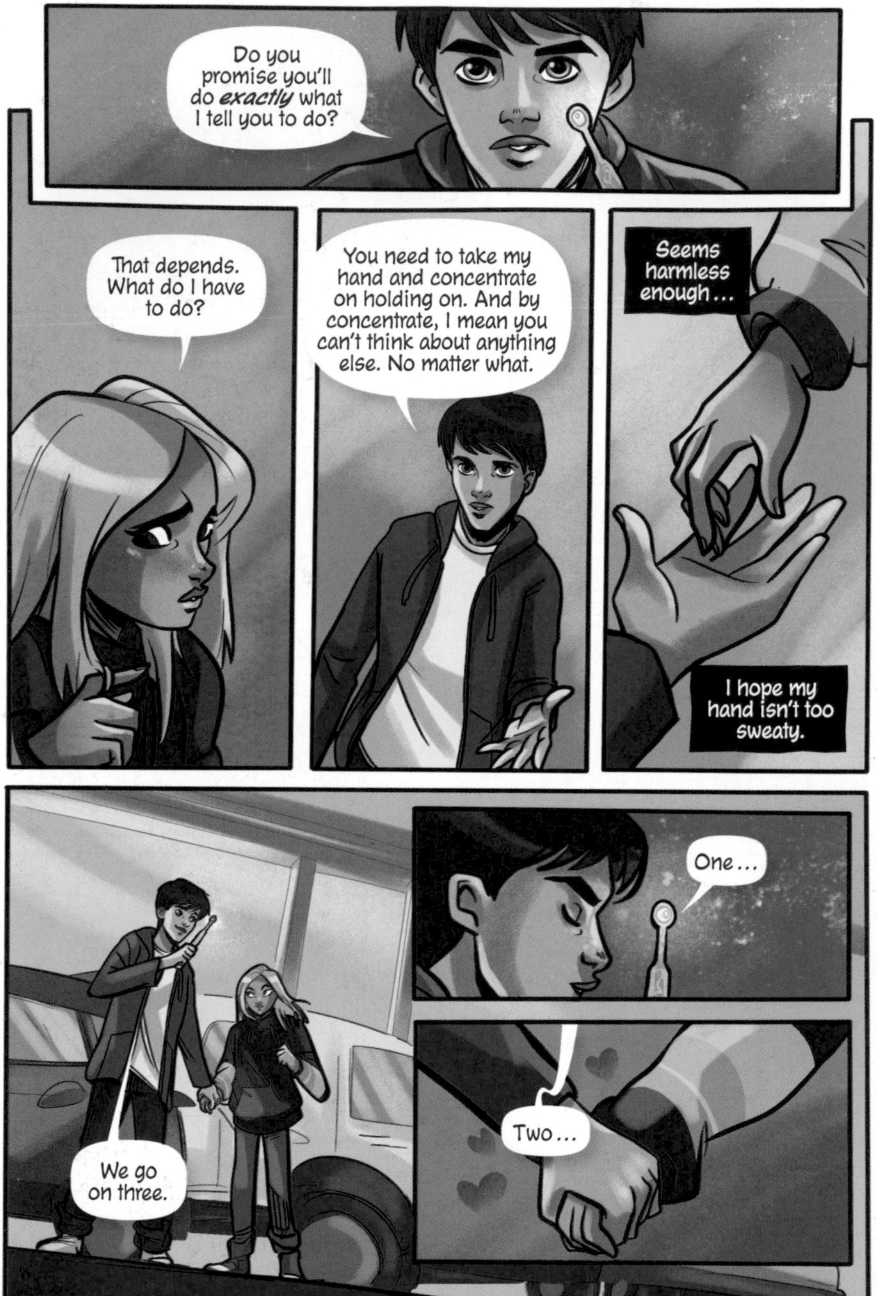

Do you promise you'll do *exactly* what I tell you to do?
That depends. What do I have to do?
You need to take my hand and concentrate on holding on. And by concentrate, I mean you can't think about anything else. No matter what.
Seems harmless enough...
I hope my hand isn't too sweaty.
We go on three.
One...
Two...

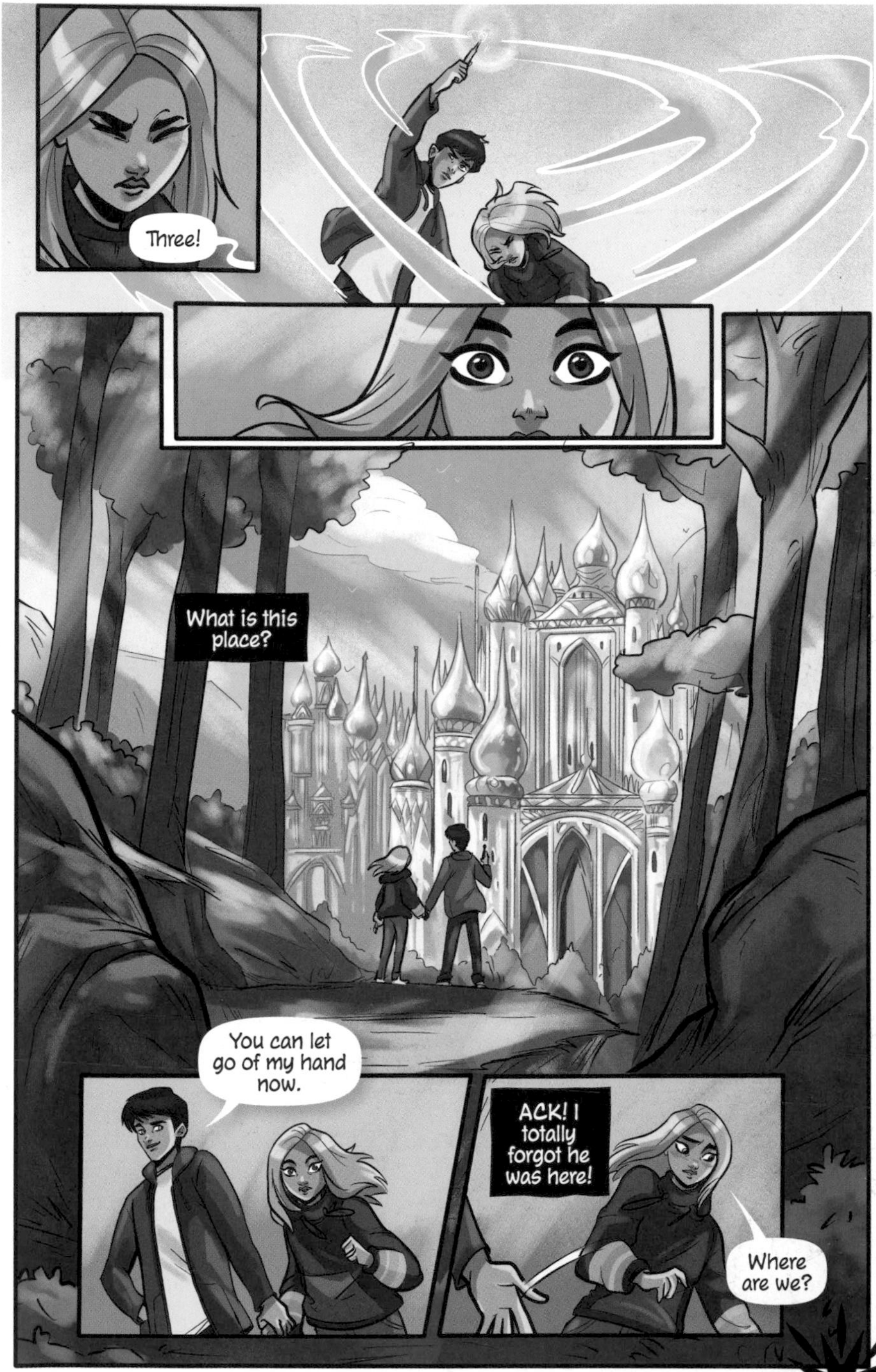

Three!
What is this place?
You can let go of my hand now.
ACK! I totally forgot he was here!
Where are we?

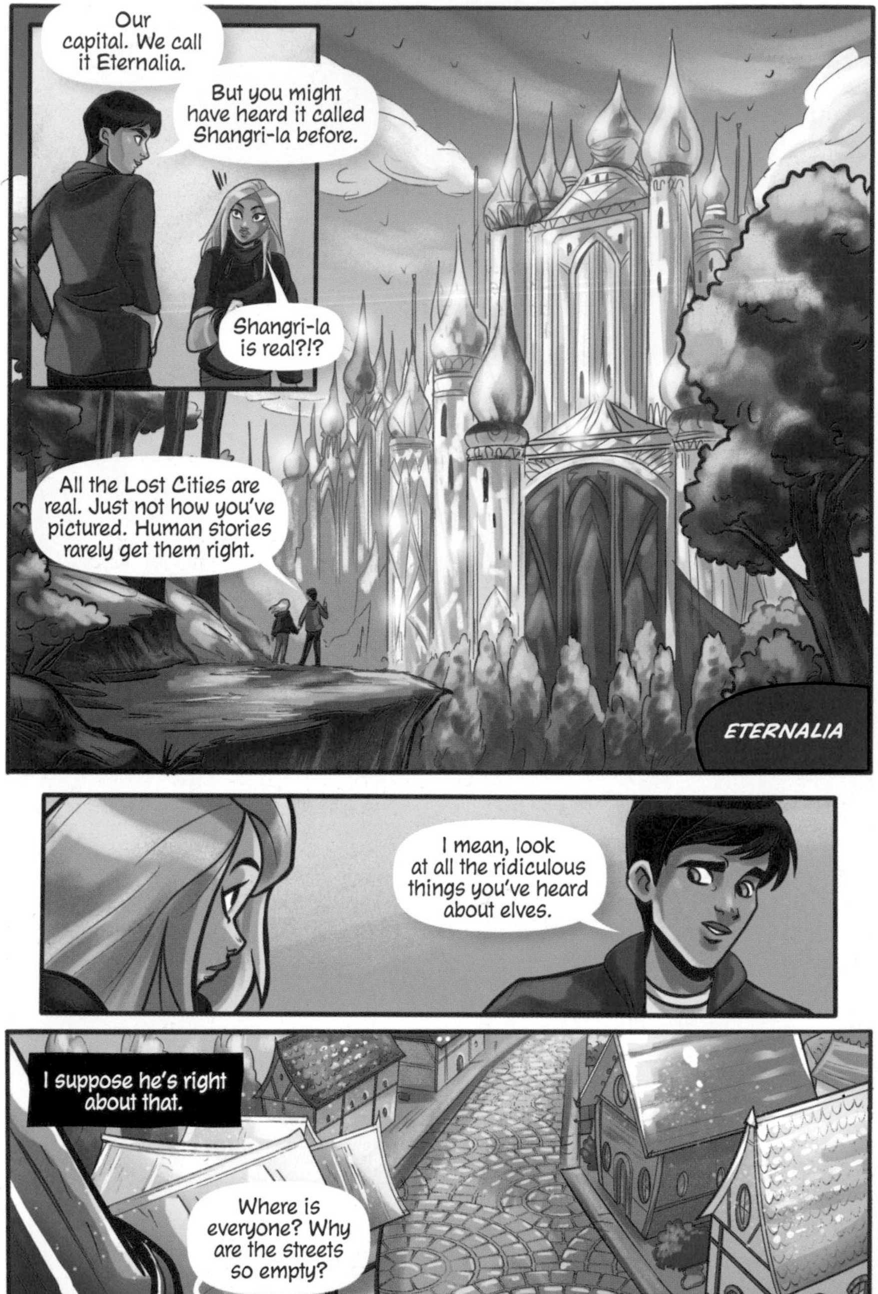
Our capital. We call it Eternalia.
But you might have heard it called Shangri-la before.
Shangri-la is real?!?
All the Lost Cities are real. Just not how you've pictured. Human stories rarely get them right.
ETERNALIA
I mean, look at all the ridiculous things you've heard about elves.
I suppose he's right about that.
Where is everyone? Why are the streets so empty?

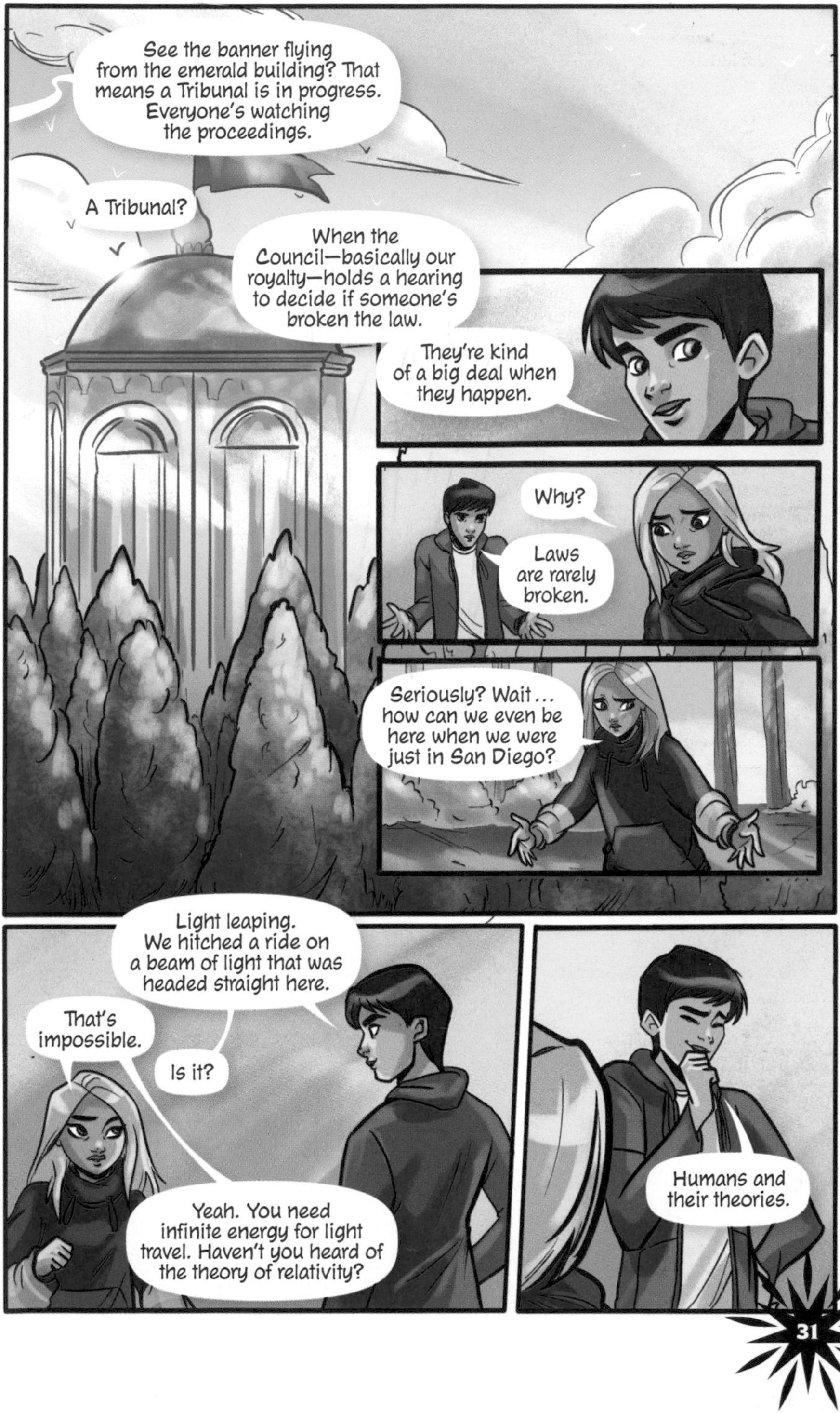
See the banner flying from the emerald building? That means a Tribunal is in progress. Everyone's watching the proceedings.
A Tribunal?
When the Council—basically our royalty—holds a hearing to decide if someone's broken the law.
They're kind of a big deal when they happen.
Why?
Laws are rarely broken.
Seriously? Wait... how can we even be here when we were just in San Diego?
Light leaping. We hitched a ride on a beam of light that was headed straight here.
That's impossible.
Is it?
Yeah. You need infinite energy for light travel. Haven't you heard of the theory of relativity?
Humans and their theories.

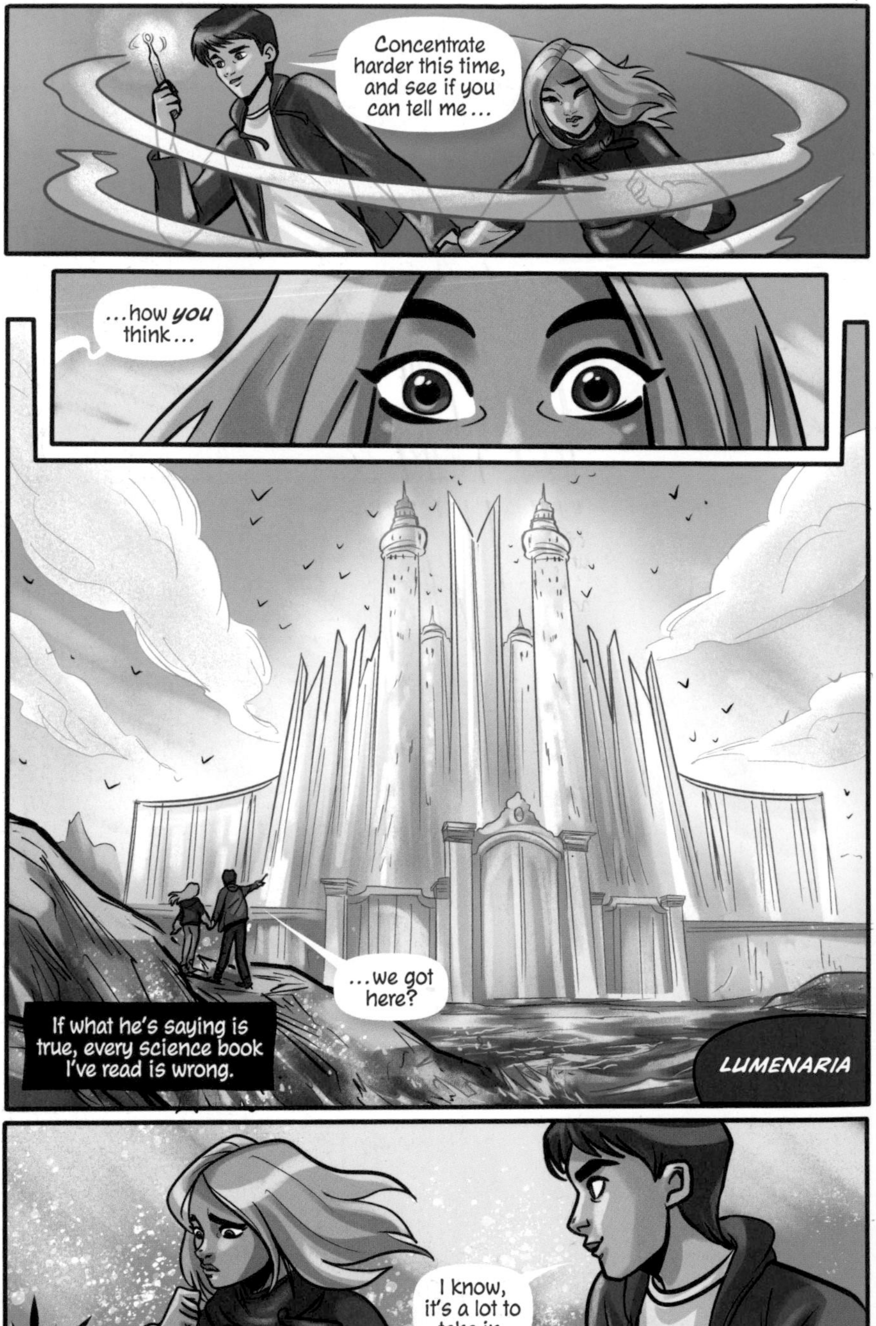
Concentrate harder this time, and see if you can tell me…
…how *you* think…
If what he's saying is true, every science book I've read is wrong.
…we got here?
LUMENARIA
I know, it's a lot to take in.

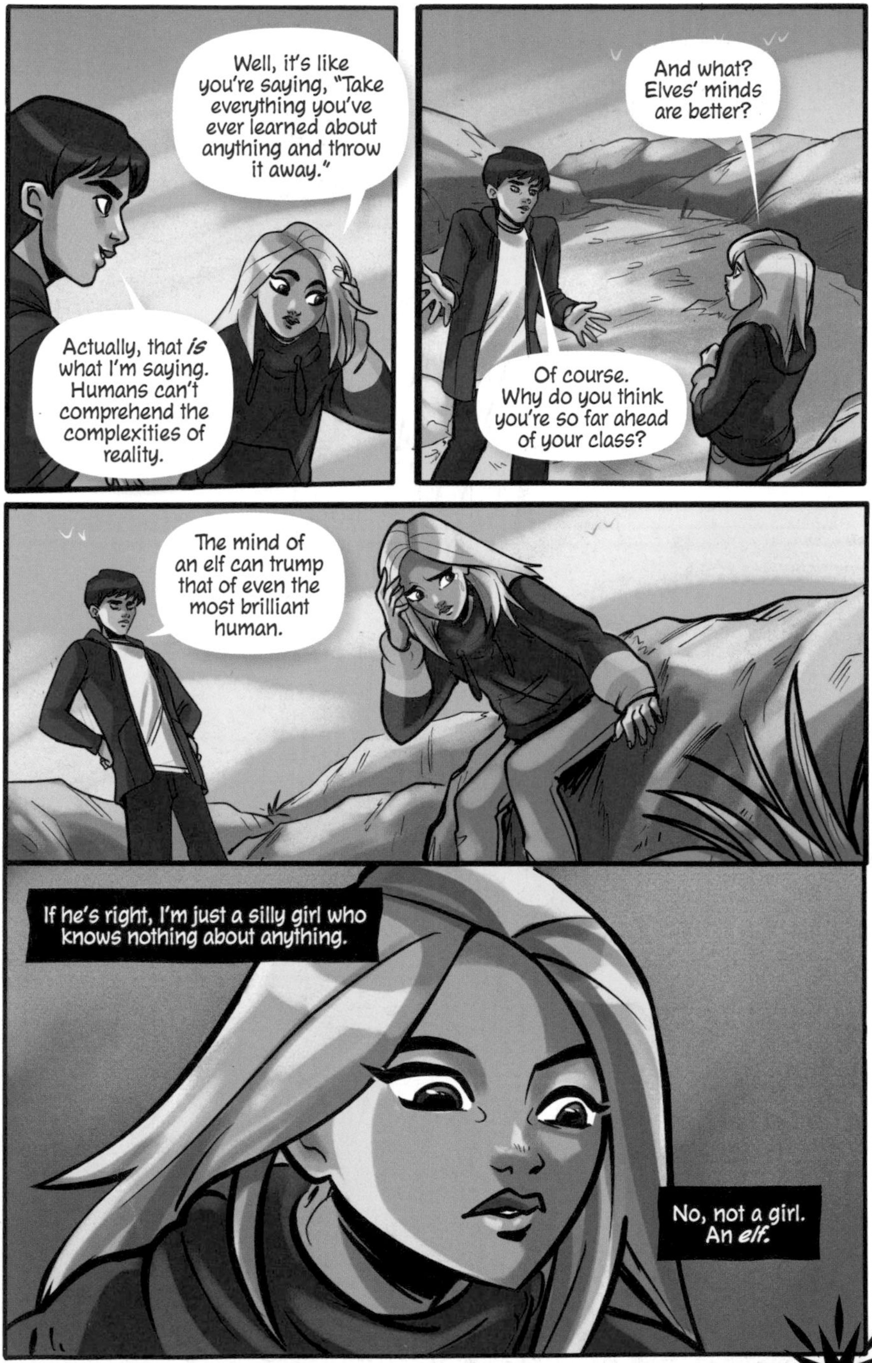
Well, it's like you're saying, "Take everything you've ever learned about anything and throw it away."
Actually, that *is* what I'm saying. Humans can't comprehend the complexities of reality.
And what? Elves' minds are better?
Of course. Why do you think you're so far ahead of your class?
The mind of an elf can trump that of even the most brilliant human.
If he's right, I'm just a silly girl who knows nothing about anything.
No, not a girl. An *elf*.

CHAPTER FOUR

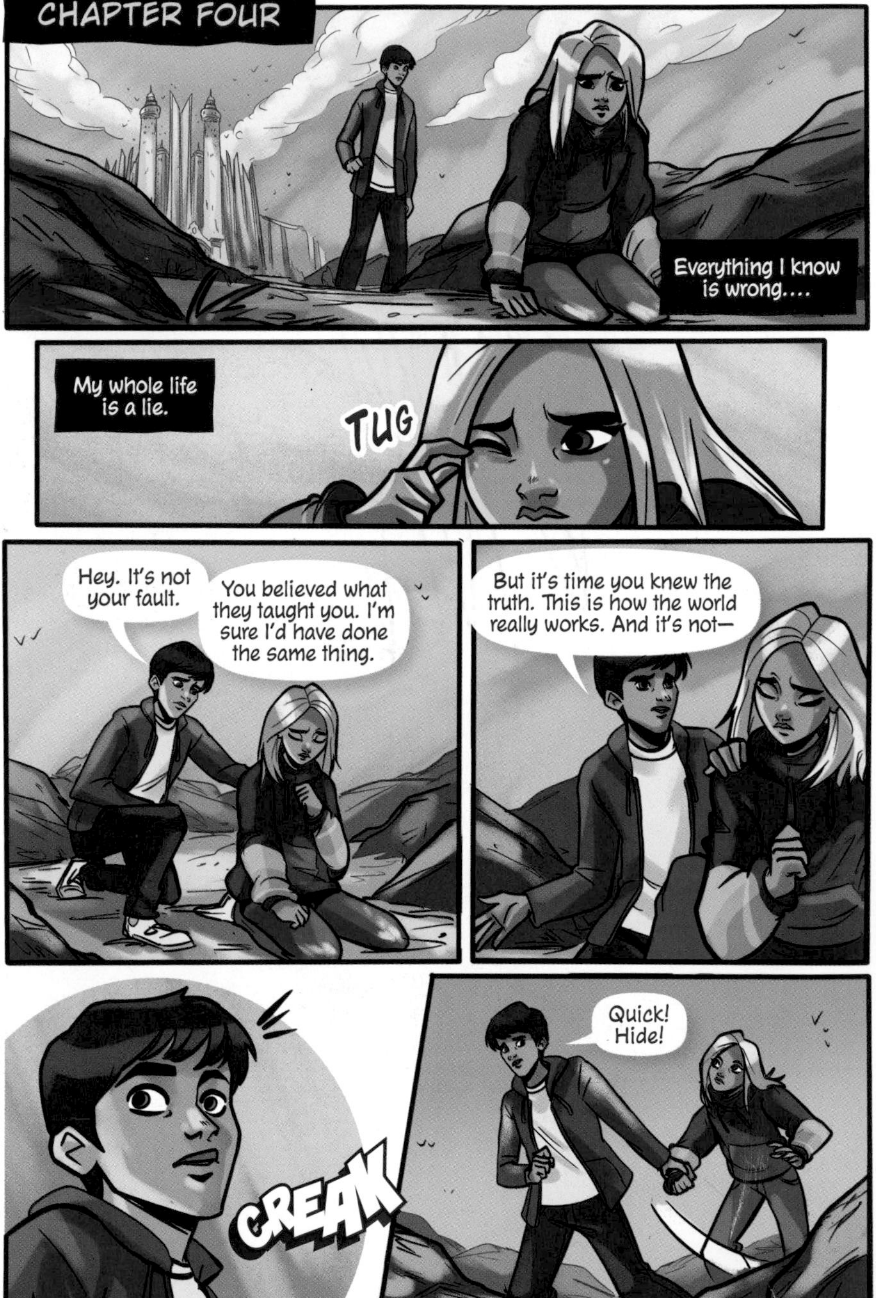

Everything I know is wrong....
My whole life is a lie.
TUG
Hey. It's not your fault.
You believed what they taught you. I'm sure I'd have done the same thing.
But it's time you knew the truth. This is how the world really works. And it's not—
CREAK
Quick! Hide!

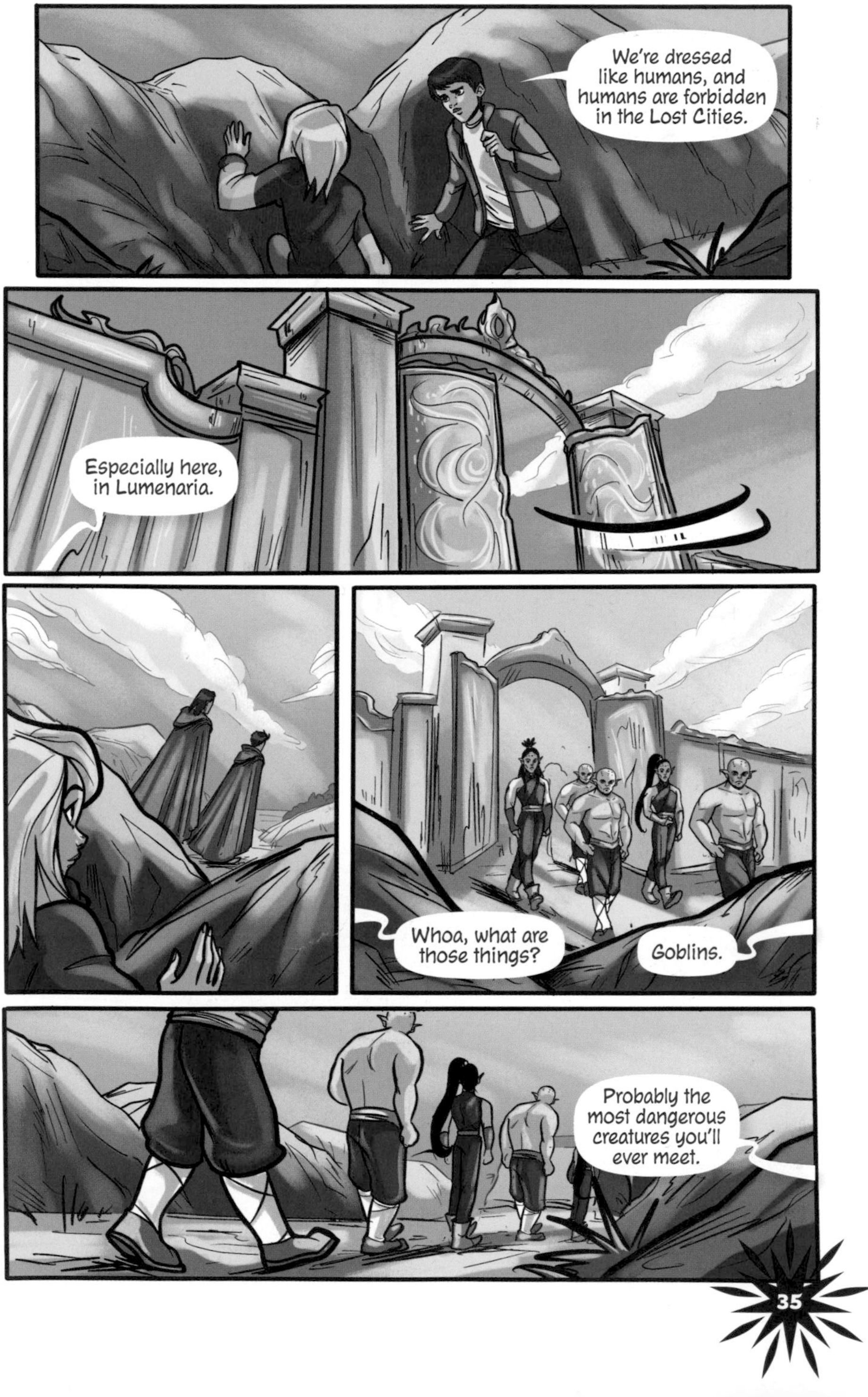

We're dressed like humans, and humans are forbidden in the Lost Cities.
Especially here, in Lumenaria.
Whoa, what are those things?
Goblins.
Probably the most dangerous creatures you'll ever meet.

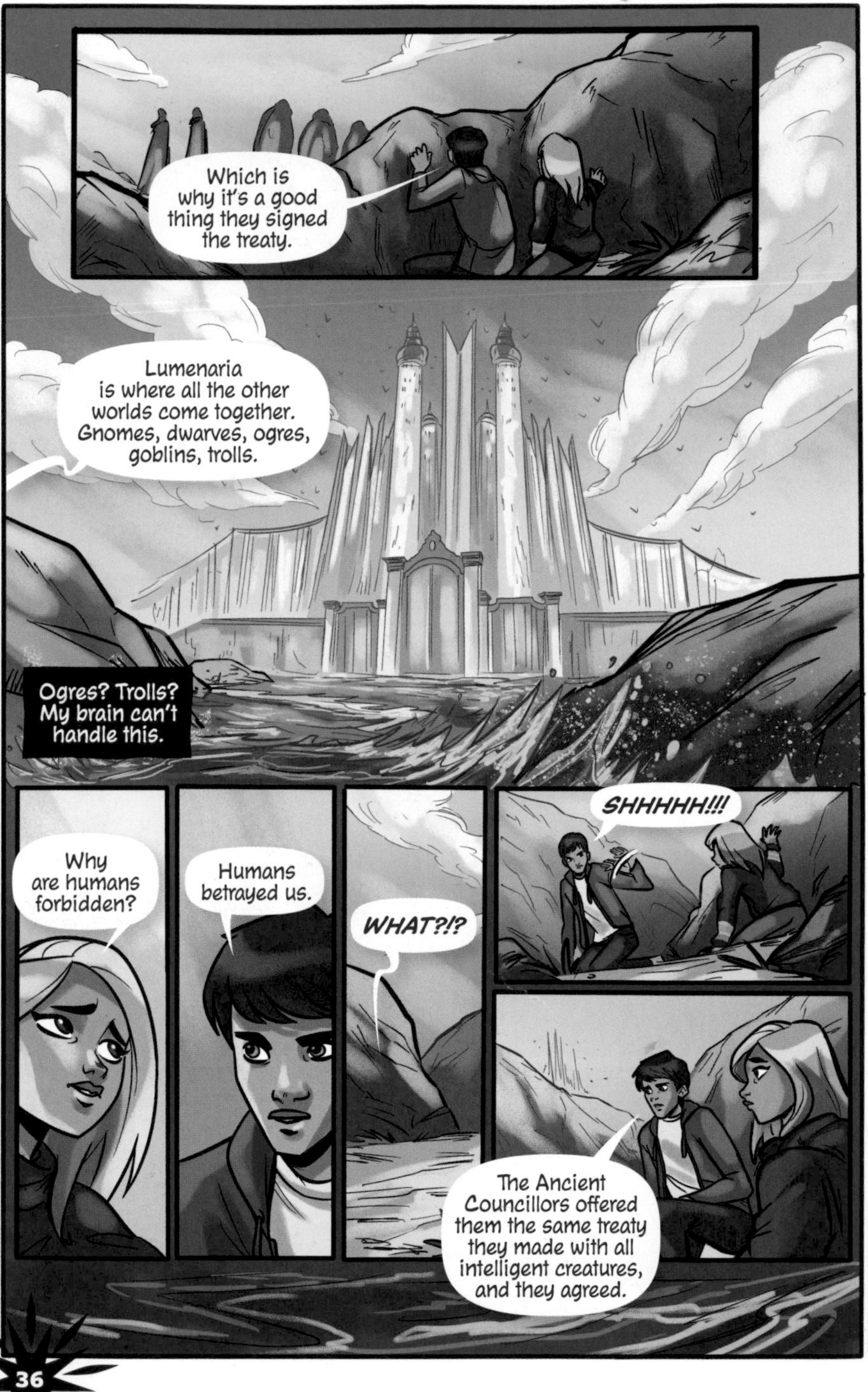
Which is why it's a good thing they signed the treaty.
Lumenaria is where all the other worlds come together. Gnomes, dwarves, ogres, goblins, trolls.
Ogres? Trolls? My brain can't handle this.
Why are humans forbidden?
Humans betrayed us.
WHAT?!?
SHHHHH!!!
The Ancient Councillors offered them the same treaty they made with all intelligent creatures, and they agreed.

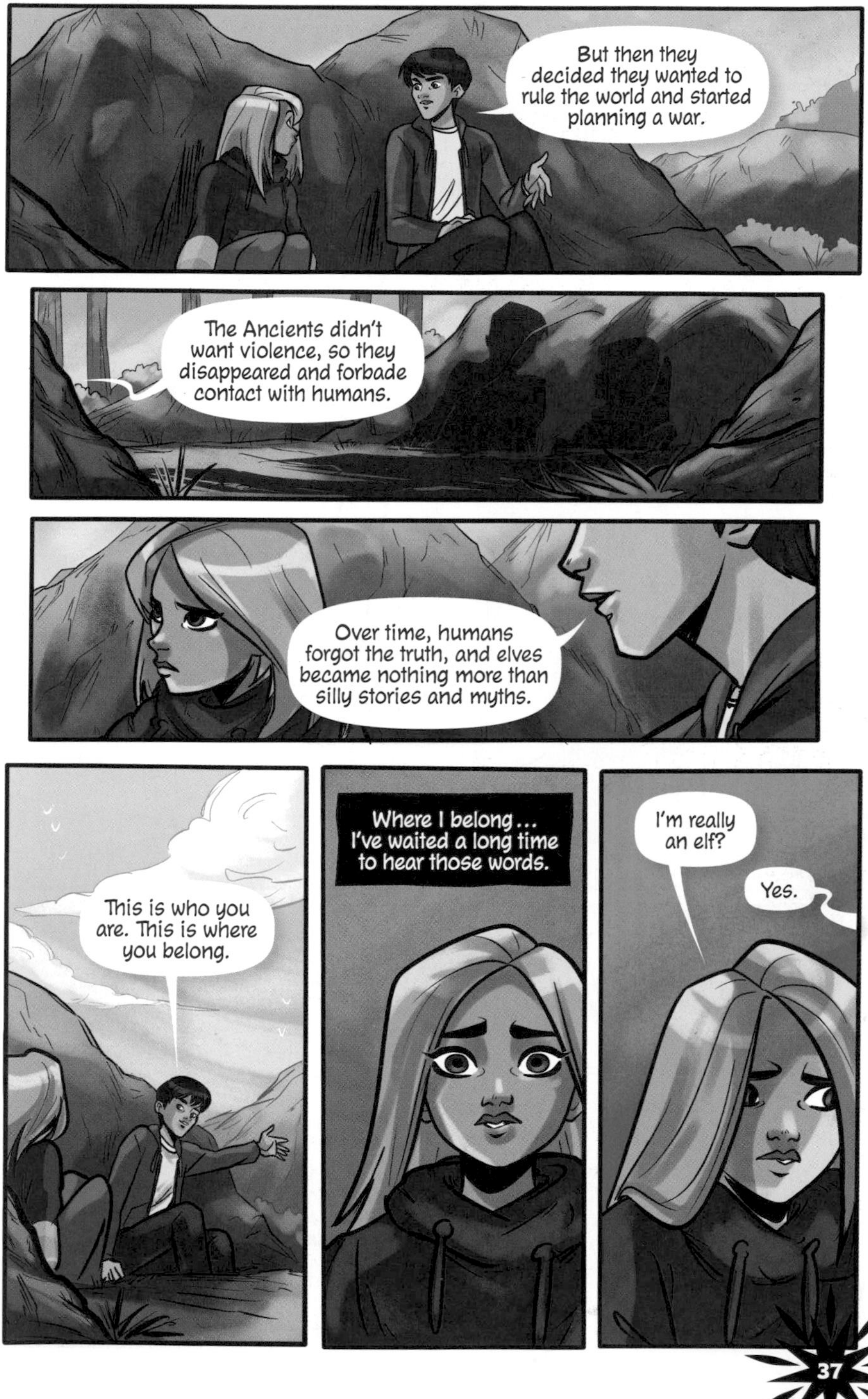

But then they decided they wanted to rule the world and started planning a war.
The Ancients didn't want violence, so they disappeared and forbade contact with humans.
Over time, humans forgot the truth, and elves became nothing more than silly stories and myths.
This is who you are. This is where you belong.
Where I belong... I've waited a long time to hear those words.
I'm really an elf?
Yes.

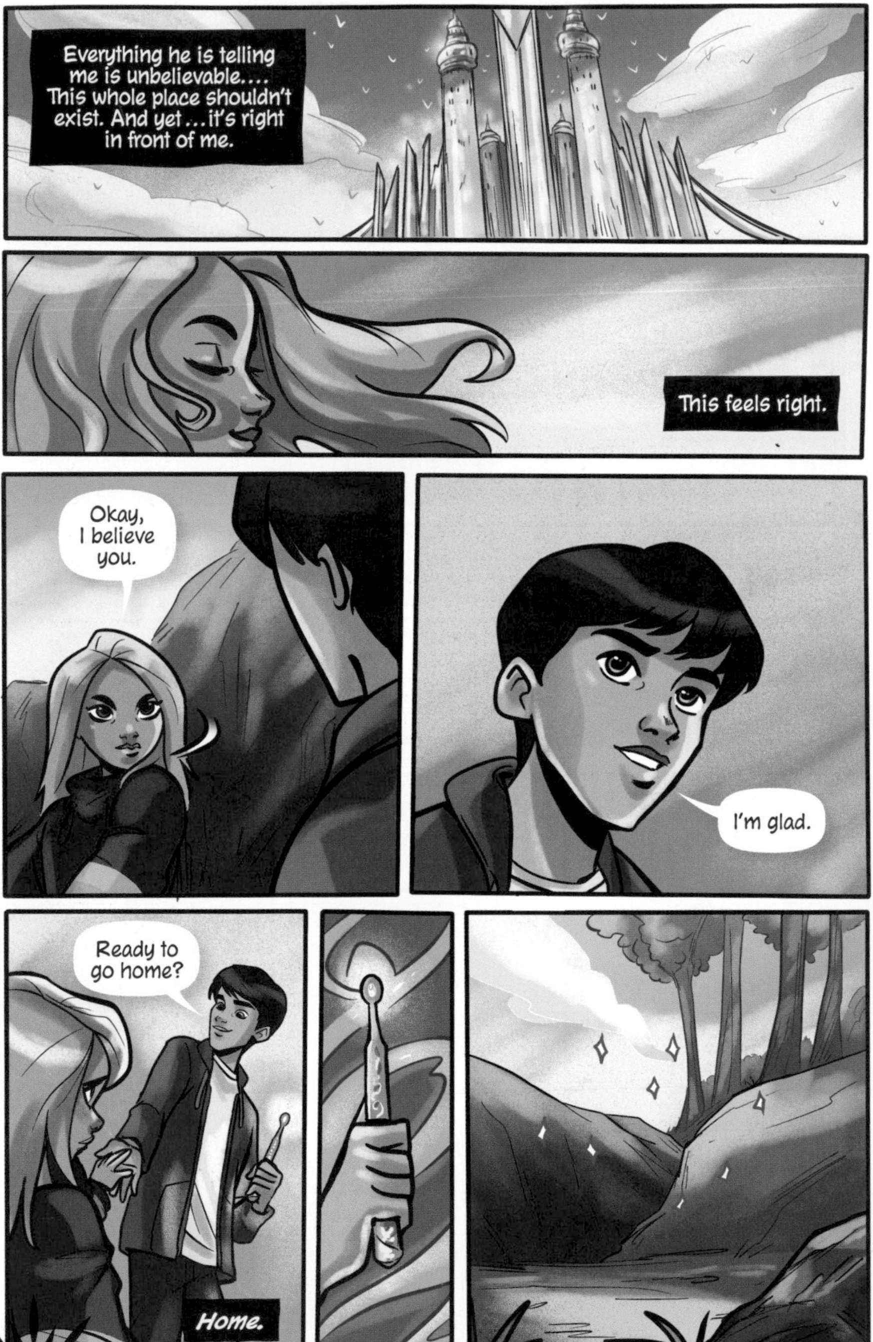

Everything he is telling me is unbelievable.... This whole place shouldn't exist. And yet...it's right in front of me.
This feels right.
Okay, I believe you.
I'm glad.
Ready to go home?
Home.

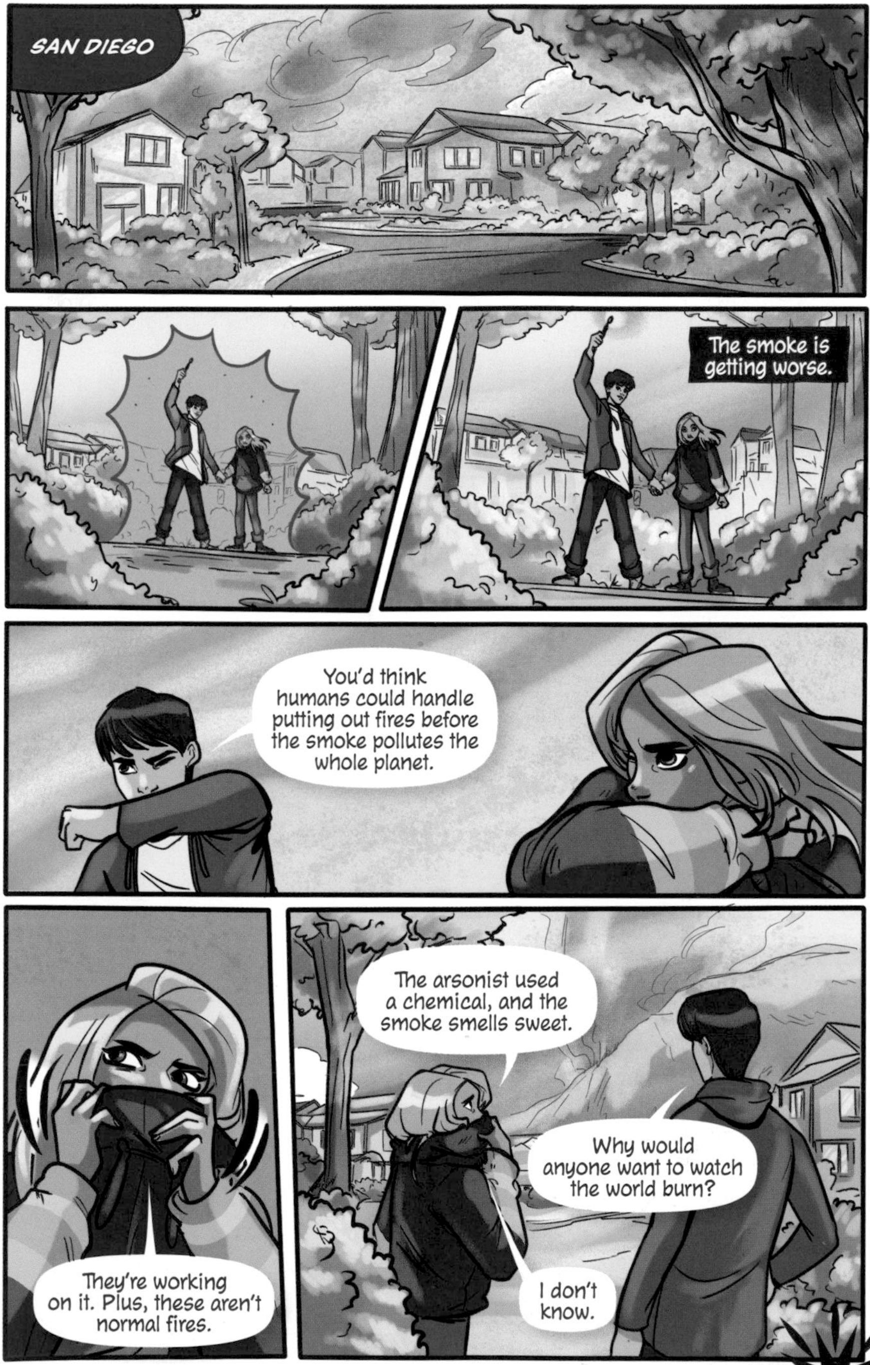
SAN DIEGO
The smoke is getting worse.
You'd think humans could handle putting out fires before the smoke pollutes the whole planet.
They're working on it. Plus, these aren't normal fires.
The arsonist used a chemical, and the smoke smells sweet.
Why would anyone want to watch the world burn?
I don't know.

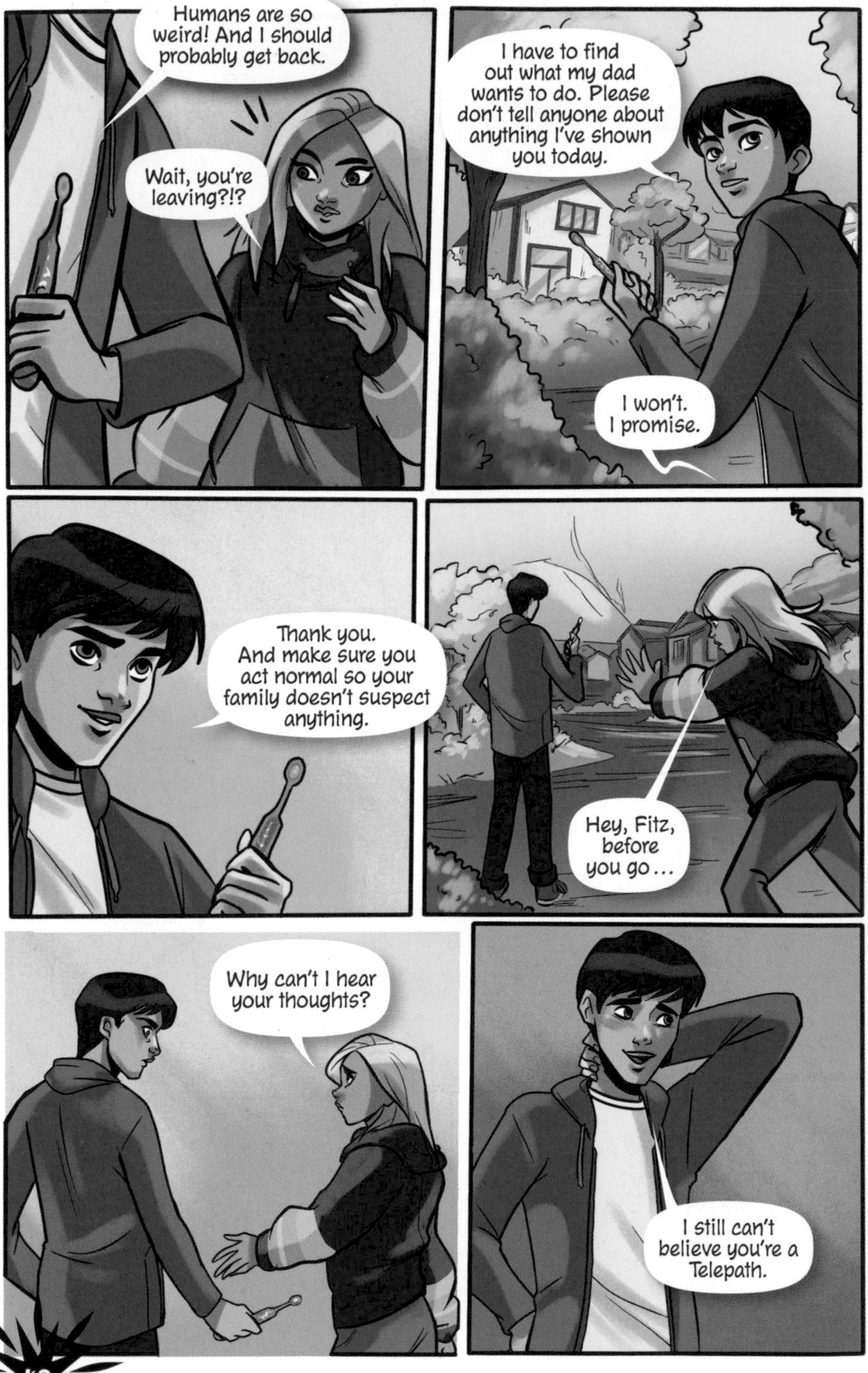
Humans are so weird! And I should probably get back.
Wait, you're leaving?!?
I have to find out what my dad wants to do. Please don't tell anyone about anything I've shown you today.
I won't. I promise.
Thank you. And make sure you act normal so your family doesn't suspect anything.
Hey, Fitz, before you go...
Why can't I hear your thoughts?
I still can't believe you're a Telepath.

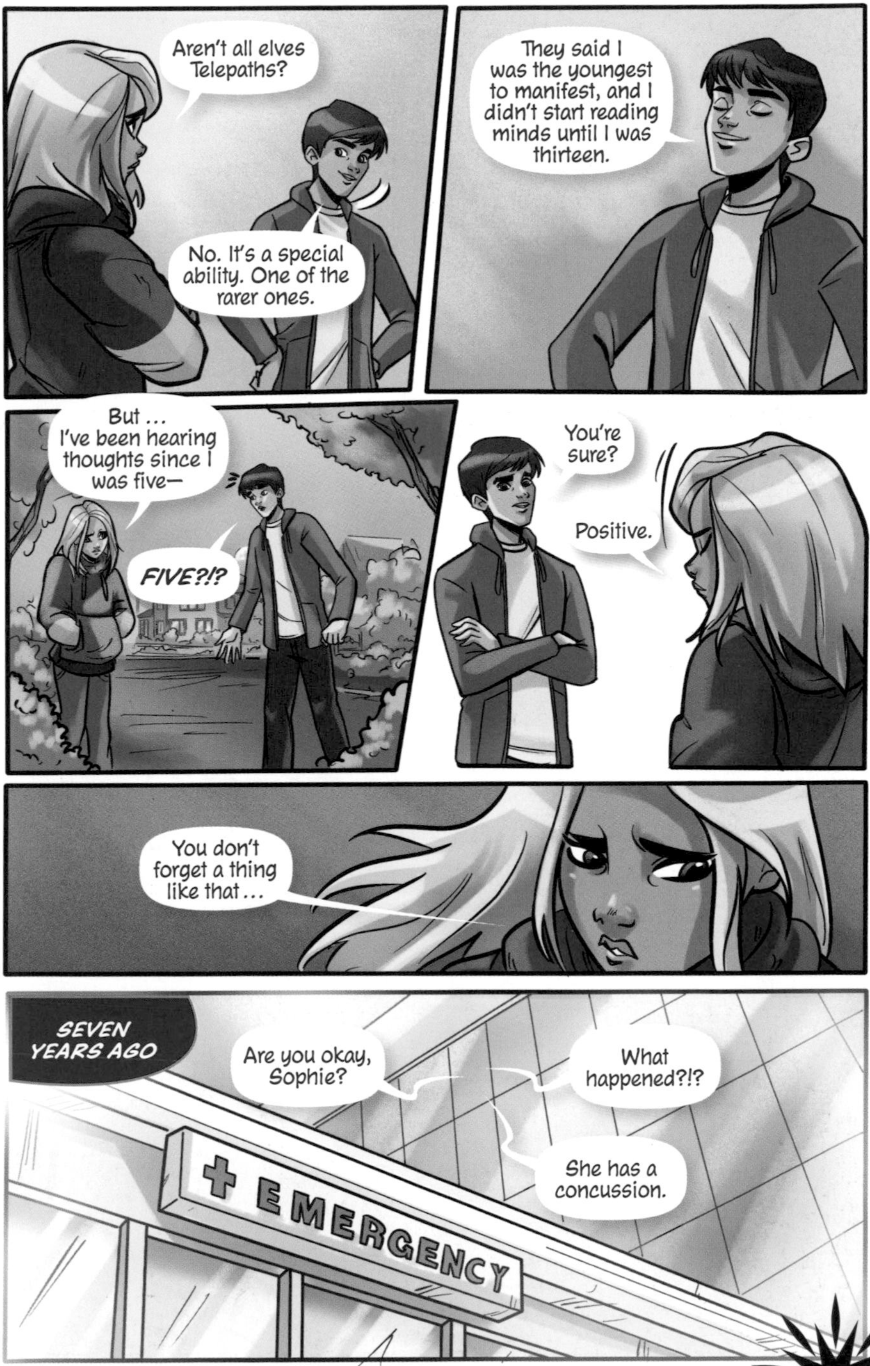
Aren't all elves Telepaths?
No. It's a special ability. One of the rarer ones.
They said I was the youngest to manifest, and I didn't start reading minds until I was thirteen.
But … I've been hearing thoughts since I was five—
FIVE?!?
You're sure?
Positive.
You don't forget a thing like that …
SEVEN YEARS AGO
Are you okay, Sophie?
What happened?!?
She has a concussion.
EMERGENCY

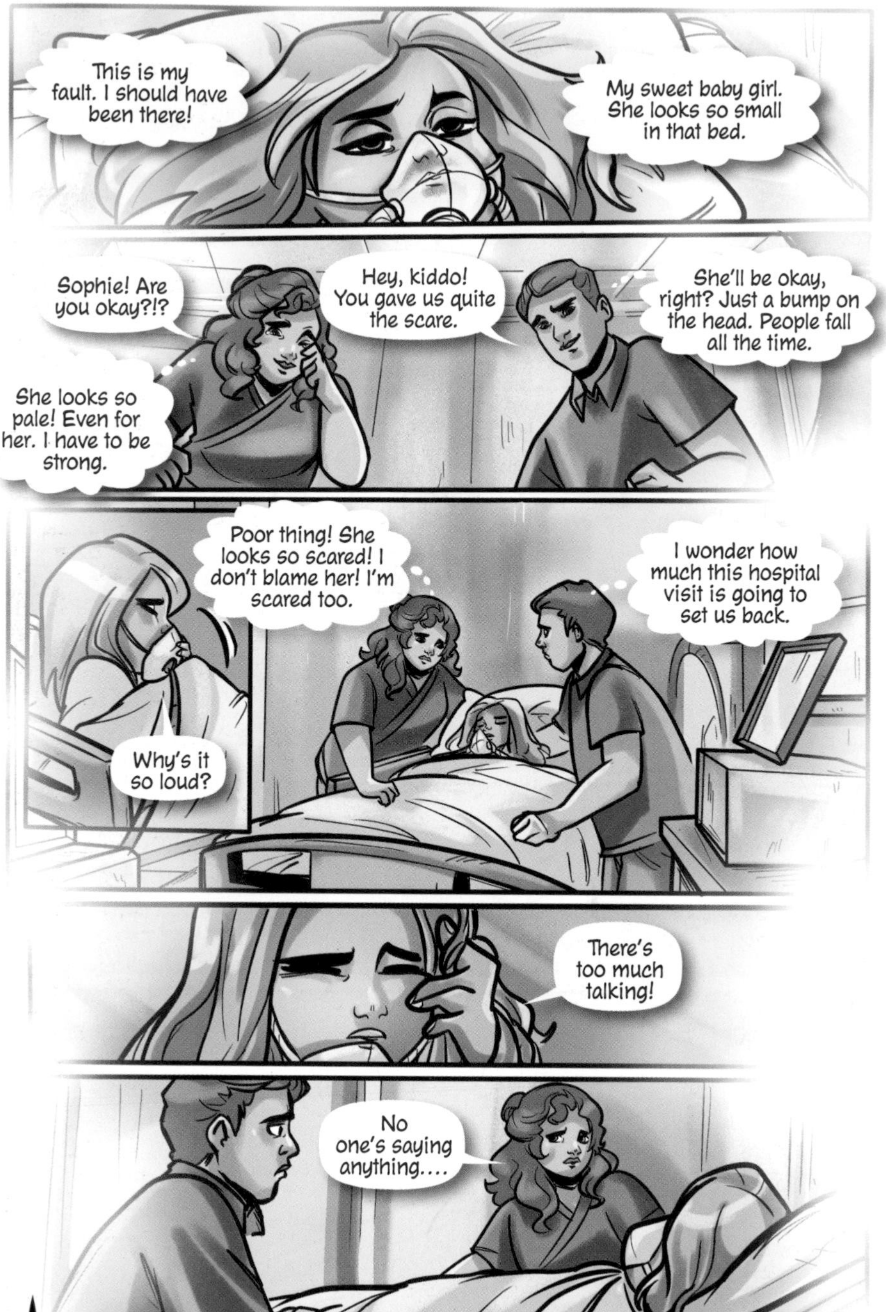
This is my fault. I should have been there!
My sweet baby girl. She looks so small in that bed.
Sophie! Are you okay?!?
Hey, kiddo! You gave us quite the scare.
She'll be okay, right? Just a bump on the head. People fall all the time.
She looks so pale! Even for her. I have to be strong.
Poor thing! She looks so scared! I don't blame her! I'm scared too.
I wonder how much this hospital visit is going to set us back.
Why's it so loud?
There's too much talking!
No one's saying anything....

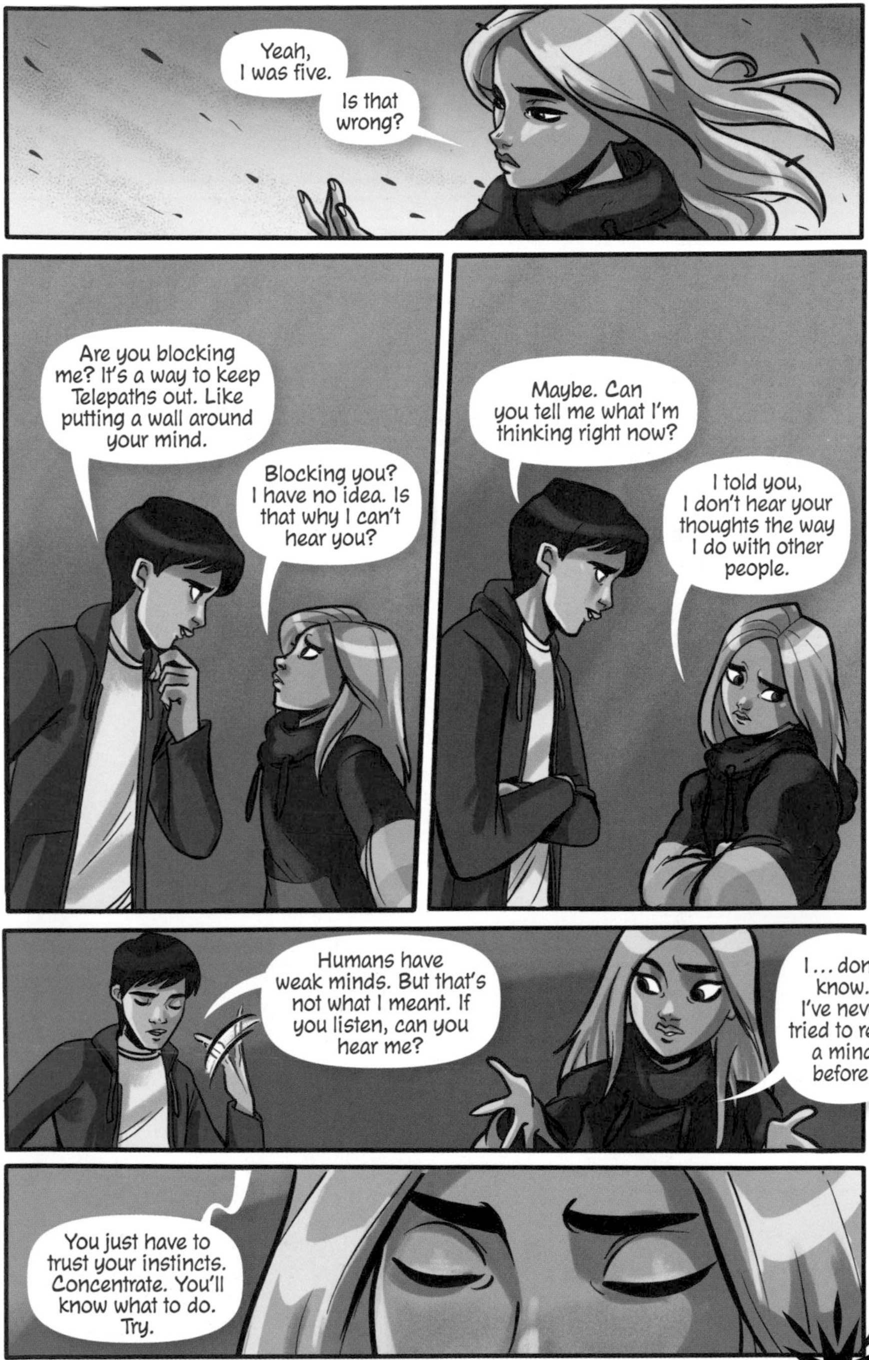
Yeah, I was five.
Is that wrong?
Are you blocking me? It's a way to keep Telepaths out. Like putting a wall around your mind.
Blocking you? I have no idea. Is that why I can't hear you?
Maybe. Can you tell me what I'm thinking right now?
I told you, I don't hear your thoughts the way I do with other people.
Humans have weak minds. But that's not what I meant. If you listen, can you hear me?
I... don't know. I've never tried to read a mind before.
You just have to trust your instincts. Concentrate. You'll know what to do. Try.

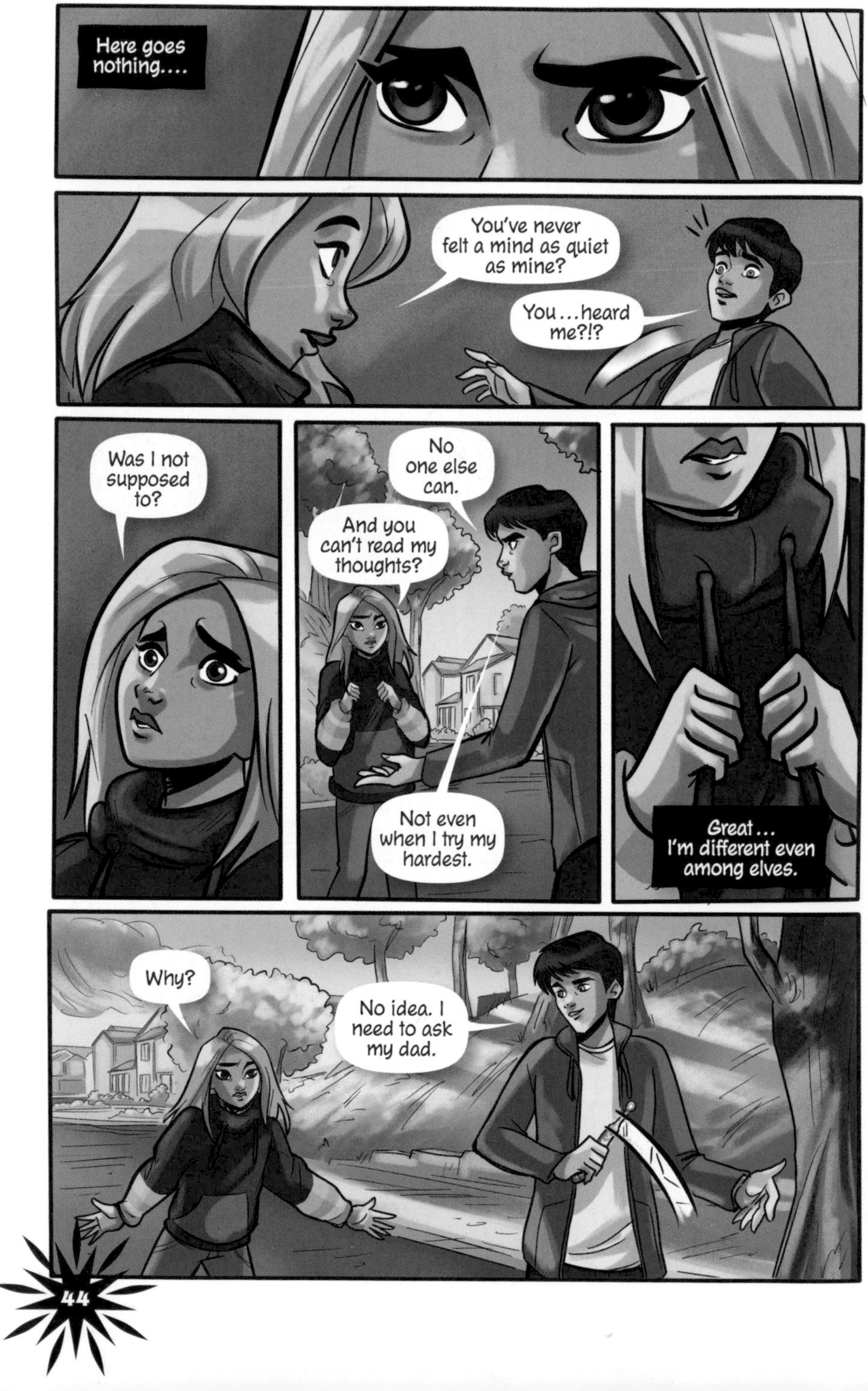
Here goes nothing....
You've never felt a mind as quiet as mine?
You...heard me?!?
Was I not supposed to?
No one else can.
And you can't read my thoughts?
Not even when I try my hardest.
Great... I'm different even among elves.
Why?
No idea. I need to ask my dad.

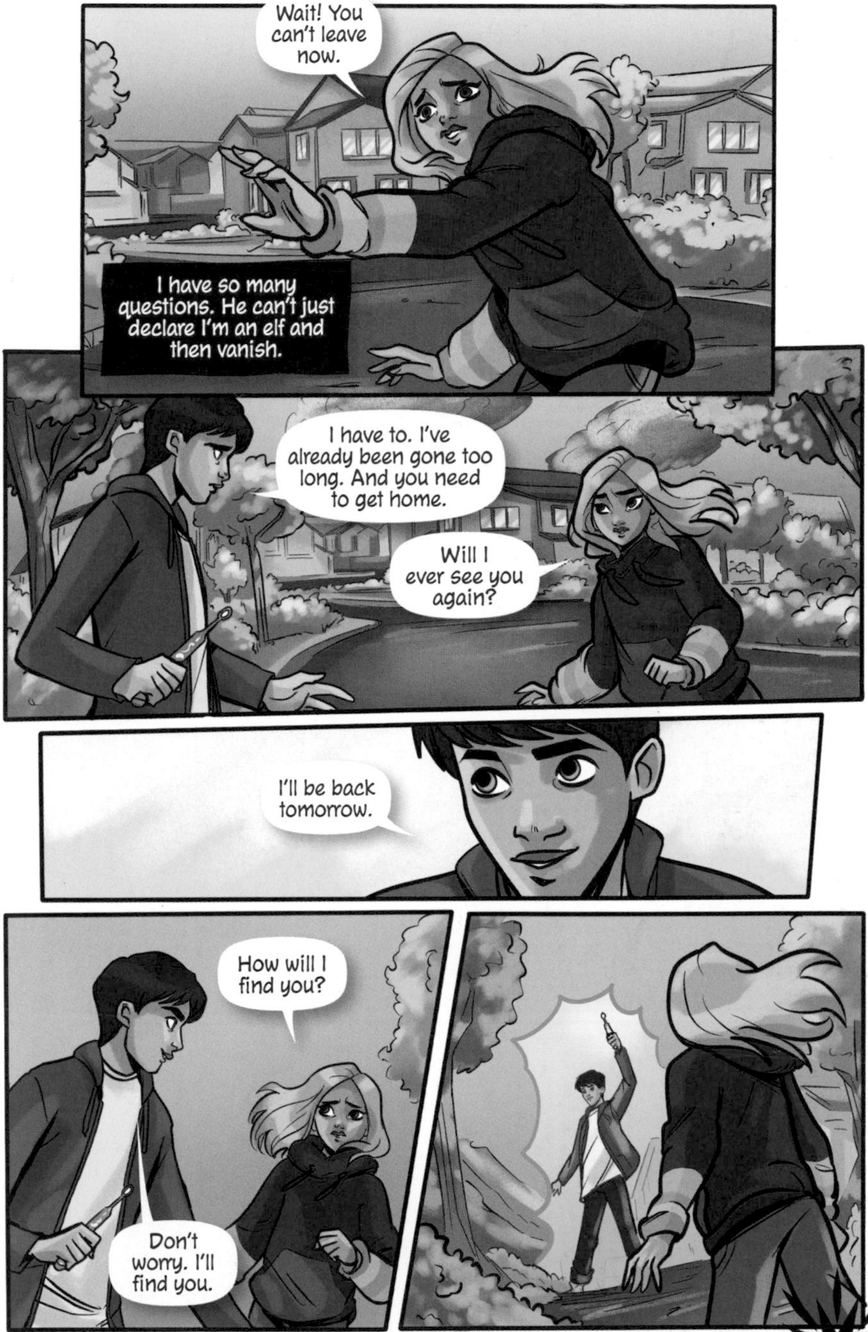
Wait! You can't leave now.
I have so many questions. He can't just declare I'm an elf and then vanish.
I have to. I've already been gone too long. And you need to get home.
Will I ever see you again?
I'll be back tomorrow.
How will I find you?
Don't worry. I'll find you.

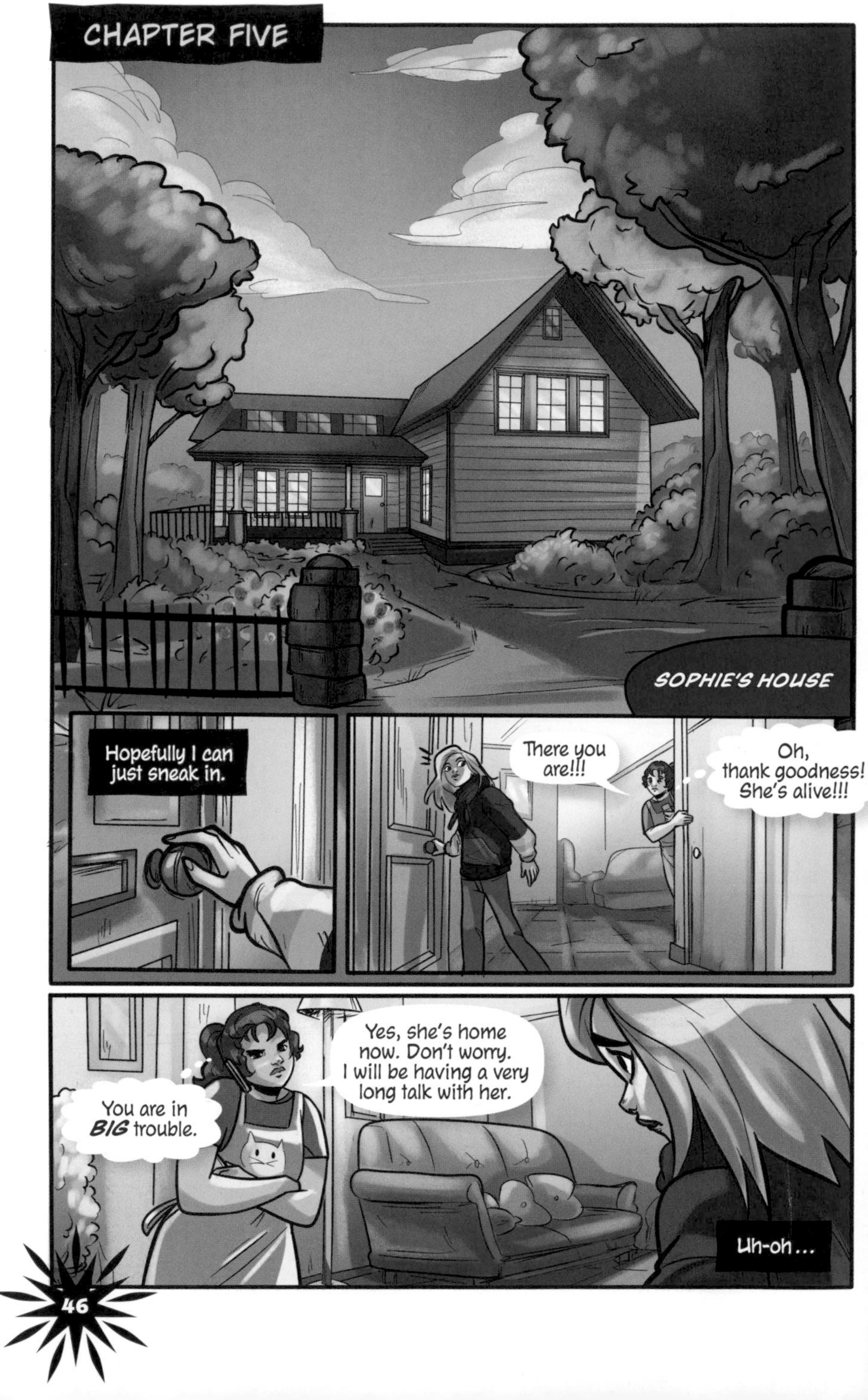

CHAPTER FIVE
SOPHIE'S HOUSE
Hopefully I can just sneak in.
There you are!!!
Oh, thank goodness! She's alive!!!
You are in BIG trouble.
Yes, she's home now. Don't worry. I will be having a very long talk with her.
Uh-oh...

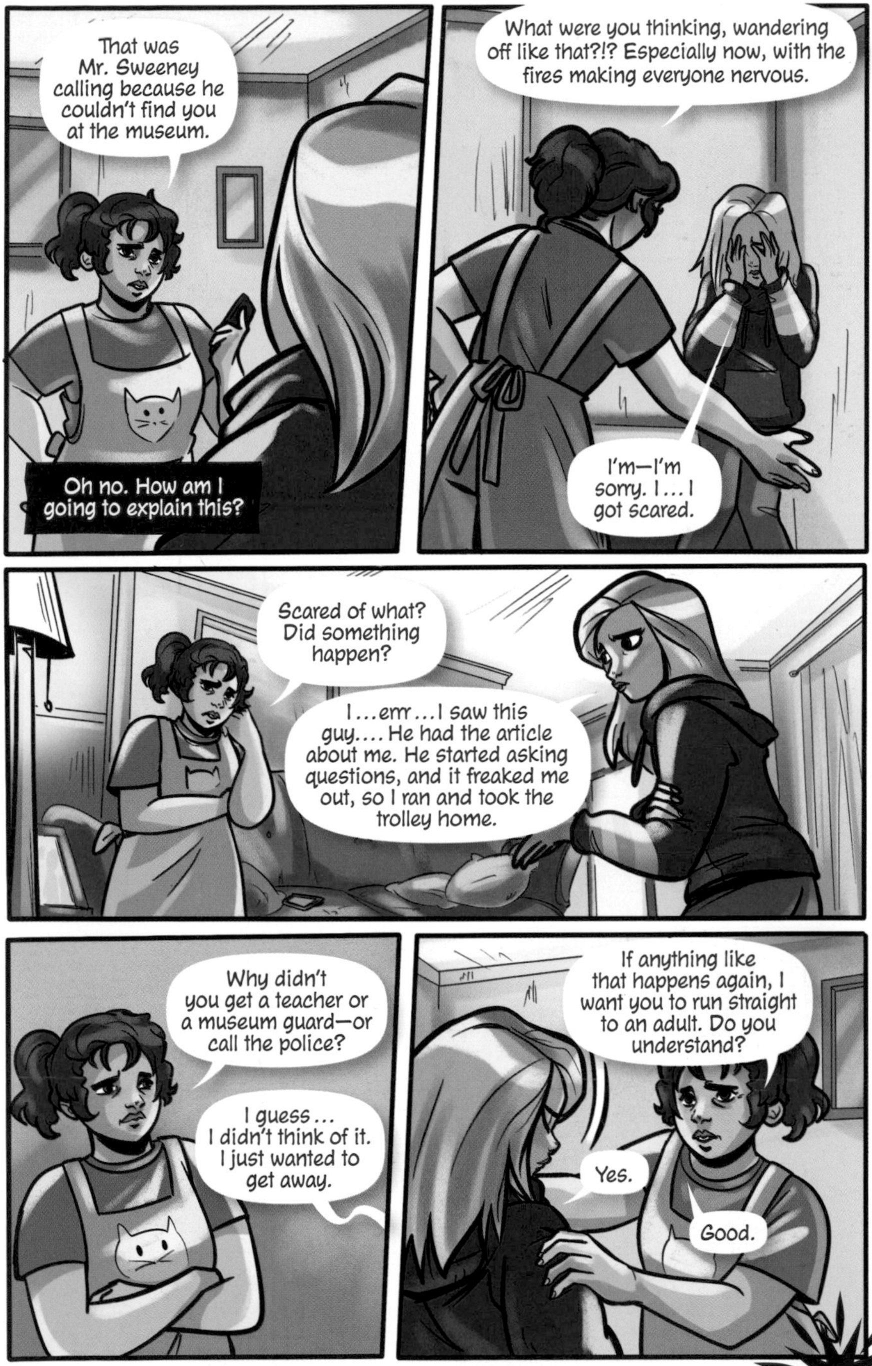
That was Mr. Sweeney calling because he couldn't find you at the museum.
Oh no. How am I going to explain this?
What were you thinking, wandering off like that?!? Especially now, with the fires making everyone nervous.
I'm—I'm sorry. I . . . I got scared.
Scared of what? Did something happen?
I . . . errr . . . I saw this guy. . . . He had the article about me. He started asking questions, and it freaked me out, so I ran and took the trolley home.
Why didn't you get a teacher or a museum guard—or call the police?
I guess . . . I didn't think of it. I just wanted to get away.
If anything like that happens again, I want you to run straight to an adult. Do you understand?
Yes.
Good.

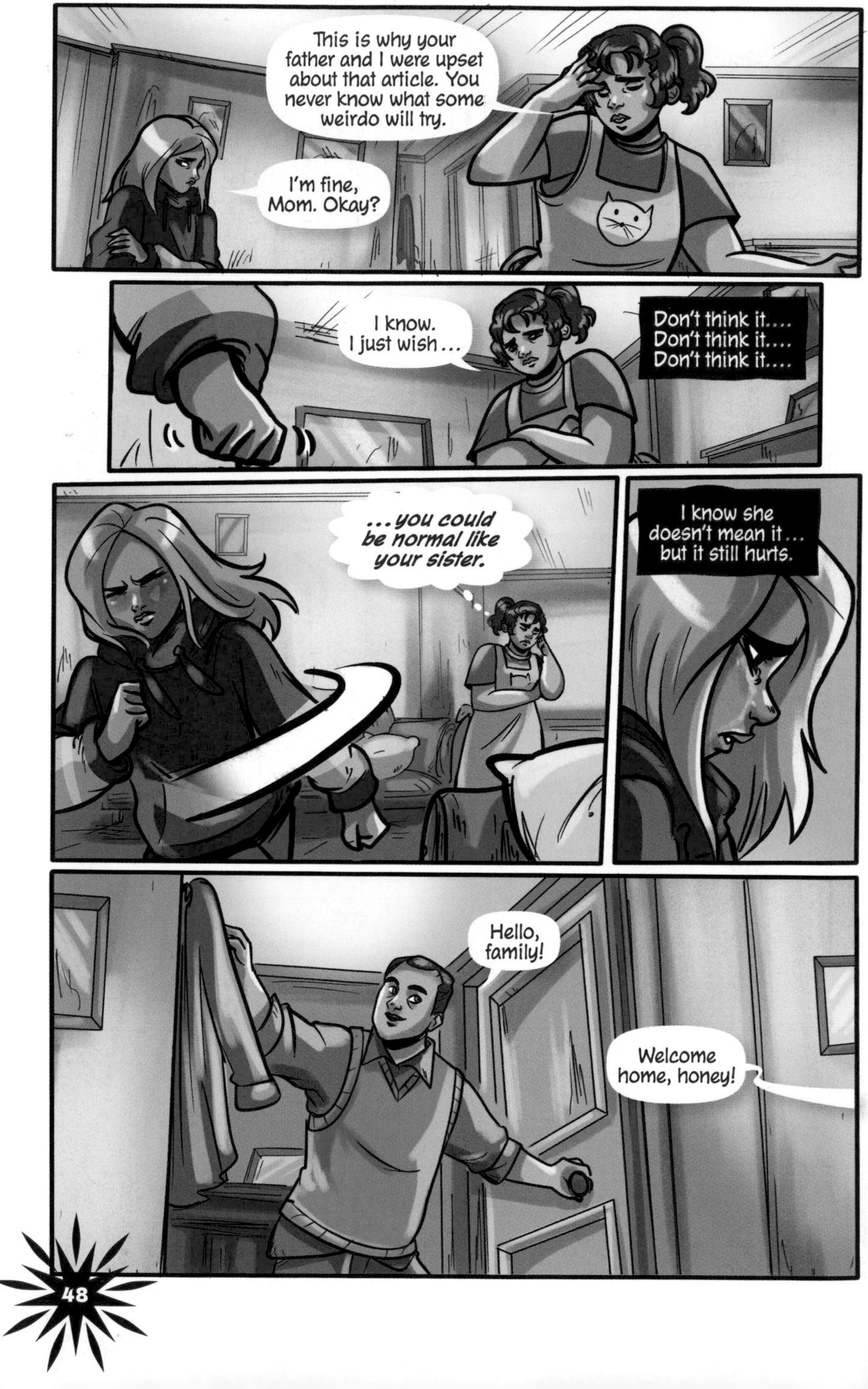
This is why your father and I were upset about that article. You never know what some weirdo will try.
I'm fine, Mom. Okay?
I know. I just wish...
Don't think it.... Don't think it.... Don't think it....
...you could be normal like your sister.
I know she doesn't mean it... but it still hurts.
Hello, family!
Welcome home, honey!

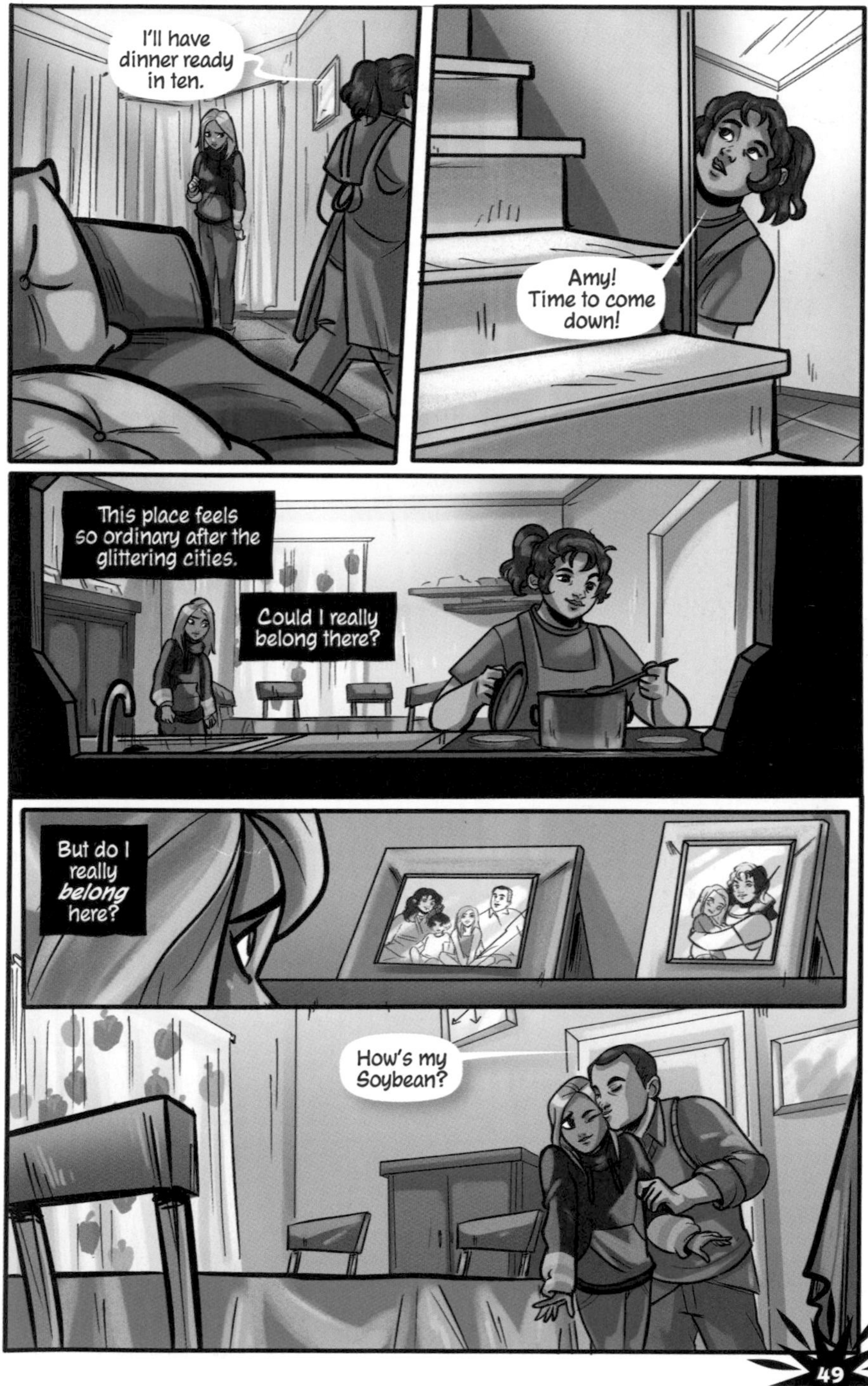
I'll have dinner ready in ten.
Amy! Time to come down!
This place feels so ordinary after the glittering cities.
Could I really belong there?
But do I really *belong* here?
How's my Soybean?

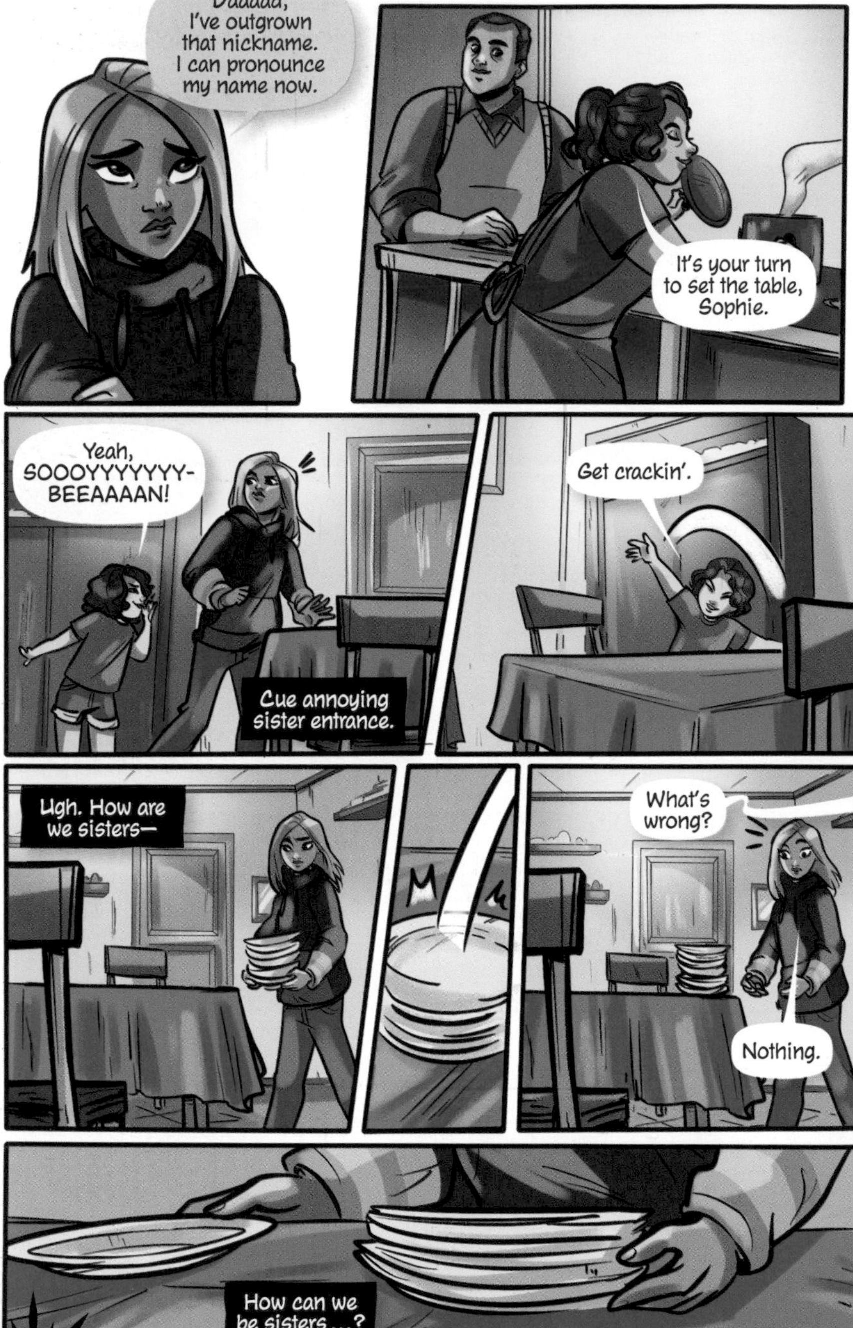

Daaaad, I've outgrown that nickname. I can pronounce my name now.
It's your turn to set the table, Sophie.
Yeah, SOOOYYYYYYY-BEEAAAAN!
Cue annoying sister entrance.
Get crackin'.
Ugh. How are we sisters—
What's wrong?
Nothing.
How can we be sisters . . . ?

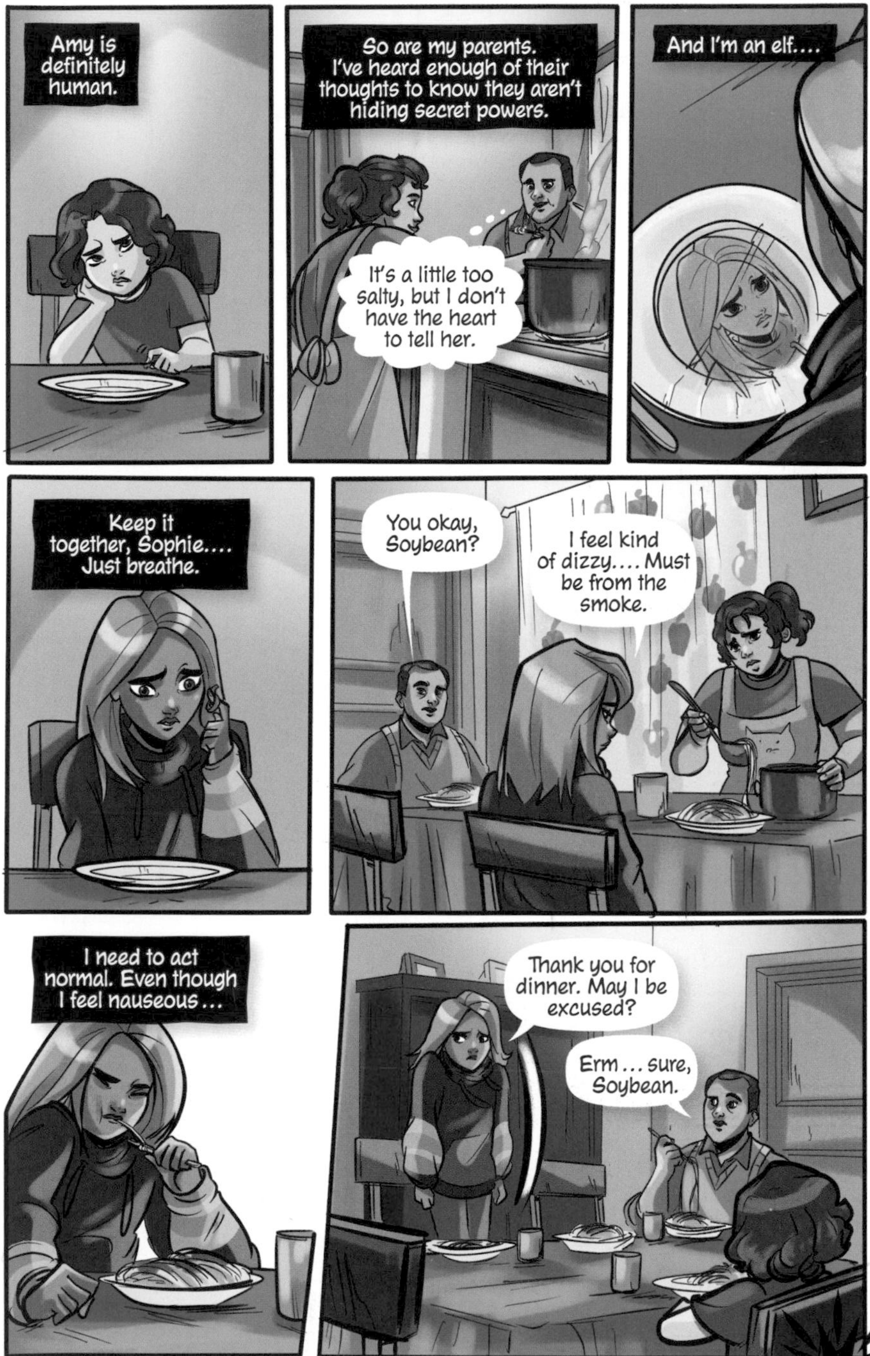

Amy is definitely human.
So are my parents. I've heard enough of their thoughts to know they aren't hiding secret powers.
It's a little too salty, but I don't have the heart to tell her.
And I'm an elf....
Keep it together, Sophie.... Just breathe.
You okay, Soybean?
I feel kind of dizzy.... Must be from the smoke.
I need to act normal. Even though I feel nauseous...
Thank you for dinner. May I be excused?
Erm... sure, Soybean.

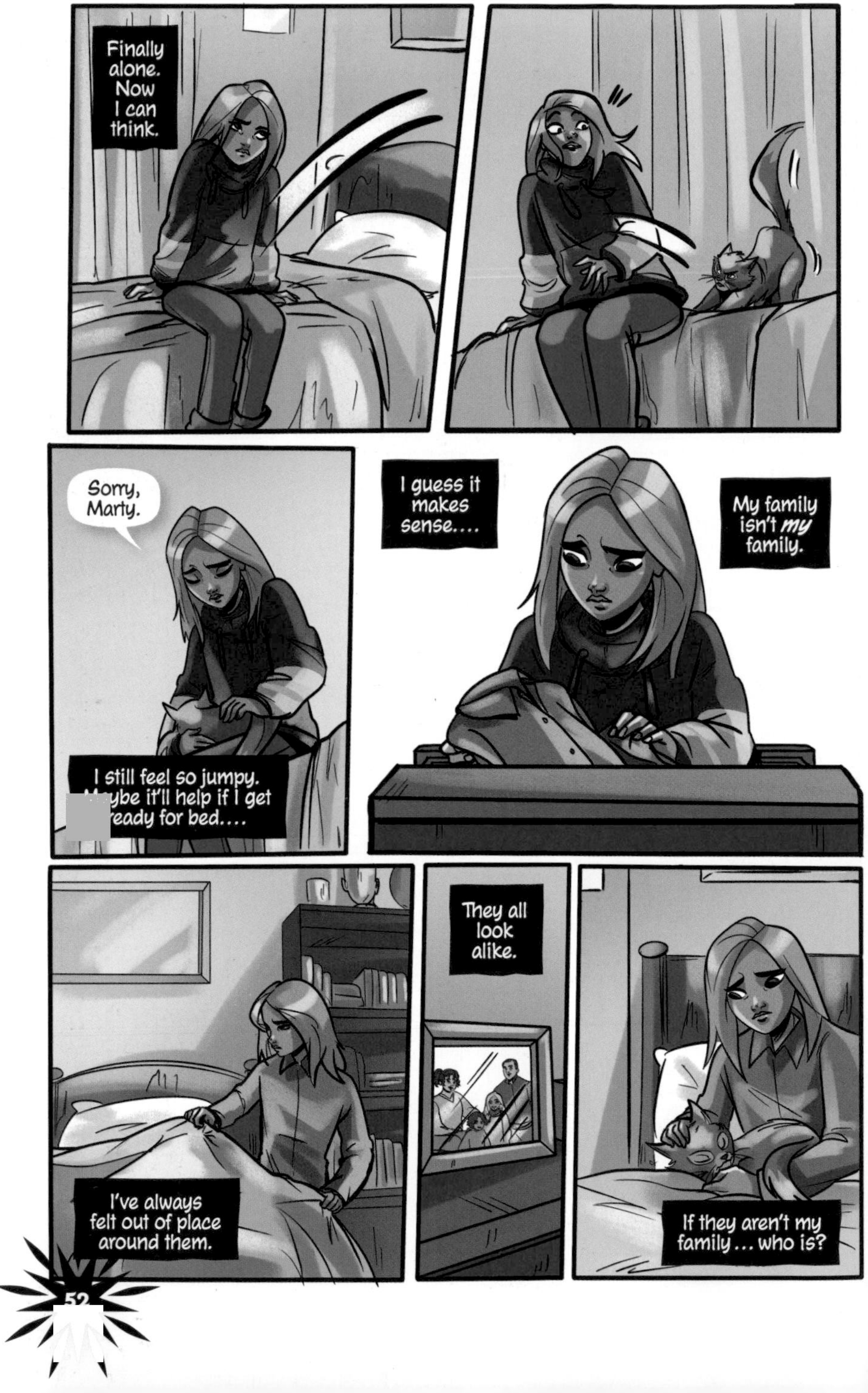
Finally alone. Now I can think.
Sorry, Marty.
I still feel so jumpy. Maybe it'll help if I get ready for bed....
I guess it makes sense....
My family isn't *my* family.
I've always felt out of place around them.
They all look alike.
If they aren't my family... who is?

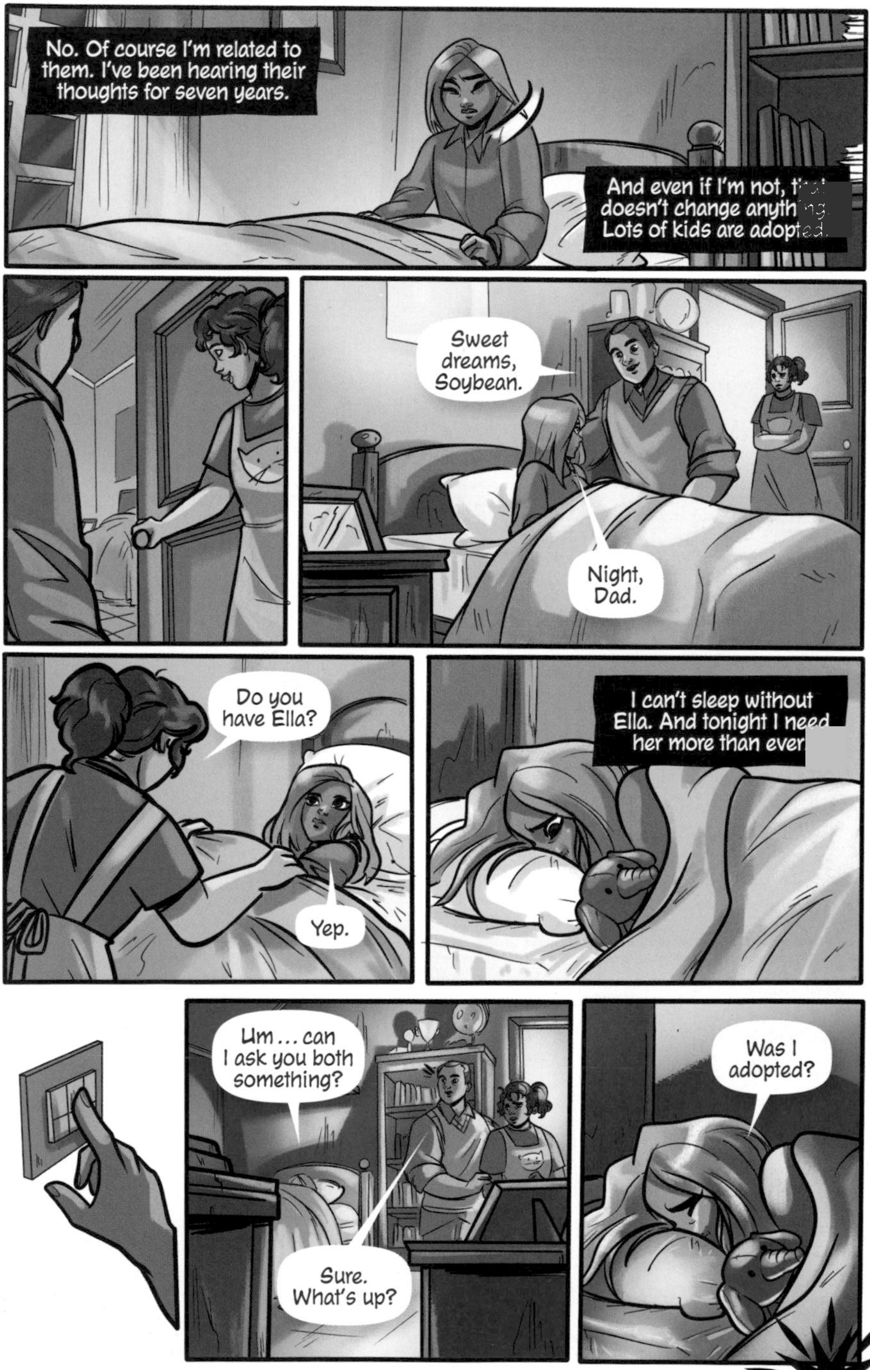
No. Of course I'm related to them. I've been hearing their thoughts for seven years.
And even if I'm not, that doesn't change anything. Lots of kids are adopted.
Sweet dreams, Soybean.
Night, Dad.
Do you have Ella?
Yep.
I can't sleep without Ella. And tonight I need her more than ever.
Um… can I ask you both something?
Sure. What's up?
Was I adopted?

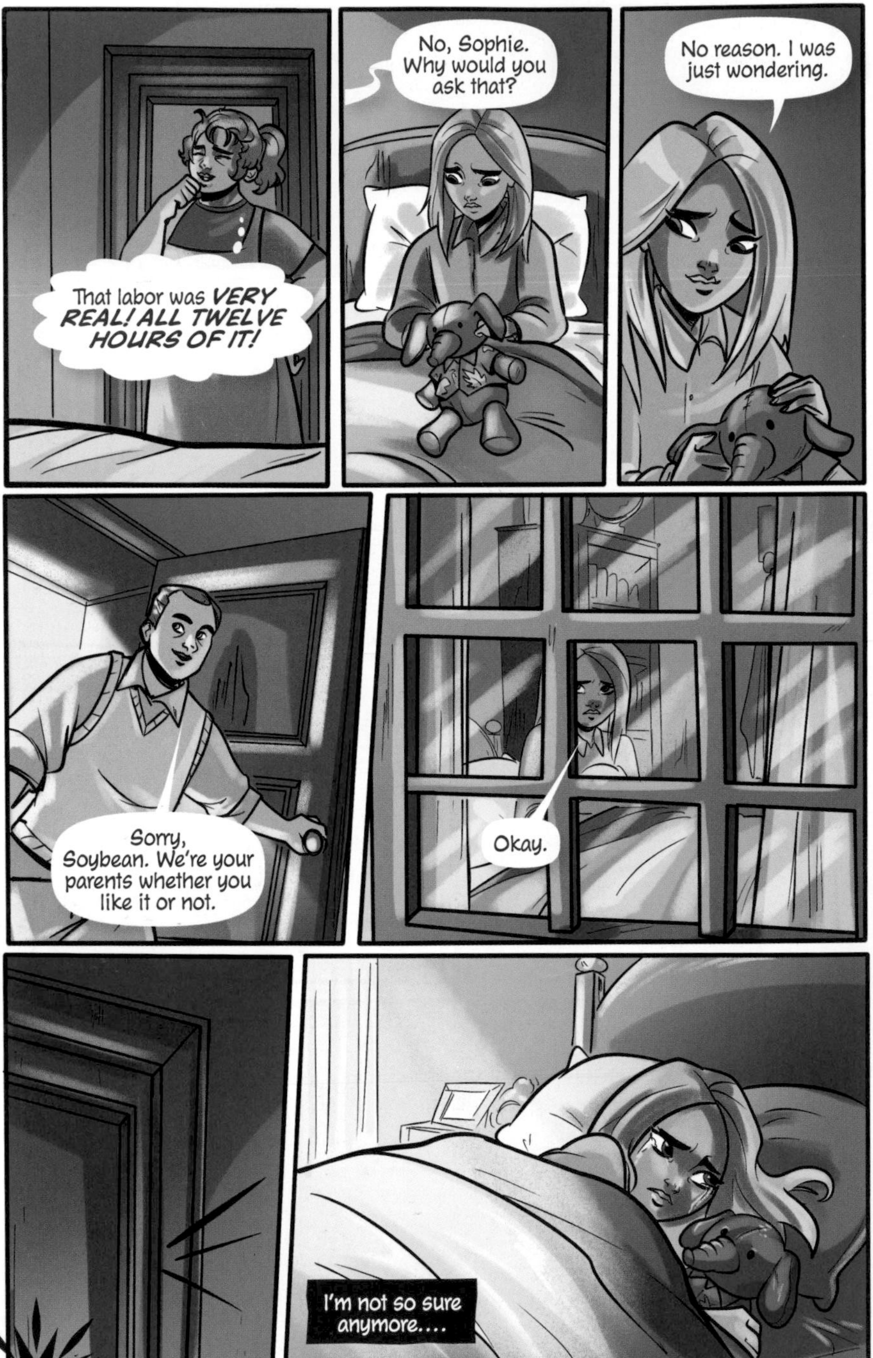
That labor was **VERY REAL! ALL TWELVE HOURS OF IT!**
No, Sophie. Why would you ask that?
No reason. I was just wondering.
Sorry, Soybean. We're your parents whether you like it or not.
Okay.
I'm not so sure anymore....

CHAPTER SIX

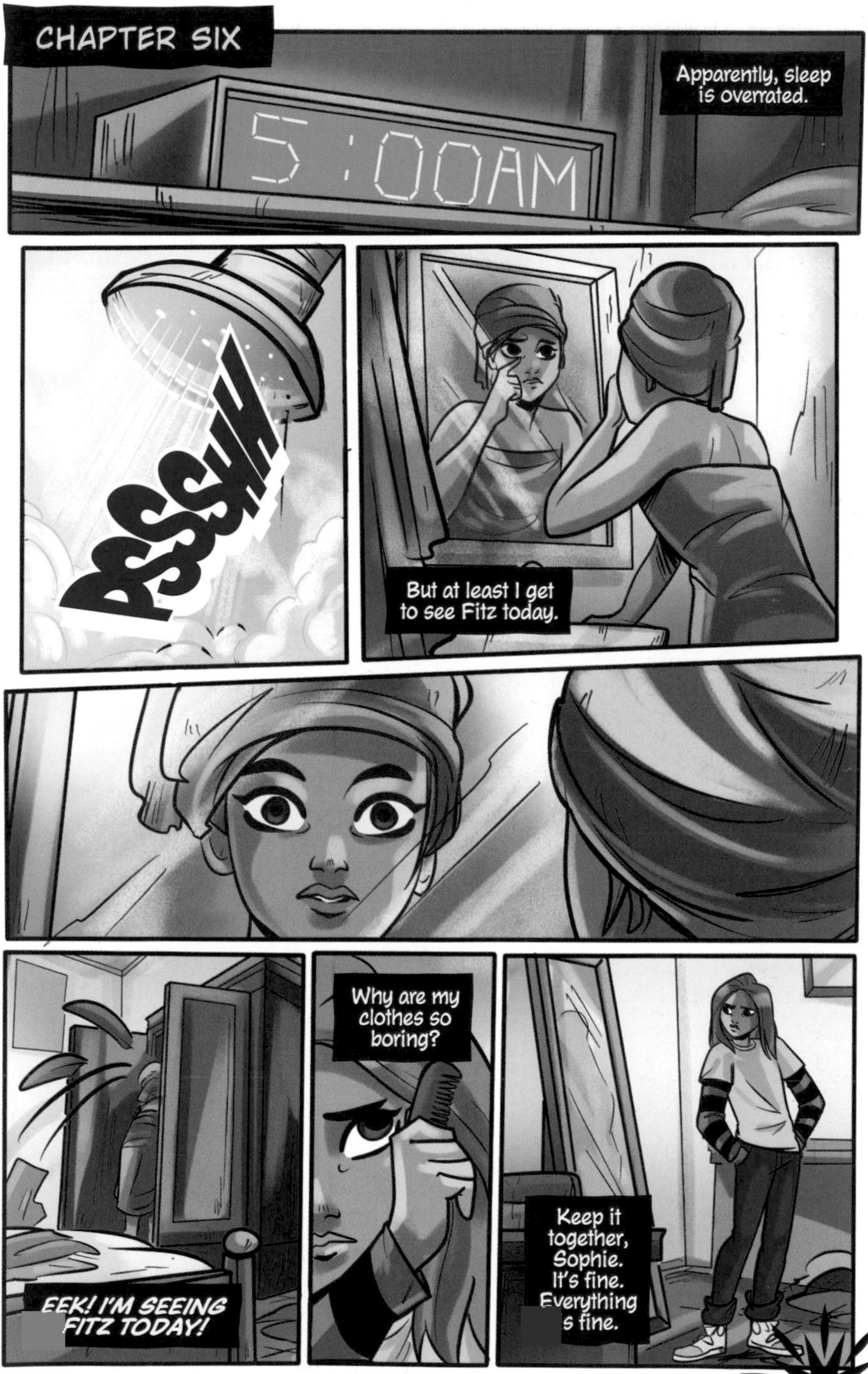
5:00AM
Apparently, sleep is overrated.
PSSSHH
But at least I get to see Fitz today.
EEK! I'M SEEING FITZ TODAY!
Why are my clothes so boring?
Keep it together, Sophie. It's fine. Everything
s fine.

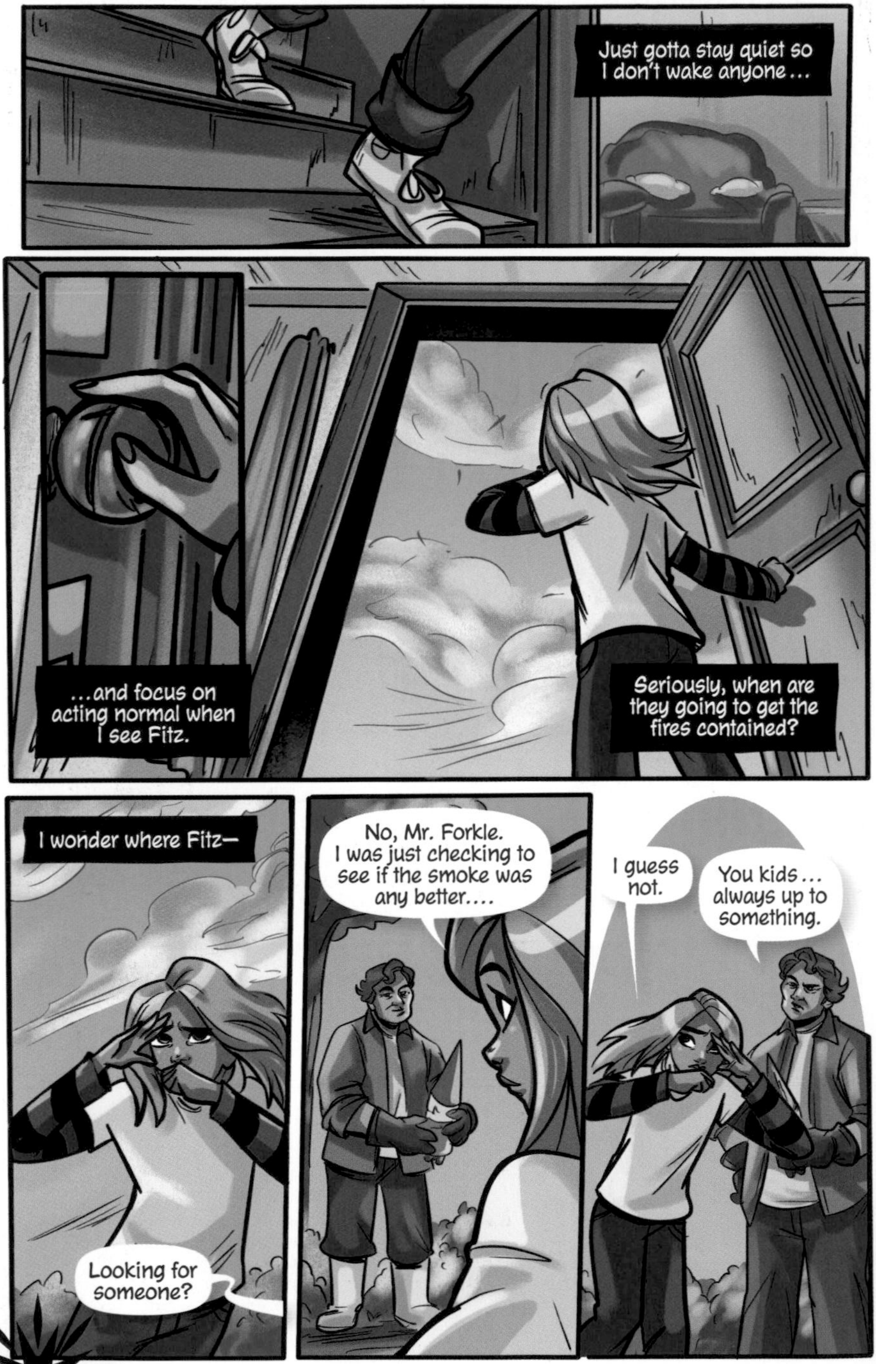
Just gotta stay quiet so I don't wake anyone...
...and focus on acting normal when I see Fitz.
Seriously, when are they going to get the fires contained?
I wonder where Fitz—
Looking for someone?
No, Mr. Forkle. I was just checking to see if the smoke was any better....
I guess not.
You kids... always up to something.

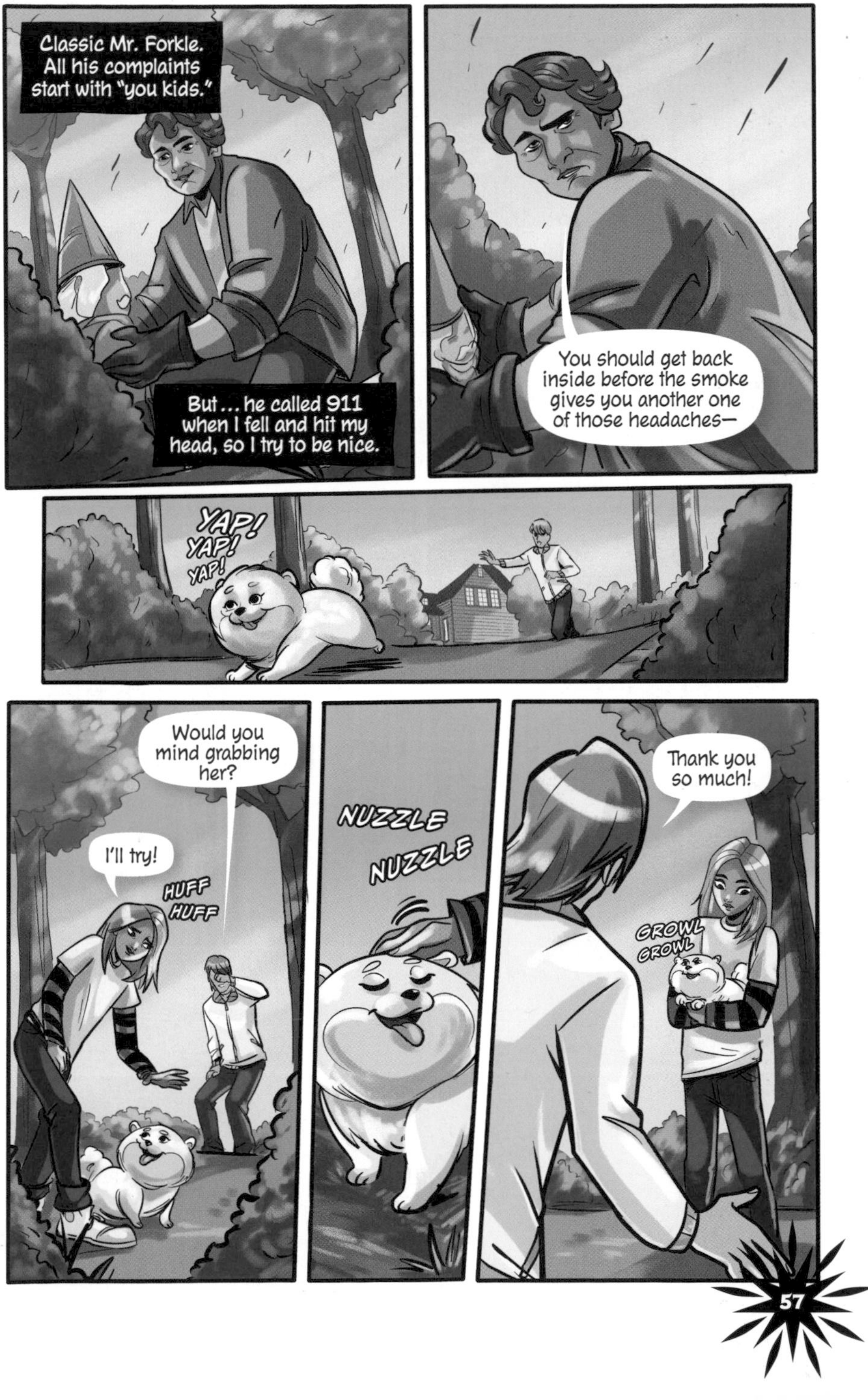
Classic Mr. Forkle. All his complaints start with "you kids."
But... he called 911 when I fell and hit my head, so I try to be nice.
You should get back inside before the smoke gives you another one of those headaches—
YAP!
YAP!
YAP!
Would you mind grabbing her?
I'll try!
HUFF
HUFF
NUZZLE
NUZZLE
Thank you so much!
GROWL
GROWL

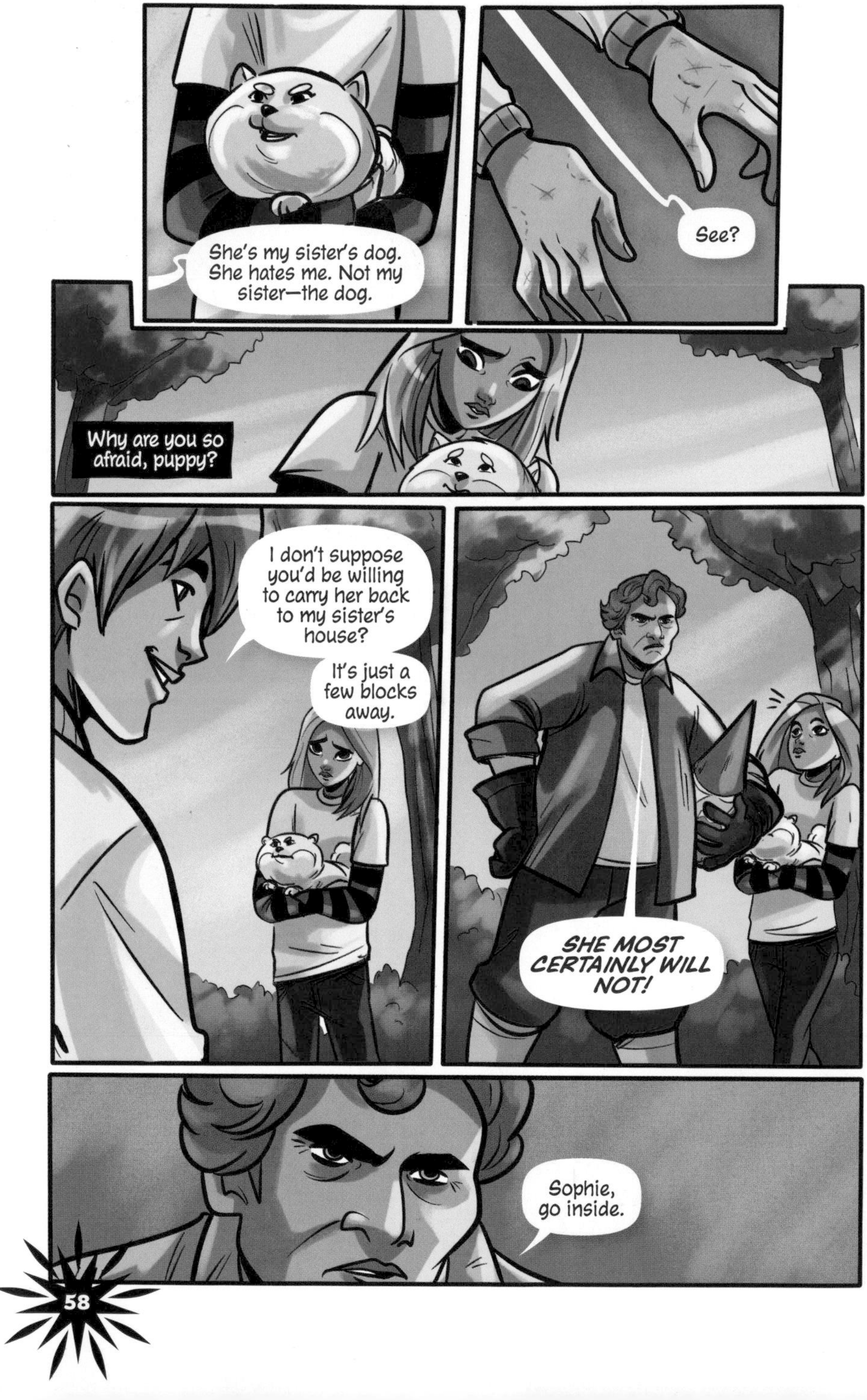

She's my sister's dog. She hates me. Not my sister—the dog.
See?
Why are you so afraid, puppy?
I don't suppose you'd be willing to carry her back to my sister's house?
It's just a few blocks away.
SHE MOST CERTAINLY WILL NOT!
Sophie, go inside.

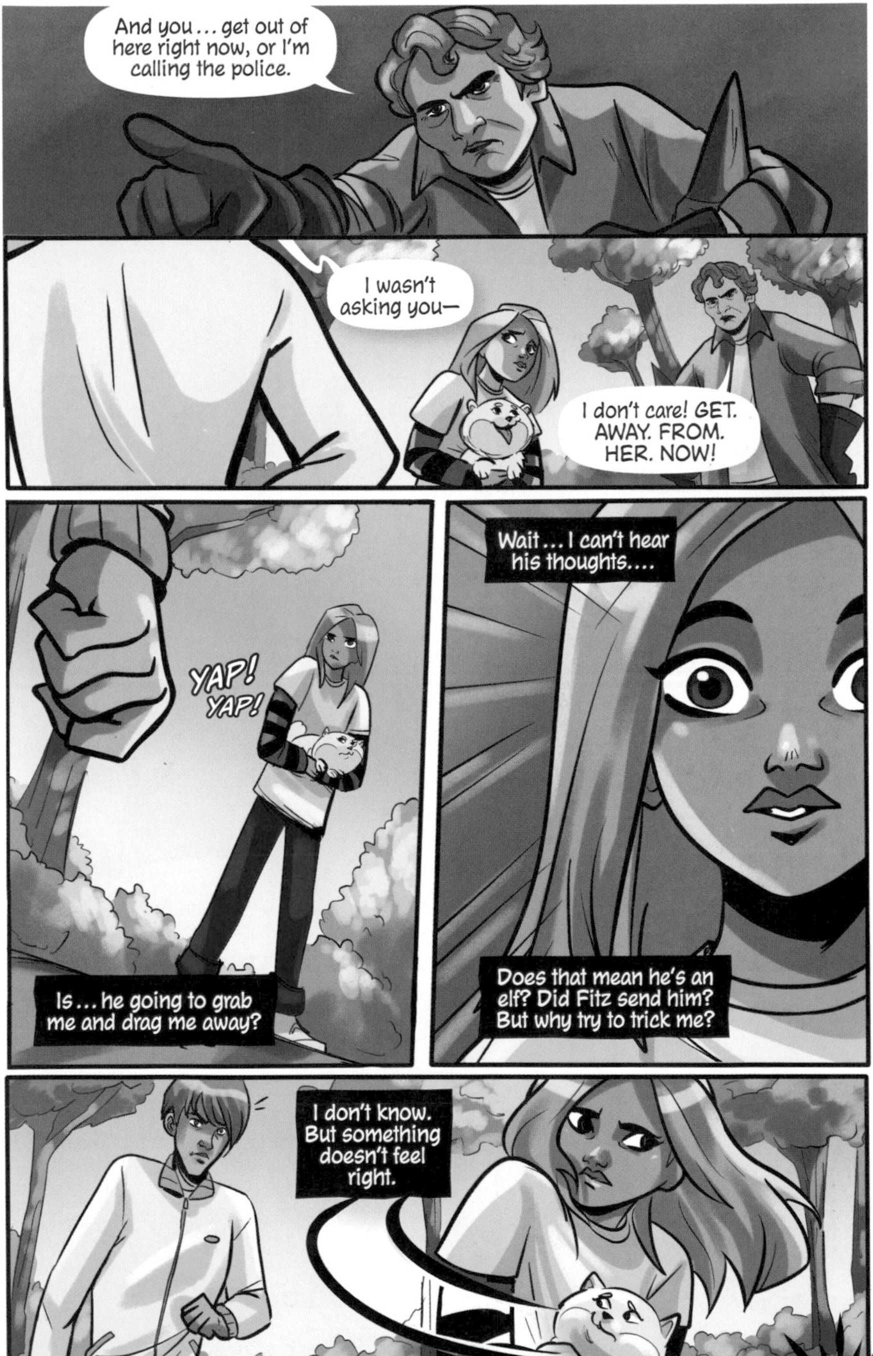
And you... get out of here right now, or I'm calling the police.
I wasn't asking you—
I don't care! GET. AWAY. FROM. HER. NOW!
YAP! YAP!
Is... he going to grab me and drag me away?
Wait... I can't hear his thoughts....
Does that mean he's an elf? Did Fitz send him? But why try to trick me?
I don't know. But something doesn't feel right.

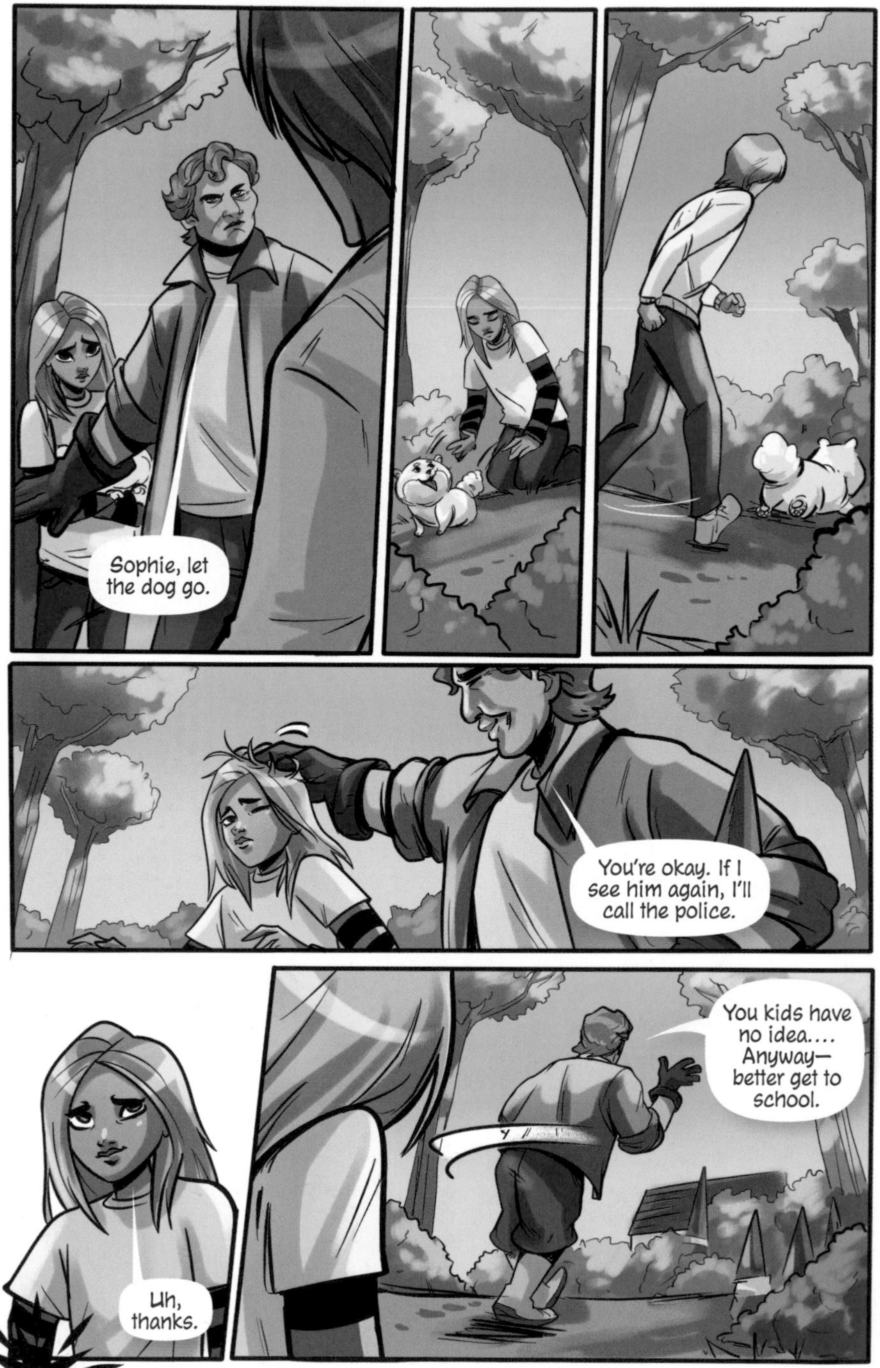
Sophie, let the dog go.
You're okay. If I see him again, I'll call the police.
Uh, thanks.
You kids have no idea.... Anyway— better get to school.

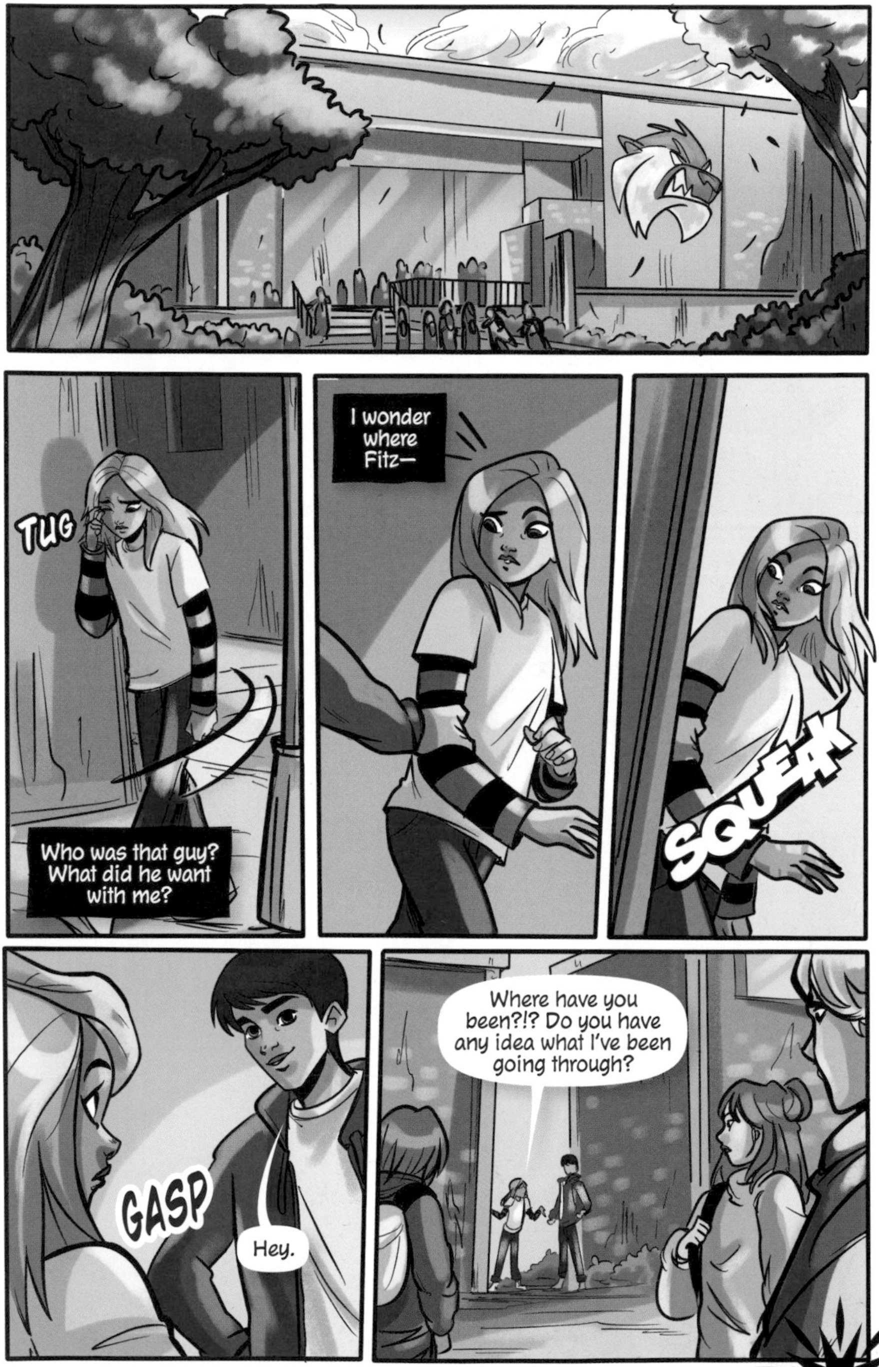
TUG
Who was that guy? What did he want with me?
I wonder where Fitz—
SQUEAK
GASP
Hey.
Where have you been?!? Do you have any idea what I've been going through?

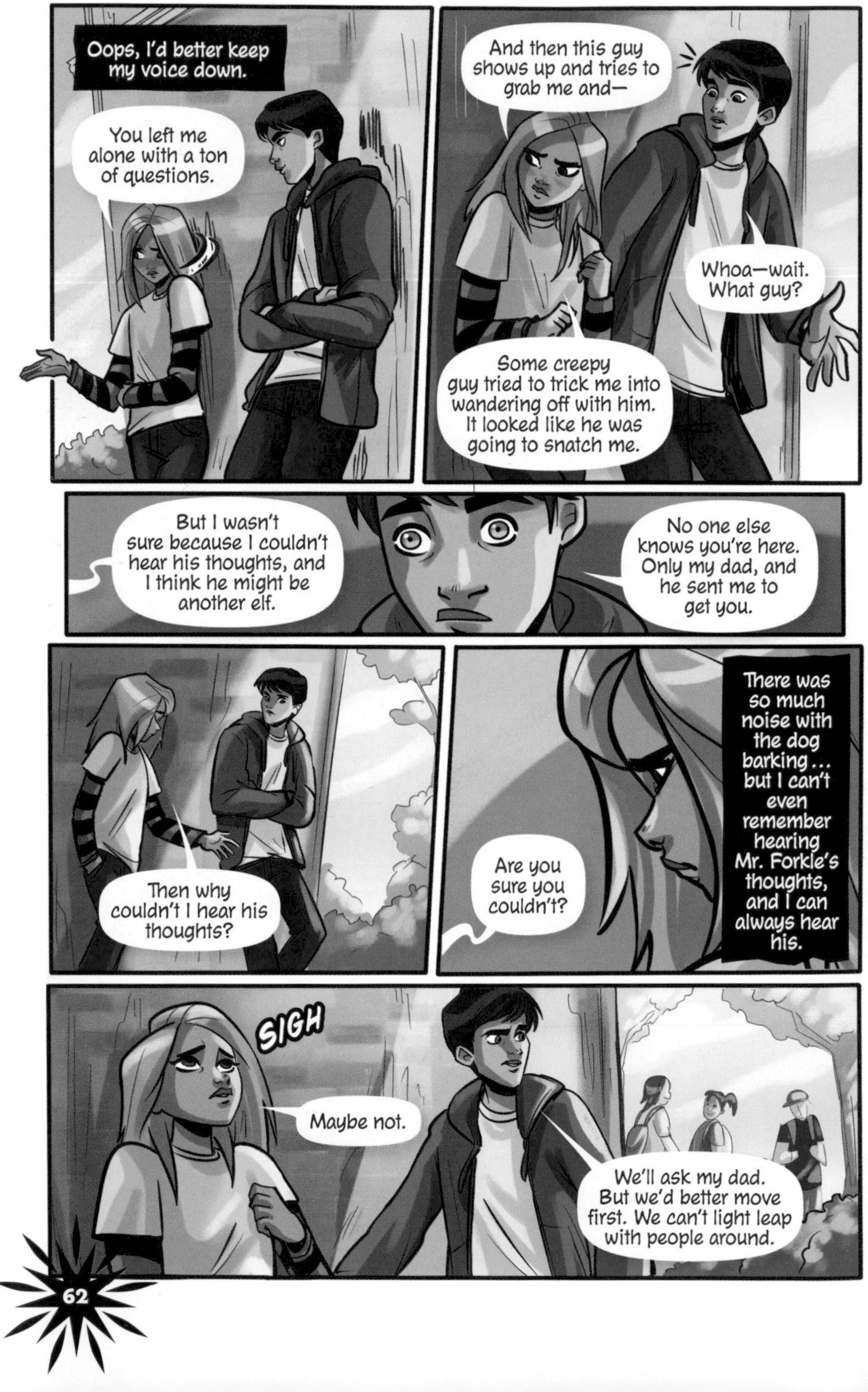
Oops, I'd better keep my voice down.
You left me alone with a ton of questions.
And then this guy shows up and tries to grab me and—
Whoa—wait. What guy?
Some creepy guy tried to trick me into wandering off with him. It looked like he was going to snatch me.
But I wasn't sure because I couldn't hear his thoughts, and I think he might be another elf.
No one else knows you're here. Only my dad, and he sent me to get you.
Then why couldn't I hear his thoughts?
Are you sure you couldn't?
There was so much noise with the dog barking... but I can't even remember hearing Mr. Forkle's thoughts, and I can always hear his.
SIGH
Maybe not.
We'll ask my dad. But we'd better move first. We can't light leap with people around.

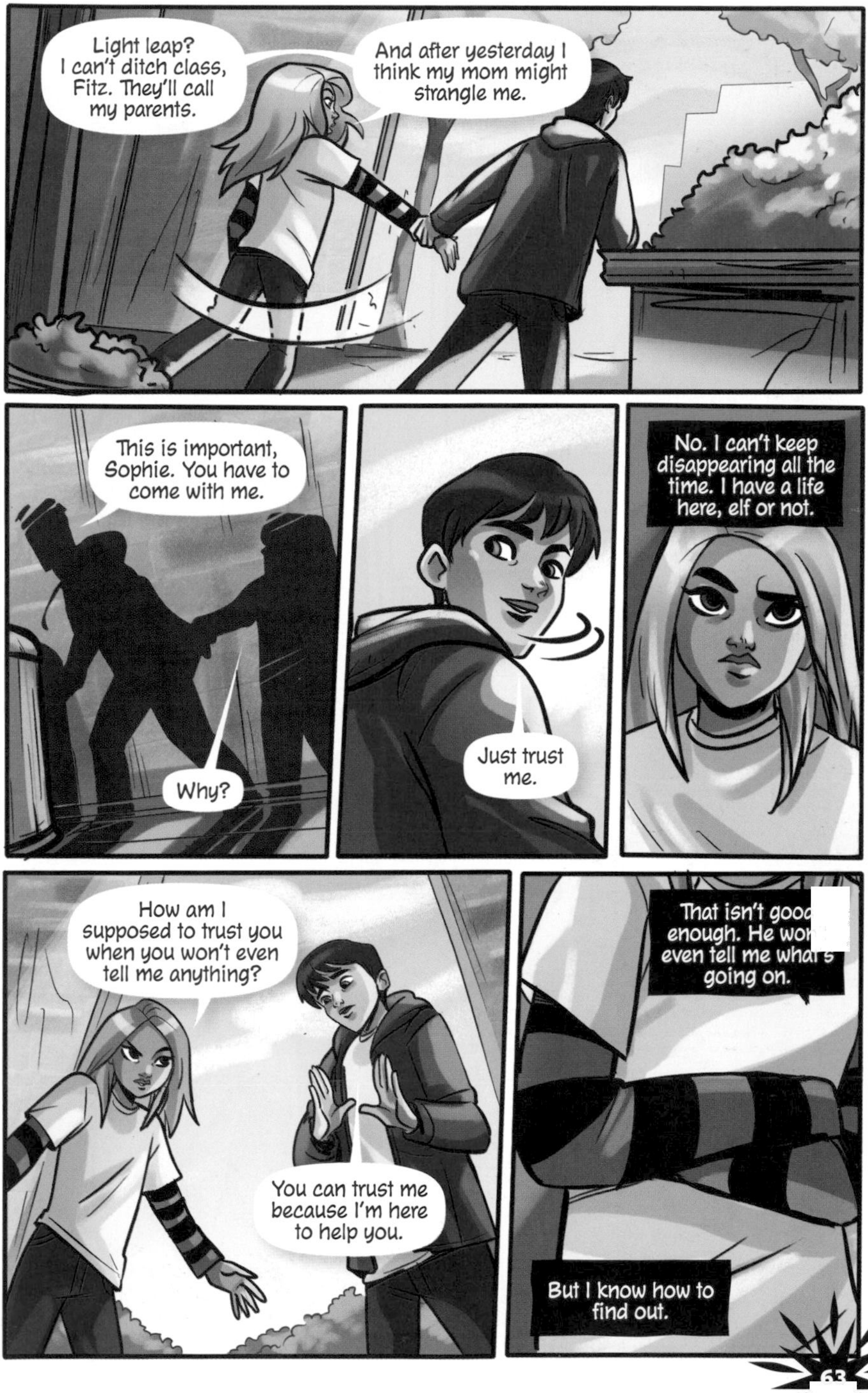
Light leap? I can't ditch class, Fitz. They'll call my parents.
And after yesterday I think my mom might strangle me.
This is important, Sophie. You have to come with me.
Why?
Just trust me.
No. I can't keep disappearing all the time. I have a life here, elf or not.
How am I supposed to trust you when you won't even tell me anything?
You can trust me because I'm here to help you.
That isn't good enough. He wor even tell me wha going on.
But I know how to find out.

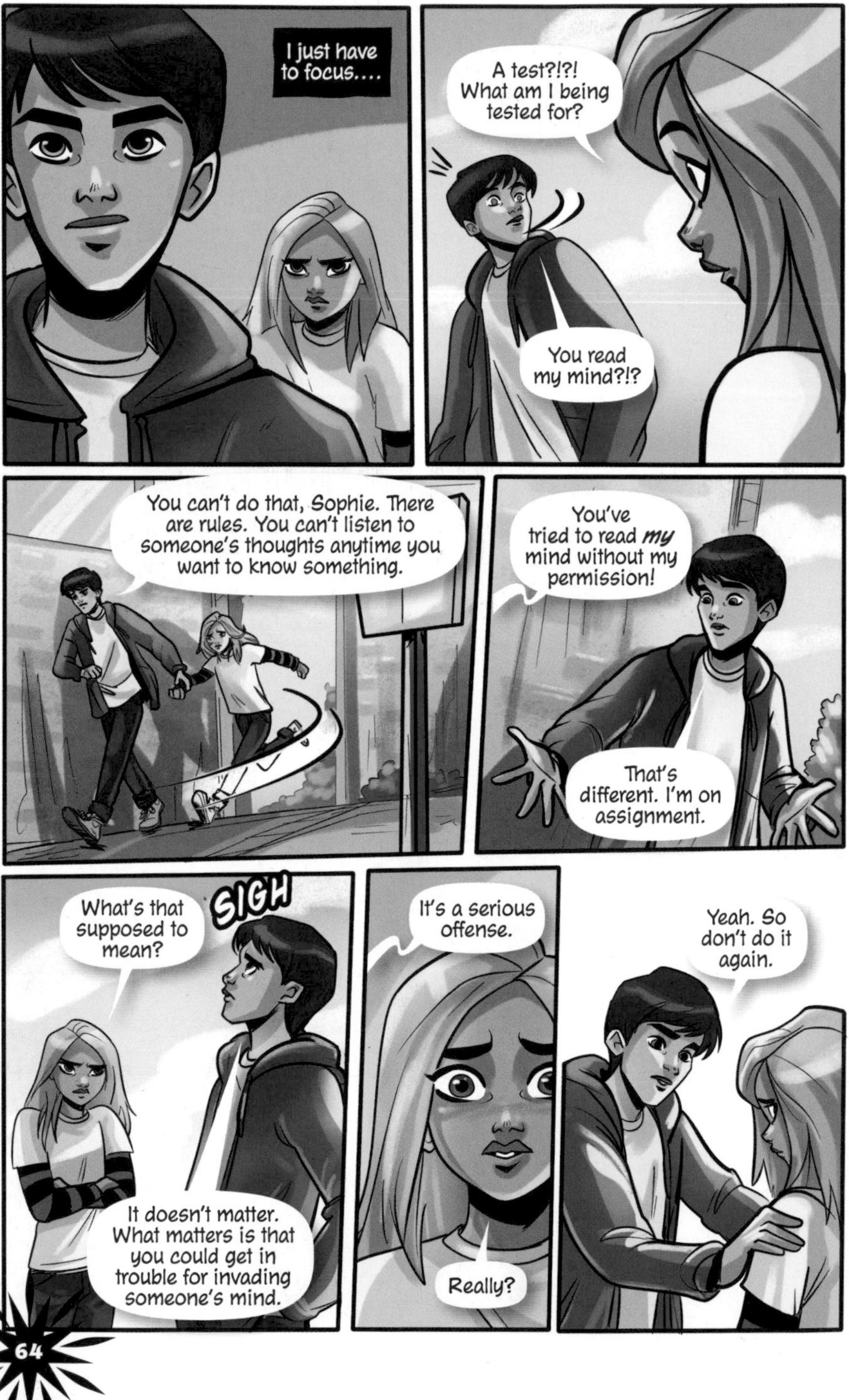
I just have to focus....
A test?!?! What am I being tested for?
You read my mind?!?
You can't do that, Sophie. There are rules. You can't listen to someone's thoughts anytime you want to know something.
You've tried to read *my* mind without my permission!
That's different. I'm on assignment.
What's that supposed to mean?
SIGH
It doesn't matter. What matters is that you could get in trouble for invading someone's mind.
It's a serious offense.
Really?
Yeah. So don't do it again.

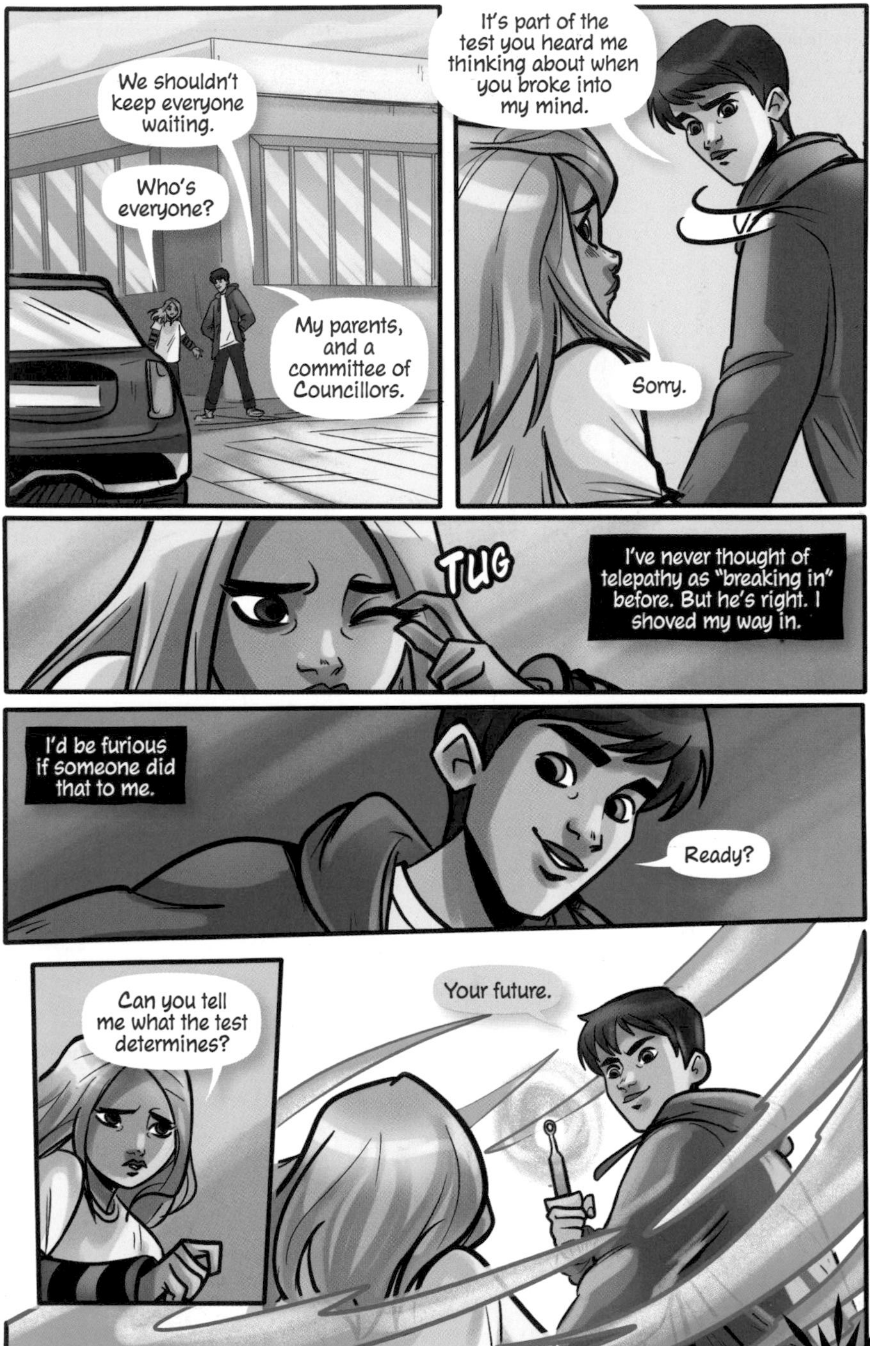

We shouldn't keep everyone waiting.
Who's everyone?
My parents, and a committee of Councillors.
It's part of the test you heard me thinking about when you broke into my mind.
Sorry.
TUG
I've never thought of telepathy as "breaking in" before. But he's right. I shoved my way in.
I'd be furious if someone did that to me.
Ready?
Can you tell me what the test determines?
Your future.

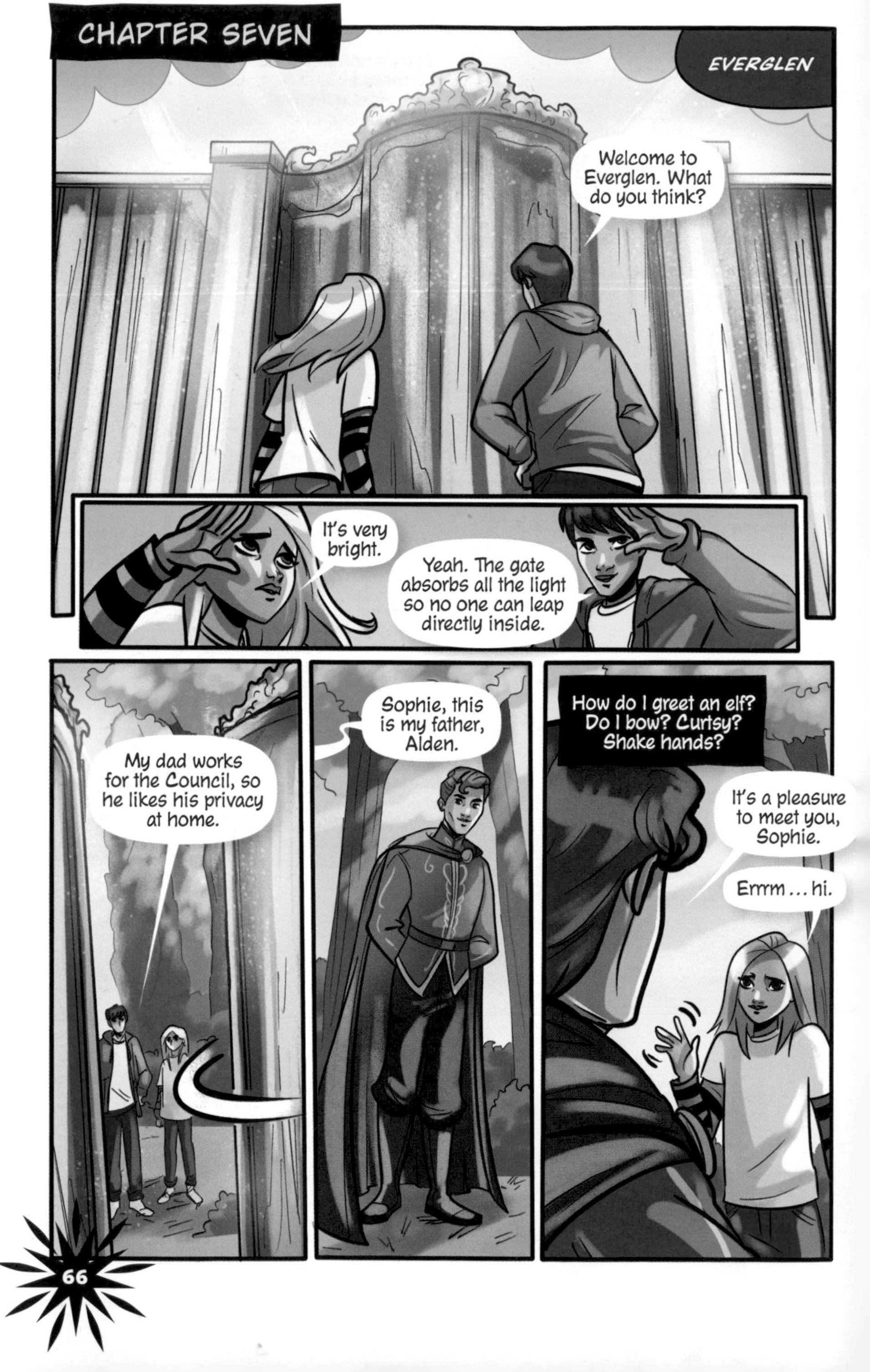
CHAPTER SEVEN
EVERGLEN
Welcome to Everglen. What do you think?
It's very bright.
Yeah. The gate absorbs all the light so no one can leap directly inside.
My dad works for the Council, so he likes his privacy at home.
Sophie, this is my father, Alden.
How do I greet an elf? Do I bow? Curtsy? Shake hands?
It's a pleasure to meet you, Sophie.
Errrm ... hi.

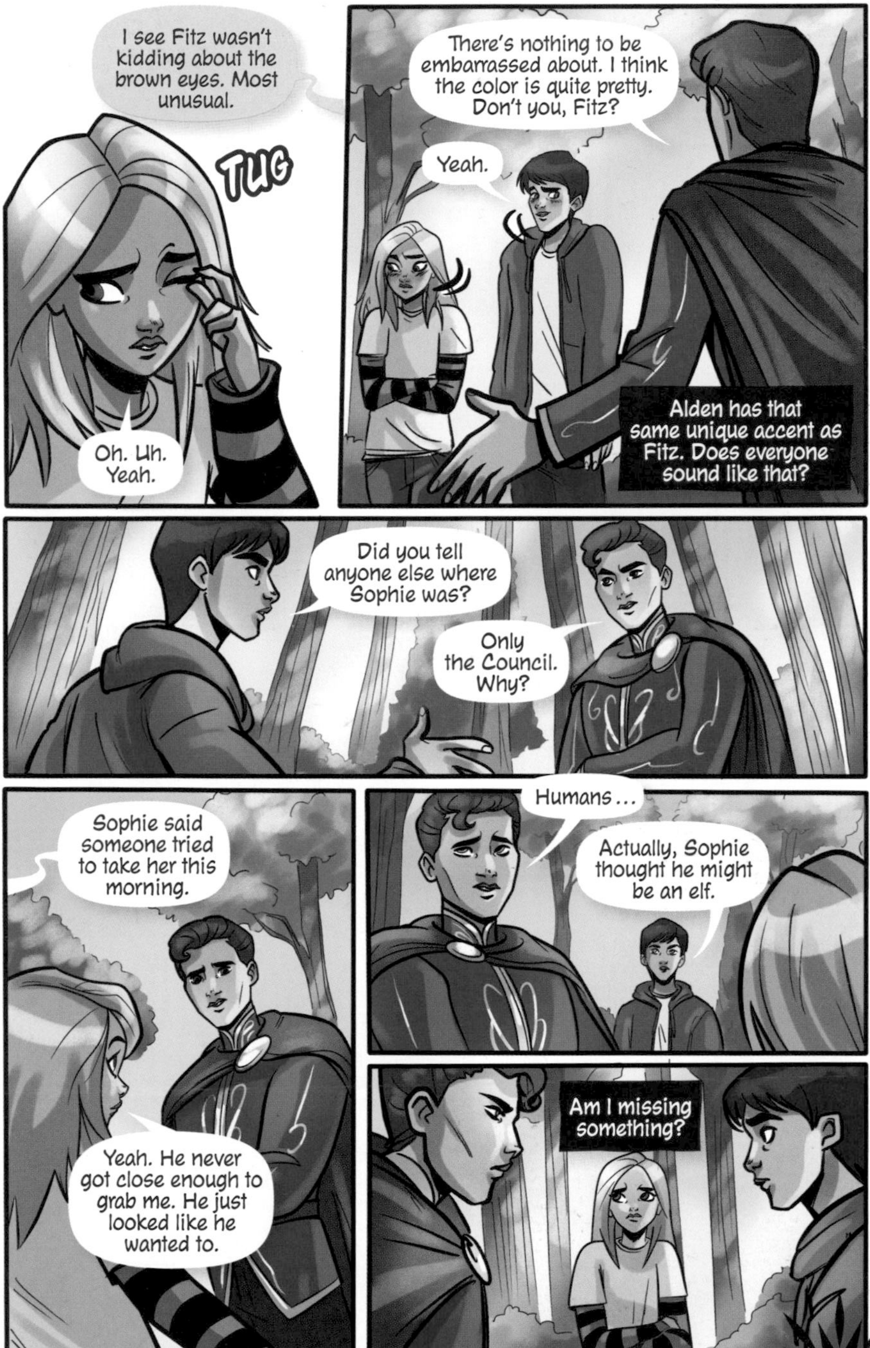
I see Fitz wasn't kidding about the brown eyes. Most unusual.
TUG
Oh. Uh. Yeah.
There's nothing to be embarrassed about. I think the color is quite pretty. Don't you, Fitz?
Yeah.
Alden has that same unique accent as Fitz. Does everyone sound like that?
Did you tell anyone else where Sophie was?
Only the Council. Why?
Sophie said someone tried to take her this morning.
Yeah. He never got close enough to grab me. He just looked like he wanted to.
Humans…
Actually, Sophie thought he might be an elf.
Am I missing something?

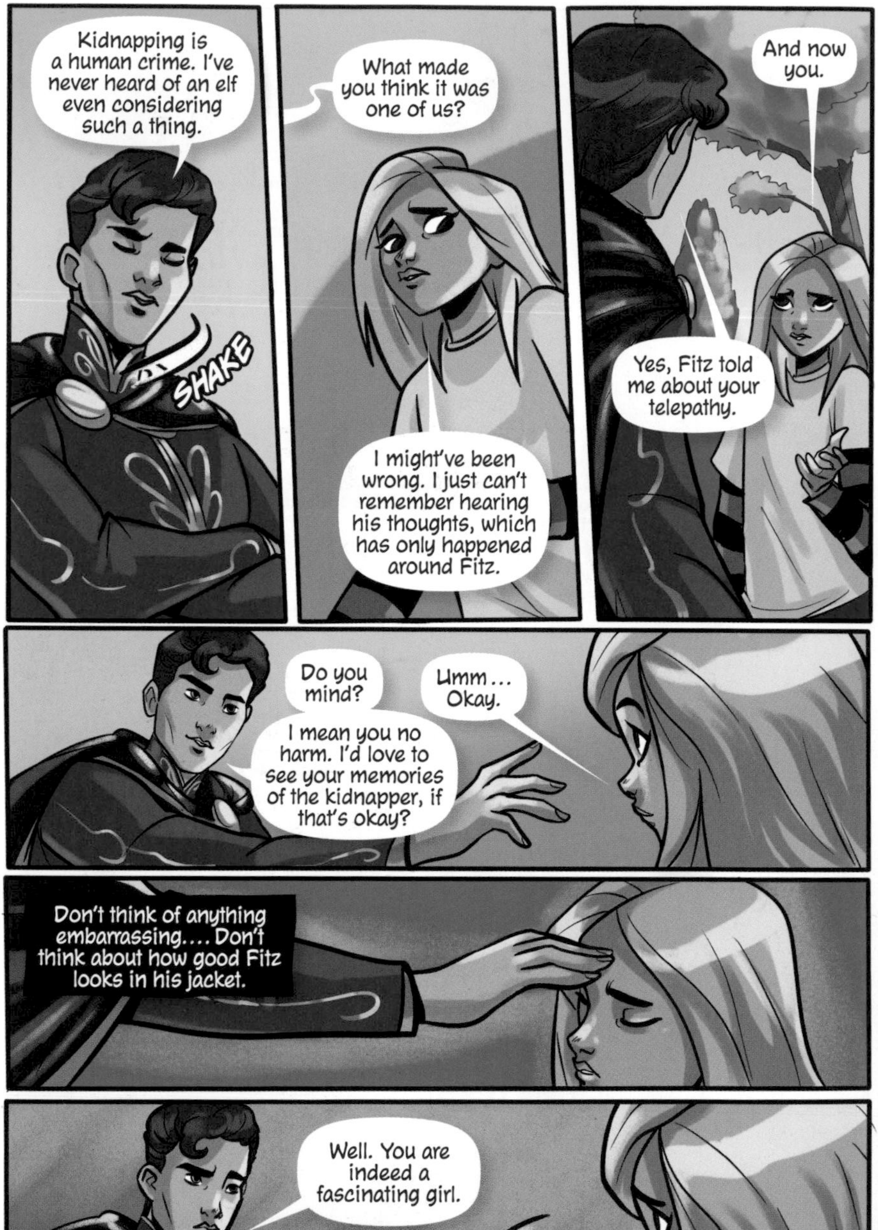
Kidnapping is a human crime. I've never heard of an elf even considering such a thing.
SHAKE
What made you think it was one of us?
I might've been wrong. I just can't remember hearing his thoughts, which has only happened around Fitz.
And now you.
Yes, Fitz told me about your telepathy.
Do you mind?
I mean you no harm. I'd love to see your memories of the kidnapper, if that's okay?
Umm... Okay.
Don't think of anything embarrassing.... Don't think about how good Fitz looks in his jacket.
Well. You are indeed a fascinating girl.

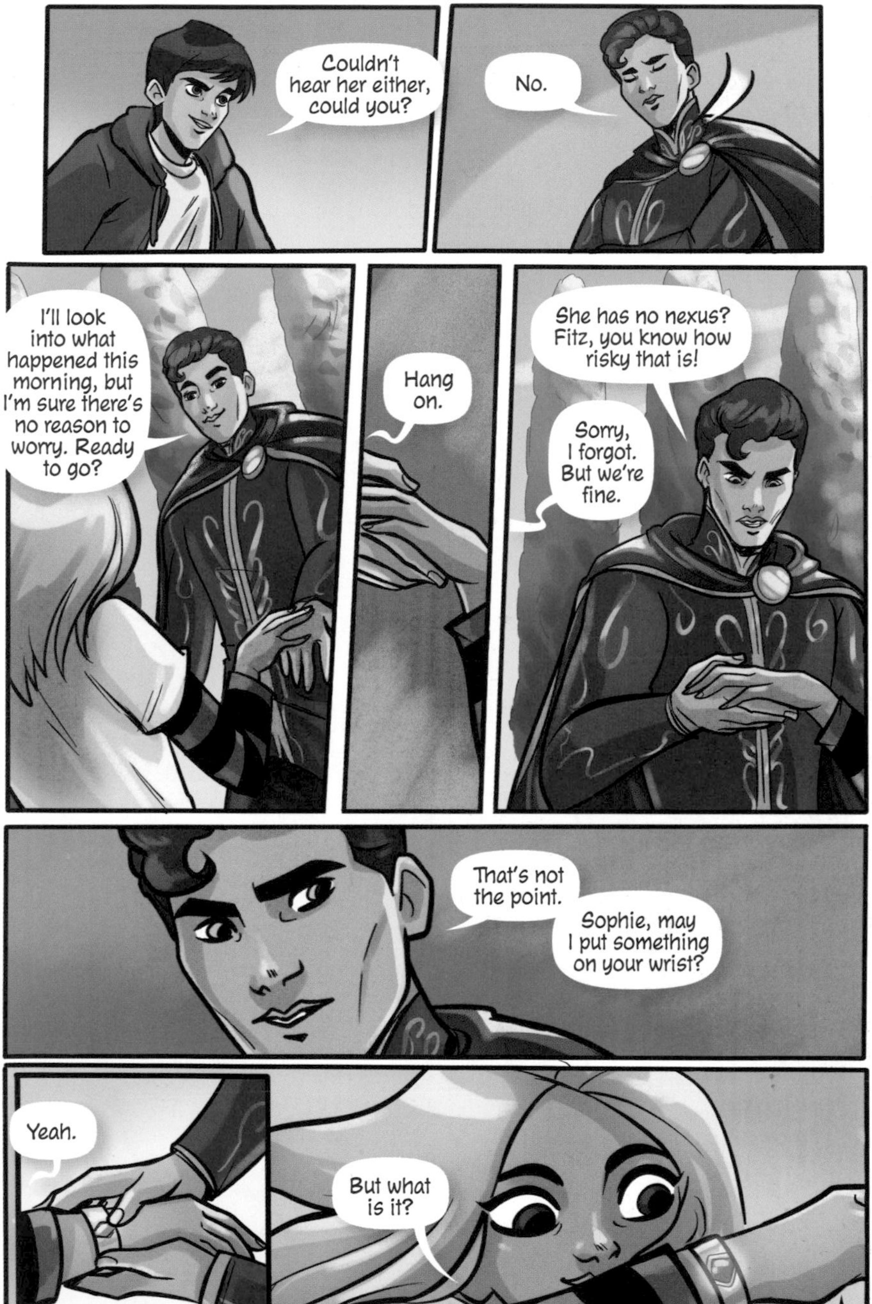
Couldn't hear her either, could you?
No.
I'll look into what happened this morning, but I'm sure there's no reason to worry. Ready to go?
Hang on.
She has no nexus? Fitz, you know how risky that is!
Sorry, I forgot. But we're fine.
That's not the point.
Sophie, may I put something on your wrist?
Yeah.
But what is it?

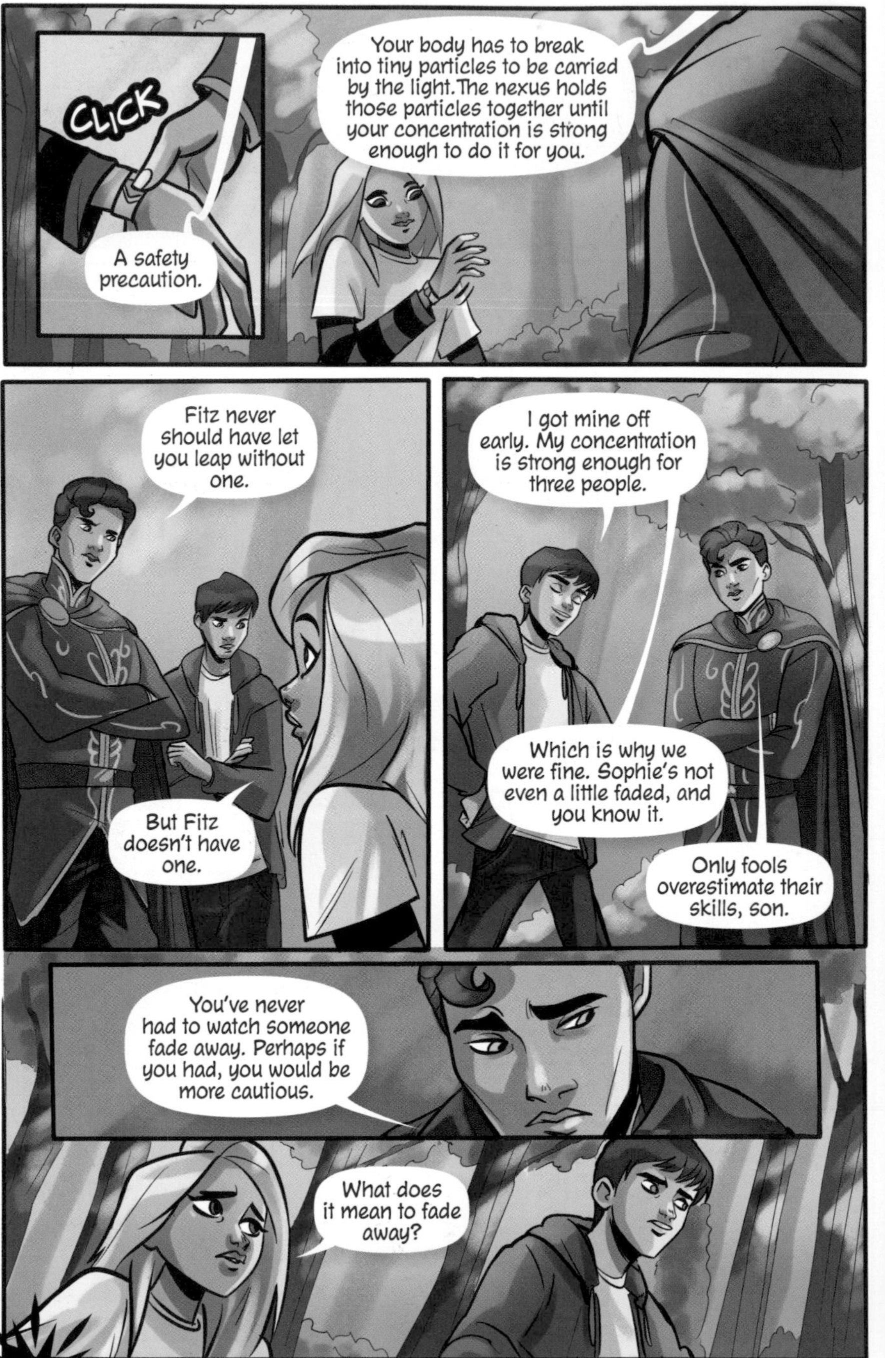
CLICK
A safety precaution.
Your body has to break into tiny particles to be carried by the light. The nexus holds those particles together until your concentration is strong enough to do it for you.
Fitz never should have let you leap without one.
But Fitz doesn't have one.
I got mine off early. My concentration is strong enough for three people.
Which is why we were fine. Sophie's not even a little faded, and you know it.
Only fools overestimate their skills, son.
You've never had to watch someone fade away. Perhaps if you had, you would be more cautious.
What does it mean to fade away?

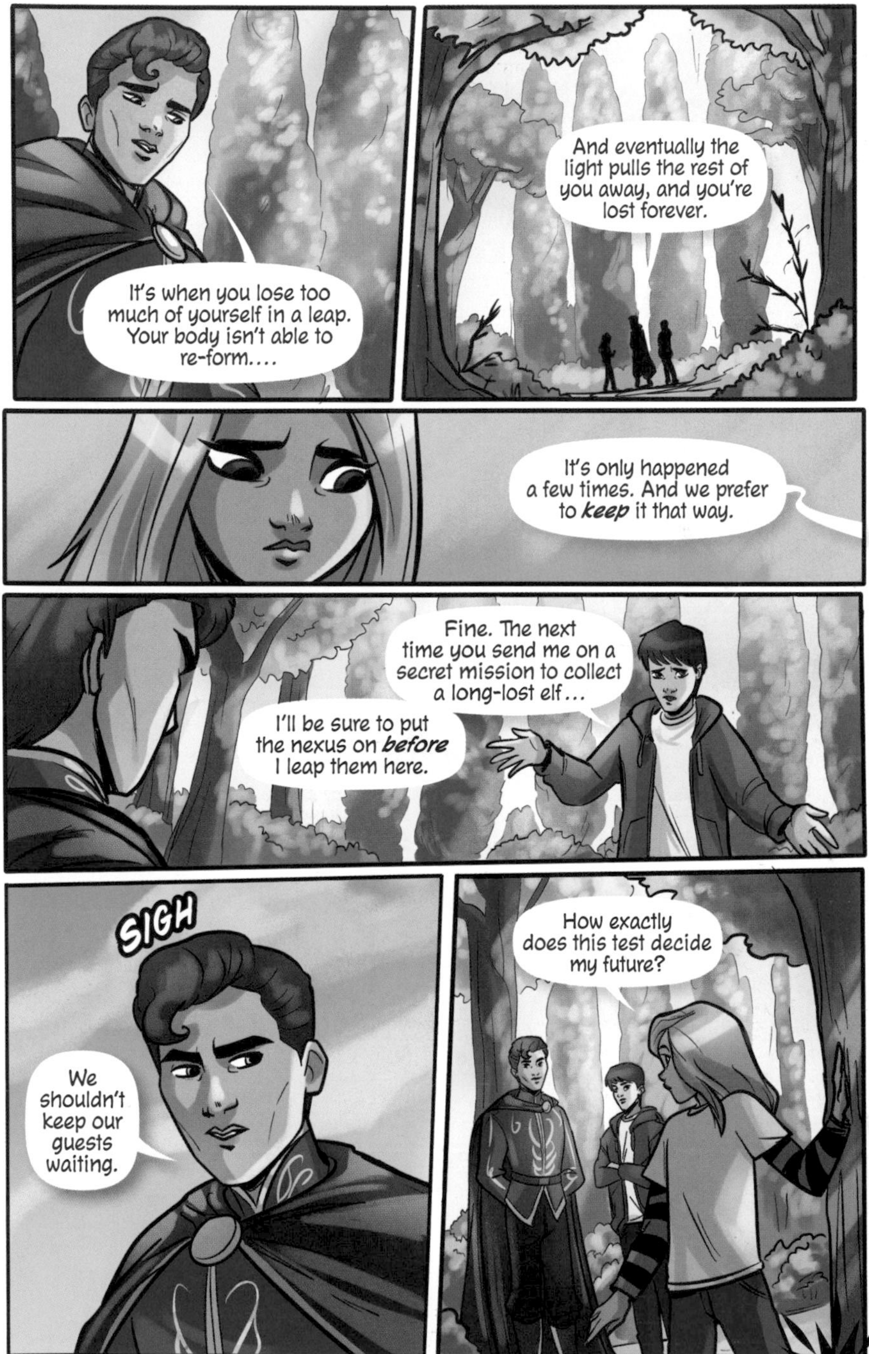
It's when you lose too much of yourself in a leap. Your body isn't able to re-form....
And eventually the light pulls the rest of you away, and you're lost forever.
It's only happened a few times. And we prefer to *keep* it that way.
Fine. The next time you send me on a secret mission to collect a long-lost elf...
I'll be sure to put the nexus on *before* I leap them here.
SIGH
We shouldn't keep our guests waiting.
How exactly does this test decide my future?

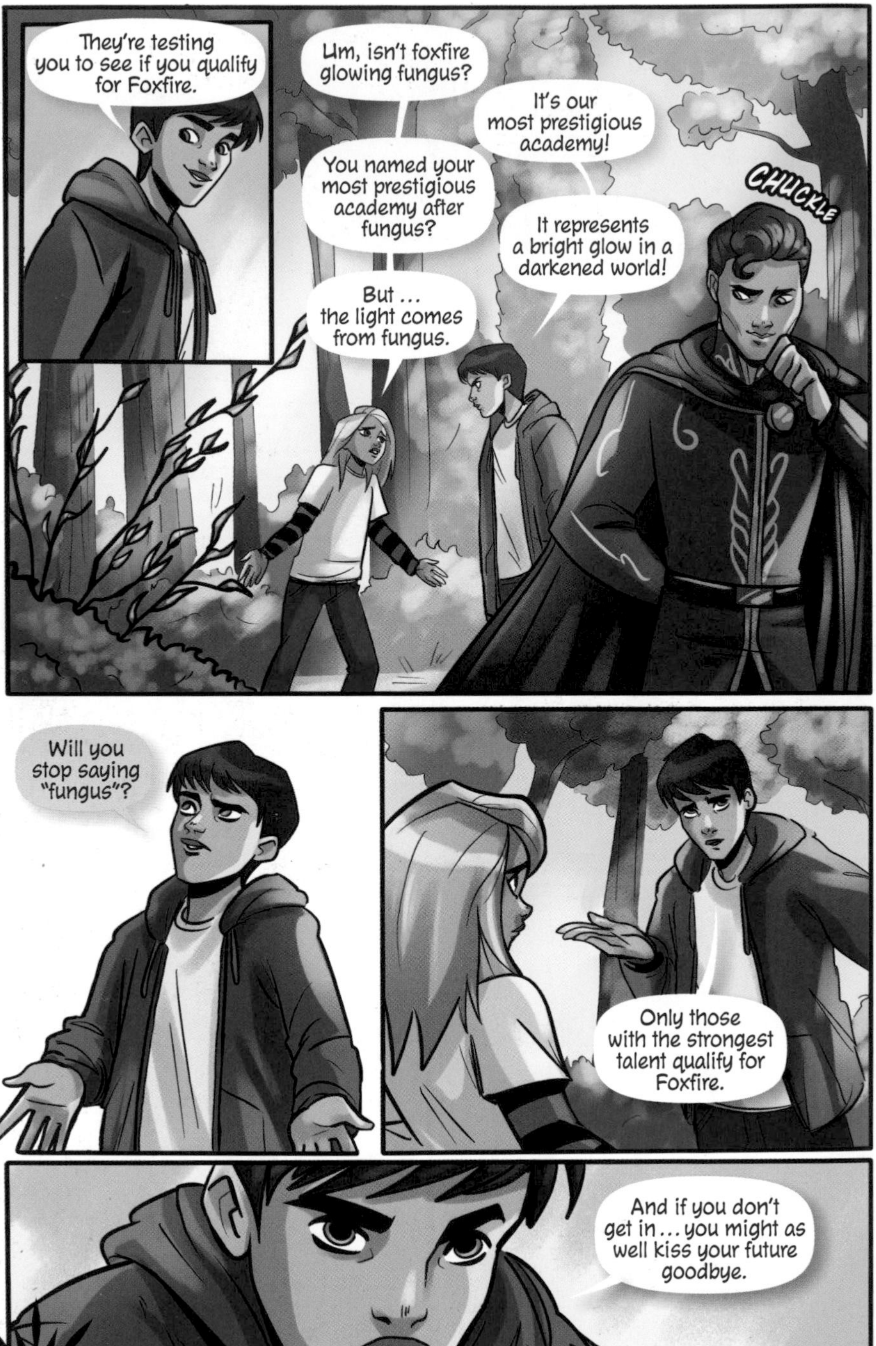
They're testing you to see if you qualify for Foxfire.
Um, isn't foxfire glowing fungus?
You named your most prestigious academy after fungus?
It's our most prestigious academy!
It represents a bright glow in a darkened world!
CHUCKLE
But … the light comes from fungus.
Will you stop saying "fungus"?
Only those with the strongest talent qualify for Foxfire.
And if you don't get in … you might as well kiss your future goodbye.

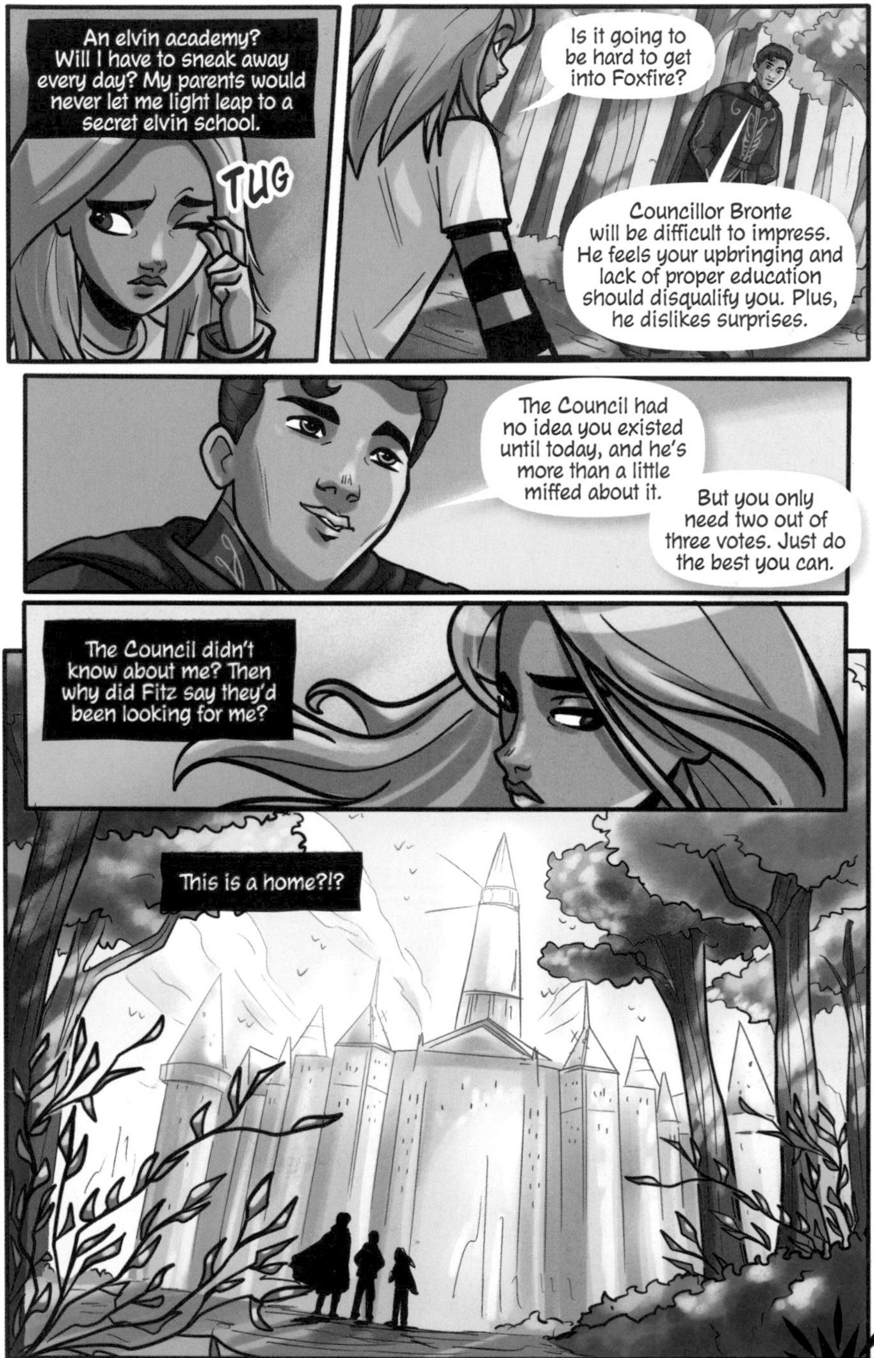
An elvin academy? Will I have to sneak away every day? My parents would never let me light leap to a secret elvin school.
TUG
Is it going to be hard to get into Foxfire?
Councillor Bronte will be difficult to impress. He feels your upbringing and lack of proper education should disqualify you. Plus, he dislikes surprises.
The Council had no idea you existed until today, and he's more than a little miffed about it.
But you only need two out of three votes. Just do the best you can.
The Council didn't know about me? Then why did Fitz say they'd been looking for me?
This is a home?!?

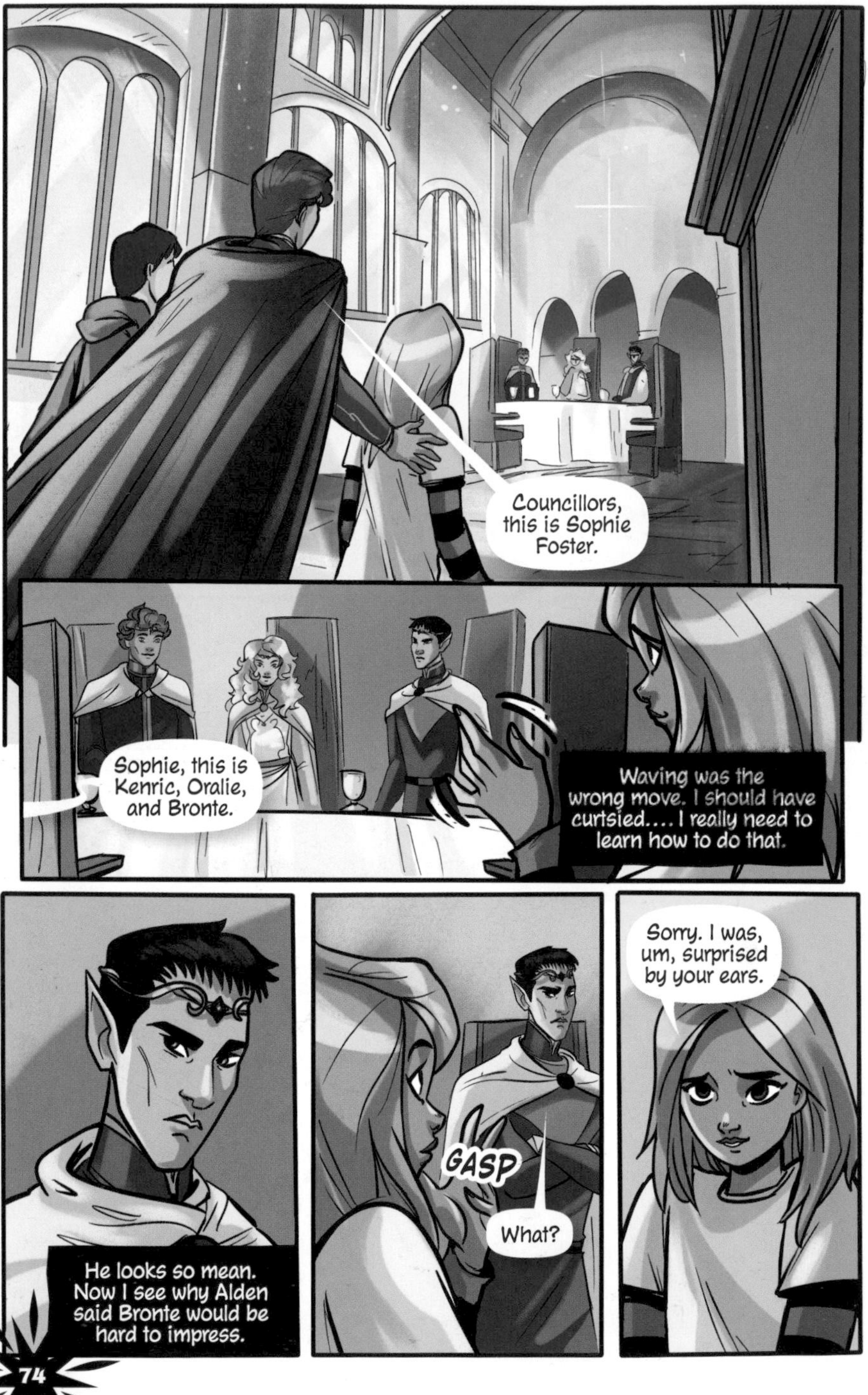
Councillors, this is Sophie Foster.
Sophie, this is Kenric, Oralie, and Bronte.
Waving was the wrong move. I should have curtsied.... I really need to learn how to do that.
He looks so mean. Now I see why Alden said Bronte would be hard to impress.
GASP
What?
Sorry. I was, um, surprised by your ears.

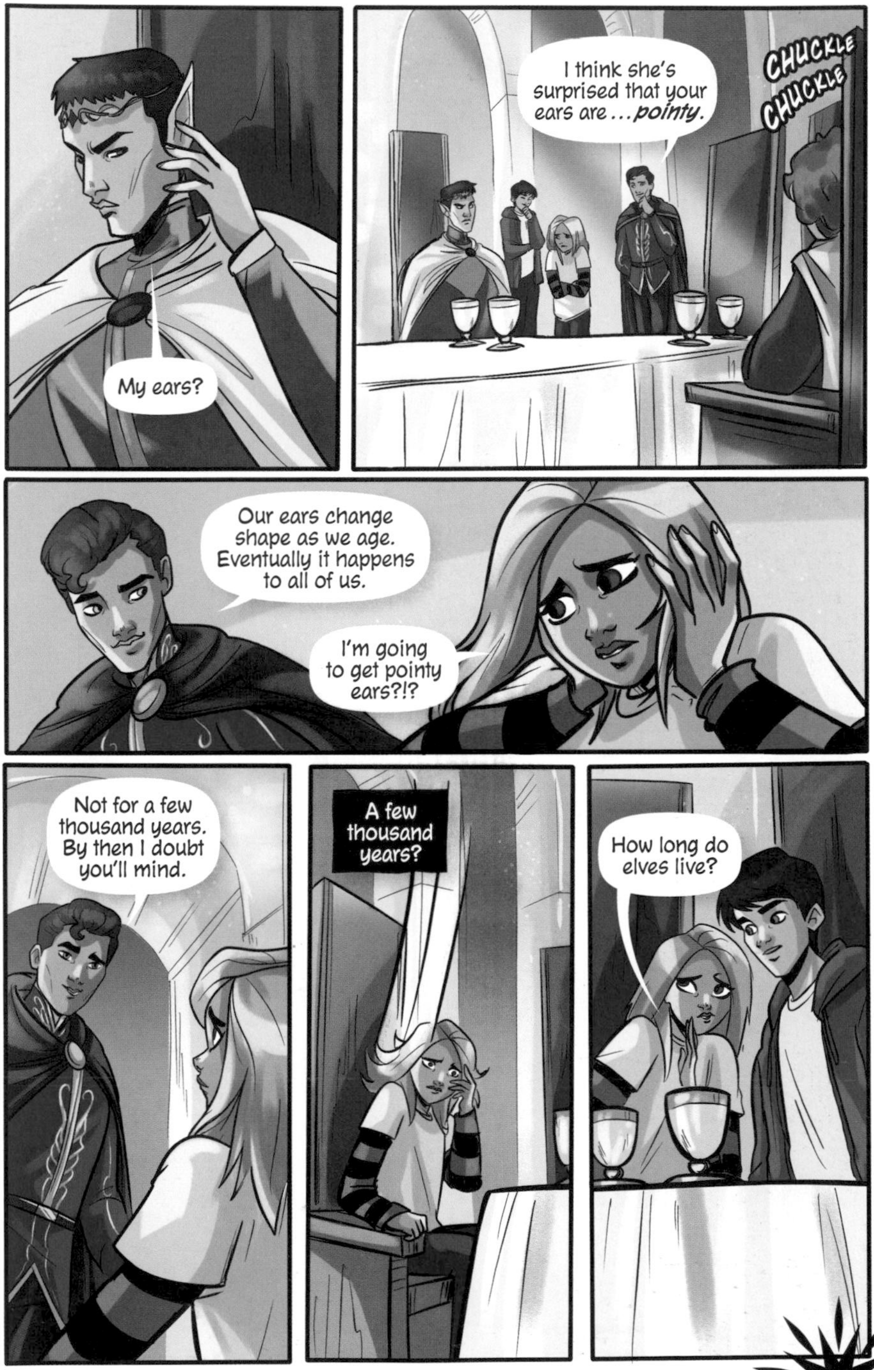
My ears?
I think she's surprised that your ears are ... *pointy*.
CHUCKLE CHUCKLE
Our ears change shape as we age. Eventually it happens to all of us.
I'm going to get pointy ears?!?
Not for a few thousand years. By then I doubt you'll mind.
A few thousand years?
How long do elves live?

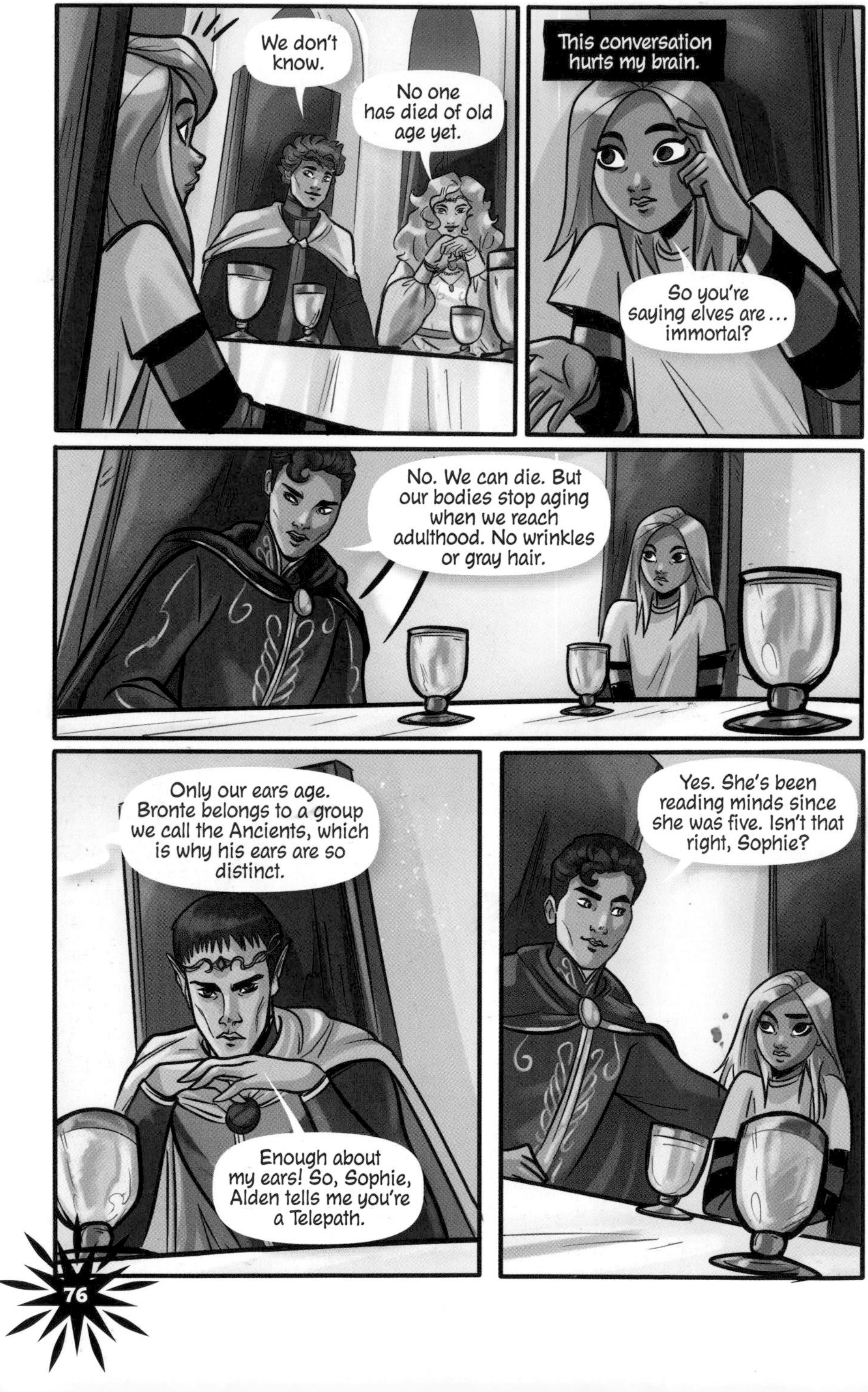
We don't know.
No one has died of old age yet.
This conversation hurts my brain.
So you're saying elves are... immortal?
No. We can die. But our bodies stop aging when we reach adulthood. No wrinkles or gray hair.
Only our ears age. Bronte belongs to a group we call the Ancients, which is why his ears are so distinct.
Enough about my ears! So, Sophie, Alden tells me you're a Telepath.
Yes. She's been reading minds since she was five. Isn't that right, Sophie?

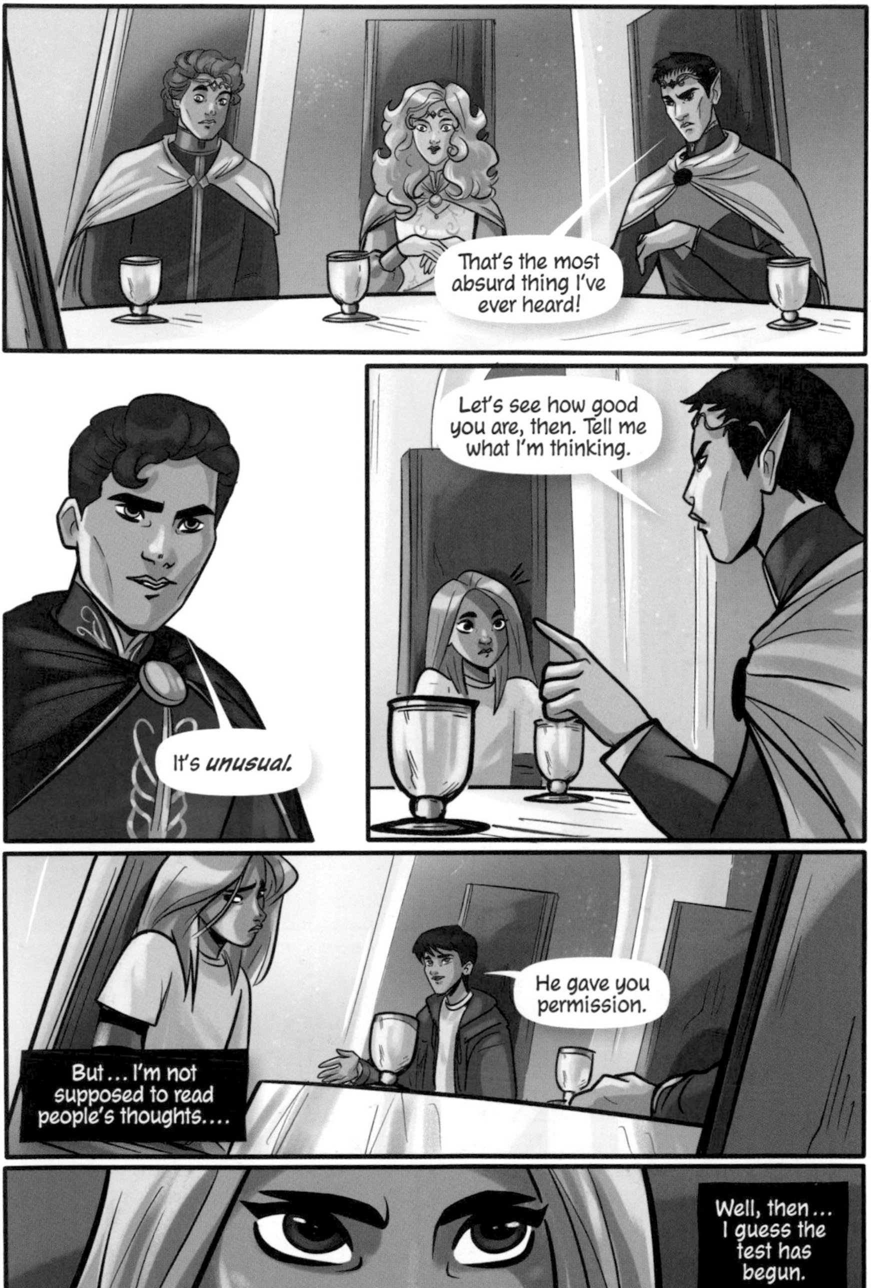
That's the most absurd thing I've ever heard!
It's *unusual.*
Let's see how good you are, then. Tell me what I'm thinking.
But... I'm not supposed to read people's thoughts....
He gave you permission.
Well, then... I guess the test has begun.

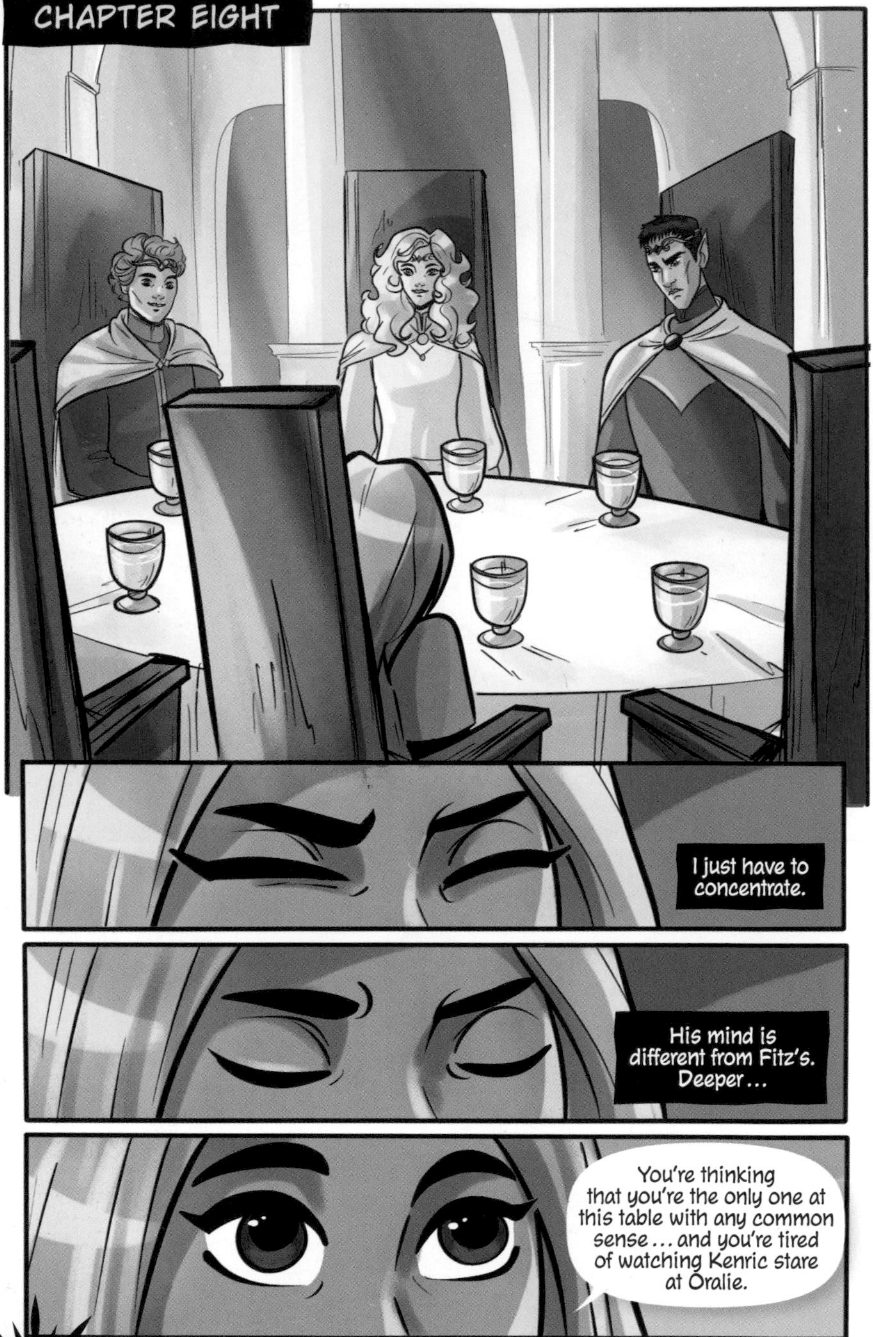
CHAPTER EIGHT
I just have to concentrate.
His mind is different from Fitz's. Deeper...
You're thinking that you're the only one at this table with any common sense... and you're tired of watching Kenric stare at Oralie.

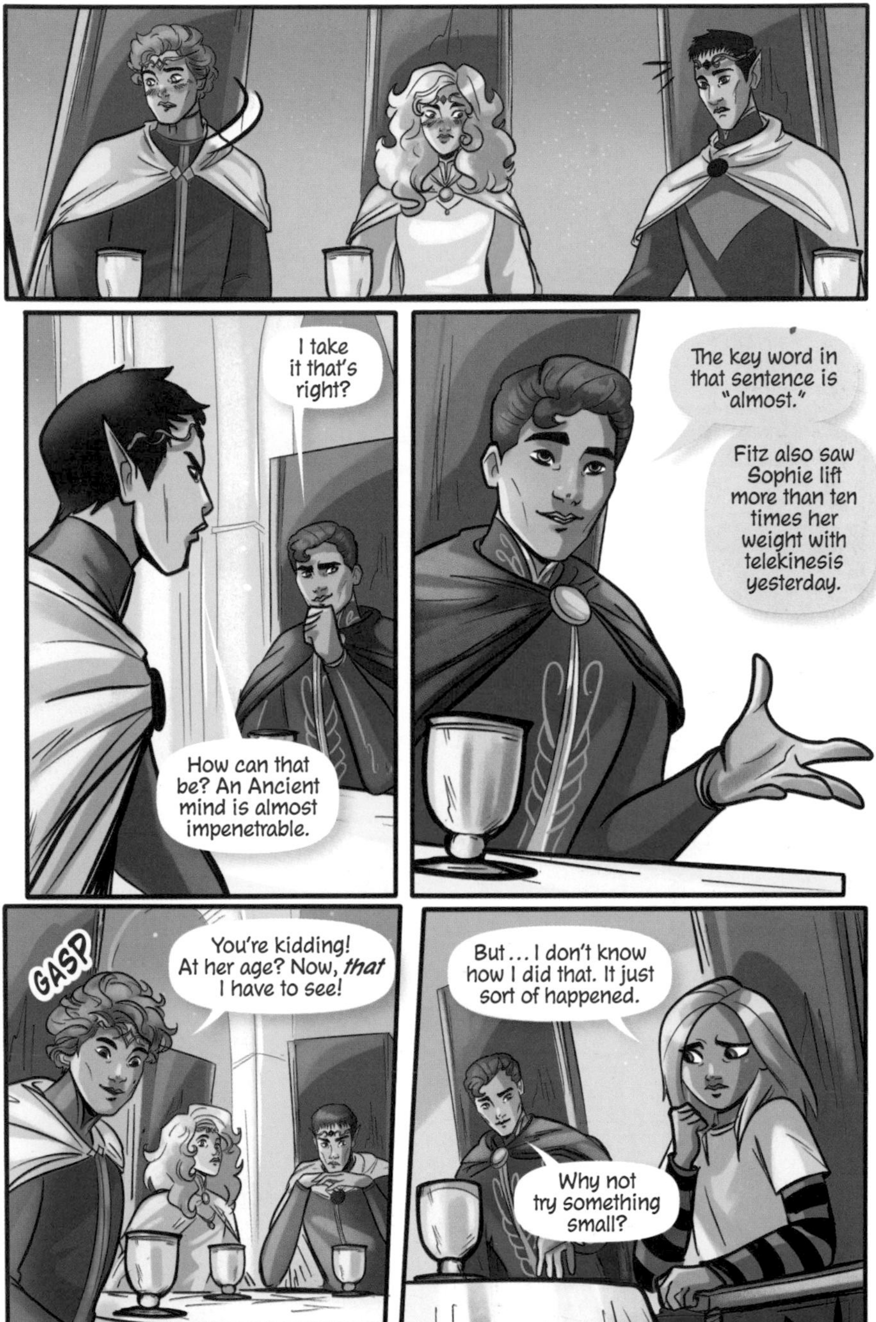
I take it that's right?
How can that be? An Ancient mind is almost impenetrable.
The key word in that sentence is "almost."
Fitz also saw Sophie lift more than ten times her weight with telekinesis yesterday.
GASP
You're kidding! At her age? Now, *that* I have to see!
But... I don't know how I did that. It just sort of happened.
Why not try something small?

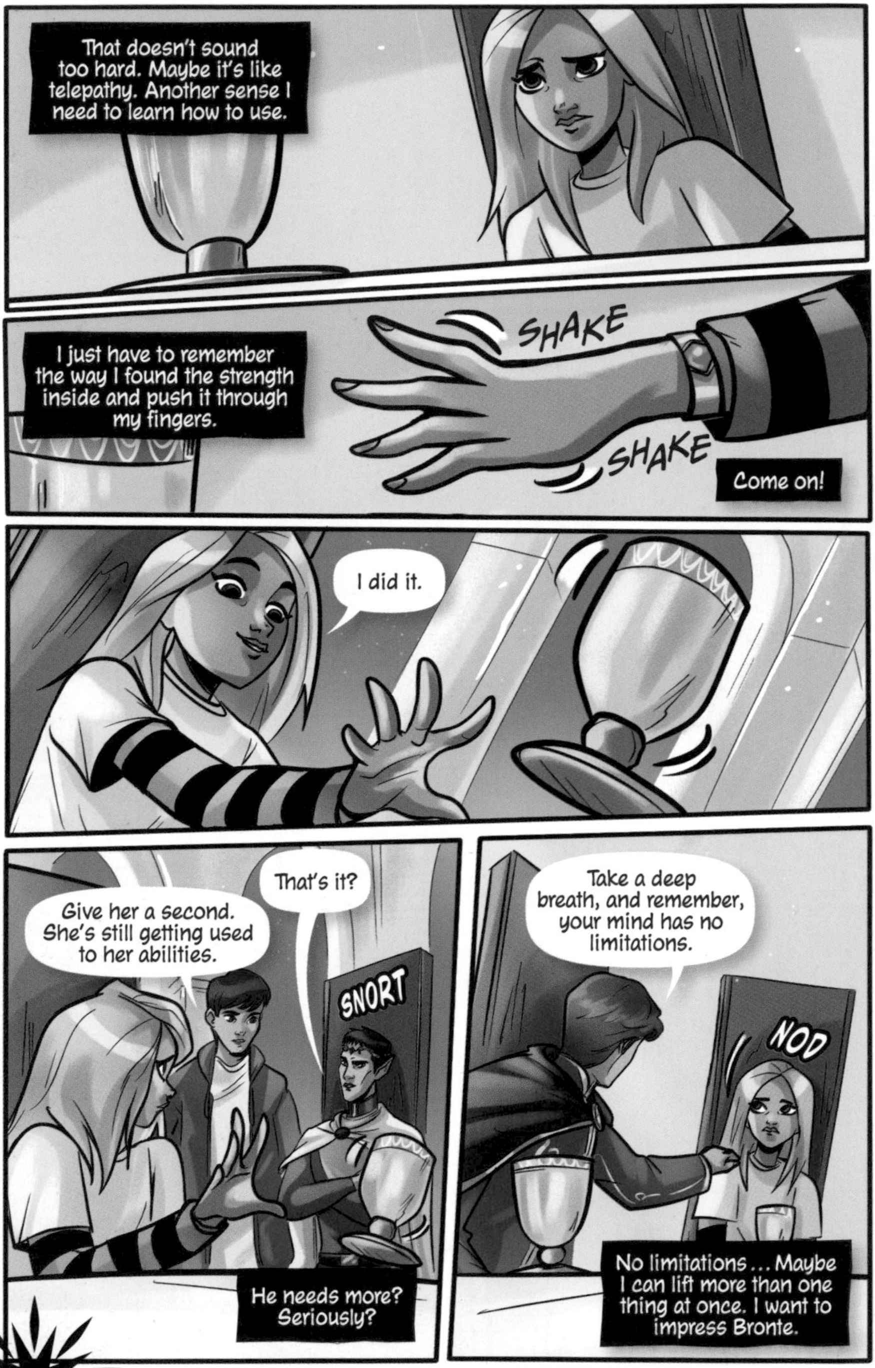
That doesn't sound too hard. Maybe it's like telepathy. Another sense I need to learn how to use.
I just have to remember the way I found the strength inside and push it through my fingers.
SHAKE
SHAKE
Come on!
I did it.
That's it?
Give her a second. She's still getting used to her abilities.
SNORT
He needs more? Seriously?
Take a deep breath, and remember, your mind has no limitations.
NOD
No limitations... Maybe I can lift more than one thing at once. I want to impress Bronte.

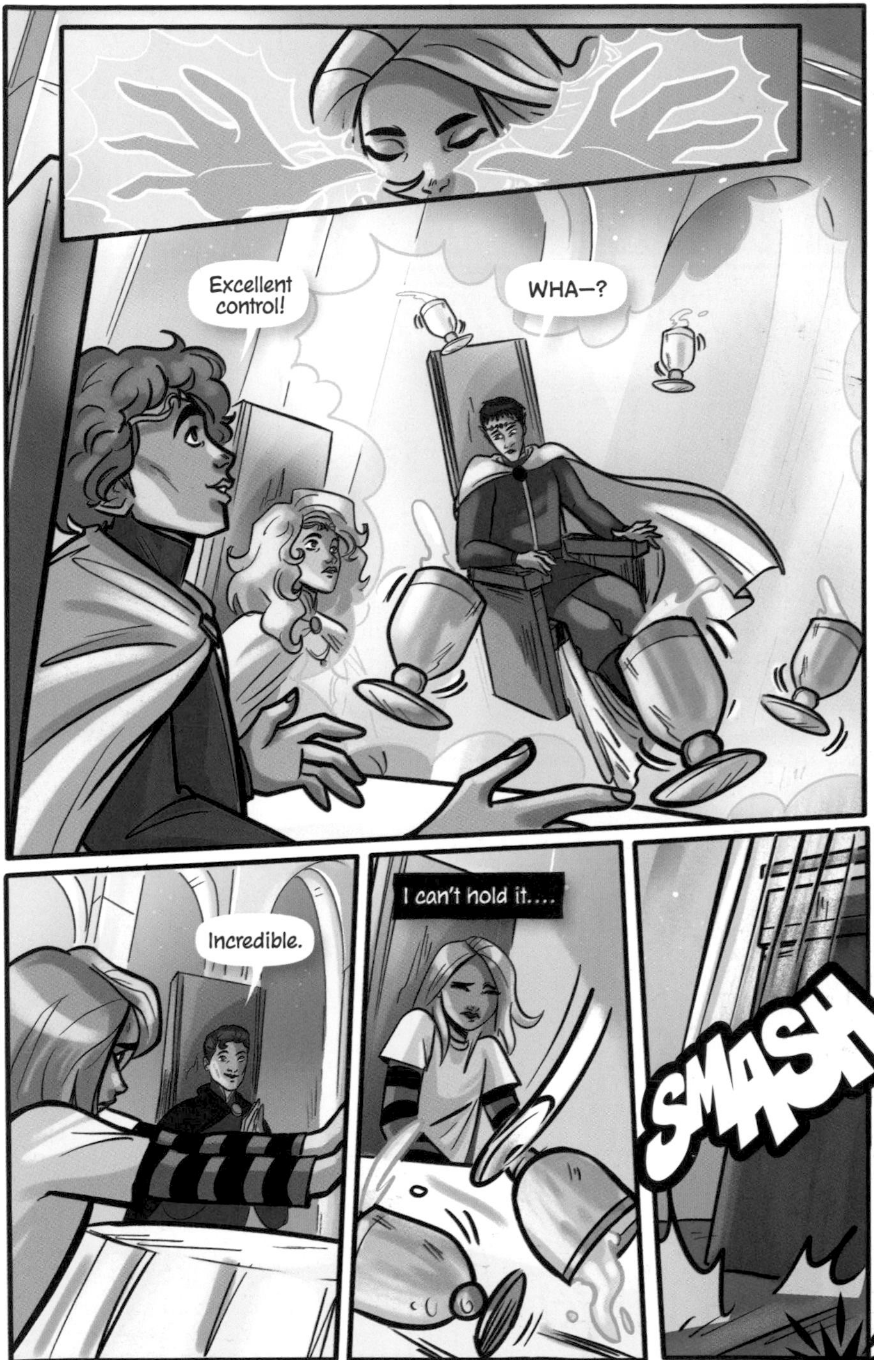
Excellent control!
WHA—?
Incredible.
I can't hold it....
SMASH

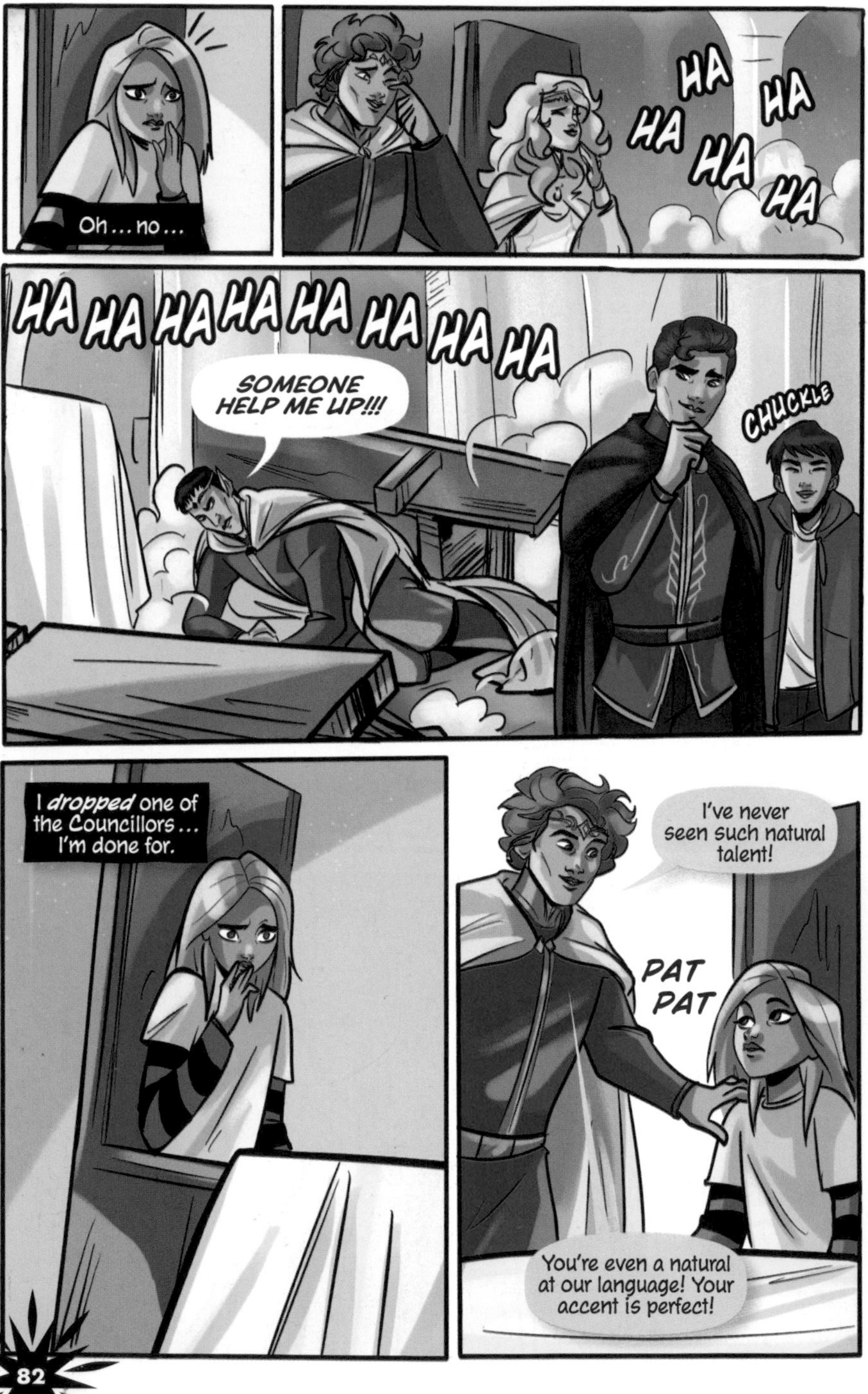

Oh... no...
HA HA HA HA HA HA
HA HA HA HA HA HA HA HA
SOMEONE HELP ME UP!!!
CHUCKLE
I *dropped* one of the Councillors... I'm done for.
I've never seen such natural talent!
PAT PAT
You're even a natural at our language! Your accent is perfect!

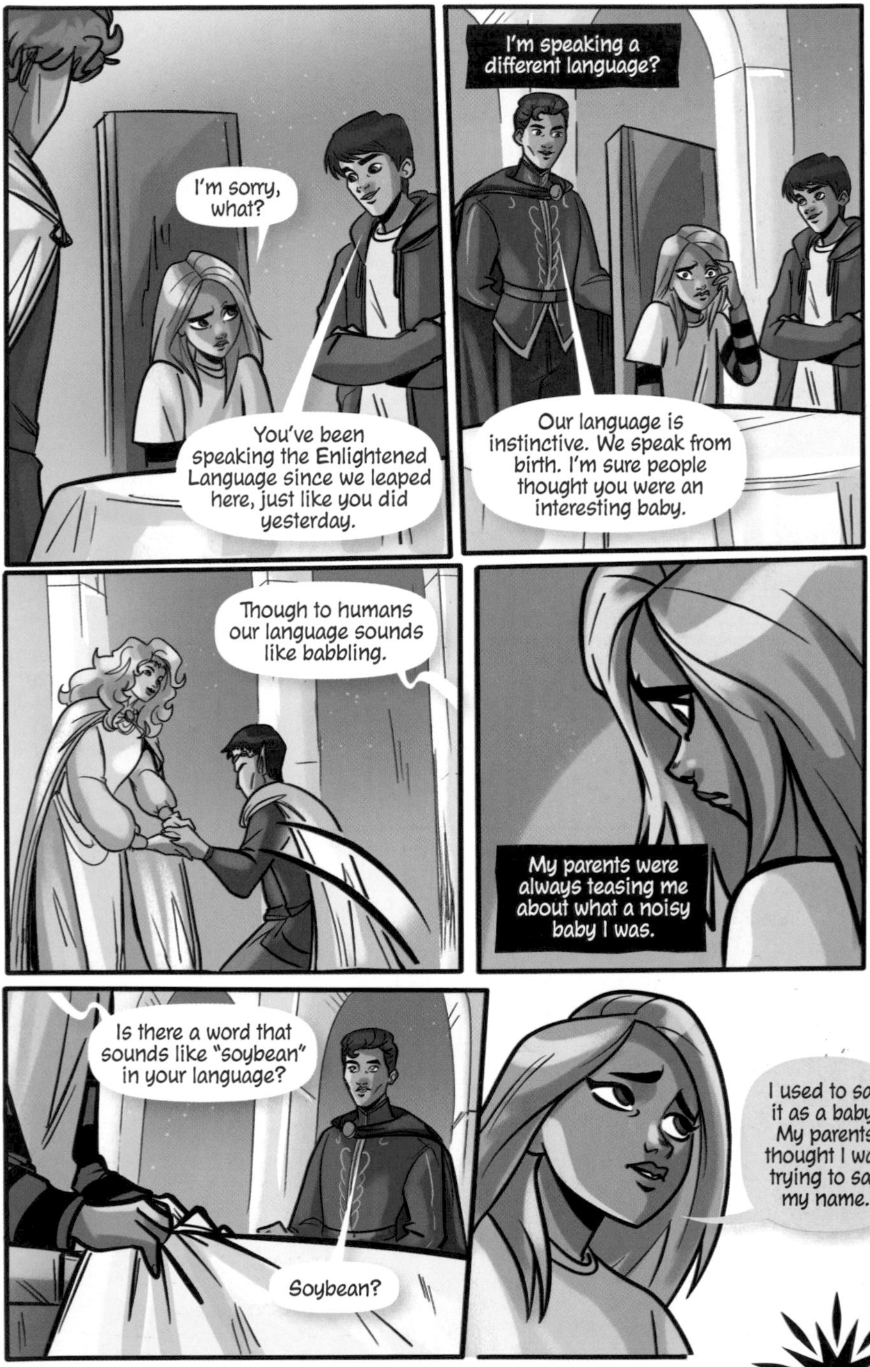
I'm sorry, what?
You've been speaking the Enlightened Language since we leaped here, just like you did yesterday.
I'm speaking a different language?
Our language is instinctive. We speak from birth. I'm sure people thought you were an interesting baby.
Though to humans our language sounds like babbling.
My parents were always teasing me about what a noisy baby I was.
Is there a word that sounds like "soybean" in your language?
Soybean?
I used to say it as a baby. My parents thought I was trying to say my name.

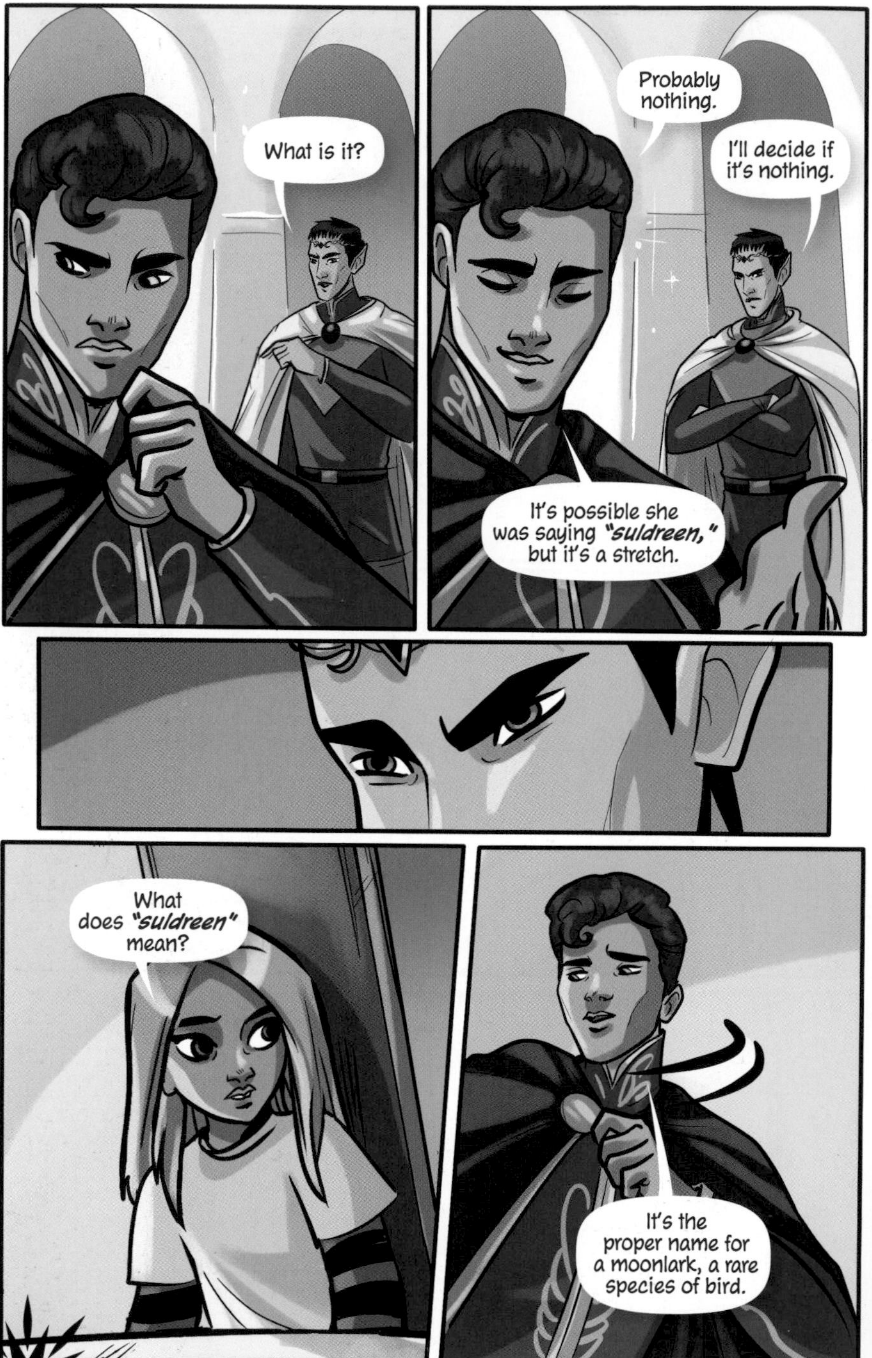

What is it?
Probably nothing.
I'll decide if it's nothing.
It's possible she was saying "*suldreen,*" but it's a stretch.
What does "*suldreen*" mean?
It's the proper name for a moonlark, a rare species of bird.

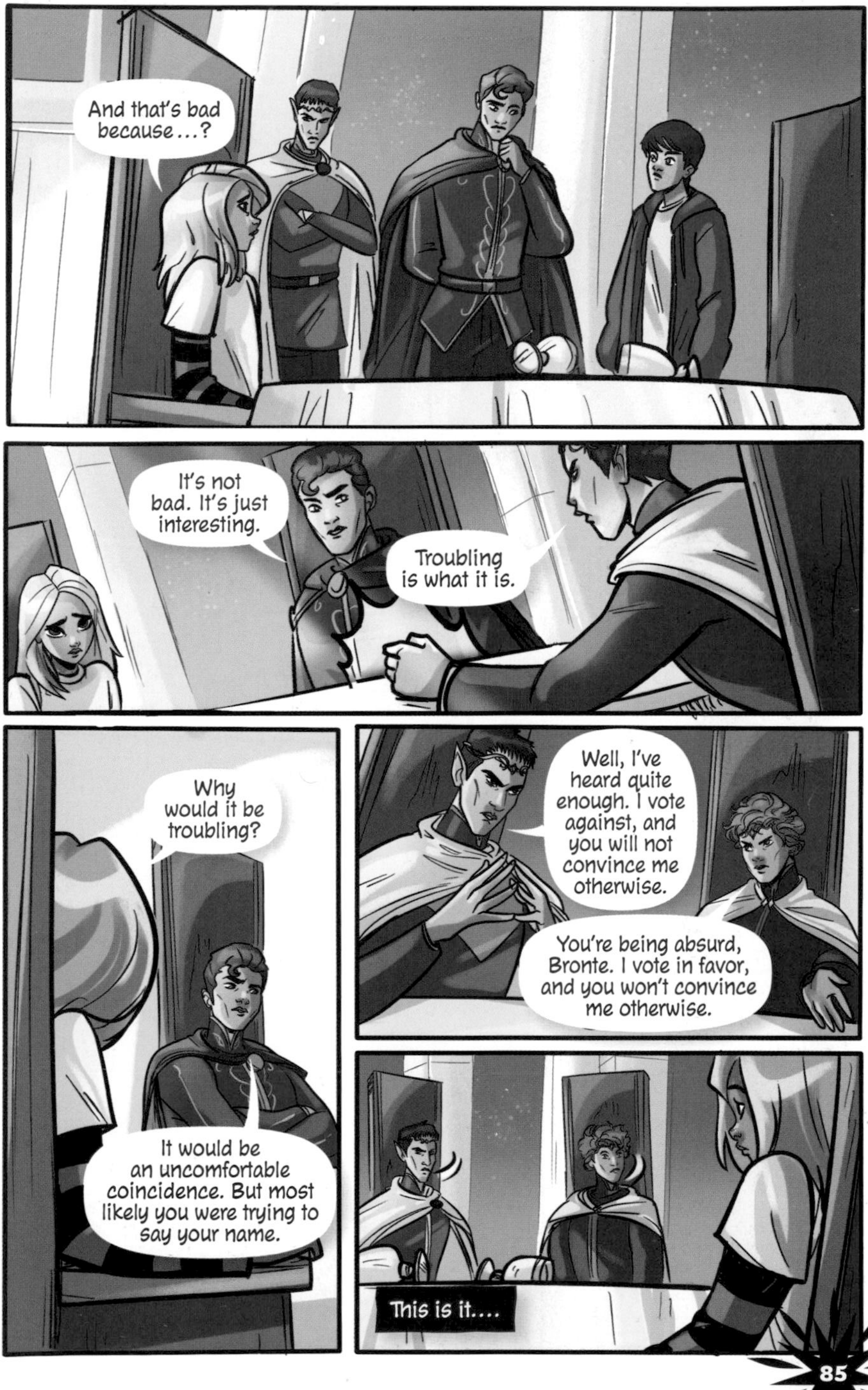
And that's bad because...?
It's not bad. It's just interesting.
Troubling is what it is.
Why would it be troubling?
It would be an uncomfortable coincidence. But most likely you were trying to say your name.
Well, I've heard quite enough. I vote against, and you will not convince me otherwise.
You're being absurd, Bronte. I vote in favor, and you won't convince me otherwise.
This is it....

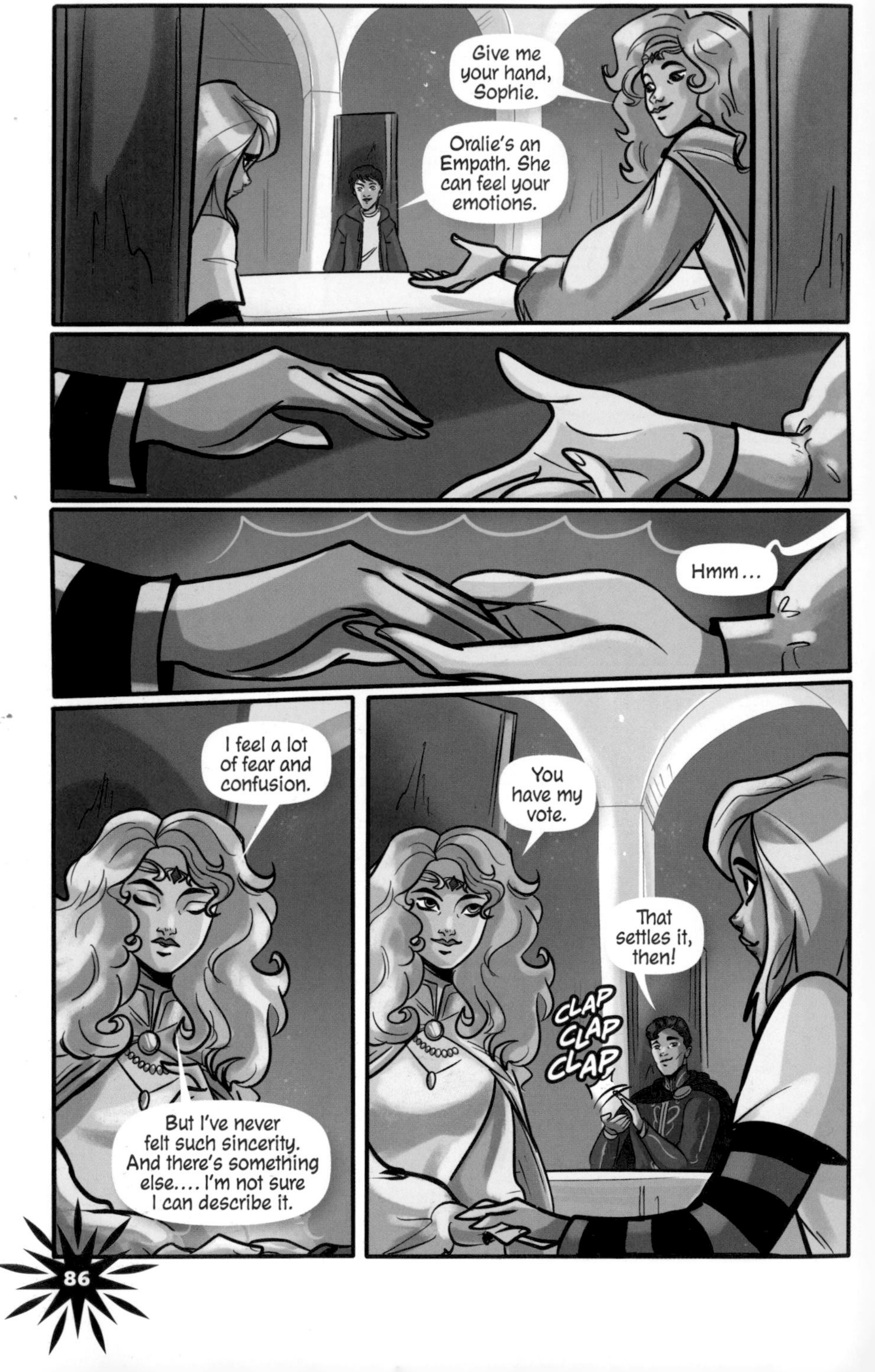
Give me your hand, Sophie.
Oralie's an Empath. She can feel your emotions.
Hmm...
I feel a lot of fear and confusion.
But I've never felt such sincerity. And there's something else.... I'm not sure I can describe it.
You have my vote.
That settles it, then!
CLAP CLAP CLAP

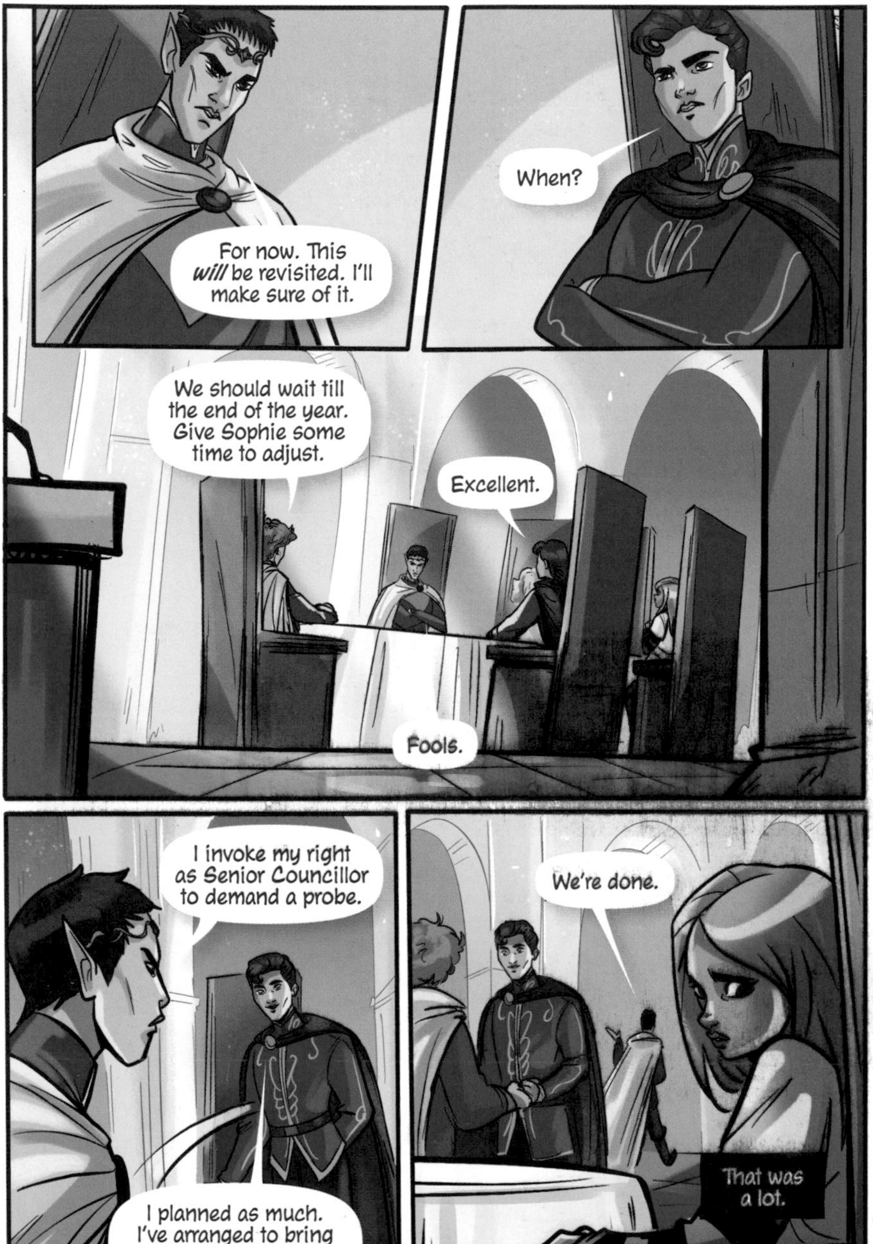
For now. This *will* be revisited. I'll make sure of it.
When?
We should wait till the end of the year. Give Sophie some time to adjust.
Excellent.
Fools.
I invoke my right as Senior Councillor to demand a probe.
I planned as much. I've arranged to bring her to Quinlin as soon as we're done here.
We're done.
That was a lot.

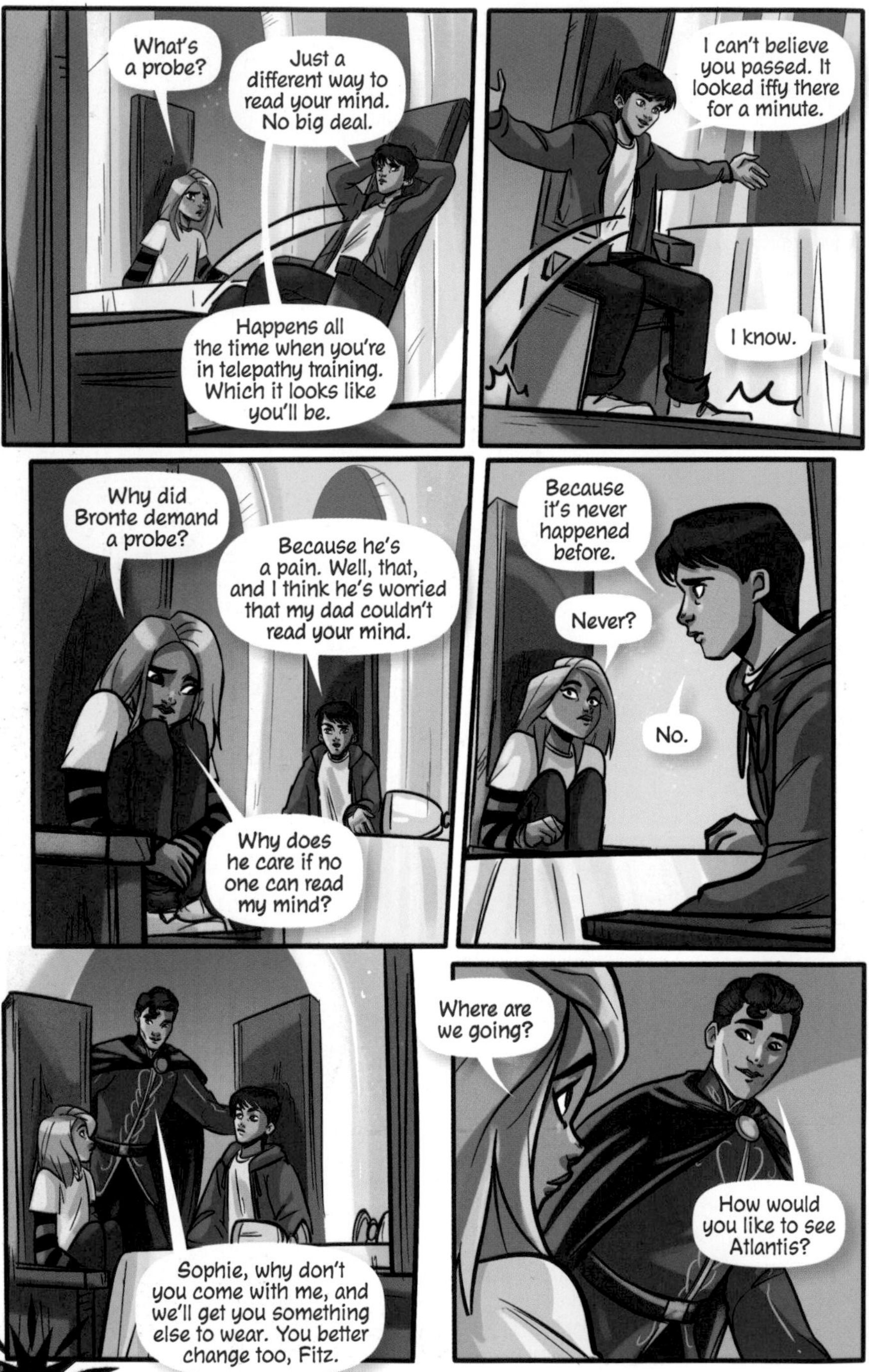
What's a probe?
Just a different way to read your mind. No big deal.
Happens all the time when you're in telepathy training. Which it looks like you'll be.
I can't believe you passed. It looked iffy there for a minute.
I know.
Why did Bronte demand a probe?
Because he's a pain. Well, that, and I think he's worried that my dad couldn't read your mind.
Why does he care if no one can read my mind?
Because it's never happened before.
Never?
No.
Sophie, why don't you come with me, and we'll get you something else to wear. You better change too, Fitz.
Where are we going?
How would you like to see Atlantis?

CHAPTER NINE

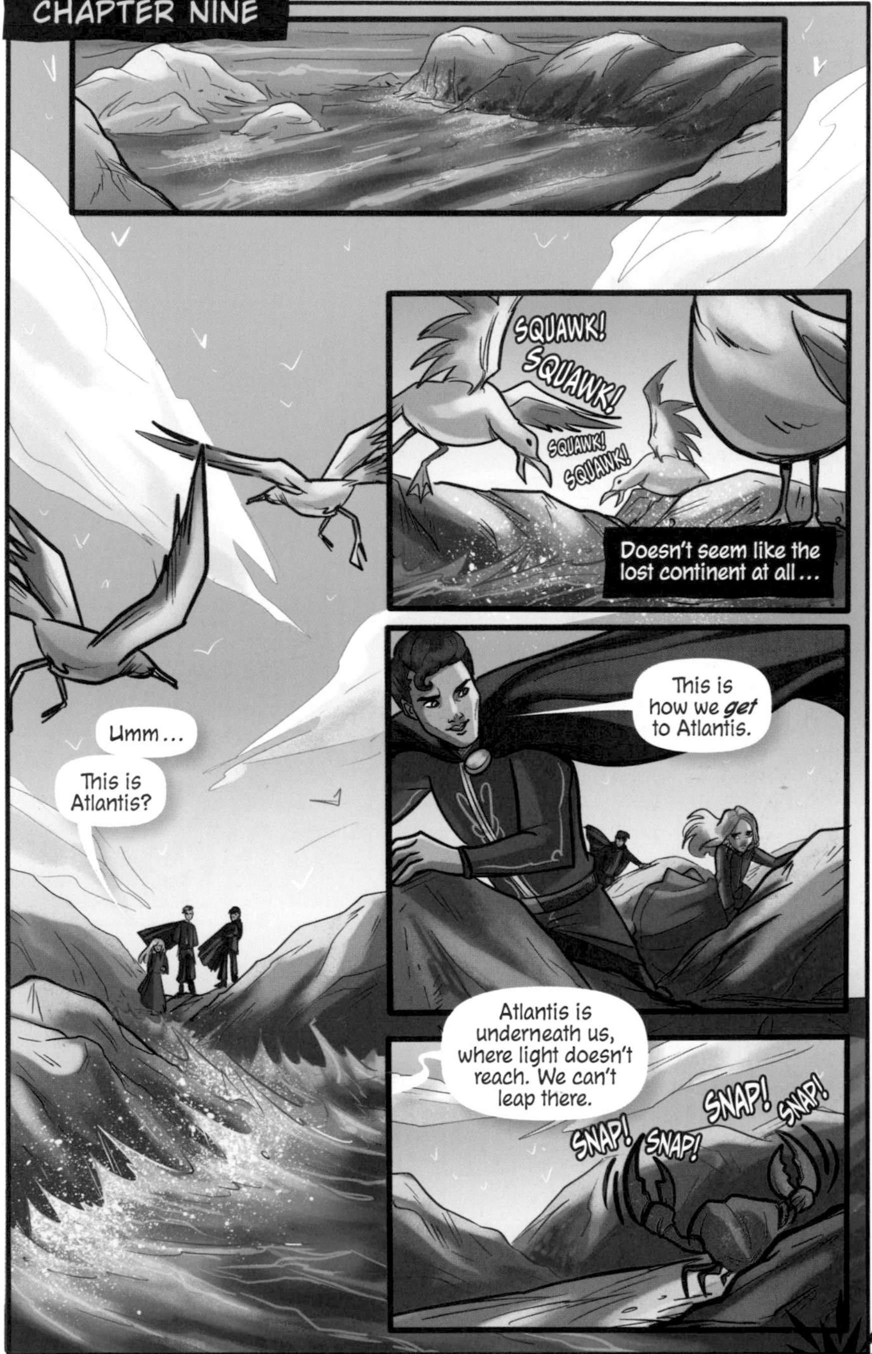

SQUAWK!
SQUAWK!
SQUAWK!
SQUAWK!
Doesn't seem like the lost continent at all…
Umm…
This is Atlantis?
This is how we *get* to Atlantis.
Atlantis is underneath us, where light doesn't reach. We can't leap there.
SNAP!
SNAP!
SNAP!
SNAP!

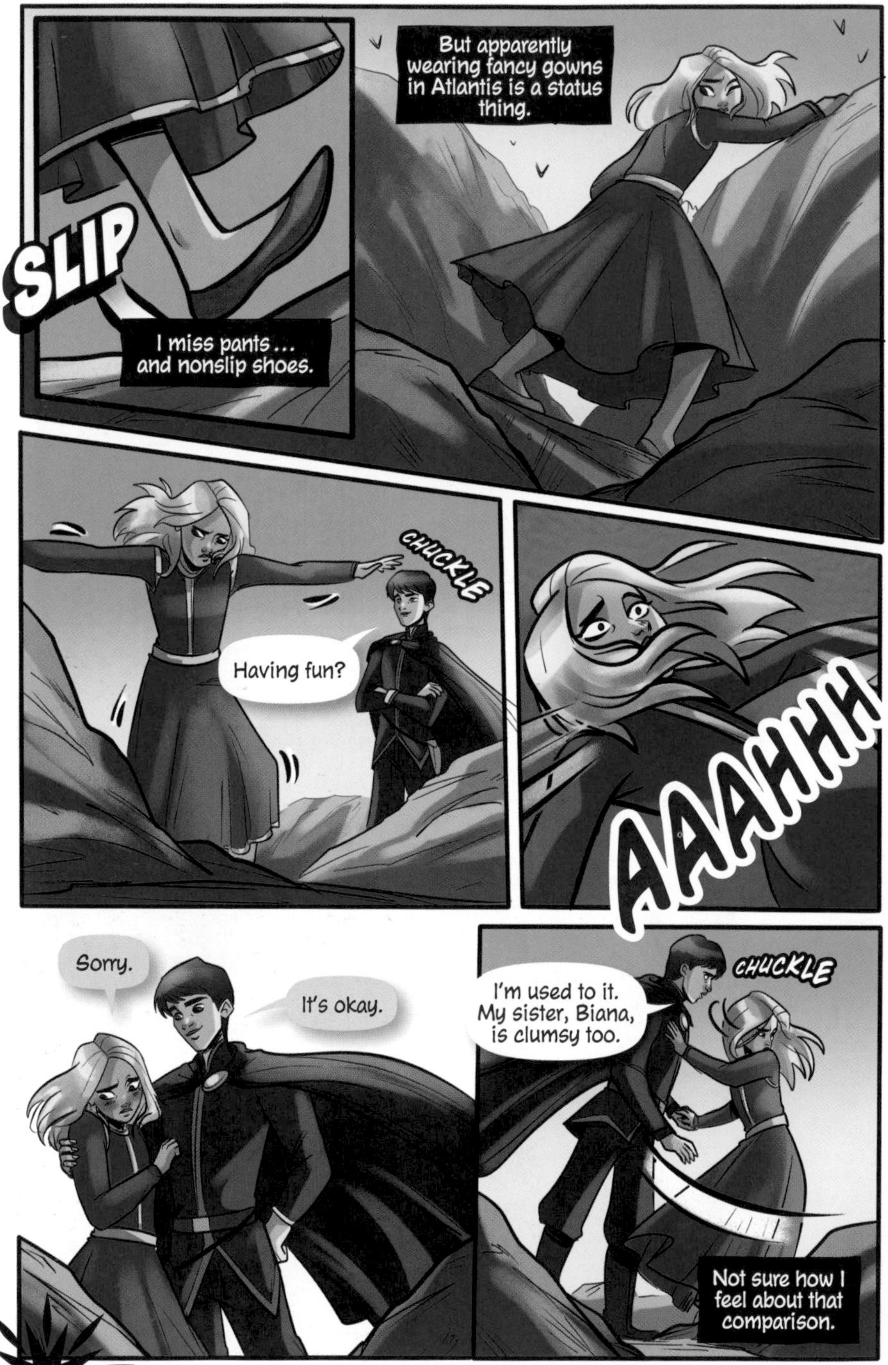
SLIP
I miss pants . . .
and nonslip shoes.
But apparently wearing fancy gowns in Atlantis is a status thing.
CHUCKLE
Having fun?
AAAHHH
Sorry.
It's okay.
I'm used to it. My sister, Biana, is clumsy too.
CHUCKLE
Not sure how I feel about that comparison.

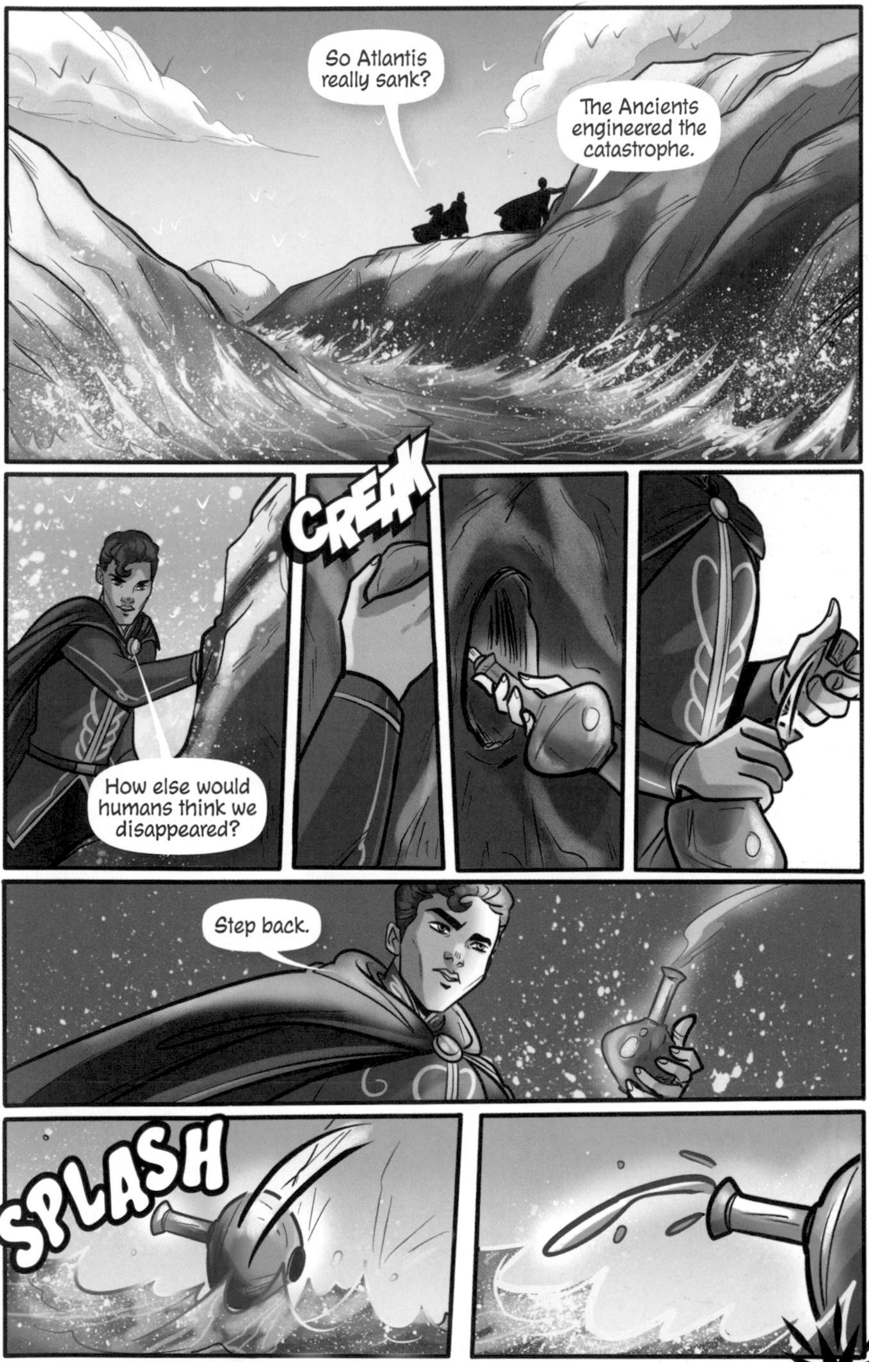
So Atlantis really sank?
The Ancients engineered the catastrophe.
How else would humans think we disappeared?
CREAK
Step back.
SPLASH

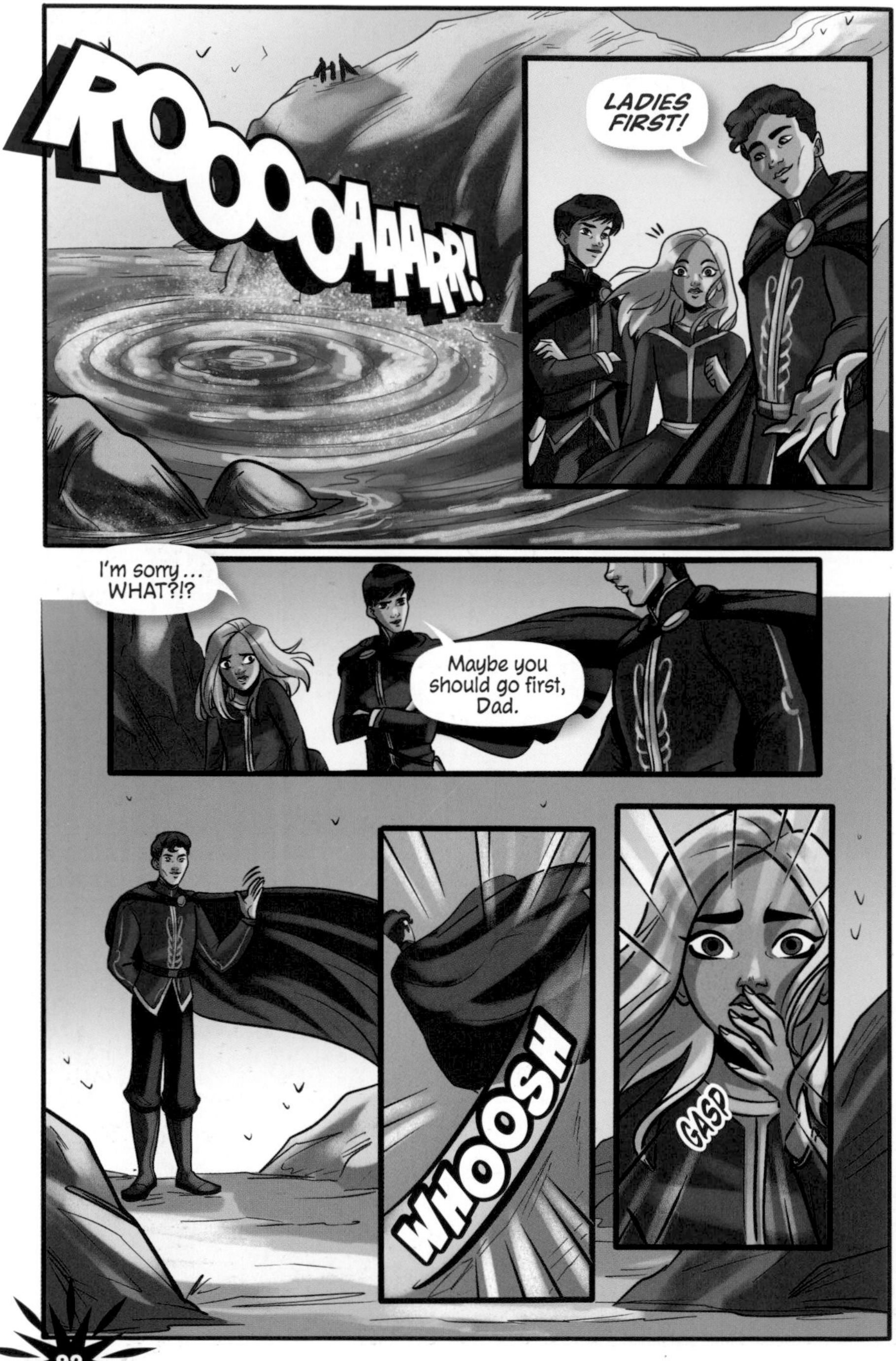
ROOOOAAARR!
LADIES FIRST!
I'm sorry... WHAT?!?
Maybe you should go first, Dad.
WHOOSH
GASP

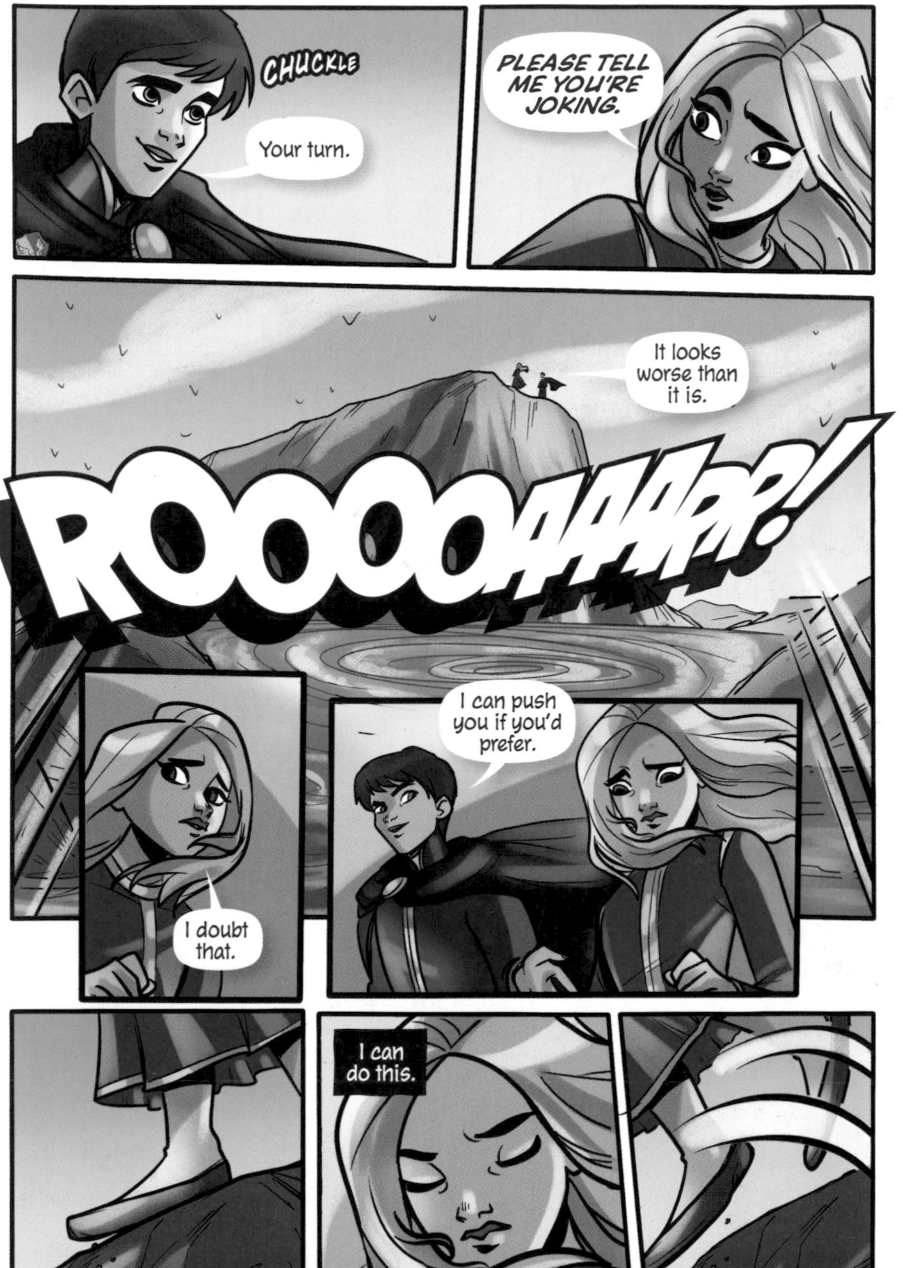
CHUCKLE
Your turn.
PLEASE TELL ME YOU'RE JOKING.
It looks worse than it is.
ROOOOAAARR!
I doubt that.
I can push you if you'd prefer.
Okay, okay.
I can do this.

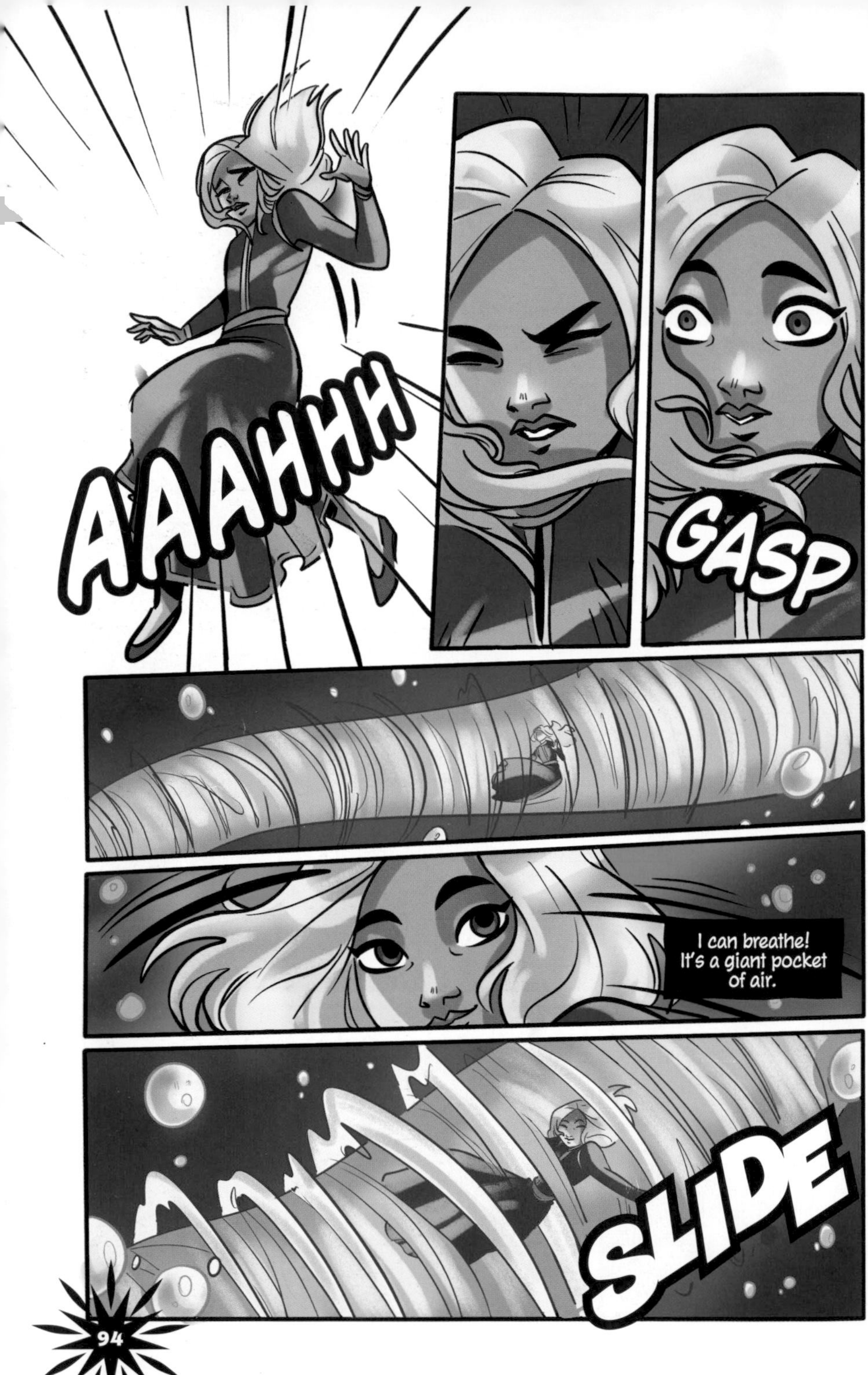
AAAHHH
GASP
I can breathe! It's a giant pocket of air.
SLIDE

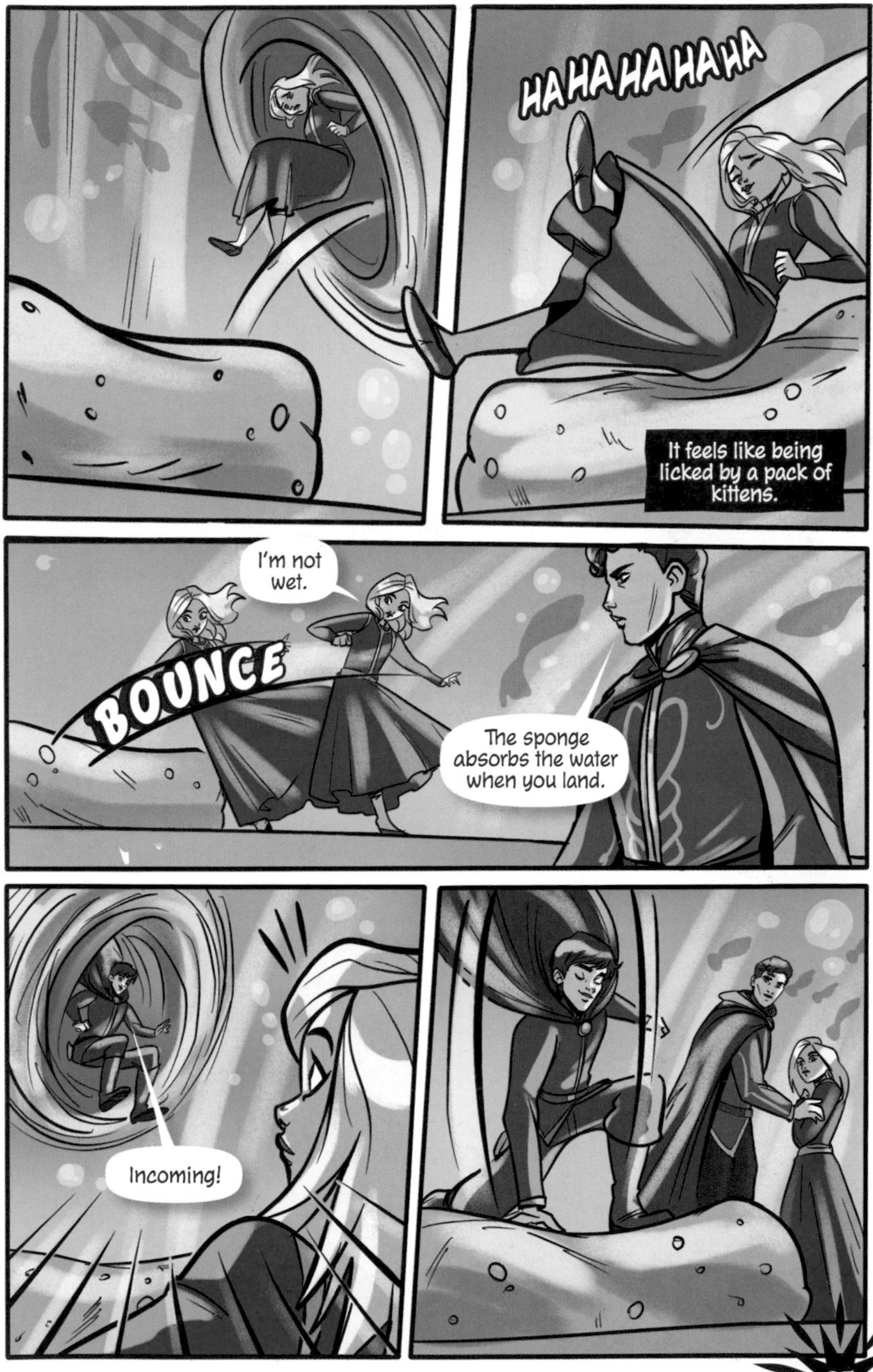
HAHAHAHAHA
It feels like being licked by a pack of kittens.
I'm not wet.
BOUNCE
The sponge absorbs the water when you land.
Incoming!

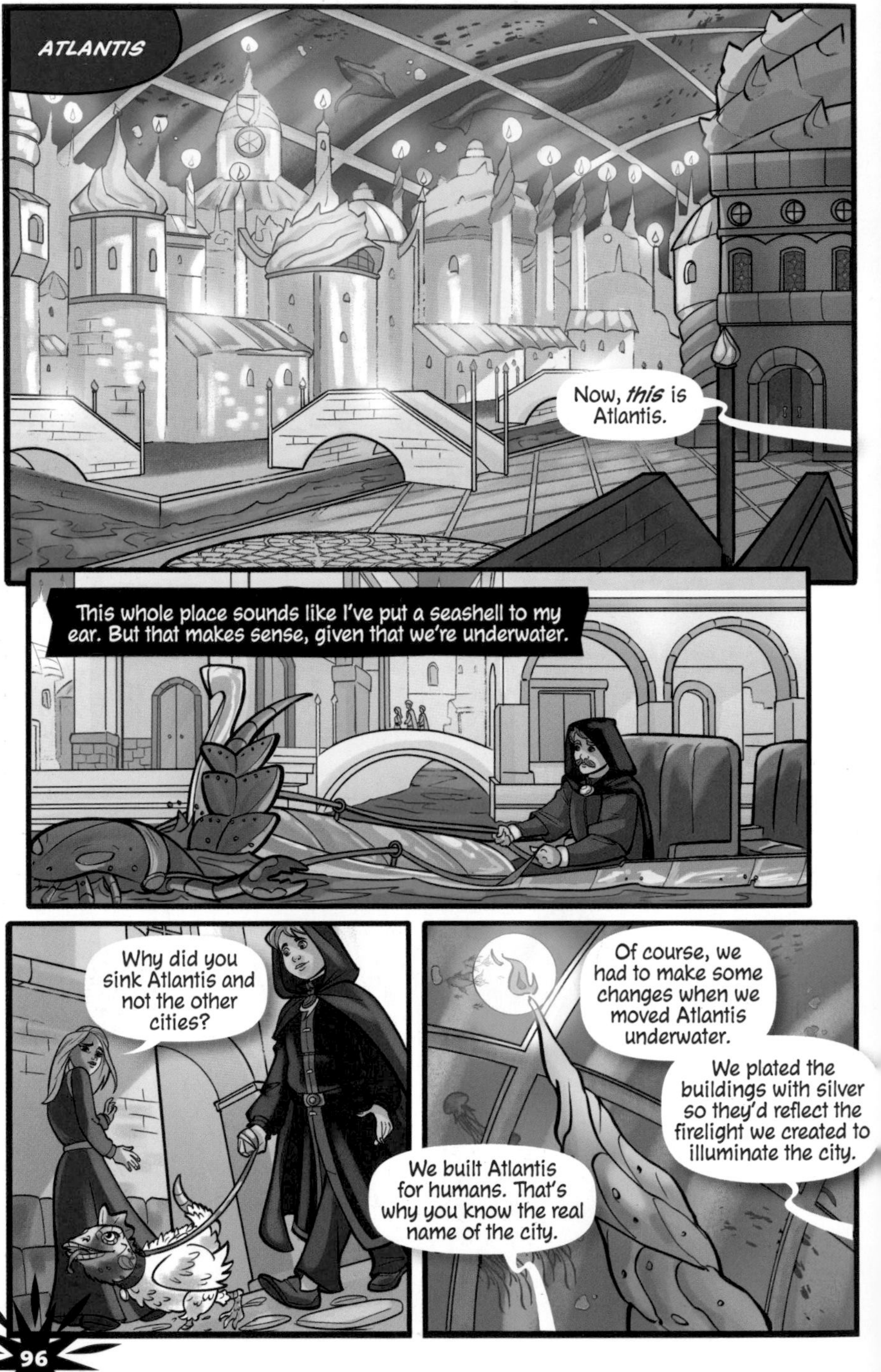
ATLANTIS
Now, *this* is Atlantis.
This whole place sounds like I've put a seashell to my ear. But that makes sense, given that we're underwater.
Why did you sink Atlantis and not the other cities?
We built Atlantis for humans. That's why you know the real name of the city.
Of course, we had to make some changes when we moved Atlantis underwater.
We plated the buildings with silver so they'd reflect the firelight we created to illuminate the city.

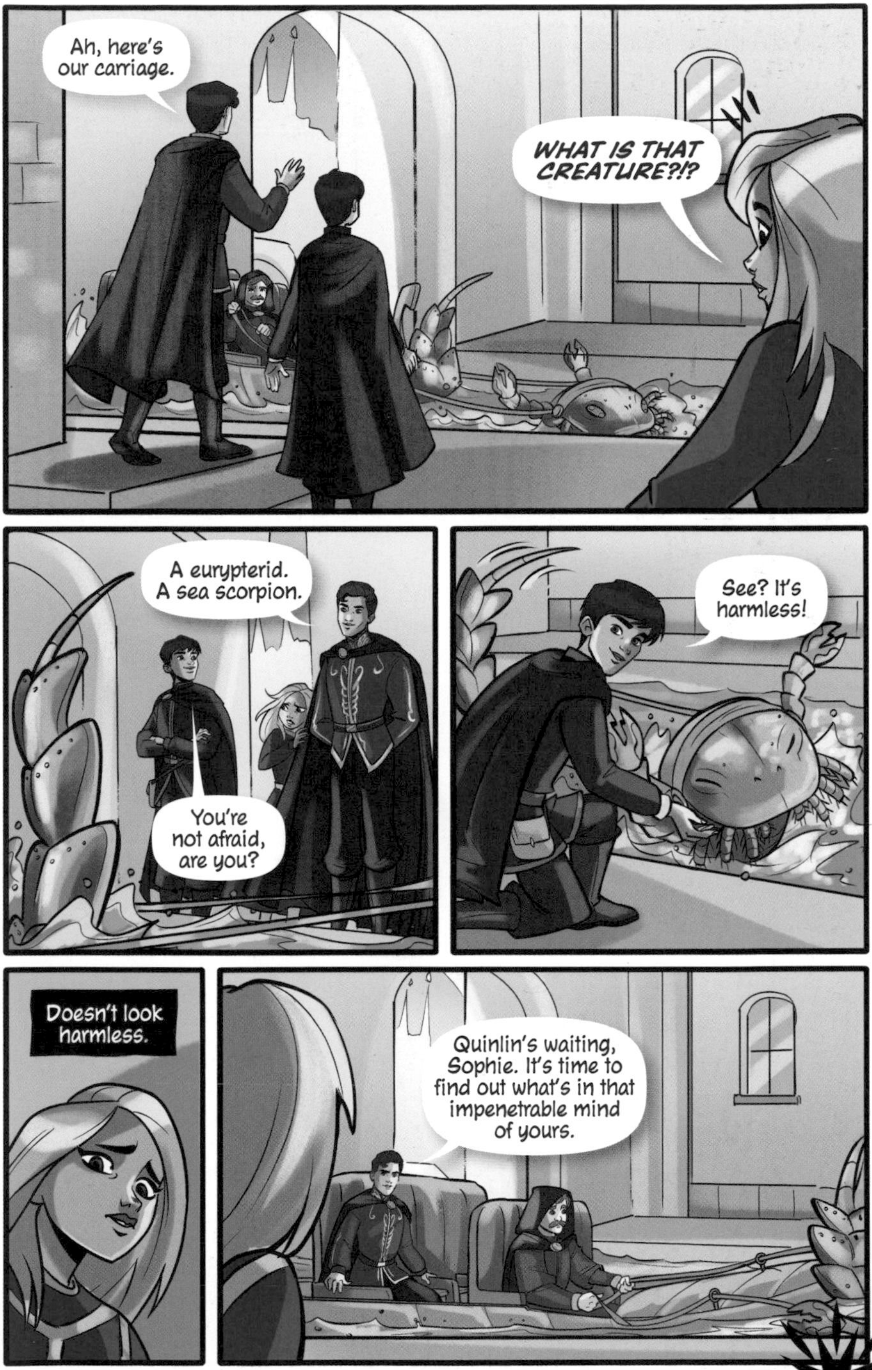
Ah, here's our carriage.
WHAT IS THAT CREATURE?!?
A eurypterid. A sea scorpion.
You're not afraid, are you?
See? It's harmless!
Doesn't look harmless.
Quinlin's waiting, Sophie. It's time to find out what's in that impenetrable mind of yours.

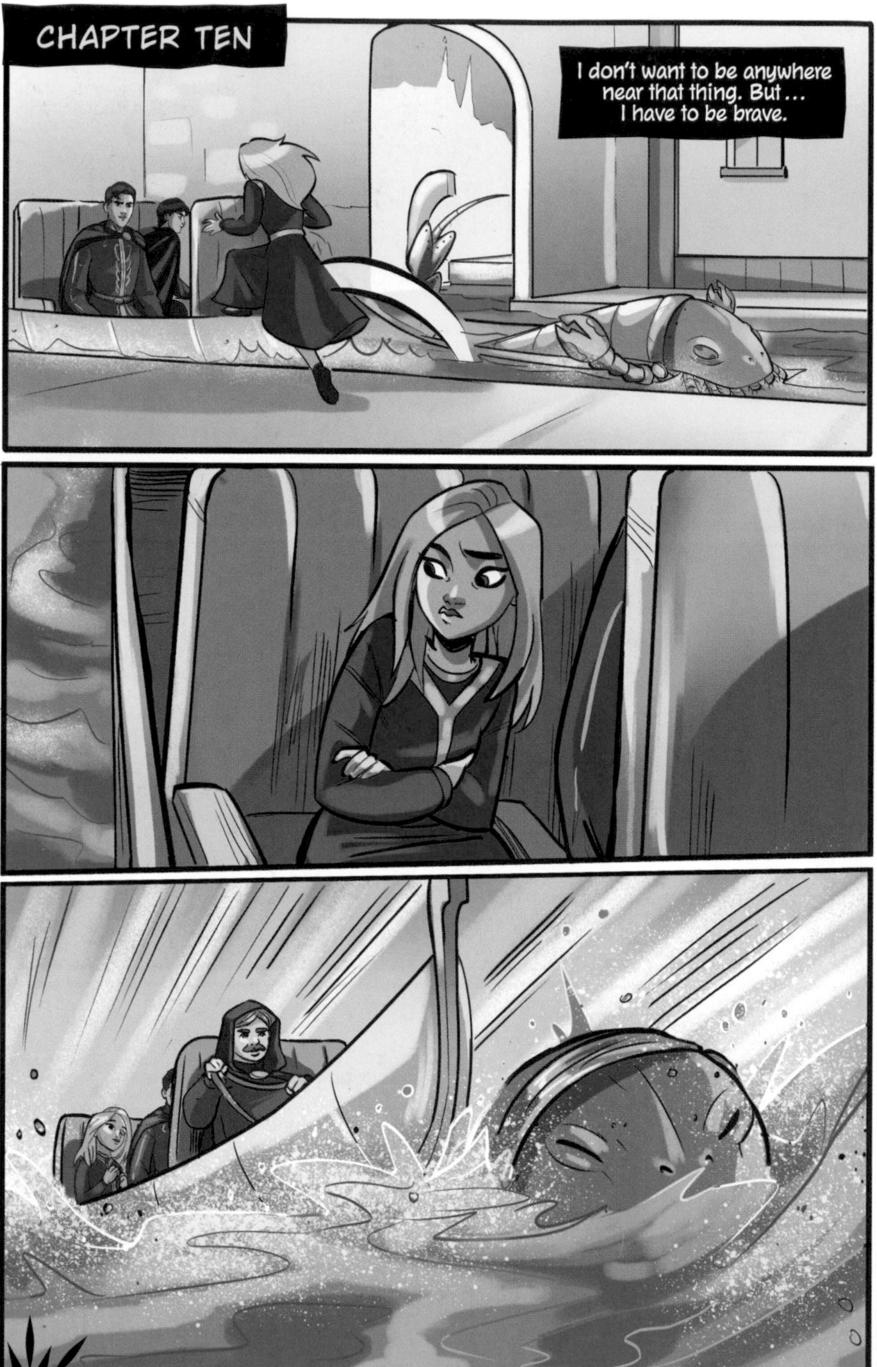
CHAPTER TEN
I don't want to be anywhere near that thing. But... I have to be brave.

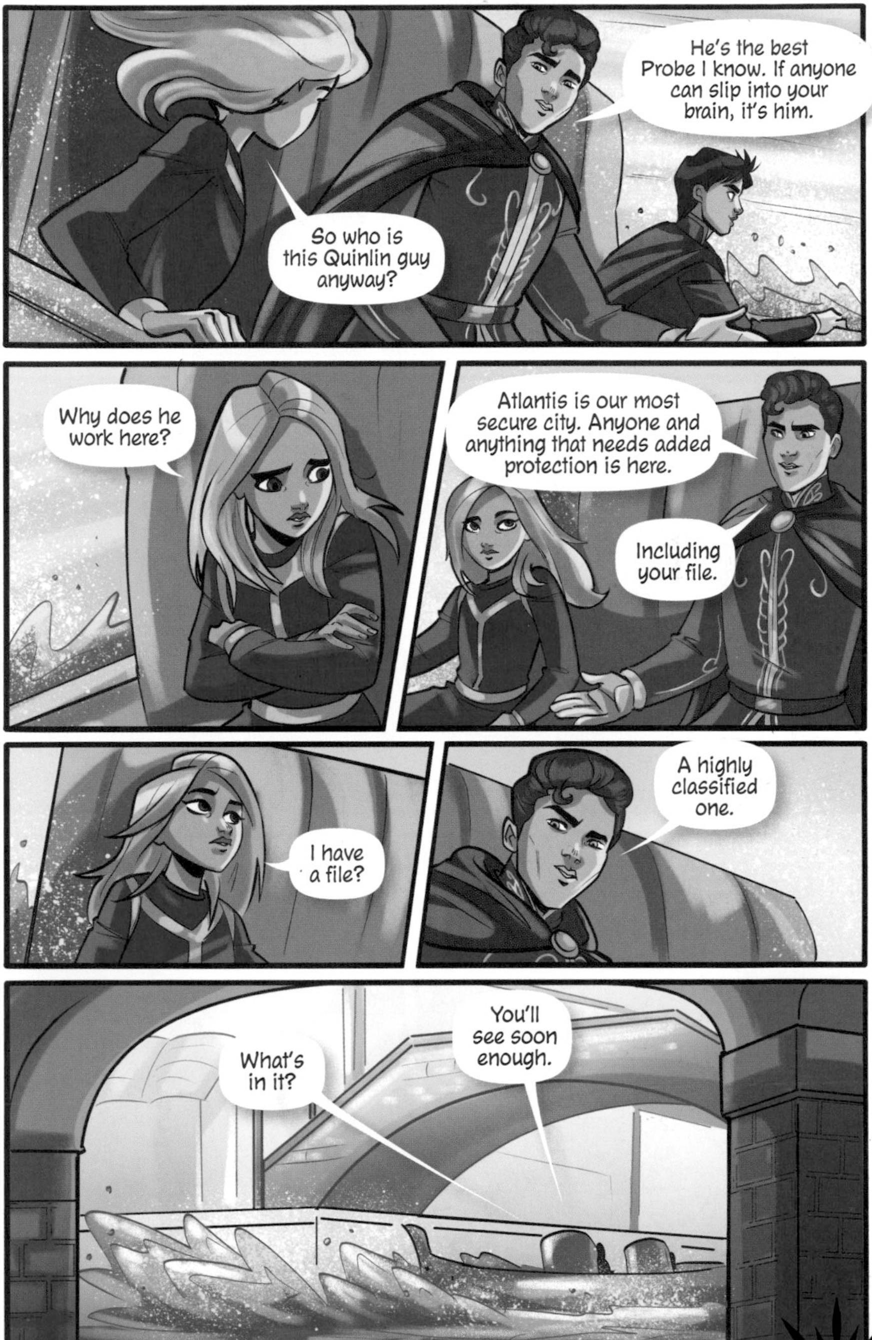
So who is this Quinlin guy anyway?
He's the best Probe I know. If anyone can slip into your brain, it's him.
Why does he work here?
Atlantis is our most secure city. Anyone and anything that needs added protection is here.
Including your file.
I have a file?
A highly classified one.
What's in it?
You'll see soon enough.

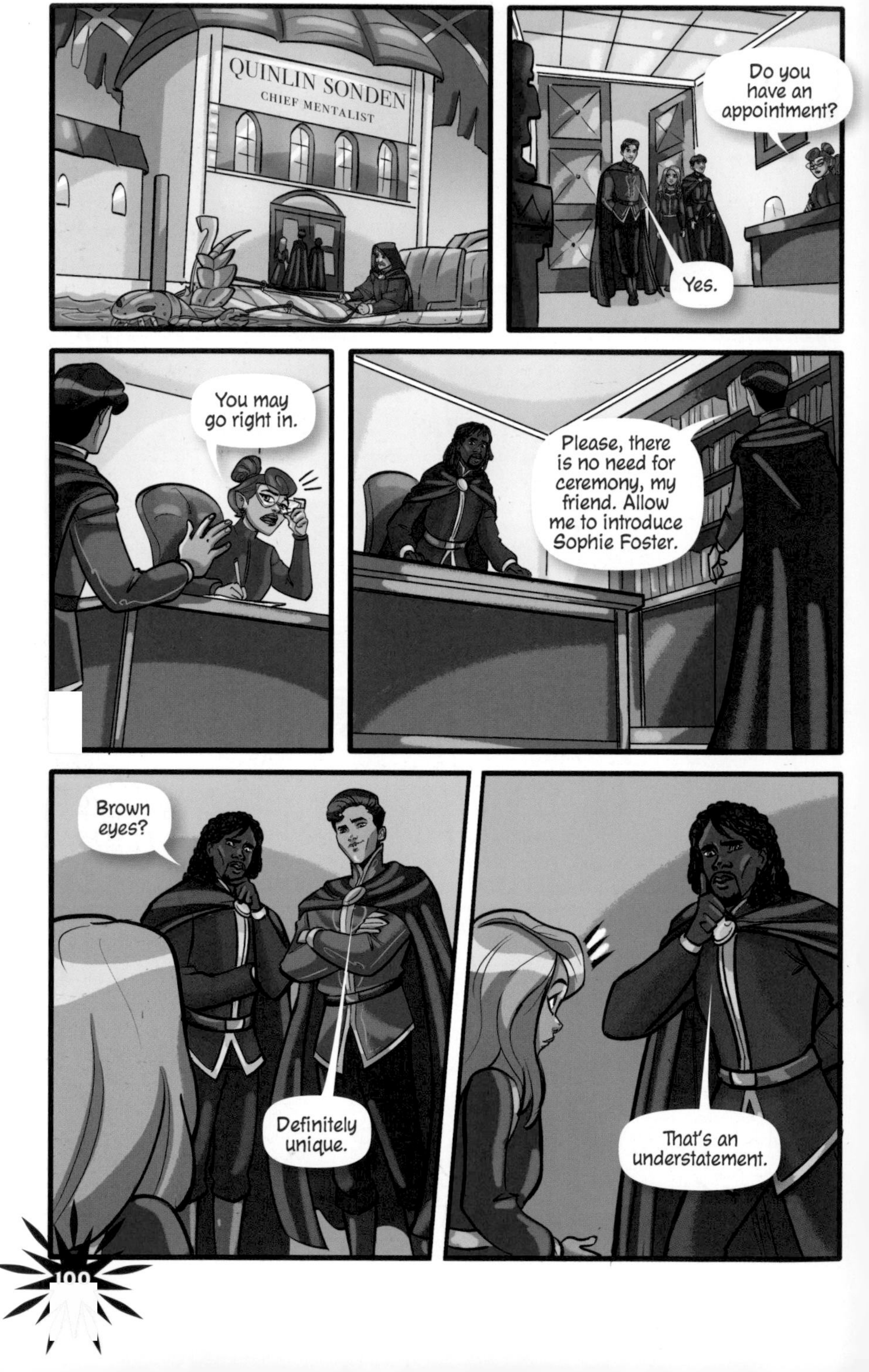
QUINLIN SONDEN
CHIEF MENTALIST
Do you have an appointment?
Yes.
You may go right in.
Please, there is no need for ceremony, my friend. Allow me to introduce Sophie Foster.
Brown eyes?
Definitely unique.
That's an understatement.

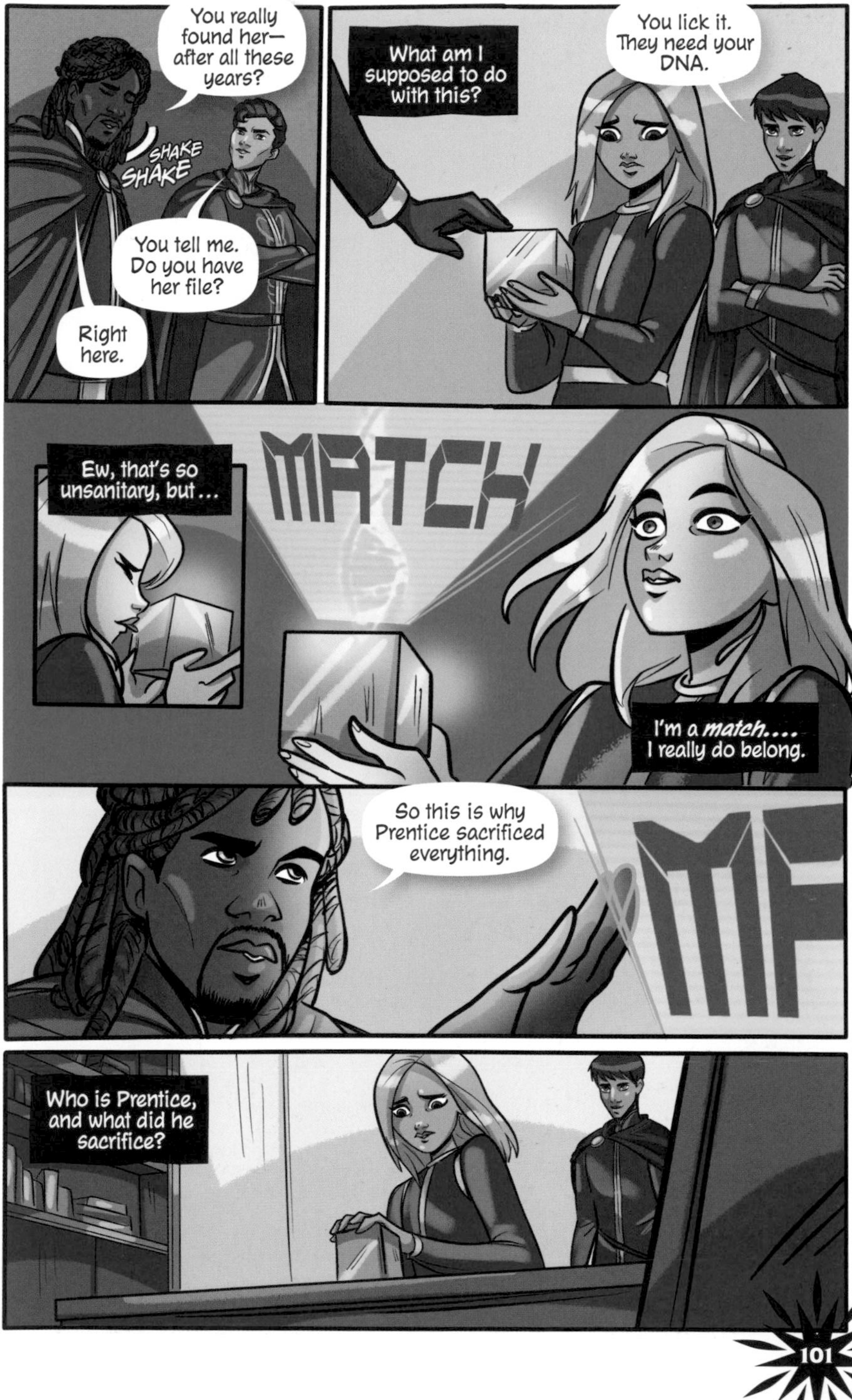
You really found her— after all these years?
SHAKE SHAKE
You tell me. Do you have her file?
Right here.
What am I supposed to do with this?
You lick it. They need your DNA.
Ew, that's so unsanitary, but...
MATCH
I'm a *match*.... I really do belong.
So this is why Prentice sacrificed everything.
Who is Prentice, and what did he sacrifice?

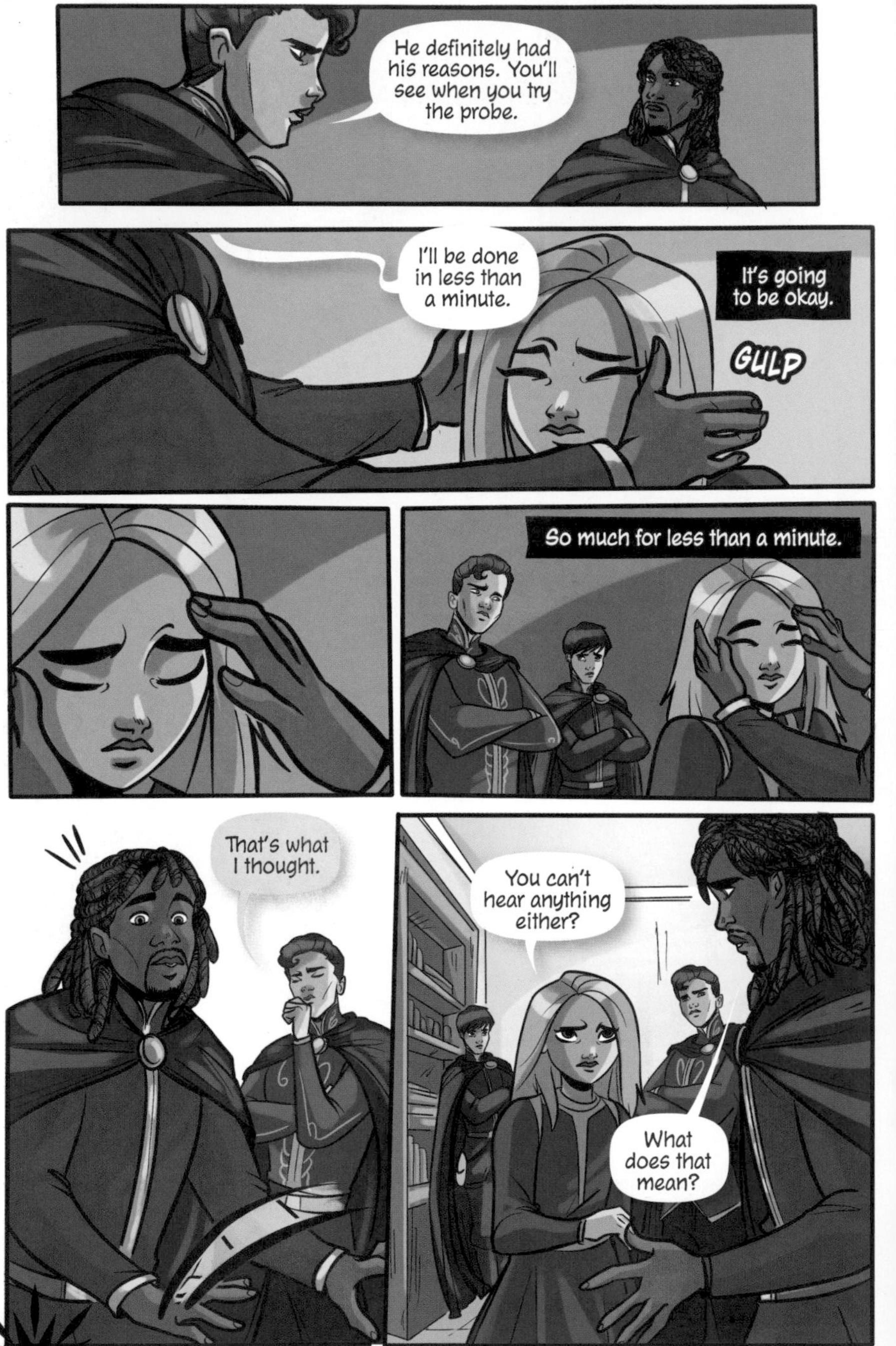
He definitely had his reasons. You'll see when you try the probe.
I'll be done in less than a minute.
It's going to be okay.
GULP
So much for less than a minute.
That's what I thought.
You can't hear anything either?
What does that mean?

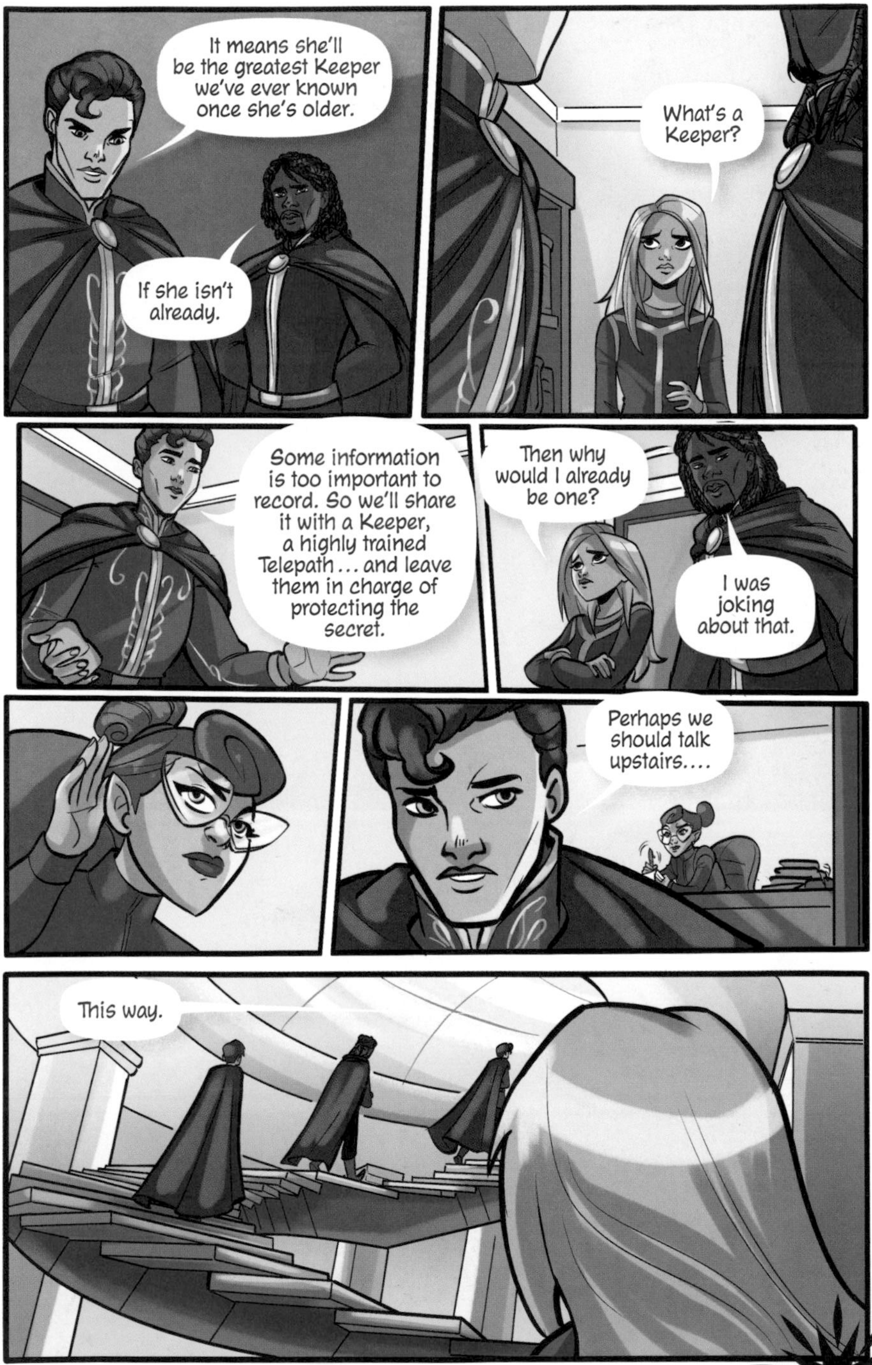
It means she'll be the greatest Keeper we've ever known once she's older.
If she isn't already.
What's a Keeper?
Some information is too important to record. So we'll share it with a Keeper, a highly trained Telepath . . . and leave them in charge of protecting the secret.
Then why would I already be one?
I was joking about that.
Perhaps we should talk upstairs. . . .
This way.

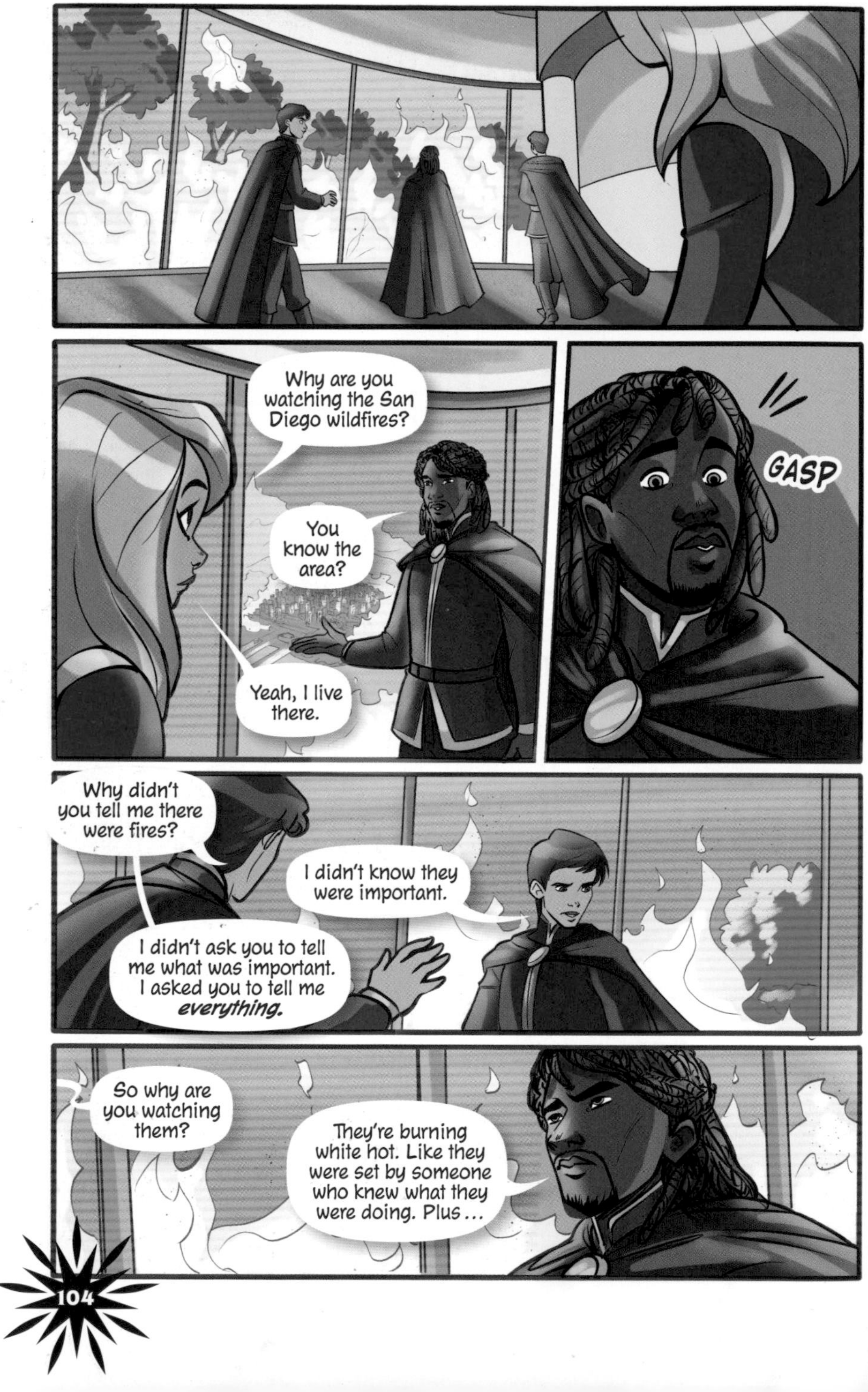
Why are you watching the San Diego wildfires?
You know the area?
Yeah, I live there.
GASP
Why didn't you tell me there were fires?
I didn't know they were important.
I didn't ask you to tell me what was important. I asked you to tell me *everything.*
So why are you watching them?
They're burning white hot. Like they were set by someone who knew what they were doing. Plus…

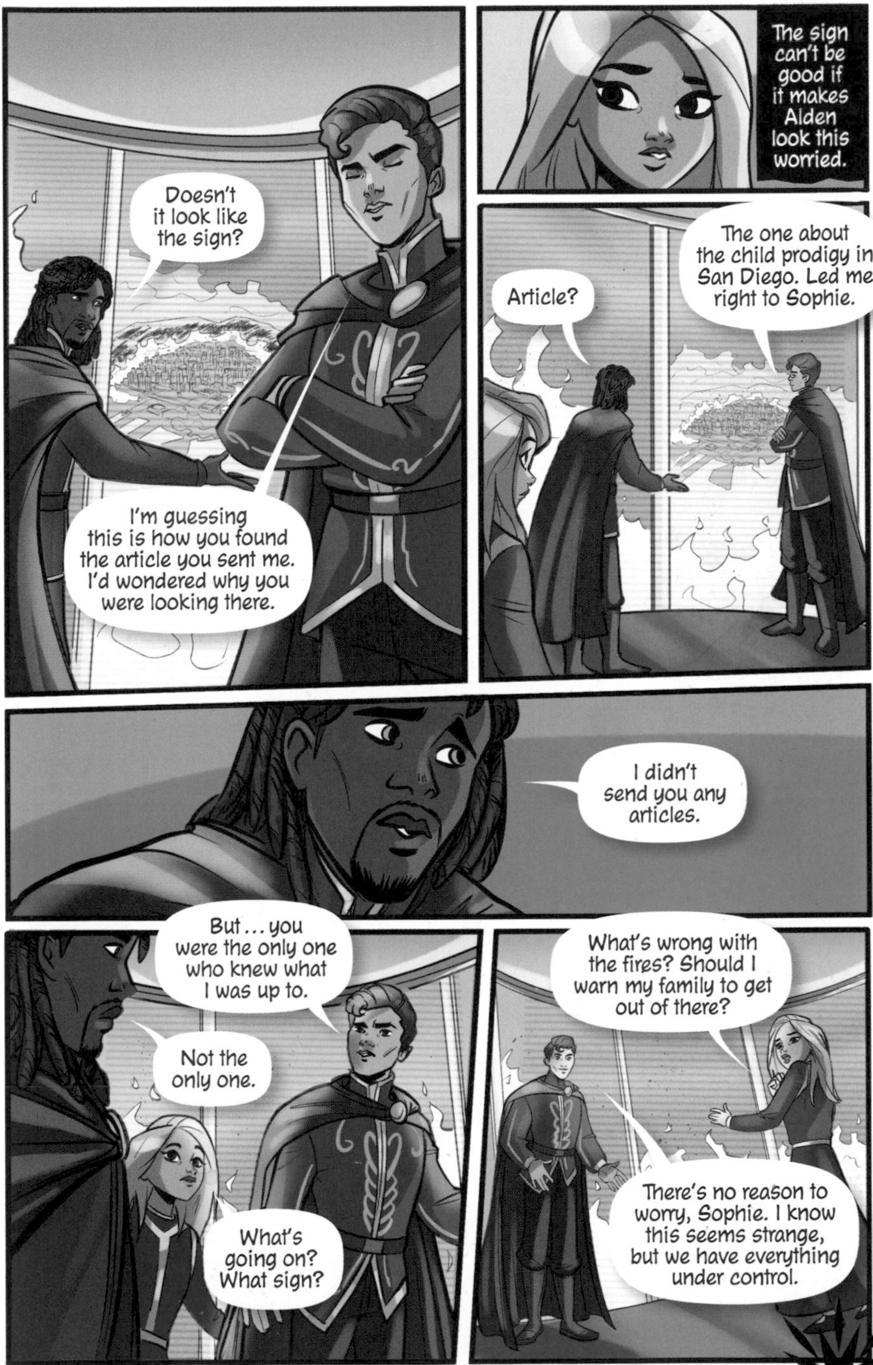
Doesn't it look like the sign?
I'm guessing this is how you found the article you sent me. I'd wondered why you were looking there.
The sign can't be good if it makes Alden look this worried.
Article?
The one about the child prodigy in San Diego. Led me right to Sophie.
I didn't send you any articles.
But... you were the only one who knew what I was up to.
Not the only one.
What's going on? What sign?
What's wrong with the fires? Should I warn my family to get out of there?
There's no reason to worry, Sophie. I know this seems strange, but we have everything under control.

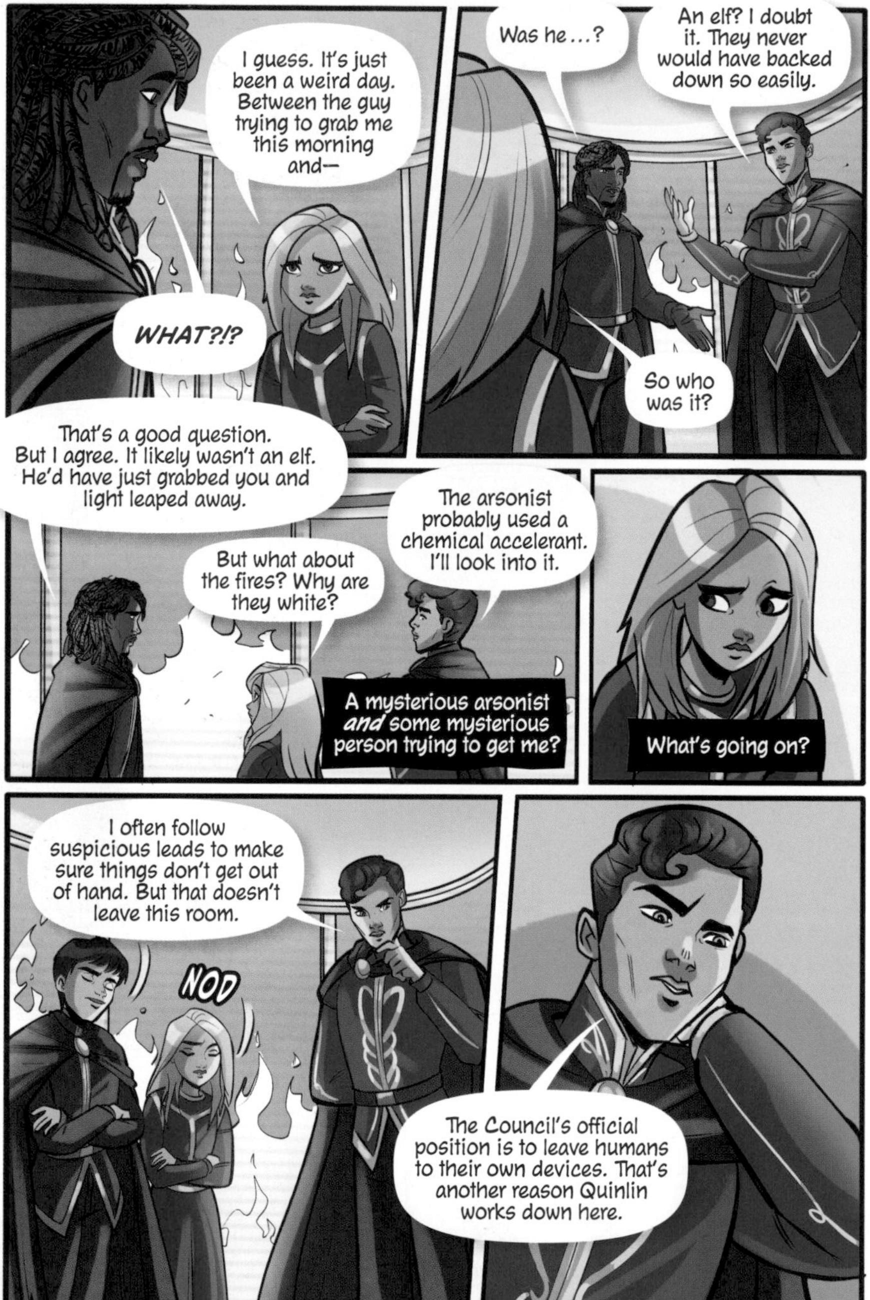
I guess. It's just been a weird day. Between the guy trying to grab me this morning and—
WHAT?!?
Was he . . . ?
An elf? I doubt it. They never would have backed down so easily.
So who was it?
That's a good question. But I agree. It likely wasn't an elf. He'd have just grabbed you and light leaped away.
But what about the fires? Why are they white?
The arsonist probably used a chemical accelerant. I'll look into it.
A mysterious arsonist *and* some mysterious person trying to get me?
What's going on?
I often follow suspicious leads to make sure things don't get out of hand. But that doesn't leave this room.
NOD
The Council's official position is to leave humans to their own devices. That's another reason Quinlin works down here.

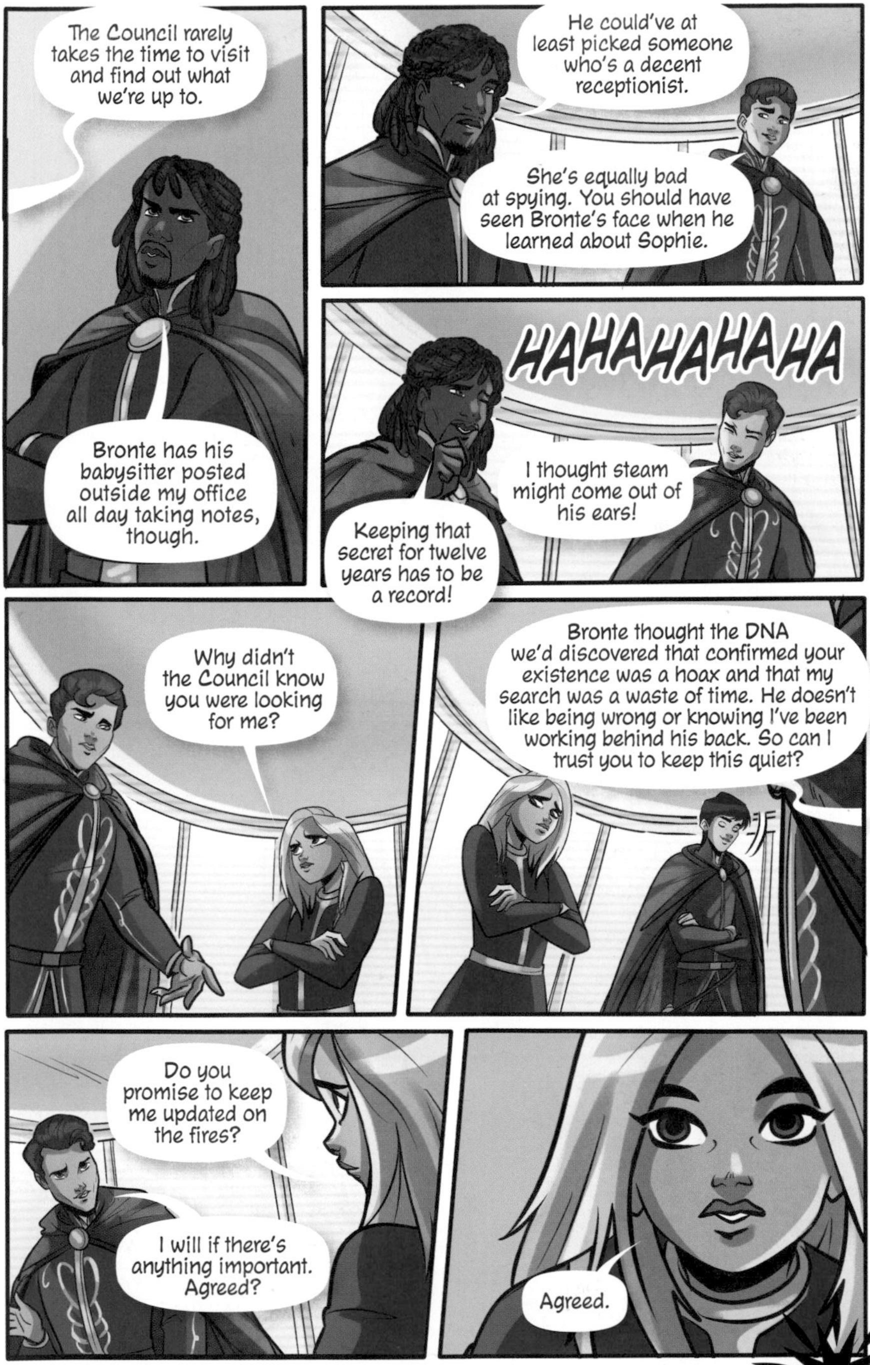
The Council rarely takes the time to visit and find out what we're up to.
Bronte has his babysitter posted outside my office all day taking notes, though.
He could've at least picked someone who's a decent receptionist.
She's equally bad at spying. You should have seen Bronte's face when he learned about Sophie.
HAHAHAHAHA
I thought steam might come out of his ears!
Keeping that secret for twelve years has to be a record!
Why didn't the Council know you were looking for me?
Bronte thought the DNA we'd discovered that confirmed your existence was a hoax and that my search was a waste of time. He doesn't like being wrong or knowing I've been working behind his back. So can I trust you to keep this quiet?
Do you promise to keep me updated on the fires?
I will if there's anything important. Agreed?
Agreed.

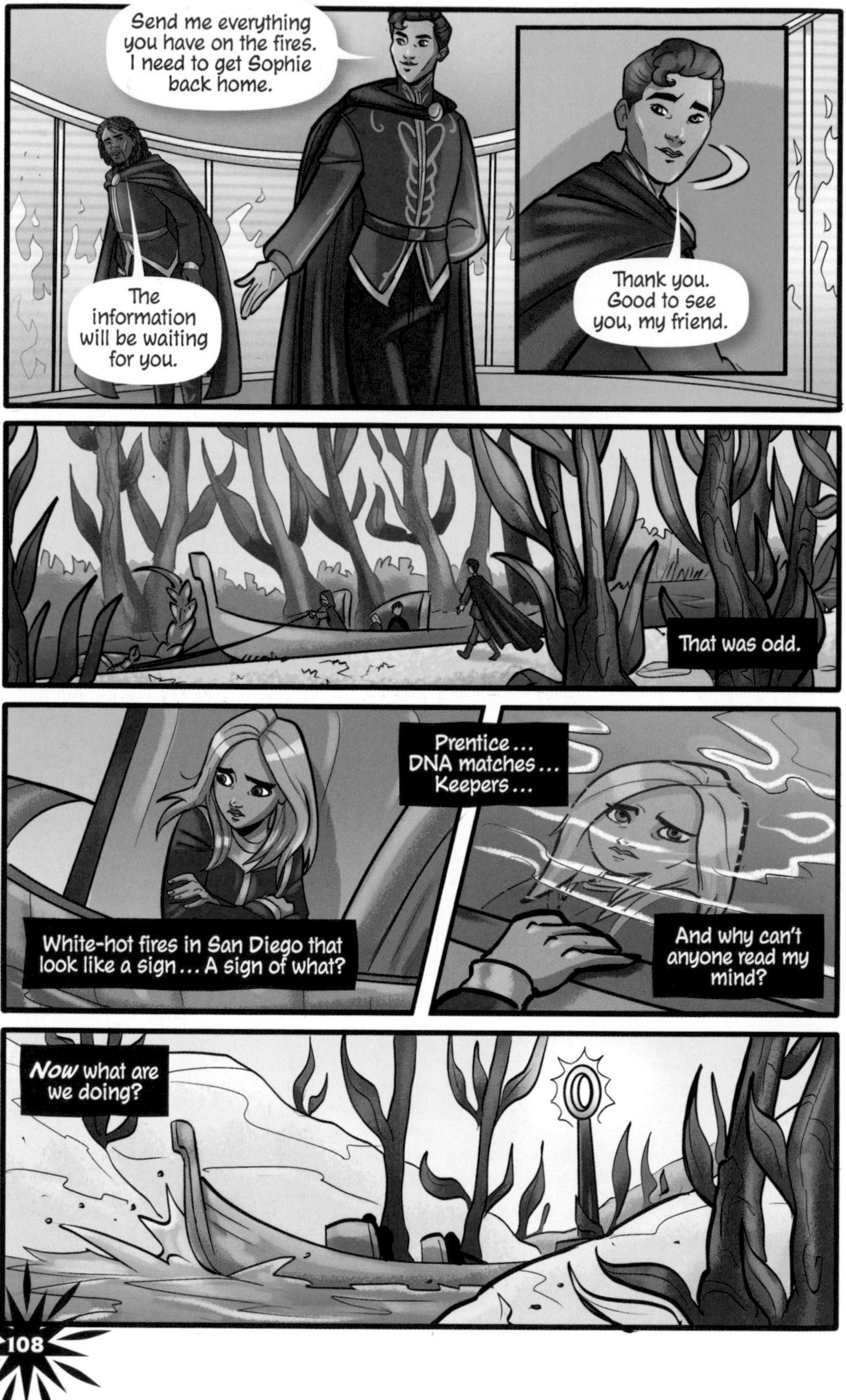

Send me everything you have on the fires. I need to get Sophie back home.
The information will be waiting for you.
Thank you. Good to see you, my friend.
That was odd.
Prentice... DNA matches... Keepers...
White-hot fires in San Diego that look like a sign... A sign of what?
And why can't anyone read my mind?
Now what are we doing?

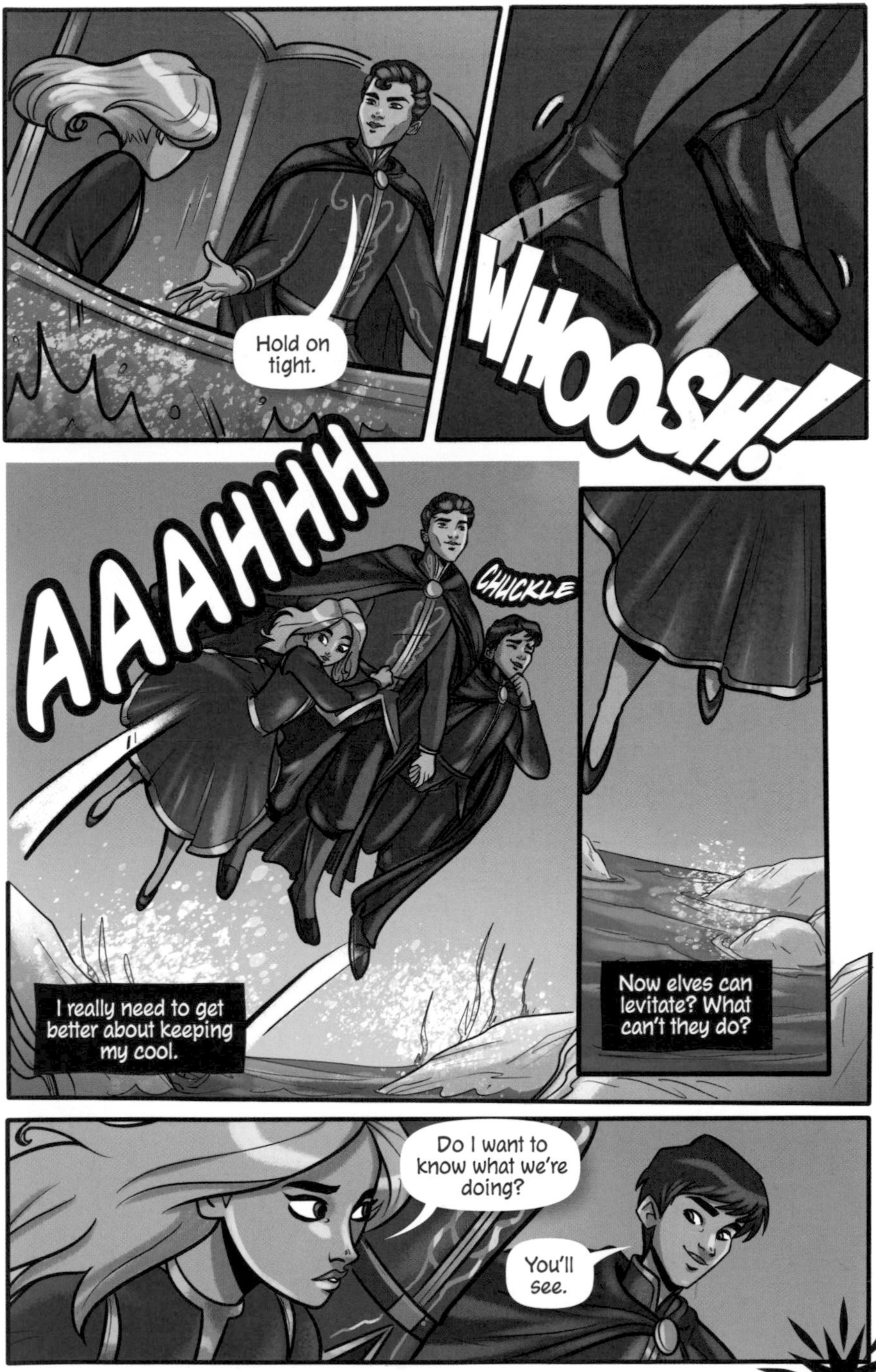
Hold on tight.
WHOOSH!
AAAHHH
CHUCKLE
I really need to get better about keeping my cool.
Now elves can levitate? What can't they do?
Do I want to know what we're doing?
You'll see.

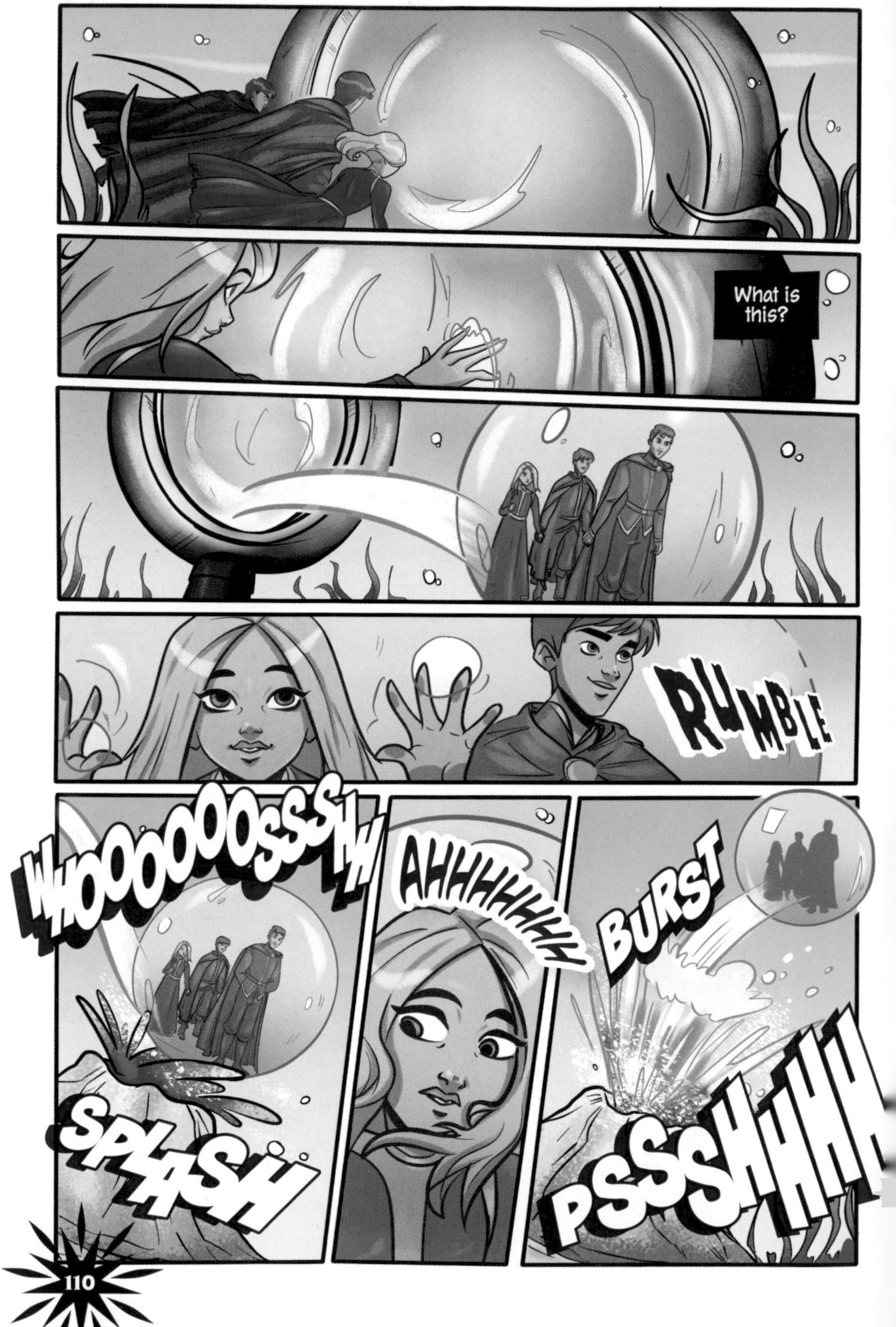
What is this?
RUMBLE
WHOOOOOOSSSHH
SPLASH
AHHHHHHH
BURST
PSSSHHHH

CHAPTER ELEVEN

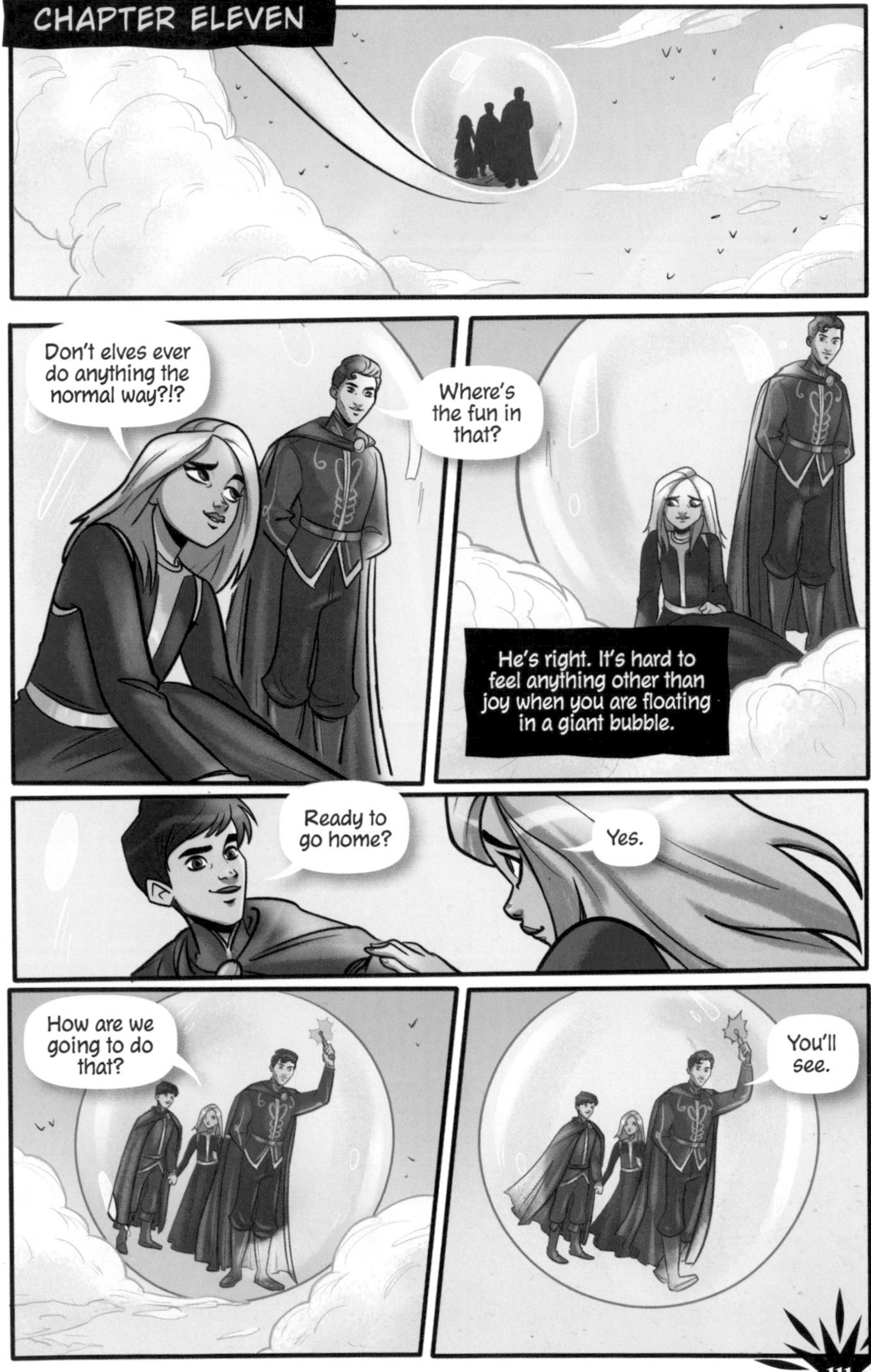
Don't elves ever do anything the normal way?!?
Where's the fun in that?
He's right. It's hard to feel anything other than joy when you are floating in a giant bubble.
Ready to go home?
Yes.
How are we going to do that?
You'll see.

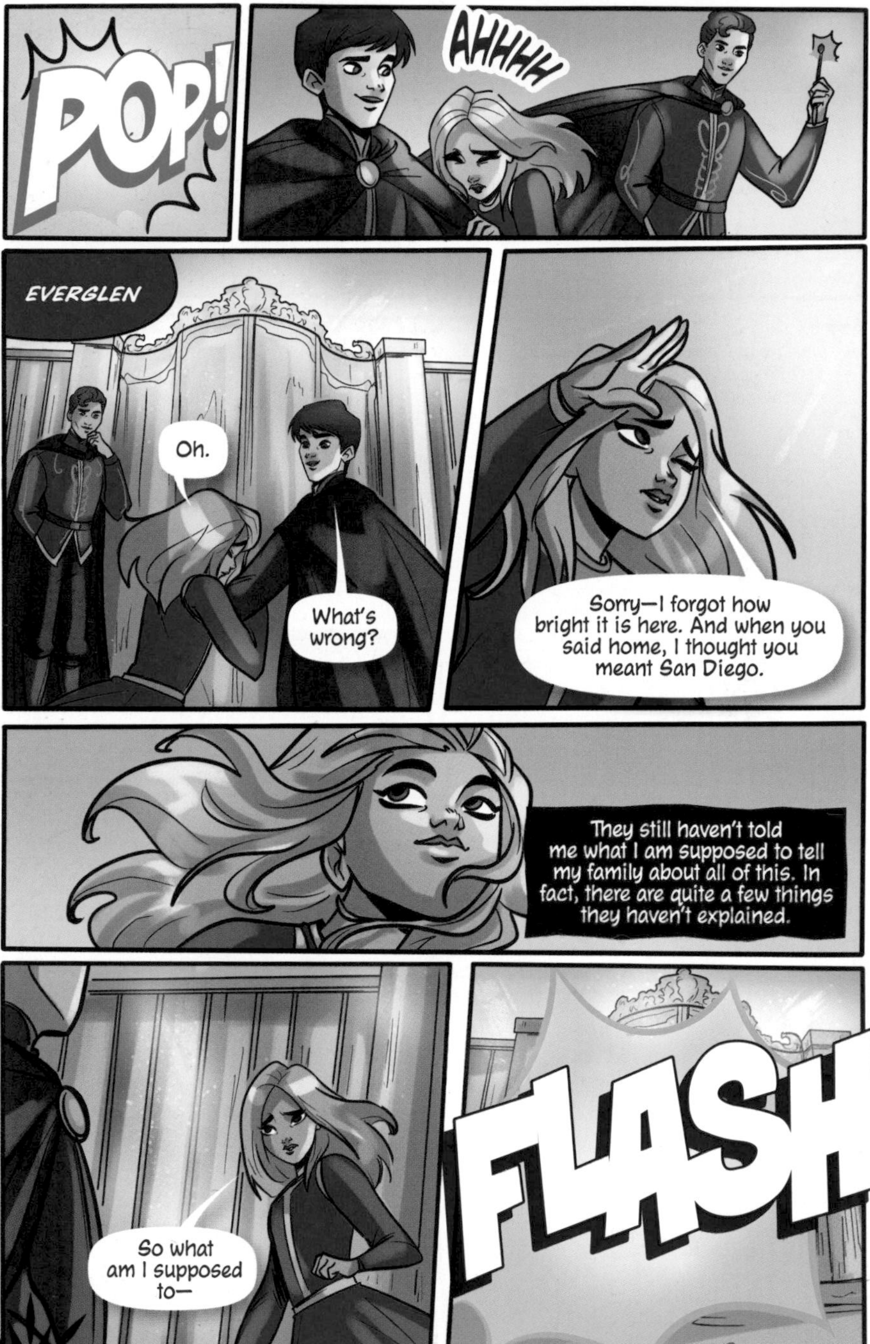
POP!
AHHHH
EVERGLEN
Oh.
What's wrong?
Sorry—I forgot how bright it is here. And when you said home, I thought you meant San Diego.
They still haven't told me what I am supposed to tell my family about all of this. In fact, there are quite a few things they haven't explained.
So what am I supposed to—
FLASH

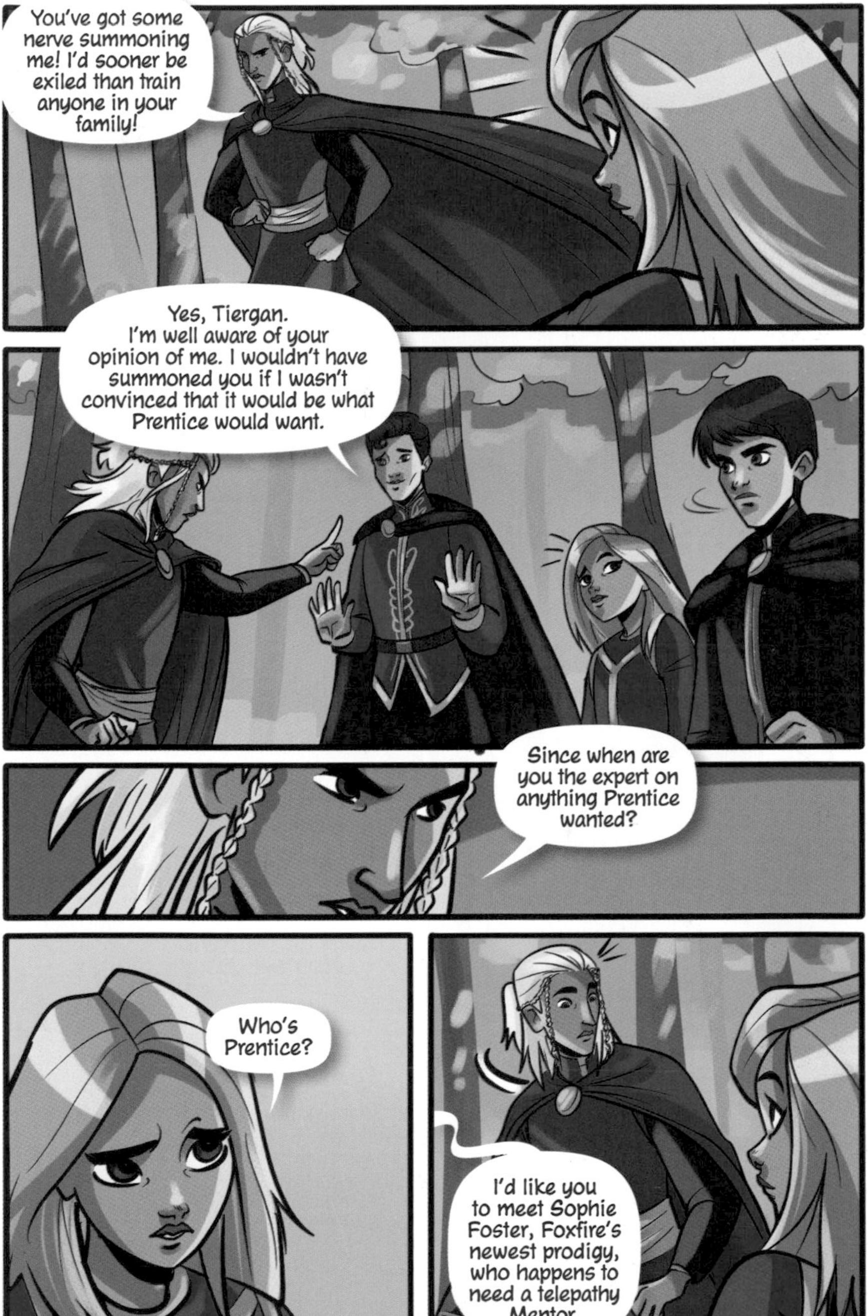
You've got some nerve summoning me! I'd sooner be exiled than train anyone in your family!
Yes, Tiergan. I'm well aware of your opinion of me. I wouldn't have summoned you if I wasn't convinced that it would be what Prentice would want.
Since when are you the expert on anything Prentice wanted?
Who's Prentice?
I'd like you to meet Sophie Foster, Foxfire's newest prodigy, who happens to need a telepathy Mentor.

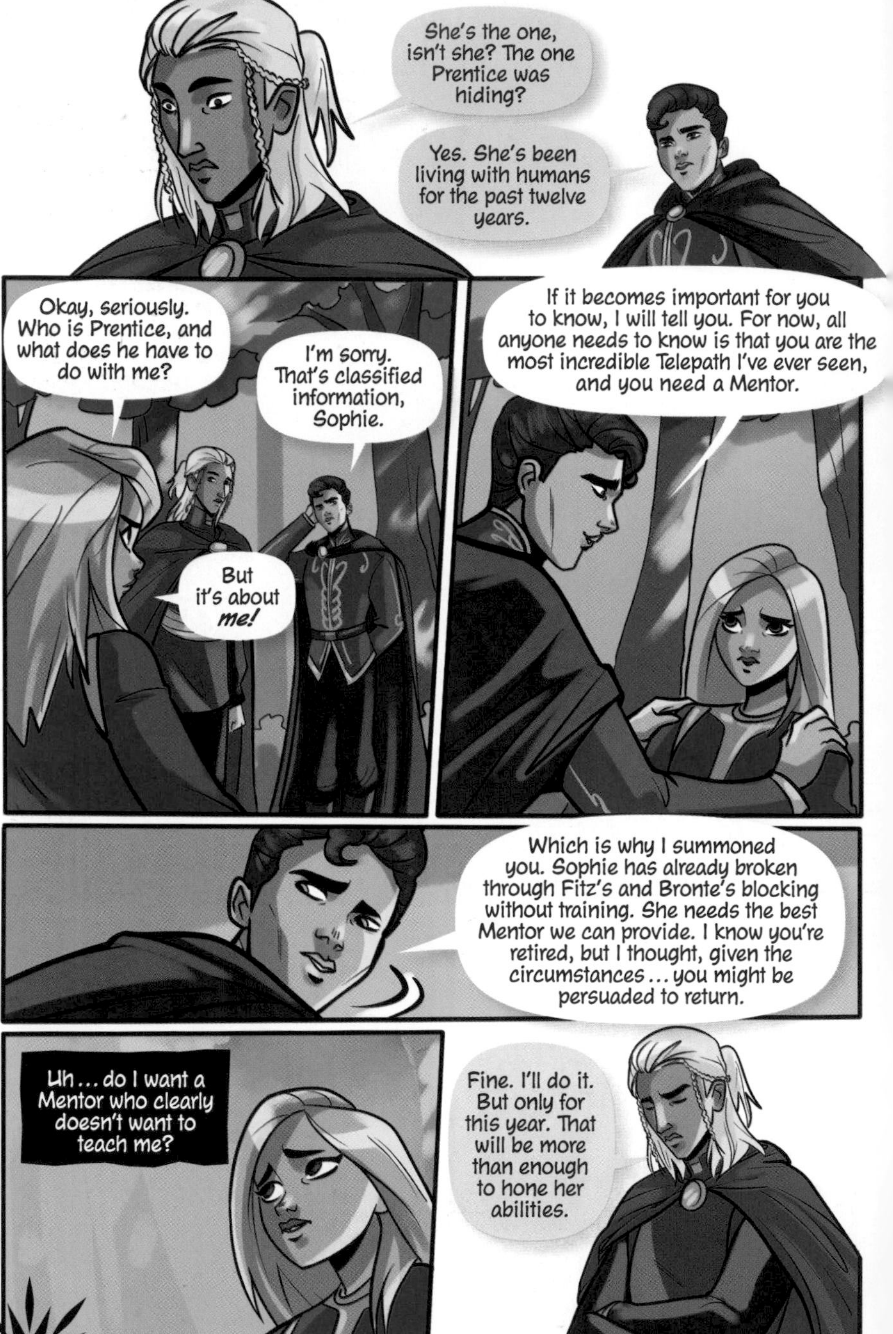
She's the one, isn't she? The one Prentice was hiding?
Yes. She's been living with humans for the past twelve years.
Okay, seriously. Who is Prentice, and what does he have to do with me?
I'm sorry. That's classified information, Sophie.
But it's about *me!*
If it becomes important for you to know, I will tell you. For now, all anyone needs to know is that you are the most incredible Telepath I've ever seen, and you need a Mentor.
Which is why I summoned you. Sophie has already broken through Fitz's and Bronte's blocking without training. She needs the best Mentor we can provide. I know you're retired, but I thought, given the circumstances... you might be persuaded to return.
Uh... do I want a Mentor who clearly doesn't want to teach me?
Fine. I'll do it. But only for this year. That will be more than enough to hone her abilities.

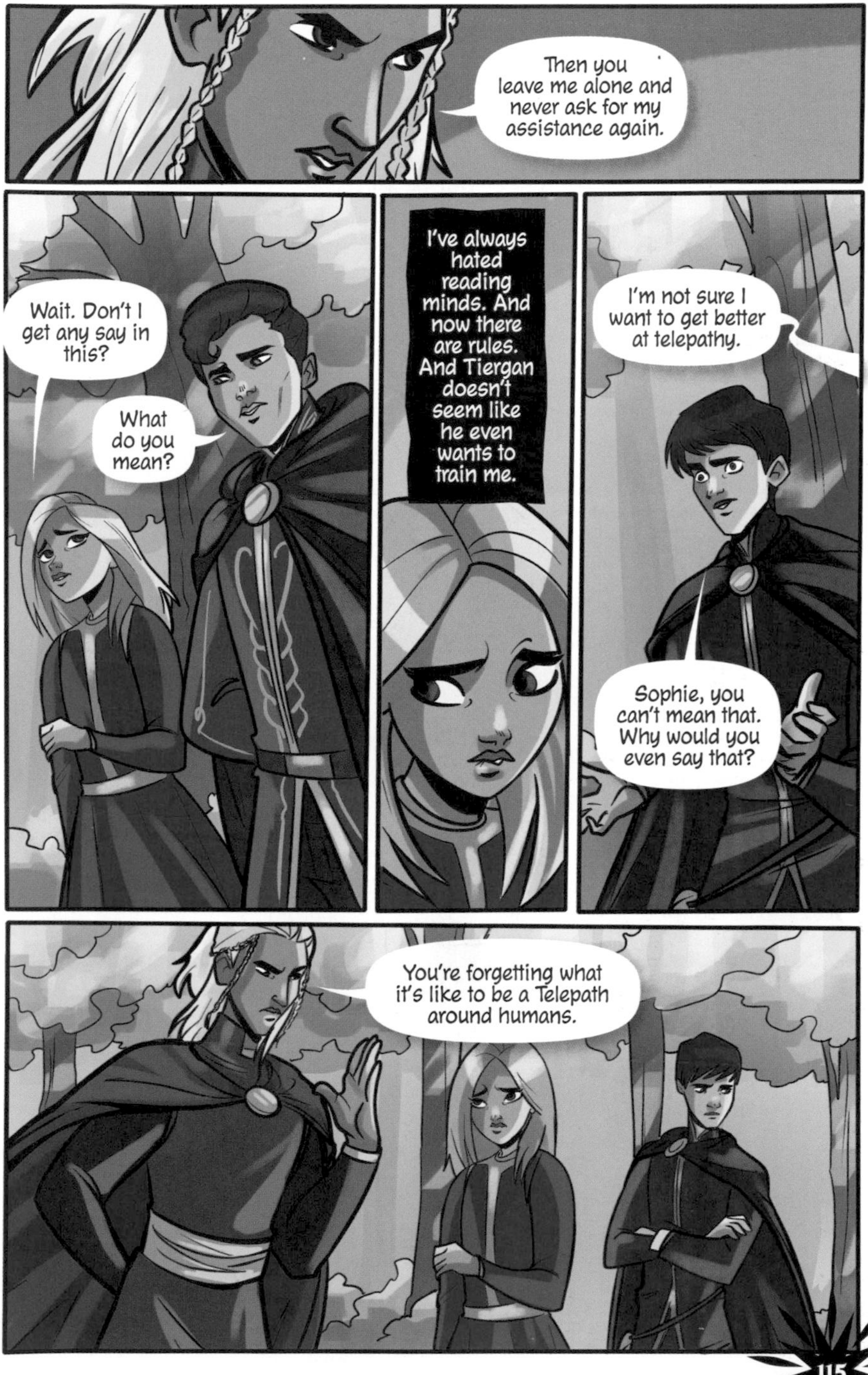

Then you leave me alone and never ask for my assistance again.
Wait. Don't I get any say in this?
What do you mean?
I've always hated reading minds. And now there are rules. And Tiergan doesn't seem like he even wants to train me.
I'm not sure I want to get better at telepathy.
Sophie, you can't mean that. Why would you even say that?
You're forgetting what it's like to be a Telepath around humans.

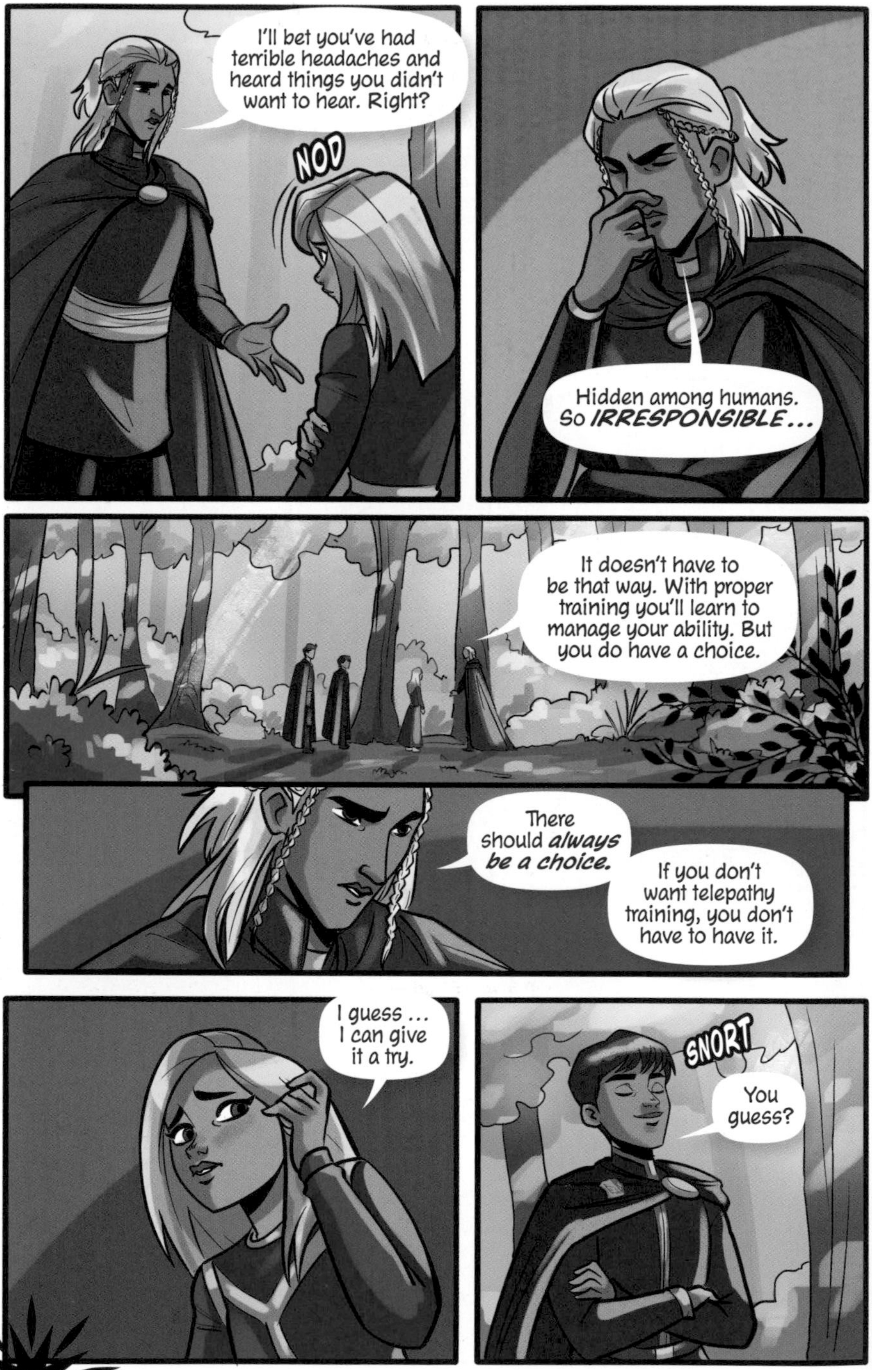
I'll bet you've had terrible headaches and heard things you didn't want to hear. Right?
NOD
Hidden among humans. So *IRRESPONSIBLE . . .*
It doesn't have to be that way. With proper training you'll learn to manage your ability. But you do have a choice.
There should *always be a choice.*
If you don't want telepathy training, you don't have to have it.
I guess . . . I can give it a try.
SNORT
You guess?

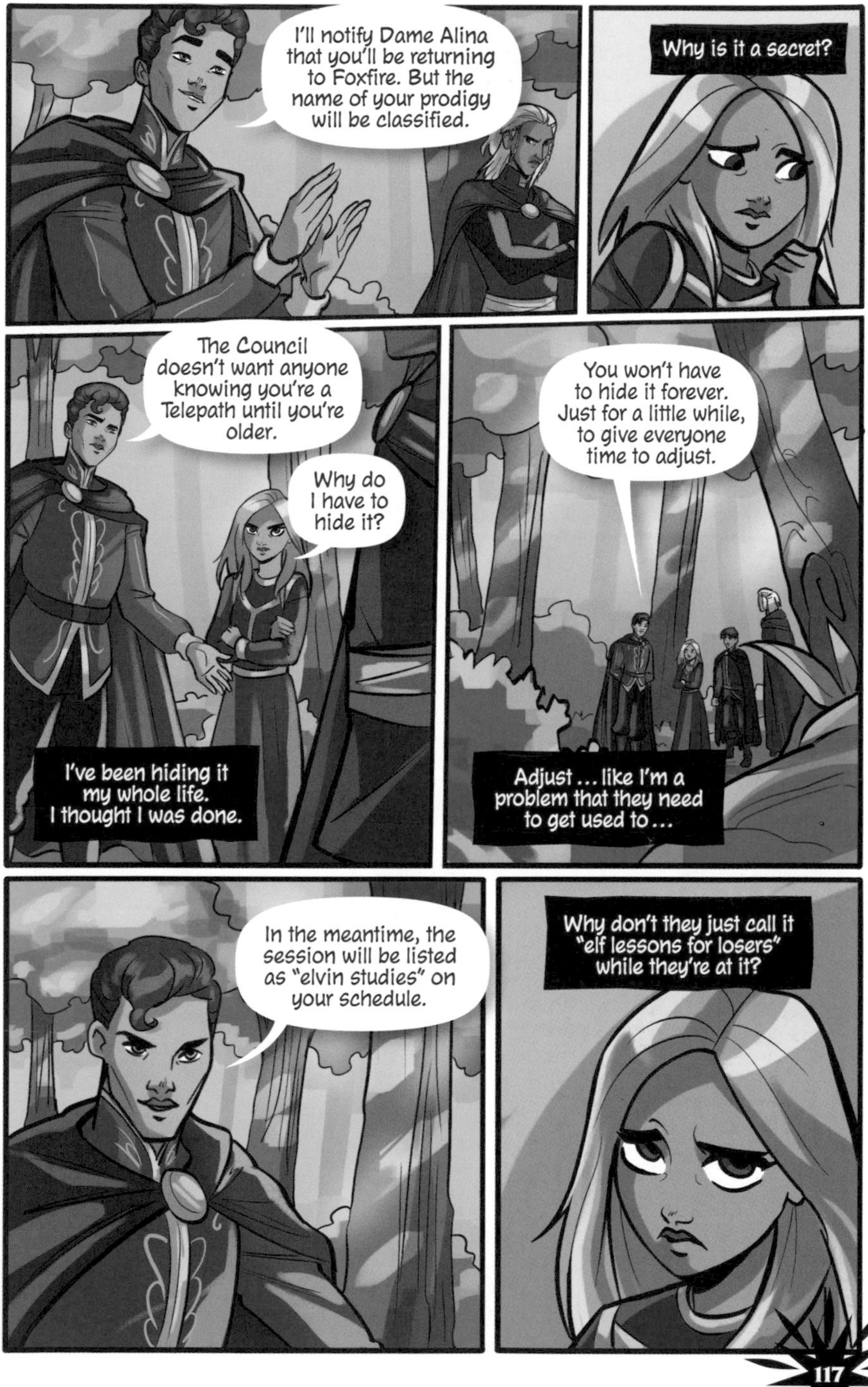
I'll notify Dame Alina that you'll be returning to Foxfire. But the name of your prodigy will be classified.
Why is it a secret?
The Council doesn't want anyone knowing you're a Telepath until you're older.
Why do I have to hide it?
I've been hiding it my whole life. I thought I was done.
You won't have to hide it forever. Just for a little while, to give everyone time to adjust.
Adjust ... like I'm a problem that they need to get used to ...
In the meantime, the session will be listed as "elvin studies" on your schedule.
Why don't they just call it "elf lessons for losers" while they're at it?

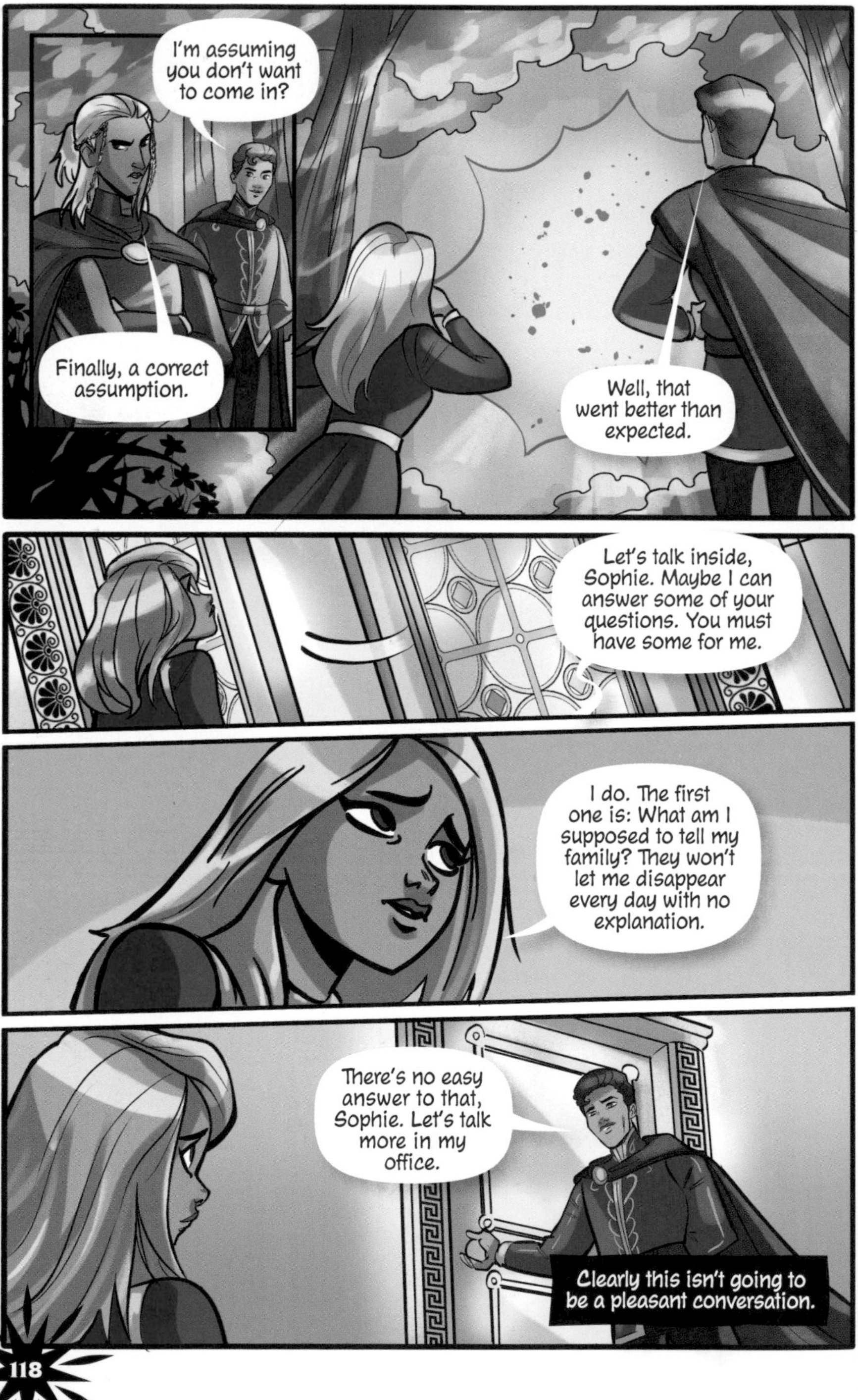
I'm assuming you don't want to come in?
Finally, a correct assumption.
Well, that went better than expected.
Let's talk inside, Sophie. Maybe I can answer some of your questions. You must have some for me.
I do. The first one is: What am I supposed to tell my family? They won't let me disappear every day with no explanation.
There's no easy answer to that, Sophie. Let's talk more in my office.
Clearly this isn't going to be a pleasant conversation.

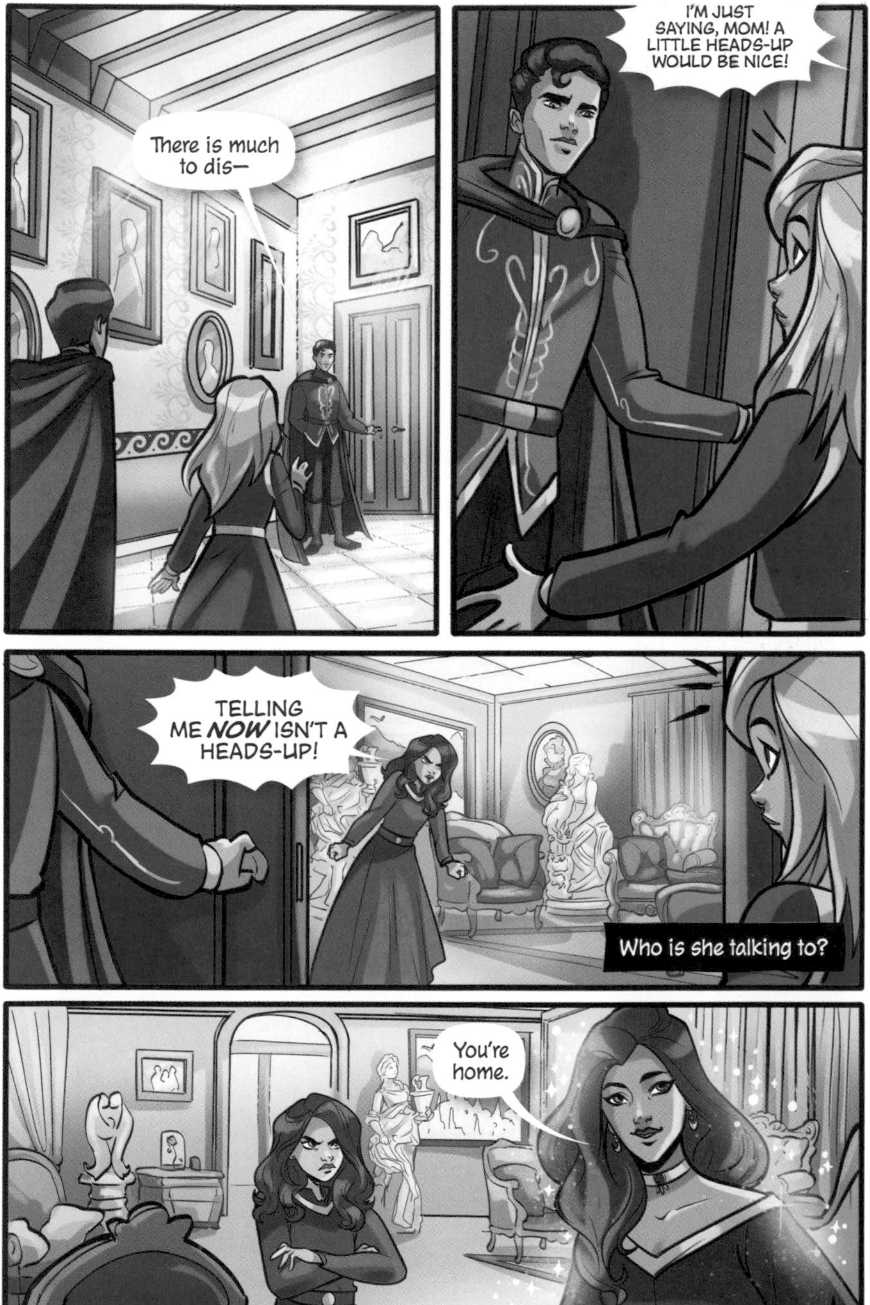
There is much to dis—
I'M JUST SAYING, MOM! A LITTLE HEADS-UP WOULD BE NICE!
TELLING ME NOW ISN'T A HEADS-UP!
Who is she talking to?
You're home.

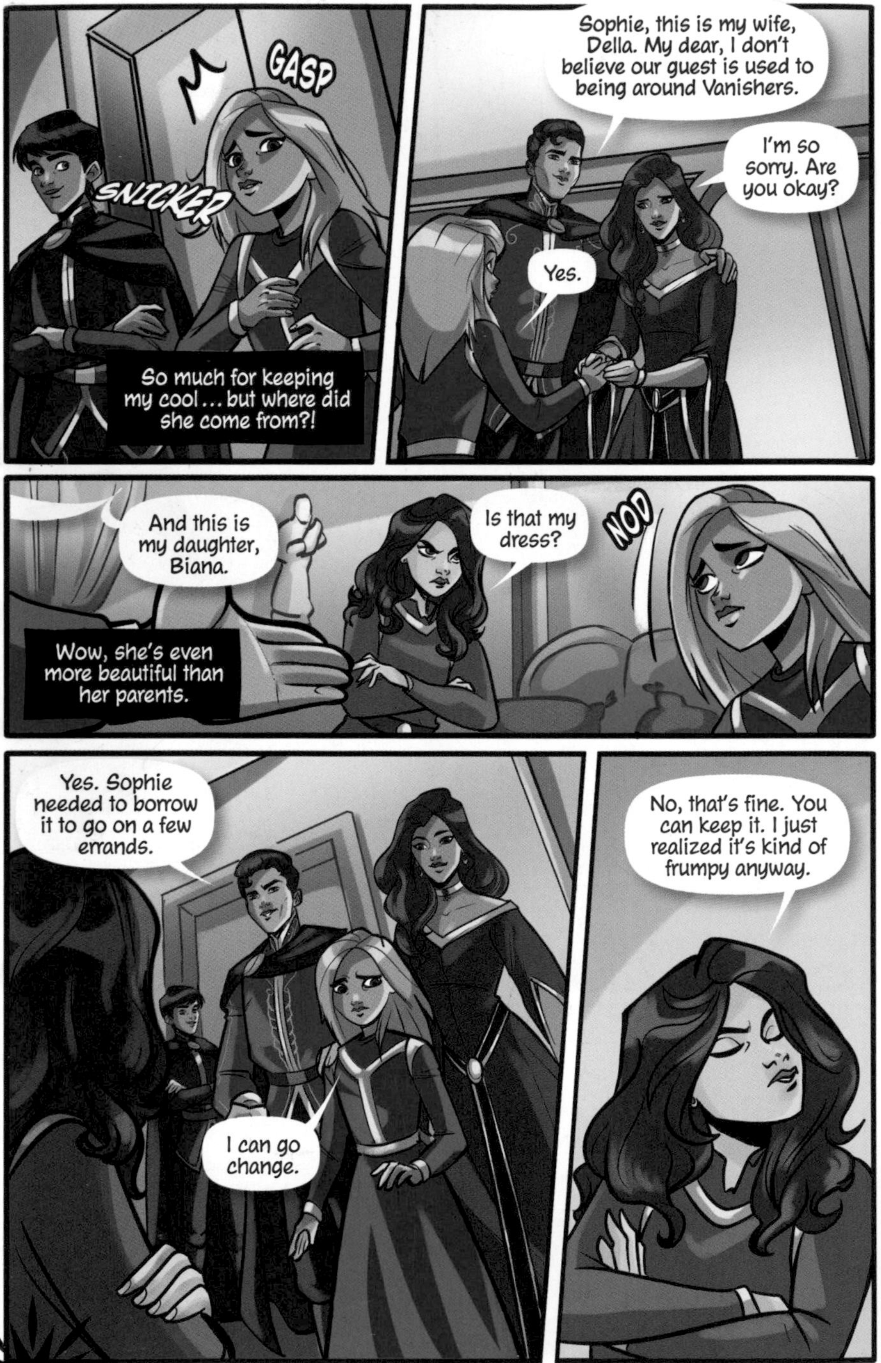
GASP
SNICKER
So much for keeping my cool... but where did she come from?!
Sophie, this is my wife, Della. My dear, I don't believe our guest is used to being around Vanishers.
I'm so sorry. Are you okay?
Yes.
And this is my daughter, Biana.
Wow, she's even more beautiful than her parents.
Is that my dress?
NOD
Yes. Sophie needed to borrow it to go on a few errands.
I can go change.
No, that's fine. You can keep it. I just realized it's kind of frumpy anyway.

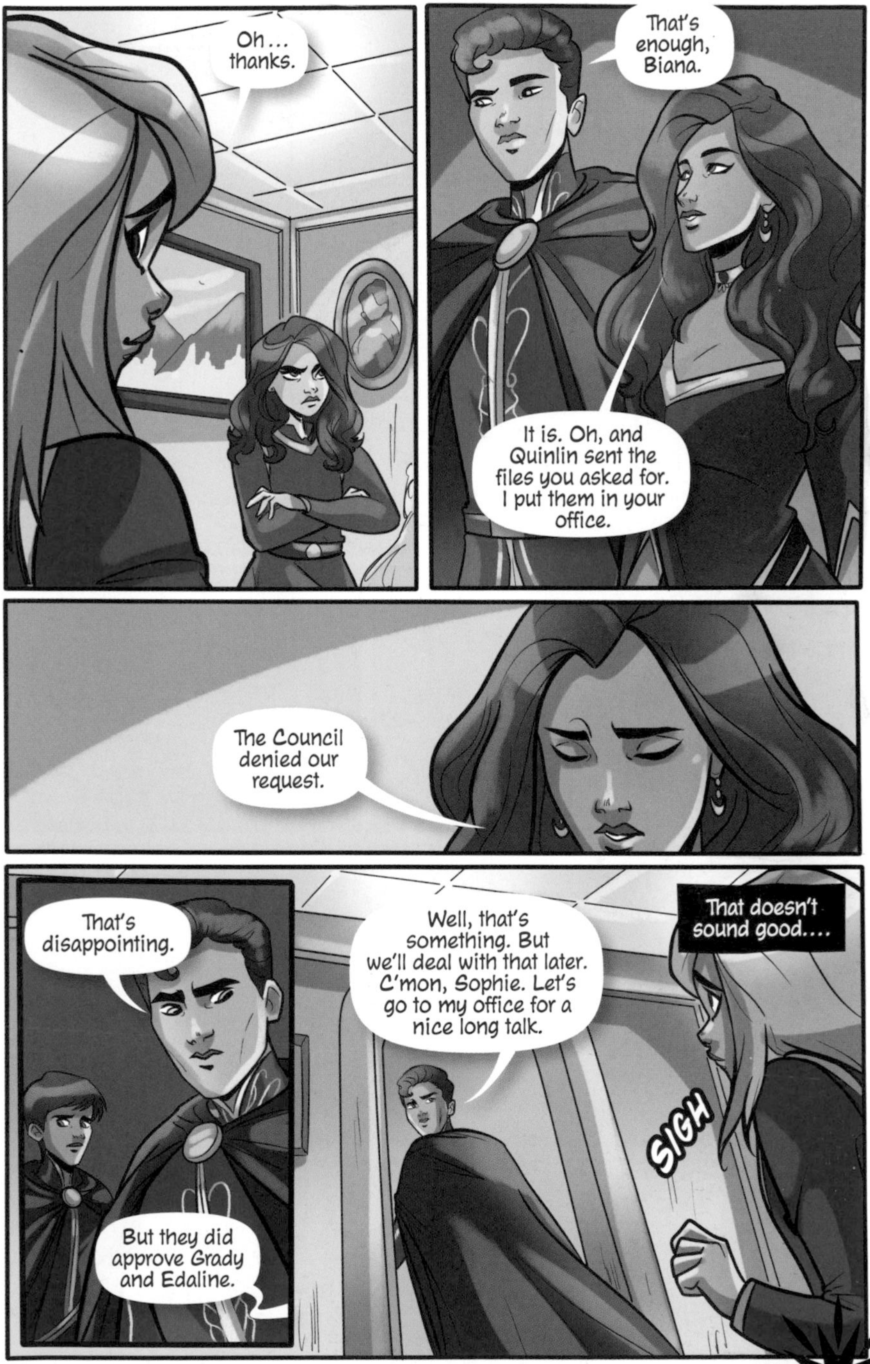
Oh... thanks.
That's enough, Biana.
It is. Oh, and Quinlin sent the files you asked for. I put them in your office.
The Council denied our request.
That's disappointing.
But they did approve Grady and Edaline.
Well, that's something. But we'll deal with that later. C'mon, Sophie. Let's go to my office for a nice long talk.
That doesn't sound good....
SIGH

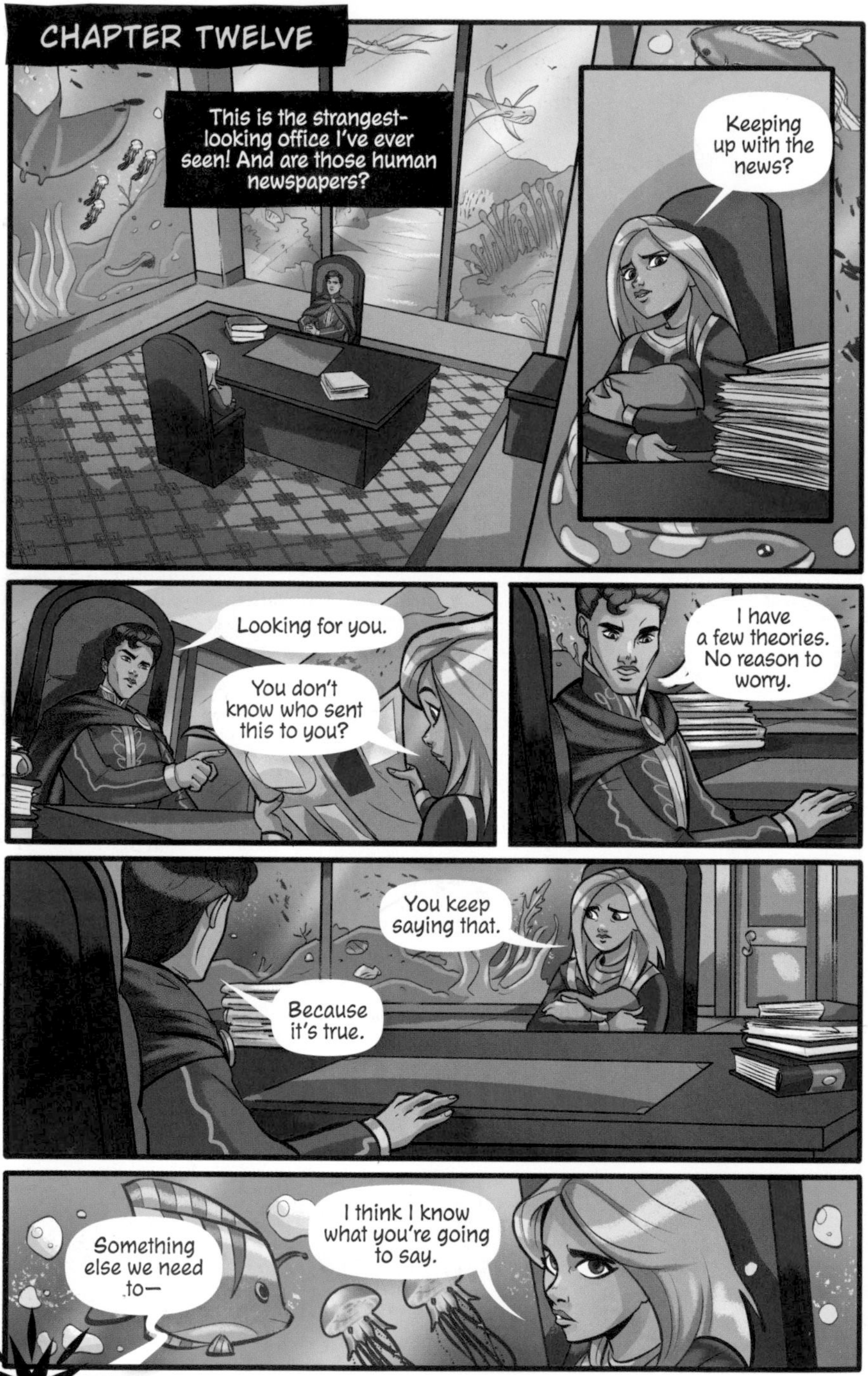
CHAPTER TWELVE
This is the strangest-looking office I've ever seen! And are those human newspapers?
Keeping up with the news?
Looking for you.
You don't know who sent this to you?
I have a few theories. No reason to worry.
You keep saying that.
Because it's true.
Something else we need to—
I think I know what you're going to say.

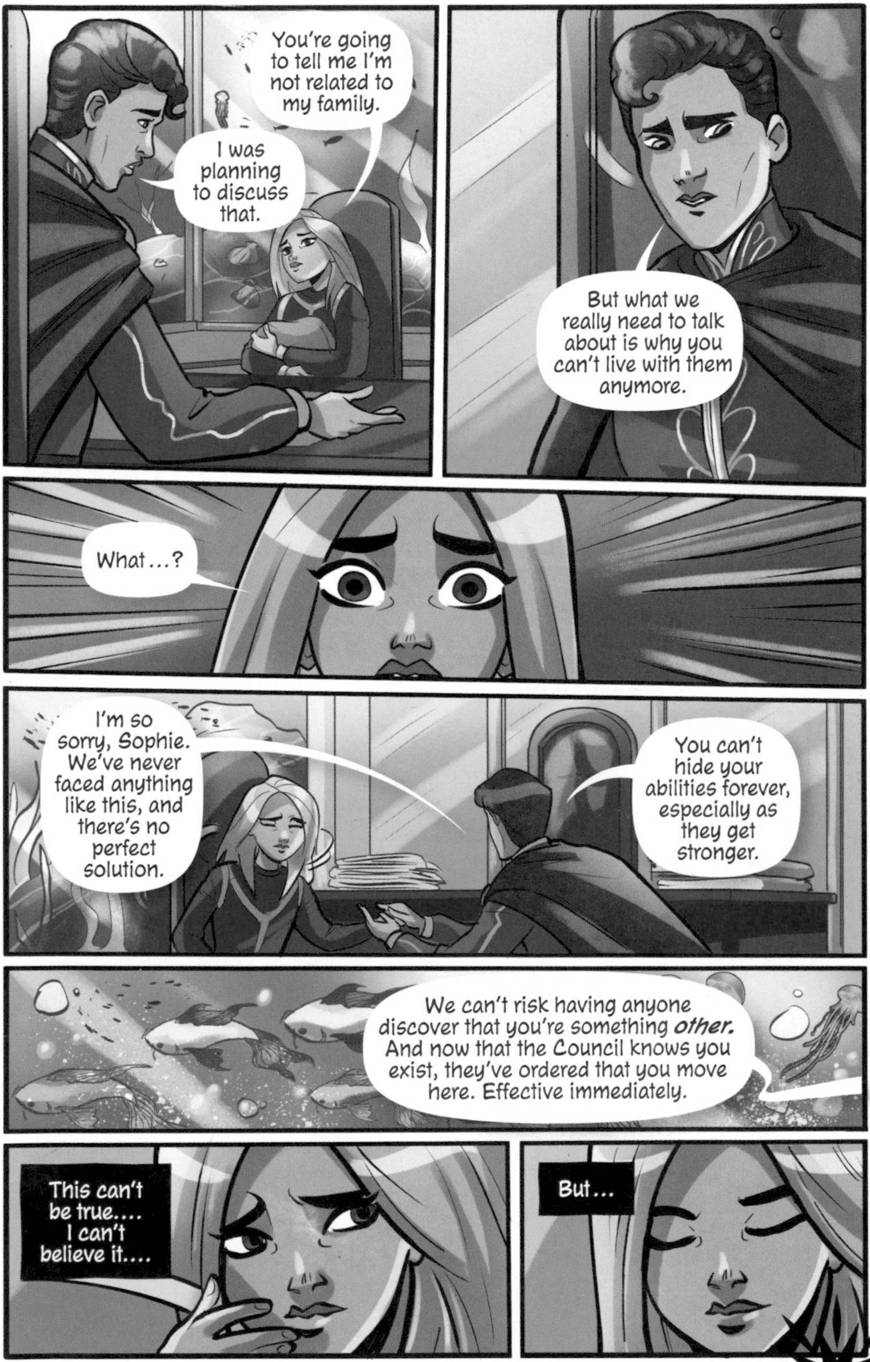
You're going to tell me I'm not related to my family.
I was planning to discuss that.
But what we really need to talk about is why you can't live with them anymore.
What...?
I'm so sorry, Sophie. We've never faced anything like this, and there's no perfect solution.
You can't hide your abilities forever, especially as they get stronger.
We can't risk having anyone discover that you're something *other.* And now that the Council knows you exist, they've ordered that you move here. Effective immediately.
This can't be true.... I can't believe it....
But...

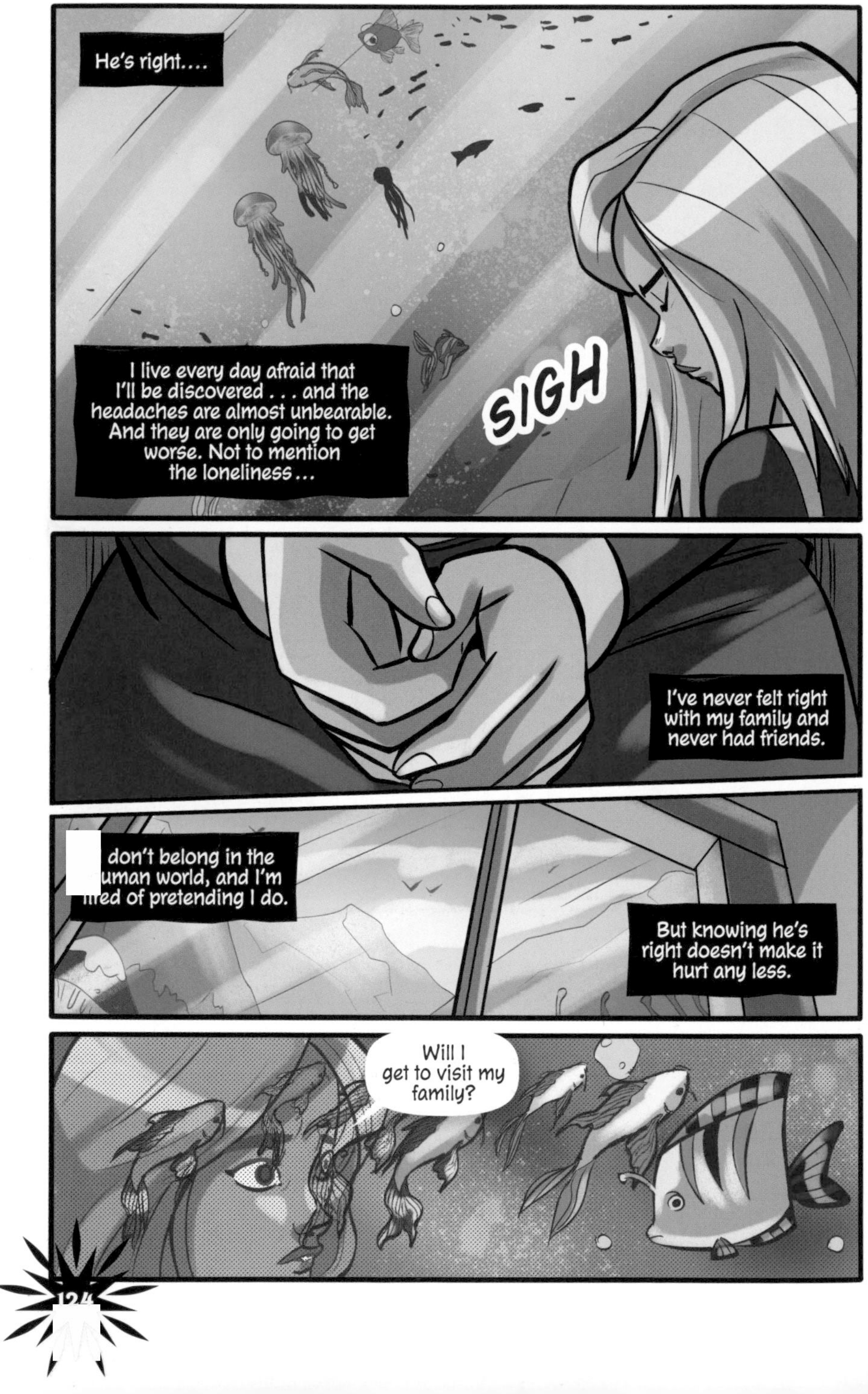
He's right....
I live every day afraid that I'll be discovered . . . and the headaches are almost unbearable. And they are only going to get worse. Not to mention the loneliness...
SIGH
I've never felt right with my family and never had friends.
don't belong in the
uman world, and I'm
ired of pretending I do.
But knowing he's right doesn't make it hurt any less.
Will I get to visit my family?

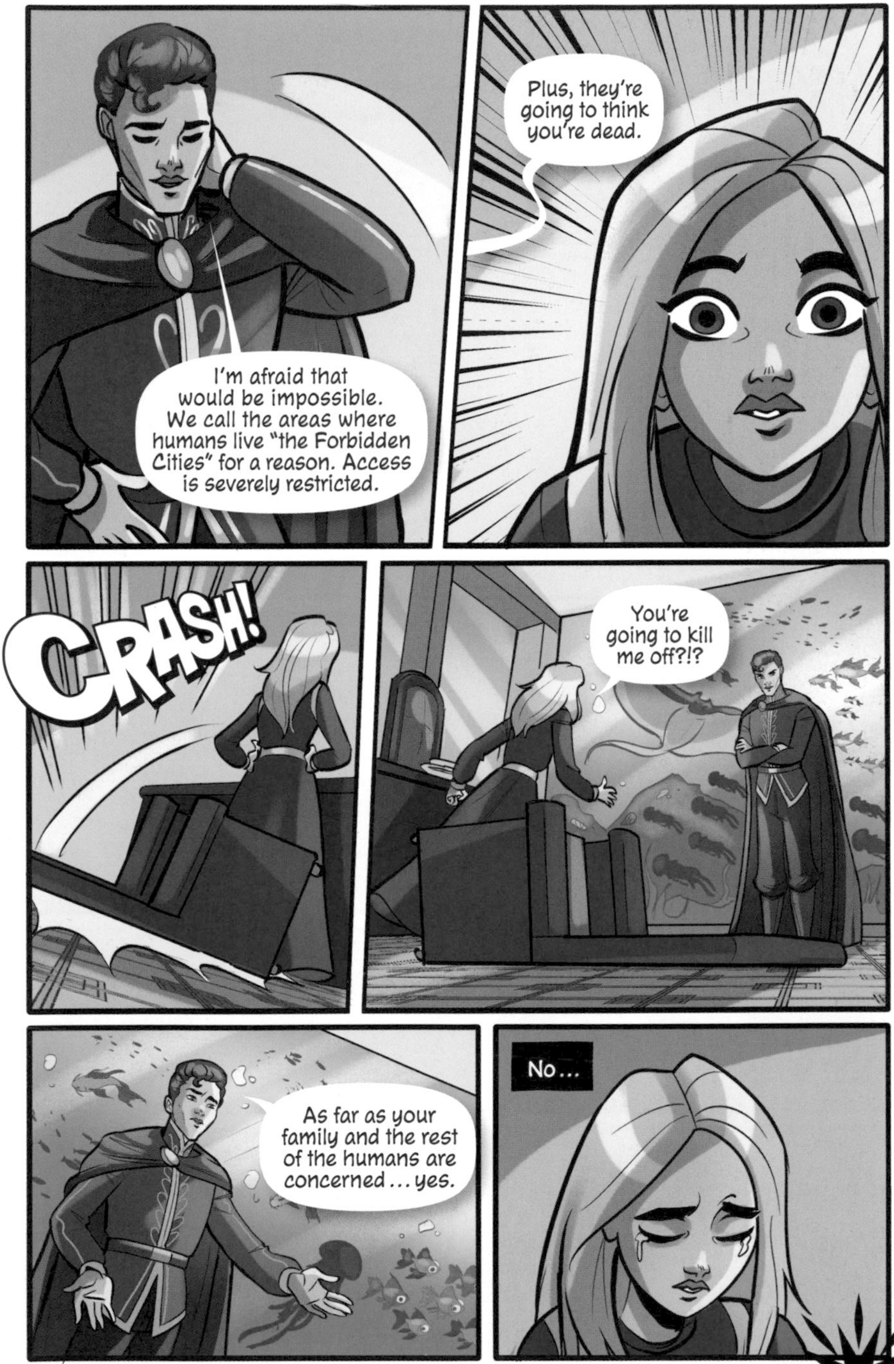
I'm afraid that would be impossible. We call the areas where humans live "the Forbidden Cities" for a reason. Access is severely restricted.
Plus, they're going to think you're dead.
CRASH!
You're going to kill me off?!?
As far as your family and the rest of the humans are concerned . . . yes.
No . . .

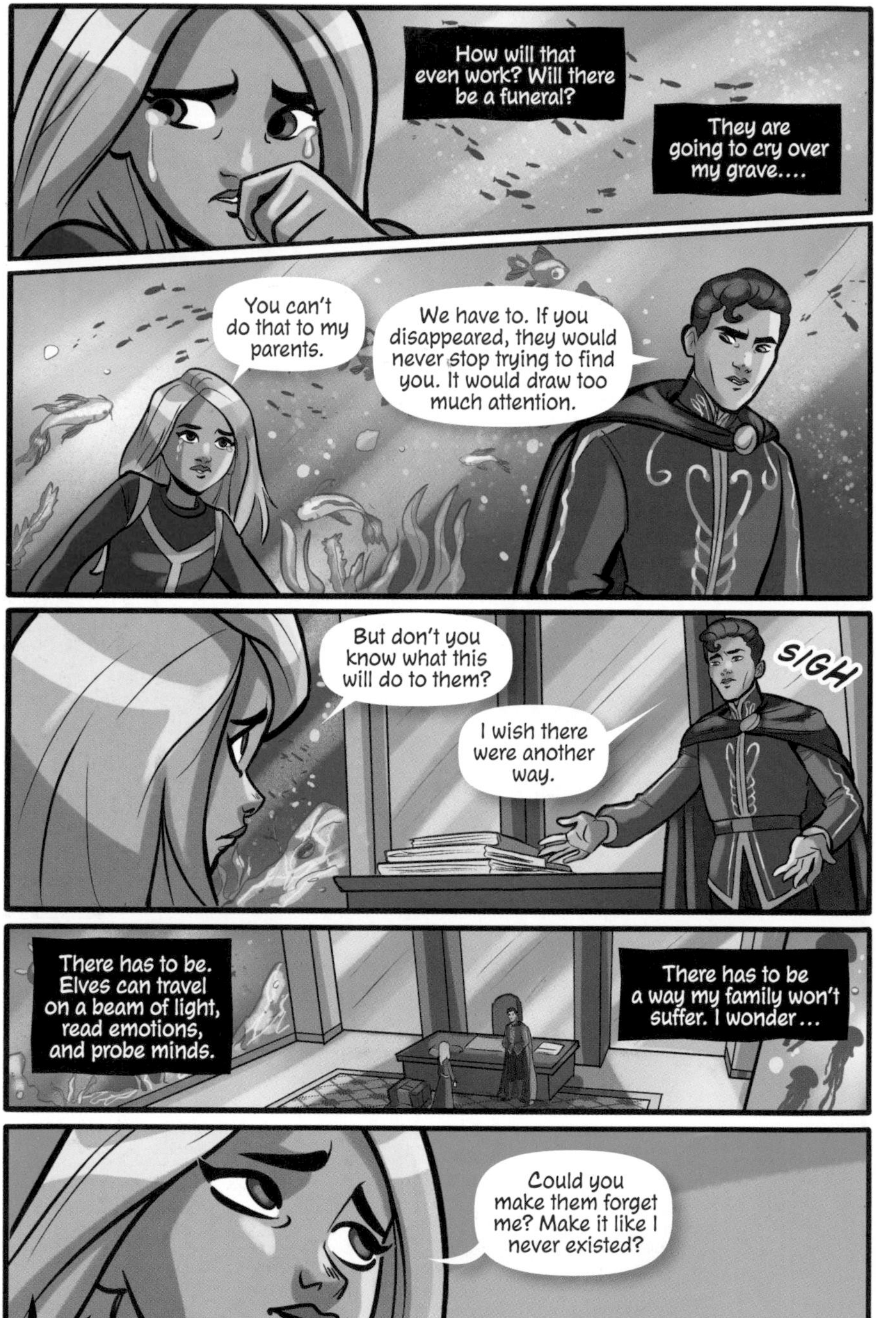
How will that even work? Will there be a funeral?
They are going to cry over my grave....
You can't do that to my parents.
We have to. If you disappeared, they would never stop trying to find you. It would draw too much attention.
But don't you know what this will do to them?
SIGH
I wish there were another way.
There has to be. Elves can travel on a beam of light, read emotions, and probe minds.
There has to be a way my family won't suffer. I wonder...
Could you make them forget me? Make it like I never existed?

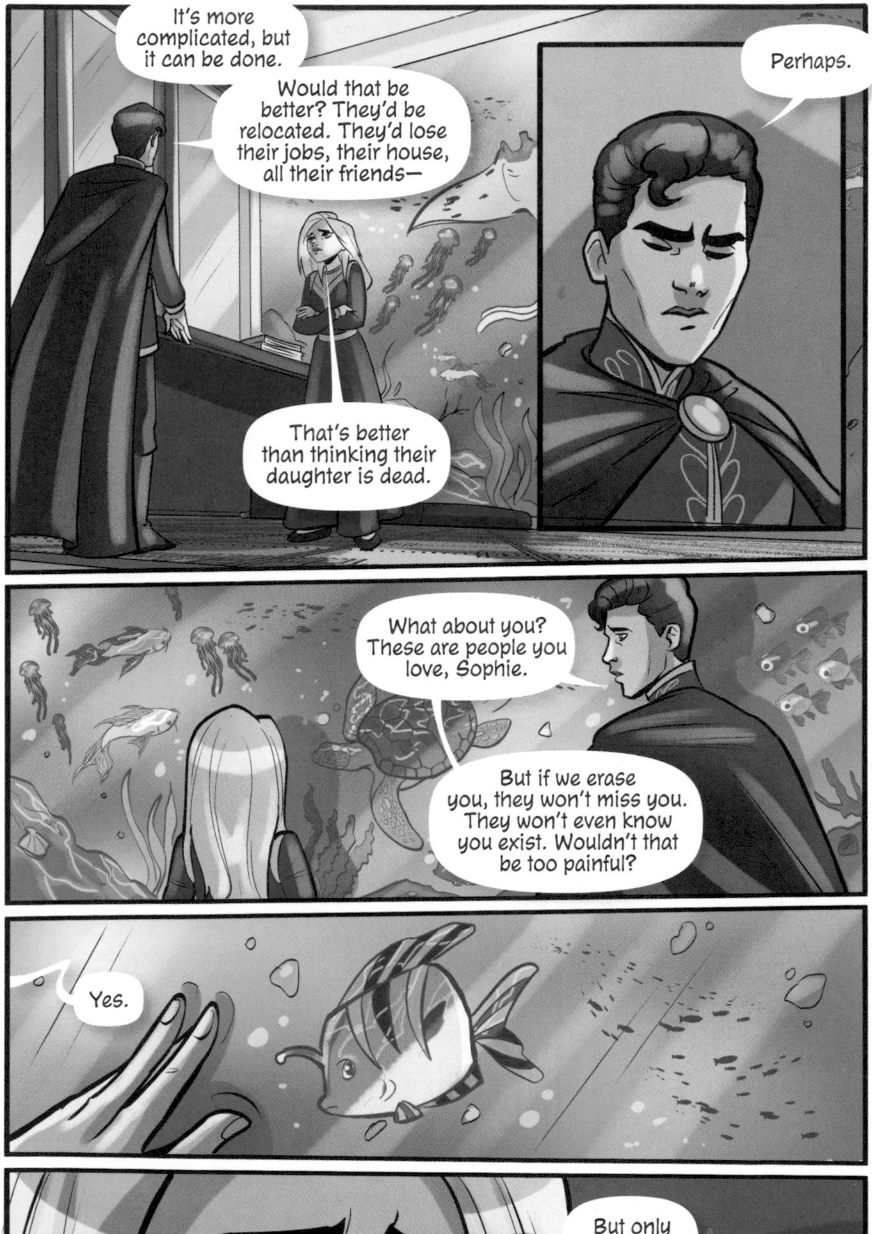
It's more complicated, but it can be done.
Would that be better? They'd be relocated. They'd lose their jobs, their house, all their friends—
That's better than thinking their daughter is dead.
Perhaps.
What about you? These are people you love, Sophie.
But if we erase you, they won't miss you. They won't even know you exist. Wouldn't that be too painful?
Yes.
But only for me. For them...

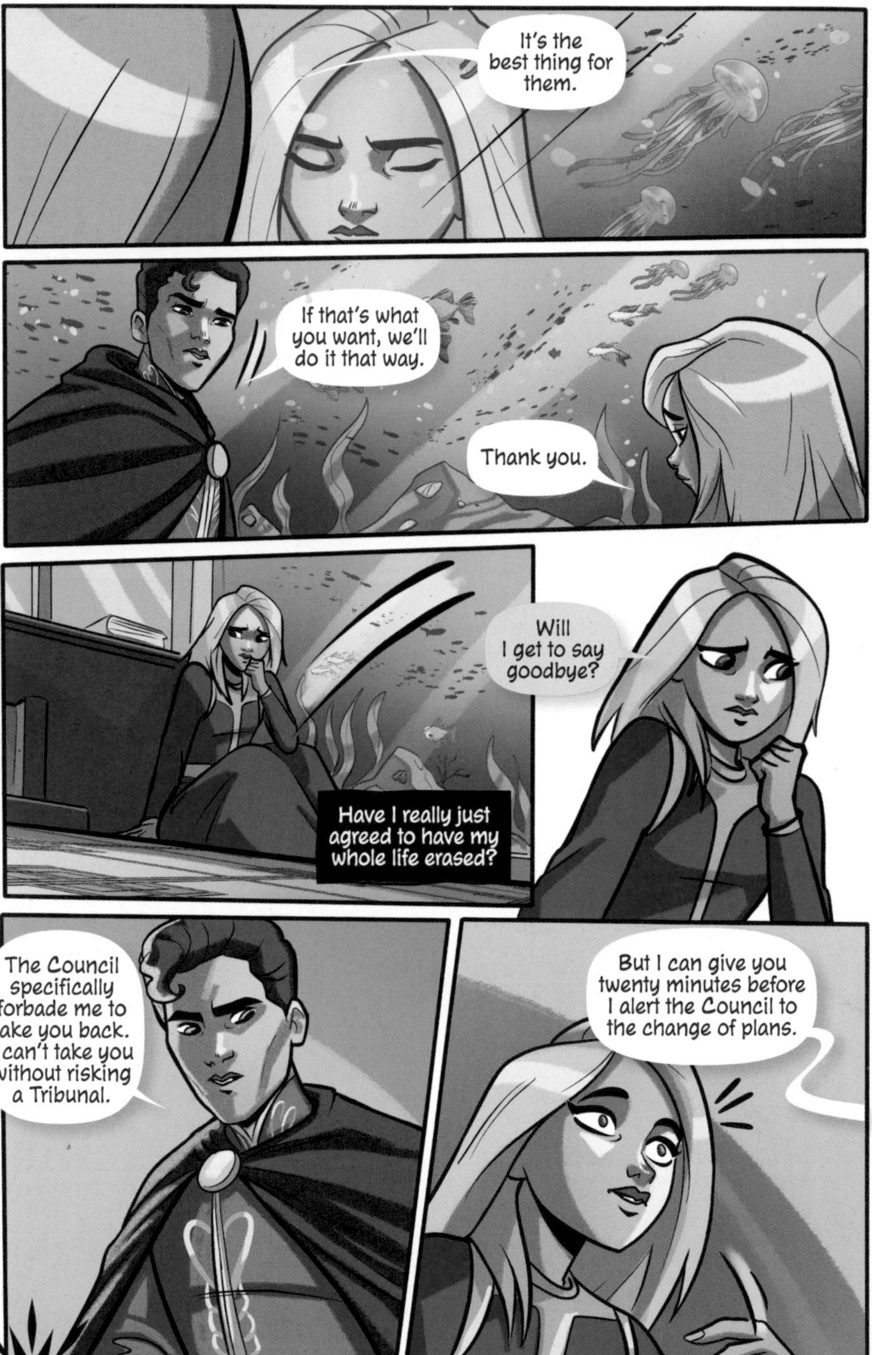
It's the best thing for them.
If that's what you want, we'll do it that way.
Thank you.
Will I get to say goodbye?
Have I really just agreed to have my whole life erased?
The Council specifically forbade me to take you back. I can't take you without risking a Tribunal.
But I can give you twenty minutes before I alert the Council to the change of plans.

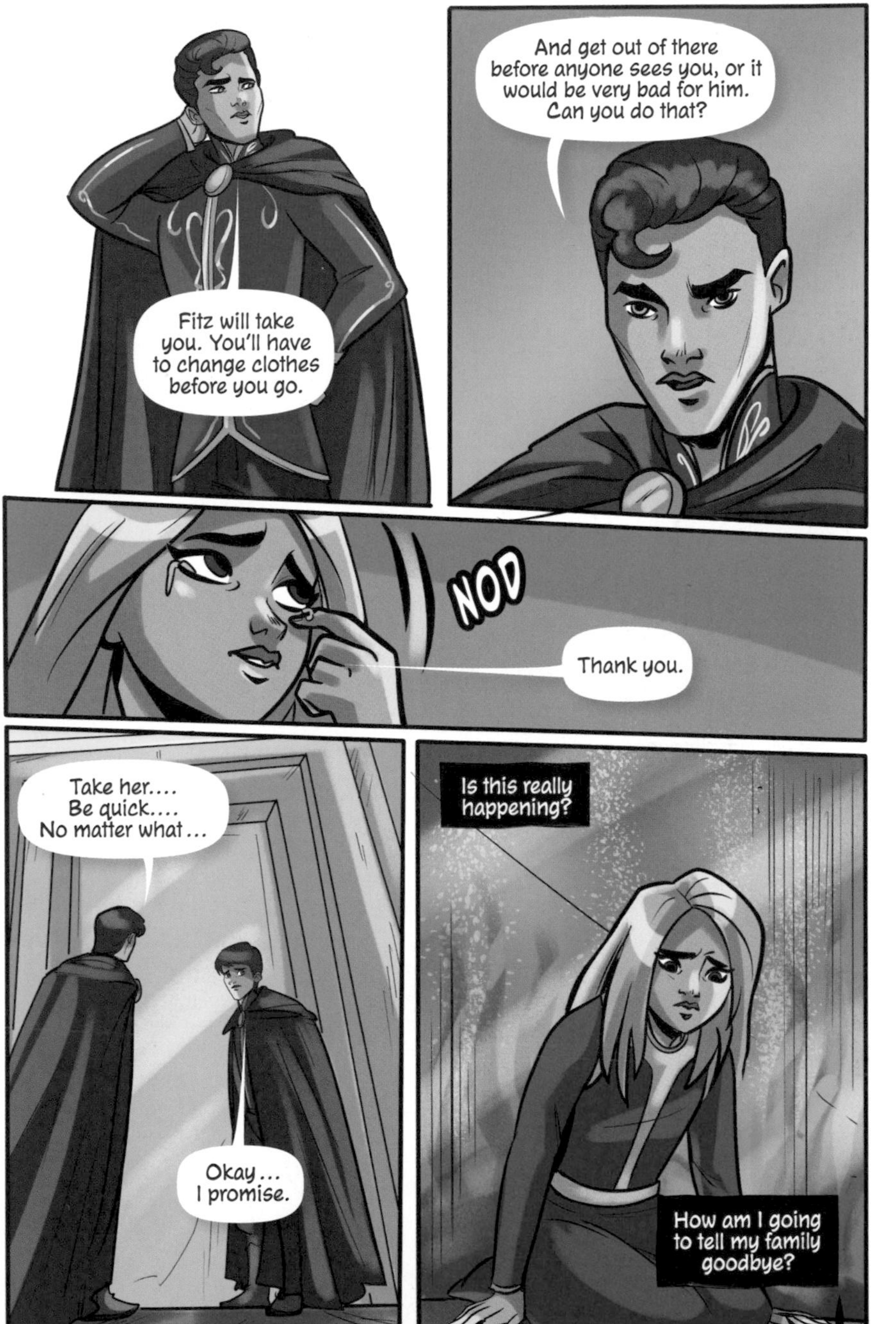
Fitz will take you. You'll have to change clothes before you go.
And get out of there before anyone sees you, or it would be very bad for him. Can you do that?
NOD
Thank you.
Take her.... Be quick.... No matter what...
Okay... I promise.
Is this really happening?
How am I going to tell my family goodbye?

CHAPTER THIRTEEN

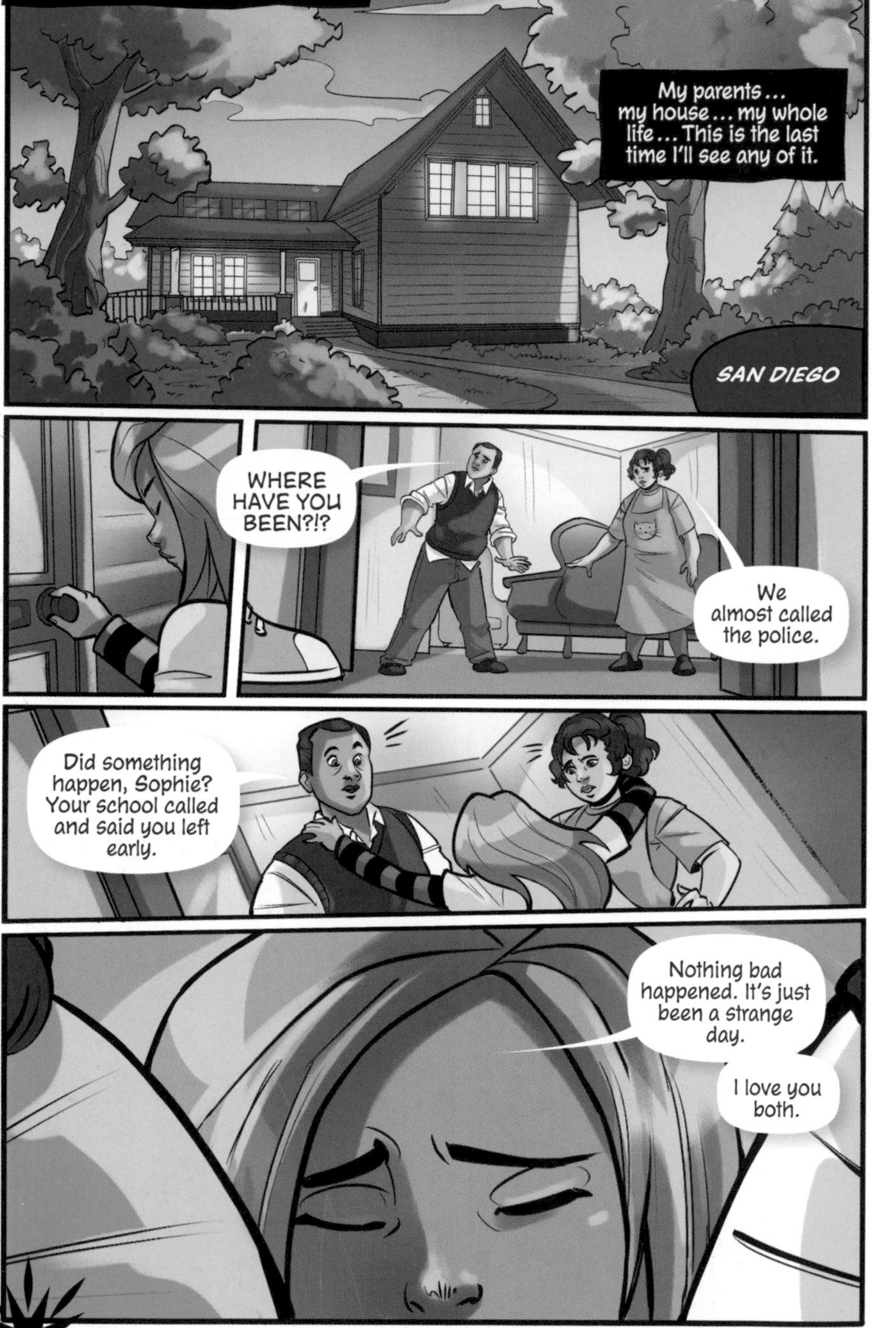
My parents... my house... my whole life... This is the last time I'll see any of it.
SAN DIEGO
WHERE HAVE YOU BEEN?!?
We almost called the police.
Did something happen, Sophie? Your school called and said you left early.
Nothing bad happened. It's just been a strange day.
I love you both.

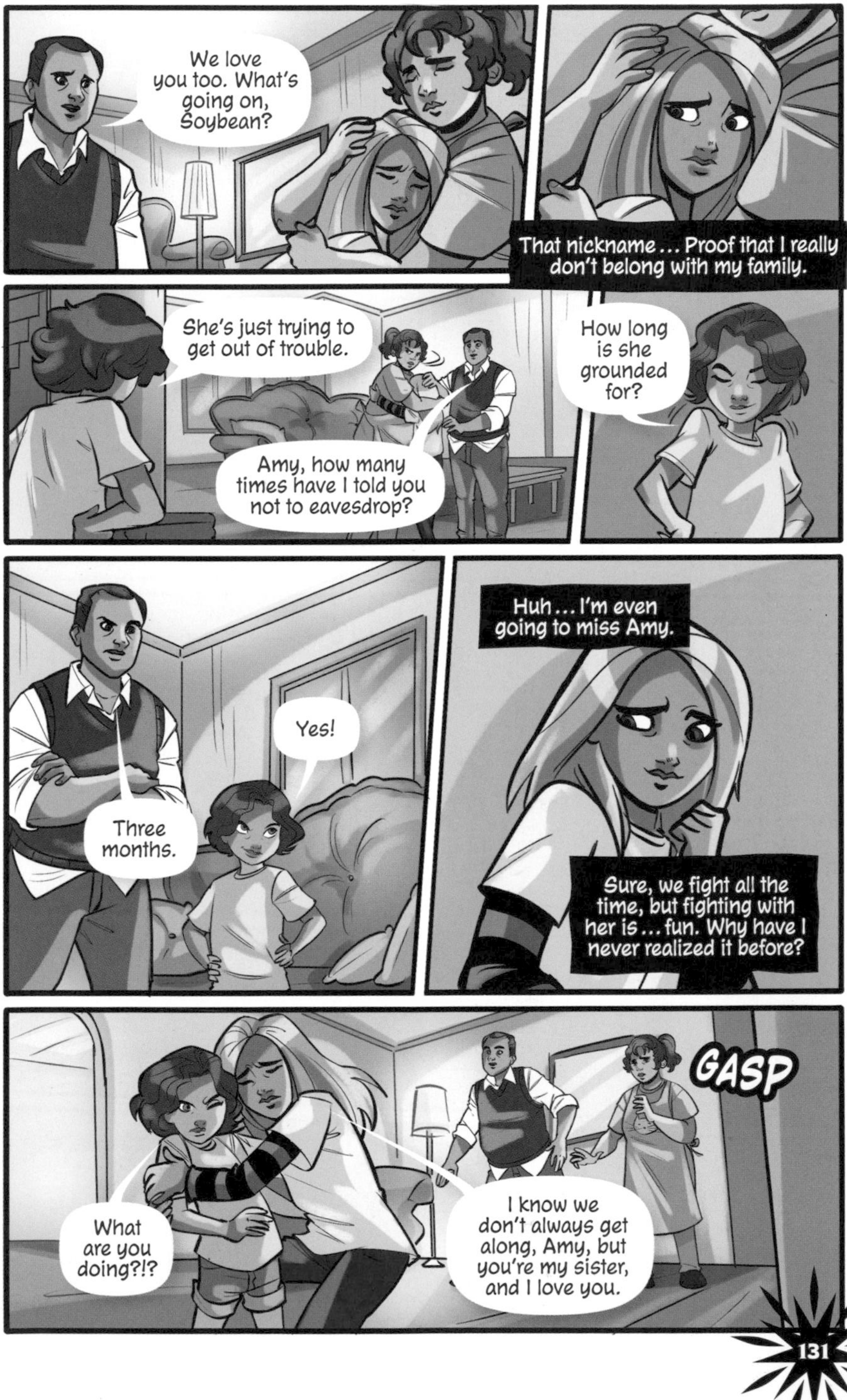
We love you too. What's going on, Soybean?
That nickname... Proof that I really don't belong with my family.
She's just trying to get out of trouble.
Amy, how many times have I told you not to eavesdrop?
How long is she grounded for?
Three months.
Yes!
Huh... I'm even going to miss Amy.
Sure, we fight all the time, but fighting with her is... fun. Why have I never realized it before?
GASP
What are you doing?!?
I know we don't always get along, Amy, but you're my sister, and I love you.

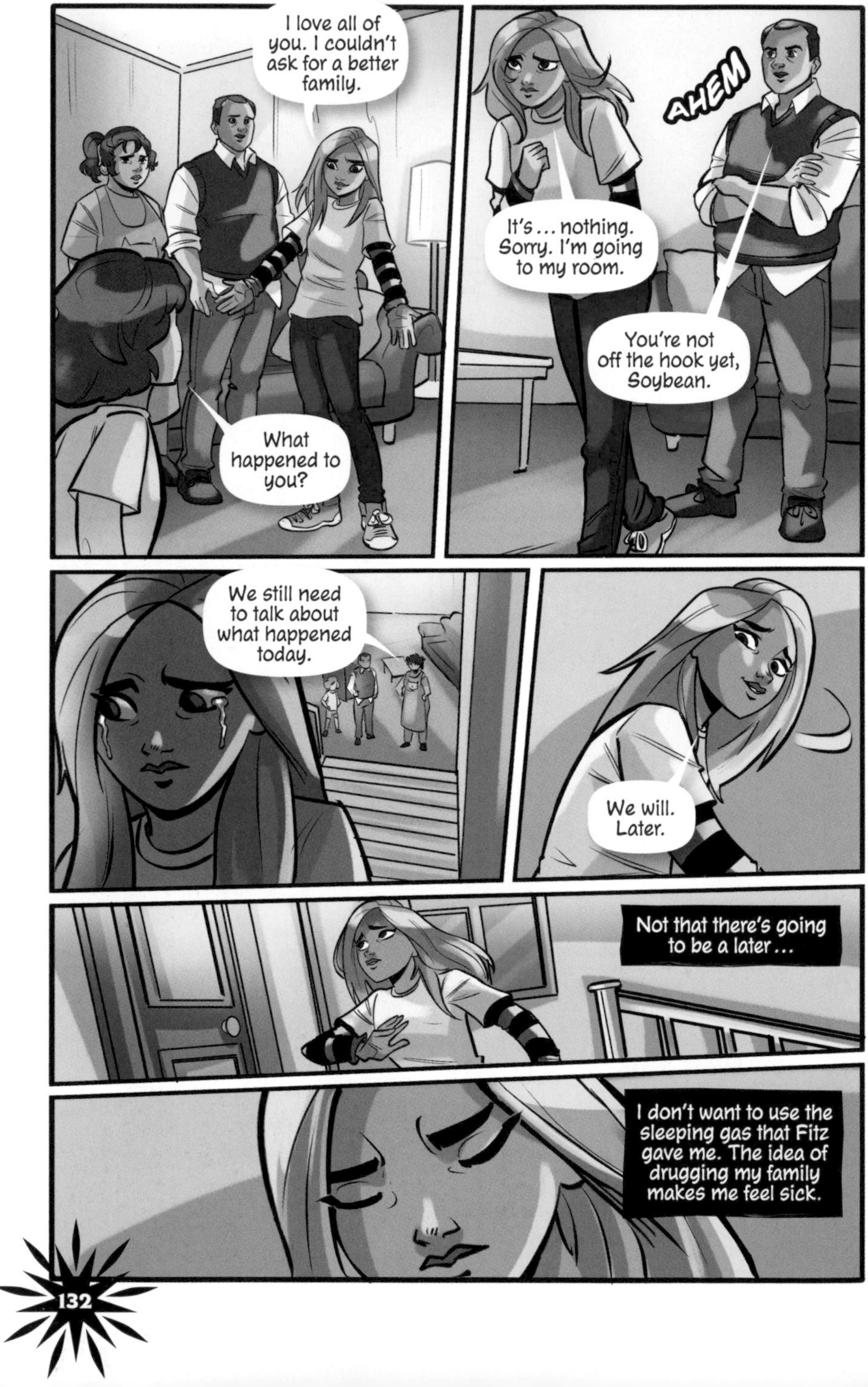
I love all of you. I couldn't ask for a better family.
What happened to you?
AHEM
It's... nothing. Sorry. I'm going to my room.
You're not off the hook yet, Soybean.
We still need to talk about what happened today.
We will. Later.
Not that there's going to be a later...
I don't want to use the sleeping gas that Fitz gave me. The idea of drugging my family makes me feel sick.

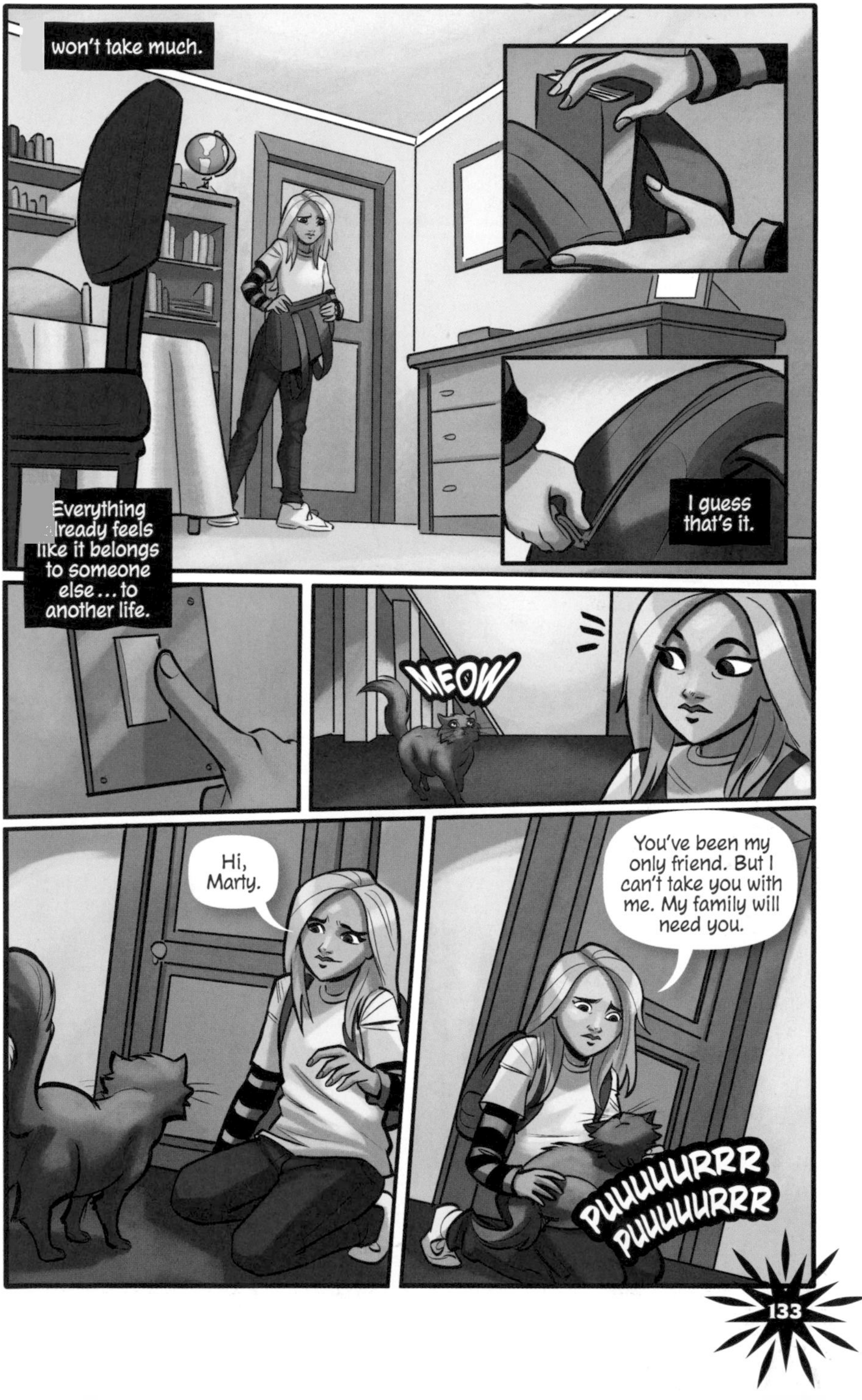
won't take much.
I guess that's it.
Everything already feels like it belongs to someone else... to another life.
MEOW
Hi, Marty.
You've been my only friend. But I can't take you with me. My family will need you.
PUUUUURRR PUUUUURRR

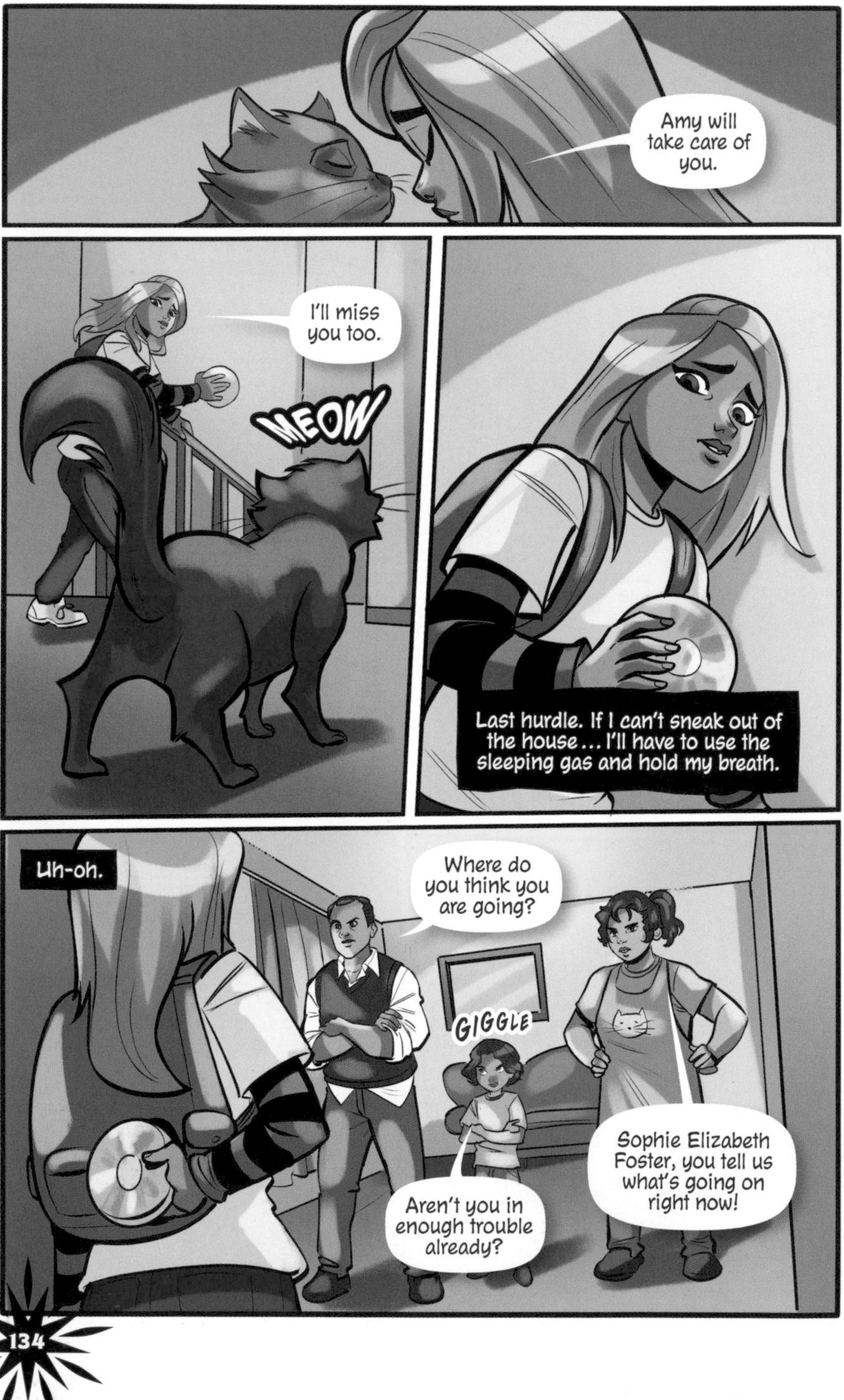
Amy will take care of you.
I'll miss you too.
MEOW
Last hurdle. If I can't sneak out of the house... I'll have to use the sleeping gas and hold my breath.
Uh-oh.
Where do you think you are going?
GIGGLE
Aren't you in enough trouble already?
Sophie Elizabeth Foster, you tell us what's going on right now!

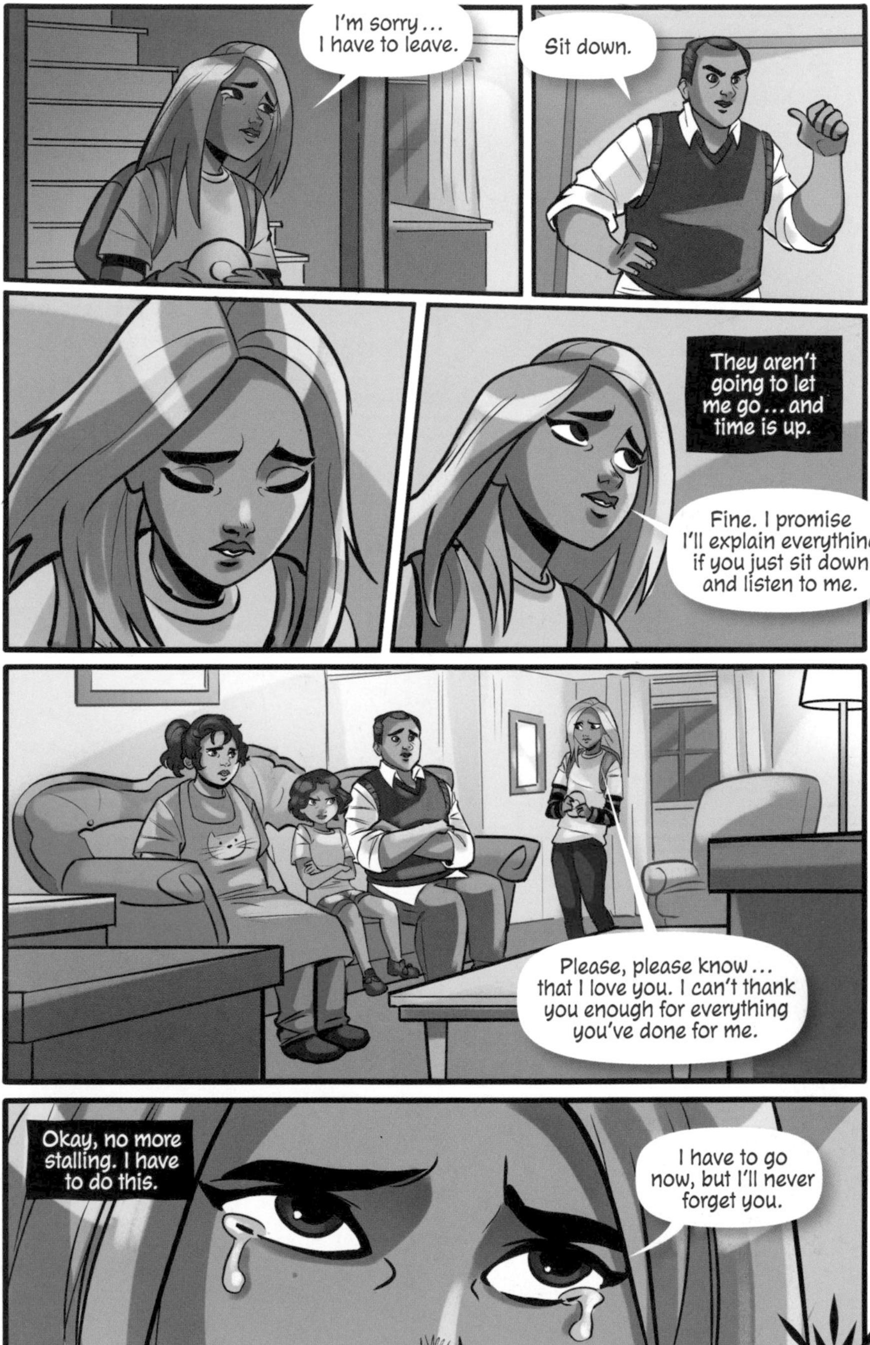
I'm sorry... I have to leave.
Sit down.
They aren't going to let me go... and time is up.
Fine. I promise I'll explain everything if you just sit down and listen to me.
Please, please know... that I love you. I can't thank you enough for everything you've done for me.
Okay, no more stalling. I have to do this.
I have to go now, but I'll never forget you.

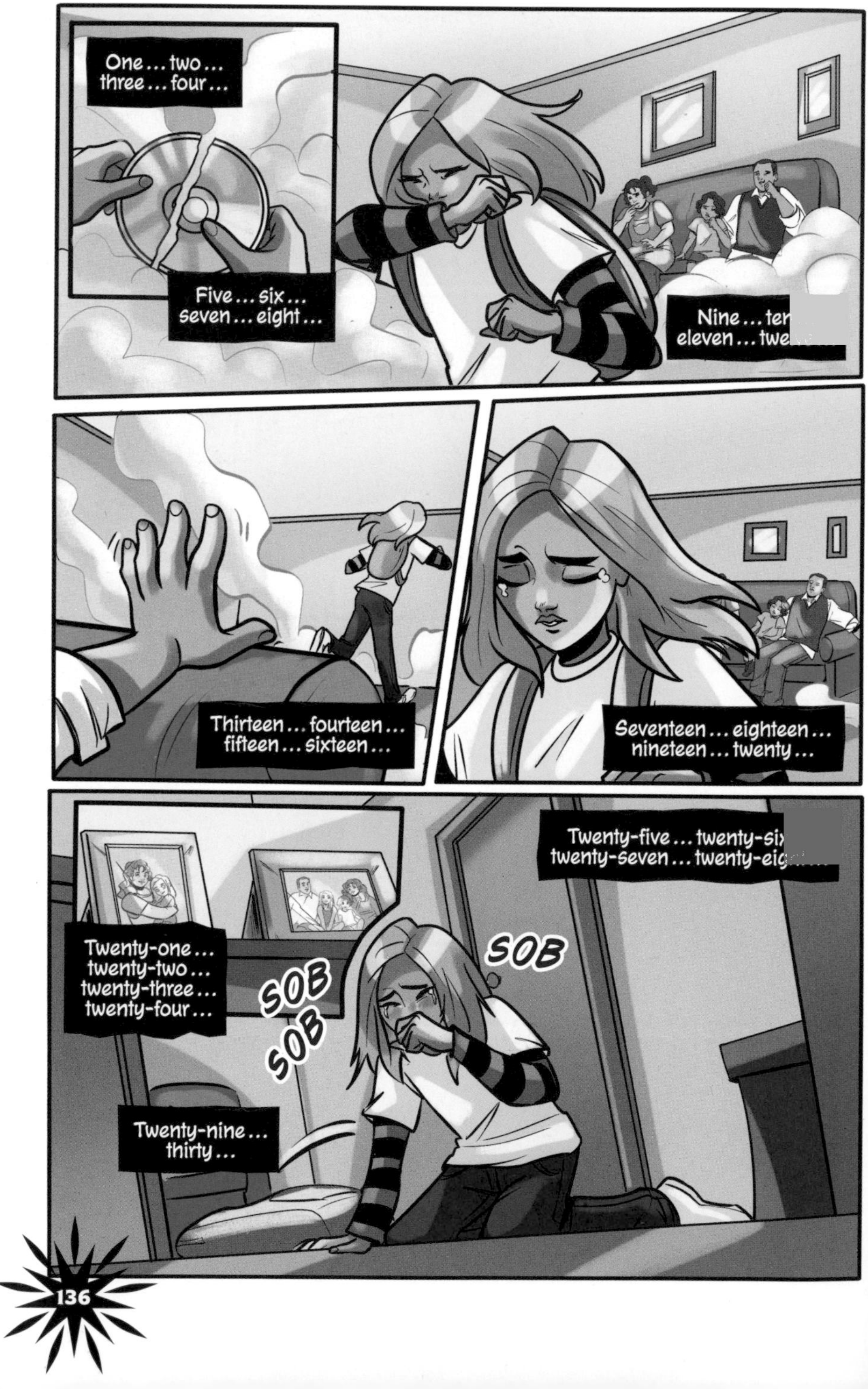
One… two… three… four…
Five… six… seven… eight…
Nine… te
eleven… twe
Thirteen… fourteen… fifteen… sixteen…
Seventeen… eighteen… nineteen… twenty…
Twenty-one… twenty-two… twenty-three… twenty-four…
Twenty-five… twenty-si
twenty-seven… twenty-eig
SOB SOB
SOB
Twenty-nine… thirty…

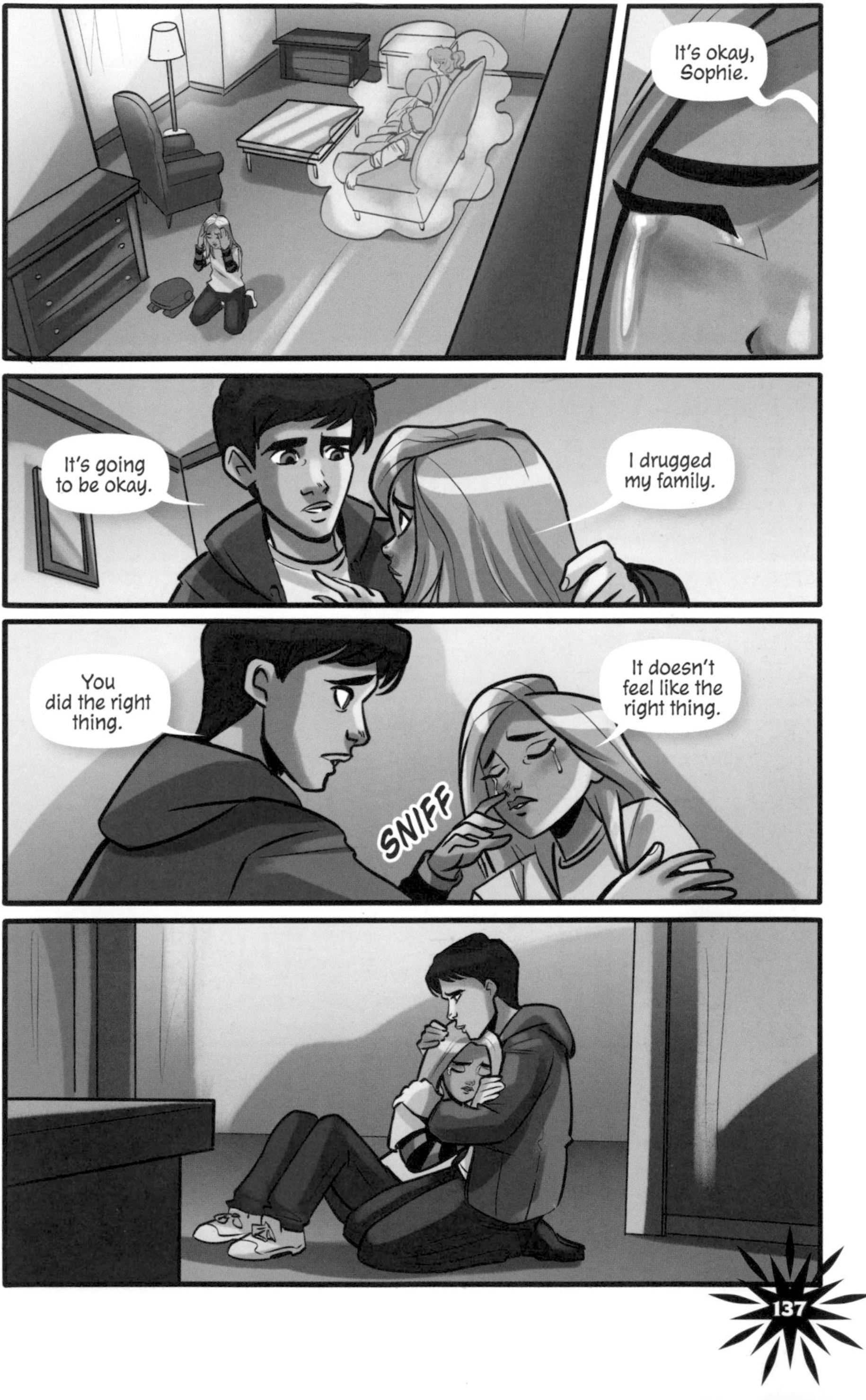
It's okay, Sophie.
It's going to be okay.
I drugged my family.
You did the right thing.
It doesn't feel like the right thing.
SNIFF

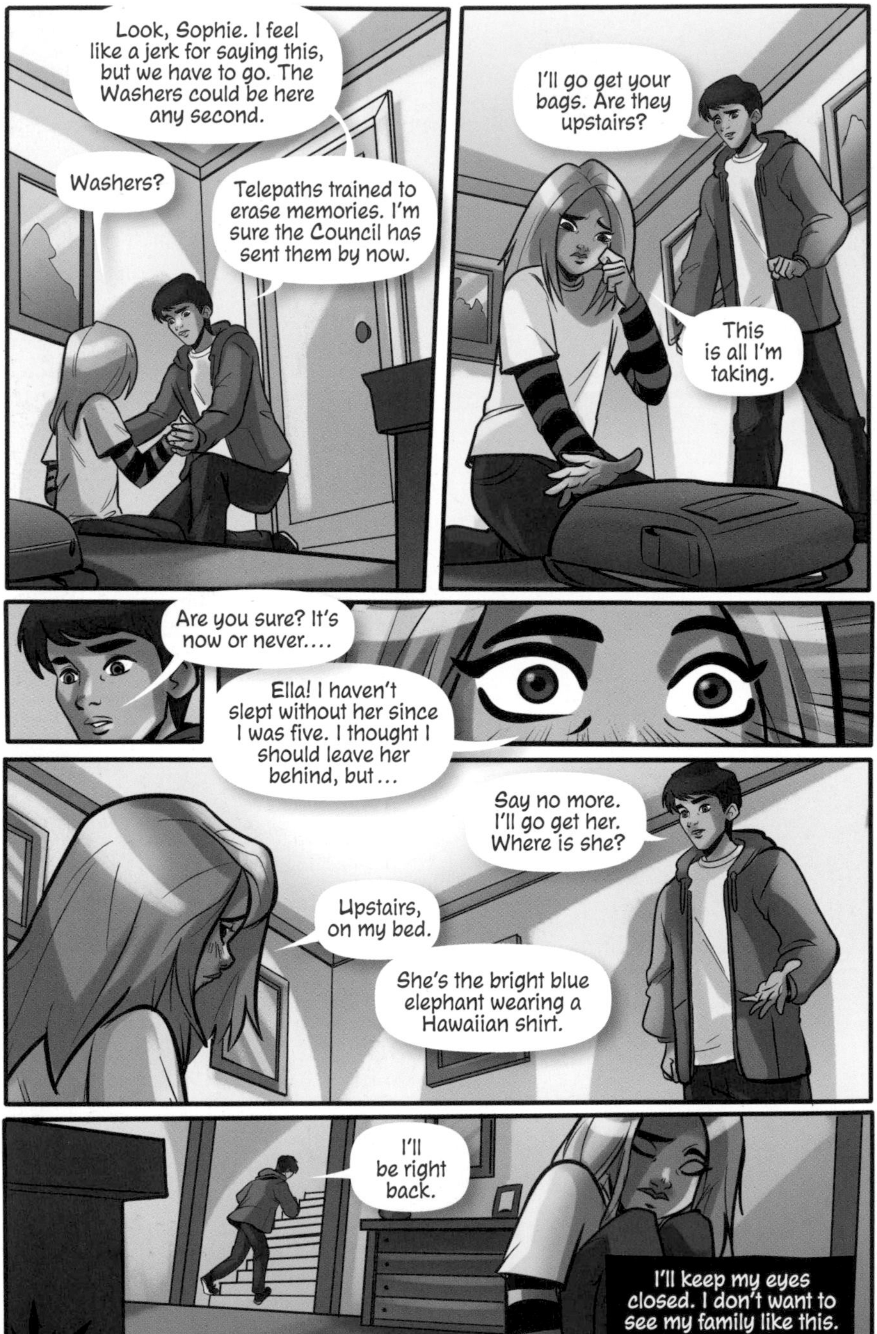

Look, Sophie. I feel like a jerk for saying this, but we have to go. The Washers could be here any second.
Washers?
Telepaths trained to erase memories. I'm sure the Council has sent them by now.
I'll go get your bags. Are they upstairs?
This is all I'm taking.
Are you sure? It's now or never....
Ella! I haven't slept without her since I was five. I thought I should leave her behind, but...
Say no more. I'll go get her. Where is she?
Upstairs, on my bed.
She's the bright blue elephant wearing a Hawaiian shirt.
I'll be right back.
I'll keep my eyes closed. I don't want to see my family like this.

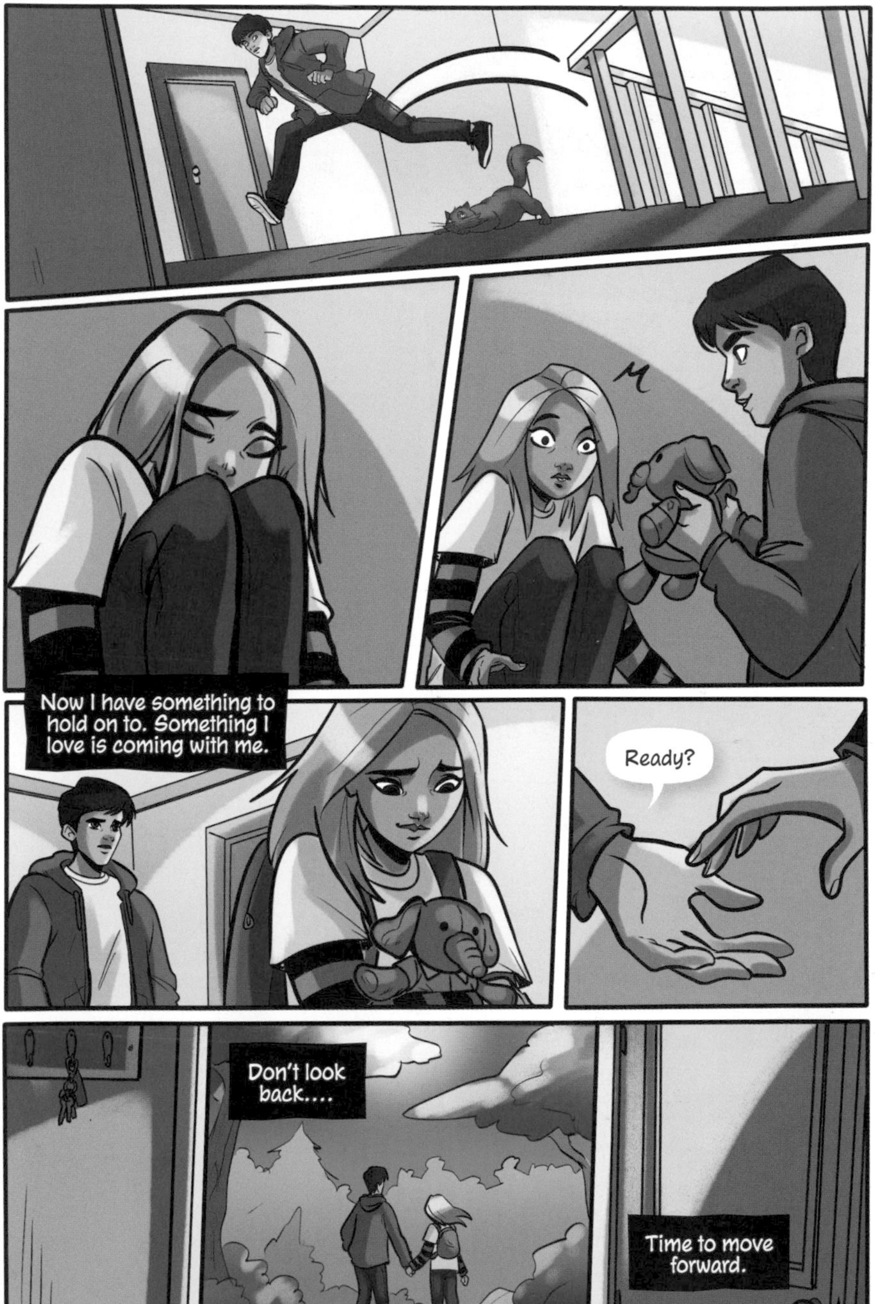
M
Now I have something to hold on to. Something I love is coming with me.
Ready?
Don't look back....
Time to move forward.

CHAPTER FOURTEEN

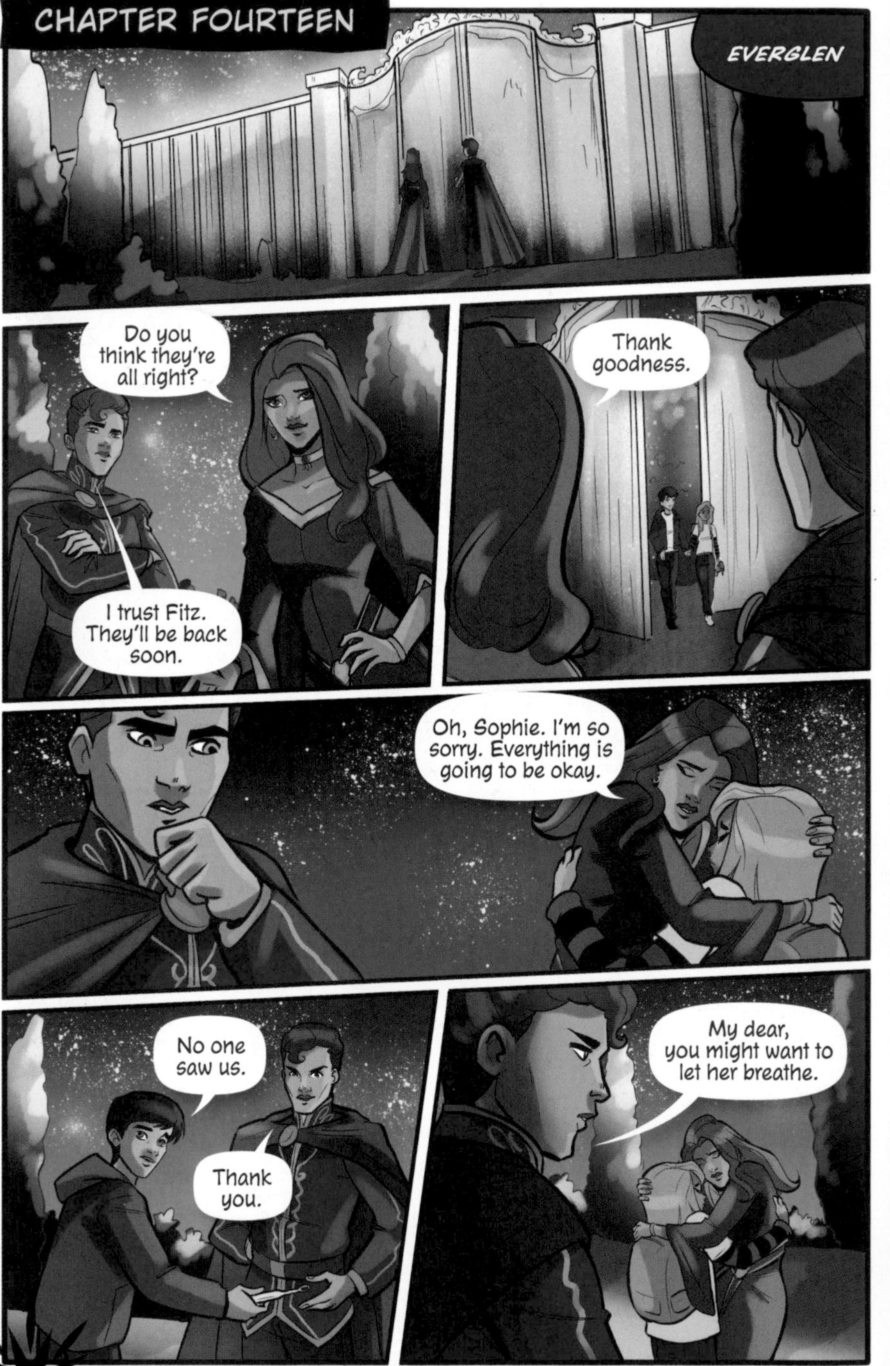
EVERGLEN
Do you think they're all right?
I trust Fitz. They'll be back soon.
Thank goodness.
Oh, Sophie. I'm so sorry. Everything is going to be okay.
No one saw us.
Thank you.
My dear, you might want to let her breathe.

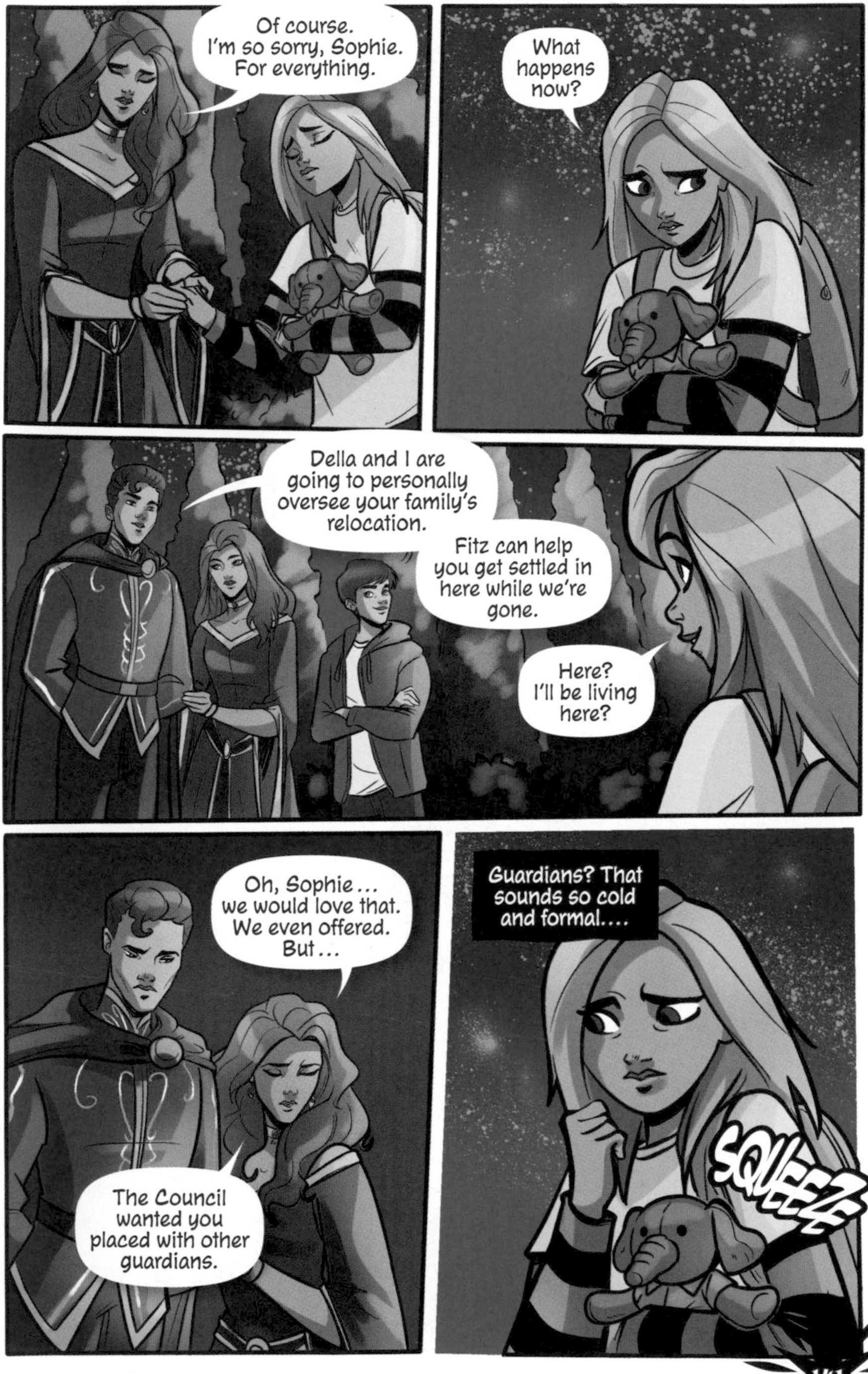
Of course. I'm so sorry, Sophie. For everything.
What happens now?
Della and I are going to personally oversee your family's relocation.
Fitz can help you get settled in here while we're gone.
Here? I'll be living here?
Oh, Sophie... we would love that. We even offered. But...
The Council wanted you placed with other guardians.
Guardians? That sounds so cold and formal....
SQUEEZE

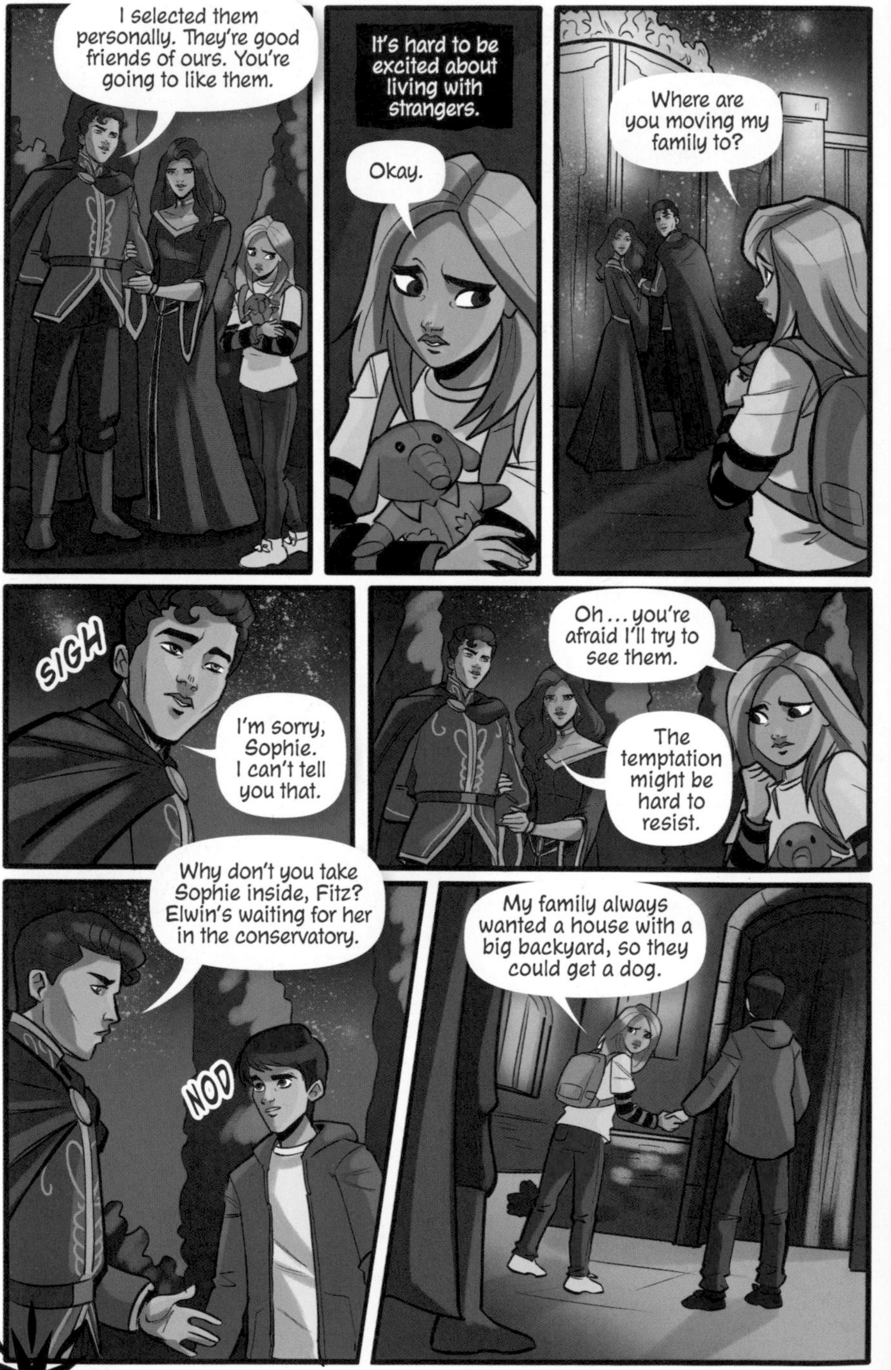
I selected them personally. They're good friends of ours. You're going to like them.
It's hard to be excited about living with strangers.
Okay.
Where are you moving my family to?
SIGH
I'm sorry, Sophie. I can't tell you that.
Oh... you're afraid I'll try to see them.
The temptation might be hard to resist.
Why don't you take Sophie inside, Fitz? Elwin's waiting for her in the conservatory.
NOD
My family always wanted a house with a big backyard, so they could get a dog.

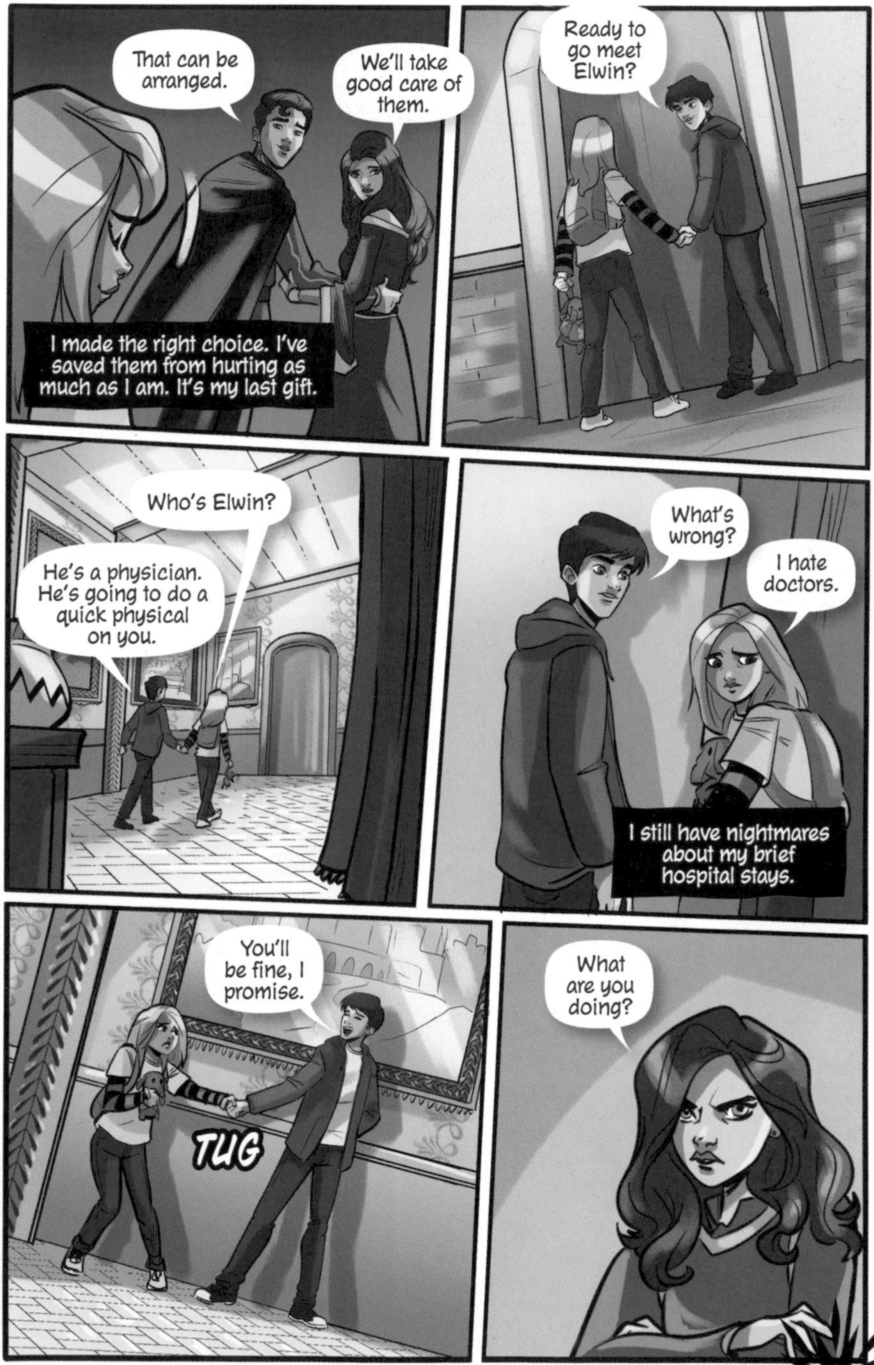
That can be arranged.
We'll take good care of them.
I made the right choice. I've saved them from hurting as much as I am. It's my last gift.
Ready to go meet Elwin?
Who's Elwin?
He's a physician. He's going to do a quick physical on you.
What's wrong?
I hate doctors.
I still have nightmares about my brief hospital stays.
You'll be fine, I promise.
TUG
What are you doing?

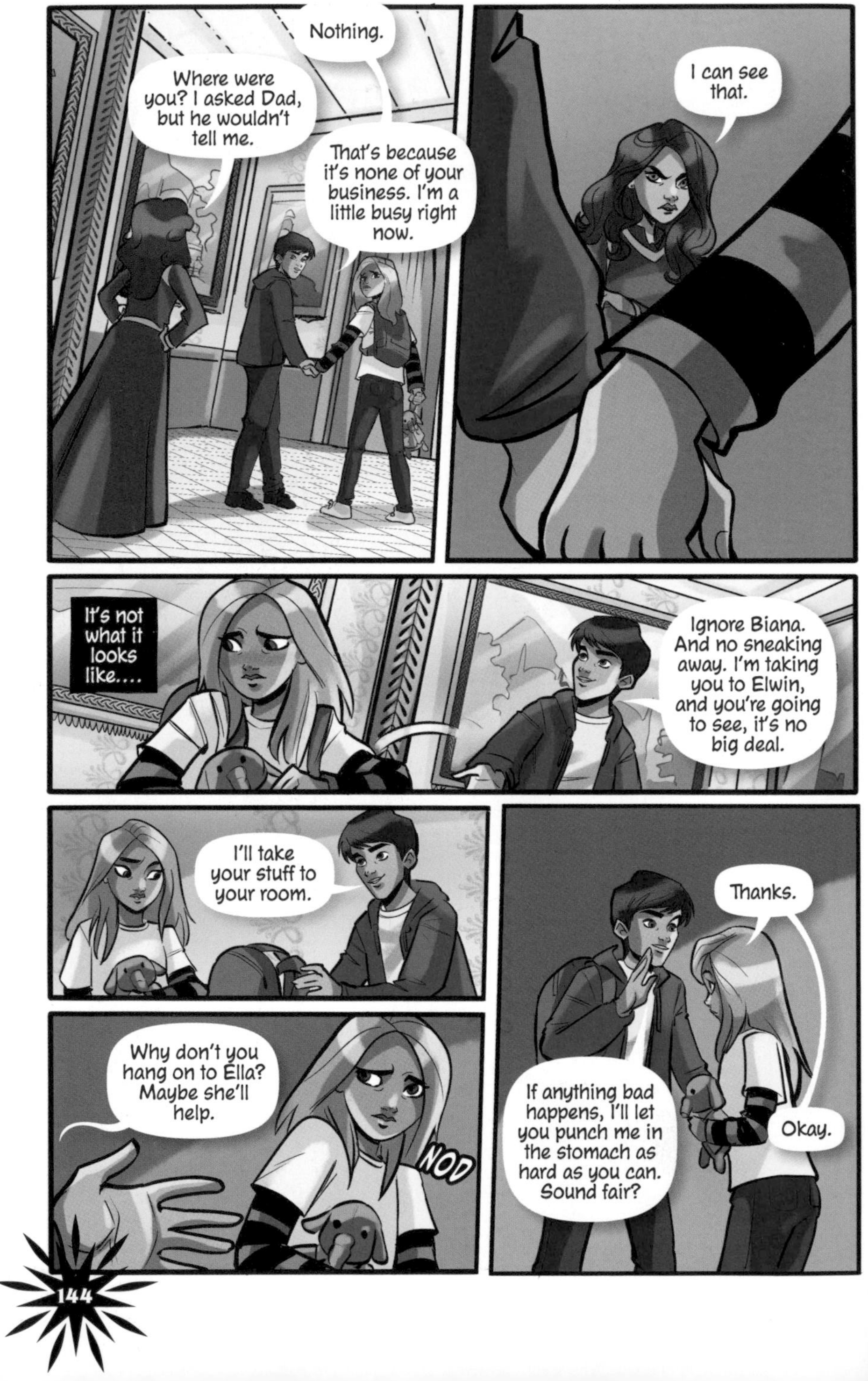
Where were you? I asked Dad, but he wouldn't tell me.
Nothing.
That's because it's none of your business. I'm a little busy right now.
I can see that.
It's not what it looks like....
Ignore Biana. And no sneaking away. I'm taking you to Elwin, and you're going to see, it's no big deal.
I'll take your stuff to your room.
Why don't you hang on to Ella? Maybe she'll help.
NOD
Thanks.
If anything bad happens, I'll let you punch me in the stomach as hard as you can. Sound fair?
Okay.

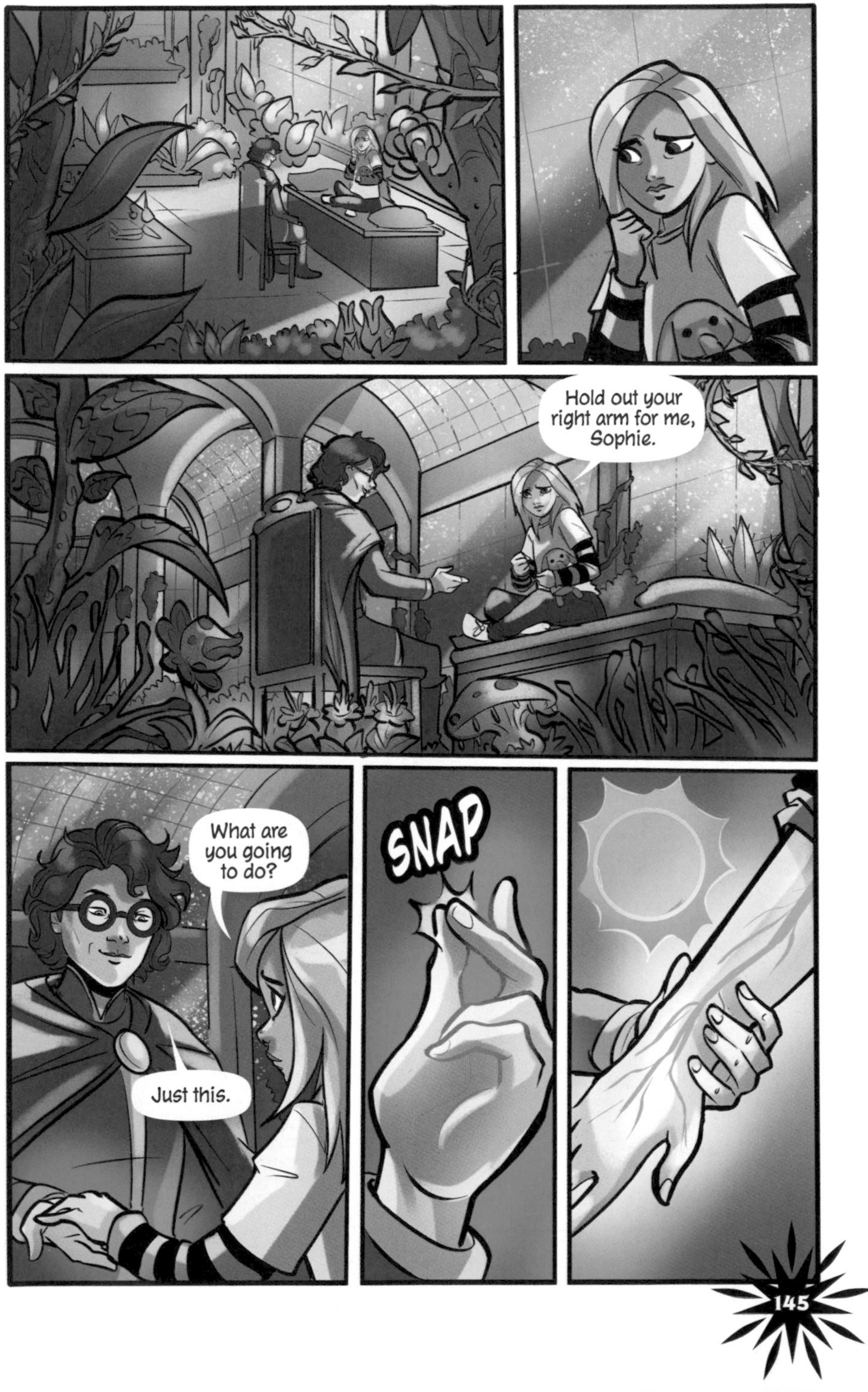
Hold out your right arm for me, Sophie.
What are you going to do?
Just this.
SNAP

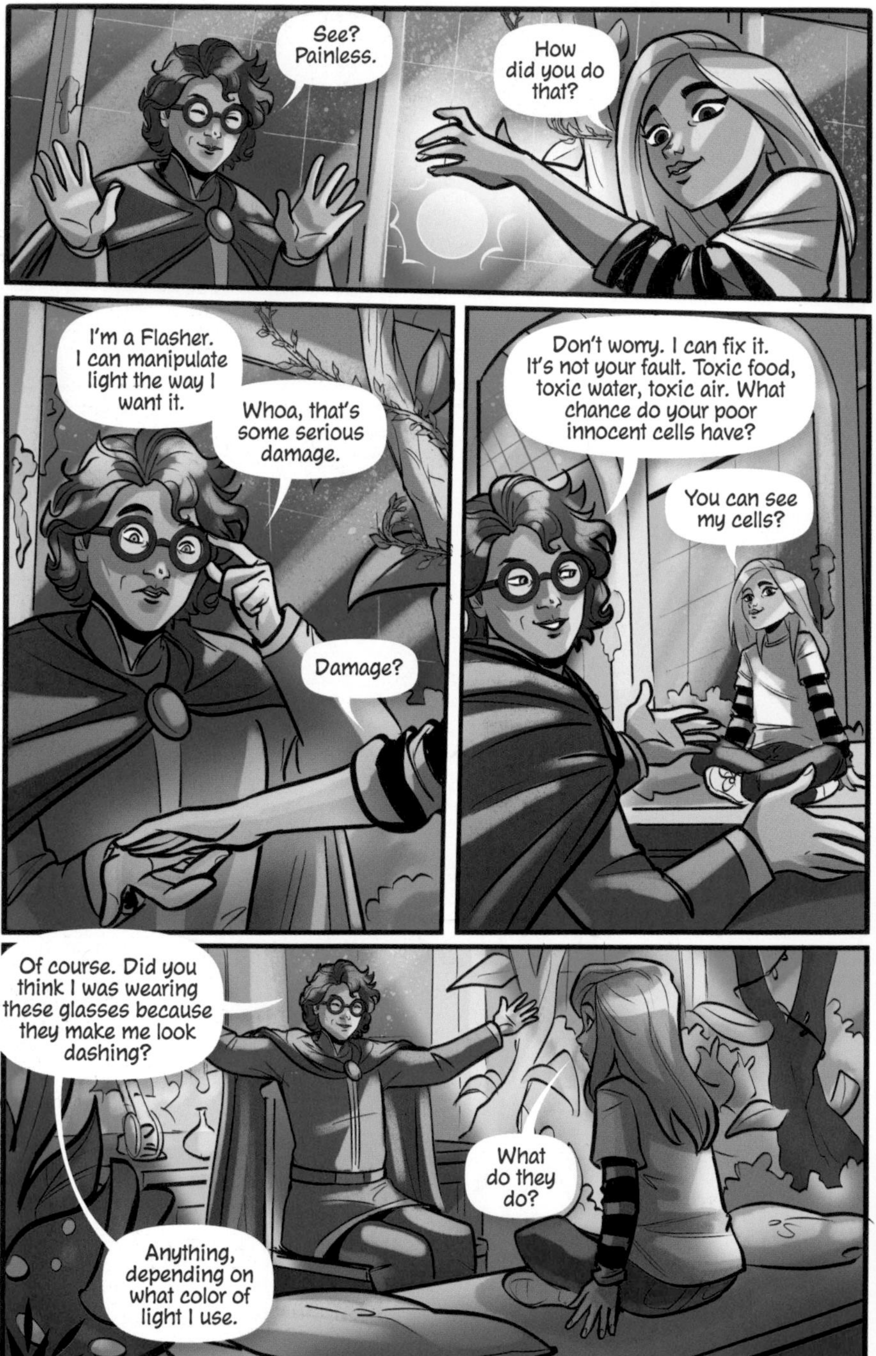
See? Painless.
How did you do that?
I'm a Flasher. I can manipulate light the way I want it.
Whoa, that's some serious damage.
Damage?
Don't worry. I can fix it. It's not your fault. Toxic food, toxic water, toxic air. What chance do your poor innocent cells have?
You can see my cells?
Of course. Did you think I was wearing these glasses because they make me look dashing?
What do they do?
Anything, depending on what color of light I use.

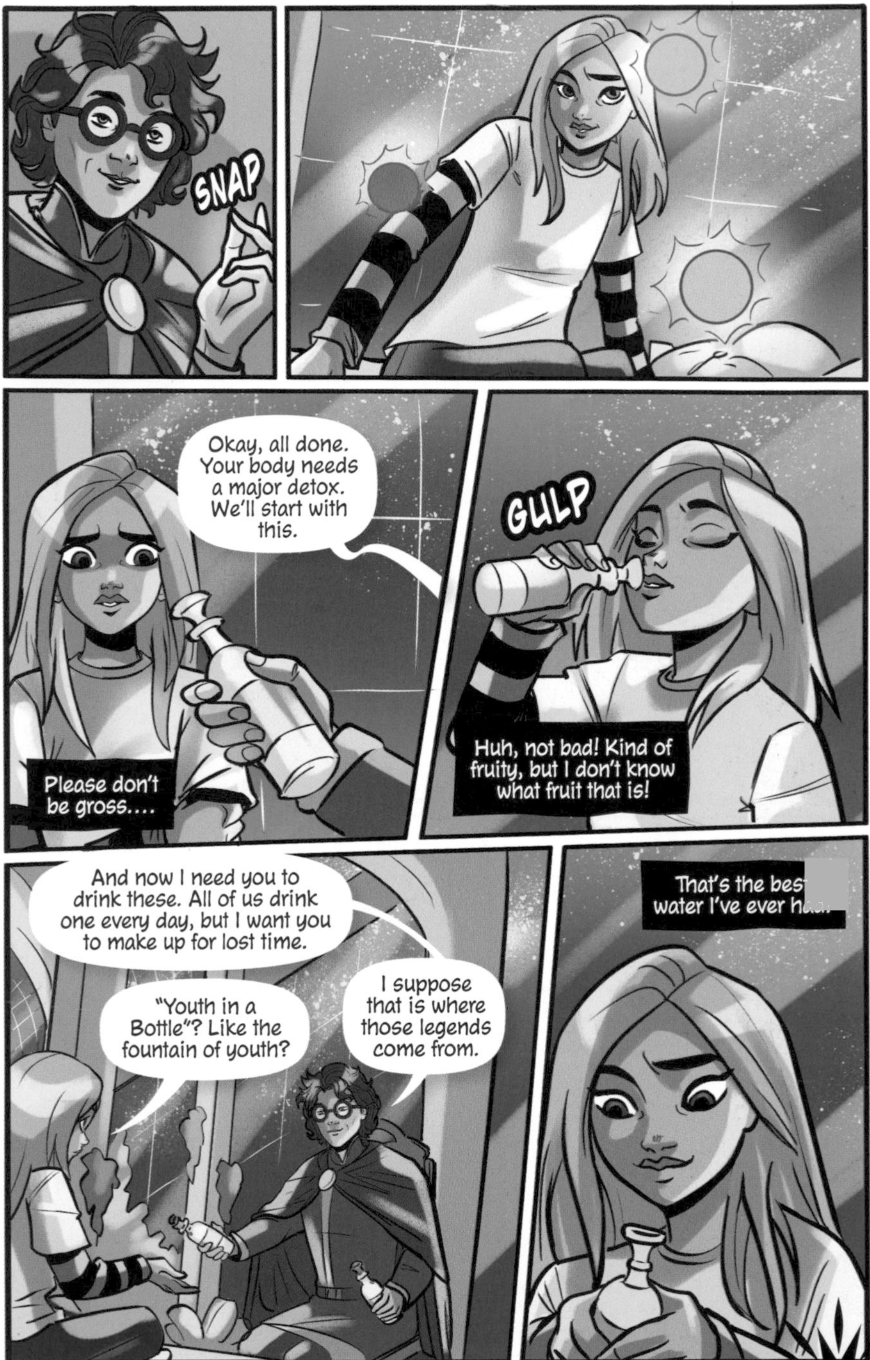
SNAP
Okay, all done. Your body needs a major detox. We'll start with this.
Please don't be gross....
GULP
Huh, not bad! Kind of fruity, but I don't know what fruit that is!
And now I need you to drink these. All of us drink one every day, but I want you to make up for lost time.
"Youth in a Bottle"? Like the fountain of youth?
I suppose that is where those legends come from.
That's the bes
water I've ever h

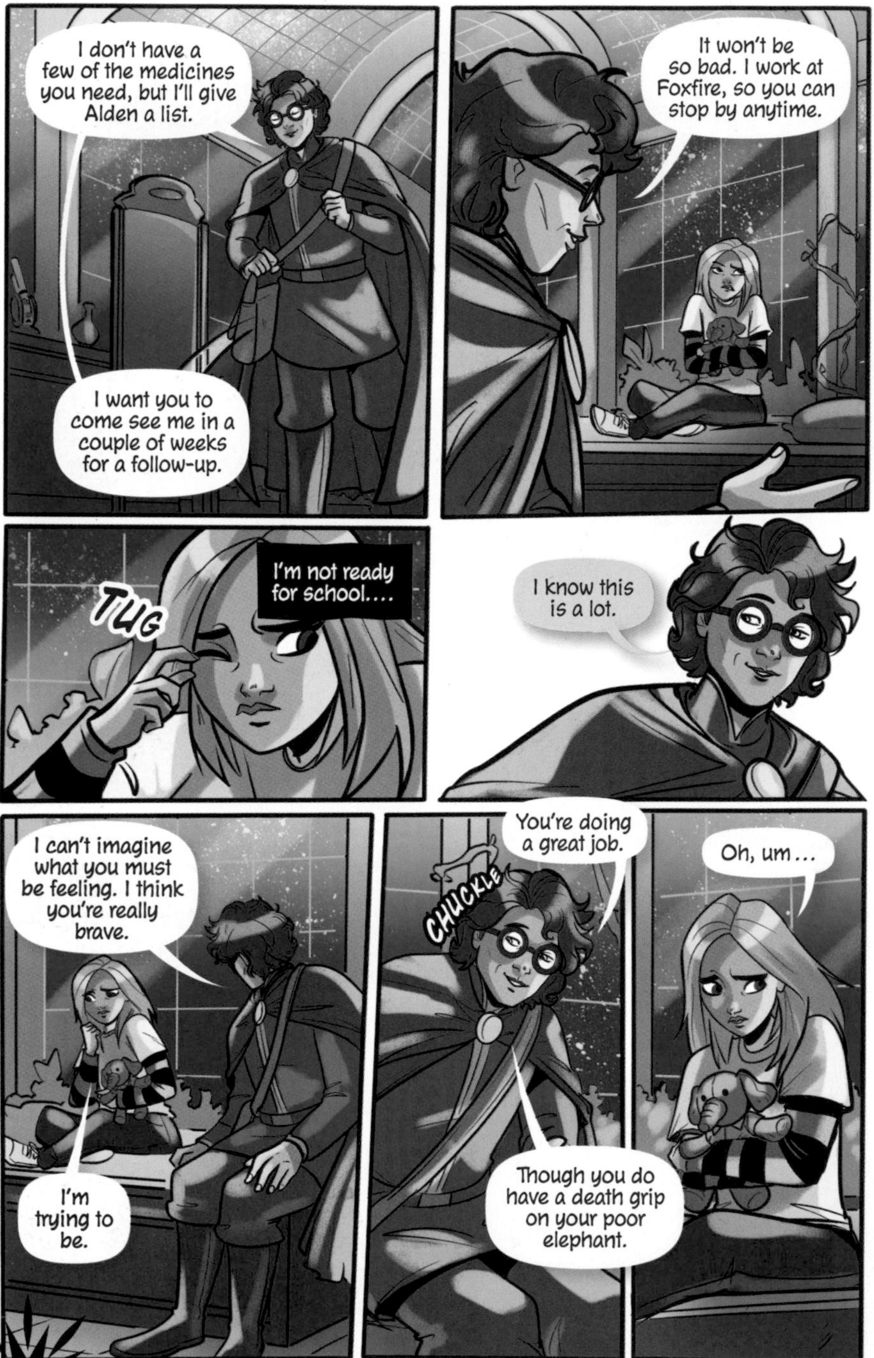
I don't have a few of the medicines you need, but I'll give Alden a list.
I want you to come see me in a couple of weeks for a follow-up.
It won't be so bad. I work at Foxfire, so you can stop by anytime.
TUG
I'm not ready for school....
I know this is a lot.
I can't imagine what you must be feeling. I think you're really brave.
I'm trying to be.
CHUCKLE
You're doing a great job.
Though you do have a death grip on your poor elephant.
Oh, um...

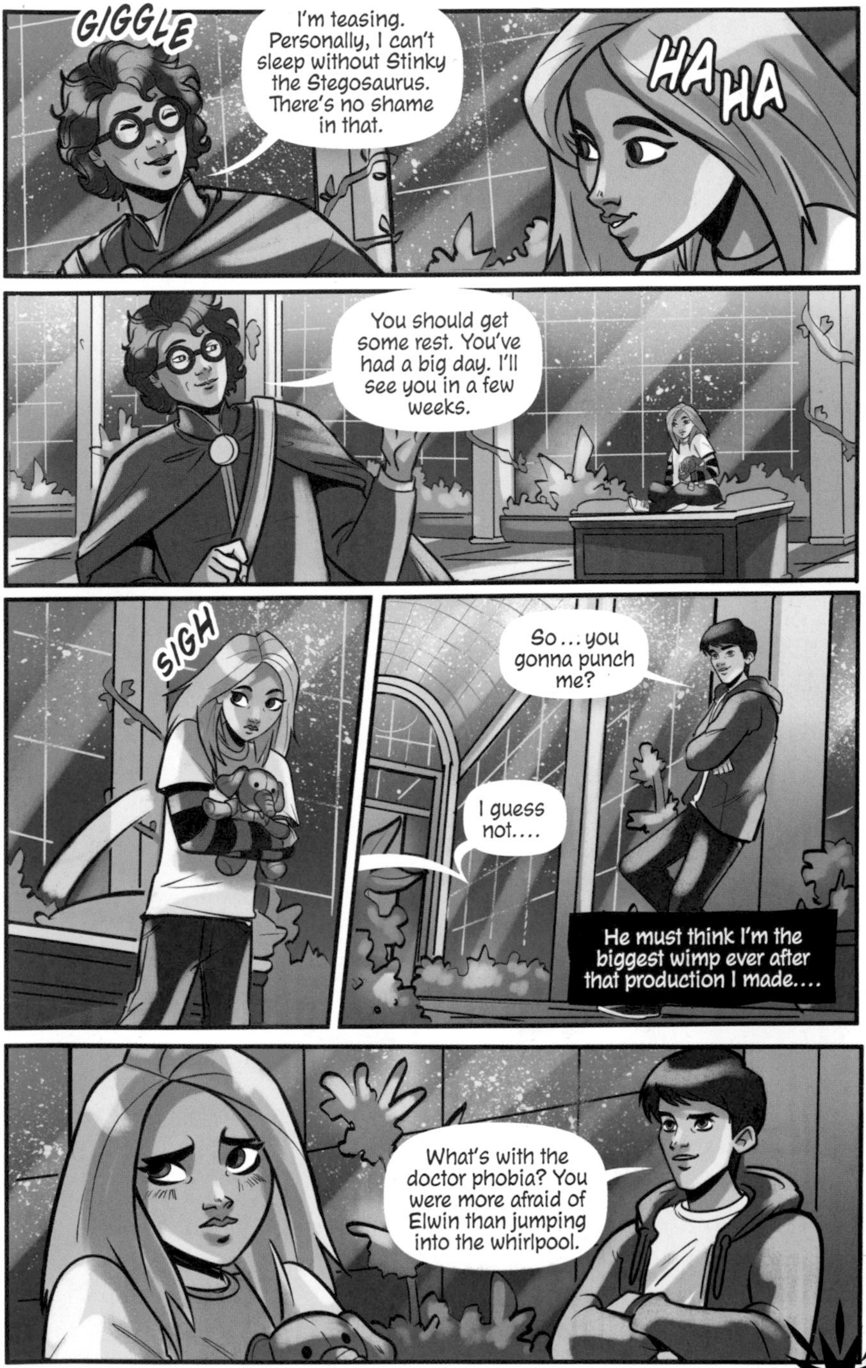
GIGGLE
I'm teasing. Personally, I can't sleep without Stinky the Stegosaurus. There's no shame in that.
HA HA
You should get some rest. You've had a big day. I'll see you in a few weeks.
SIGH
So... you gonna punch me?
I guess not....
He must think I'm the biggest wimp ever after that production I made....
What's with the doctor phobia? You were more afraid of Elwin than jumping into the whirlpool.

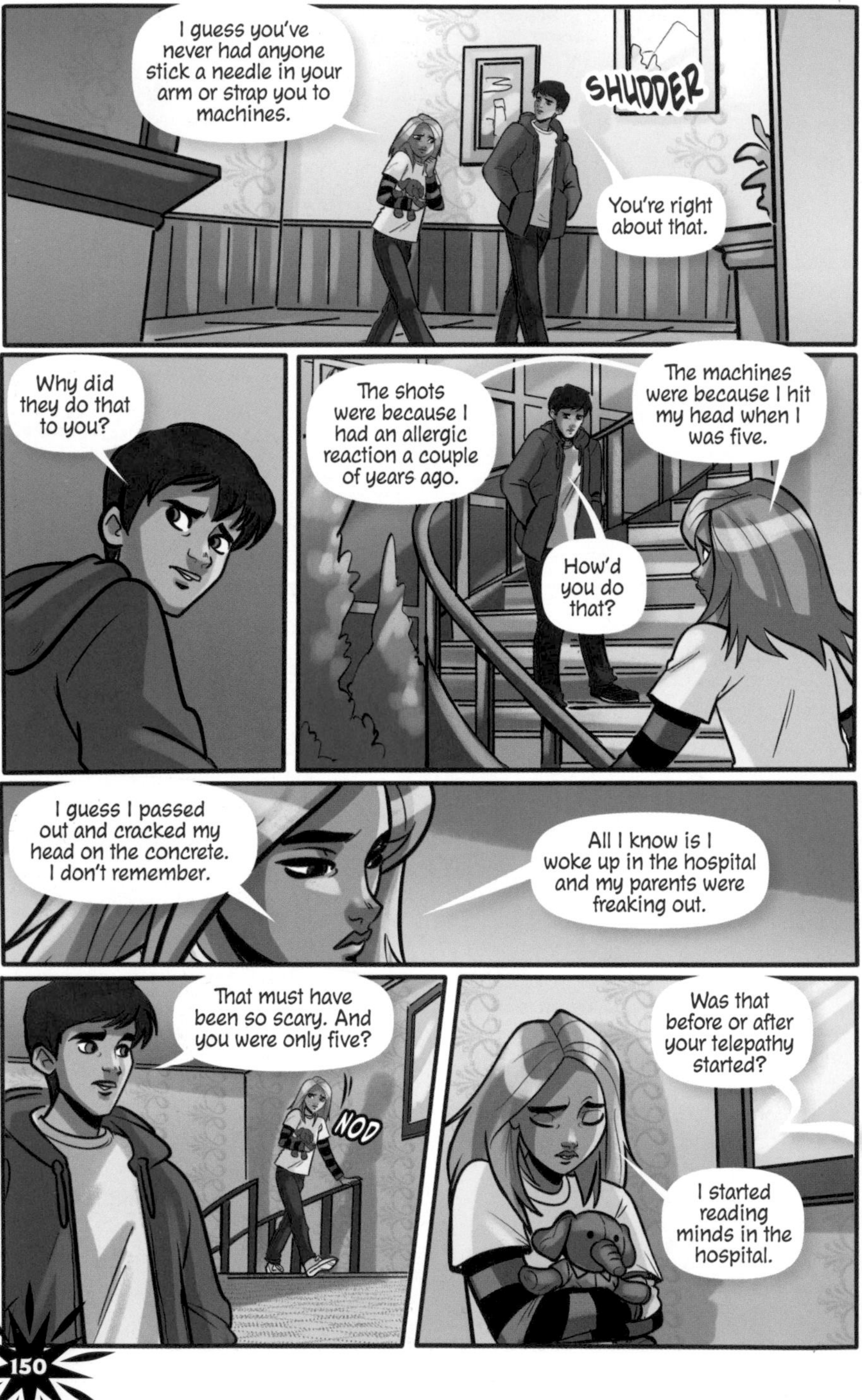
I guess you've never had anyone stick a needle in your arm or strap you to machines.
SHUDDER
You're right about that.
Why did they do that to you?
The shots were because I had an allergic reaction a couple of years ago.
The machines were because I hit my head when I was five.
How'd you do that?
I guess I passed out and cracked my head on the concrete. I don't remember.
All I know is I woke up in the hospital and my parents were freaking out.
That must have been so scary. And you were only five?
NOD
Was that before or after your telepathy started?
I started reading minds in the hospital.

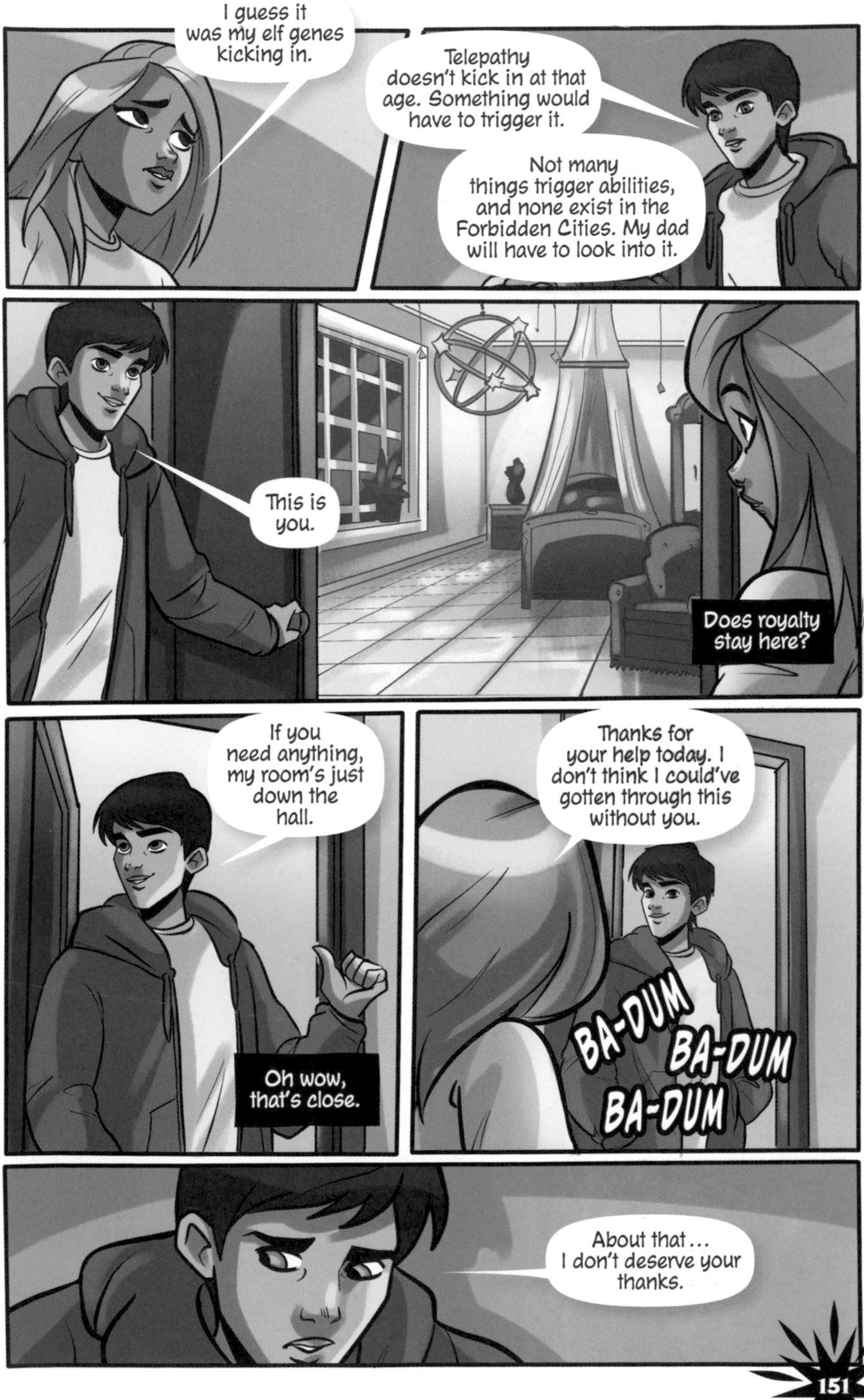
I guess it was my elf genes kicking in.
Telepathy doesn't kick in at that age. Something would have to trigger it.
Not many things trigger abilities, and none exist in the Forbidden Cities. My dad will have to look into it.
This is you.
Does royalty stay here?
If you need anything, my room's just down the hall.
Oh wow, that's close.
Thanks for your help today. I don't think I could've gotten through this without you.
BA-DUM
BA-DUM
BA-DUM
About that . . . I don't deserve your thanks.

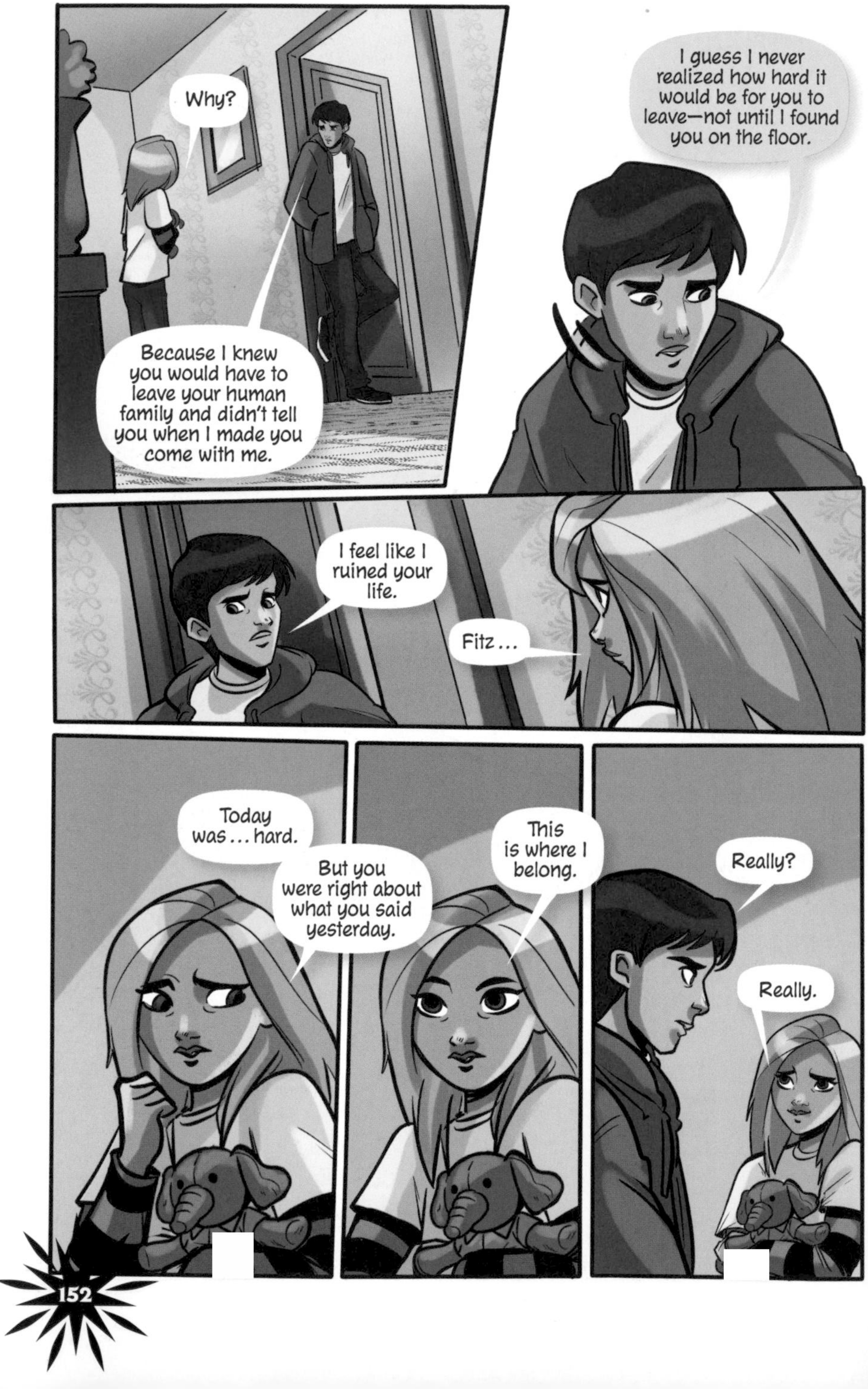
Why?
Because I knew you would have to leave your human family and didn't tell you when I made you come with me.
I guess I never realized how hard it would be for you to leave—not until I found you on the floor.
I feel like I ruined your life.
Fitz...
Today was... hard.
But you were right about what you said yesterday.
This is where I belong.
Really?
Really.

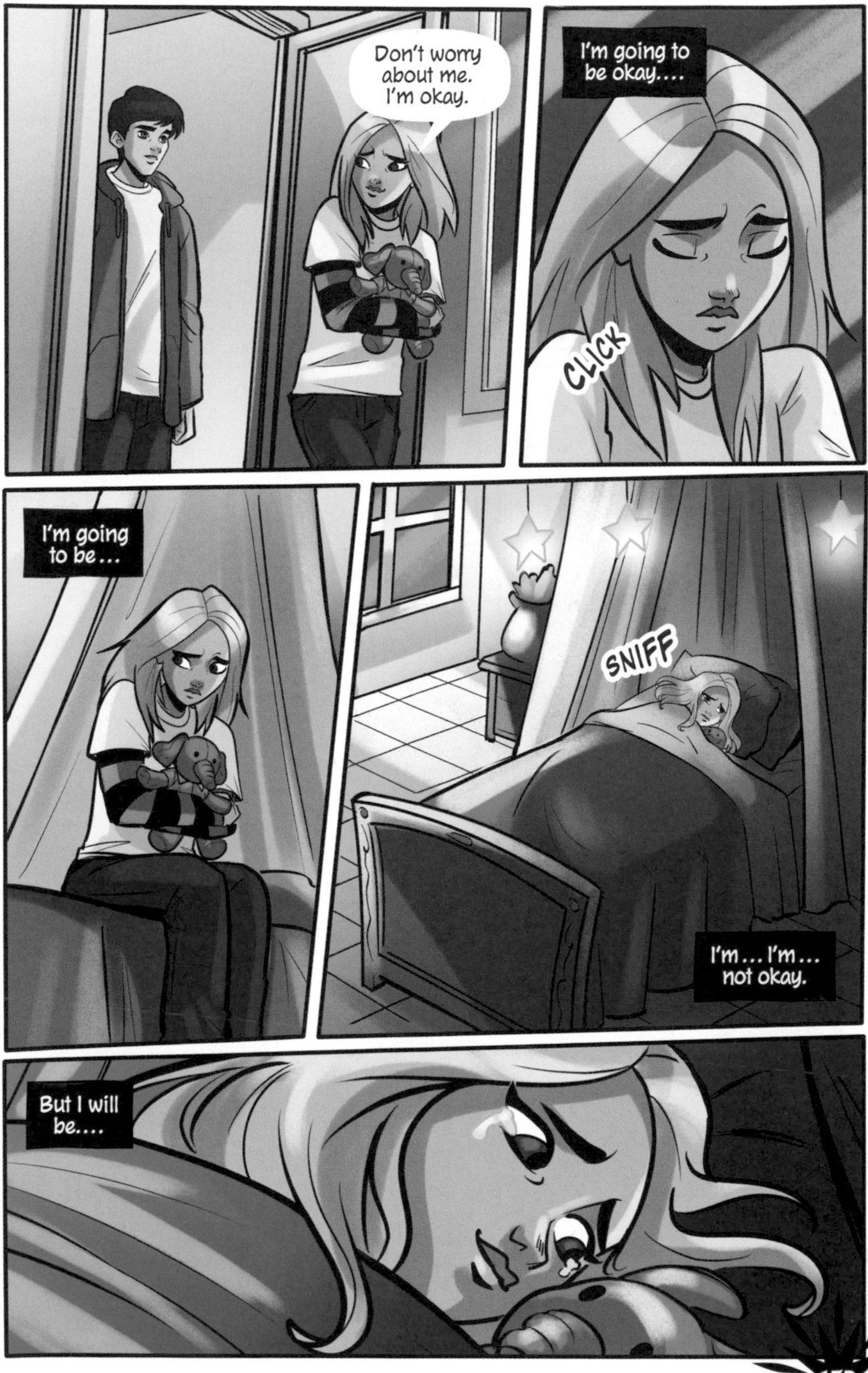
Don't worry about me. I'm okay.
I'm going to be okay....
CLICK
I'm going to be...
SNIFF
I'm... I'm... not okay.
But I will be....

CHAPTER FIFTEEN

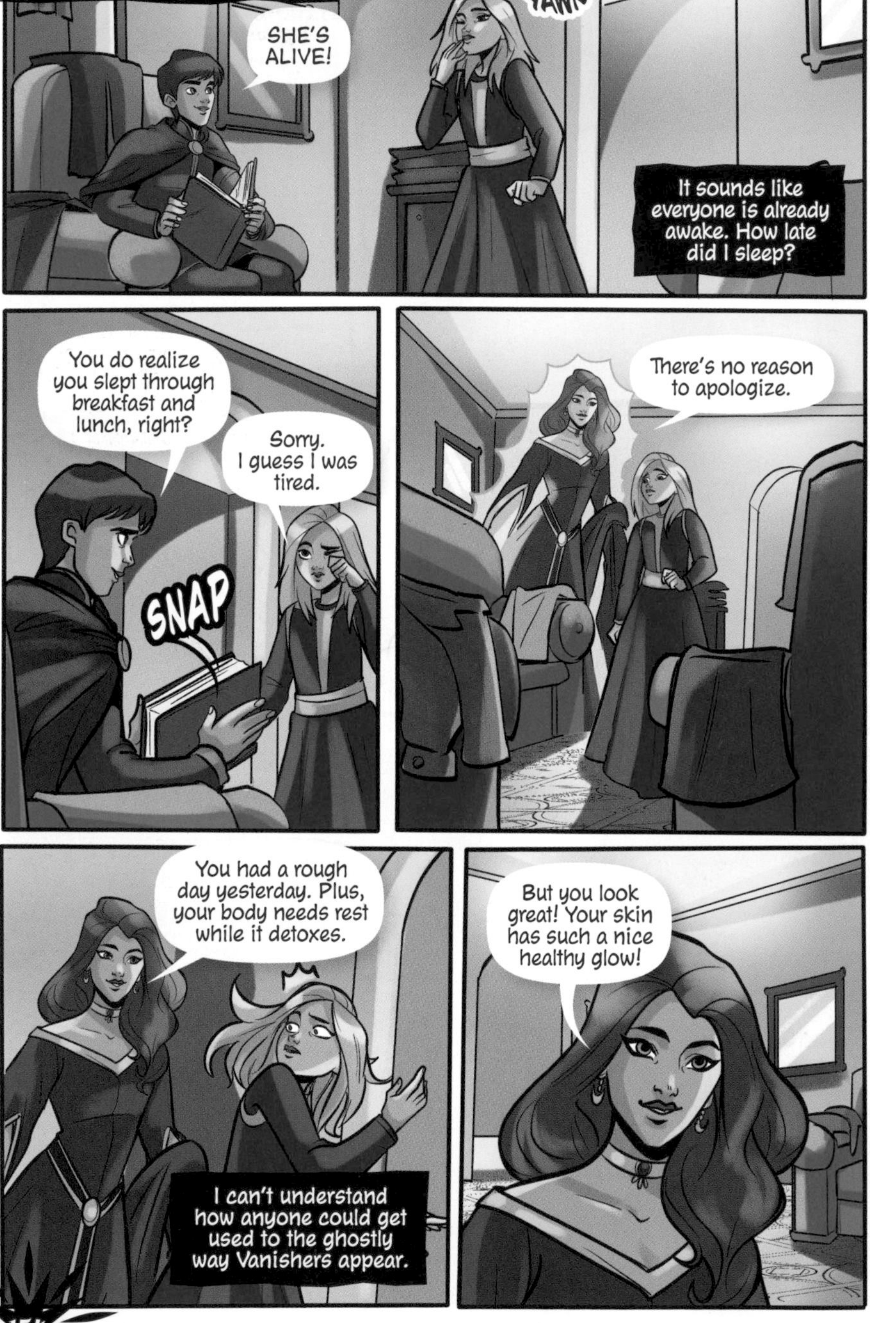
SHE'S ALIVE!
YAWN
It sounds like everyone is already awake. How late did I sleep?
You do realize you slept through breakfast and lunch, right?
Sorry. I guess I was tired.
SNAP
There's no reason to apologize.
You had a rough day yesterday. Plus, your body needs rest while it detoxes.
I can't understand how anyone could get used to the ghostly way Vanishers appear.
But you look great! Your skin has such a nice healthy glow!

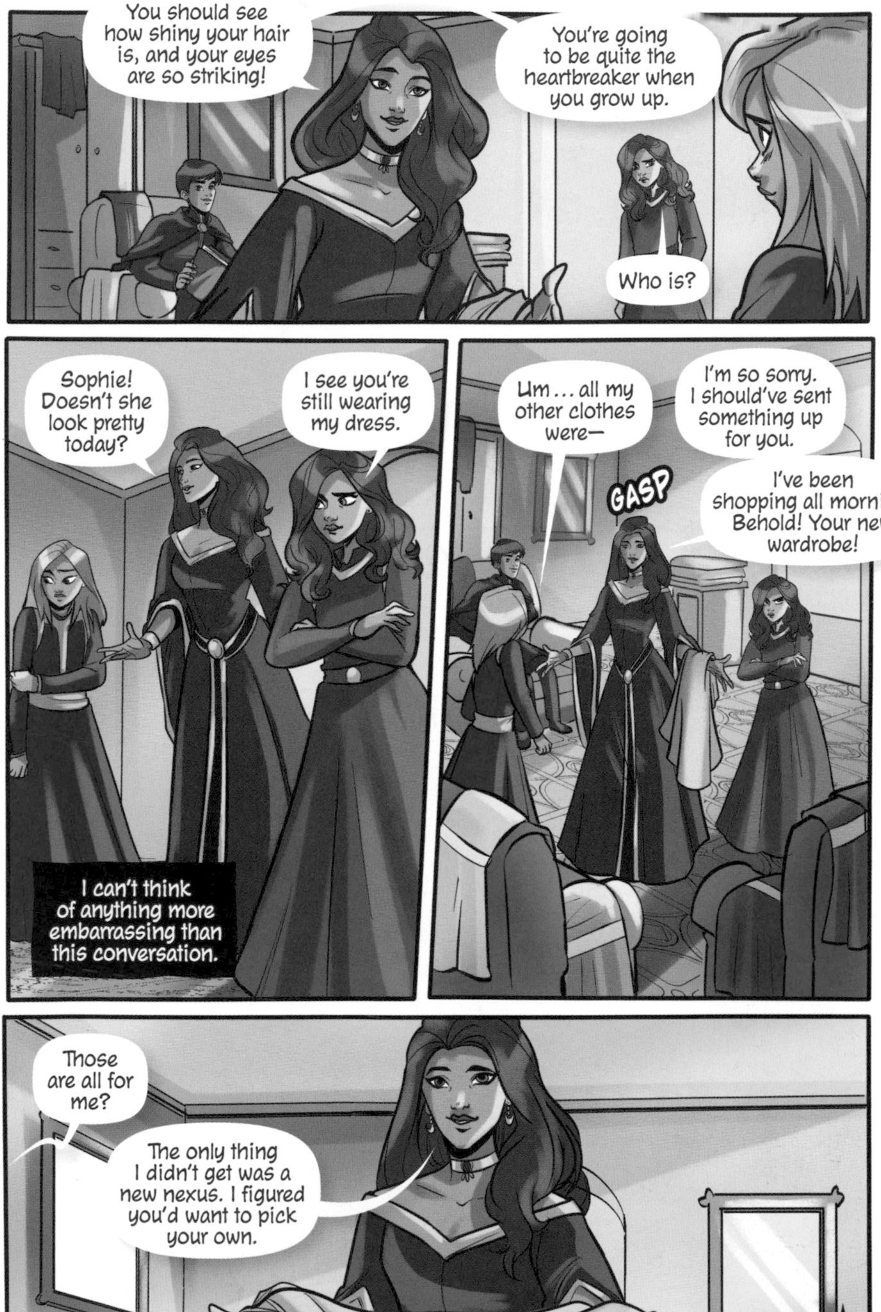
You should see how shiny your hair is, and your eyes are so striking!
You're going to be quite the heartbreaker when you grow up.
Who is?
Sophie! Doesn't she look pretty today?
I see you're still wearing my dress.
I can't think of anything more embarrassing than this conversation.
Um . . . all my other clothes were—
I'm so sorry. I should've sent something up for you.
GASP
I've been shopping all morning. Behold! Your new wardrobe!
Those are all for me?
The only thing I didn't get was a new nexus. I figured you'd want to pick your own.

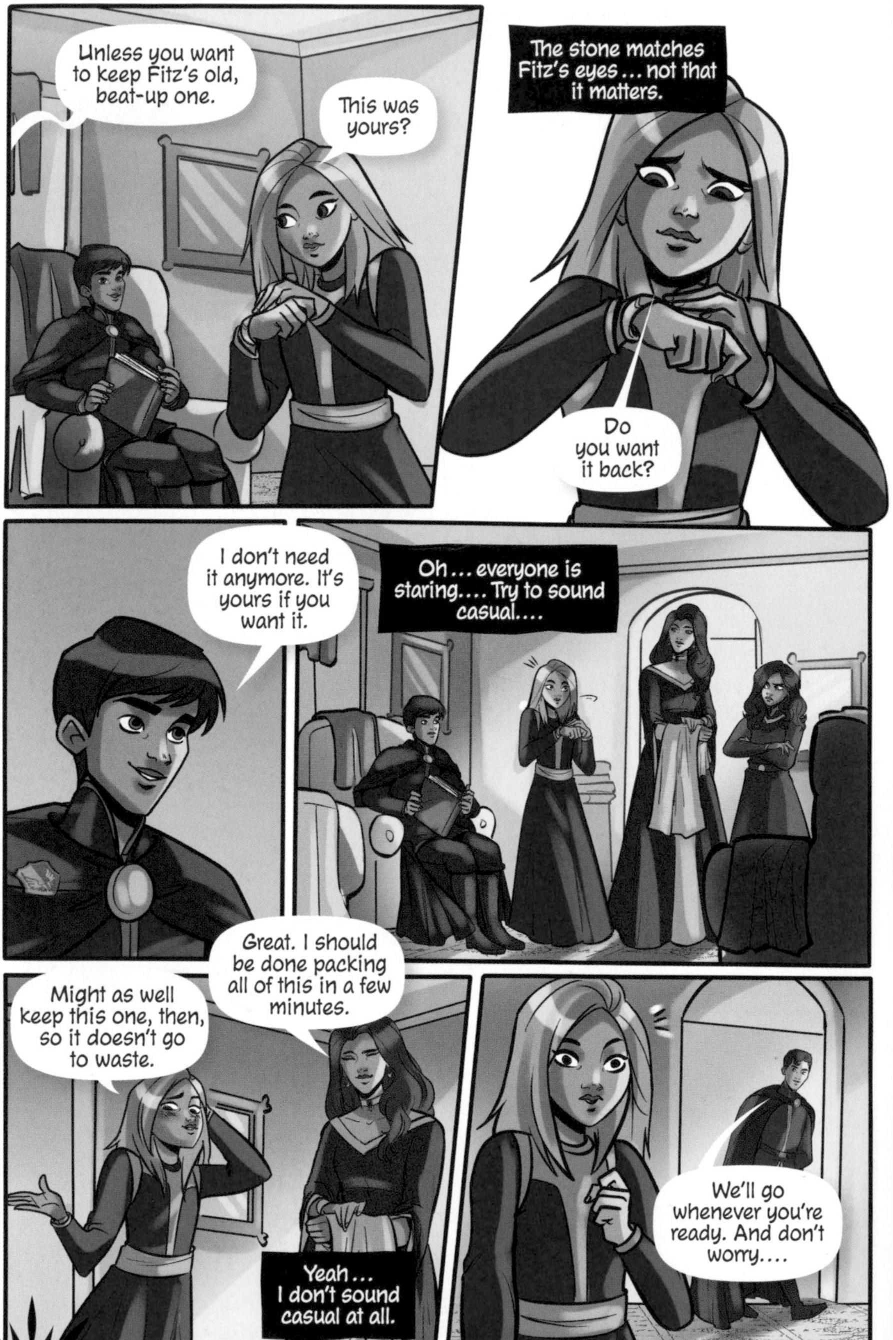

Unless you want to keep Fitz's old, beat-up one.
This was yours?
The stone matches Fitz's eyes... not that it matters.
Do you want it back?
I don't need it anymore. It's yours if you want it.
Oh... everyone is staring.... Try to sound casual....
Might as well keep this one, then, so it doesn't go to waste.
Great. I should be done packing all of this in a few minutes.
Yeah... I don't sound casual at all.
We'll go whenever you're ready. And don't worry....

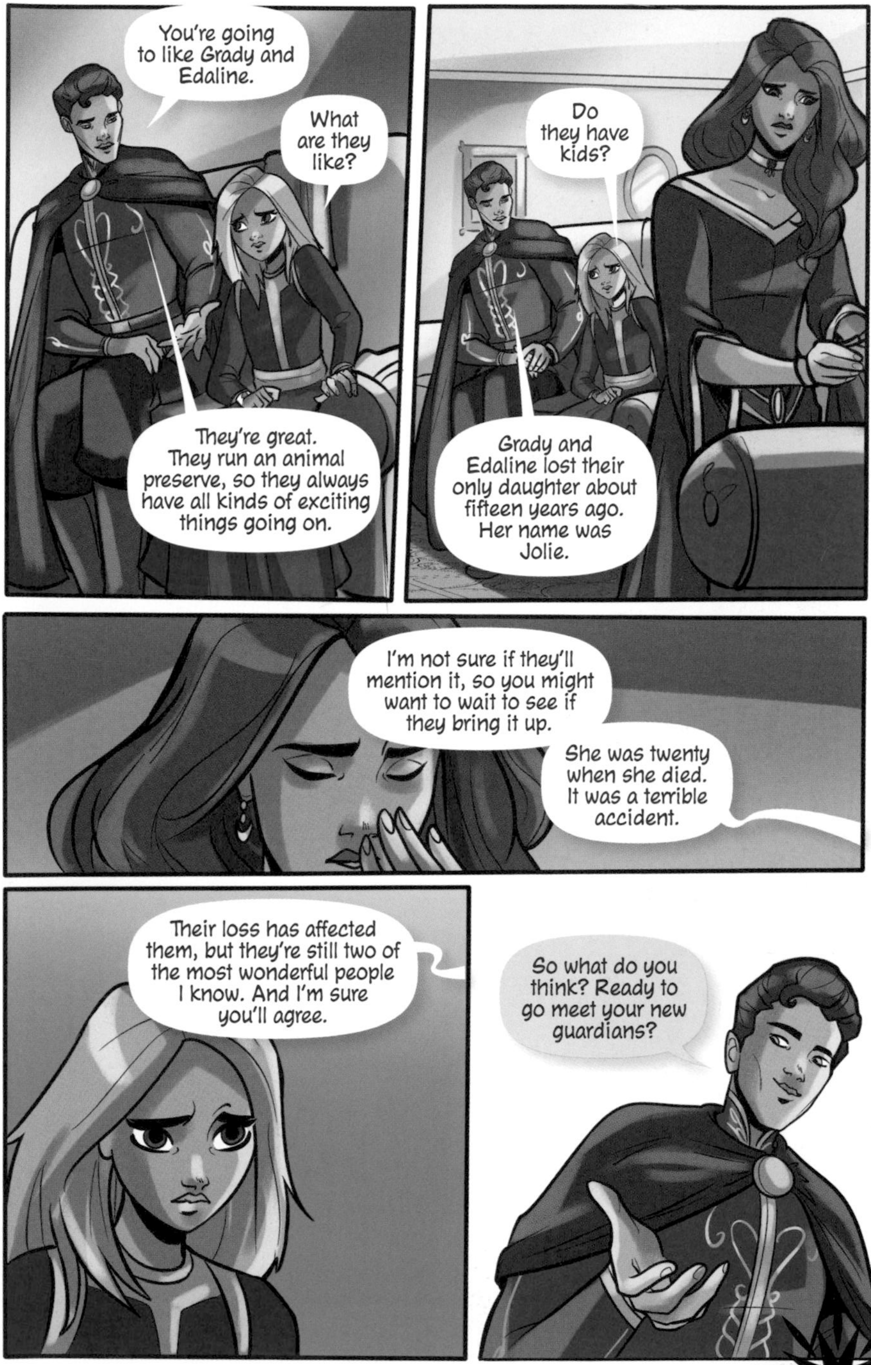
You're going to like Grady and Edaline.
What are they like?
They're great. They run an animal preserve, so they always have all kinds of exciting things going on.
Do they have kids?
Grady and Edaline lost their only daughter about fifteen years ago. Her name was Jolie.
I'm not sure if they'll mention it, so you might want to wait to see if they bring it up.
She was twenty when she died. It was a terrible accident.
Their loss has affected them, but they're still two of the most wonderful people I know. And I'm sure you'll agree.
So what do you think? Ready to go meet your new guardians?

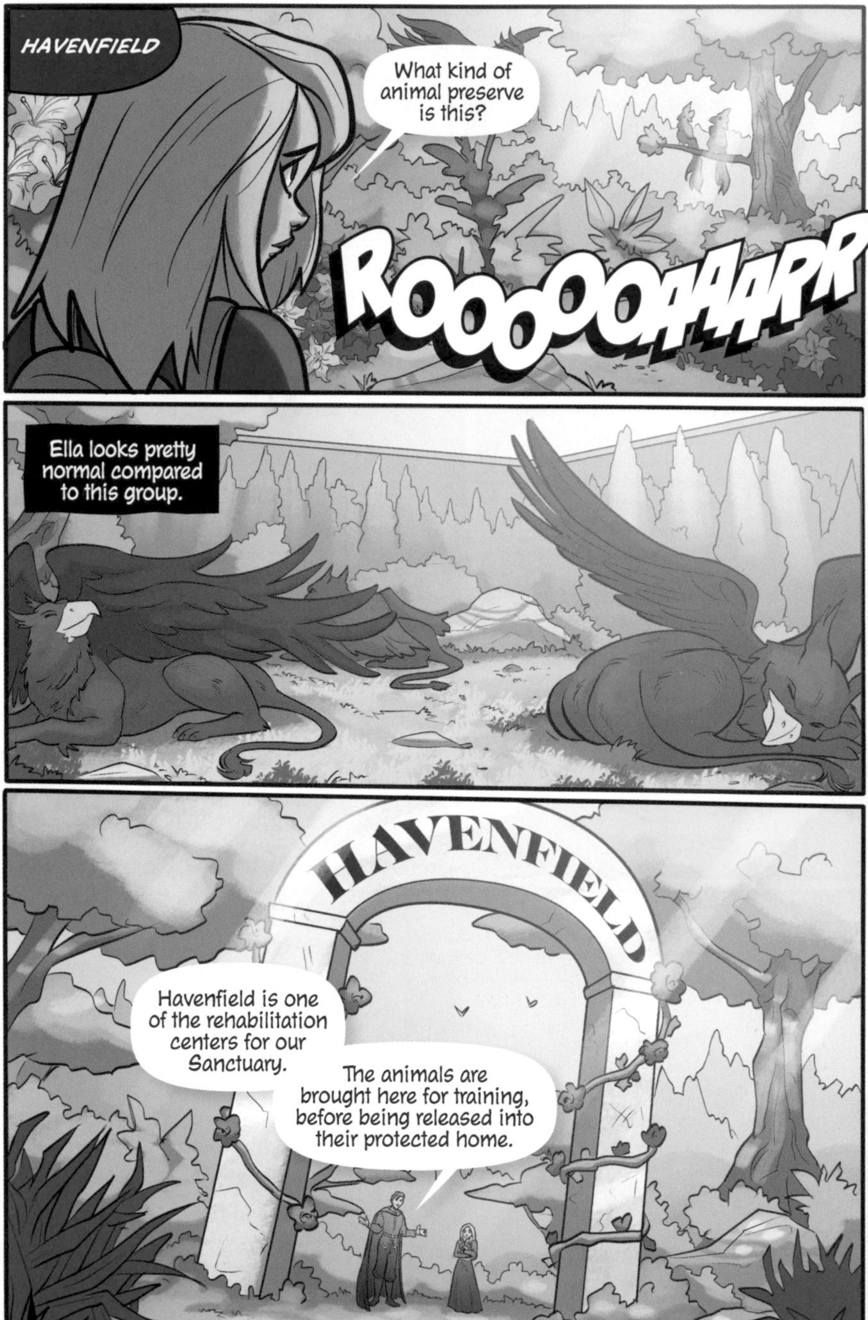
HAVENFIELD
What kind of animal preserve is this?
ROOOOOOAAARR
Ella looks pretty normal compared to this group.
HAVENFIELD
Havenfield is one of the rehabilitation centers for our Sanctuary.
The animals are brought here for training, before being released into their protected home.

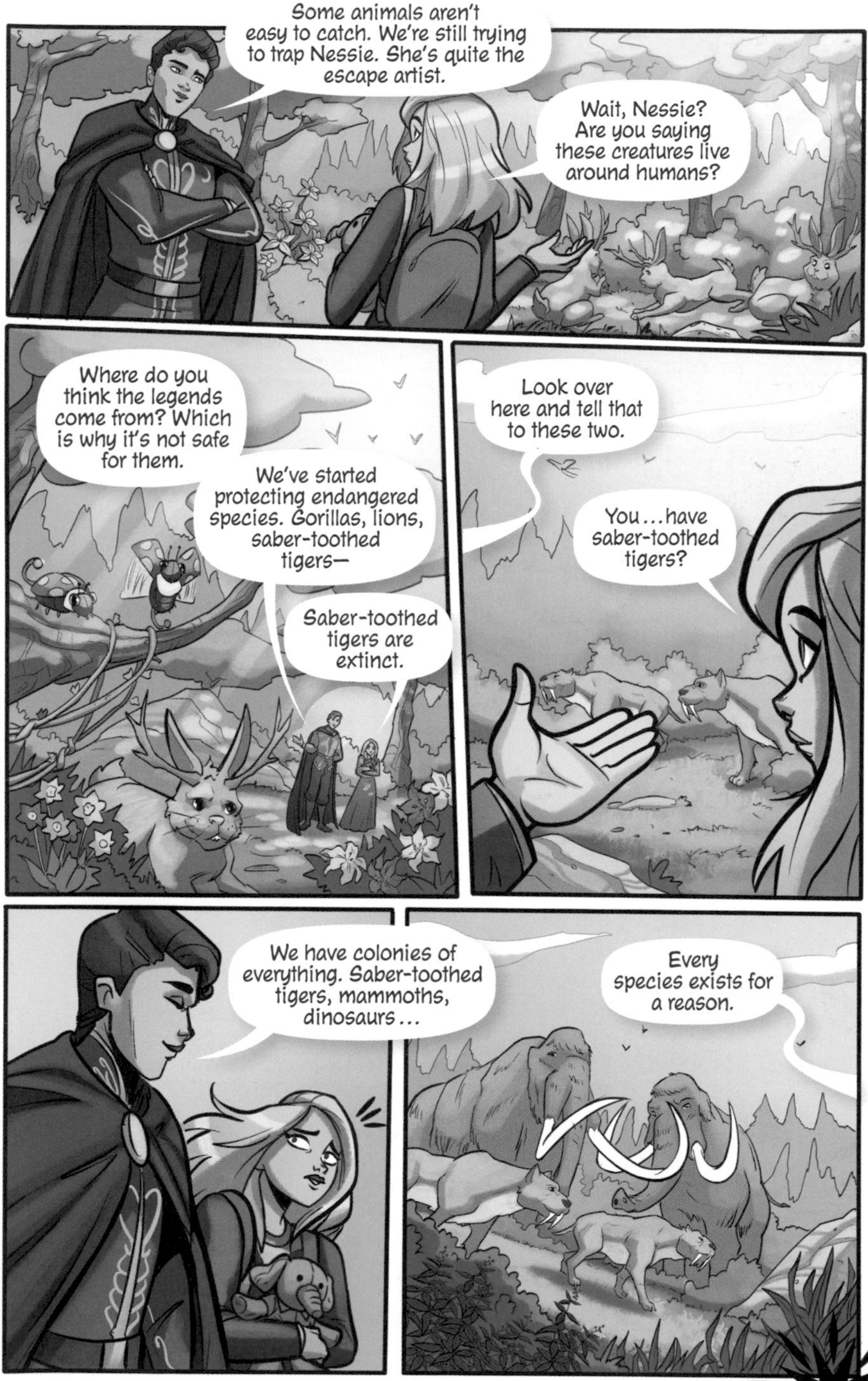
Some animals aren't easy to catch. We're still trying to trap Nessie. She's quite the escape artist.
Wait, Nessie? Are you saying these creatures live around humans?
Where do you think the legends come from? Which is why it's not safe for them.
We've started protecting endangered species. Gorillas, lions, saber-toothed tigers—
Saber-toothed tigers are extinct.
Look over here and tell that to these two.
You...have saber-toothed tigers?
We have colonies of everything. Saber-toothed tigers, mammoths, dinosaurs...
Every species exists for a reason.

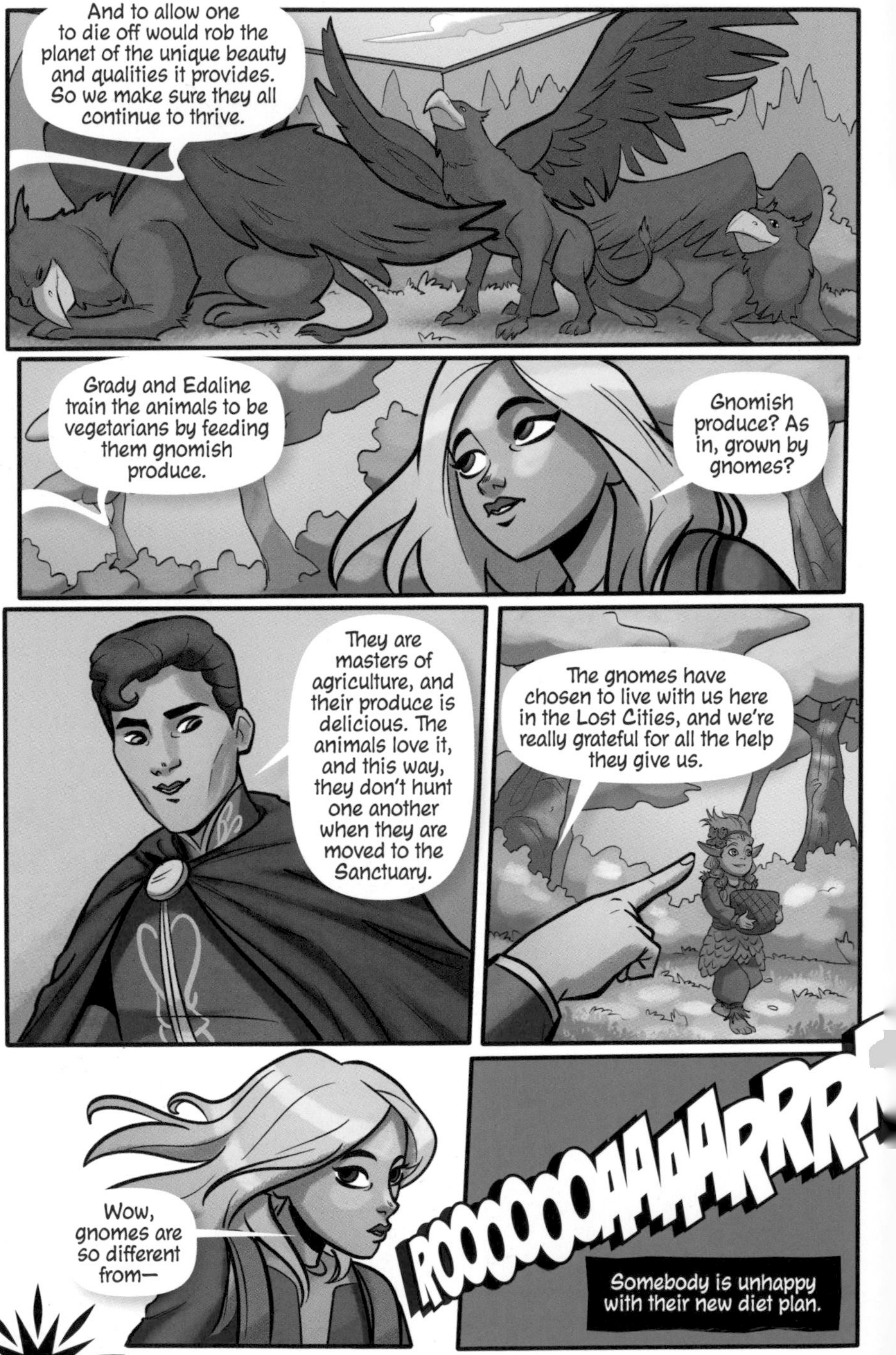

And to allow one to die off would rob the planet of the unique beauty and qualities it provides. So we make sure they all continue to thrive.
Grady and Edaline train the animals to be vegetarians by feeding them gnomish produce.
Gnomish produce? As in, grown by gnomes?
They are masters of agriculture, and their produce is delicious. The animals love it, and this way, they don't hunt one another when they are moved to the Sanctuary.
The gnomes have chosen to live with us here in the Lost Cities, and we're really grateful for all the help they give us.
Wow, gnomes are so different from—
ROOOOOOAAAARRR
Somebody is unhappy with their new diet plan.

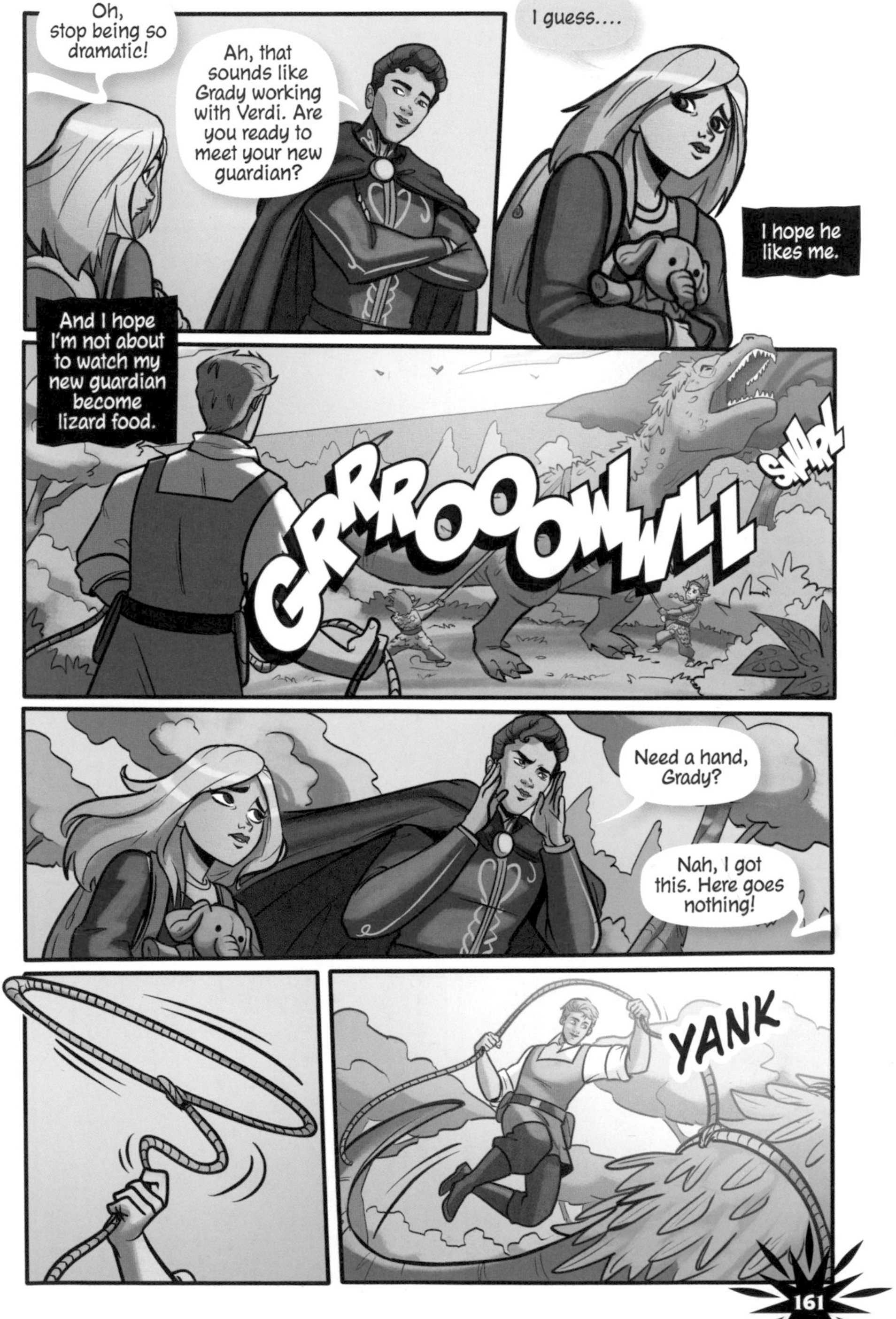
Oh, stop being so dramatic!
Ah, that sounds like Grady working with Verdi. Are you ready to meet your new guardian?
I guess....
I hope he likes me.
And I hope I'm not about to watch my new guardian become lizard food.
GRRROOOOWLL
SNARL
Need a hand, Grady?
Nah, I got this. Here goes nothing!
YANK

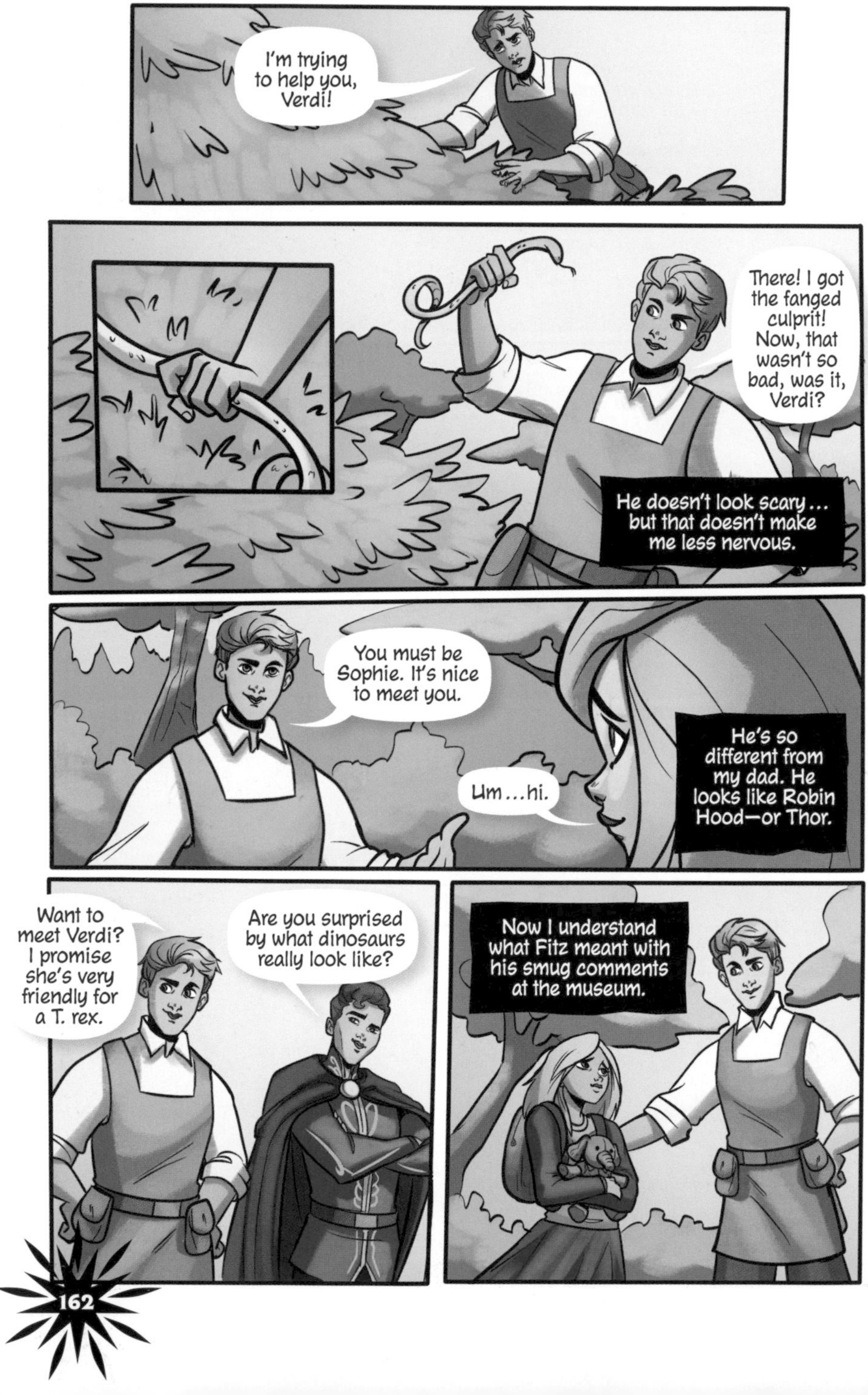
I'm trying to help you, Verdi!
There! I got the fanged culprit! Now, that wasn't so bad, was it, Verdi?
He doesn't look scary... but that doesn't make me less nervous.
You must be Sophie. It's nice to meet you.
Um...hi.
He's so different from my dad. He looks like Robin Hood—or Thor.
Want to meet Verdi? I promise she's very friendly for a T. rex.
Are you surprised by what dinosaurs really look like?
Now I understand what Fitz meant with his smug comments at the museum.

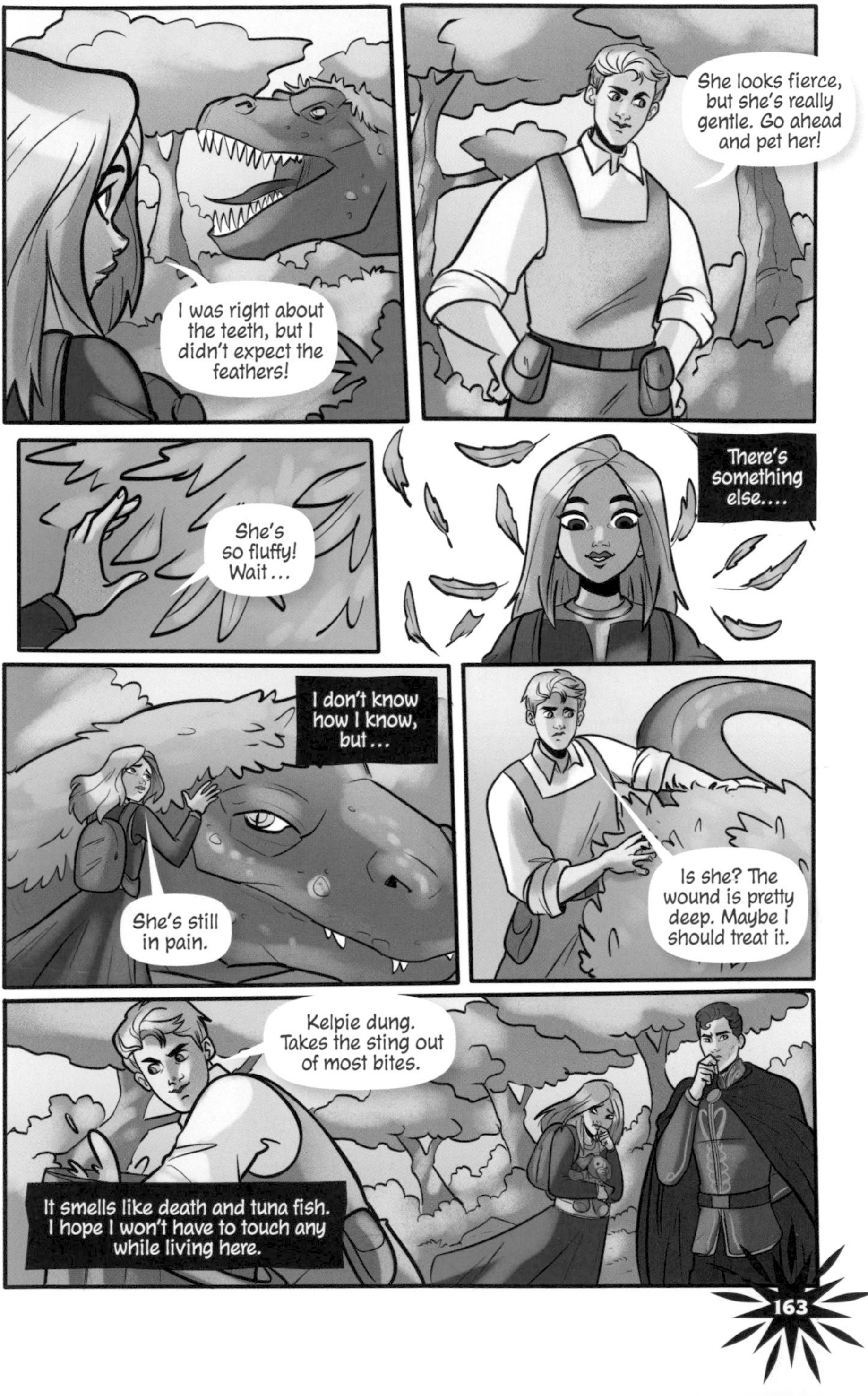
I was right about the teeth, but I didn't expect the feathers!
She looks fierce, but she's really gentle. Go ahead and pet her!
She's so fluffy! Wait…
There's something else….
I don't know how I know, but…
She's still in pain.
Is she? The wound is pretty deep. Maybe I should treat it.
Kelpie dung. Takes the sting out of most bites.
It smells like death and tuna fish. I hope I won't have to touch any while living here.

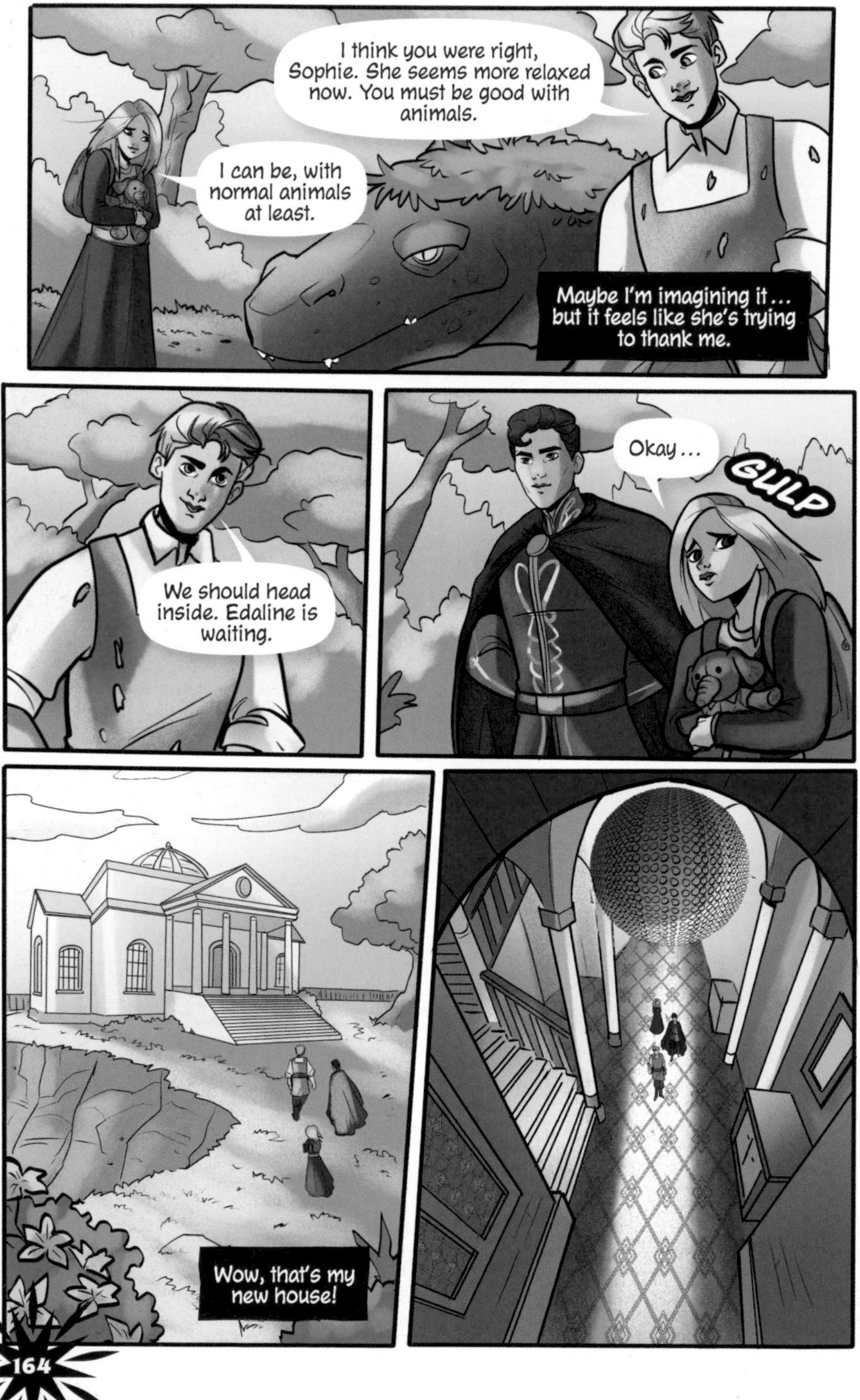

I think you were right, Sophie. She seems more relaxed now. You must be good with animals.
I can be, with normal animals at least.
Maybe I'm imagining it… but it feels like she's trying to thank me.
We should head inside. Edaline is waiting.
Okay…
GULP
Wow, that's my new house!

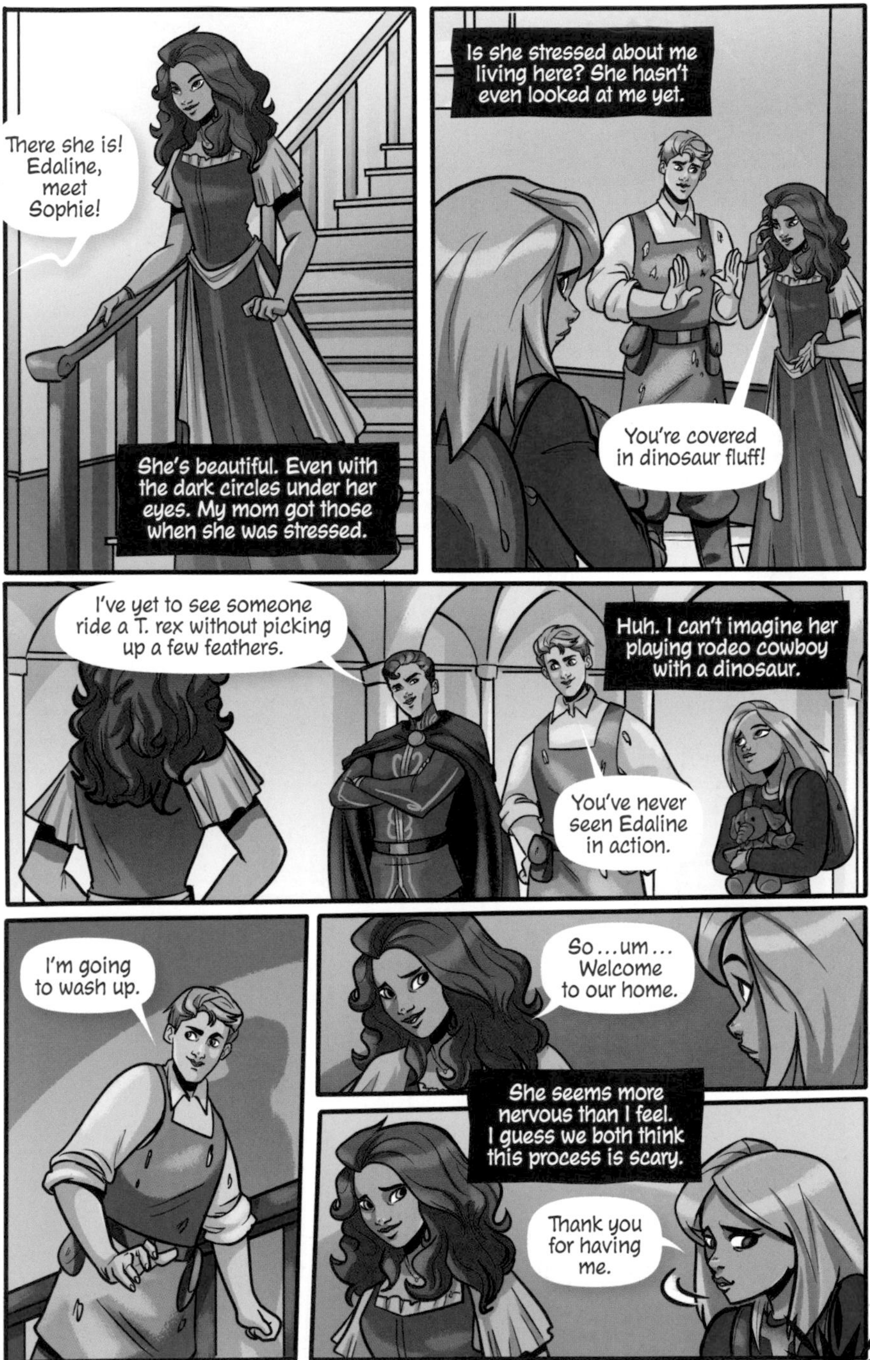
There she is! Edaline, meet Sophie!
She's beautiful. Even with the dark circles under her eyes. My mom got those when she was stressed.
Is she stressed about me living here? She hasn't even looked at me yet.
You're covered in dinosaur fluff!
I've yet to see someone ride a T. rex without picking up a few feathers.
Huh. I can't imagine her playing rodeo cowboy with a dinosaur.
You've never seen Edaline in action.
I'm going to wash up.
So...um... Welcome to our home.
She seems more nervous than I feel. I guess we both think this process is scary.
Thank you for having me.

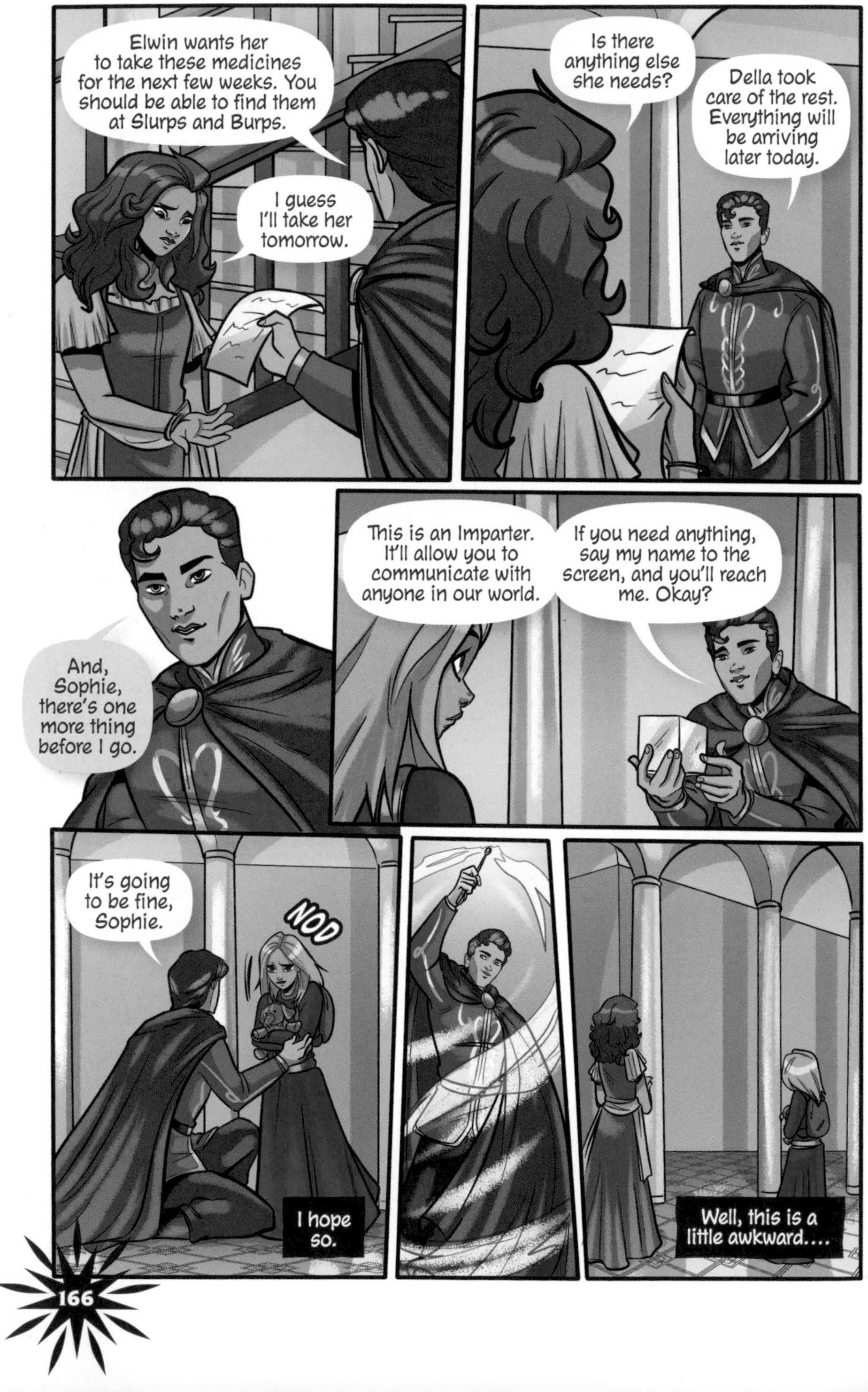
Elwin wants her to take these medicines for the next few weeks. You should be able to find them at Slurps and Burps.
I guess I'll take her tomorrow.
Is there anything else she needs?
Della took care of the rest. Everything will be arriving later today.
And, Sophie, there's one more thing before I go.
This is an Imparter. It'll allow you to communicate with anyone in our world.
If you need anything, say my name to the screen, and you'll reach me. Okay?
It's going to be fine, Sophie.
NOD
I hope so.
Well, this is a little awkward....

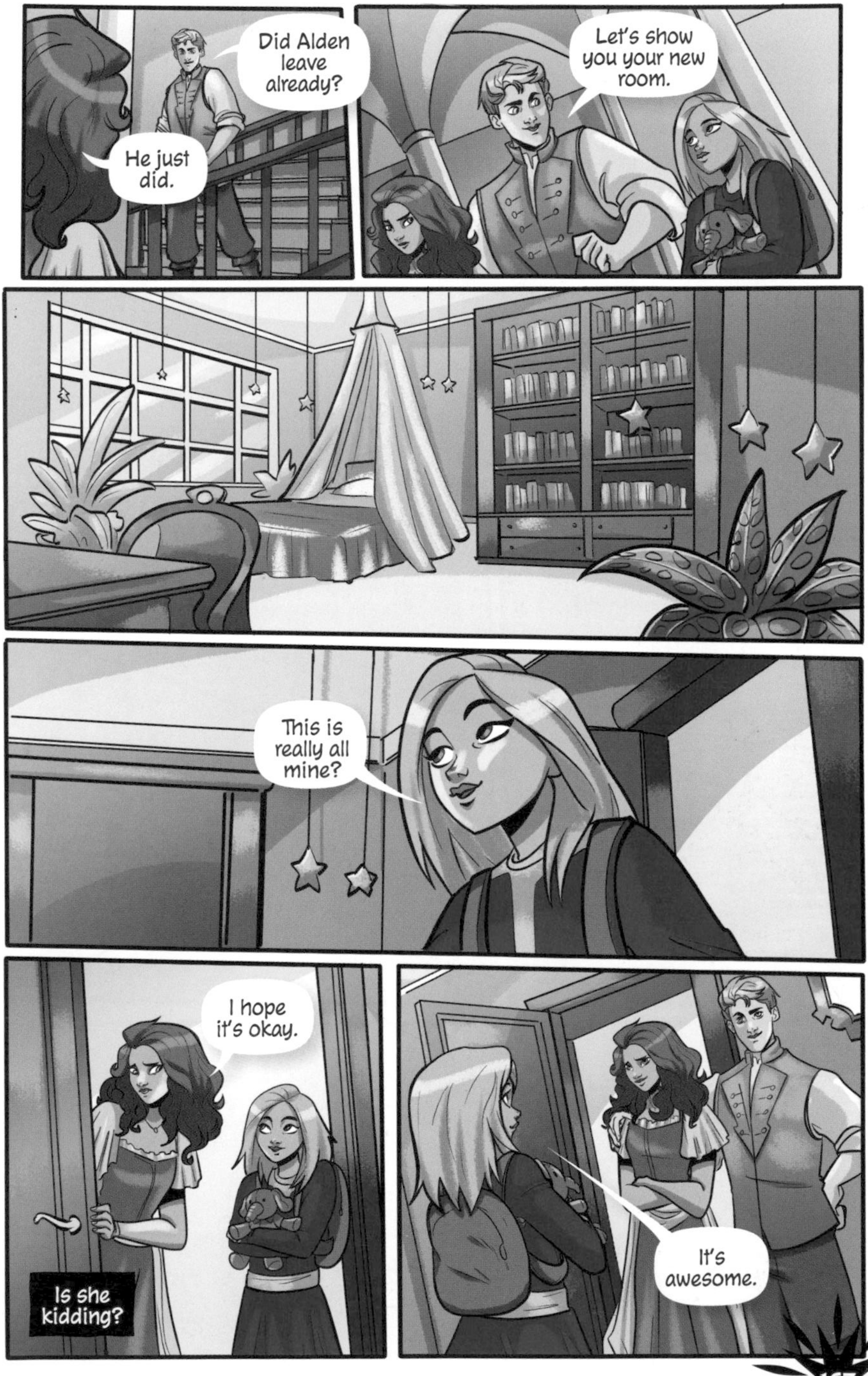
Did Alden leave already?
He just did.
Let's show you your new room.
This is really all mine?
I hope it's okay.
Is she kidding?
It's awesome.

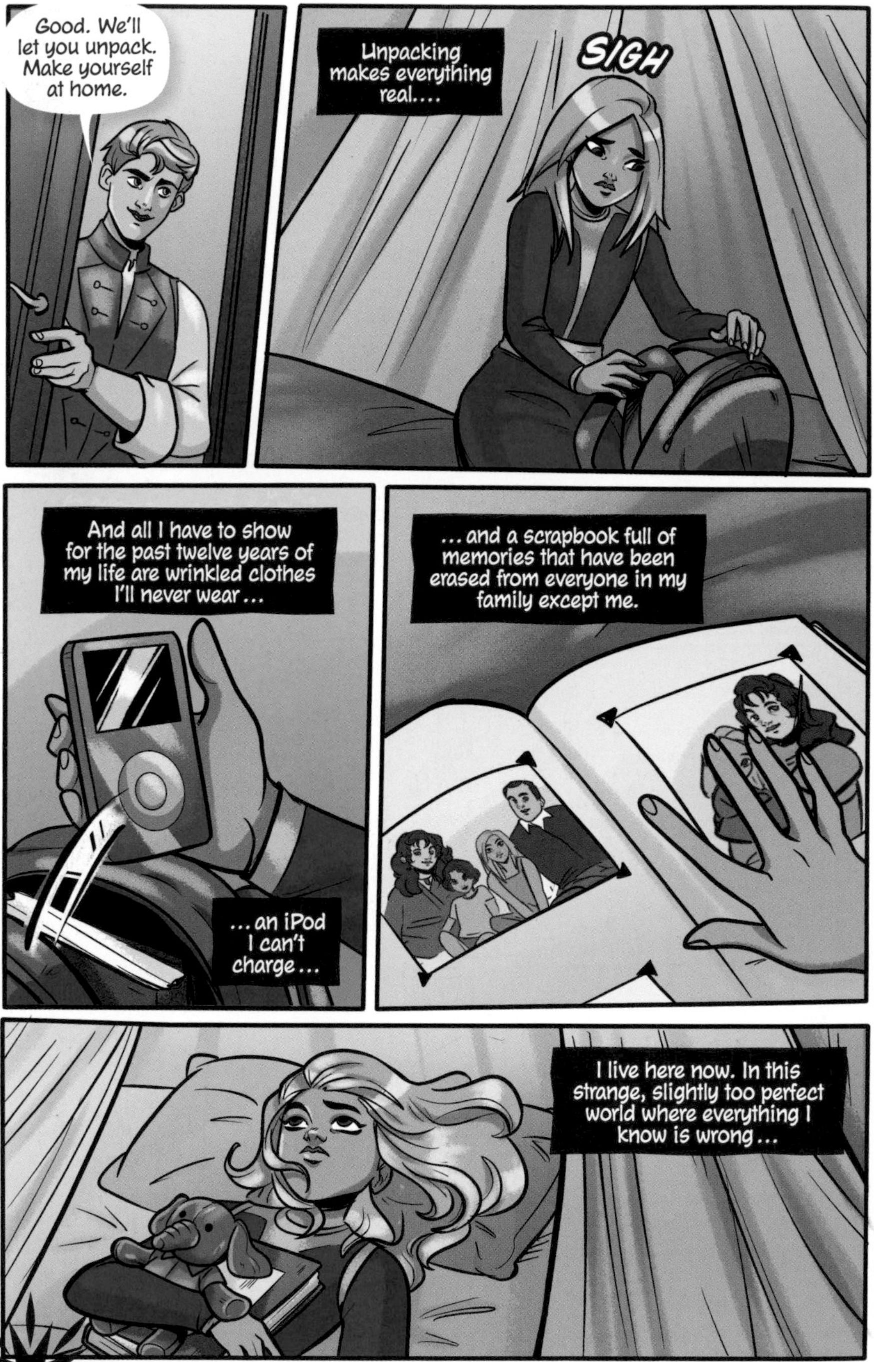
Good. We'll let you unpack. Make yourself at home.
Unpacking makes everything real....
SIGH
And all I have to show for the past twelve years of my life are wrinkled clothes I'll never wear...
...an iPod I can't charge...
...and a scrapbook full of memories that have been erased from everyone in my family except me.
I live here now. In this strange, slightly too perfect world where everything I know is wrong...

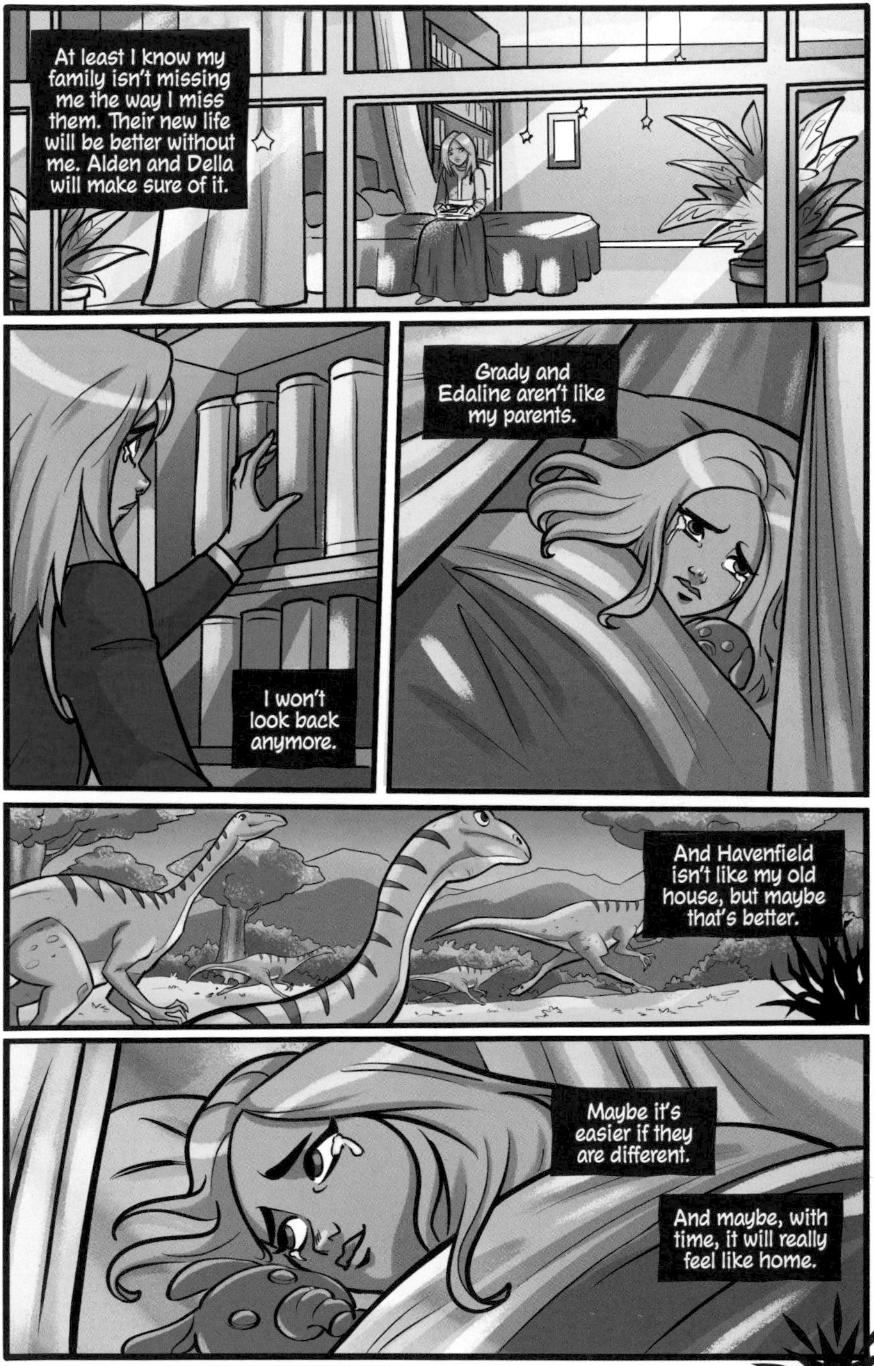
At least I know my family isn't missing me the way I miss them. Their new life will be better without me. Alden and Della will make sure of it.
I won't look back anymore.
Grady and Edaline aren't like my parents.
And Havenfield isn't like my old house, but maybe that's better.
Maybe it's easier if they are different.
And maybe, with time, it will really feel like home.

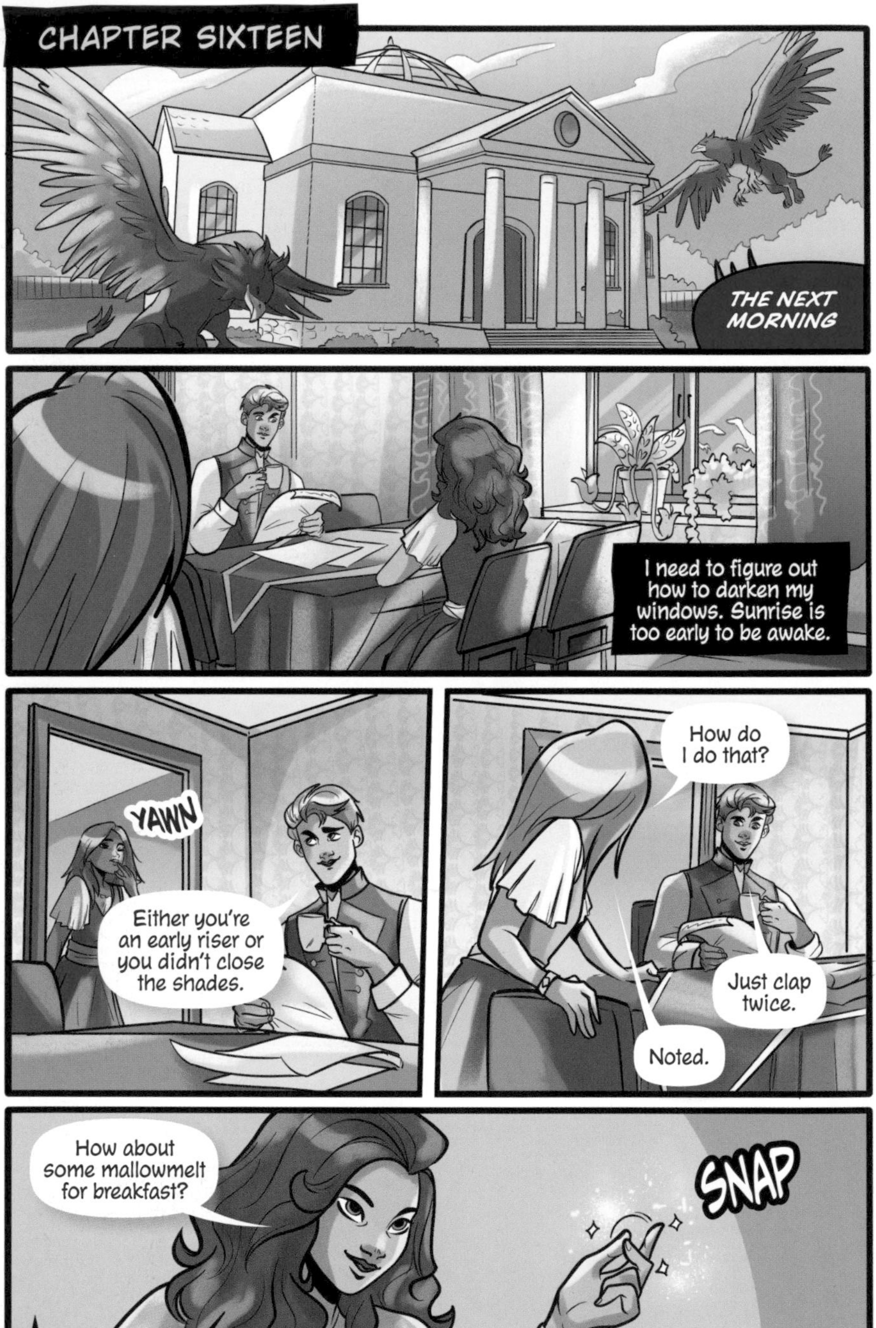
CHAPTER SIXTEEN
THE NEXT MORNING
I need to figure out how to darken my windows. Sunrise is too early to be awake.
YAWN
Either you're an early riser or you didn't close the shades.
How do I do that?
Just clap twice.
Noted.
How about some mallowmelt for breakfast?
SNAP

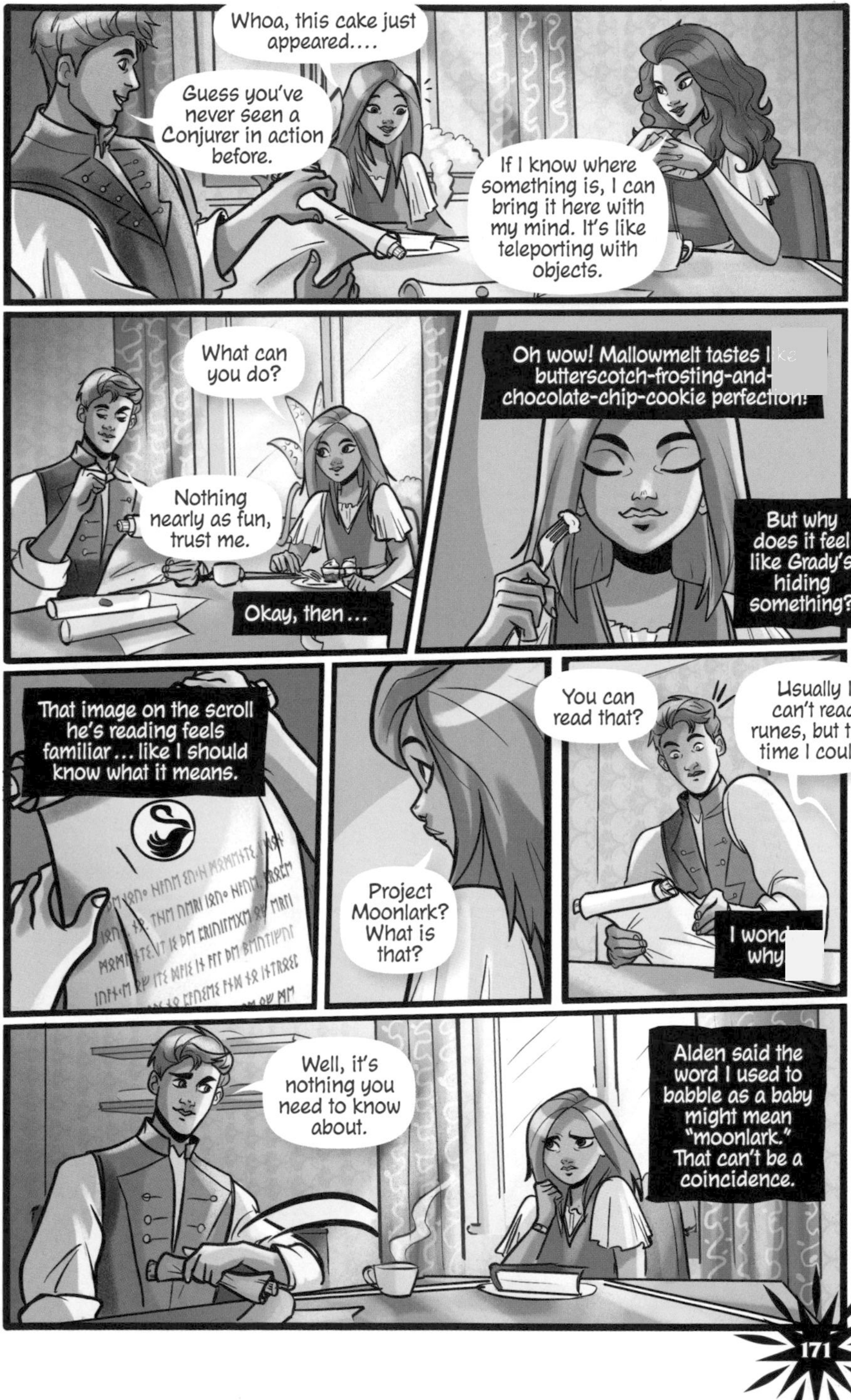
Whoa, this cake just appeared....
Guess you've never seen a Conjurer in action before.
If I know where something is, I can bring it here with my mind. It's like teleporting with objects.
What can you do?
Nothing nearly as fun, trust me.
Okay, then...
Oh wow! Mallowmelt tastes like butterscotch-frosting-and-chocolate-chip-cookie perfection!
But why does it feel like Grady's hiding something?
That image on the scroll he's reading feels familiar... like I should know what it means.
Project Moonlark? What is that?
You can read that?
Usually I can't read runes, but this time I could.
I wond
why
Well, it's nothing you need to know about.
Alden said the word I used to babble as a baby might mean "moonlark." That can't be a coincidence.

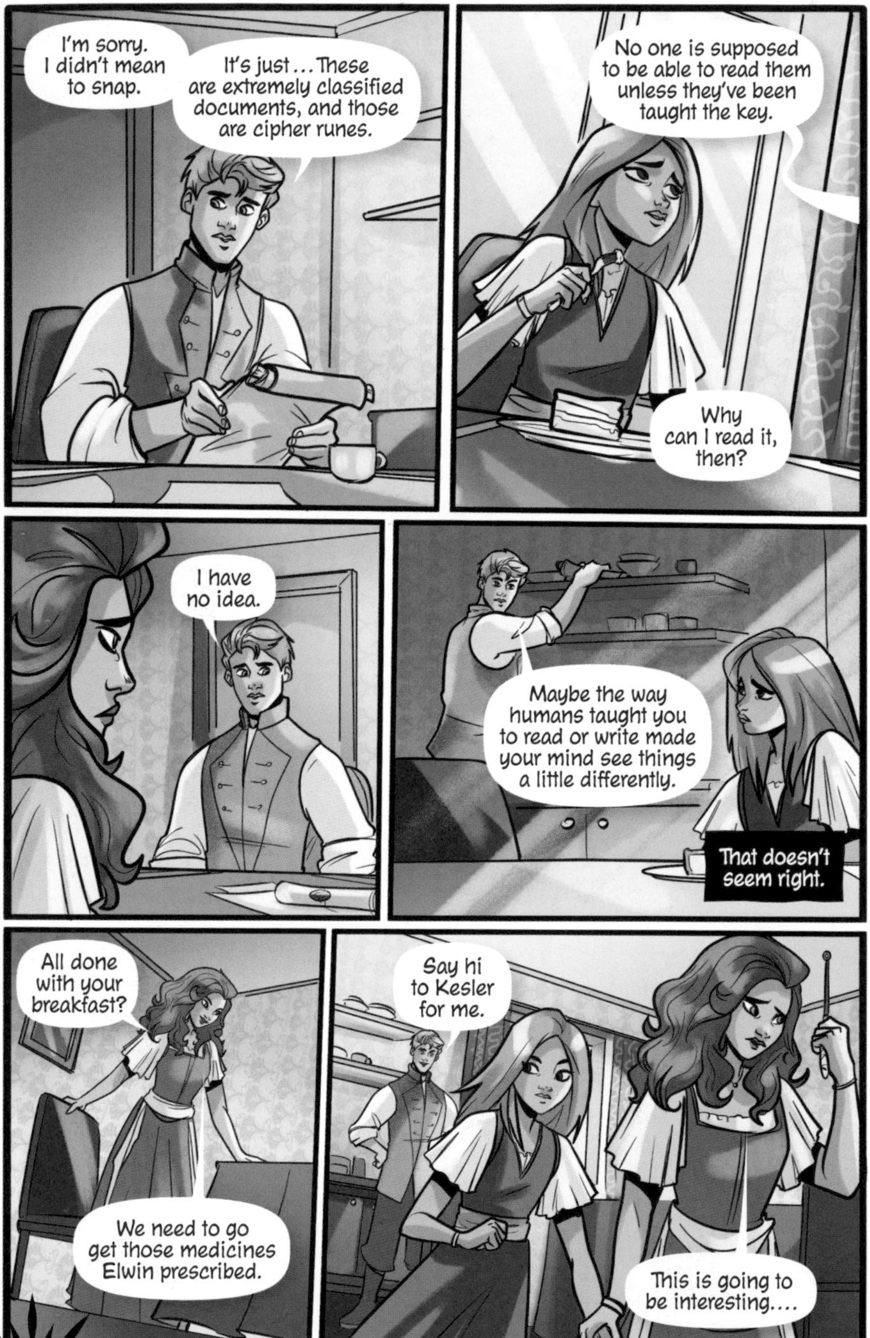
I'm sorry. I didn't mean to snap.
It's just... These are extremely classified documents, and those are cipher runes.
No one is supposed to be able to read them unless they've been taught the key.
Why can I read it, then?
I have no idea.
Maybe the way humans taught you to read or write made your mind see things a little differently.
That doesn't seem right.
All done with your breakfast?
We need to go get those medicines Elwin prescribed.
Say hi to Kesler for me.
This is going to be interesting....

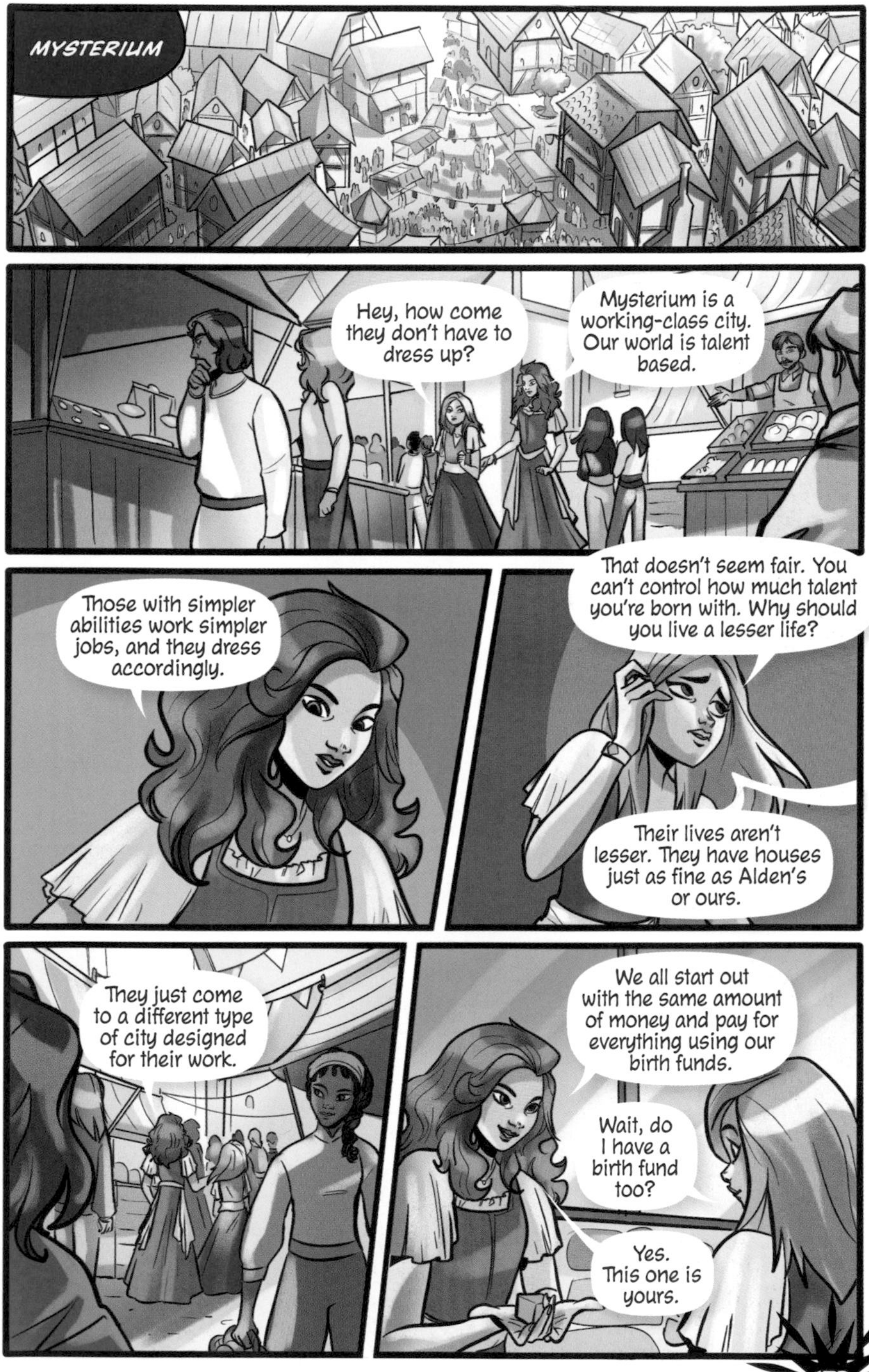
MYSTERIUM
Hey, how come they don't have to dress up?
Mysterium is a working-class city. Our world is talent based.
Those with simpler abilities work simpler jobs, and they dress accordingly.
That doesn't seem fair. You can't control how much talent you're born with. Why should you live a lesser life?
Their lives aren't lesser. They have houses just as fine as Alden's or ours.
They just come to a different type of city designed for their work.
We all start out with the same amount of money and pay for everything using our birth funds.
Wait, do I have a birth fund too?
Yes. This one is yours.

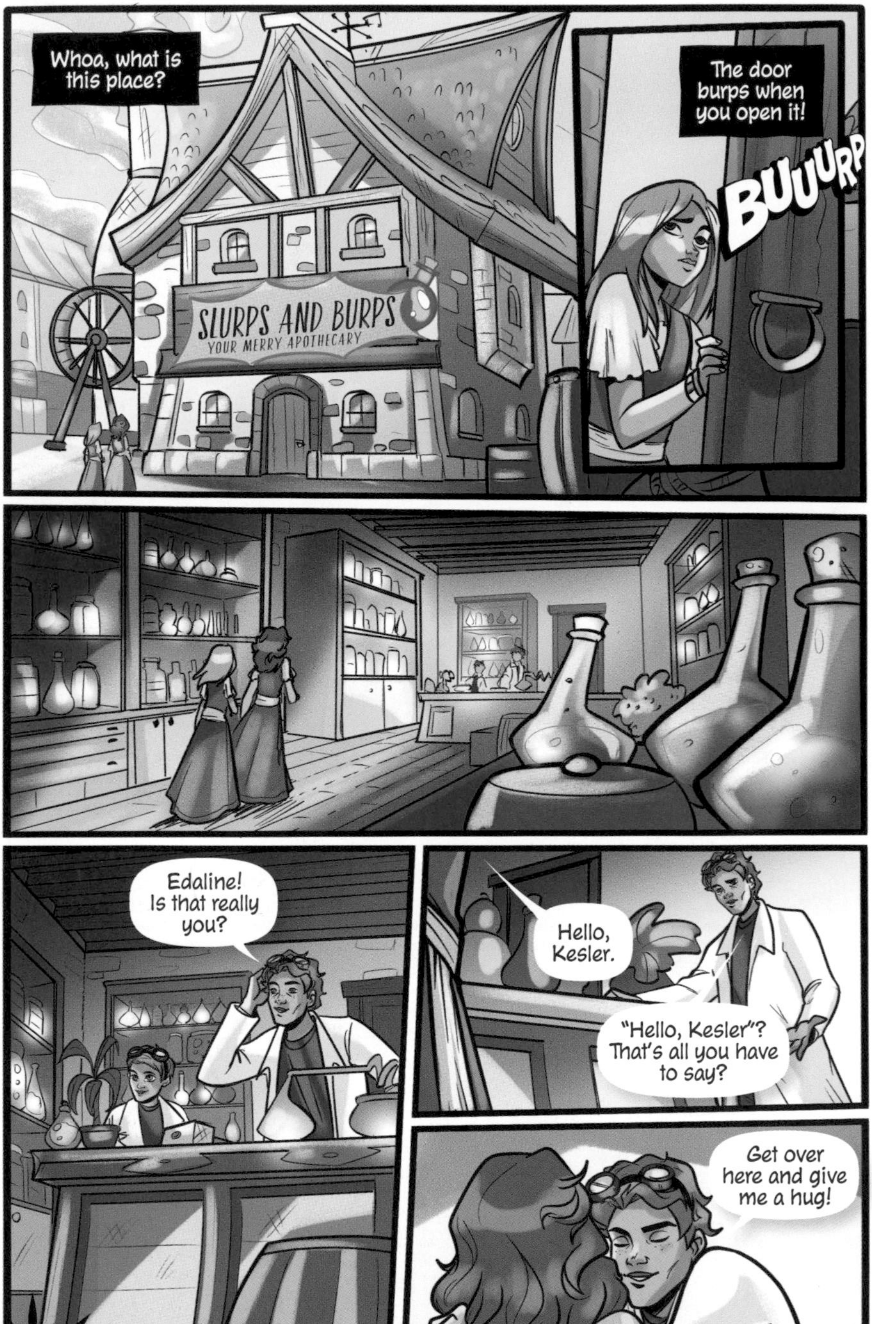
Whoa, what is this place?
SLURPS AND BURPS
YOUR MERRY APOTHECARY
The door burps when you open it!
BUUURP
Edaline! Is that really you?
Hello, Kesler.
"Hello, Kesler"? That's all you have to say?
Get over here and give me a hug!

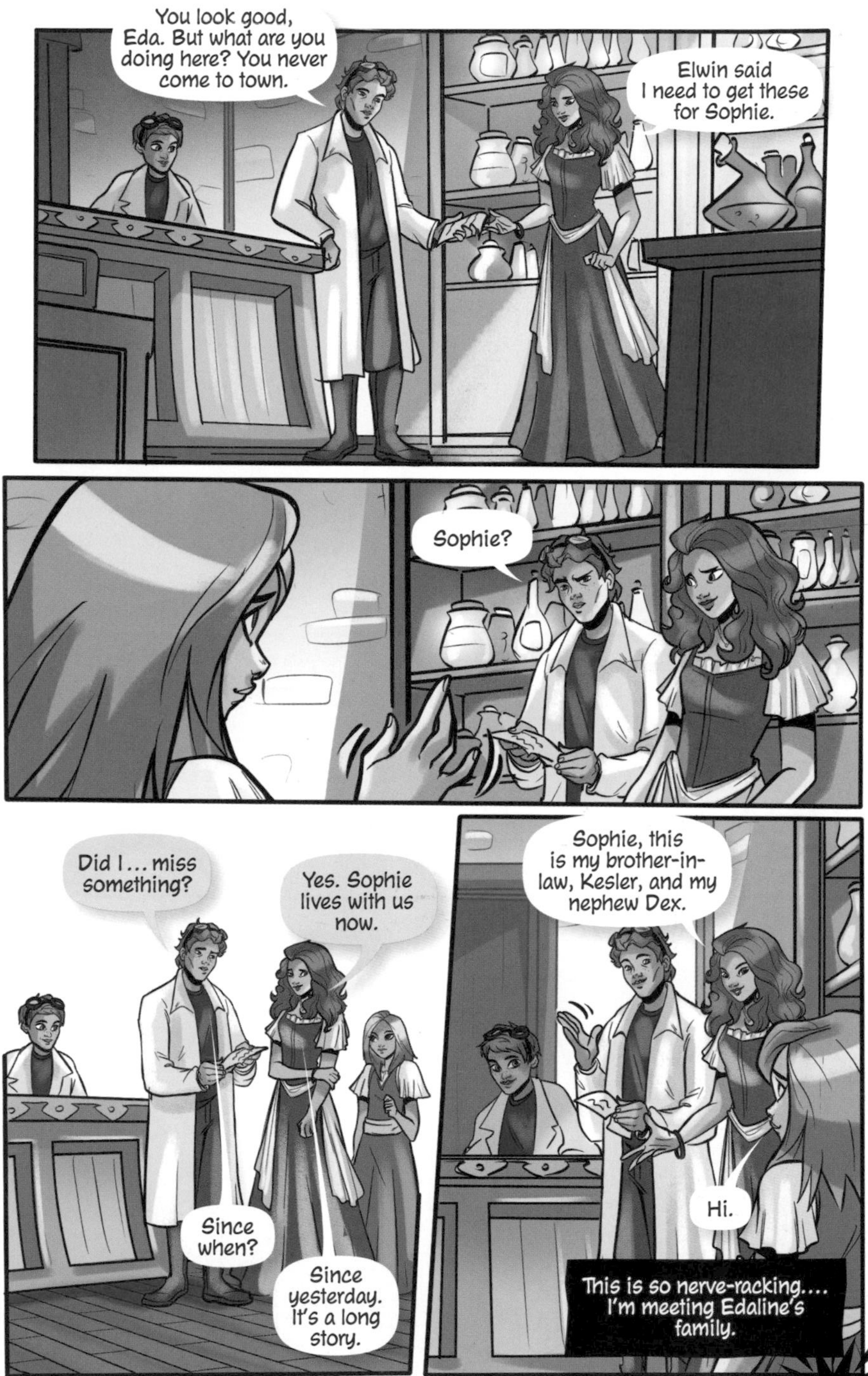
You look good, Eda. But what are you doing here? You never come to town.
Elwin said I need to get these for Sophie.
Sophie?
Did I... miss something?
Yes. Sophie lives with us now.
Since when?
Since yesterday. It's a long story.
Sophie, this is my brother-in-law, Kesler, and my nephew Dex.
Hi.
This is so nerve-racking.... I'm meeting Edaline's family.

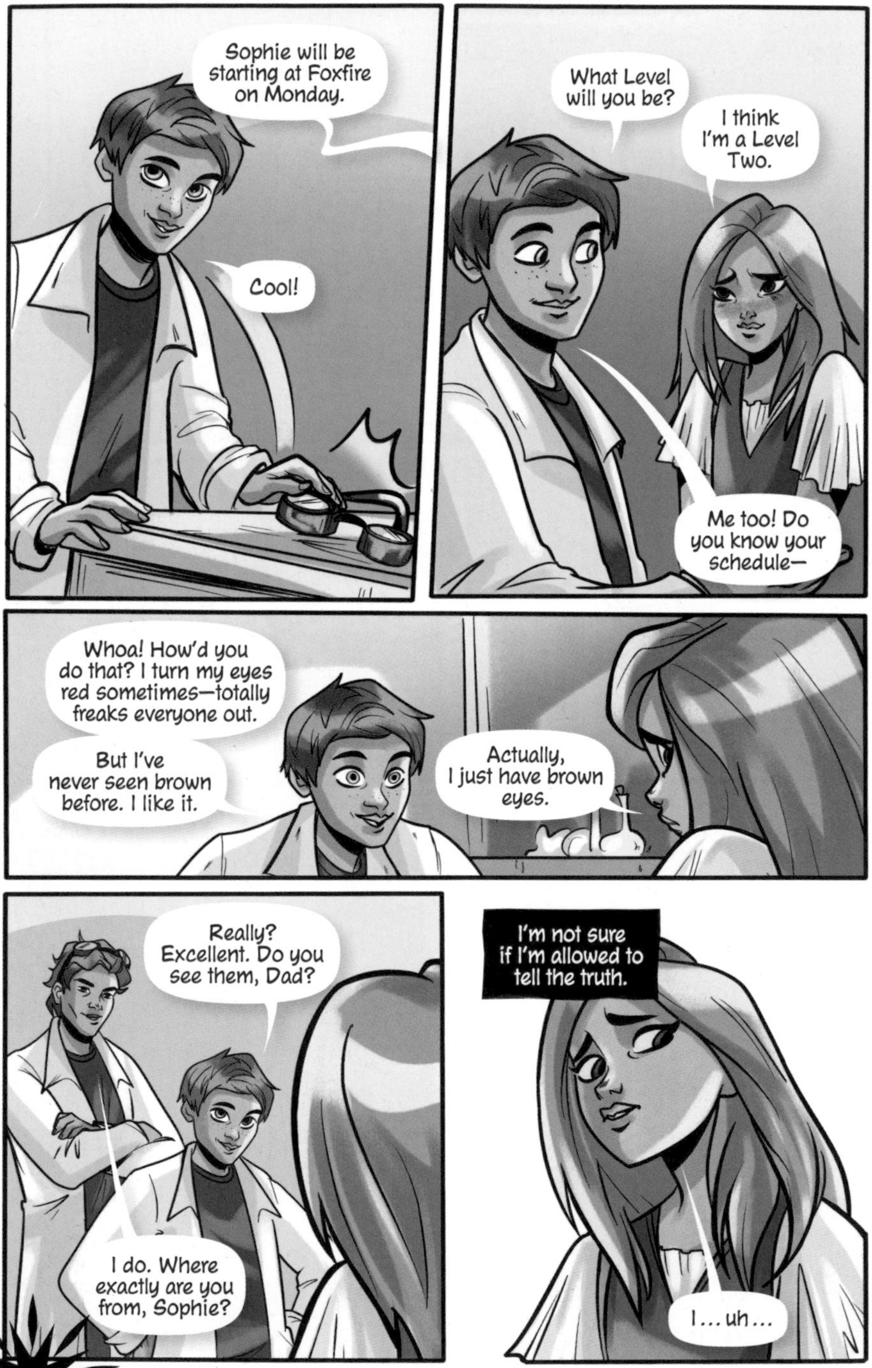
Sophie will be starting at Foxfire on Monday.
Cool!
What Level will you be?
I think I'm a Level Two.
Me too! Do you know your schedule—
Whoa! How'd you do that? I turn my eyes red sometimes—totally freaks everyone out.
But I've never seen brown before. I like it.
Actually, I just have brown eyes.
Really? Excellent. Do you see them, Dad?
I do. Where exactly are you from, Sophie?
I'm not sure if I'm allowed to tell the truth.
I... uh...

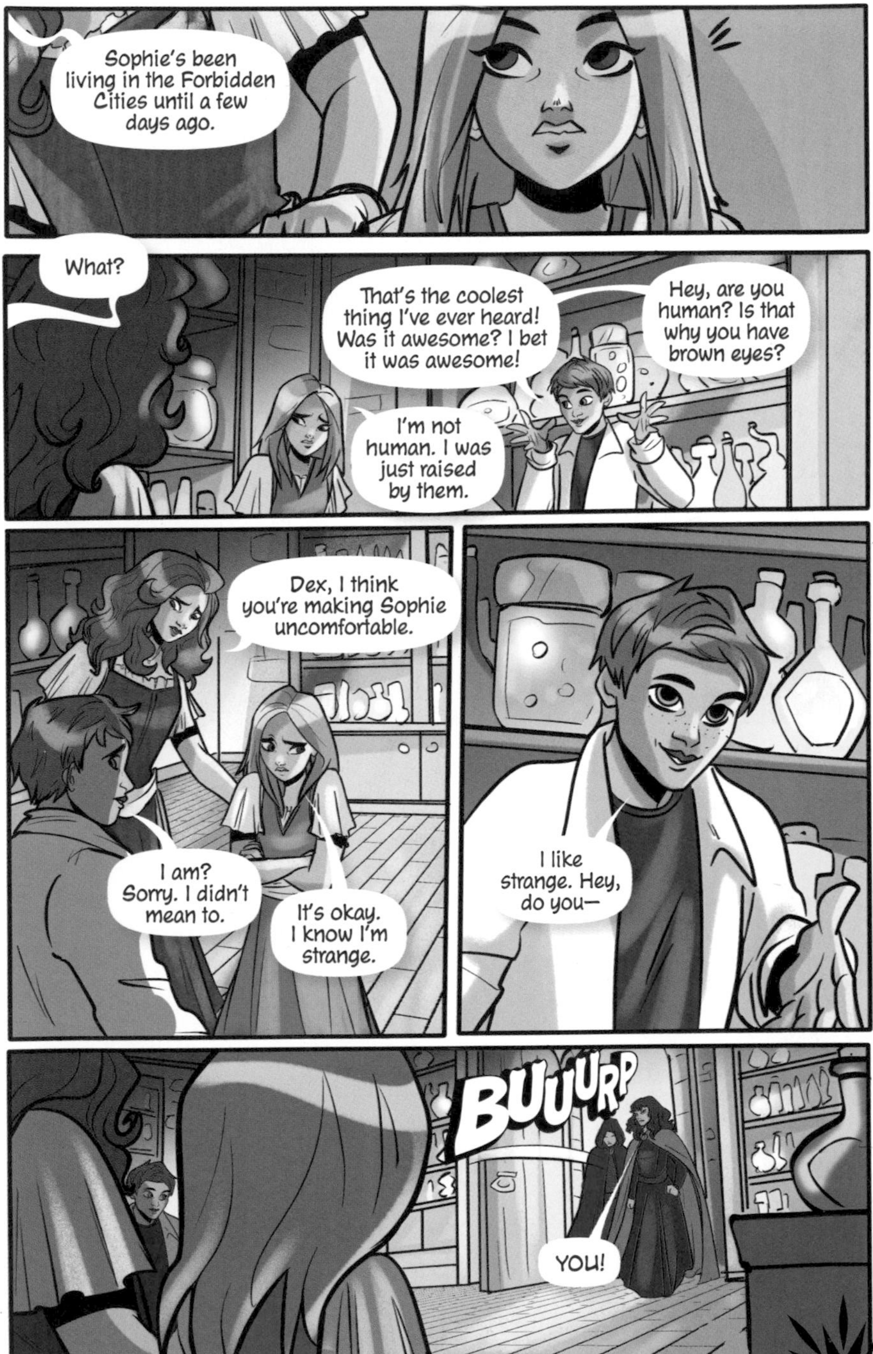
Sophie's been living in the Forbidden Cities until a few days ago.
What?
That's the coolest thing I've ever heard! Was it awesome? I bet it was awesome!
Hey, are you human? Is that why you have brown eyes?
I'm not human. I was just raised by them.
Dex, I think you're making Sophie uncomfortable.
I am? Sorry. I didn't mean to.
It's okay. I know I'm strange.
I like strange. Hey, do you—
BUUURP
YOU!

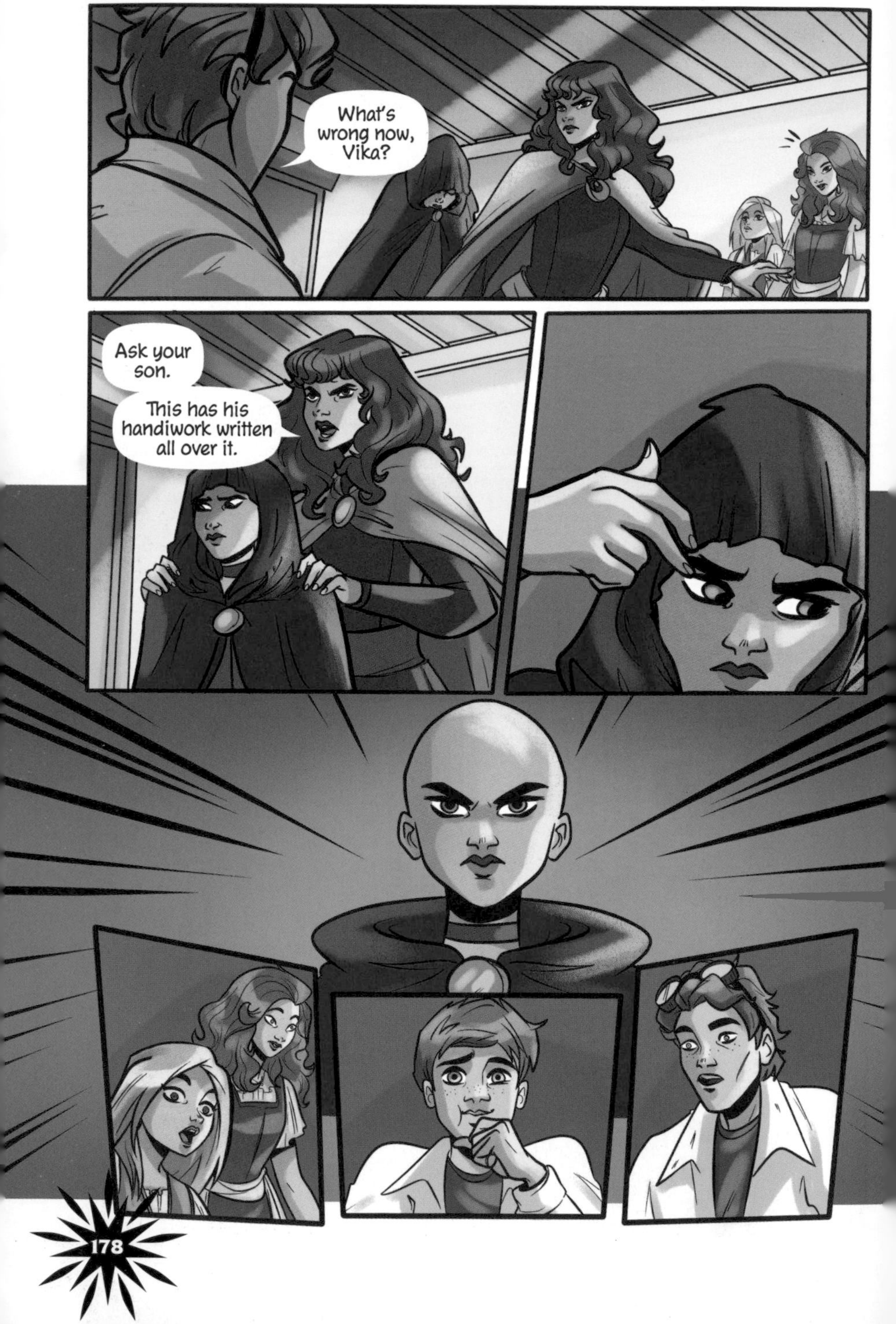
What's wrong now, Vika?
Ask your son.
This has his handiwork written all over it.

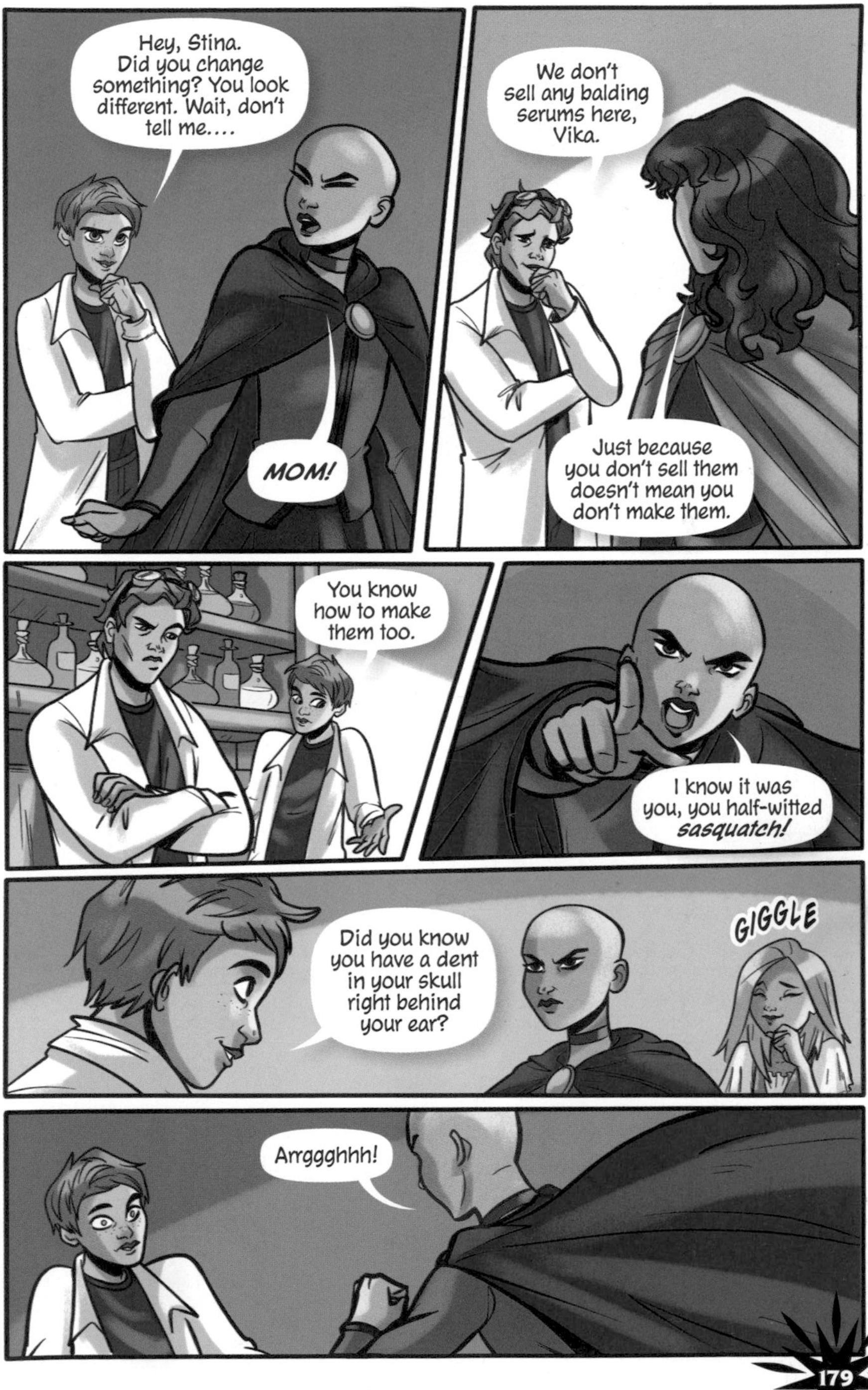
Hey, Stina. Did you change something? You look different. Wait, don't tell me....
MOM!
We don't sell any balding serums here, Vika.
Just because you don't sell them doesn't mean you don't make them.
You know how to make them too.
I know it was you, you half-witted *sasquatch!*
Did you know you have a dent in your skull right behind your ear?
GIGGLE
Arrggghhh!

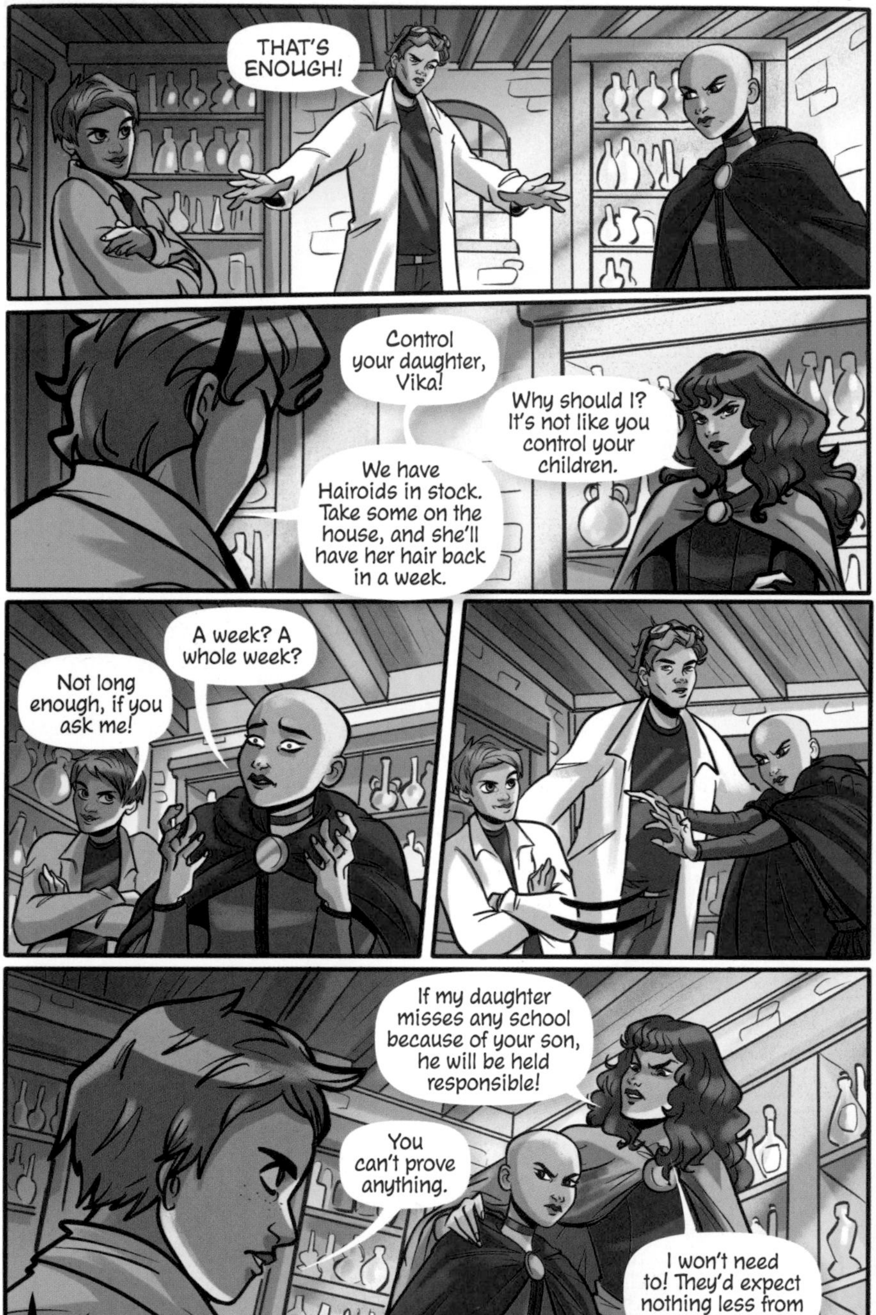
THAT'S ENOUGH!
Control your daughter, Vika!
We have Hairoids in stock. Take some on the house, and she'll have her hair back in a week.
Why should I? It's not like you control your children.
A week? A whole week?
Not long enough, if you ask me!
If my daughter misses any school because of your son, he will be held responsible!
You can't prove anything.
I won't need to! They'd expect nothing less from a bad match!

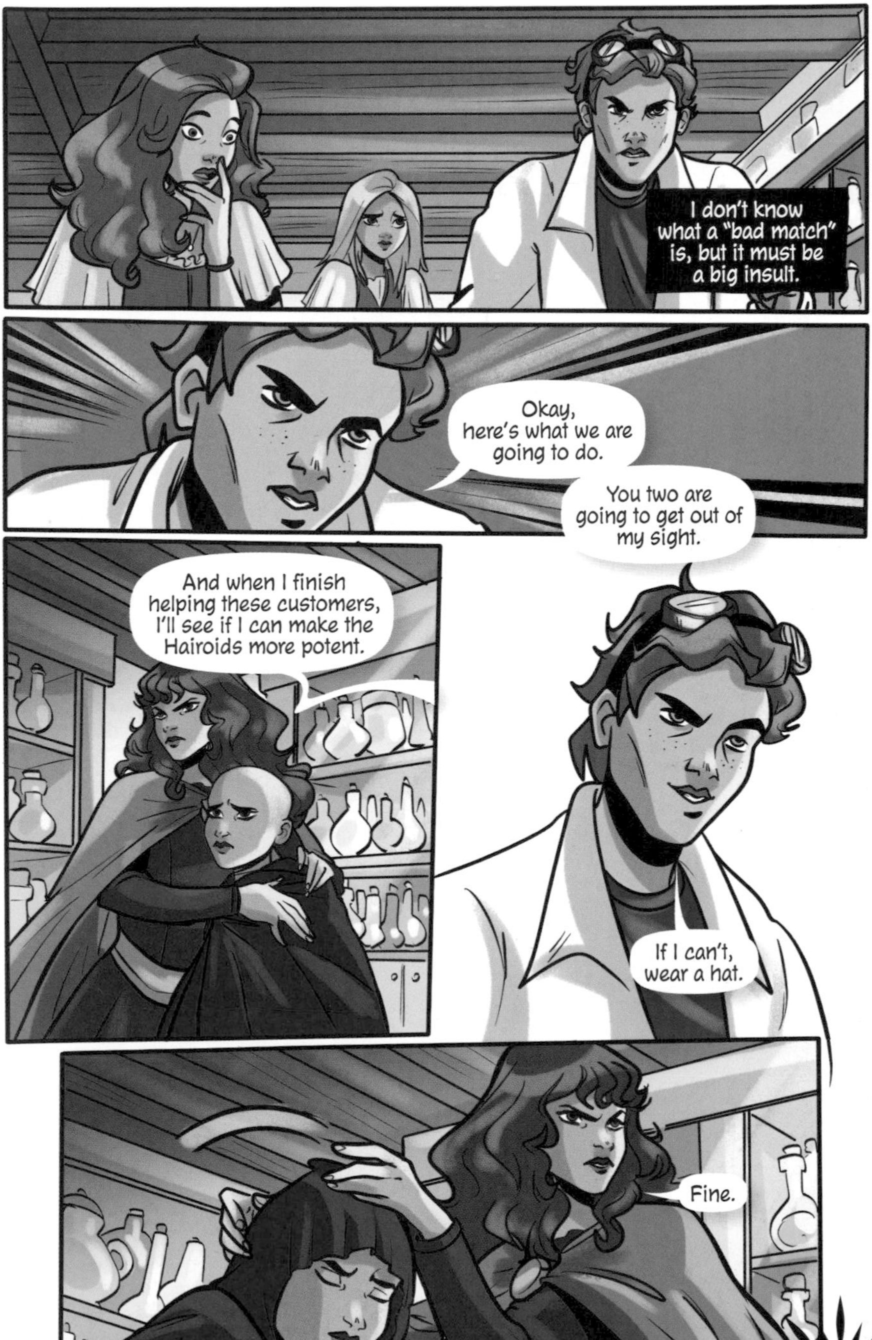
I don't know what a "bad match" is, but it must be a big insult.
Okay, here's what we are going to do.
You two are going to get out of my sight.
And when I finish helping these customers, I'll see if I can make the Hairoids more potent.
If I can't, wear a hat.
Fine.

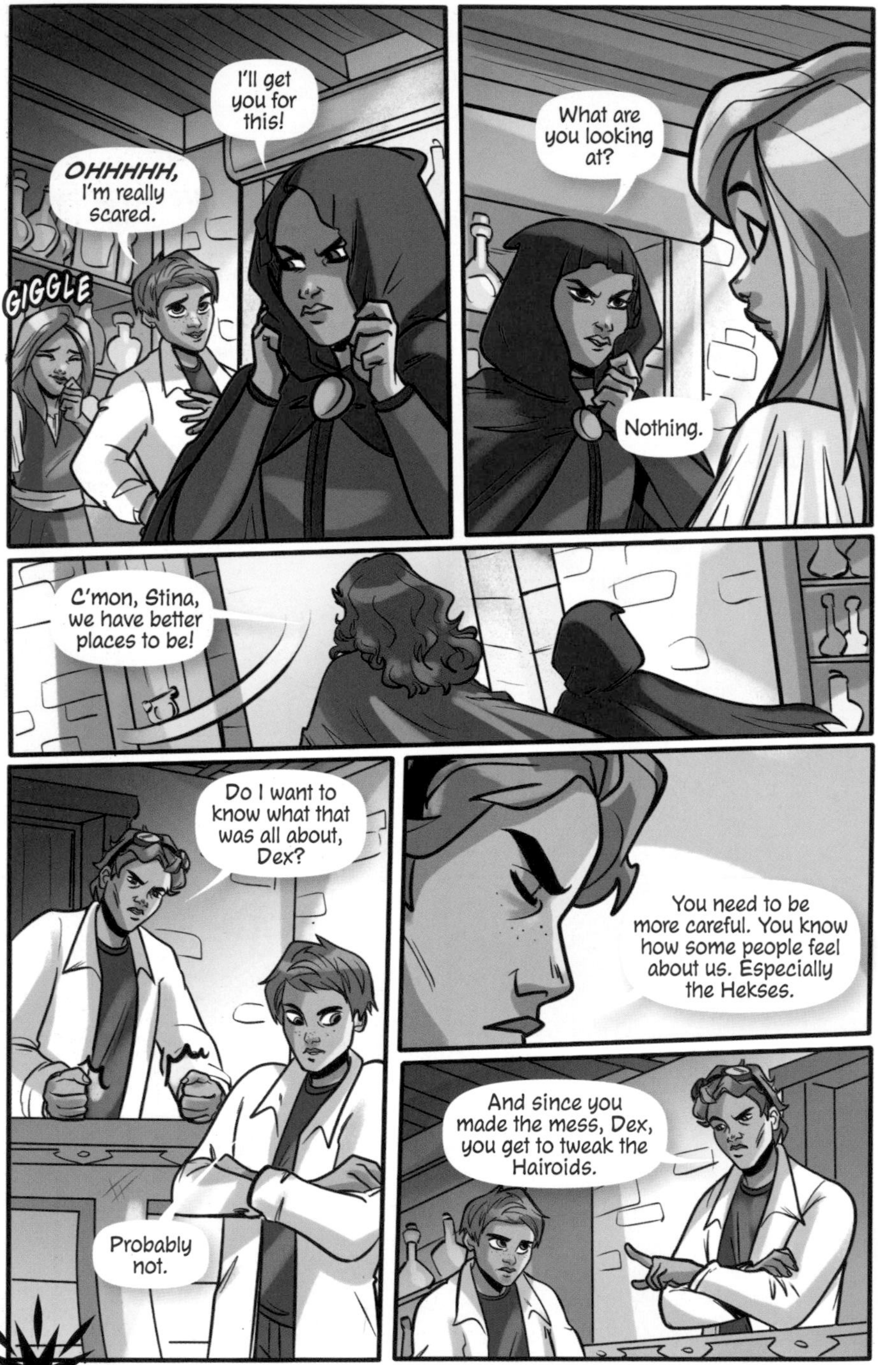
I'll get you for this!
OHHHHH, I'm really scared.
GIGGLE
What are you looking at?
Nothing.
C'mon, Stina, we have better places to be!
Do I want to know what that was all about, Dex?
Probably not.
You need to be more careful. You know how some people feel about us. Especially the Hekses.
And since you made the mess, Dex, you get to tweak the Hairoids.

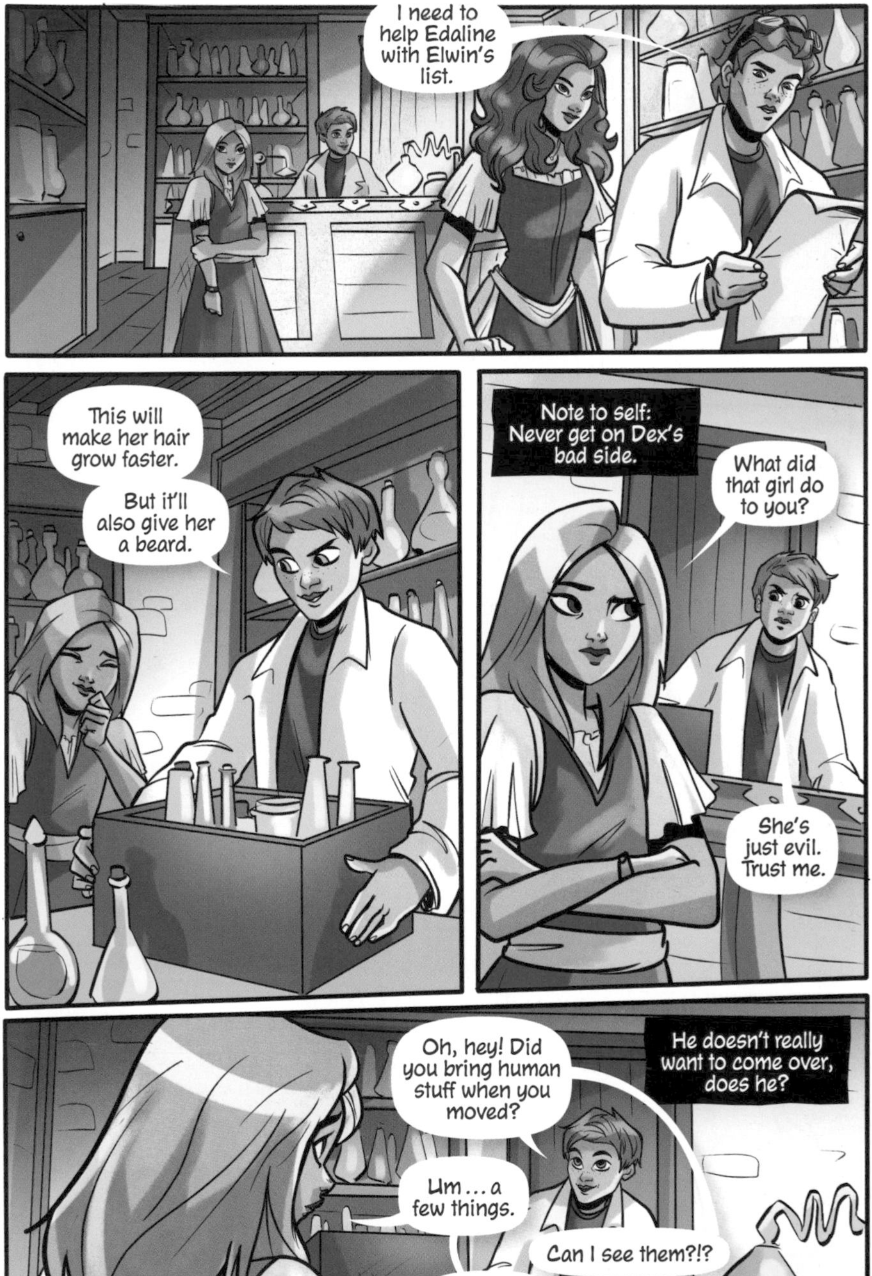
I need to help Edaline with Elwin's list.
This will make her hair grow faster.
But it'll also give her a beard.
Note to self: Never get on Dex's bad side.
What did that girl do to you?
She's just evil. Trust me.
Oh, hey! Did you bring human stuff when you moved?
He doesn't really want to come over, does he?
Um... a few things.
Can I see them?!?
Uh... sure.

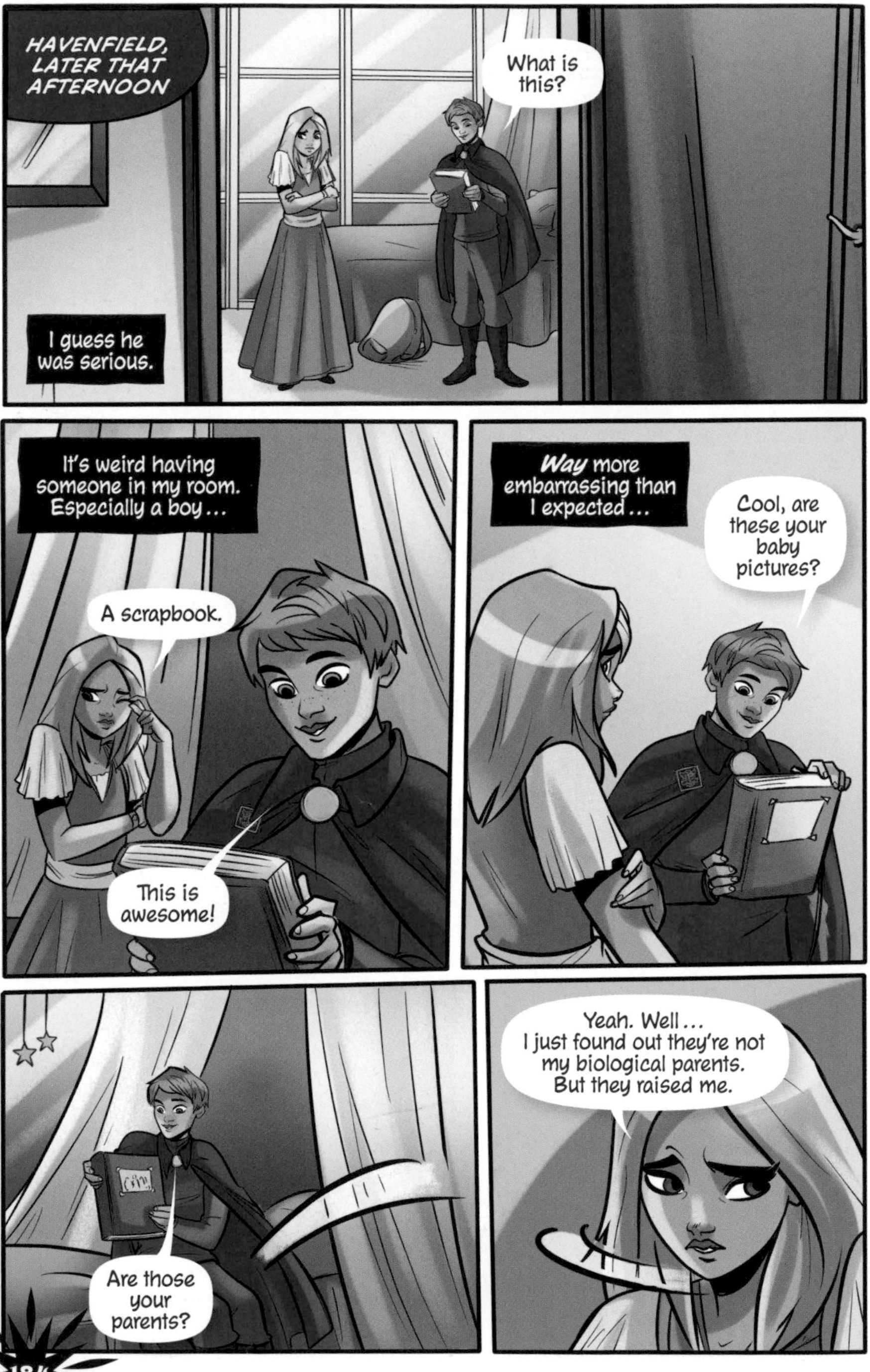
HAVENFIELD, LATER THAT AFTERNOON
What is this?
I guess he was serious.
It's weird having someone in my room. Especially a boy...
A scrapbook.
This is awesome!
Way more embarrassing than I expected...
Cool, are these your baby pictures?
Are those your parents?
Yeah. Well... I just found out they're not my biological parents. But they raised me.

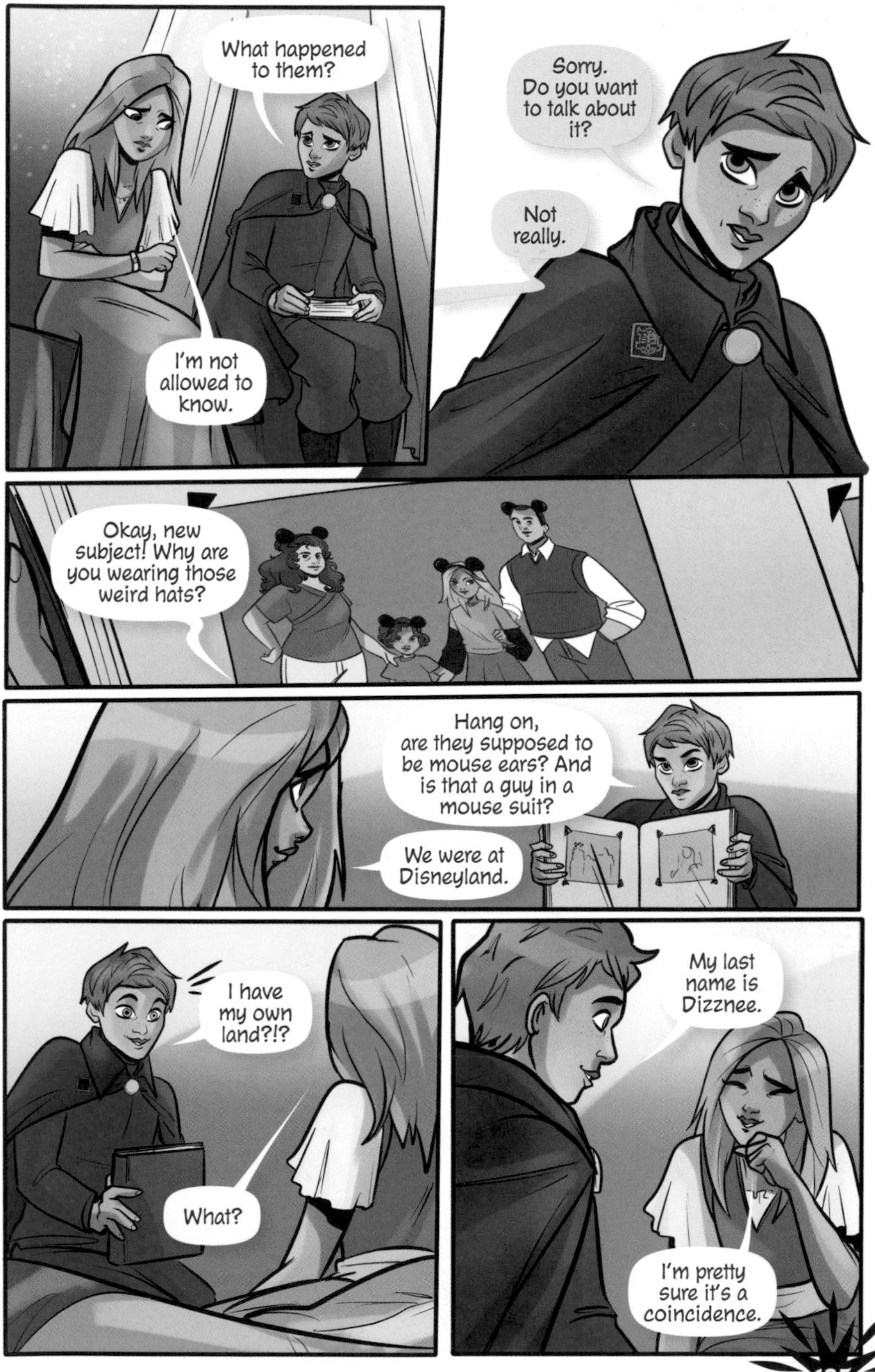
What happened to them?
I'm not allowed to know.
Sorry. Do you want to talk about it?
Not really.
Okay, new subject! Why are you wearing those weird hats?
Hang on, are they supposed to be mouse ears? And is that a guy in a mouse suit?
We were at Disneyland.
I have my own land?!?
What?
My last name is Dizznee.
I'm pretty sure it's a coincidence.

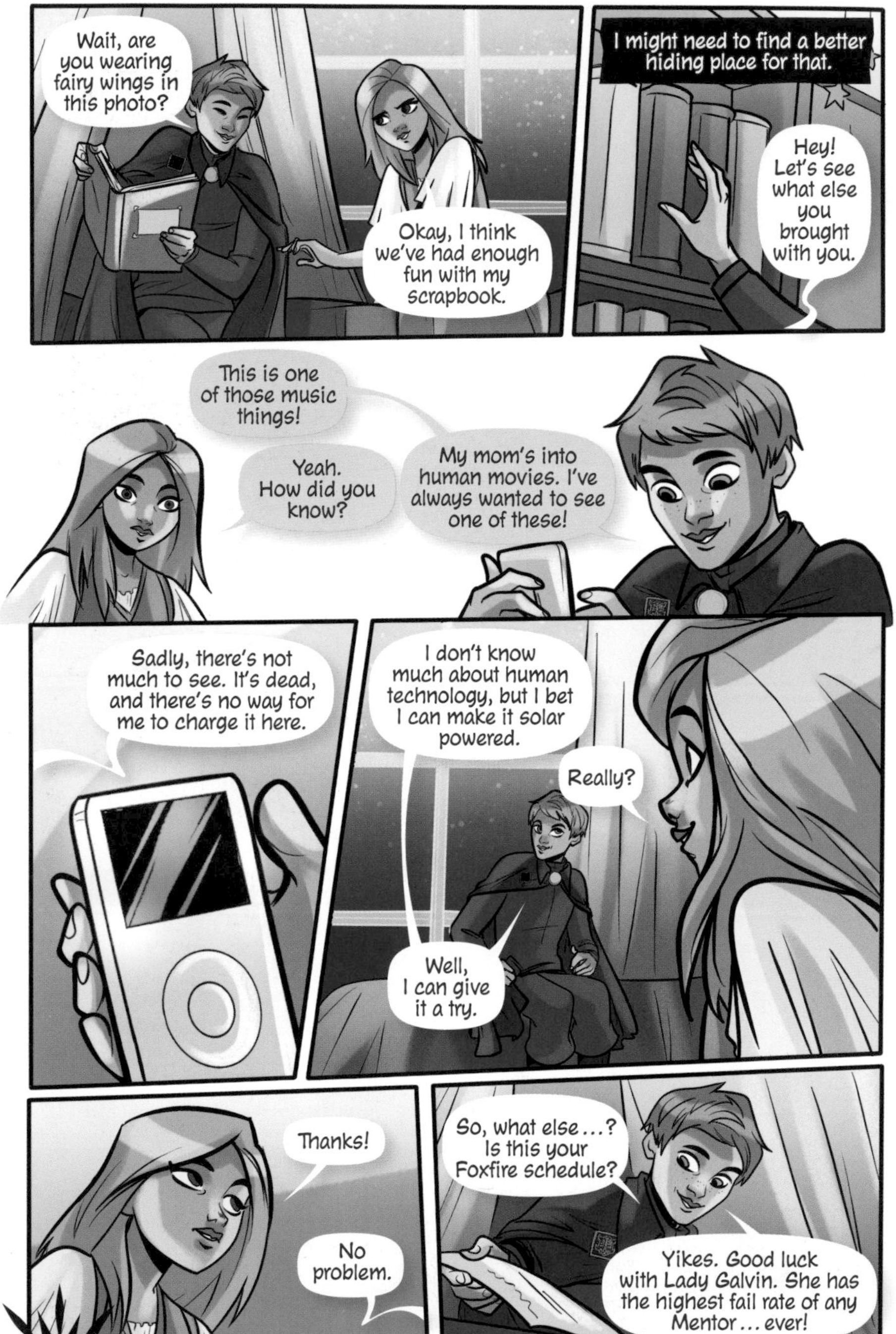
Wait, are you wearing fairy wings in this photo?
Okay, I think we've had enough fun with my scrapbook.
I might need to find a better hiding place for that.
Hey! Let's see what else you brought with you.
This is one of those music things!
Yeah. How did you know?
My mom's into human movies. I've always wanted to see one of these!
Sadly, there's not much to see. It's dead, and there's no way for me to charge it here.
I don't know much about human technology, but I bet I can make it solar powered.
Really?
Well, I can give it a try.
Thanks!
No problem.
So, what else...? Is this your Foxfire schedule?
Yikes. Good luck with Lady Galvin. She has the highest fail rate of any Mentor... ever!

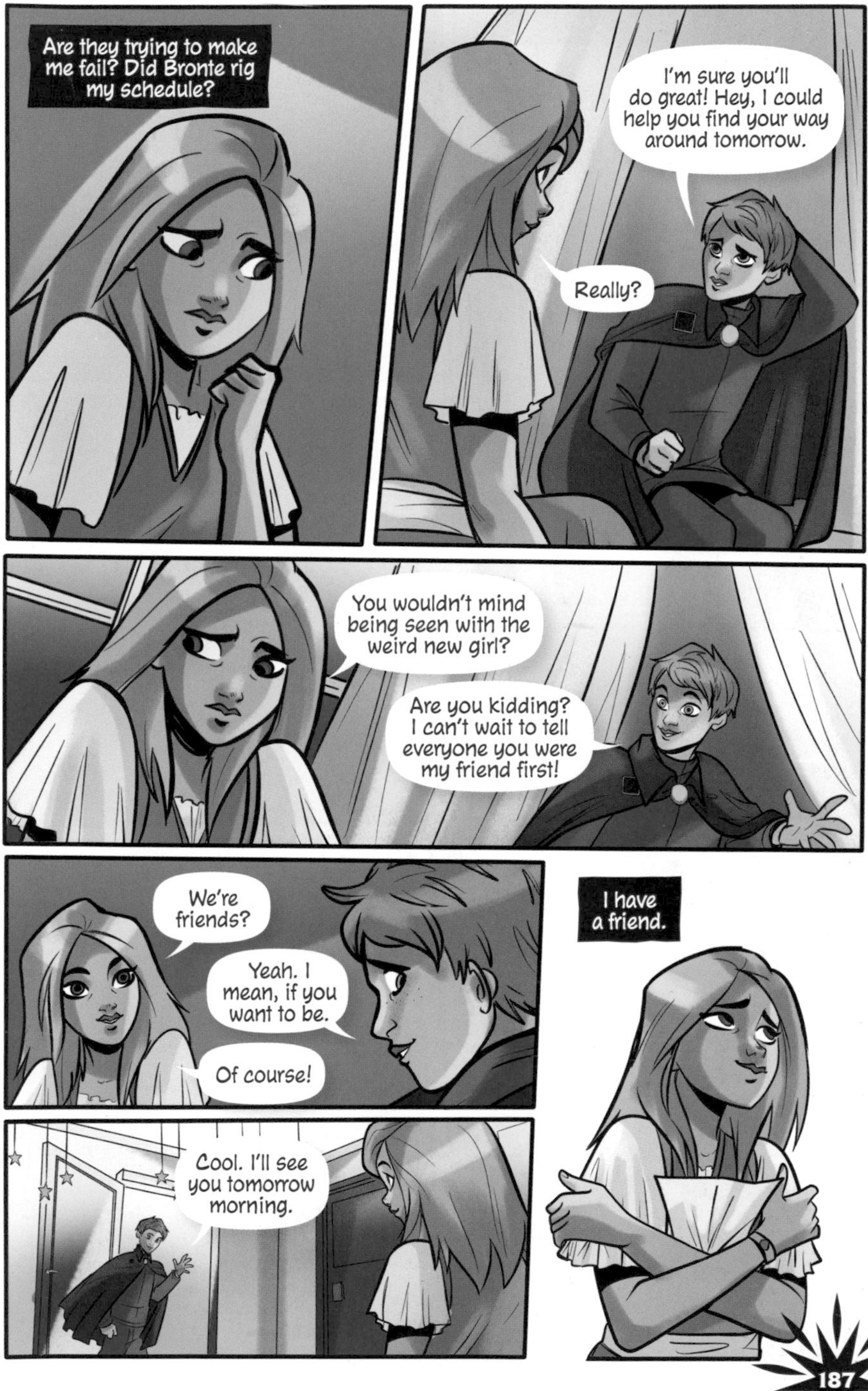
Are they trying to make me fail? Did Bronte rig my schedule?
I'm sure you'll do great! Hey, I could help you find your way around tomorrow.
Really?
You wouldn't mind being seen with the weird new girl?
Are you kidding? I can't wait to tell everyone you were my friend first!
We're friends?
Yeah. I mean, if you want to be.
Of course!
Cool. I'll see you tomorrow morning.
I have a friend.

CHAPTER SEVENTEEN

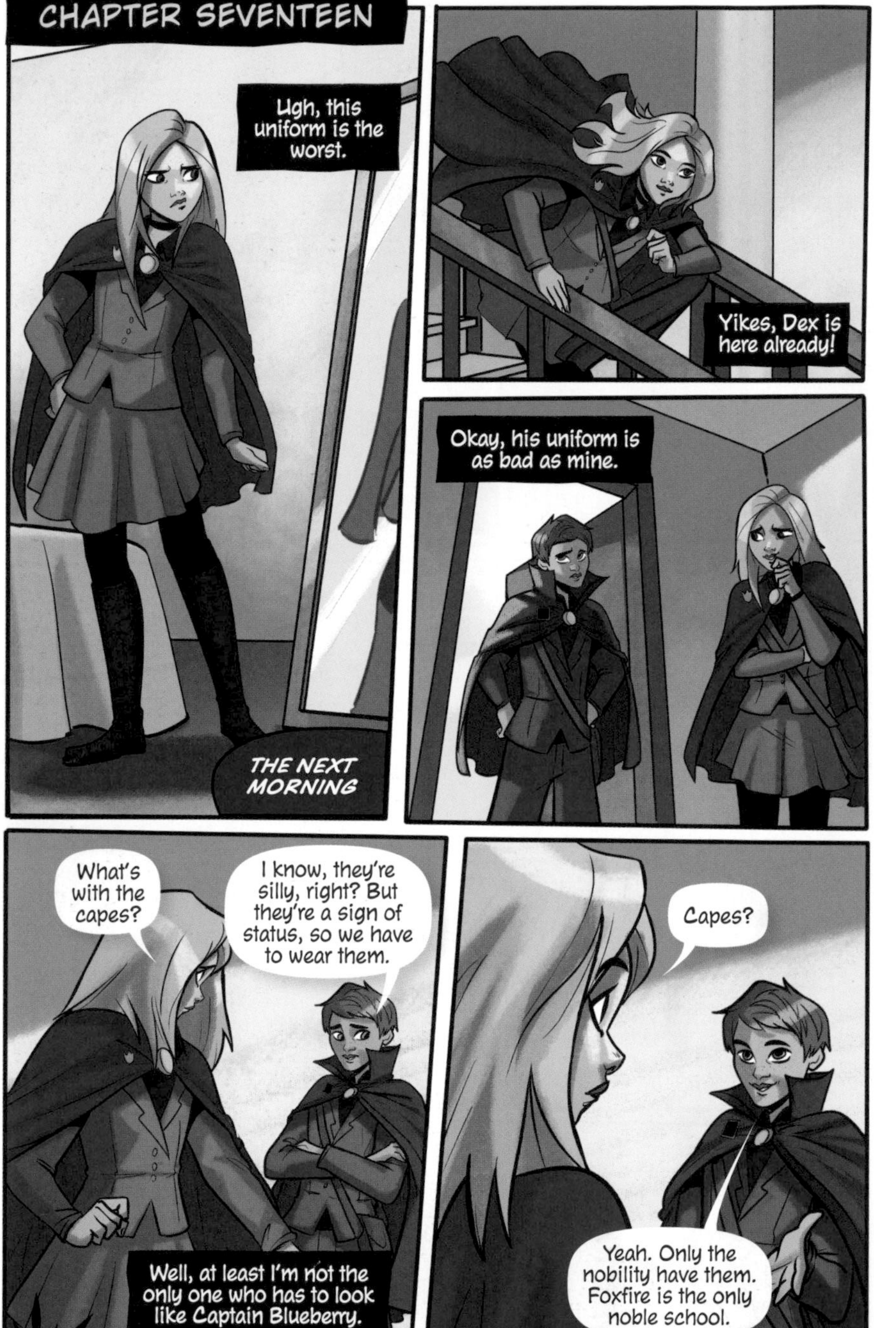

Ugh, this uniform is the worst.
THE NEXT MORNING
Yikes, Dex is here already!
Okay, his uniform is as bad as mine.
What's with the capes?
I know, they're silly, right? But they're a sign of status, so we have to wear them.
Well, at least I'm not the only one who has to look like Captain Blueberry.
Capes?
Yeah. Only the nobility have them. Foxfire is the only noble school.

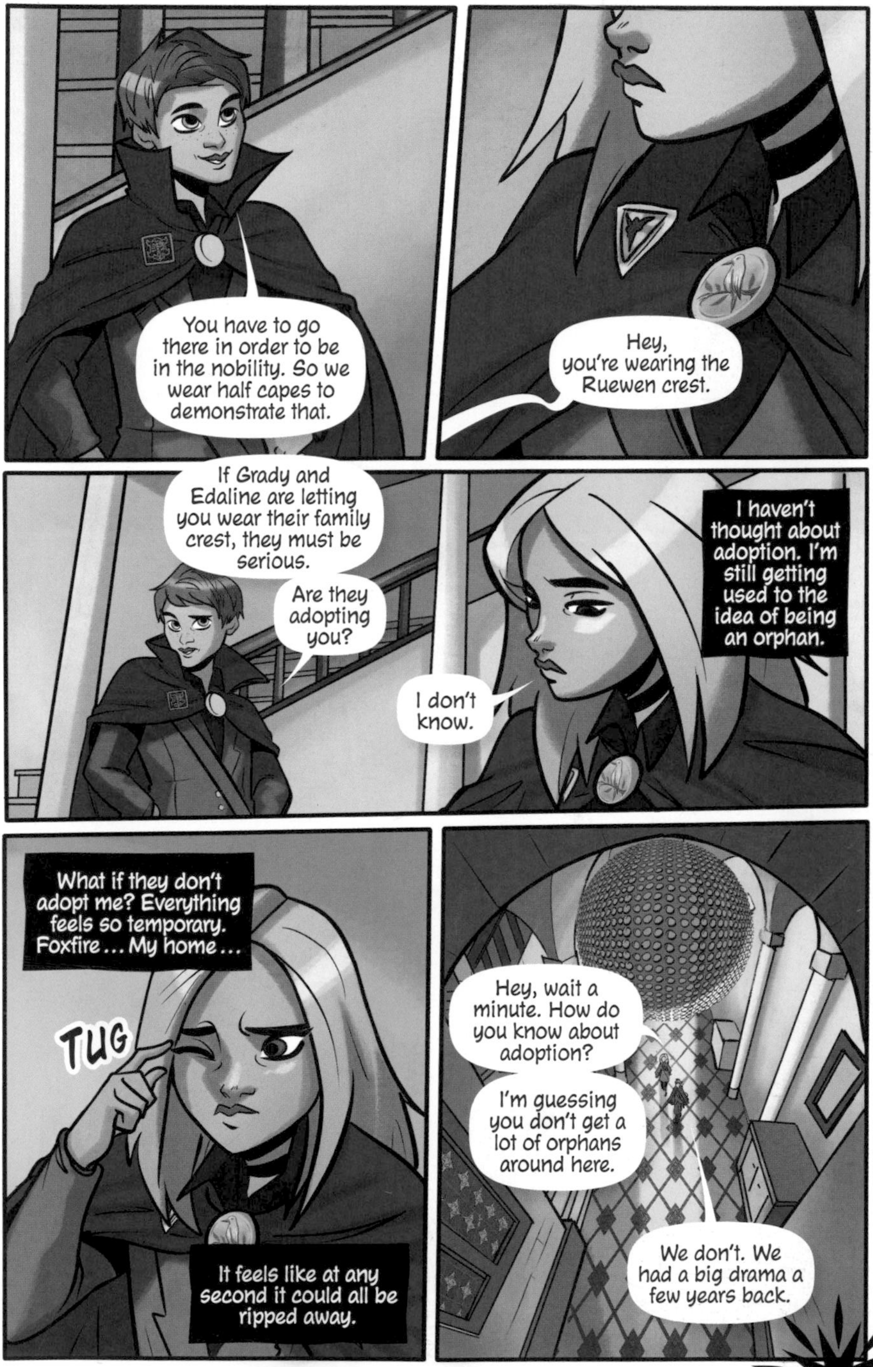
You have to go there in order to be in the nobility. So we wear half capes to demonstrate that.
Hey, you're wearing the Ruewen crest.
If Grady and Edaline are letting you wear their family crest, they must be serious.
Are they adopting you?
I don't know.
I haven't thought about adoption. I'm still getting used to the idea of being an orphan.
What if they don't adopt me? Everything feels so temporary. Foxfire... My home...
TUG
It feels like at any second it could all be ripped away.
Hey, wait a minute. How do you know about adoption?
I'm guessing you don't get a lot of orphans around here.
We don't. We had a big drama a few years back.

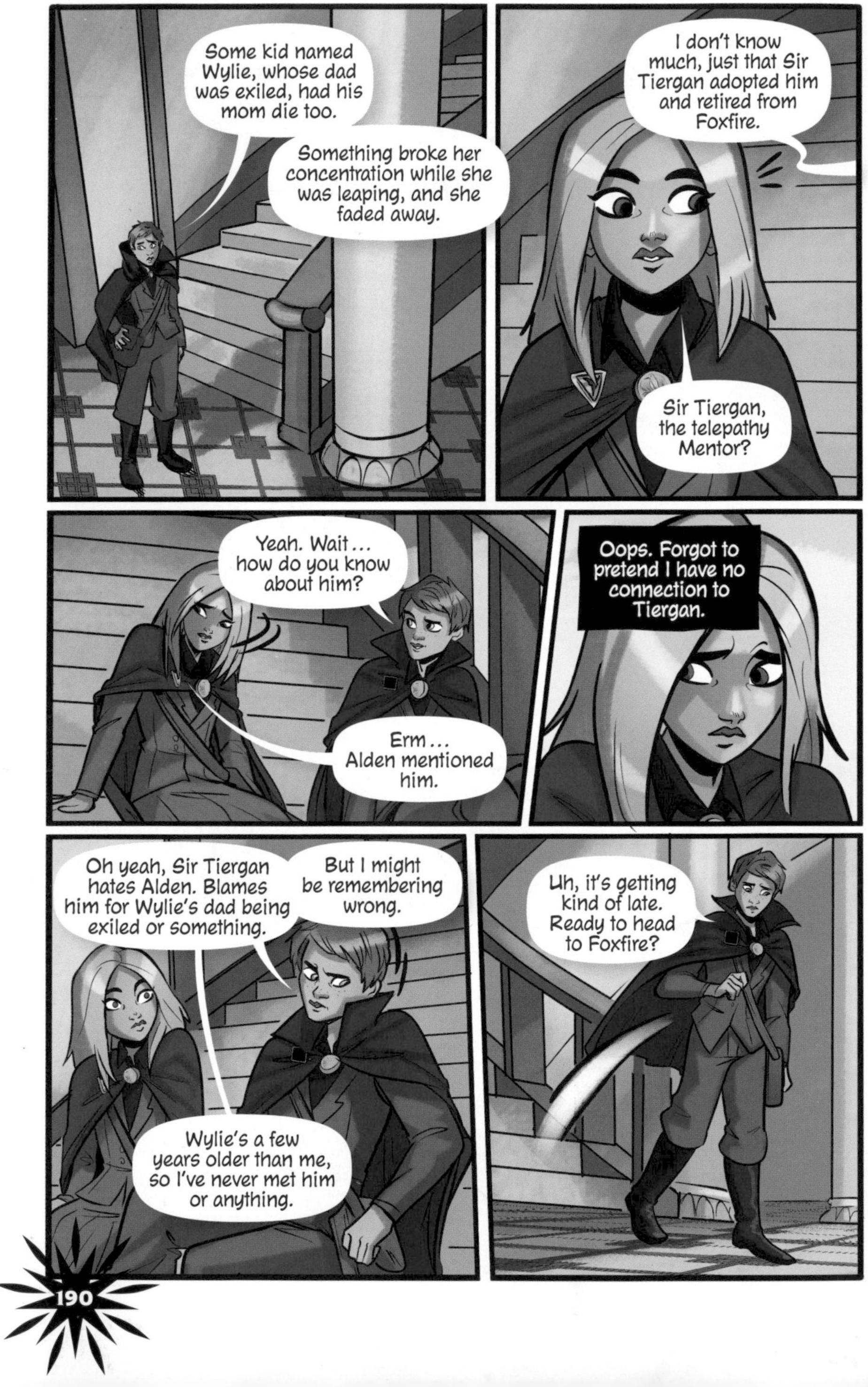
Some kid named Wylie, whose dad was exiled, had his mom die too.
Something broke her concentration while she was leaping, and she faded away.
I don't know much, just that Sir Tiergan adopted him and retired from Foxfire.
Sir Tiergan, the telepathy Mentor?
Yeah. Wait... how do you know about him?
Erm... Alden mentioned him.
Oops. Forgot to pretend I have no connection to Tiergan.
Oh yeah, Sir Tiergan hates Alden. Blames him for Wylie's dad being exiled or something.
But I might be remembering wrong.
Wylie's a few years older than me, so I've never met him or anything.
Uh, it's getting kind of late. Ready to head to Foxfire?

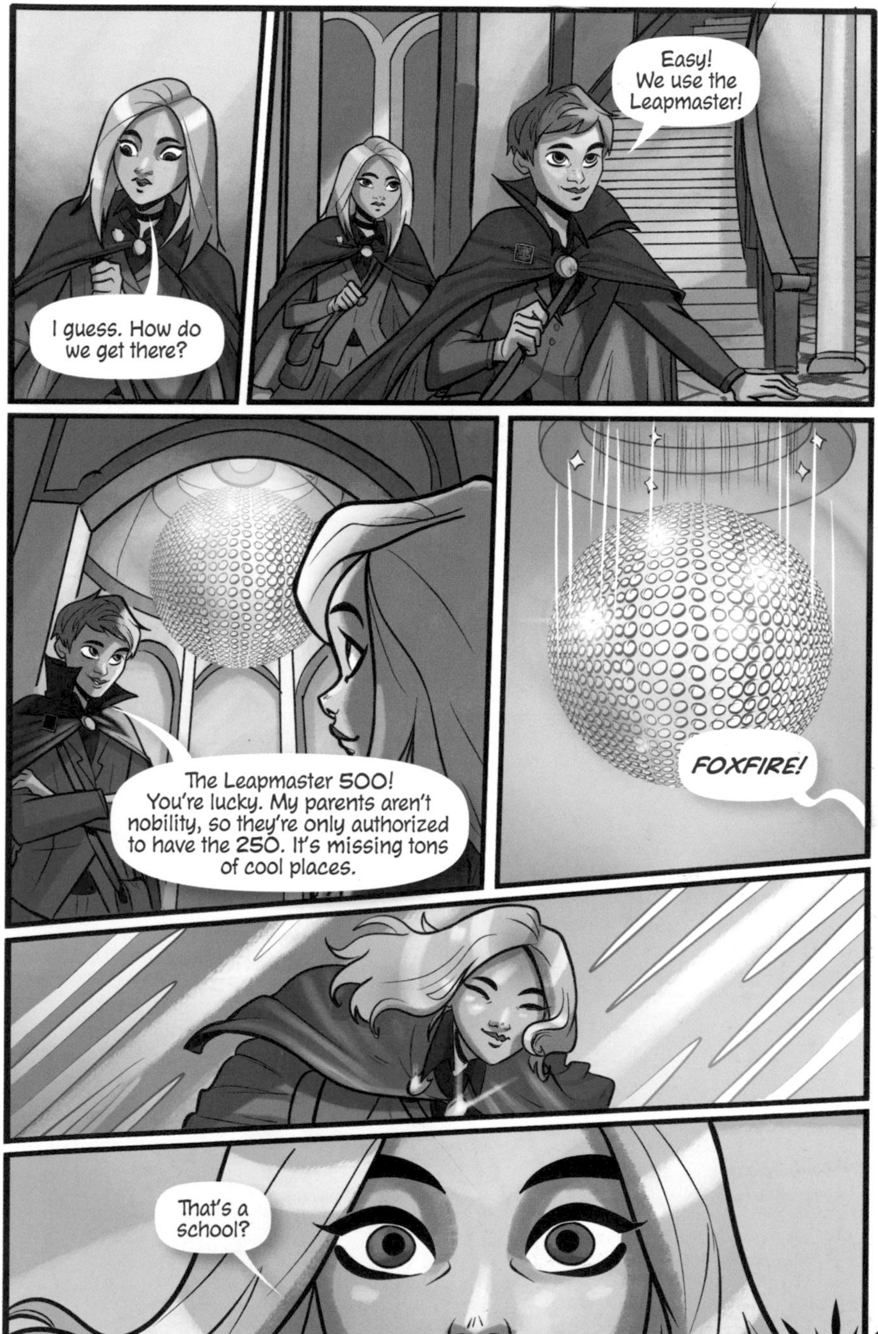
I guess. How do we get there?
Easy! We use the Leapmaster!
The Leapmaster 500! You're lucky. My parents aren't nobility, so they're only authorized to have the 250. It's missing tons of cool places.
FOXFIRE!
That's a school?

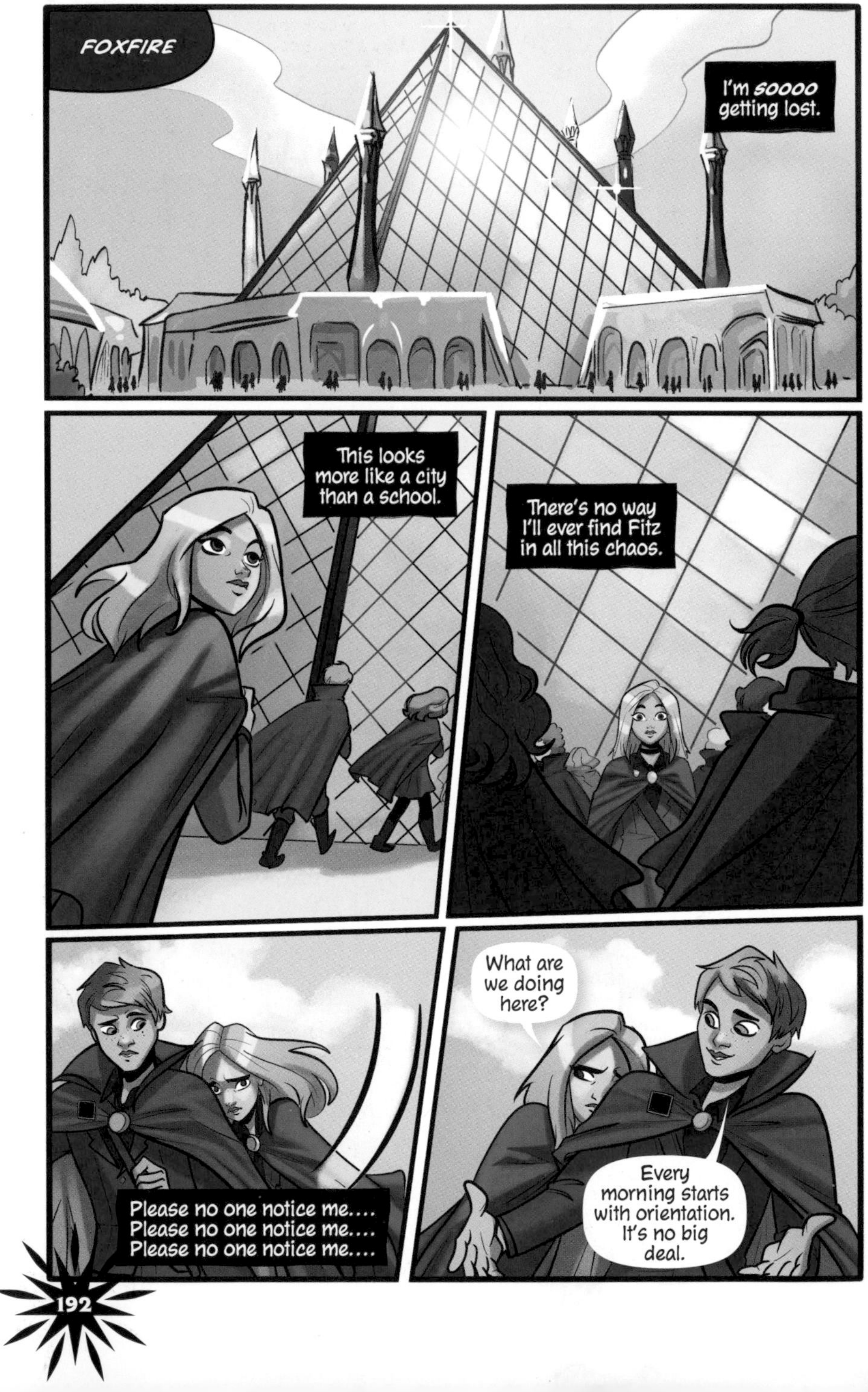
FOXFIRE
I'm sOOOO getting lost.
This looks more like a city than a school.
There's no way I'll ever find Fitz in all this chaos.
Please no one notice me....
Please no one notice me....
Please no one notice me....
What are we doing here?
Every morning starts with orientation. It's no big deal.

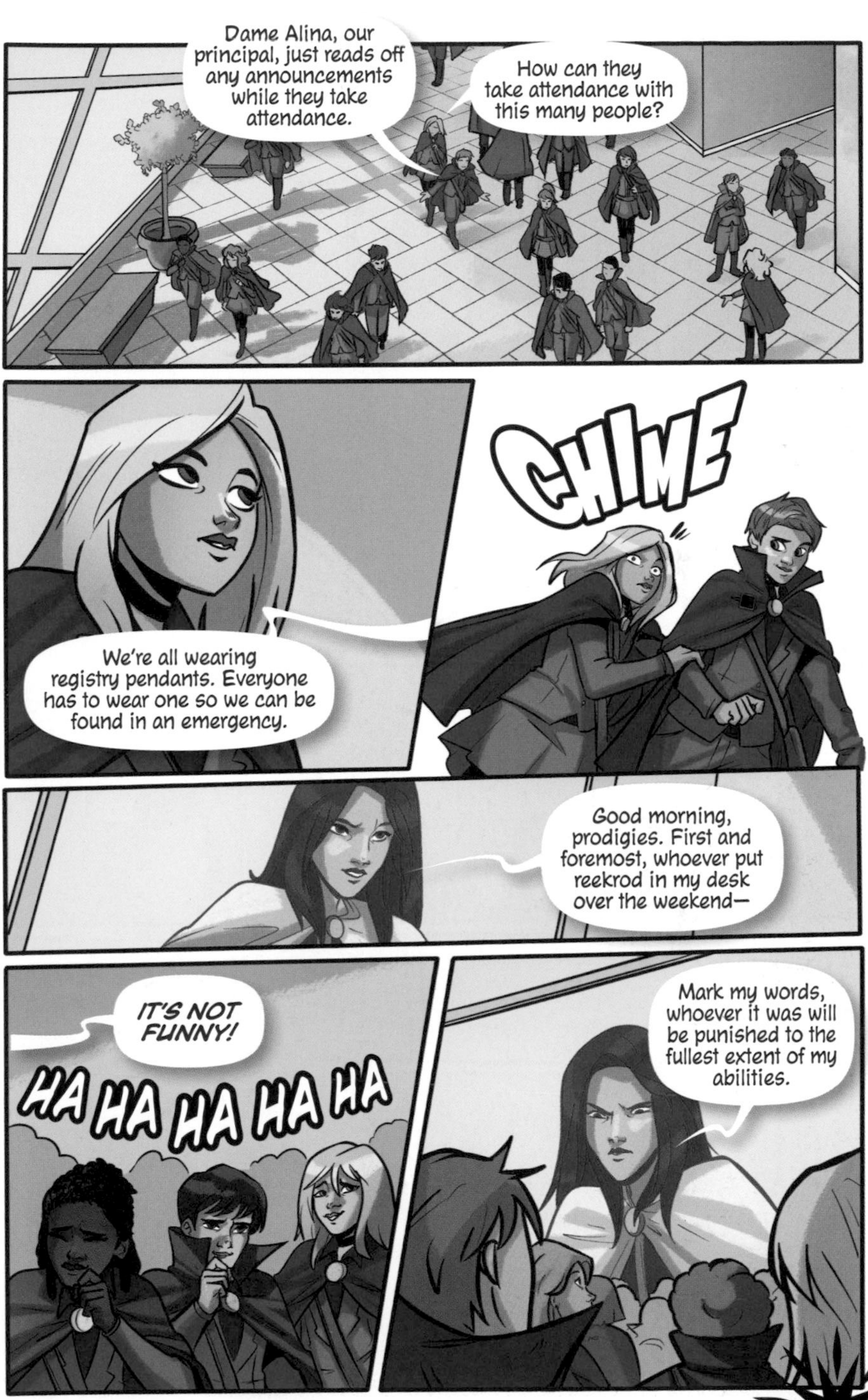
Dame Alina, our principal, just reads off any announcements while they take attendance.
How can they take attendance with this many people?
We're all wearing registry pendants. Everyone has to wear one so we can be found in an emergency.
CHIME
Good morning, prodigies. First and foremost, whoever put reekrod in my desk over the weekend—
IT'S NOT FUNNY!
HA HA HA HA HA
Mark my words, whoever it was will be punished to the fullest extent of my abilities.

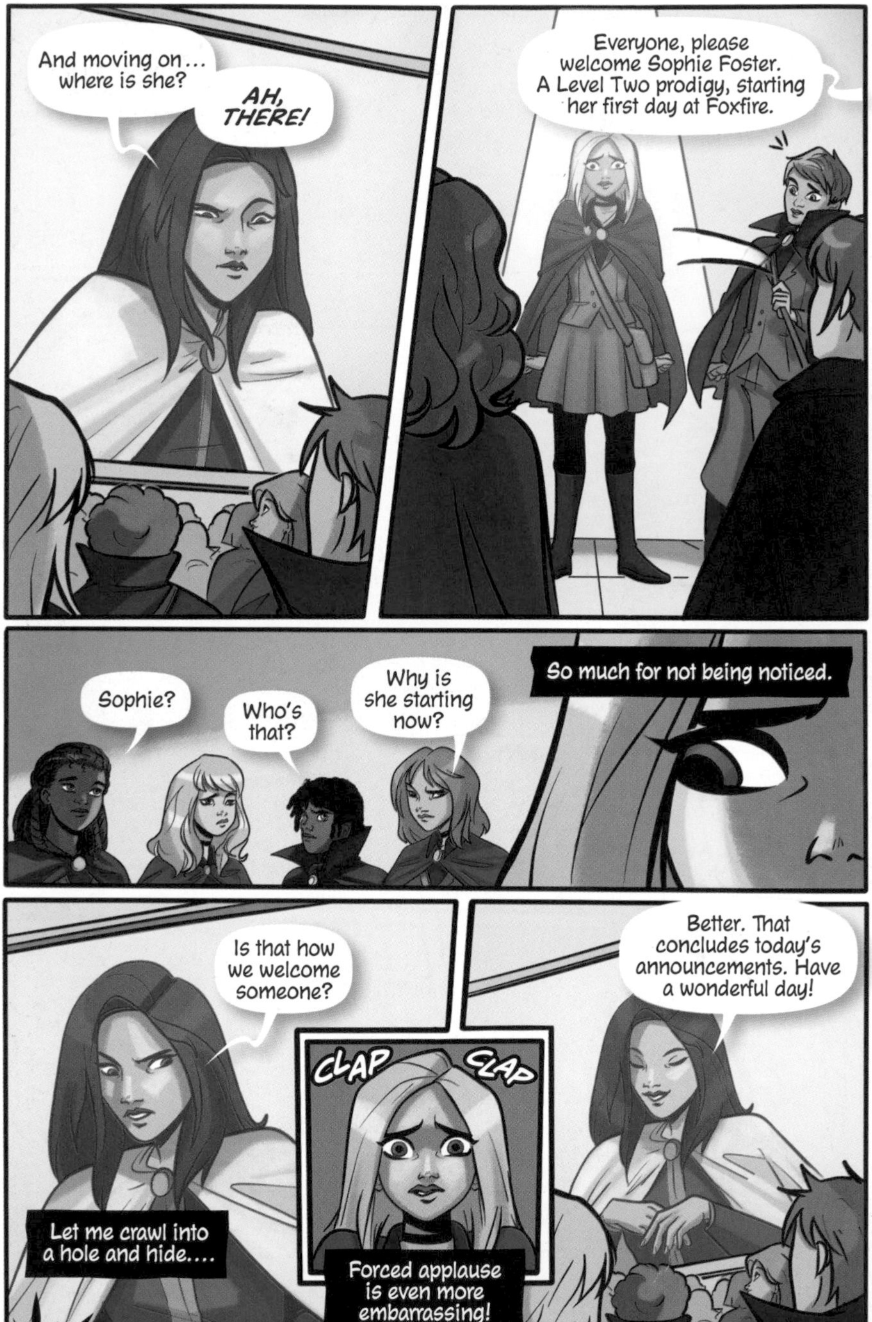

And moving on... where is she?
AH, THERE!
Everyone, please welcome Sophie Foster. A Level Two prodigy, starting her first day at Foxfire.
Sophie?
Who's that?
Why is she starting now?
So much for not being noticed.
Is that how we welcome someone?
Let me crawl into a hole and hide....
CLAP CLAP
Forced applause is even more embarrassing!
Better. That concludes today's announcements. Have a wonderful day!

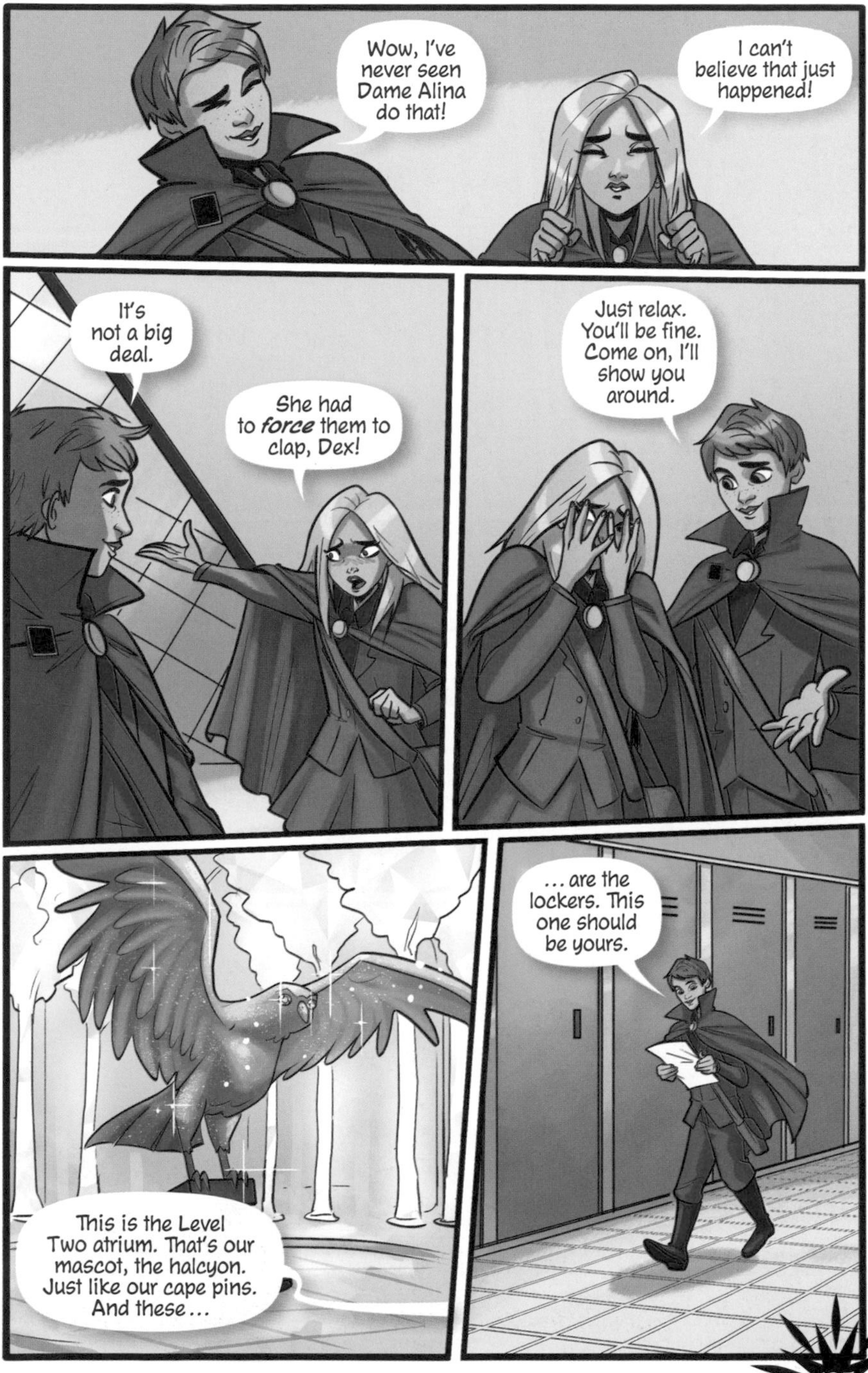
Wow, I've never seen Dame Alina do that!
I can't believe that just happened!
It's not a big deal.
She had to *force* them to clap, Dex!
Just relax. You'll be fine. Come on, I'll show you around.
This is the Level Two atrium. That's our mascot, the halcyon. Just like our cape pins. And these…
…are the lockers. This one should be yours.

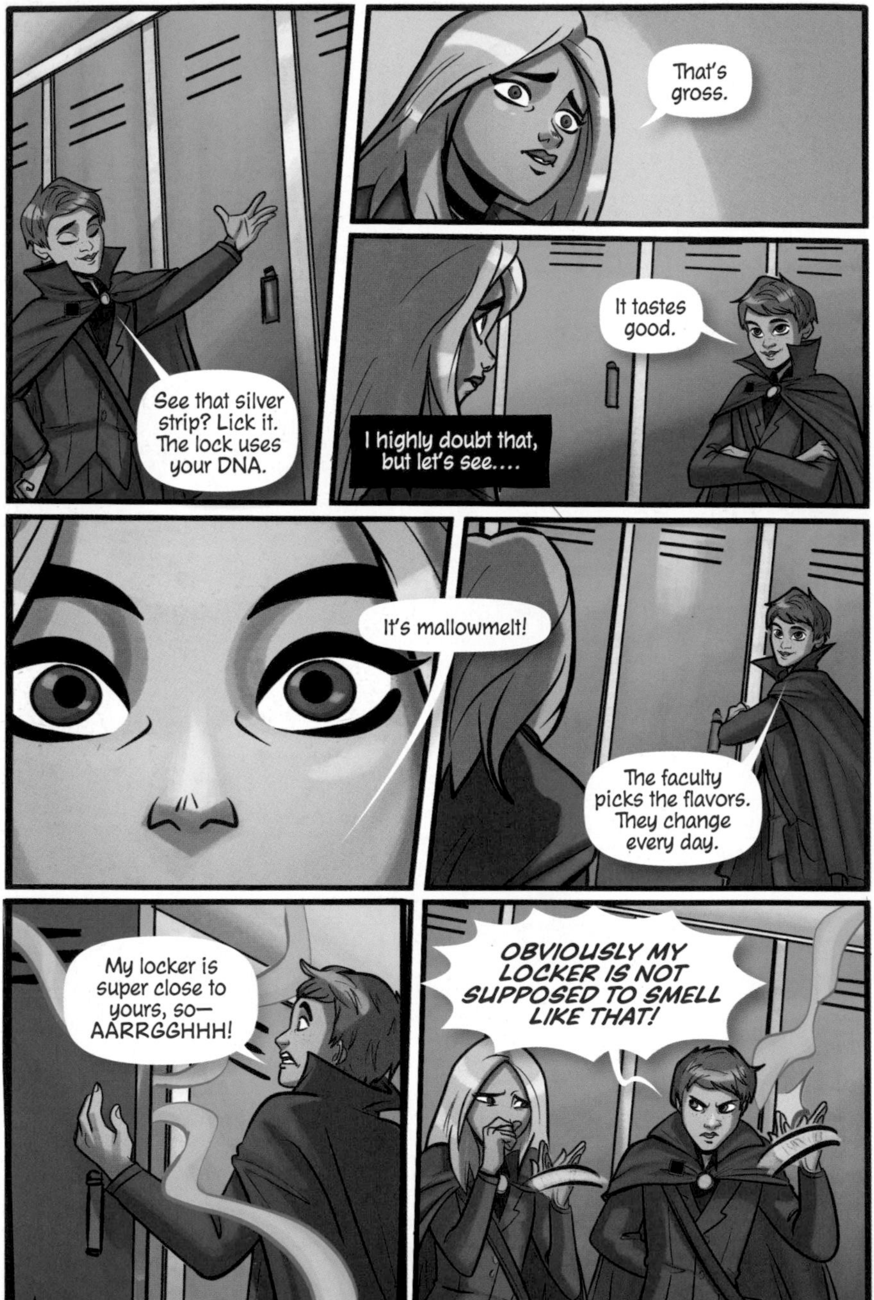
See that silver strip? Lick it. The lock uses your DNA.
That's gross.
It tastes good.
I highly doubt that, but let's see....
It's mallowmelt!
The faculty picks the flavors. They change every day.
My locker is super close to yours, so— AARRGGHHH!
OBVIOUSLY MY LOCKER IS NOT SUPPOSED TO SMELL LIKE THAT!

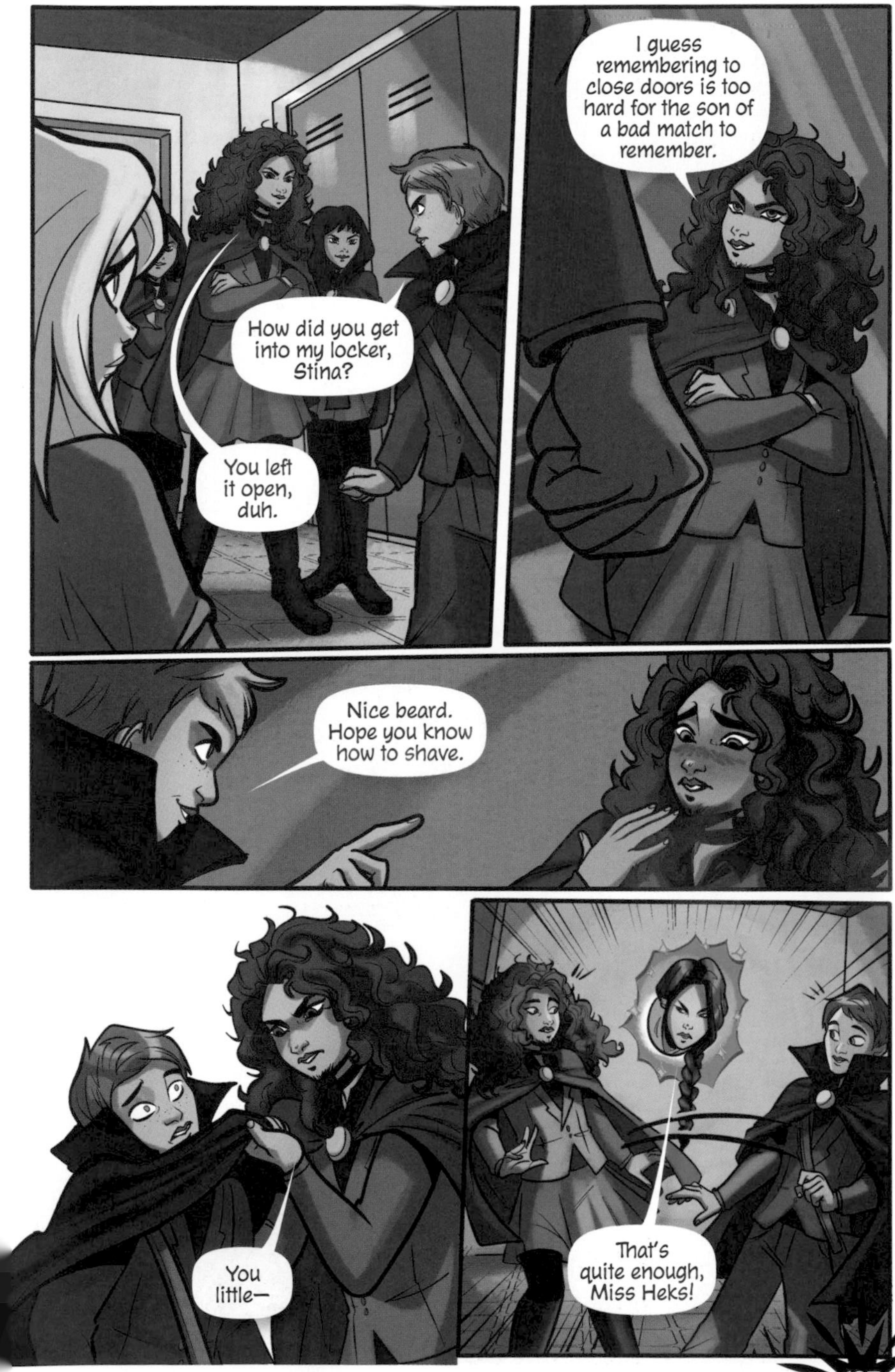
How did you get into my locker, Stina?
You left it open, duh.
I guess remembering to close doors is too hard for the son of a bad match to remember.
Nice beard. Hope you know how to shave.
You little—
That's quite enough, Miss Heks!

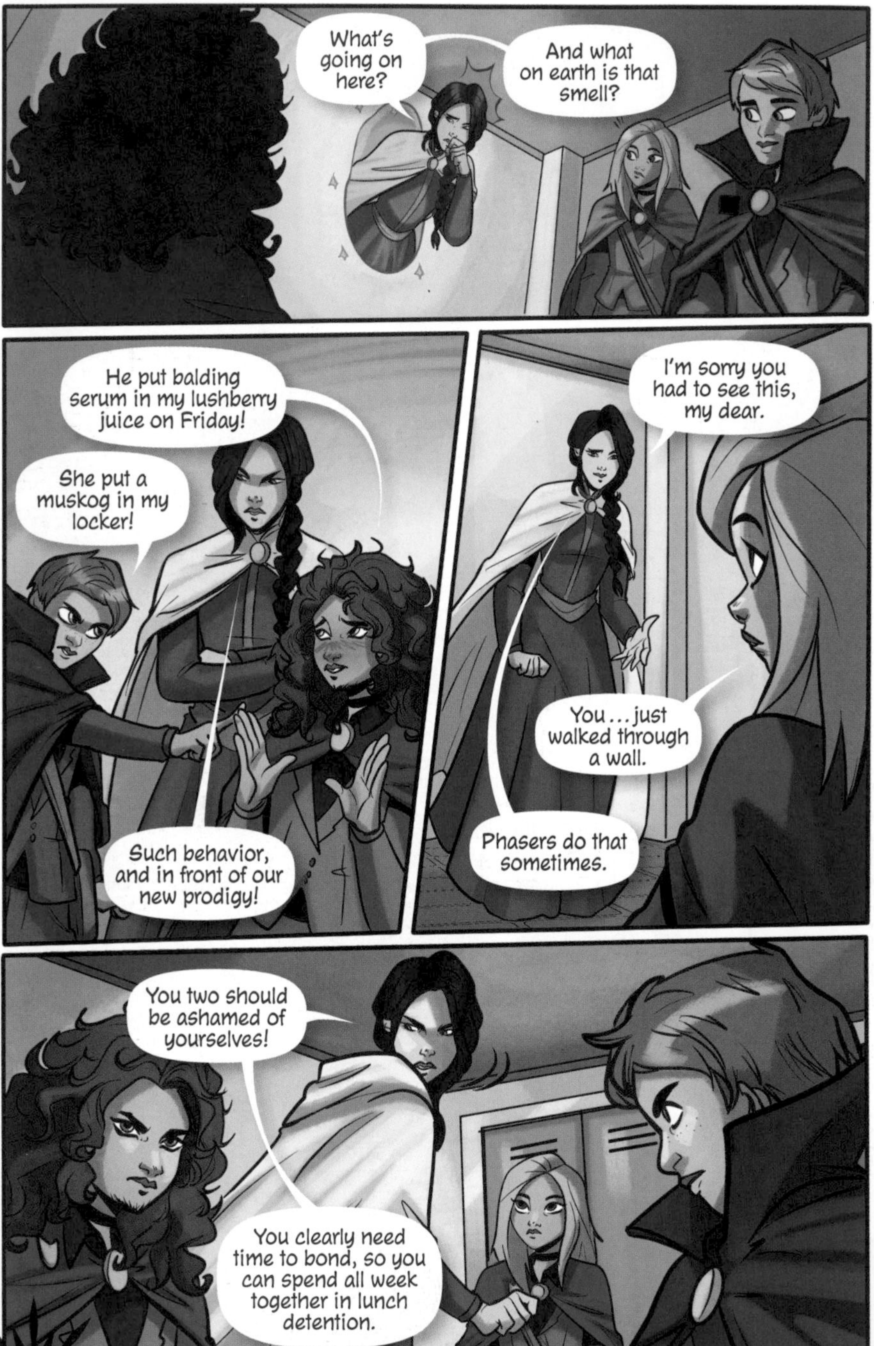
What's going on here?
And what on earth is that smell?
He put balding serum in my lushberry juice on Friday!
She put a muskog in my locker!
Such behavior, and in front of our new prodigy!
I'm sorry you had to see this, my dear.
You... just walked through a wall.
Phasers do that sometimes.
You two should be ashamed of yourselves!
You clearly need time to bond, so you can spend all week together in lunch detention.

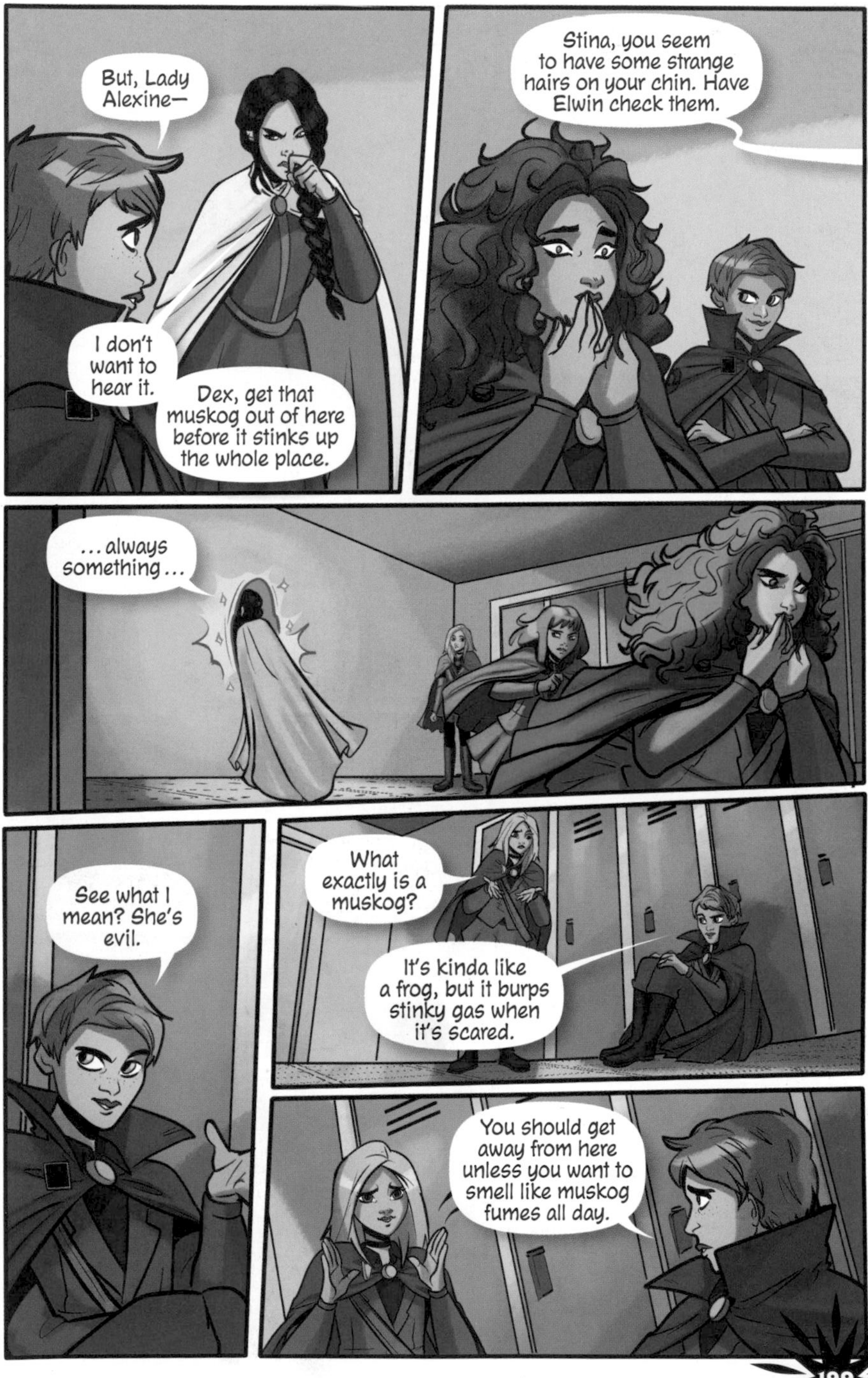
But, Lady Alexine—
I don't want to hear it.
Dex, get that muskog out of here before it stinks up the whole place.
Stina, you seem to have some strange hairs on your chin. Have Elwin check them.
...always something...
See what I mean? She's evil.
What exactly is a muskog?
It's kinda like a frog, but it burps stinky gas when it's scared.
You should get away from here unless you want to smell like muskog fumes all day.

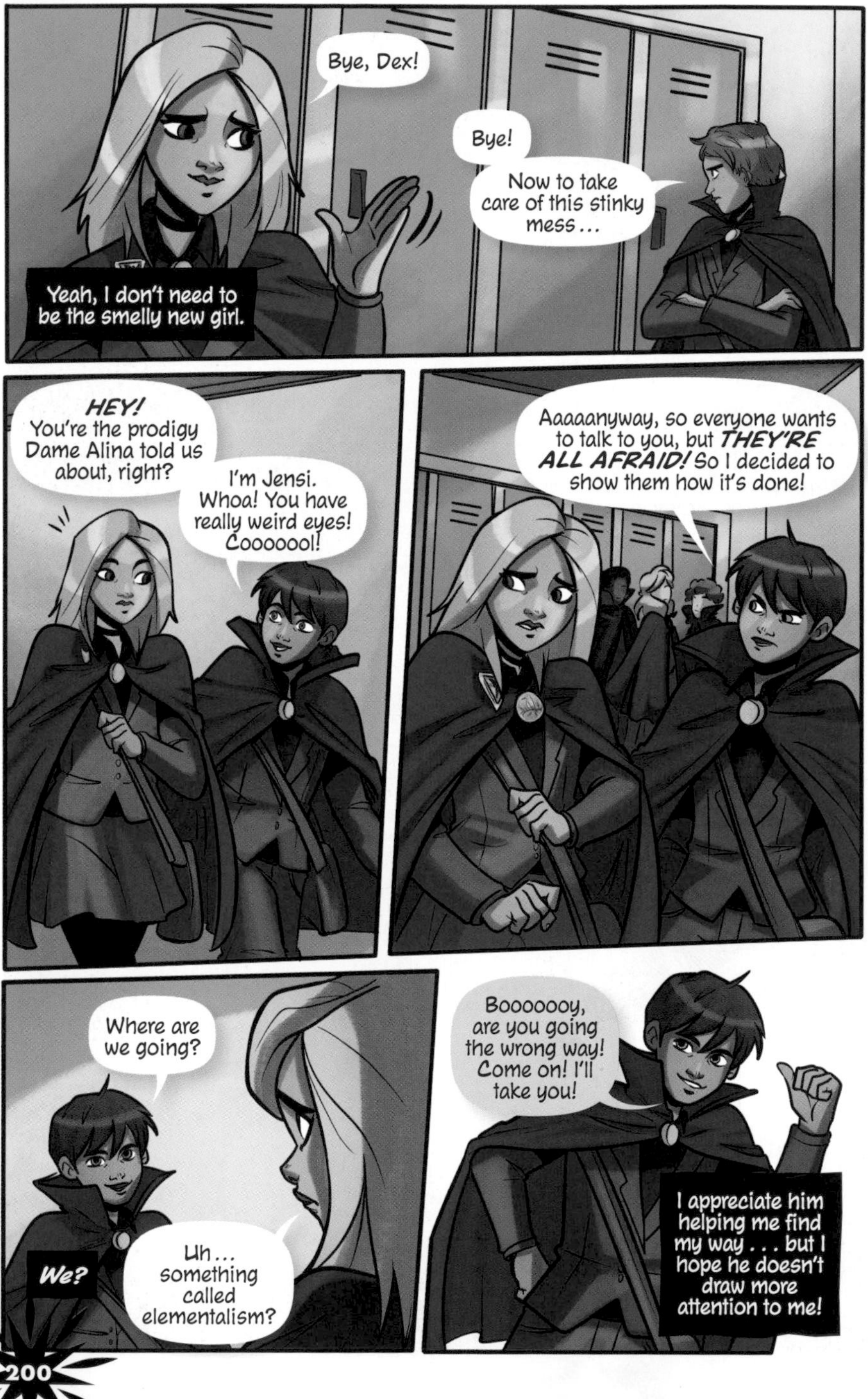
Bye, Dex!
Bye!
Now to take care of this stinky mess…
Yeah, I don't need to be the smelly new girl.
HEY! You're the prodigy Dame Alina told us about, right?
I'm Jensi. Whoa! You have really weird eyes! Cooooool!
Aaaaanyway, so everyone wants to talk to you, but THEY'RE ALL AFRAID! So I decided to show them how it's done!
Where are we going?
We?
Uh… something called elementalism?
Boooooy, are you going the wrong way! Come on! I'll take you!
I appreciate him helping me find my way . . . but I hope he doesn't draw more attention to me!

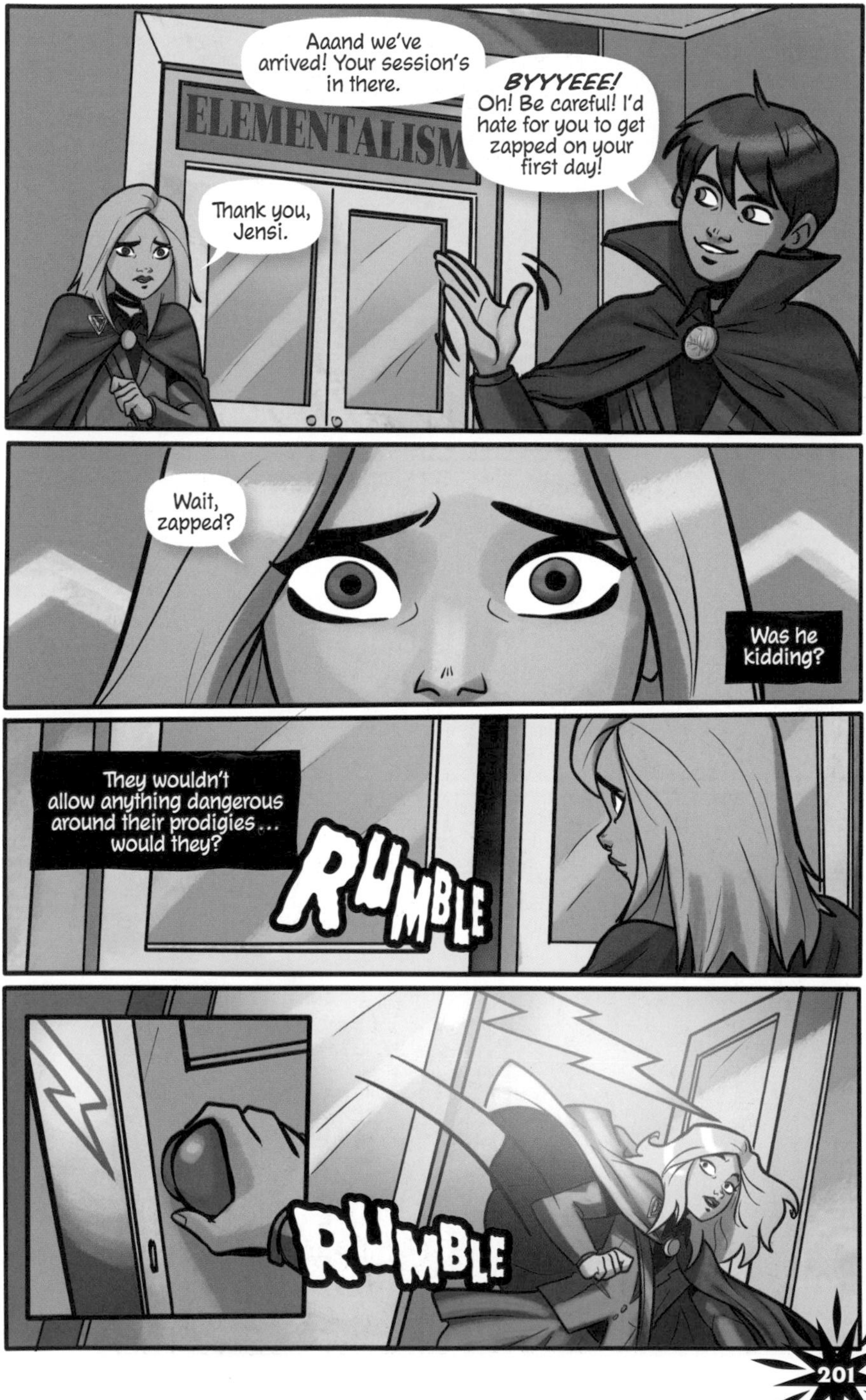
ELEMENTALISM
Aaand we've arrived! Your session's in there.
BYYYEEE! Oh! Be careful! I'd hate for you to get zapped on your first day!
Thank you, Jensi.
Wait, zapped?
Was he kidding?
They wouldn't allow anything dangerous around their prodigies... would they?
RUMBLE
RUMBLE

CHAPTER EIGHTEEN

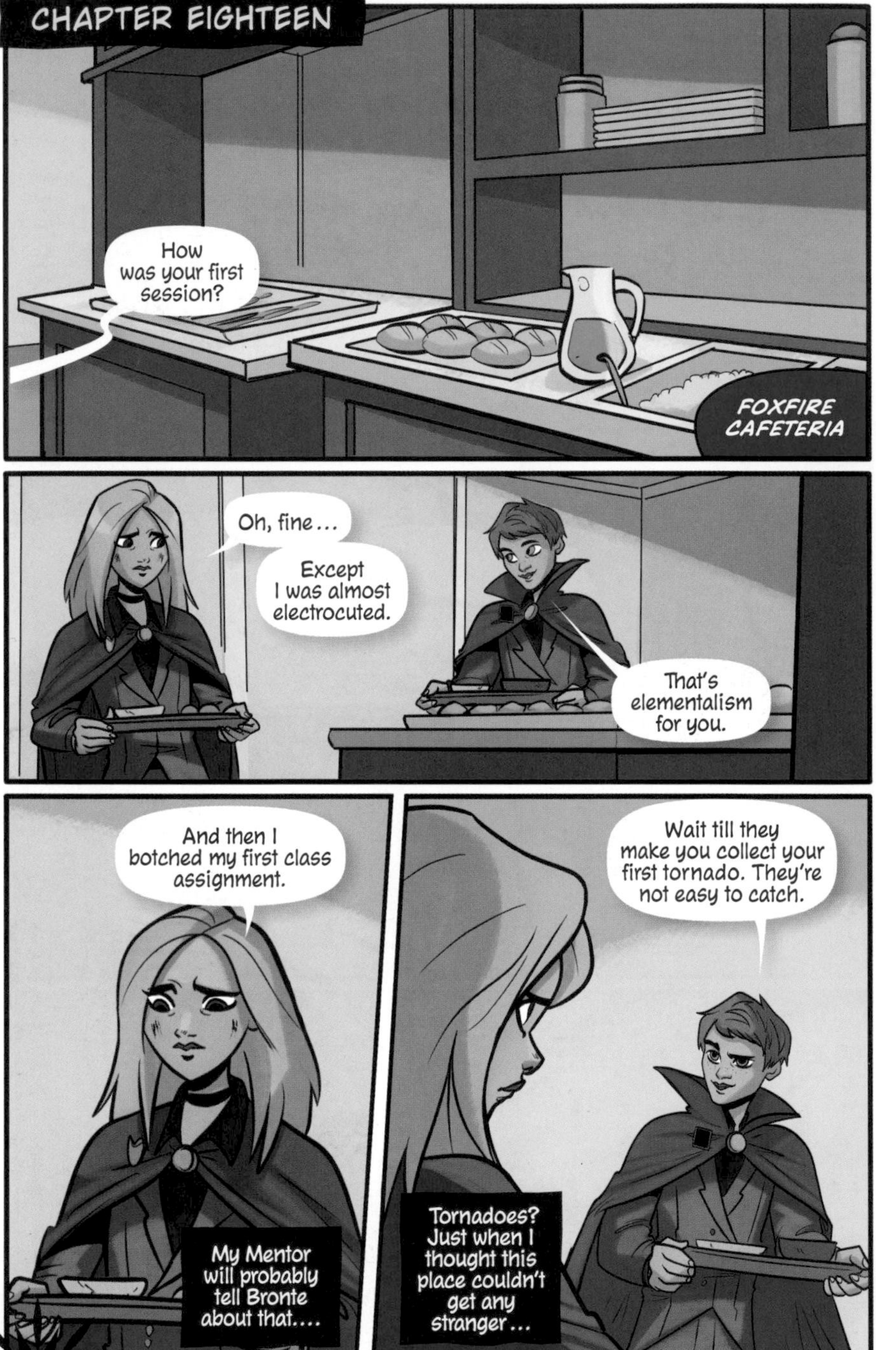

How was your first session?
FOXFIRE CAFETERIA
Oh, fine...
Except I was almost electrocuted.
That's elementalism for you.
And then I botched my first class assignment.
My Mentor will probably tell Bronte about that....
Wait till they make you collect your first tornado. They're not easy to catch.
Tornadoes? Just when I thought this place couldn't get any stranger...

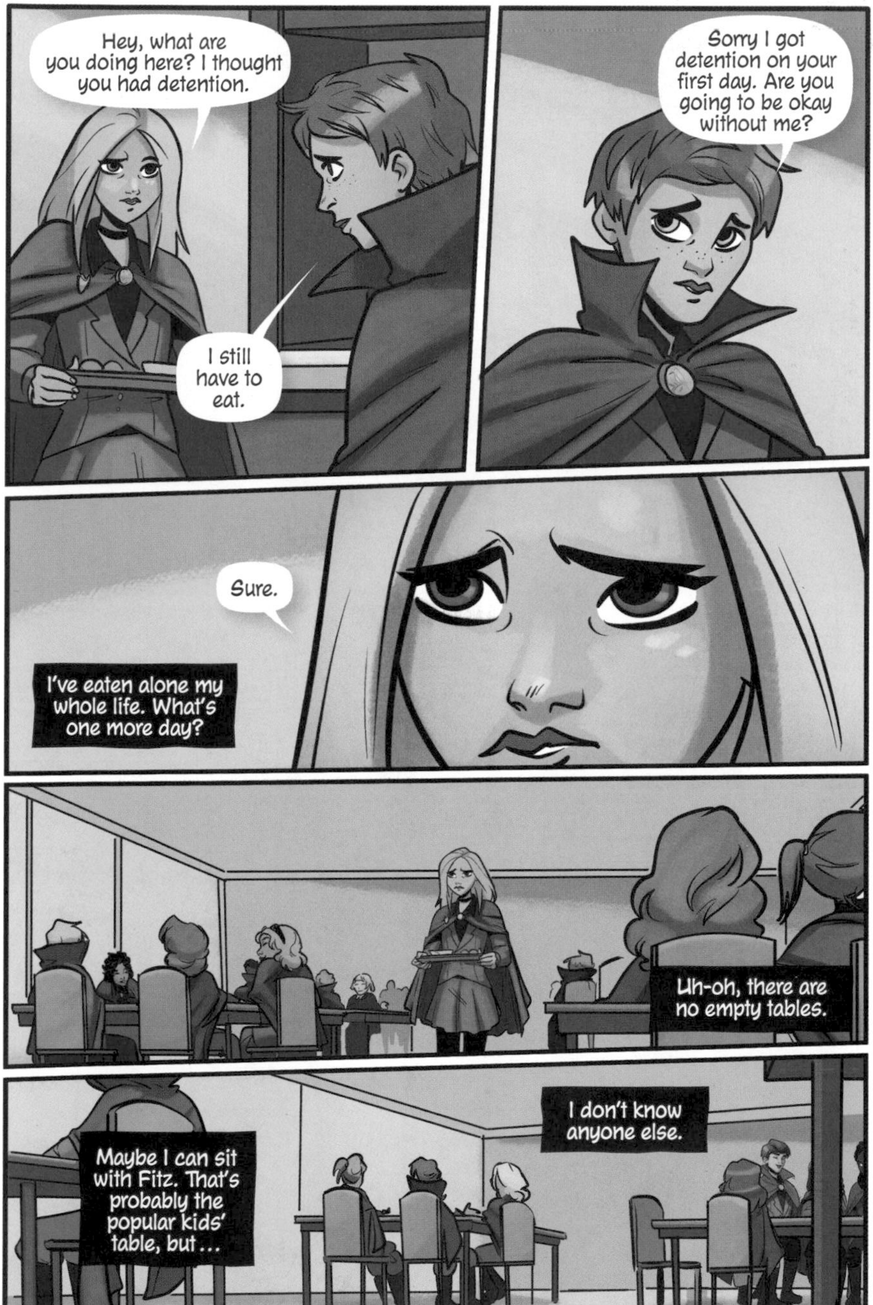
Hey, what are you doing here? I thought you had detention.
I still have to eat.
Sorry I got detention on your first day. Are you going to be okay without me?
Sure.
I've eaten alone my whole life. What's one more day?
Uh-oh, there are no empty tables.
Maybe I can sit with Fitz. That's probably the popular kids' table, but . . .
I don't know anyone else.

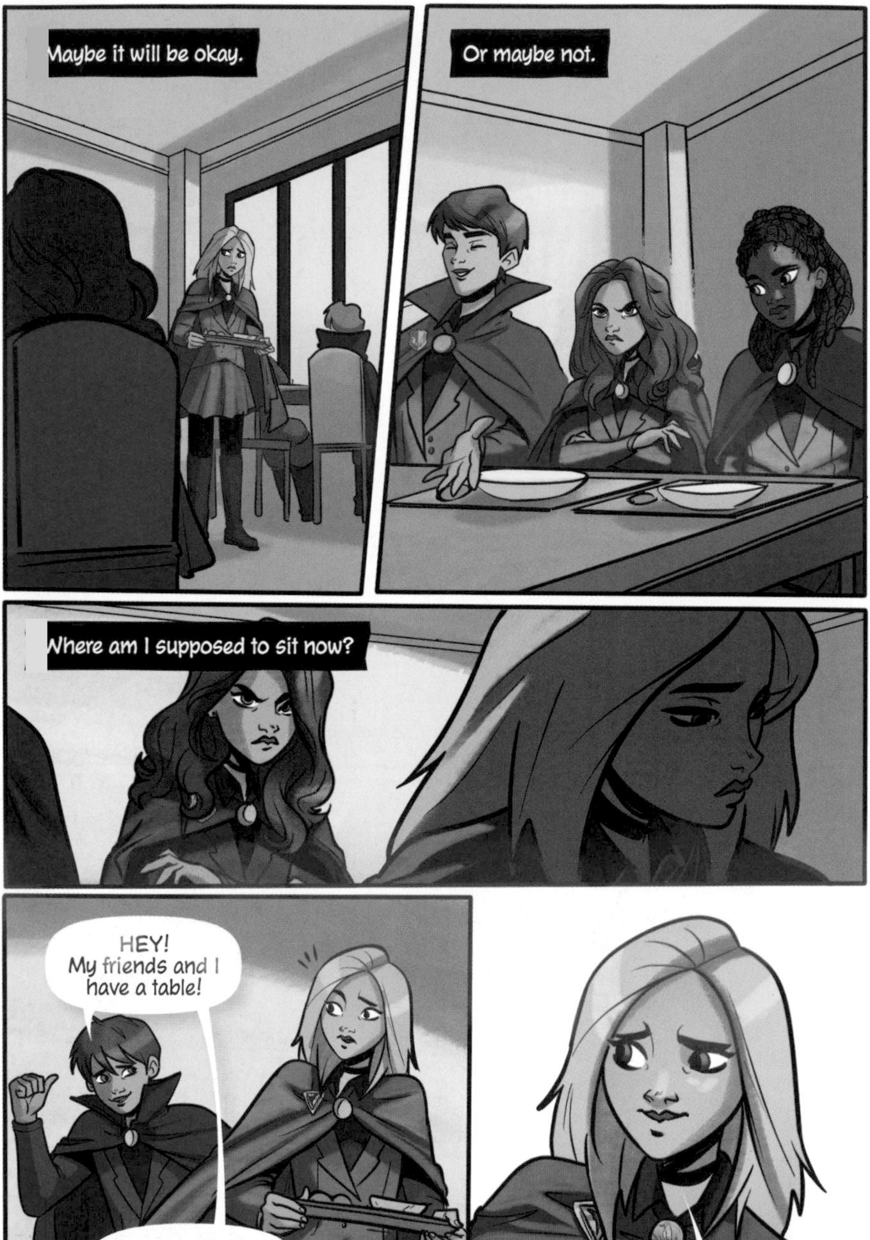
Maybe it will be okay.
Or maybe not.
Where am I supposed to sit now?
HEY! My friends and I have a table!
We're all huge nerds—but you can sit with us if you want to!
Thanks, Jensi.

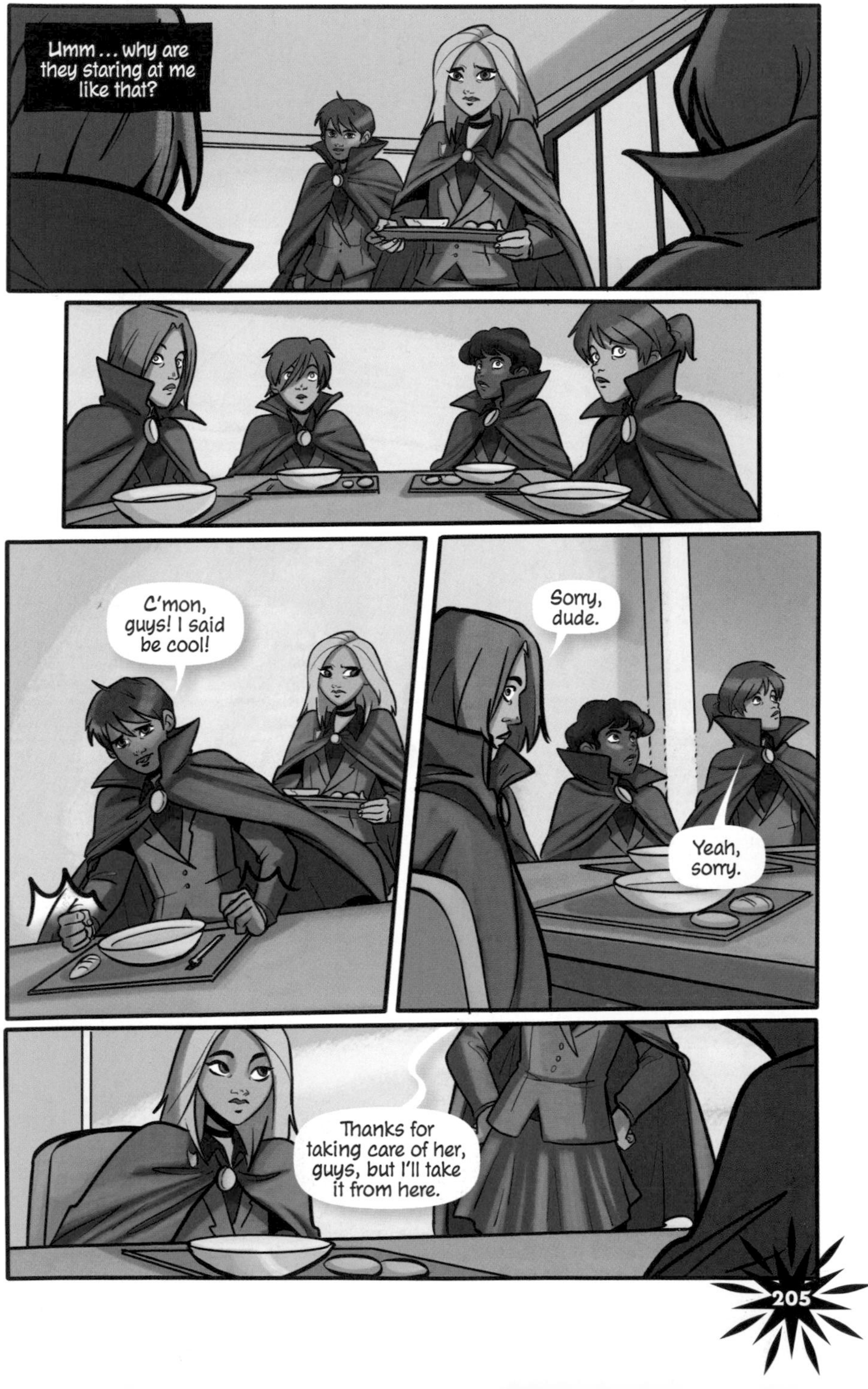
Umm... why are they staring at me like that?
C'mon, guys! I said be cool!
Sorry, dude.
Yeah, sorry.
Thanks for taking care of her, guys, but I'll take it from here.

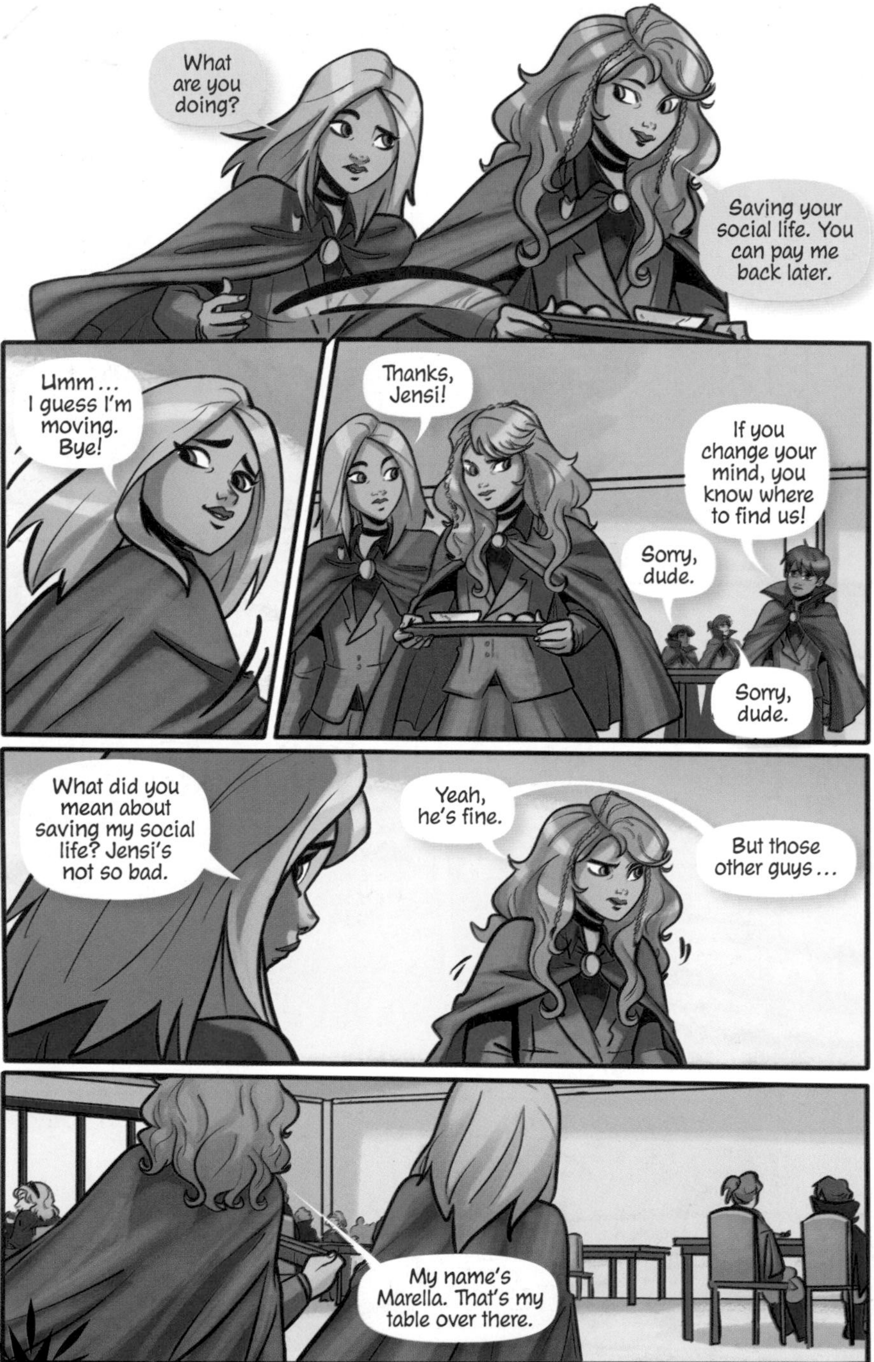
What are you doing?
Saving your social life. You can pay me back later.
Umm... I guess I'm moving. Bye!
Thanks, Jensi!
If you change your mind, you know where to find us!
Sorry, dude.
Sorry, dude.
What did you mean about saving my social life? Jensi's not so bad.
Yeah, he's fine.
But those other guys...
My name's Marella. That's my table over there.

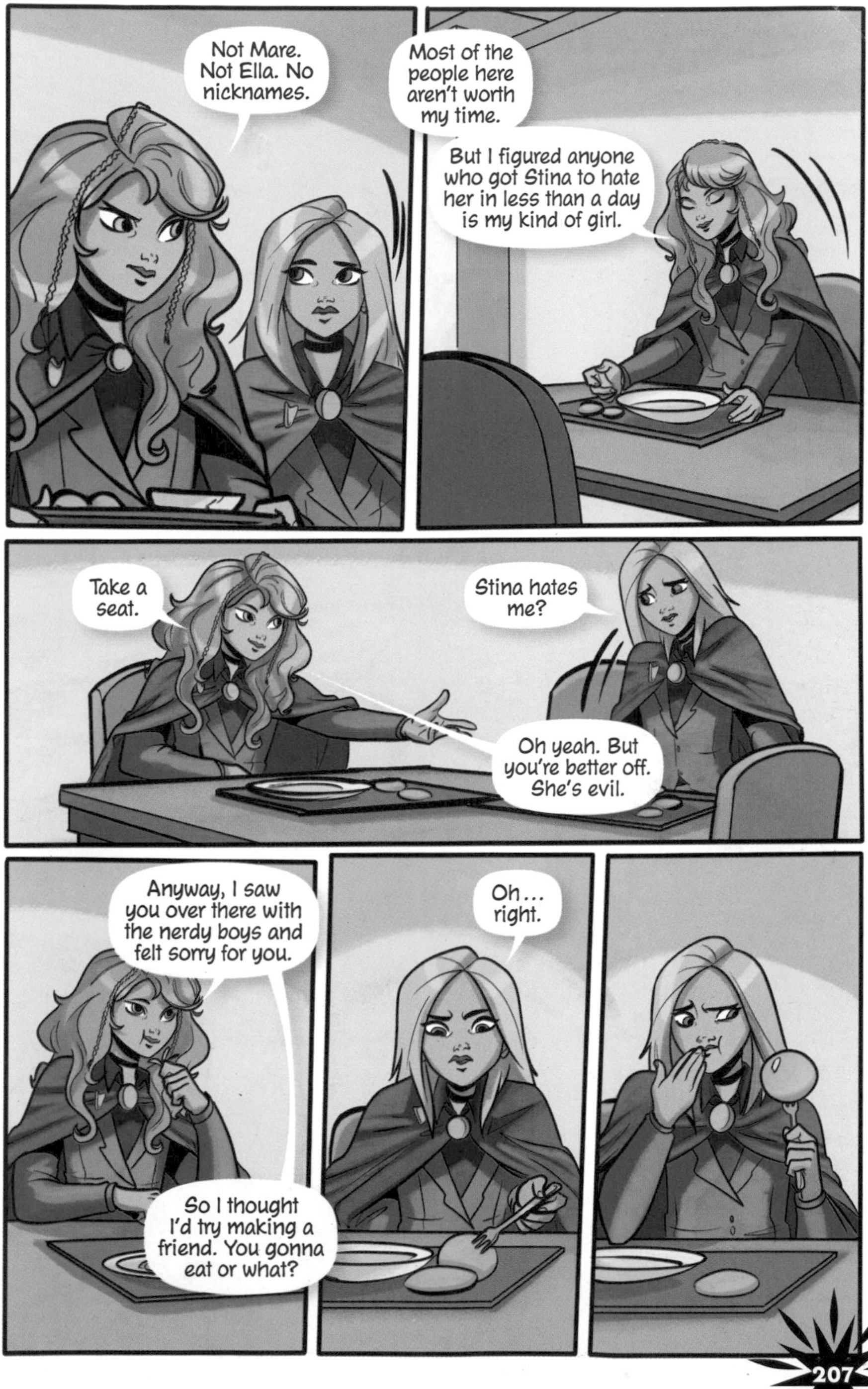
Not Mare. Not Ella. No nicknames.
Most of the people here aren't worth my time.
But I figured anyone who got Stina to hate her in less than a day is my kind of girl.
Take a seat.
Stina hates me?
Oh yeah. But you're better off. She's evil.
Anyway, I saw you over there with the nerdy boys and felt sorry for you.
So I thought I'd try making a friend. You gonna eat or what?
Oh… right.

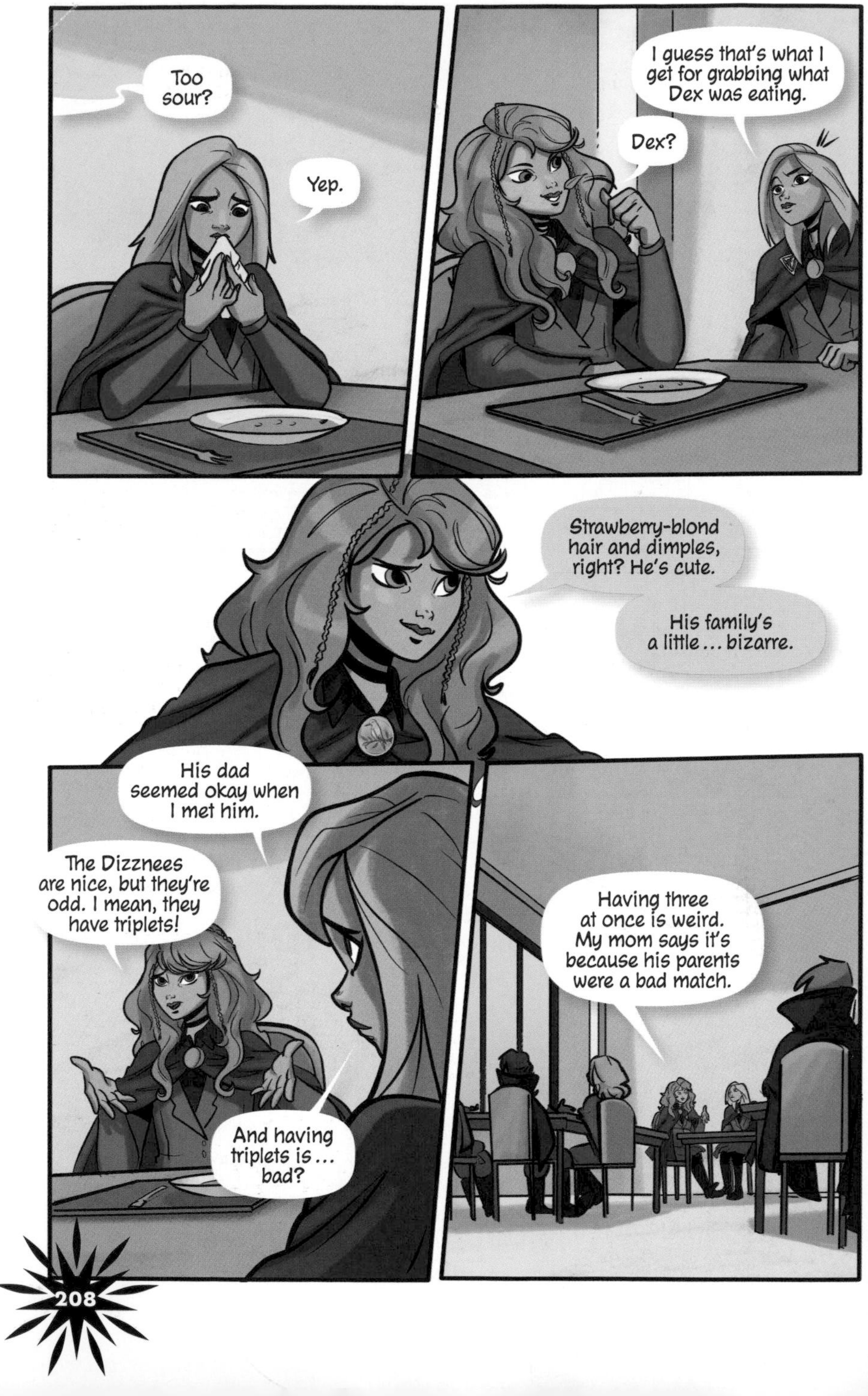
Too sour?
Yep.
I guess that's what I get for grabbing what Dex was eating.
Dex?
Strawberry-blond hair and dimples, right? He's cute.
His family's a little ... bizarre.
His dad seemed okay when I met him.
The Dizznees are nice, but they're odd. I mean, they have triplets!
And having triplets is ... bad?
Having three at once is weird. My mom says it's because his parents were a bad match.

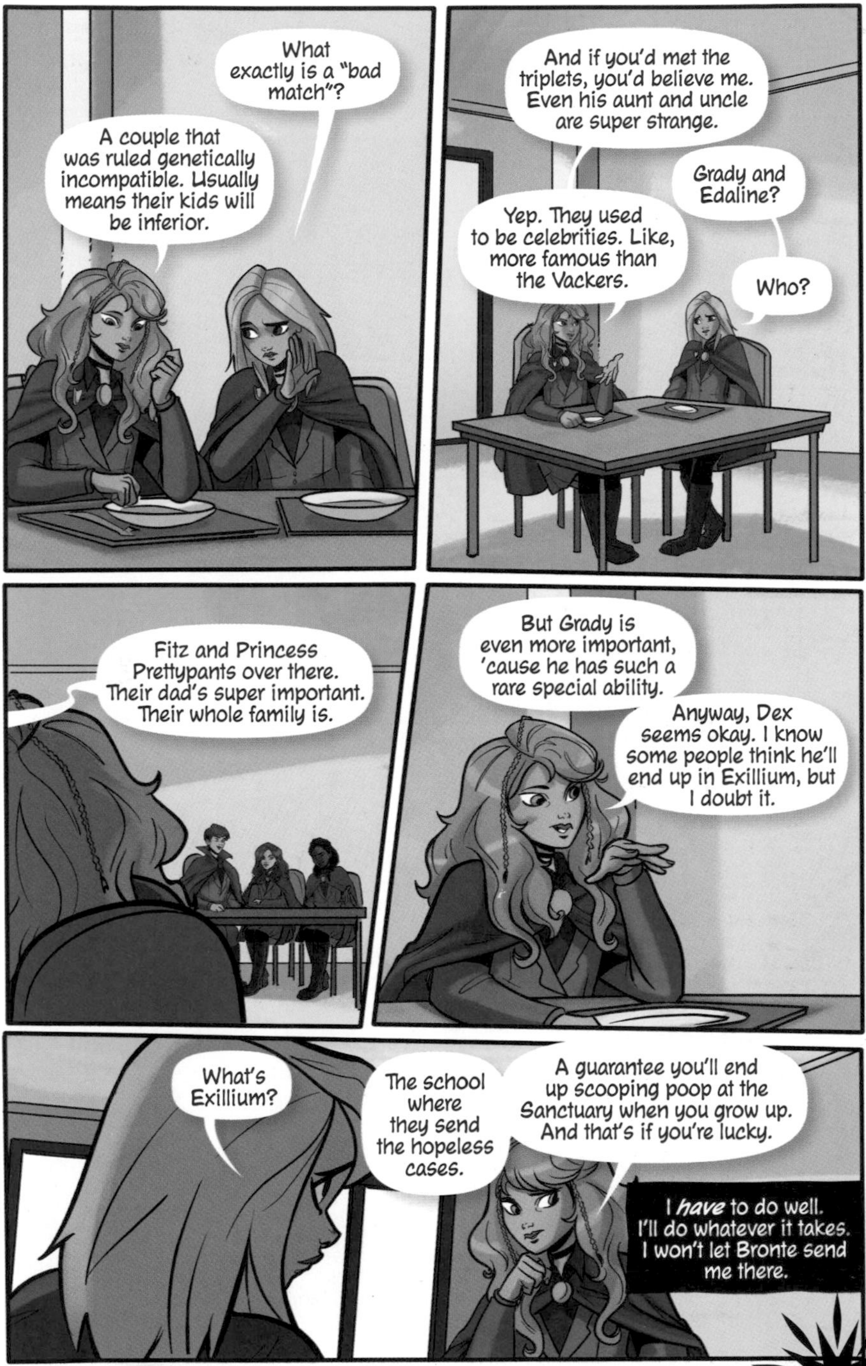
What exactly is a "bad match"?
A couple that was ruled genetically incompatible. Usually means their kids will be inferior.
And if you'd met the triplets, you'd believe me. Even his aunt and uncle are super strange.
Grady and Edaline?
Who?
Yep. They used to be celebrities. Like, more famous than the Vackers.
Fitz and Princess Prettypants over there. Their dad's super important. Their whole family is.
But Grady is even more important, 'cause he has such a rare special ability.
Anyway, Dex seems okay. I know some people think he'll end up in Exillium, but I doubt it.
What's Exillium?
The school where they send the hopeless cases.
A guarantee you'll end up scooping poop at the Sanctuary when you grow up. And that's if you're lucky.
I *have* to do well. I'll do whatever it takes. I won't let Bronte send me there.

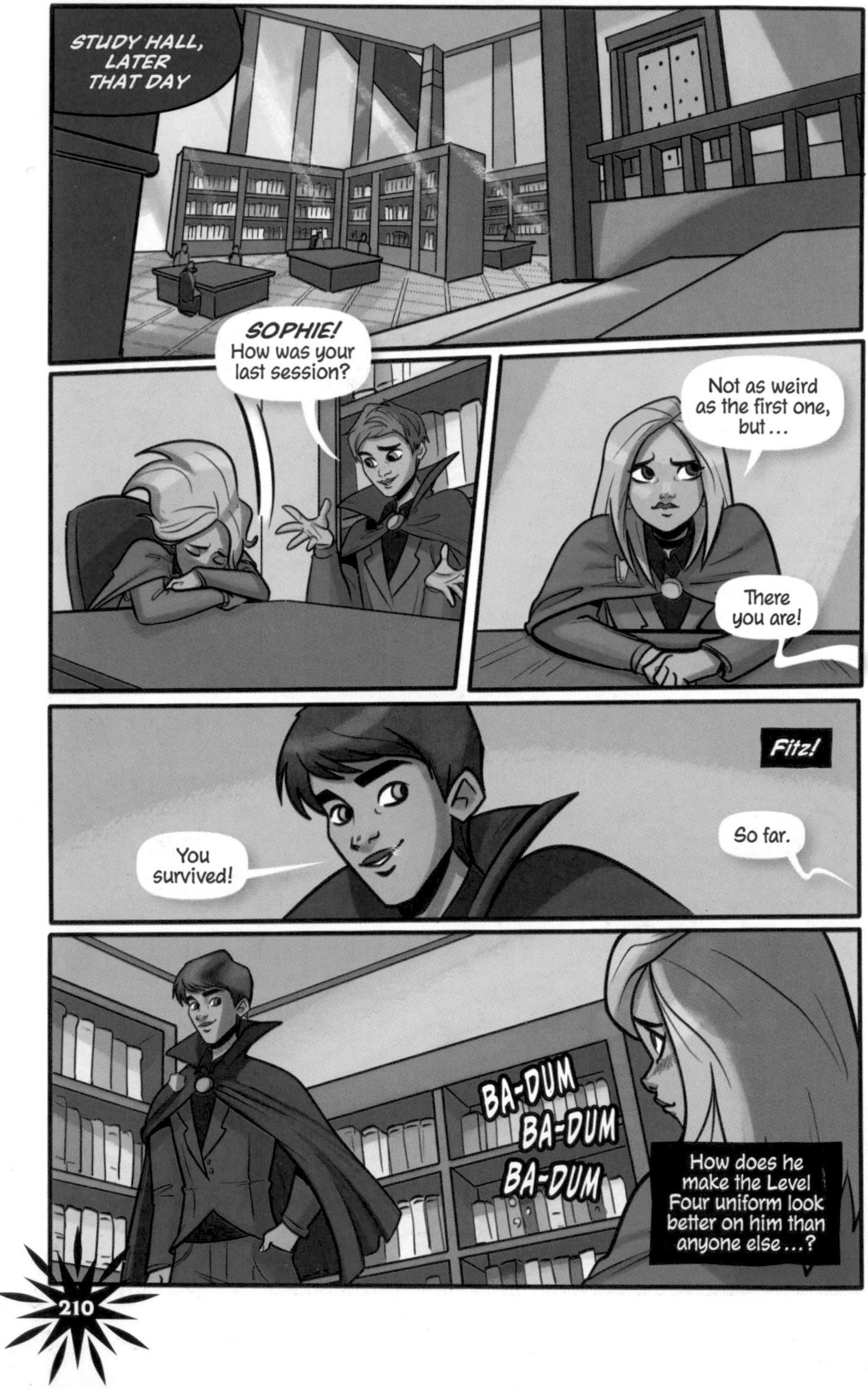
STUDY HALL, LATER THAT DAY
SOPHIE! How was your last session?
Not as weird as the first one, but...
There you are!
Fitz!
You survived!
So far.
BA-DUM
BA-DUM
BA-DUM
How does he make the Level Four uniform look better on him than anyone else...?

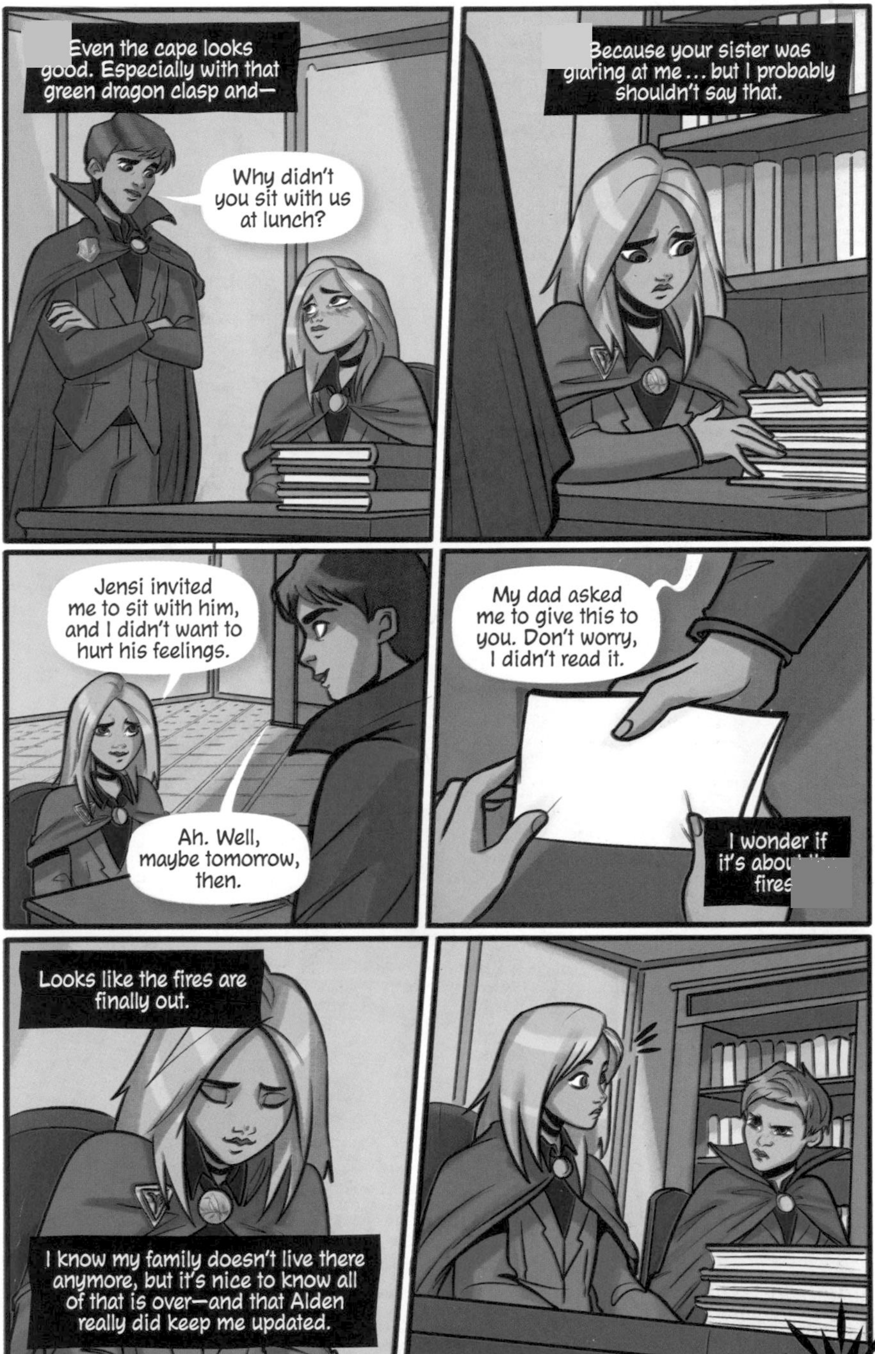

Even the cape looks good. Especially with that green dragon clasp and—
Why didn't you sit with us at lunch?
Because your sister was glaring at me . . . but I probably shouldn't say that.
Jensi invited me to sit with him, and I didn't want to hurt his feelings.
Ah. Well, maybe tomorrow, then.
My dad asked me to give this to you. Don't worry, I didn't read it.
I wonder if it's abou
Looks like the fires are finally out.
I know my family doesn't live there anymore, but it's nice to know all of that is over—and that Alden really did keep me updated.

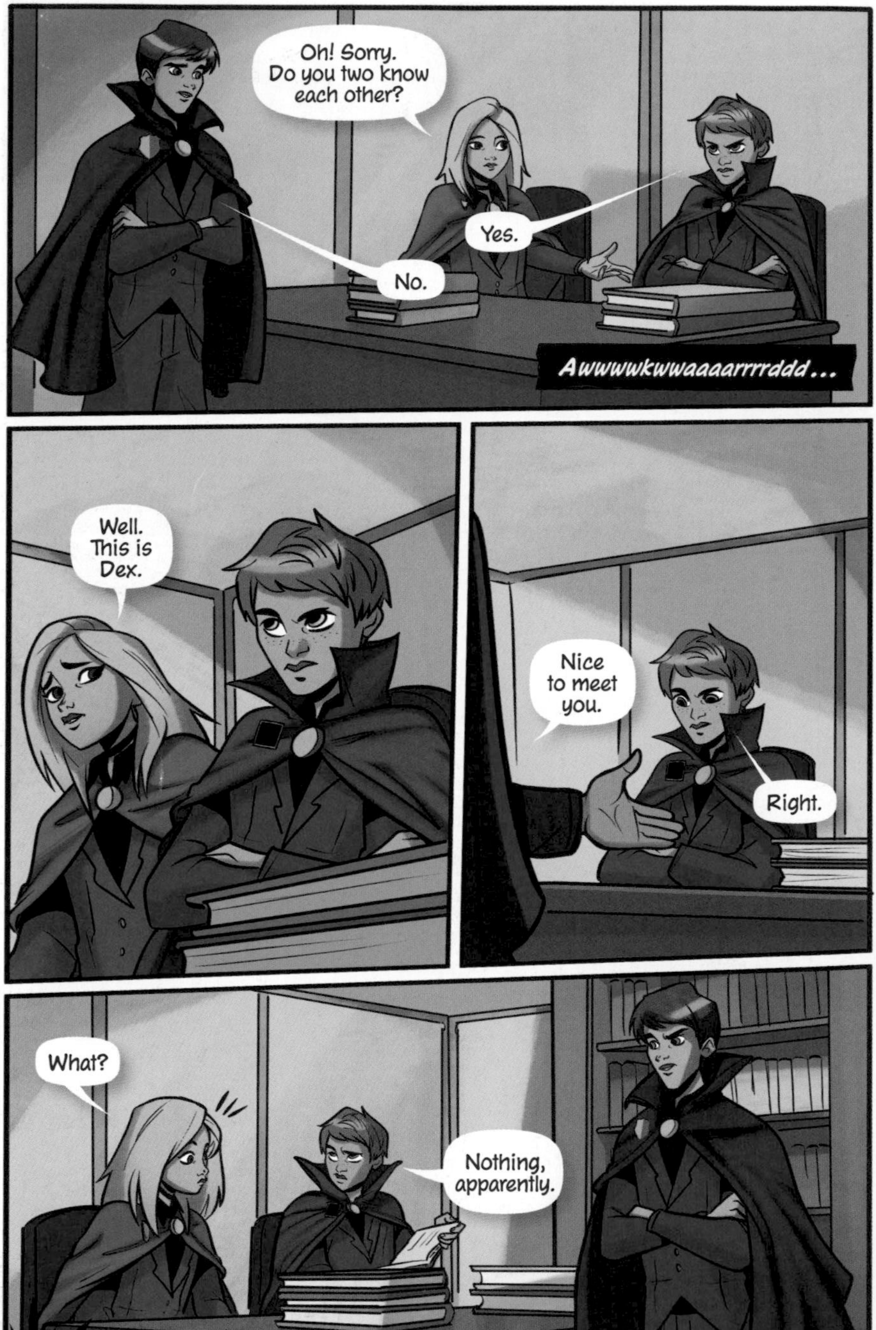
Oh! Sorry. Do you two know each other?
Yes.
No.
Awwwwkwwaaaarrrrddd...
Well. This is Dex.
Nice to meet you.
Right.
What?
Nothing, apparently.

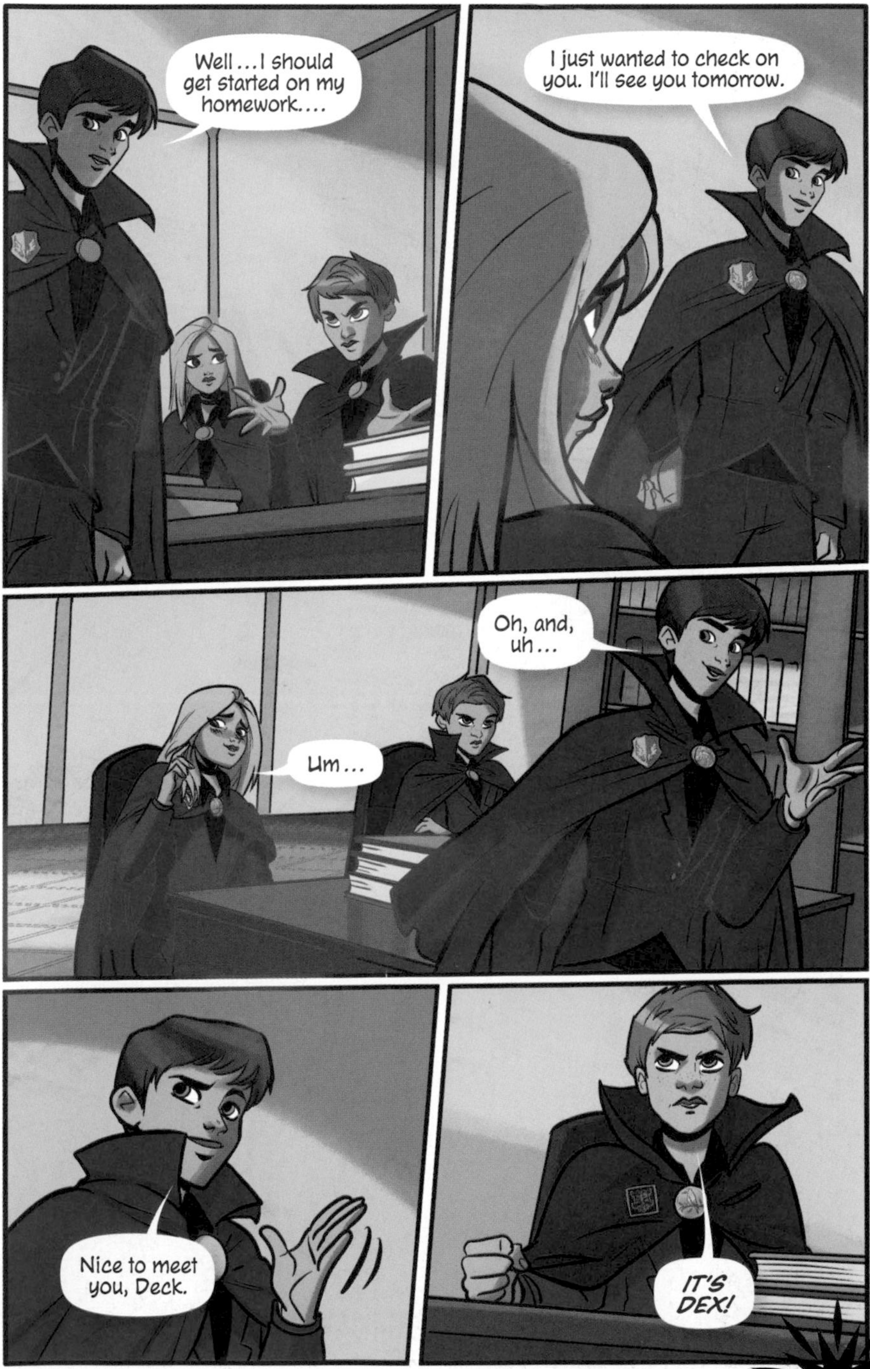
Well…I should get started on my homework….
I just wanted to check on you. I'll see you tomorrow.
Oh, and, uh…
Um…
Nice to meet you, Deck.
IT'S DEX!

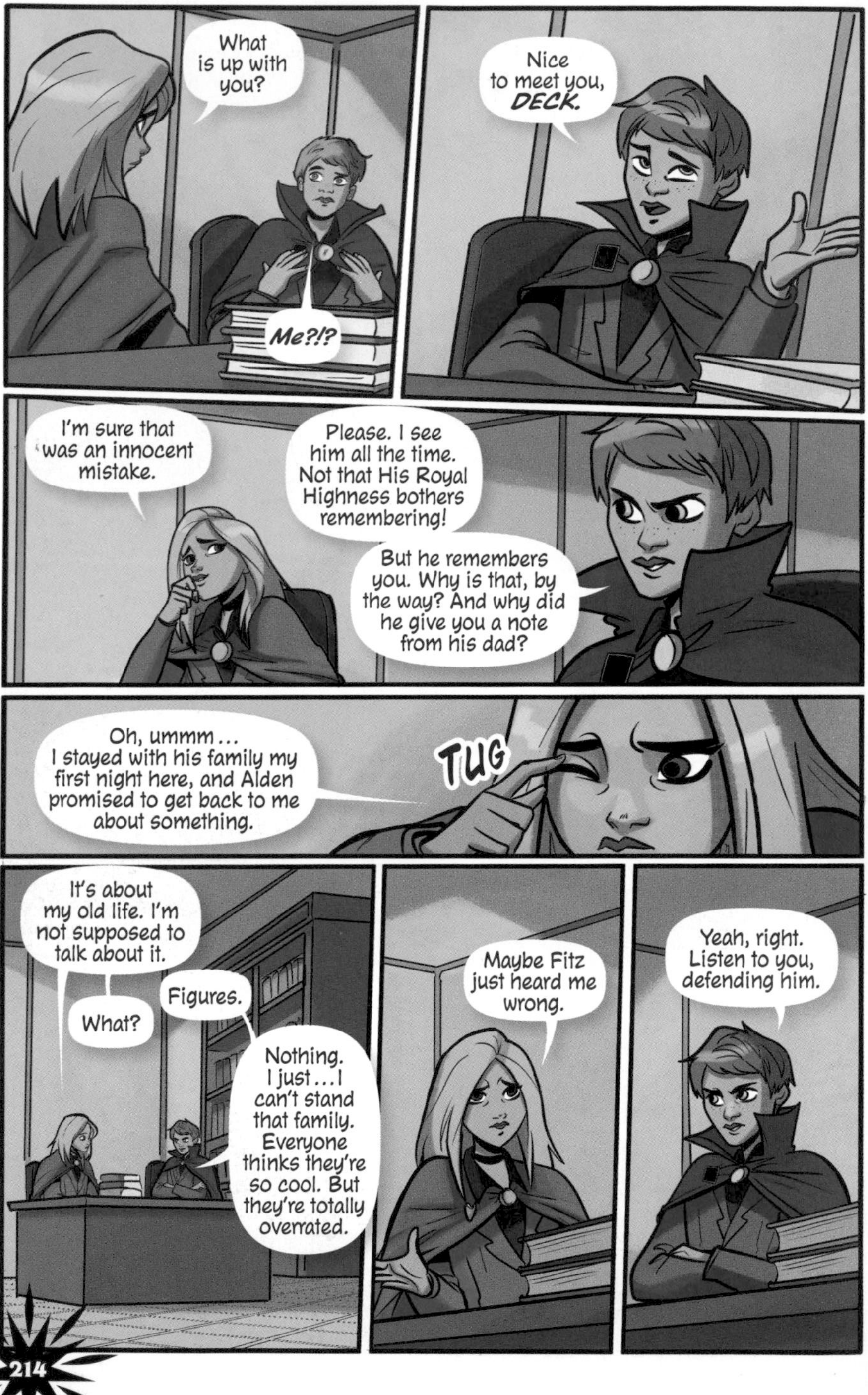
What is up with you?
Me?!?
Nice to meet you, DECK.
I'm sure that was an innocent mistake.
Please. I see him all the time. Not that His Royal Highness bothers remembering!
But he remembers you. Why is that, by the way? And why did he give you a note from his dad?
Oh, ummm… I stayed with his family my first night here, and Alden promised to get back to me about something.
TUG
It's about my old life. I'm not supposed to talk about it.
Figures.
What?
Nothing. I just… I can't stand that family. Everyone thinks they're so cool. But they're totally overrated.
Maybe Fitz just heard me wrong.
Yeah, right. Listen to you, defending him.

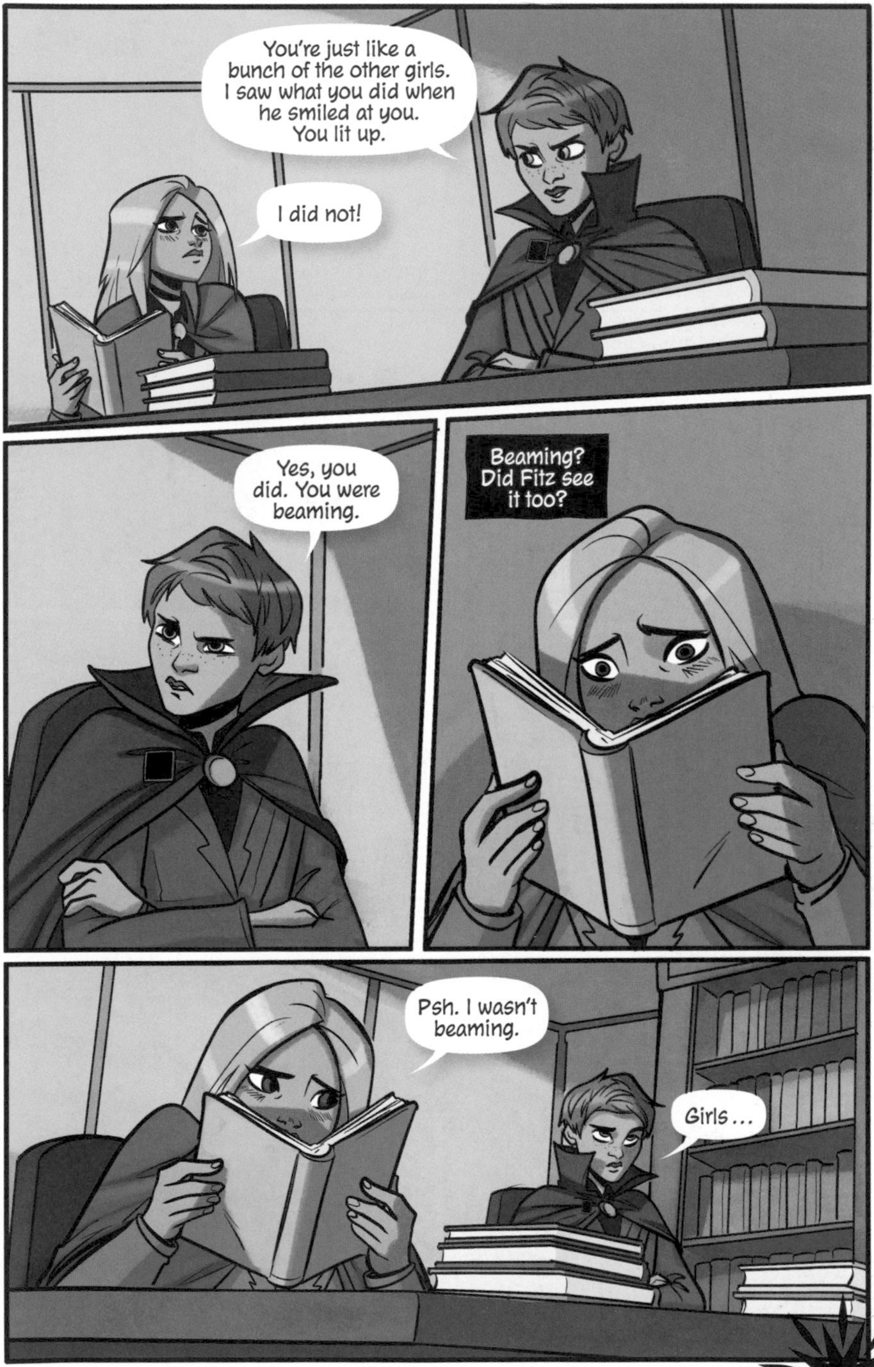
You're just like a bunch of the other girls. I saw what you did when he smiled at you. You lit up.
I did not!
Yes, you did. You were beaming.
Beaming? Did Fitz see it too?
Psh. I wasn't beaming.
Girls...

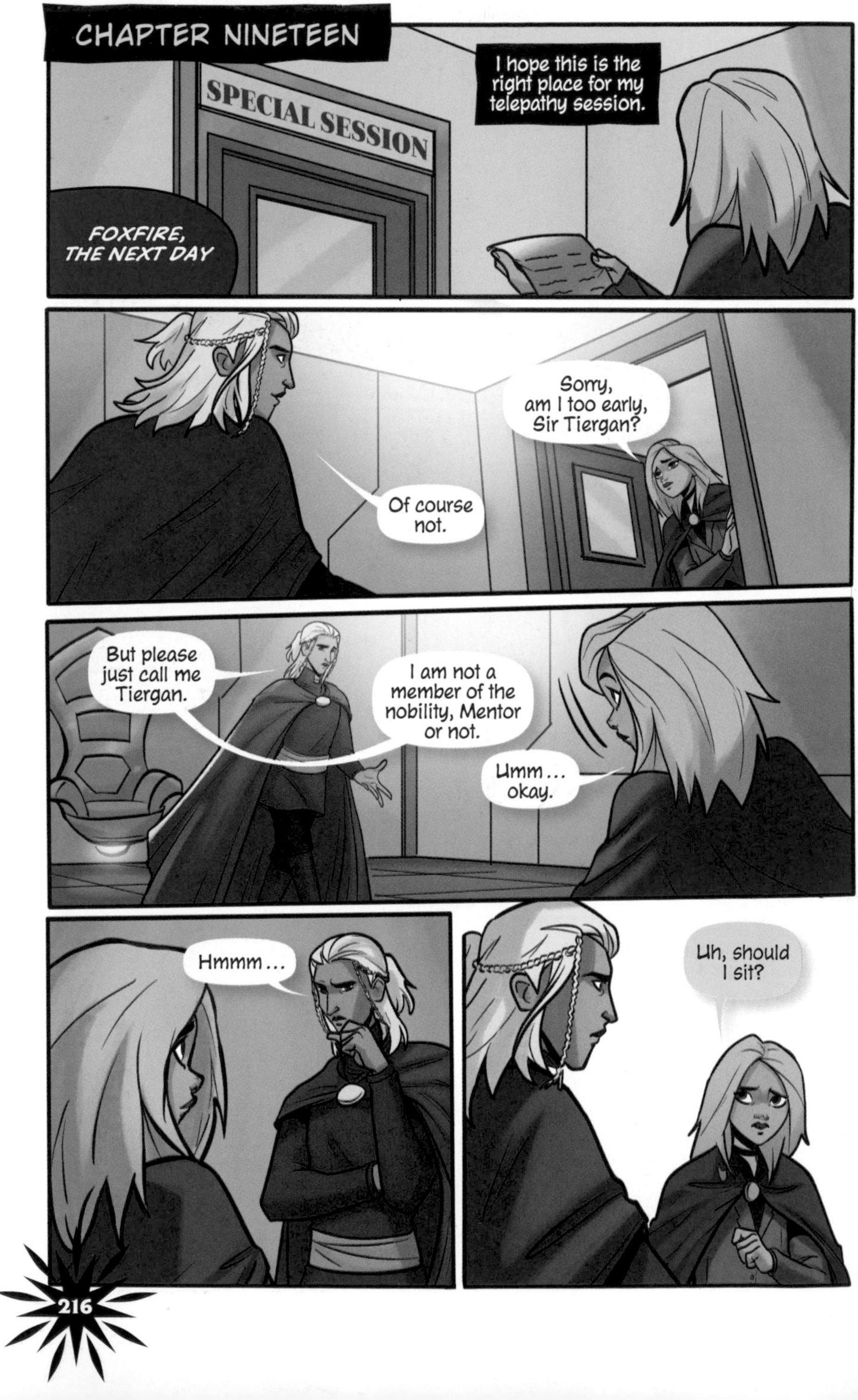
CHAPTER NINETEEN
SPECIAL SESSION
I hope this is the right place for my telepathy session.
FOXFIRE, THE NEXT DAY
Sorry, am I too early, Sir Tiergan?
Of course not.
But please just call me Tiergan.
I am not a member of the nobility, Mentor or not.
Umm... okay.
Hmmm...
Uh, should I sit?

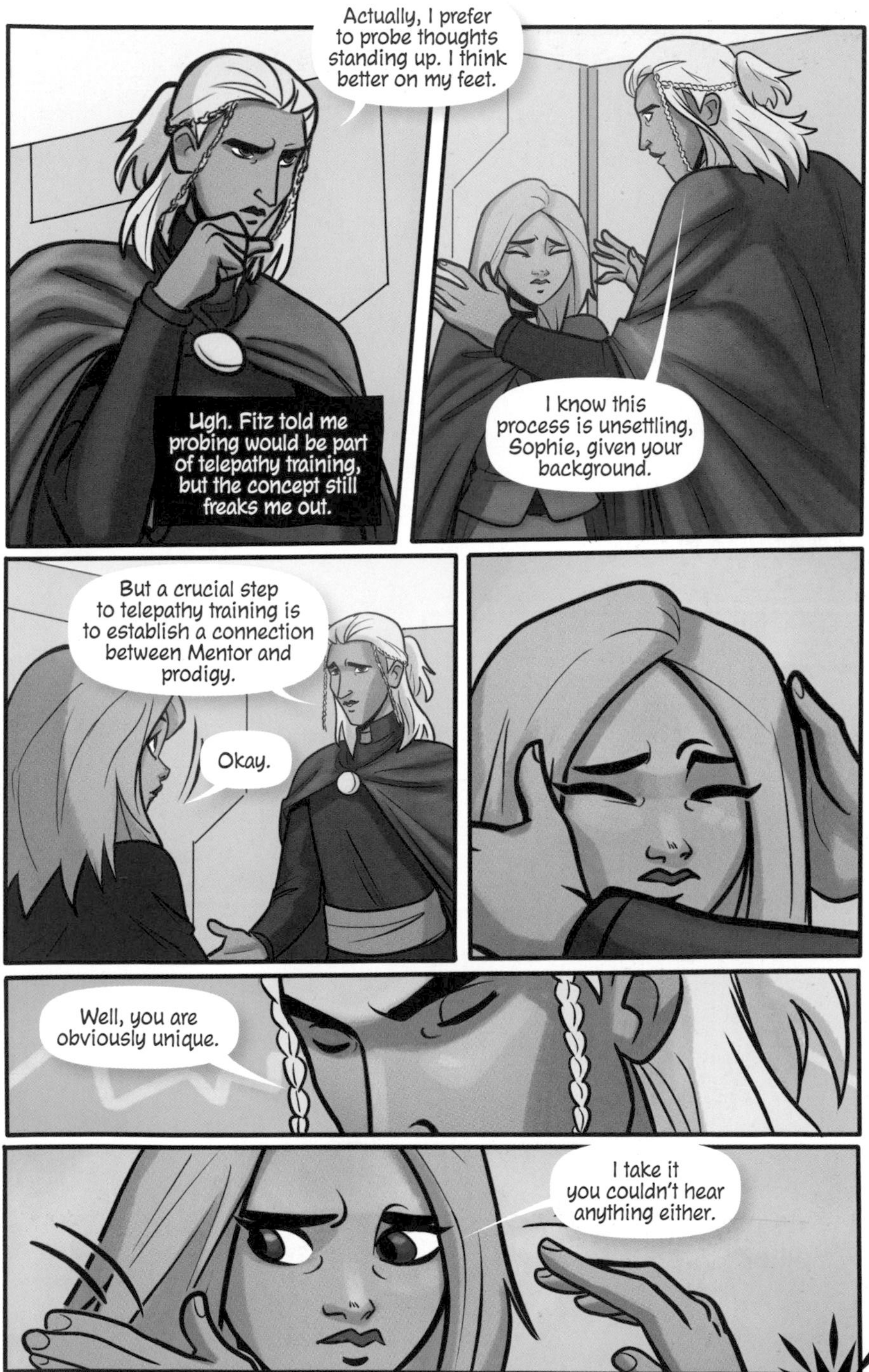
Actually, I prefer to probe thoughts standing up. I think better on my feet.
Ugh. Fitz told me probing would be part of telepathy training, but the concept still freaks me out.
I know this process is unsettling, Sophie, given your background.
But a crucial step to telepathy training is to establish a connection between Mentor and prodigy.
Okay.
Well, you are obviously unique.
I take it you couldn't hear anything either.

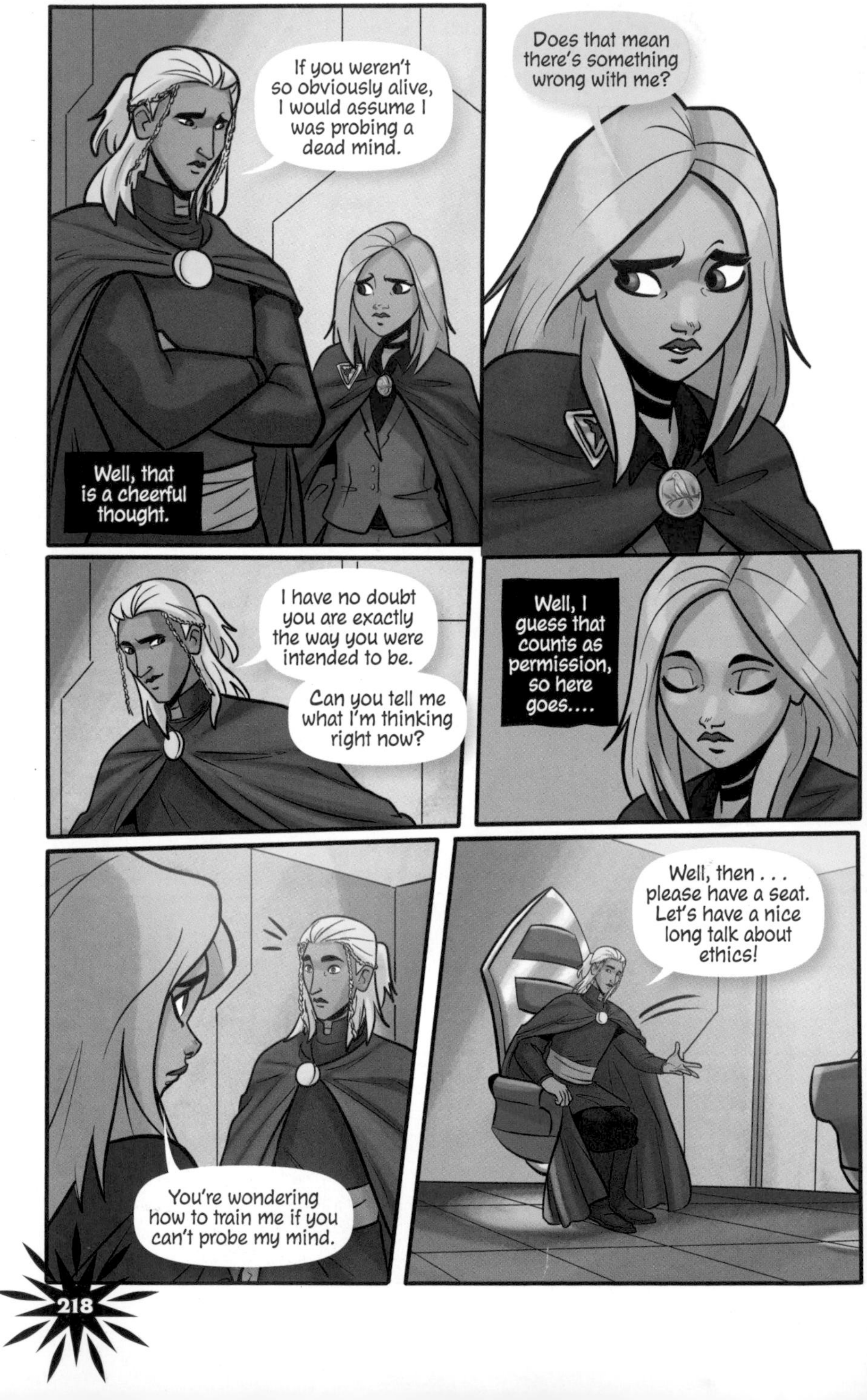

If you weren't so obviously alive, I would assume I was probing a dead mind.
Well, that is a cheerful thought.
Does that mean there's something wrong with me?
I have no doubt you are exactly the way you were intended to be.
Can you tell me what I'm thinking right now?
Well, I guess that counts as permission, so here goes....
You're wondering how to train me if you can't probe my mind.
Well, then . . . please have a seat. Let's have a nice long talk about ethics!

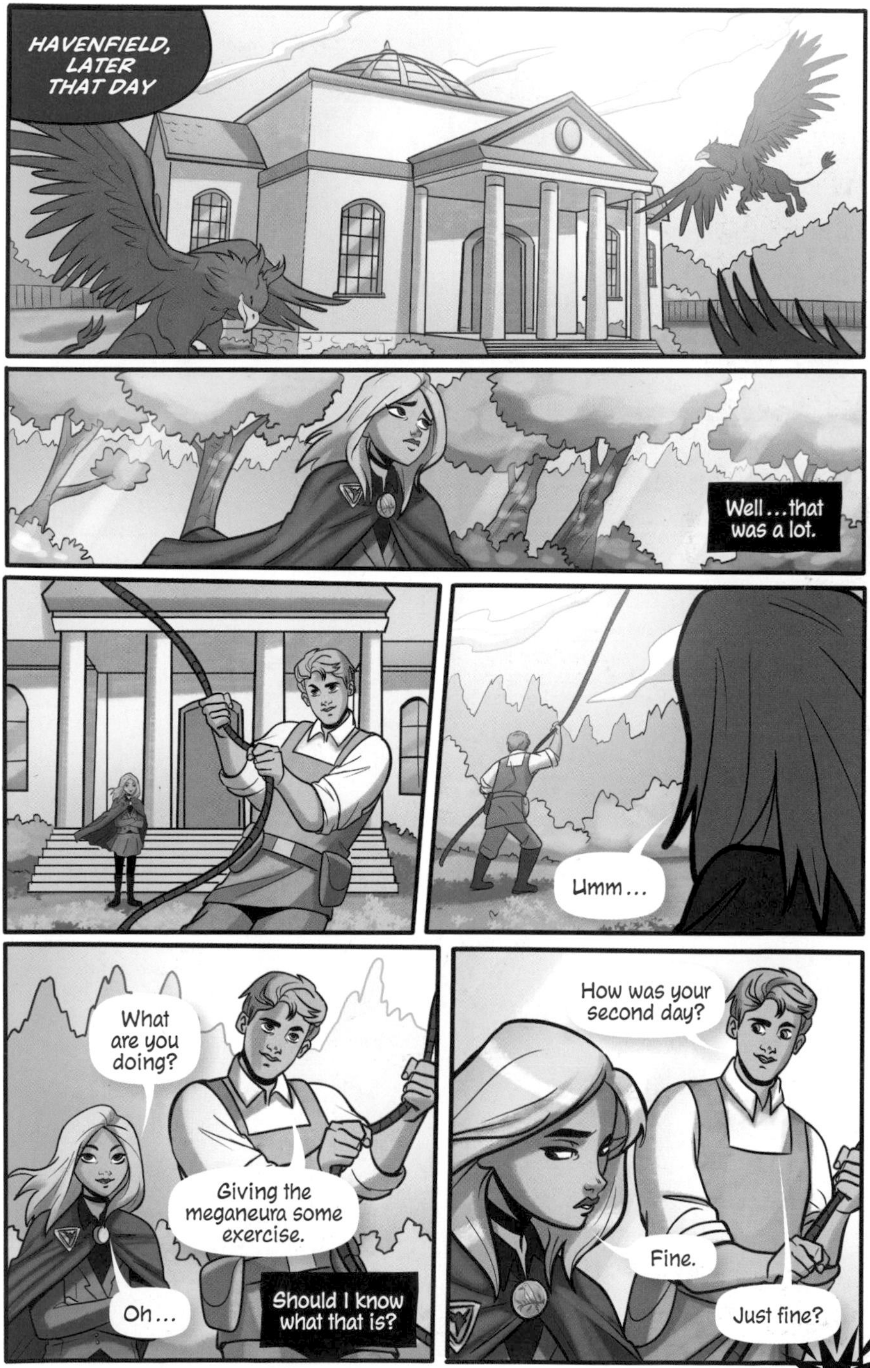

HAVENFIELD, LATER THAT DAY
Well...that was a lot.
Umm...
What are you doing?
Giving the meganeura some exercise.
Oh...
Should I know what that is?
How was your second day?
Fine.
Just fine?

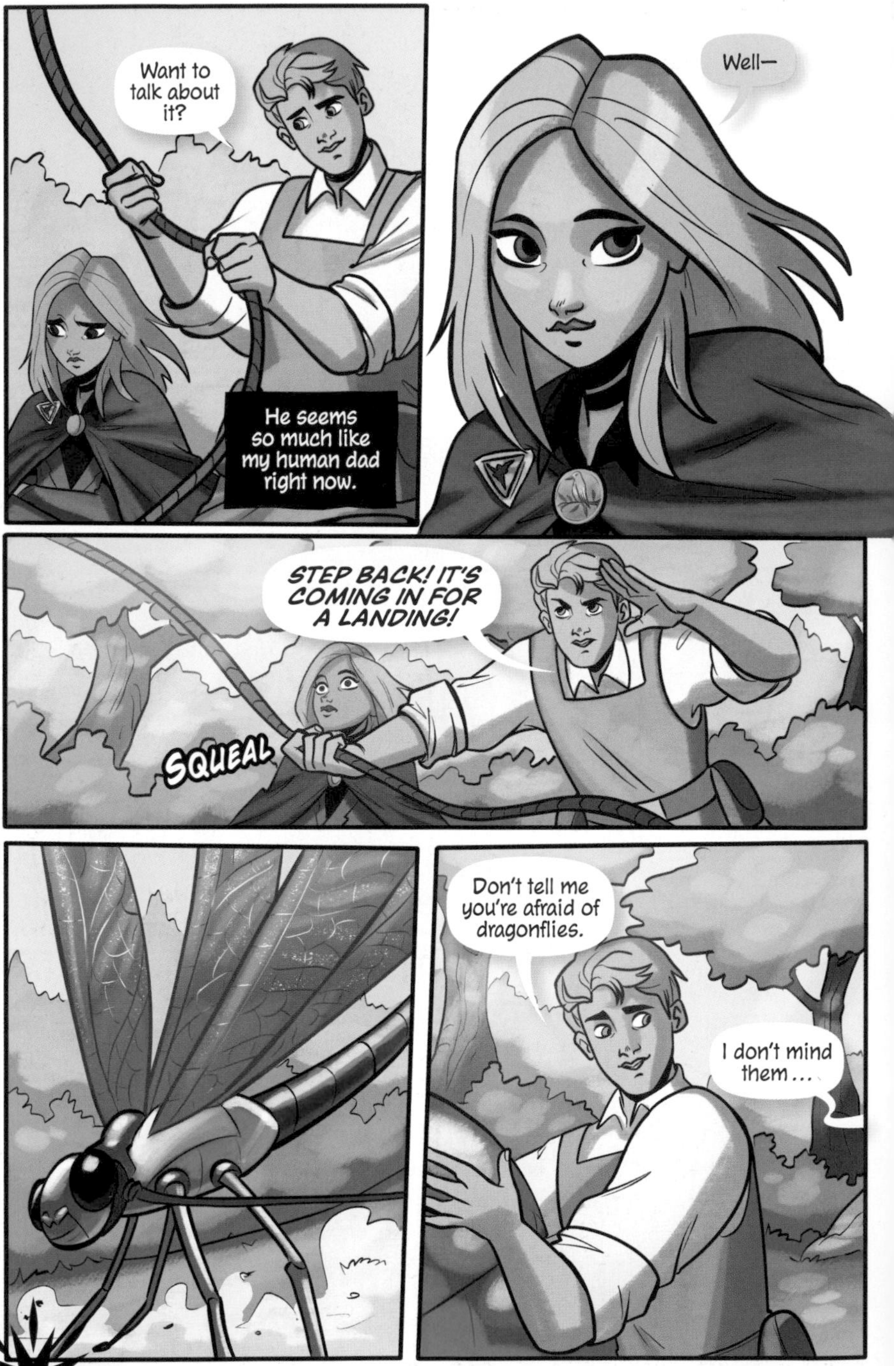
Want to talk about it?
He seems so much like my human dad right now.
Well—
STEP BACK! IT'S COMING IN FOR A LANDING!
SQUEAL
Don't tell me you're afraid of dragonflies.
I don't mind them . . .

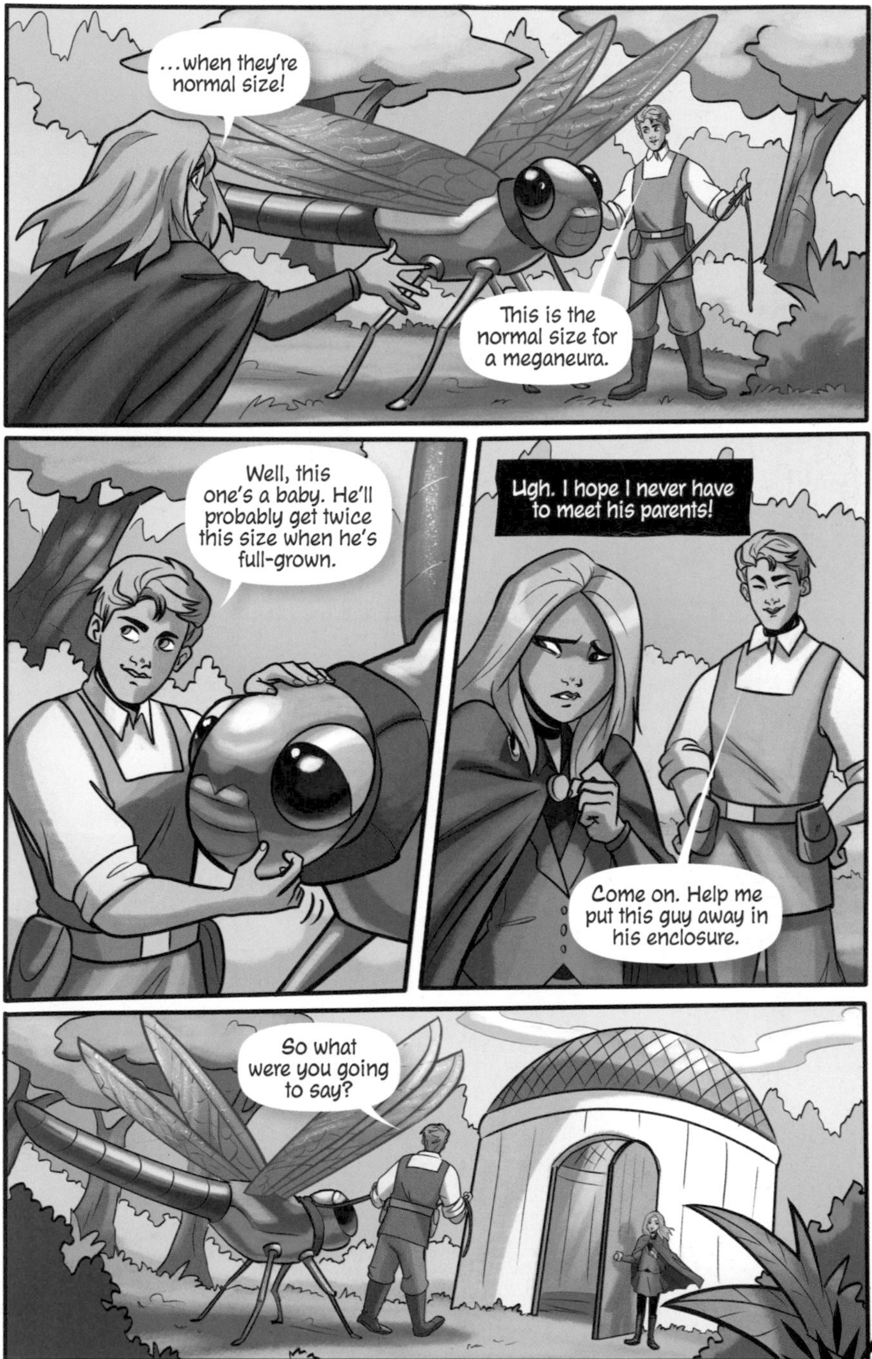
...when they're normal size!
This is the normal size for a meganeura.
Well, this one's a baby. He'll probably get twice this size when he's full-grown.
Ugh. I hope I never have to meet his parents!
Come on. Help me put this guy away in his enclosure.
So what were you going to say?

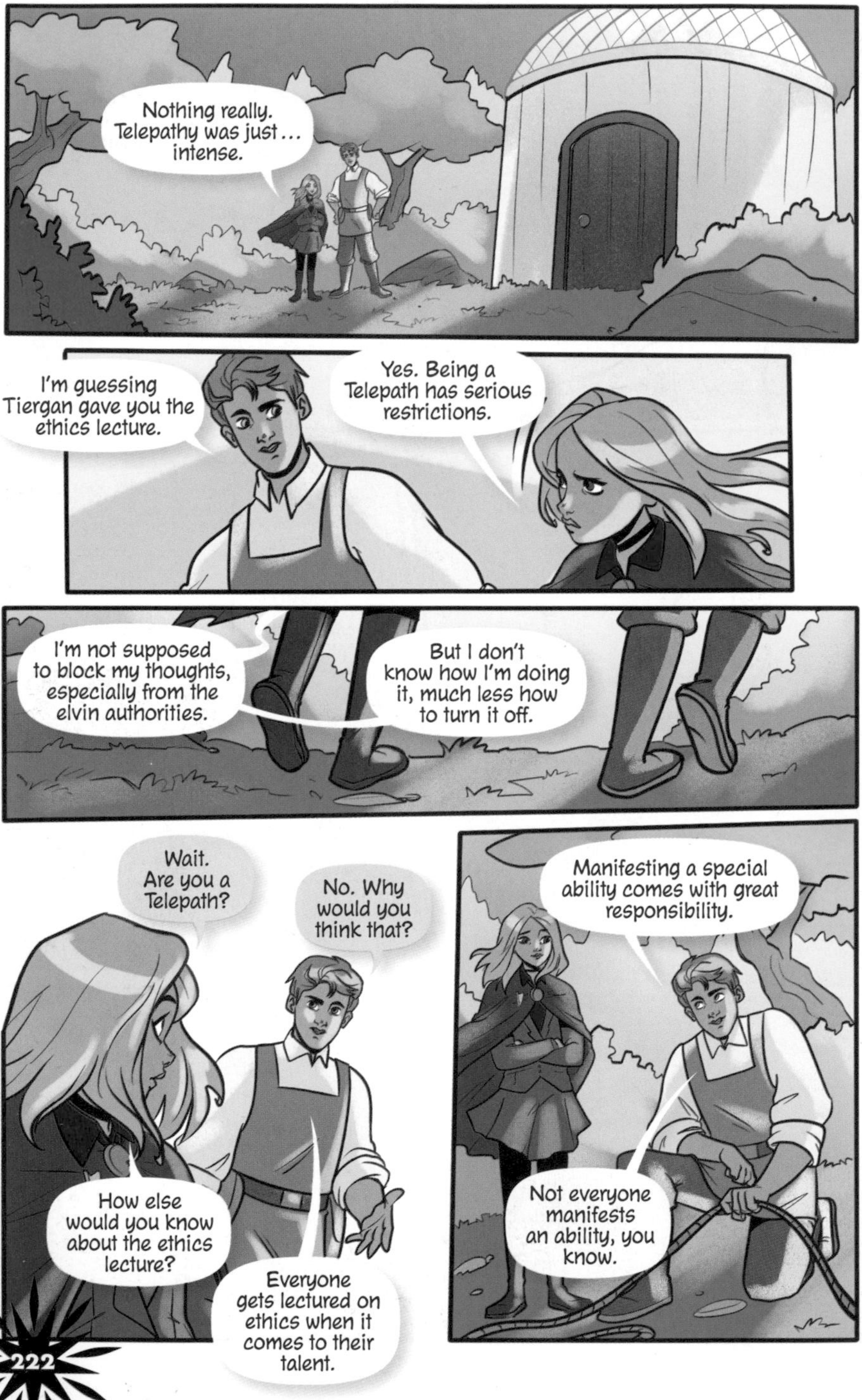

Nothing really. Telepathy was just... intense.
I'm guessing Tiergan gave you the ethics lecture.
Yes. Being a Telepath has serious restrictions.
I'm not supposed to block my thoughts, especially from the elvin authorities.
But I don't know how I'm doing it, much less how to turn it off.
Wait. Are you a Telepath?
No. Why would you think that?
How else would you know about the ethics lecture?
Everyone gets lectured on ethics when it comes to their talent.
Manifesting a special ability comes with great responsibility.
Not everyone manifests an ability, you know.

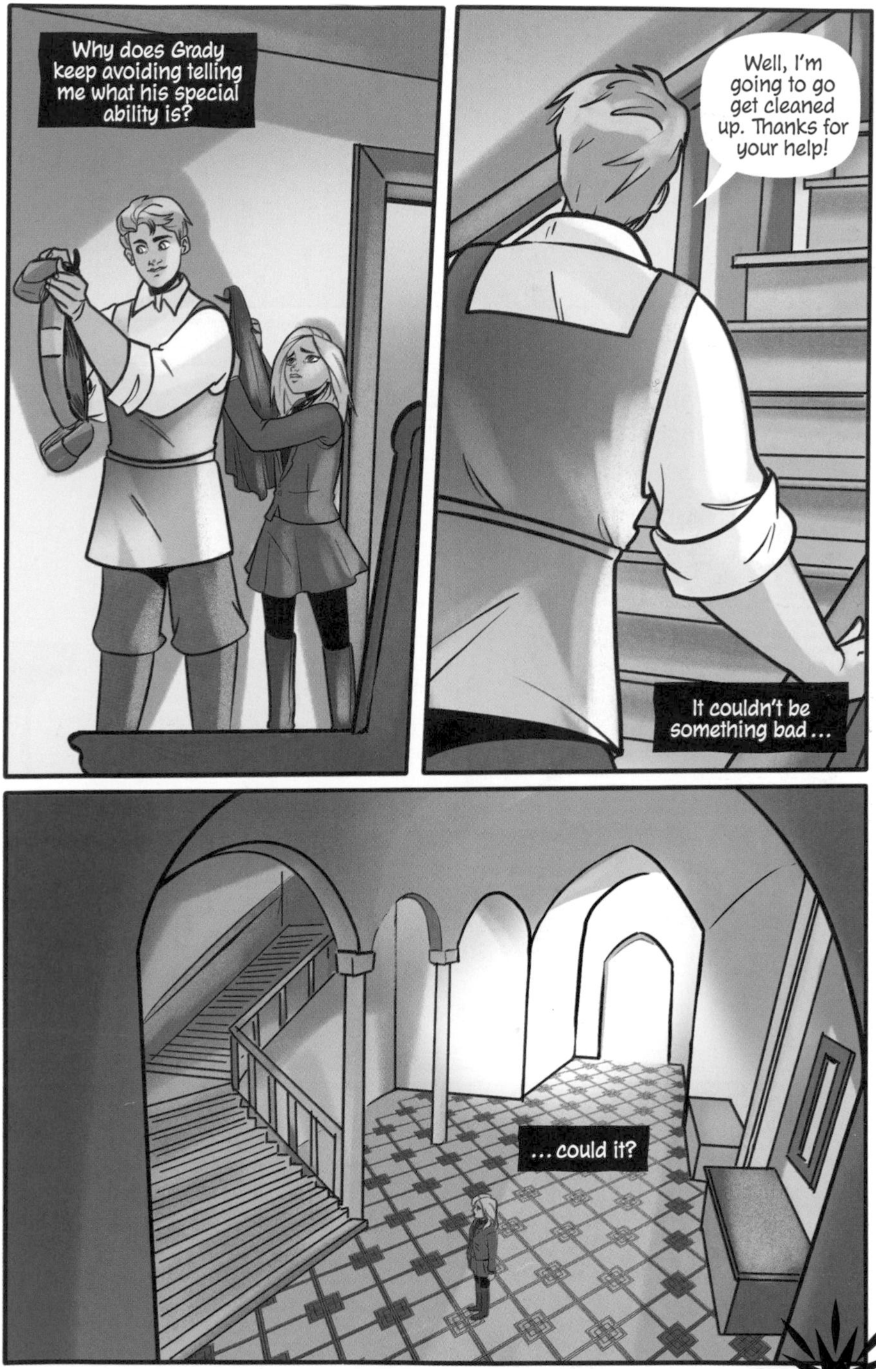
Why does Grady keep avoiding telling me what his special ability is?
Well, I'm going to go get cleaned up. Thanks for your help!
It couldn't be something bad . . .
. . . could it?

CHAPTER TWENTY

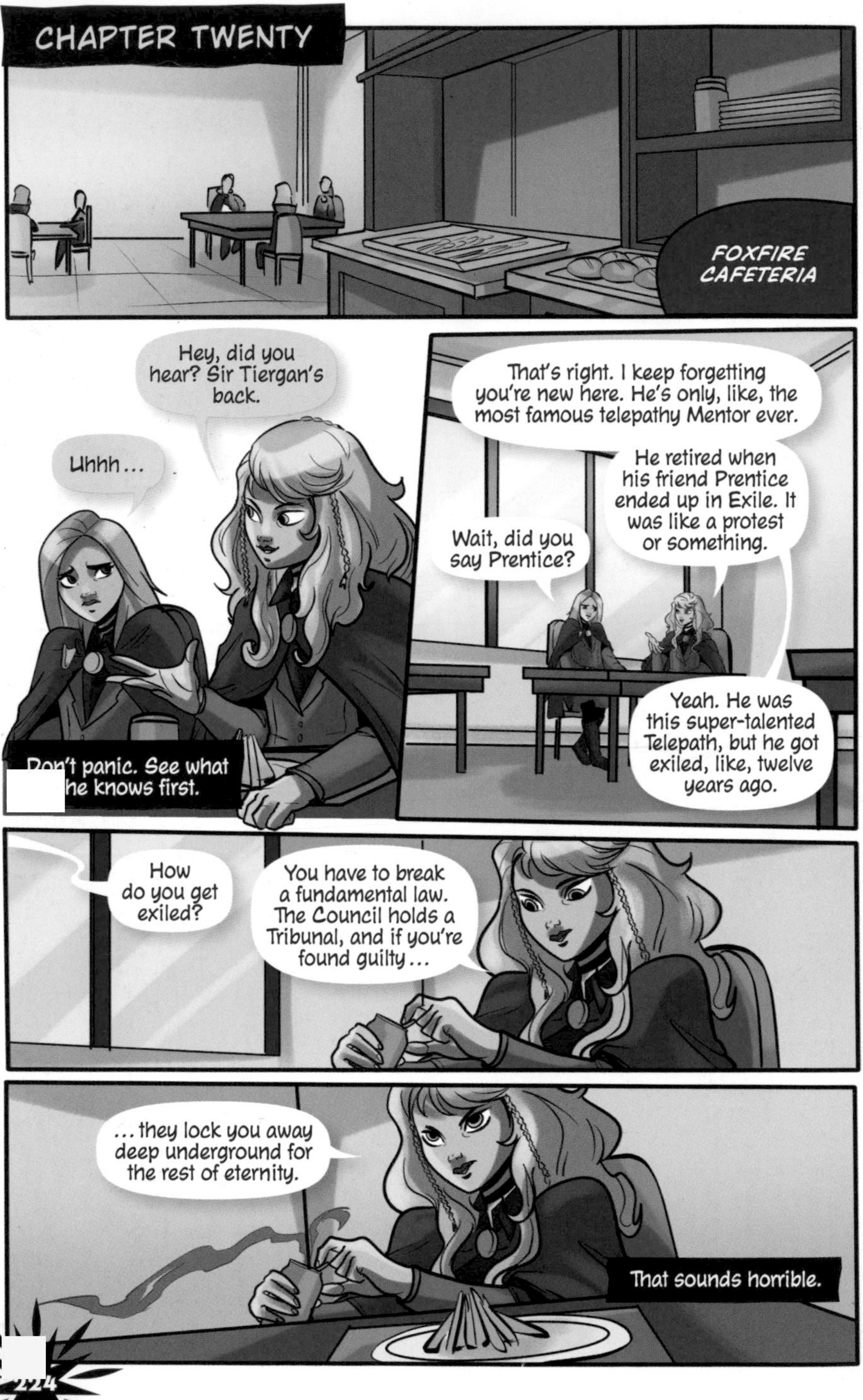
FOXFIRE CAFETERIA
Hey, did you hear? Sir Tiergan's back.
Uhhh...
Don't panic. See what
he knows first.
That's right. I keep forgetting you're new here. He's only, like, the most famous telepathy Mentor ever.
He retired when his friend Prentice ended up in Exile. It was like a protest or something.
Wait, did you say Prentice?
Yeah. He was this super-talented Telepath, but he got exiled, like, twelve years ago.
How do you get exiled?
You have to break a fundamental law. The Council holds a Tribunal, and if you're found guilty...
...they lock you away deep underground for the rest of eternity.
That sounds horrible.

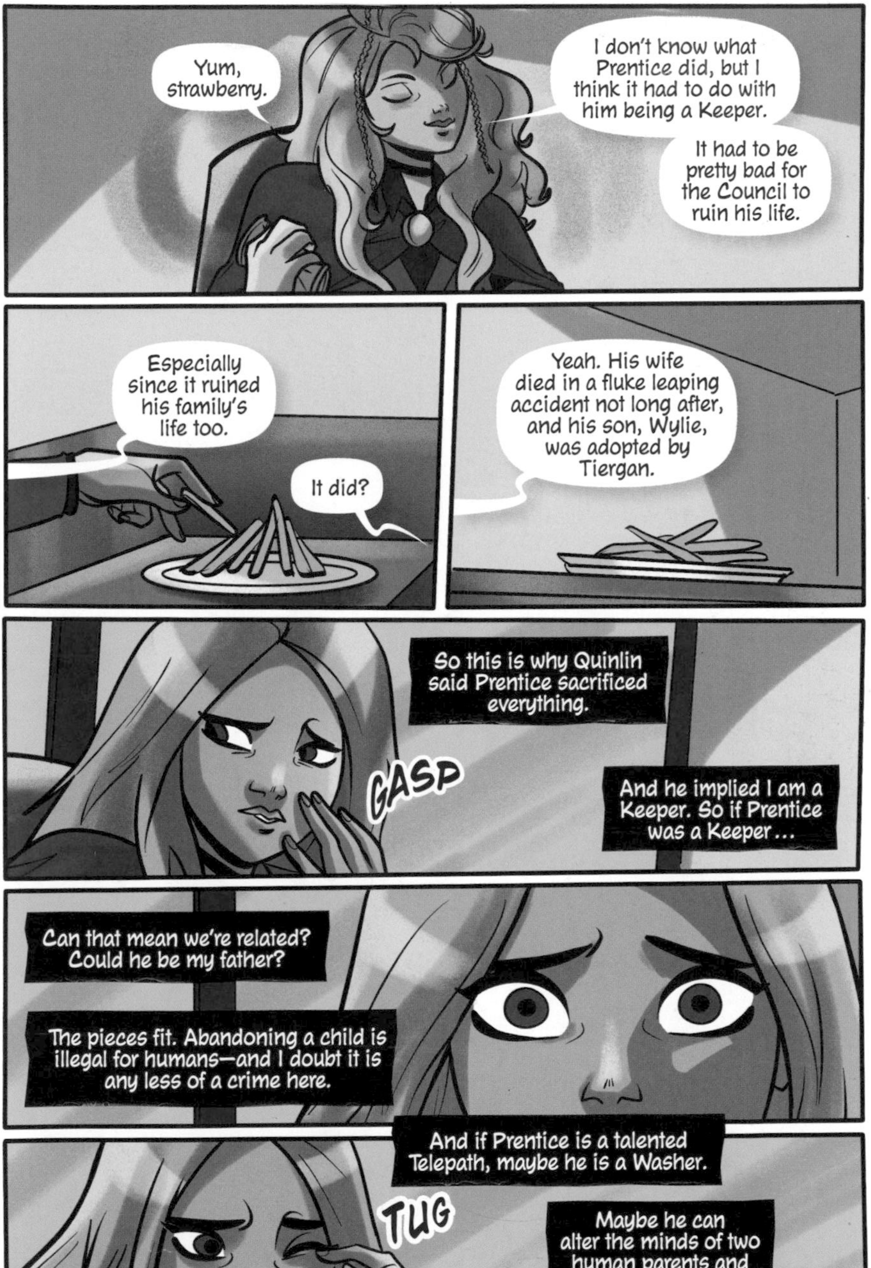
Yum, strawberry.
I don't know what Prentice did, but I think it had to do with him being a Keeper.
It had to be pretty bad for the Council to ruin his life.
Especially since it ruined his family's life too.
It did?
Yeah. His wife died in a fluke leaping accident not long after, and his son, Wylie, was adopted by Tiergan.
So this is why Quinlin said Prentice sacrificed everything.
GASP
And he implied I am a Keeper. So if Prentice was a Keeper...
Can that mean we're related? Could he be my father?
The pieces fit. Abandoning a child is illegal for humans—and I doubt it is any less of a crime here.
And if Prentice is a talented Telepath, maybe he is a Washer.
TUG
Maybe he can alter the minds of two human parents and make them believe a child is theirs.

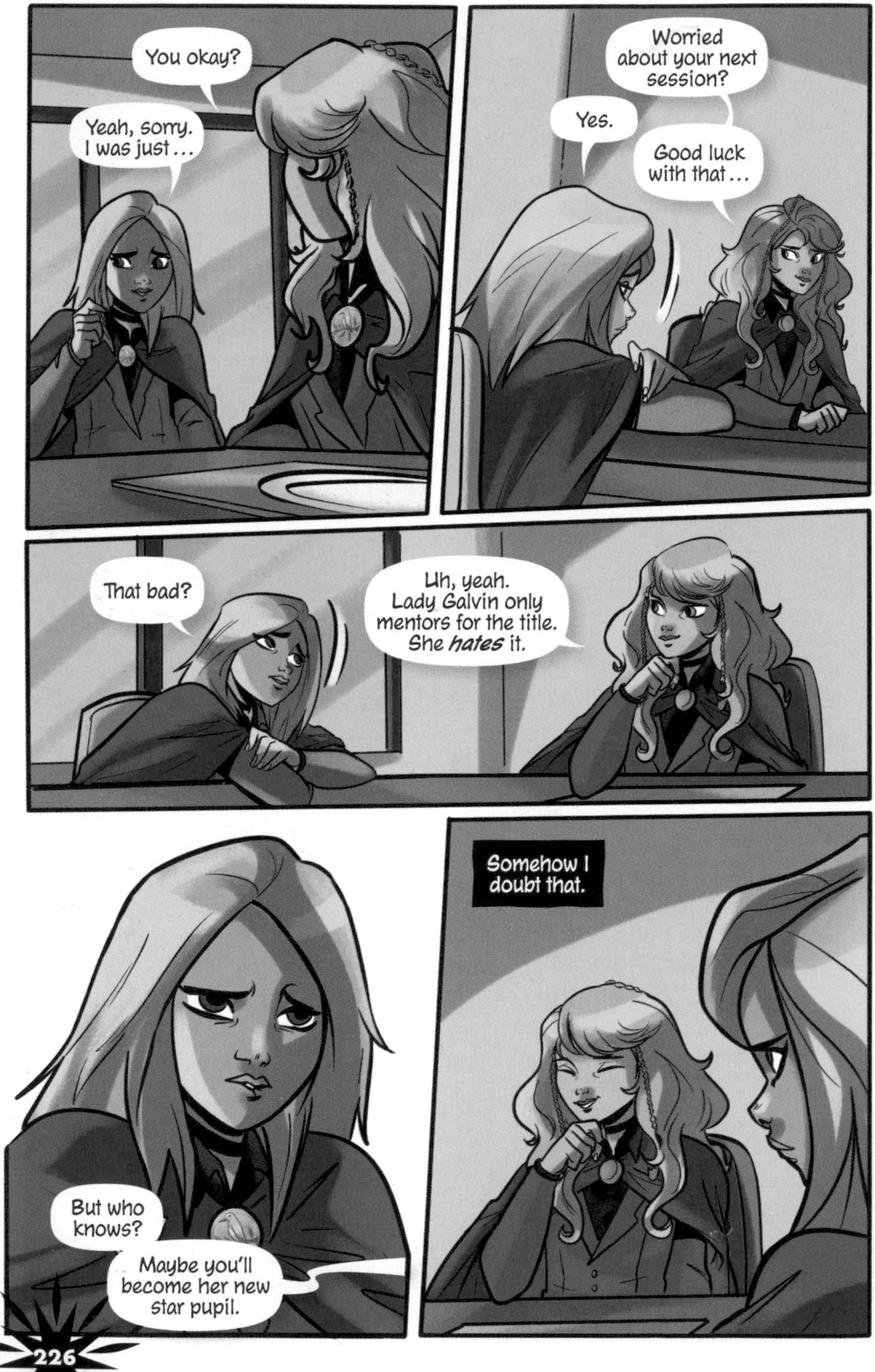
You okay?
Yeah, sorry. I was just . . .
Worried about your next session?
Yes.
Good luck with that . . .
That bad?
Uh, yeah. Lady Galvin only mentors for the title. She *hates* it.
But who knows?
Maybe you'll become her new star pupil.
Somehow I doubt that.

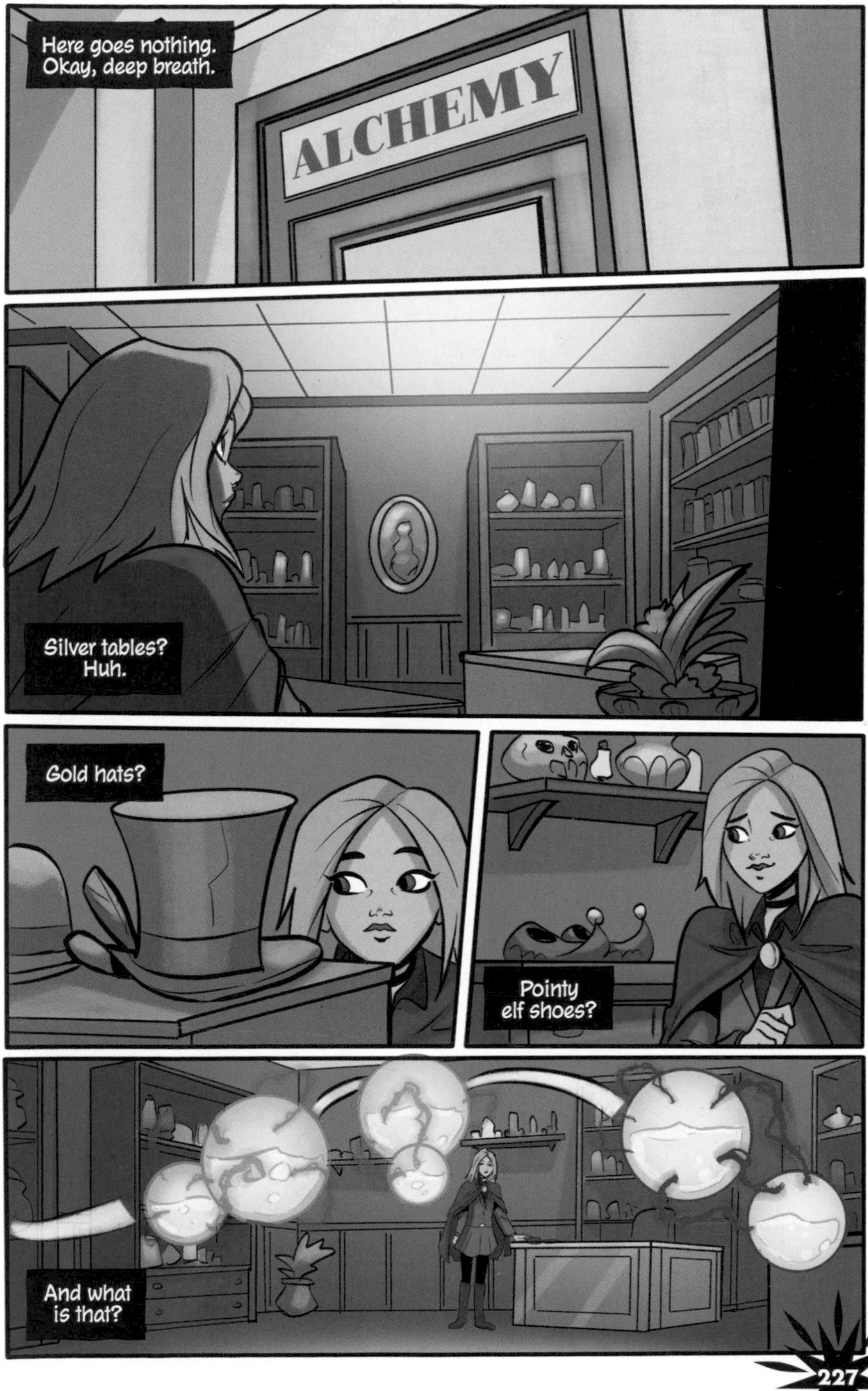
Here goes nothing. Okay, deep breath.
ALCHEMY
Silver tables? Huh.
Gold hats?
Pointy elf shoes?
And what is that?

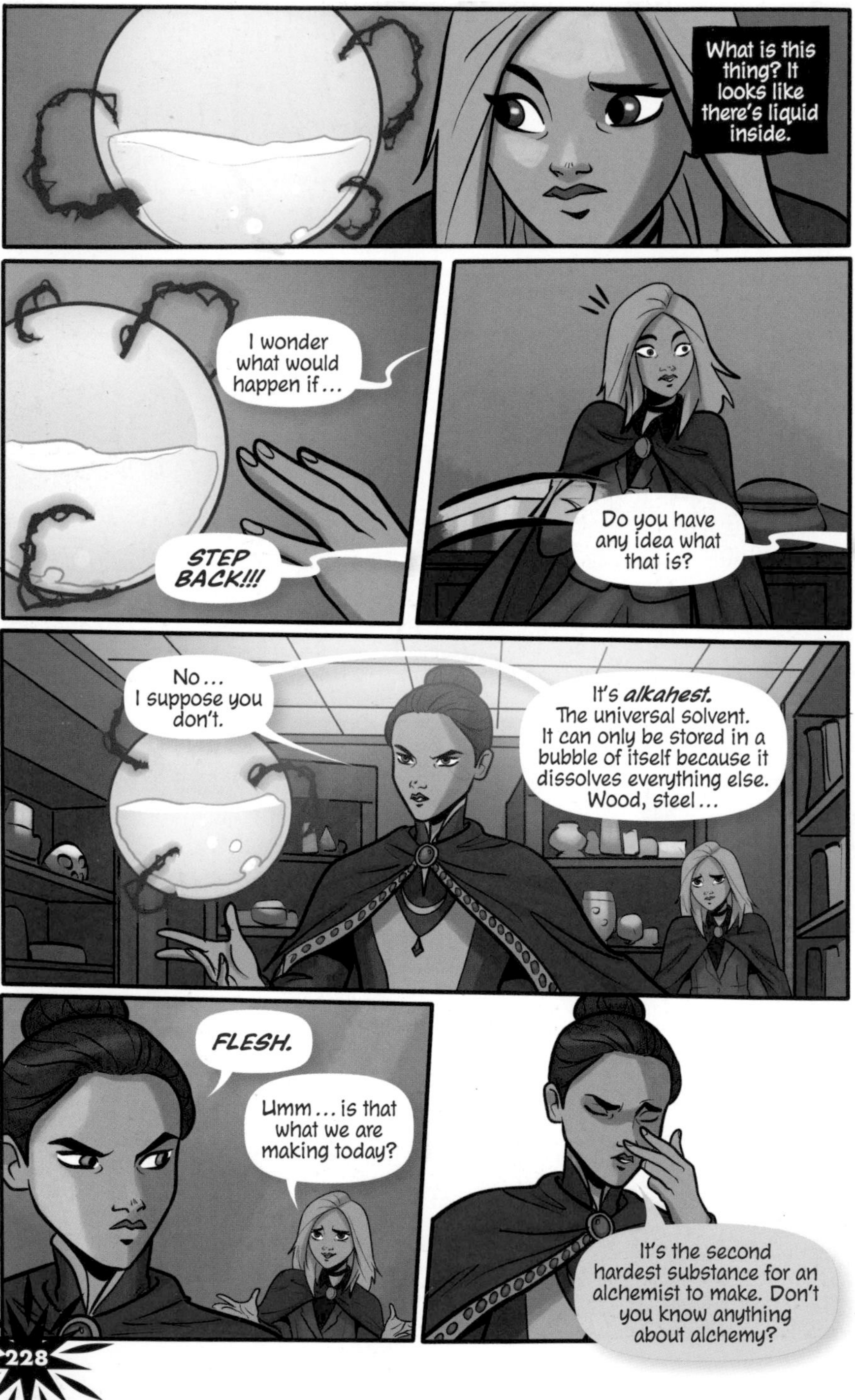
What is this thing? It looks like there's liquid inside.
I wonder what would happen if...
STEP BACK!!!
Do you have any idea what that is?
No... I suppose you don't.
It's *alkahest.* The universal solvent. It can only be stored in a bubble of itself because it dissolves everything else. Wood, steel...
FLESH.
Umm... is that what we are making today?
It's the second hardest substance for an alchemist to make. Don't you know anything about alchemy?

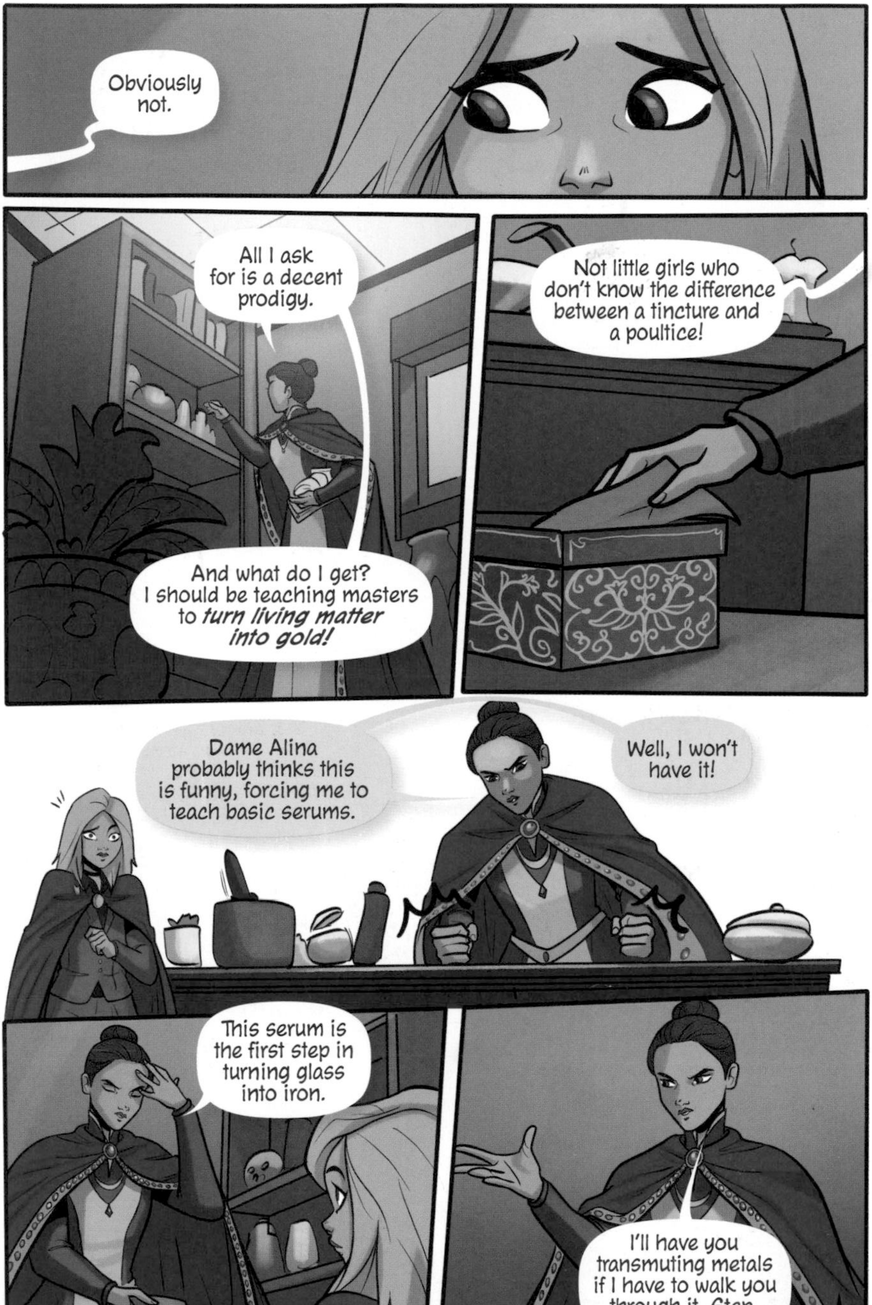
Obviously not.
All I ask for is a decent prodigy.
And what do I get? I should be teaching masters to *turn living matter into gold!*
Not little girls who don't know the difference between a tincture and a poultice!
Dame Alina probably thinks this is funny, forcing me to teach basic serums.
Well, I won't have it!
This serum is the first step in turning glass into iron.
I'll have you transmuting metals if I have to walk you through it. Step. By. Step.

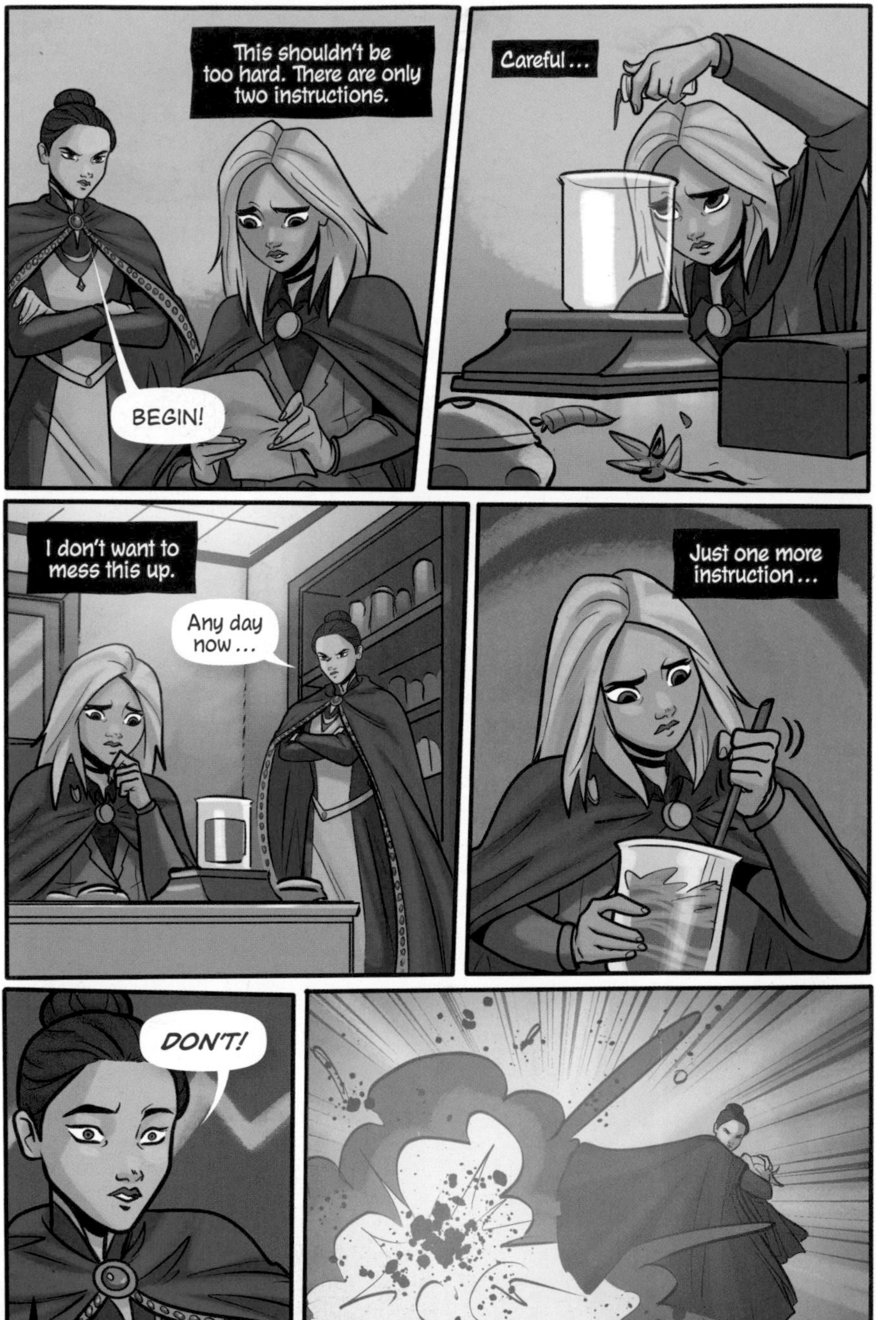
This shouldn't be too hard. There are only two instructions.
BEGIN!
Careful...
I don't want to mess this up.
Any day now...
Just one more instruction...
DON'T!

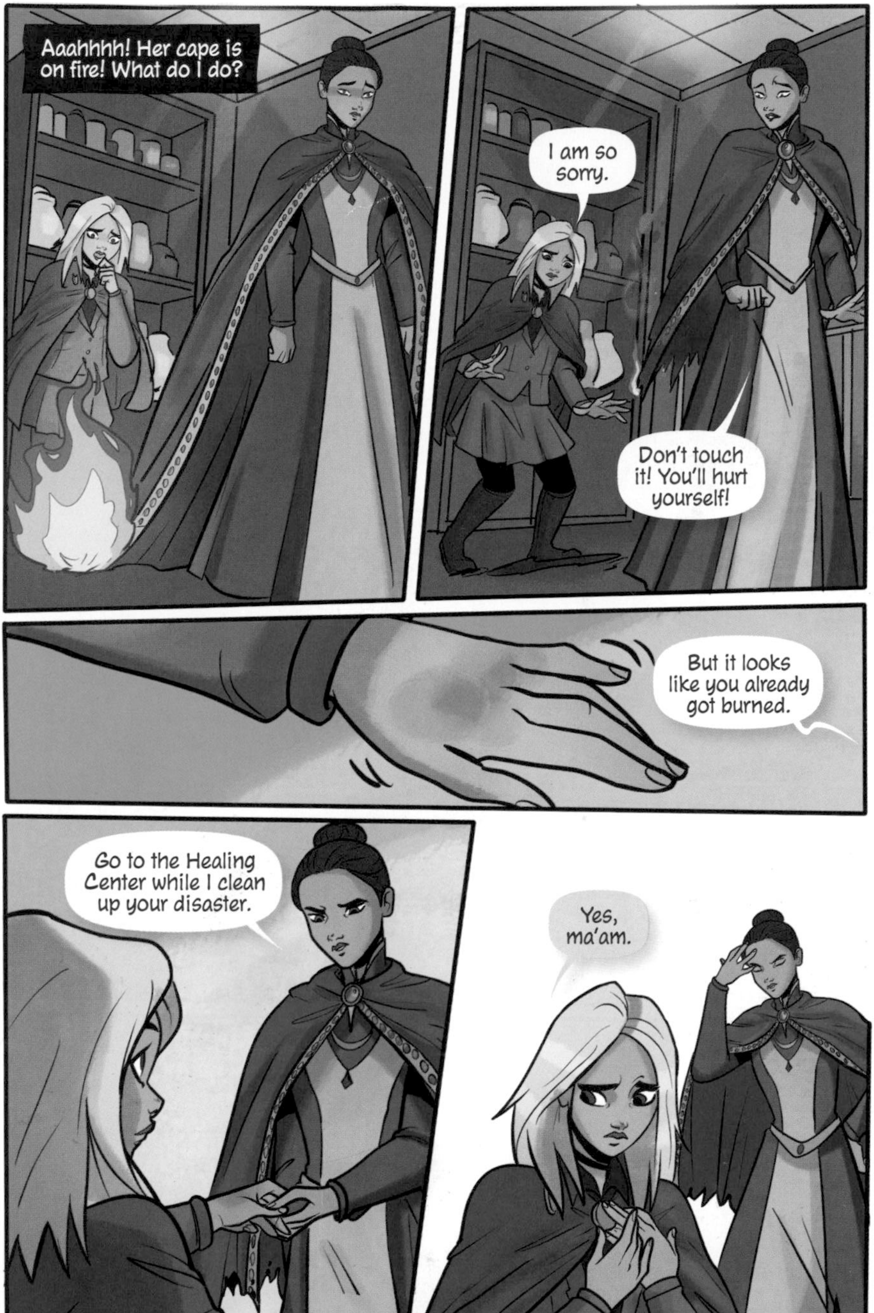
Aaahhhh! Her cape is on fire! What do I do?
I am so sorry.
Don't touch it! You'll hurt yourself!
But it looks like you already got burned.
Go to the Healing Center while I clean up your disaster.
Yes, ma'am.

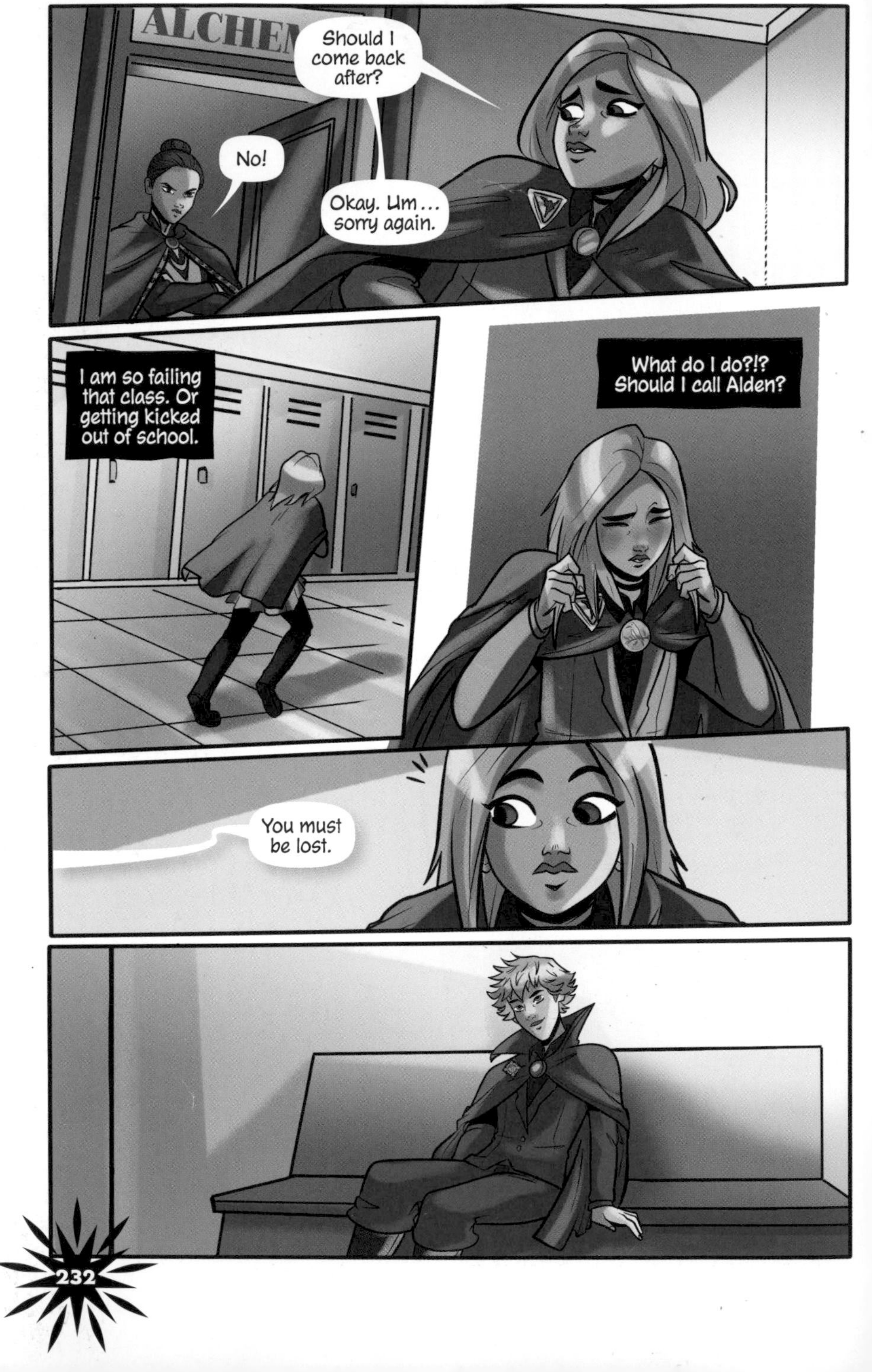
ALCHEM
Should I come back after?
No!
Okay. Um... sorry again.
I am so failing that class. Or getting kicked out of school.
What do I do?!? Should I call Alden?
You must be lost.

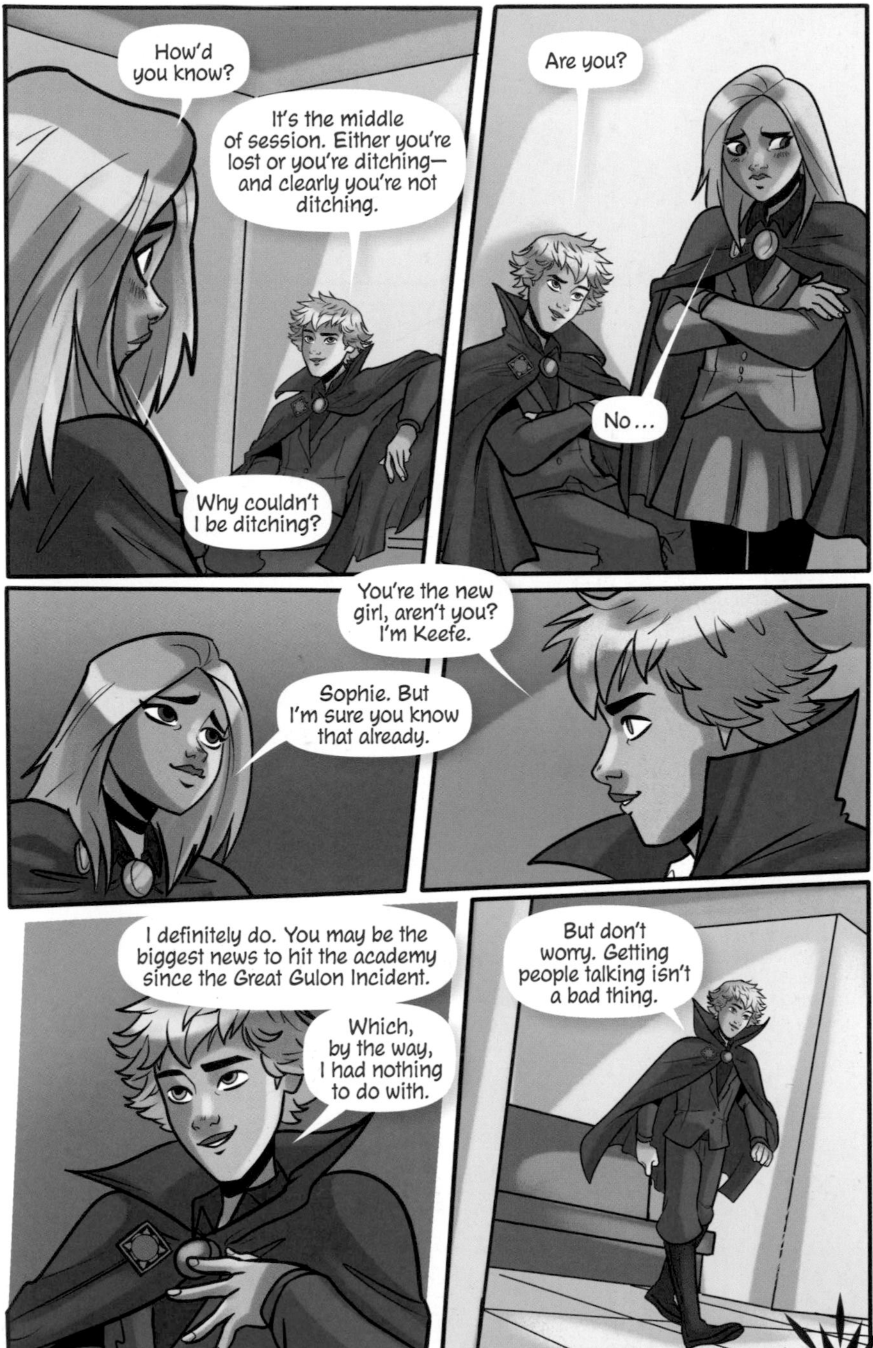
How'd you know?
It's the middle of session. Either you're lost or you're ditching—and clearly you're not ditching.
Why couldn't I be ditching?
Are you?
No...
You're the new girl, aren't you? I'm Keefe.
Sophie. But I'm sure you know that already.
I definitely do. You may be the biggest news to hit the academy since the Great Gulon Incident.
Which, by the way, I had nothing to do with.
But don't worry. Getting people talking isn't a bad thing.

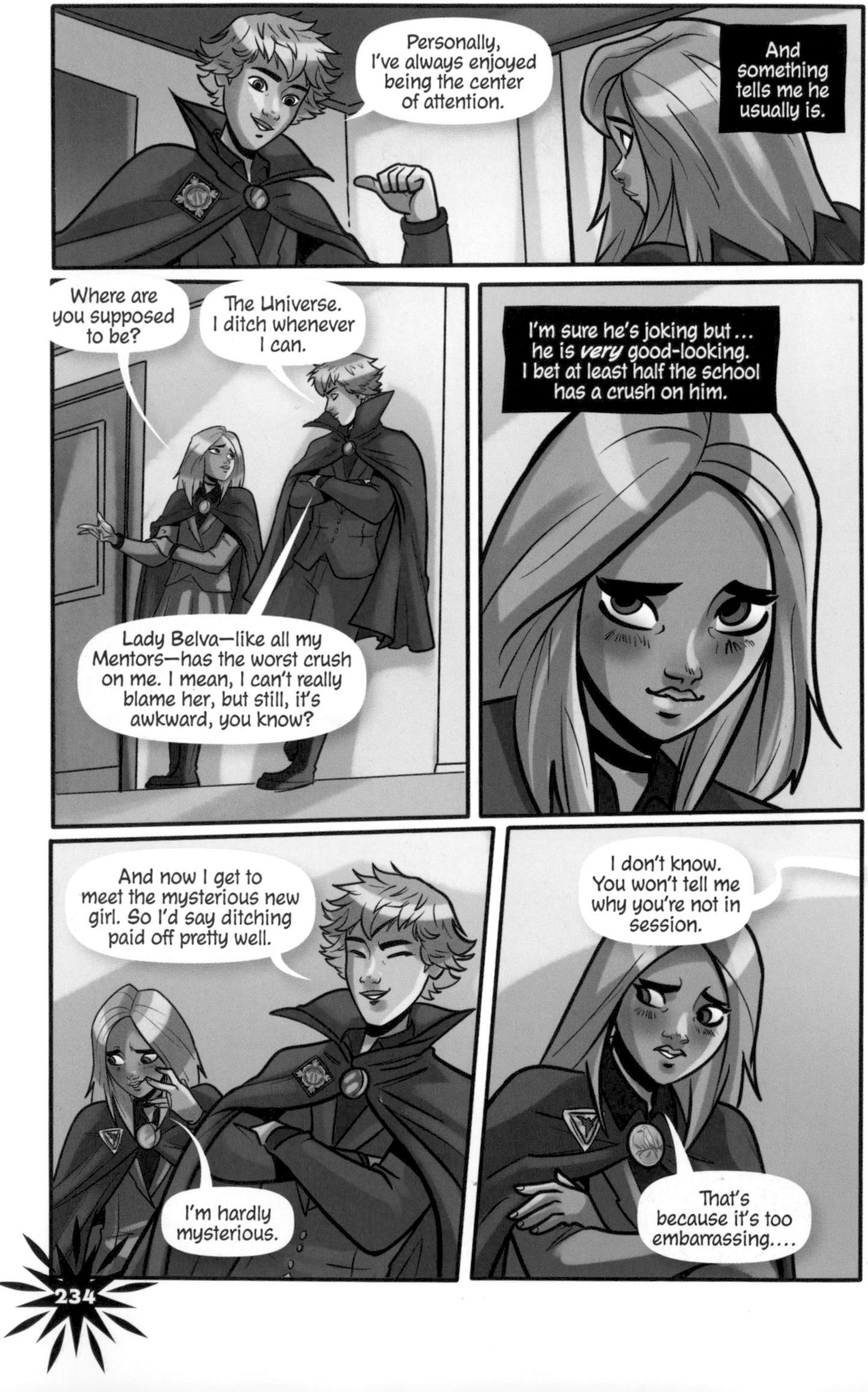

Personally, I've always enjoyed being the center of attention.
And something tells me he usually is.
Where are you supposed to be?
The Universe. I ditch whenever I can.
Lady Belva—like all my Mentors—has the worst crush on me. I mean, I can't really blame her, but still, it's awkward, you know?
I'm sure he's joking but… he is *very* good-looking. I bet at least half the school has a crush on him.
And now I get to meet the mysterious new girl. So I'd say ditching paid off pretty well.
I'm hardly mysterious.
I don't know. You won't tell me why you're not in session.
That's because it's too embarrassing….

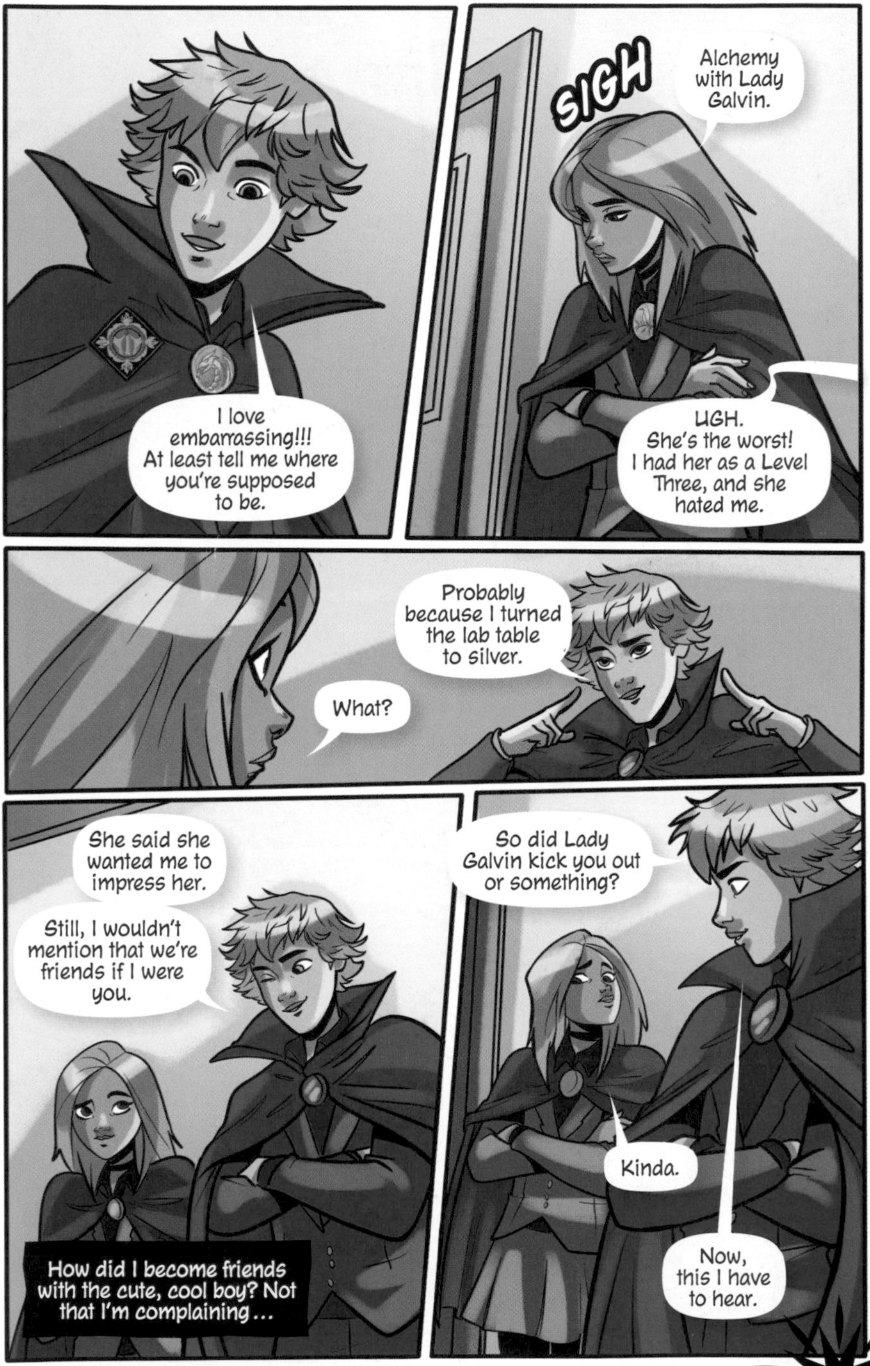
I love embarrassing!!! At least tell me where you're supposed to be.
SIGH
Alchemy with Lady Galvin.
UGH. She's the worst! I had her as a Level Three, and she hated me.
Probably because I turned the lab table to silver.
What?
She said she wanted me to impress her.
Still, I wouldn't mention that we're friends if I were you.
How did I become friends with the cute, cool boy? Not that I'm complaining…
So did Lady Galvin kick you out or something?
Kinda.
Now, this I have to hear.

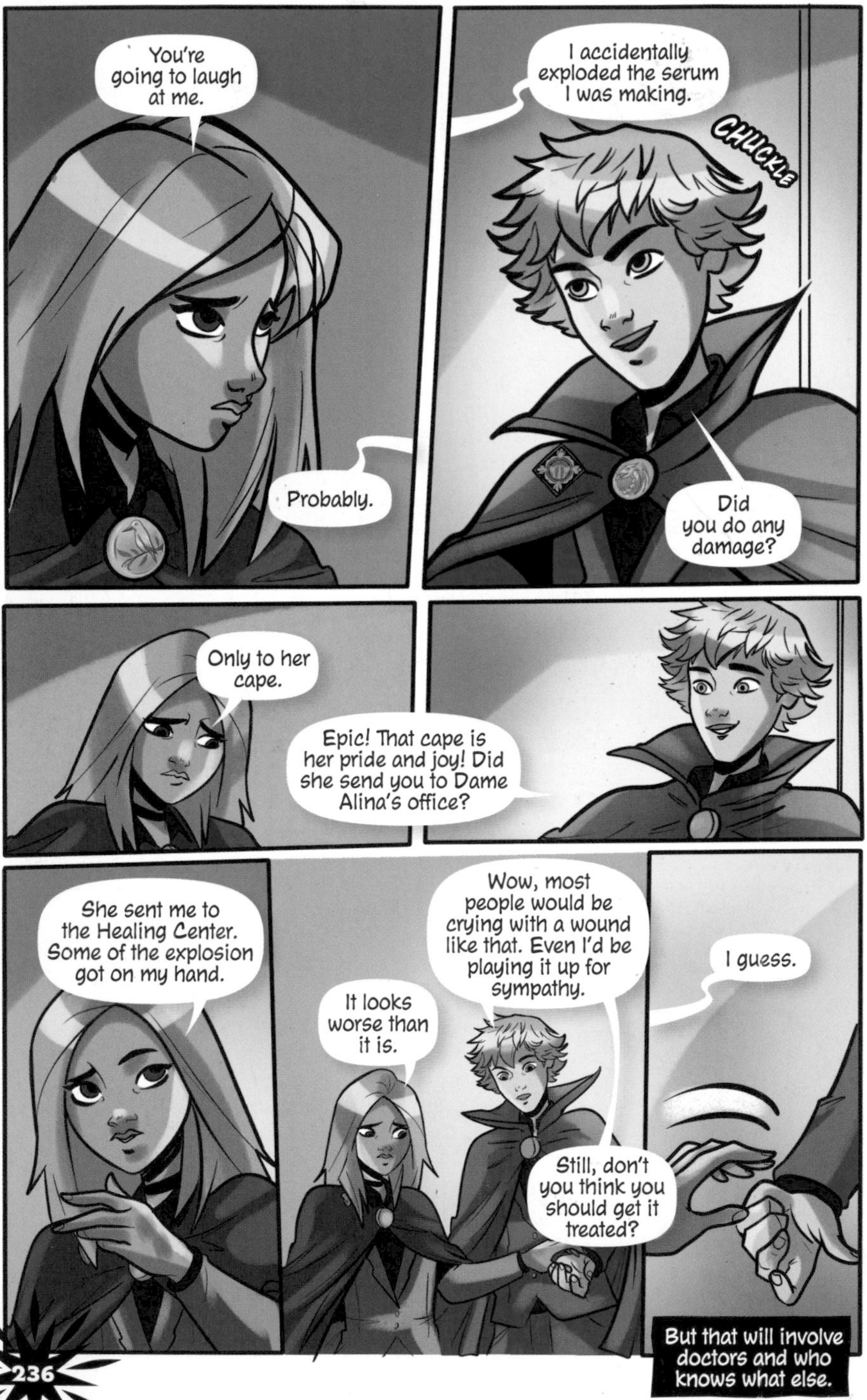
You're going to laugh at me.
I accidentally exploded the serum I was making.
CHUCKLE
Probably.
Did you do any damage?
Only to her cape.
Epic! That cape is her pride and joy! Did she send you to Dame Alina's office?
She sent me to the Healing Center. Some of the explosion got on my hand.
It looks worse than it is.
Wow, most people would be crying with a wound like that. Even I'd be playing it up for sympathy.
Still, don't you think you should get it treated?
I guess.
But that will involve doctors and who knows what else.

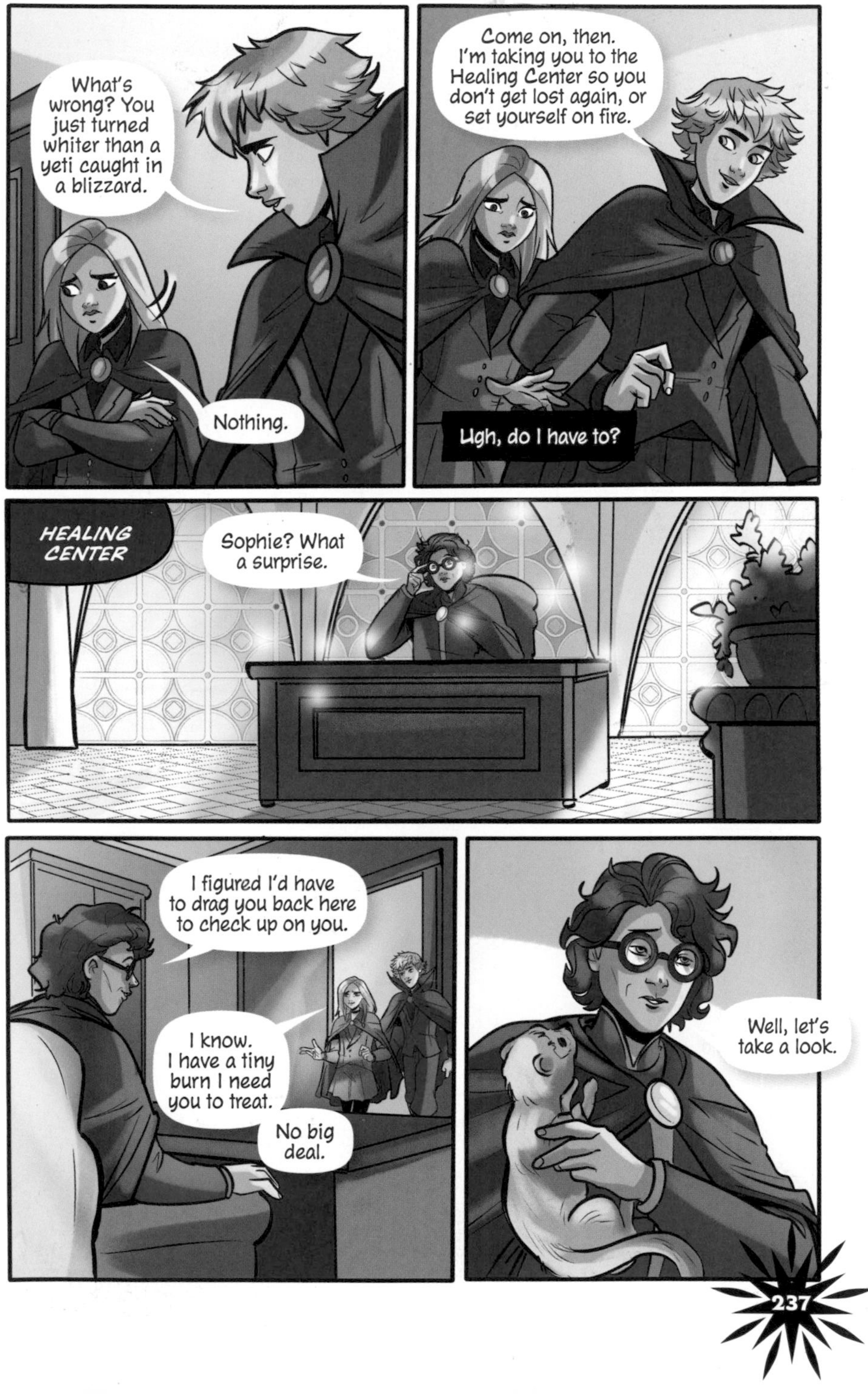

What's wrong? You just turned whiter than a yeti caught in a blizzard.
Nothing.
Come on, then. I'm taking you to the Healing Center so you don't get lost again, or set yourself on fire.
Ugh, do I have to?
HEALING CENTER
Sophie? What a surprise.
I figured I'd have to drag you back here to check up on you.
I know. I have a tiny burn I need you to treat.
No big deal.
Well, let's take a look.

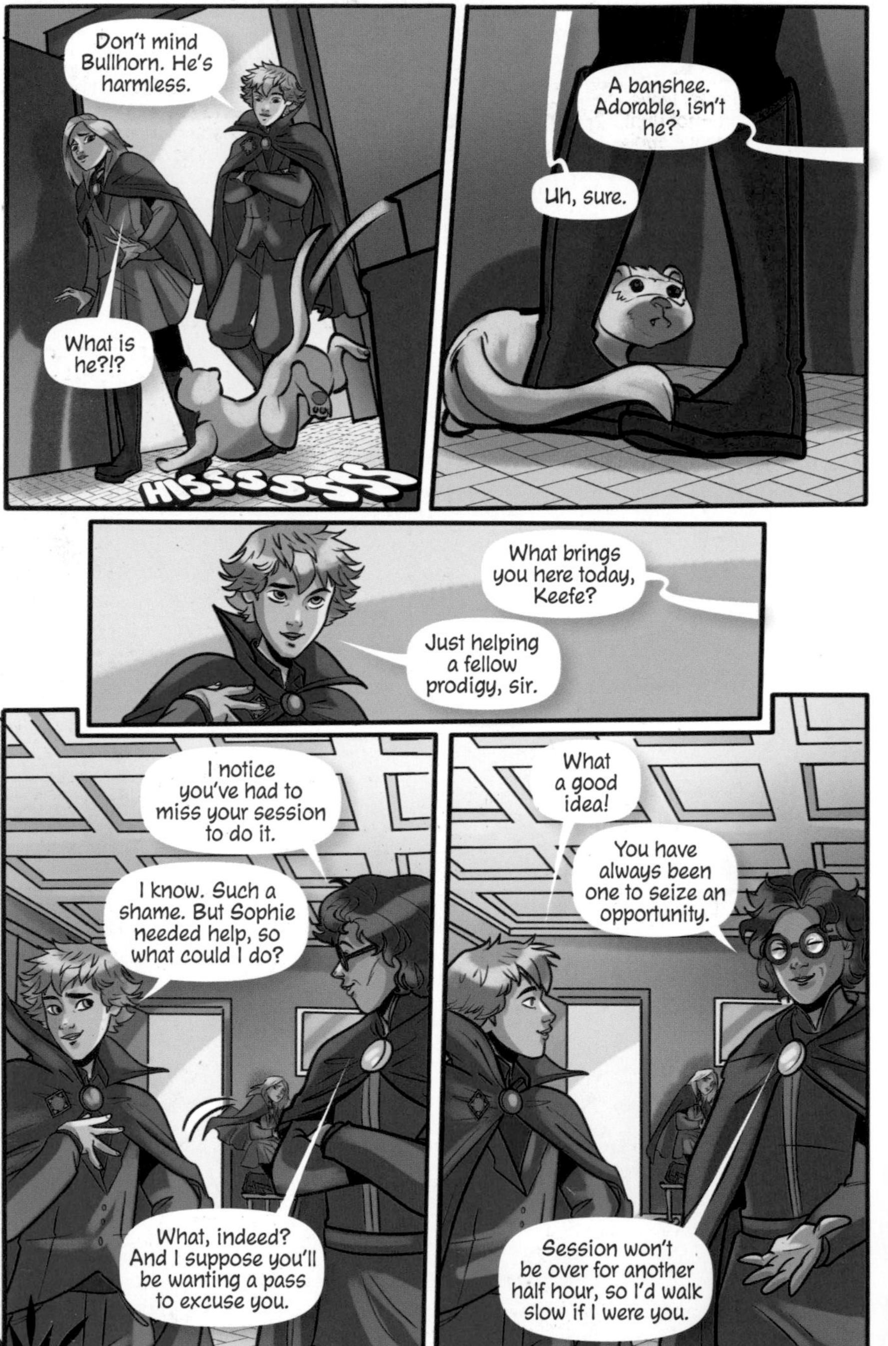
Don't mind Bullhorn. He's harmless.
What is he?!?
HISSSSSSS
A banshee. Adorable, isn't he?
Uh, sure.
What brings you here today, Keefe?
Just helping a fellow prodigy, sir.
I notice you've had to miss your session to do it.
I know. Such a shame. But Sophie needed help, so what could I do?
What, indeed? And I suppose you'll be wanting a pass to excuse you.
What a good idea!
You have always been one to seize an opportunity.
Session won't be over for another half hour, so I'd walk slow if I were you.

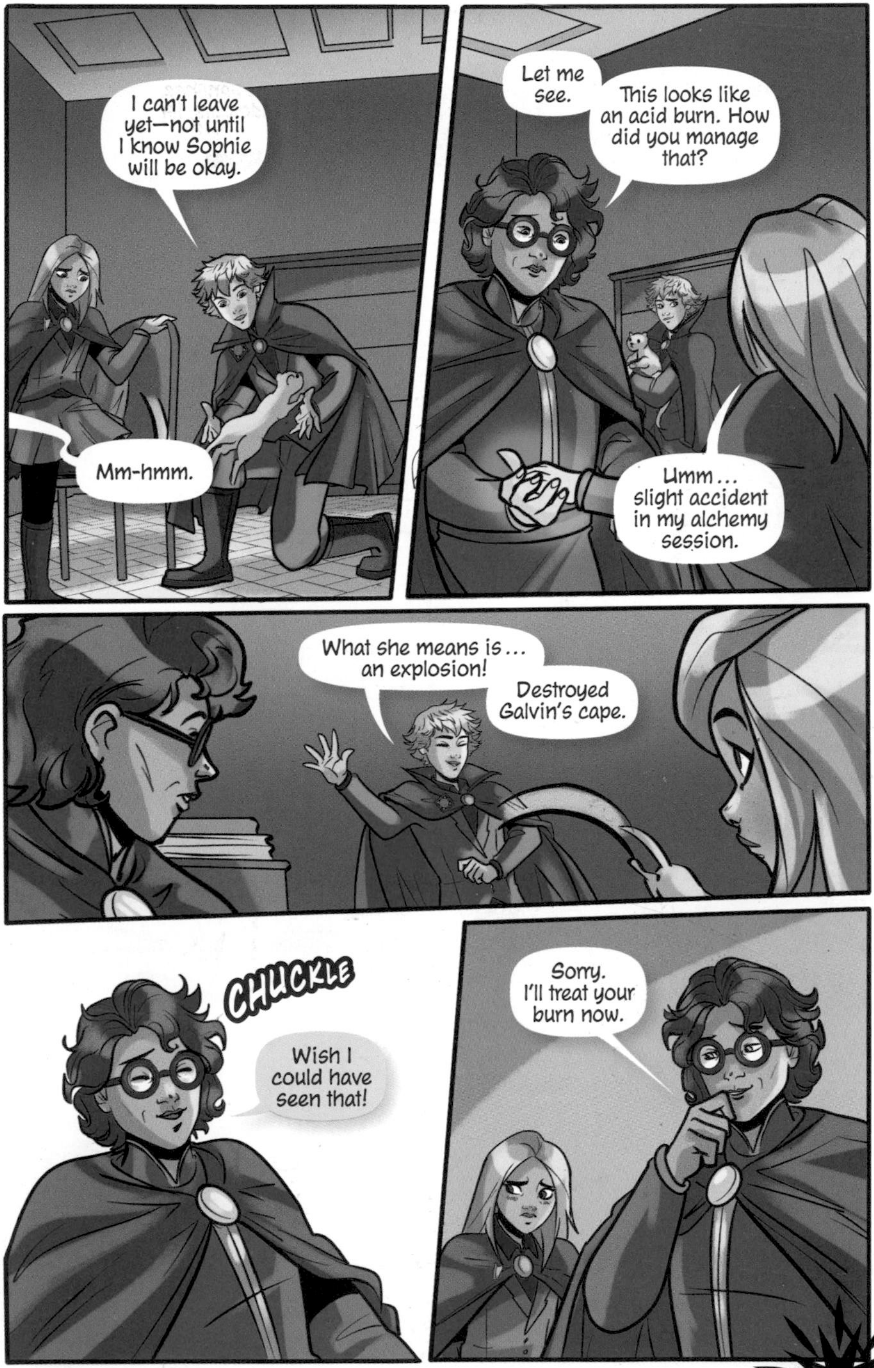
I can't leave yet—not until I know Sophie will be okay.
Mm-hmm.
Let me see.
This looks like an acid burn. How did you manage that?
Umm… slight accident in my alchemy session.
What she means is… an explosion!
Destroyed Galvin's cape.
CHUCKLE
Wish I could have seen that!
Sorry. I'll treat your burn now.

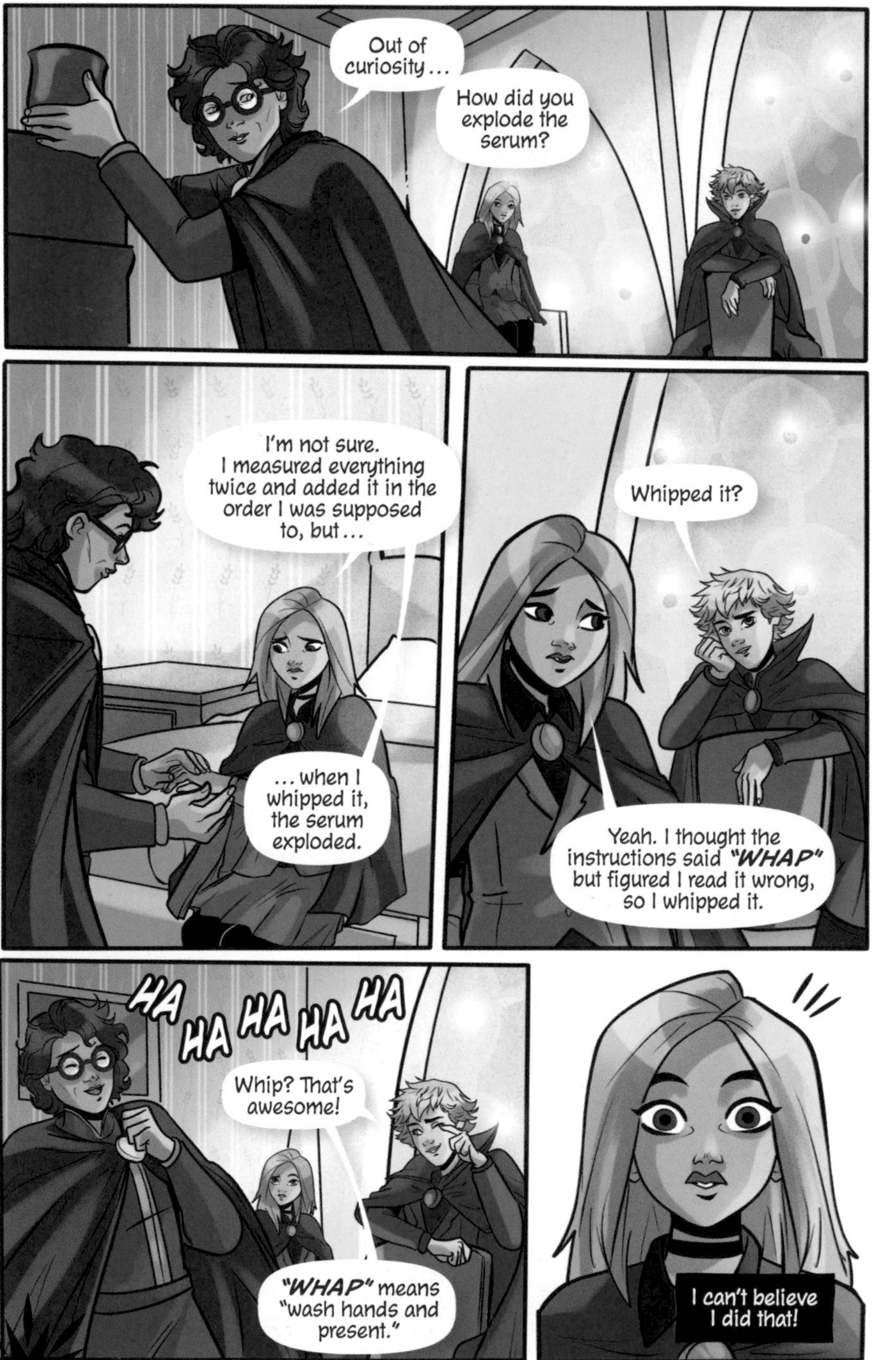
Out of curiosity . . .
How did you explode the serum?
I'm not sure. I measured everything twice and added it in the order I was supposed to, but . . .
. . . when I whipped it, the serum exploded.
Whipped it?
Yeah. I thought the instructions said "WHAP" but figured I read it wrong, so I whipped it.
HA HA HA HA HA
Whip? That's awesome!
"WHAP" means "wash hands and present."
I can't believe I did that!

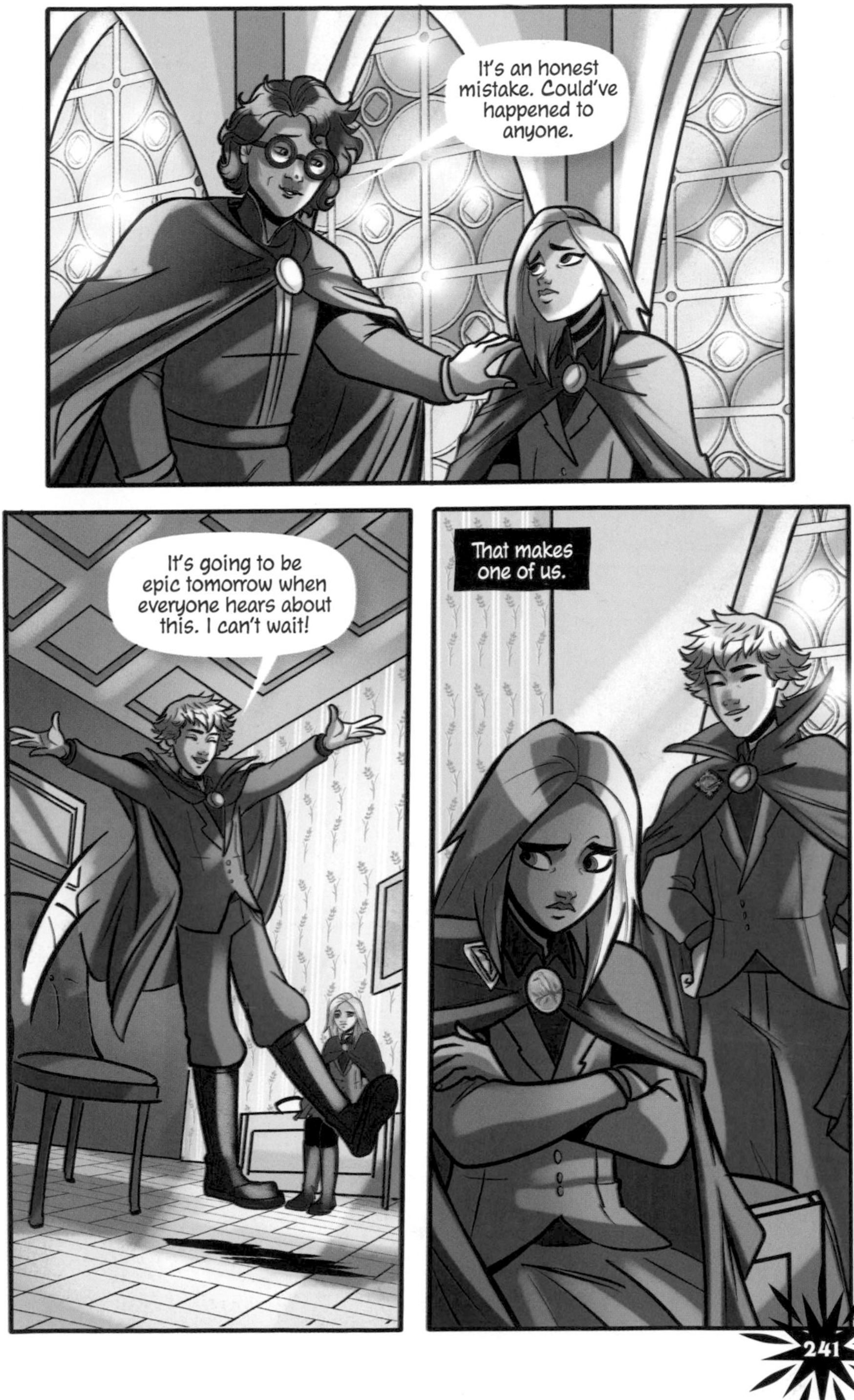
It's an honest mistake. Could've happened to anyone.
It's going to be epic tomorrow when everyone hears about this. I can't wait!
That makes one of us.

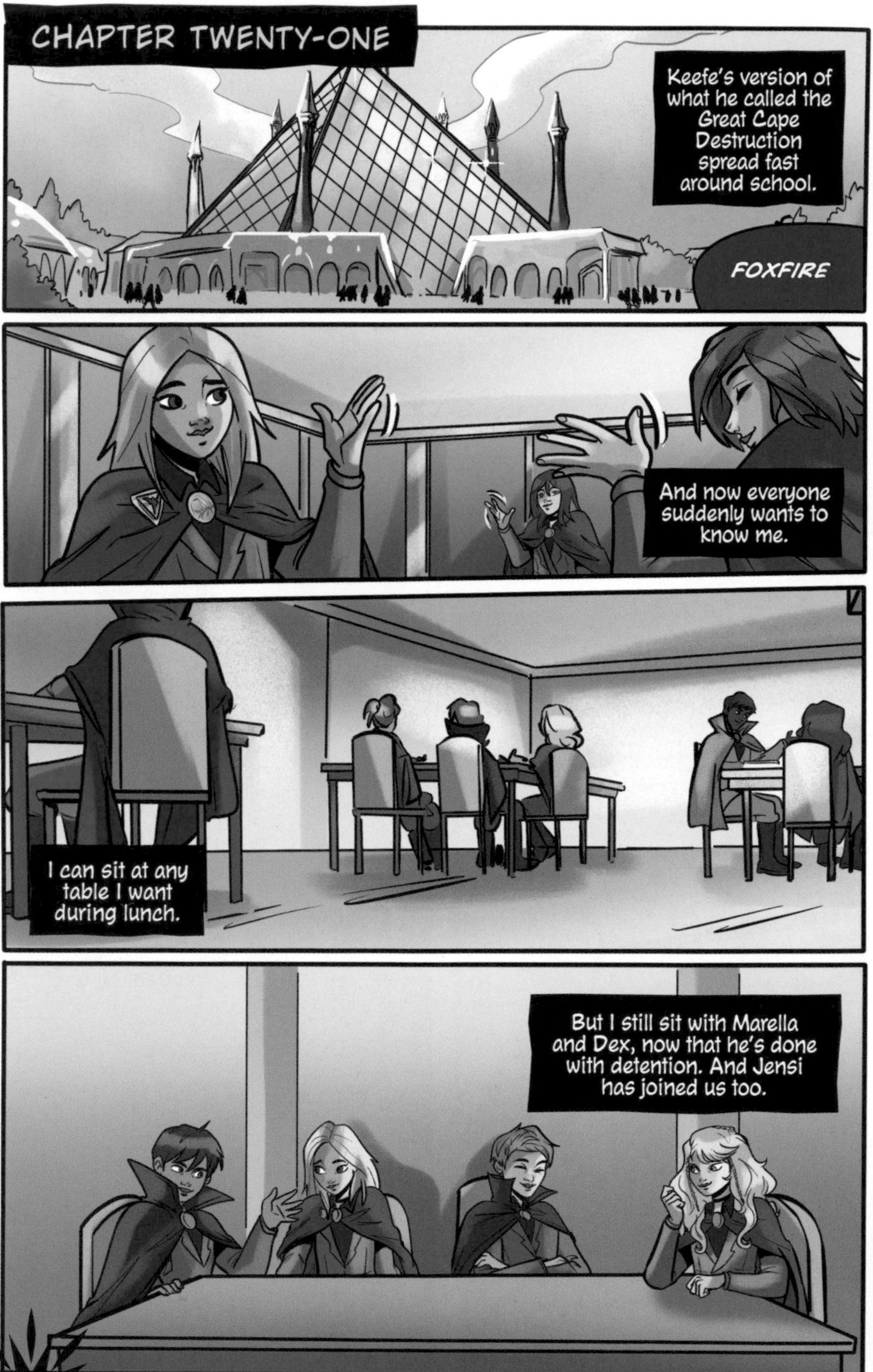
CHAPTER TWENTY-ONE
Keefe's version of what he called the Great Cape Destruction spread fast around school.
FOXFIRE
And now everyone suddenly wants to know me.
I can sit at any table I want during lunch.
But I still sit with Marella and Dex, now that he's done with detention. And Jensi has joined us too.

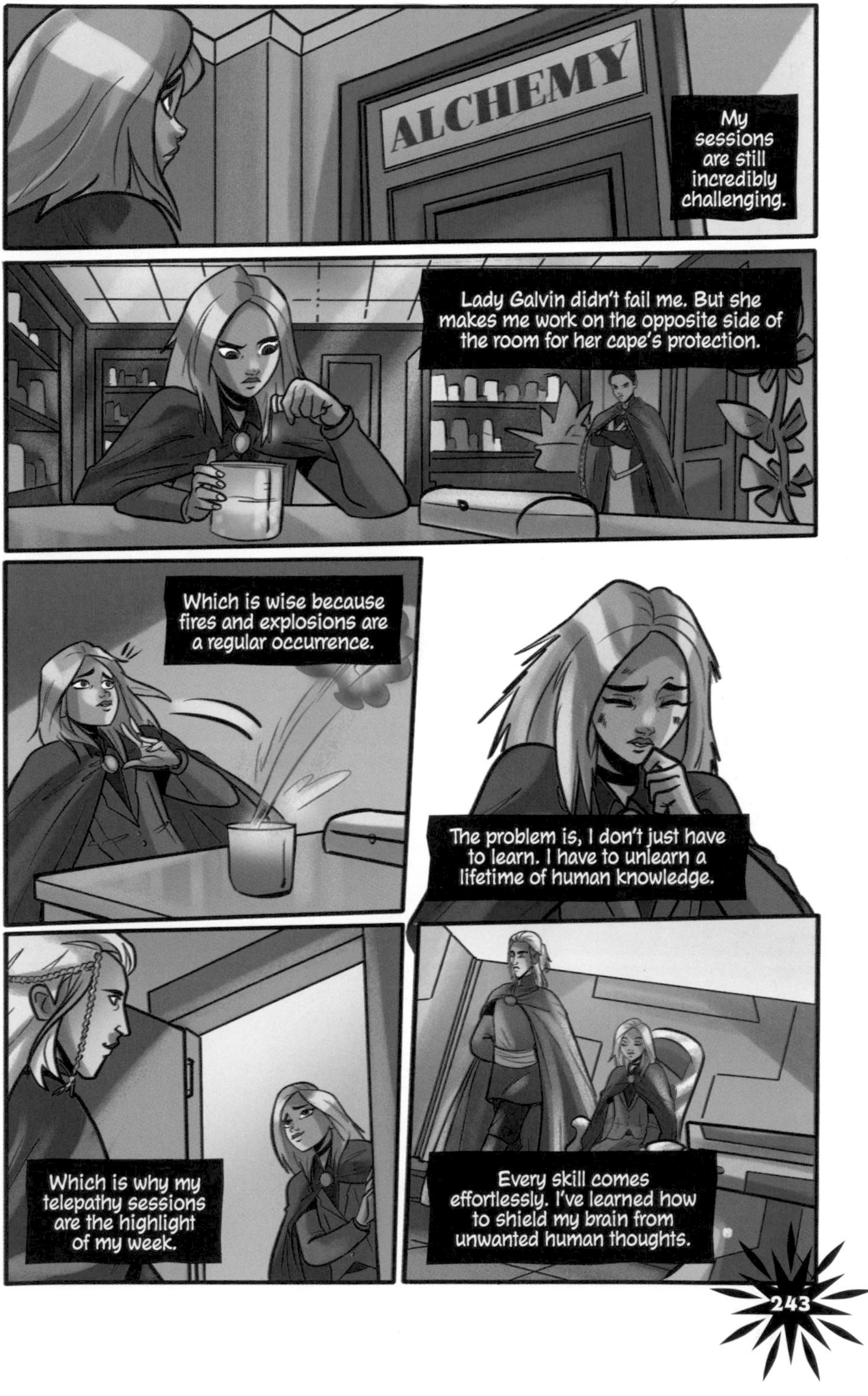
ALCHEMY
My sessions are still incredibly challenging.
Lady Galvin didn't fail me. But she makes me work on the opposite side of the room for her cape's protection.
Which is wise because fires and explosions are a regular occurrence.
The problem is, I don't just have to learn. I have to unlearn a lifetime of human knowledge.
Which is why my telepathy sessions are the highlight of my week.
Every skill comes effortlessly. I've learned how to shield my brain from unwanted human thoughts.

Fitz + Sophie

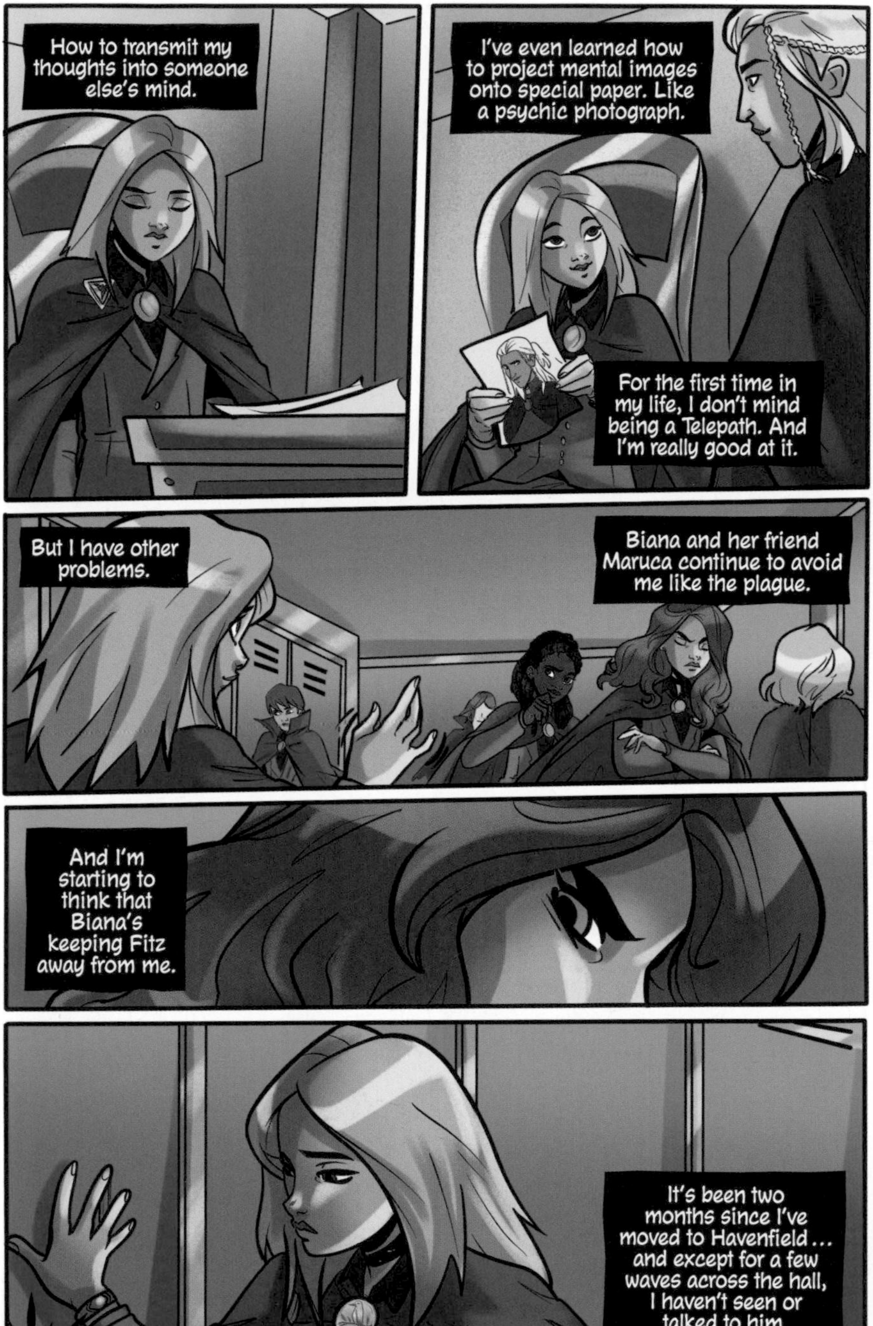
How to transmit my thoughts into someone else's mind.
I've even learned how to project mental images onto special paper. Like a psychic photograph.
For the first time in my life, I don't mind being a Telepath. And I'm really good at it.
But I have other problems.
Biana and her friend Maruca continue to avoid me like the plague.
And I'm starting to think that Biana's keeping Fitz away from me.
It's been two months since I've moved to Havenfield... and except for a few waves across the hall, I haven't seen or talked to him.

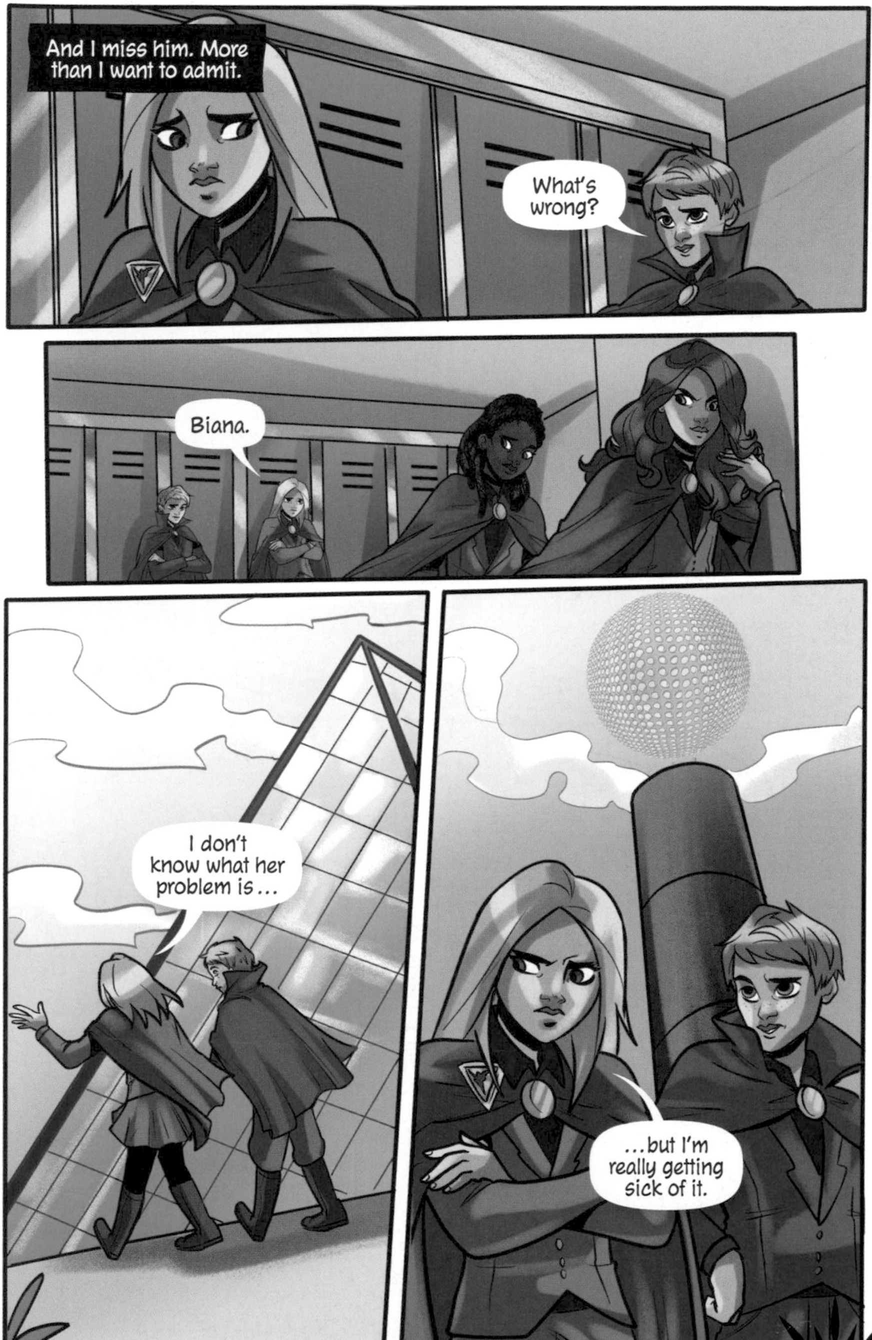

And I miss him. More than I want to admit.
What's wrong?
Biana.
I don't know what her problem is...
...but I'm really getting sick of it.

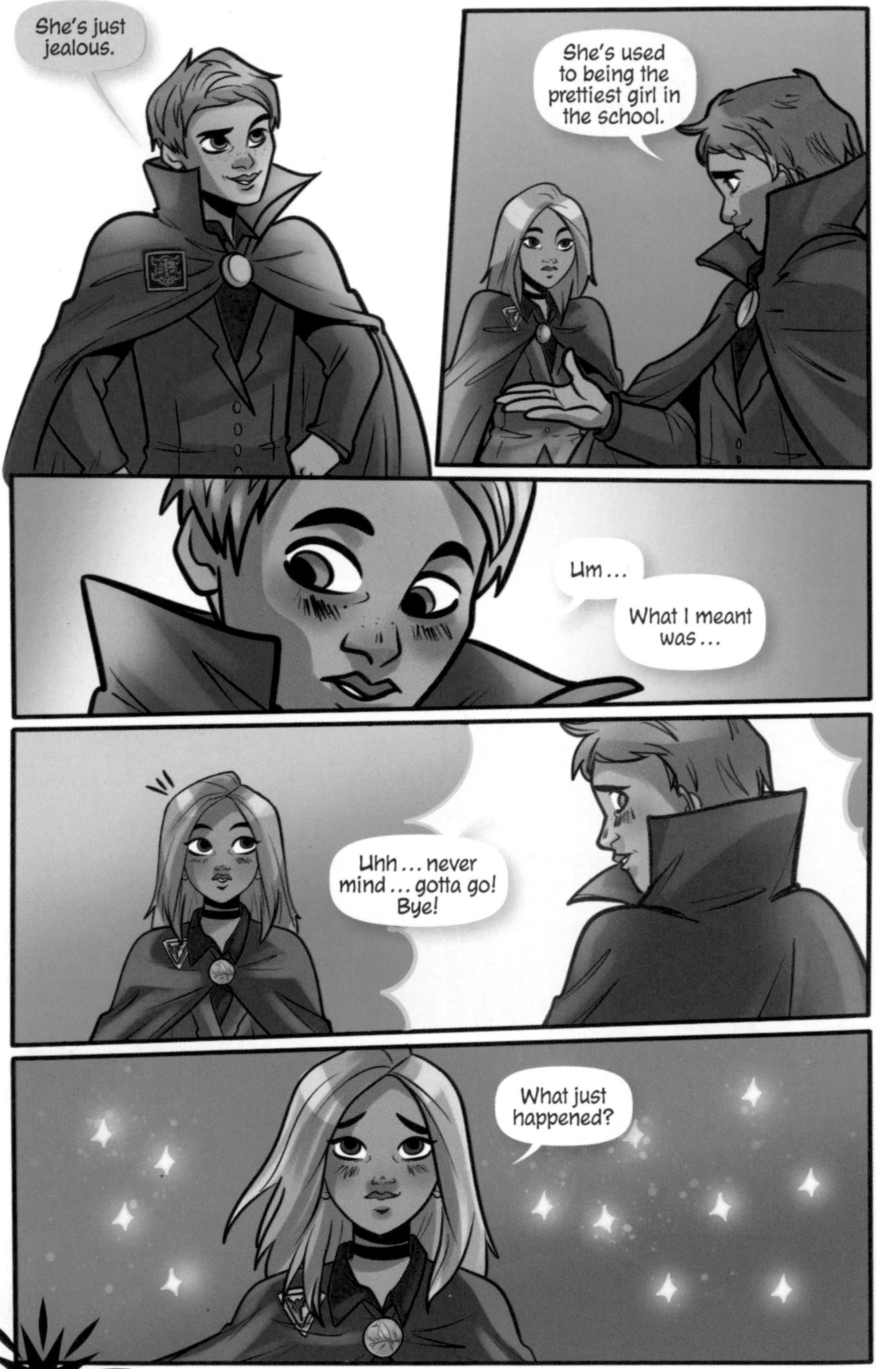
She's just jealous.
She's used to being the prettiest girl in the school.
Um...
What I meant was...
Uhh... never mind... gotta go! Bye!
What just happened?

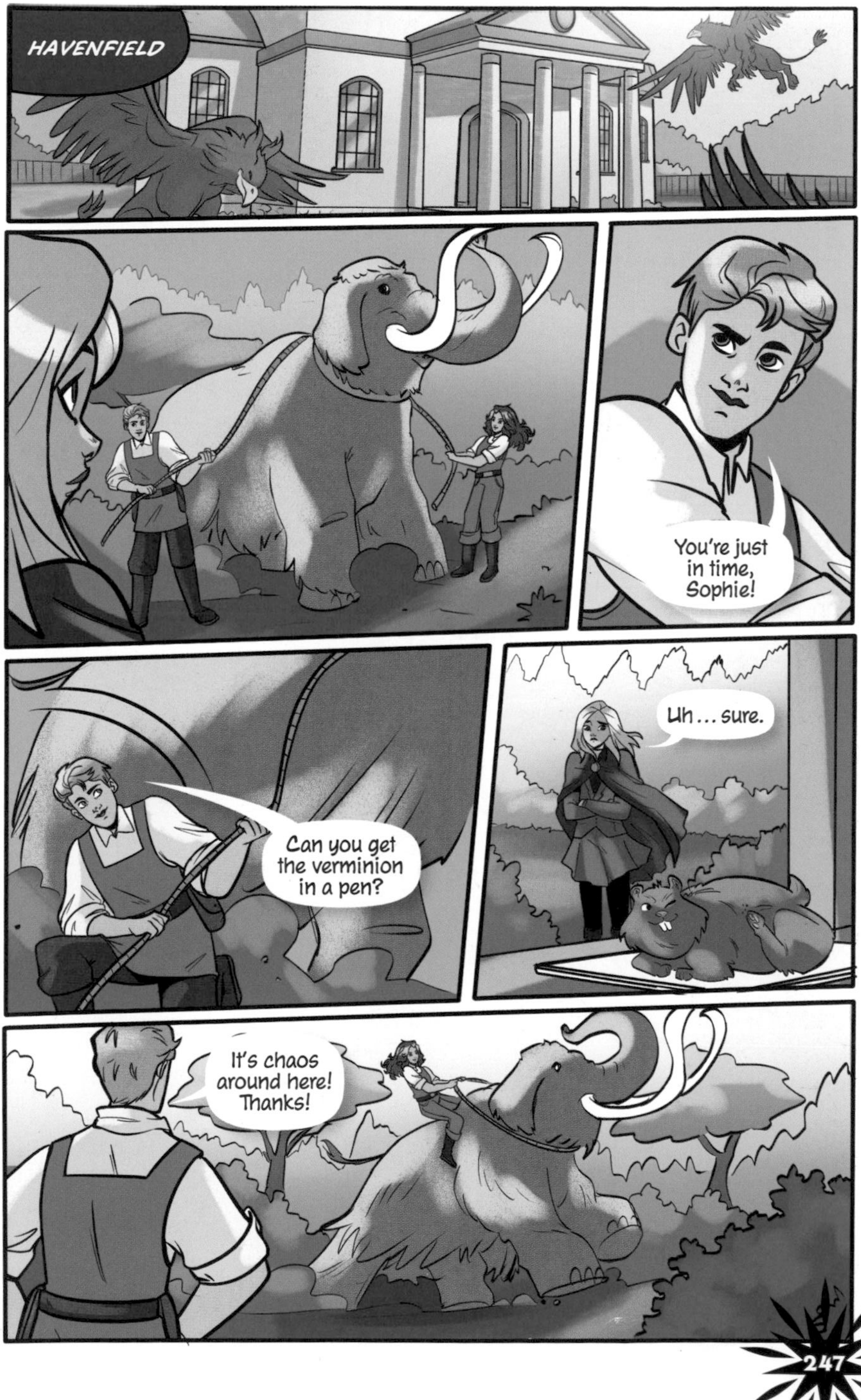
HAVENFIELD
You're just in time, Sophie!
Can you get the verminion in a pen?
Uh... sure.
It's chaos around here! Thanks!

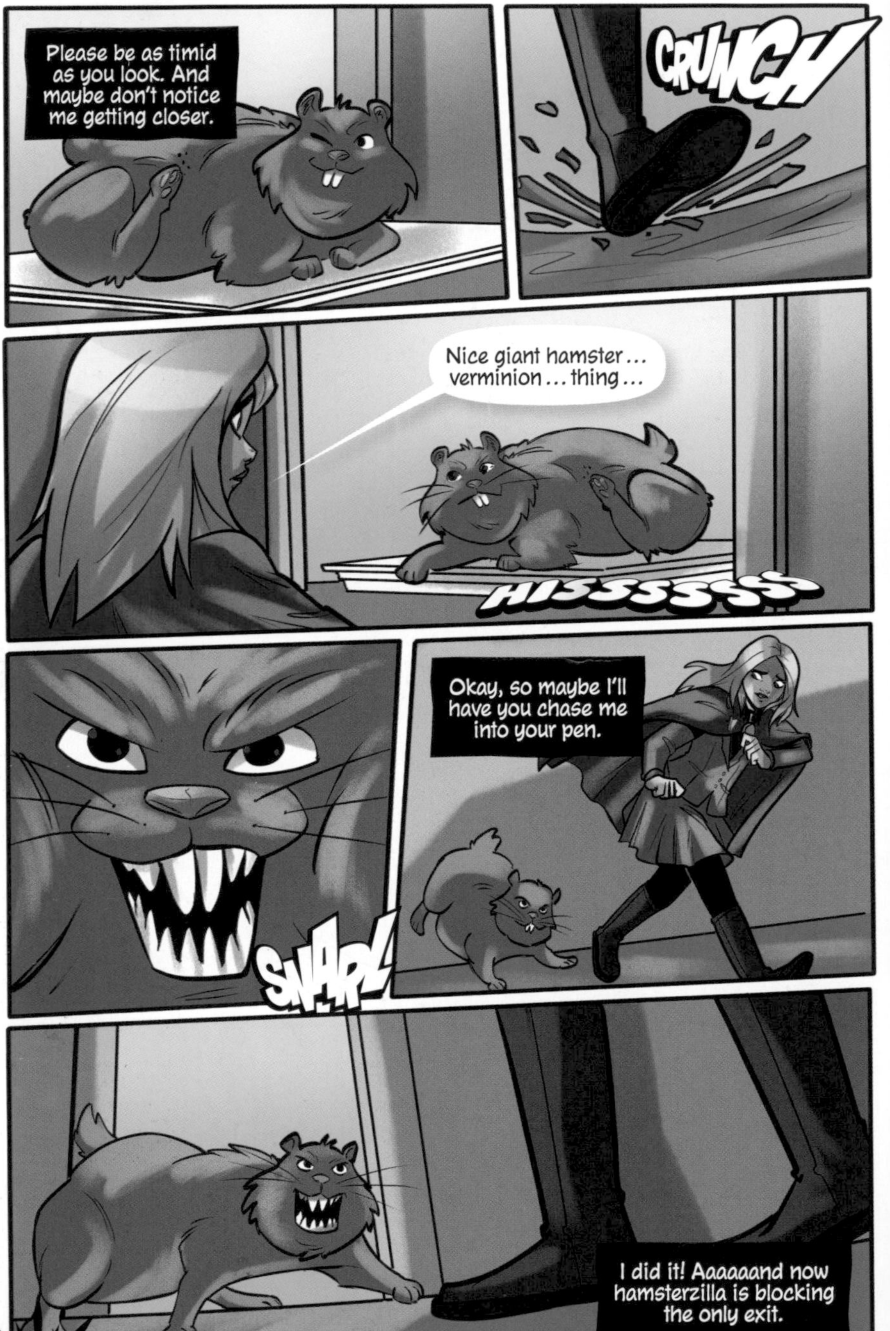

Please be as timid as you look. And maybe don't notice me getting closer.
CRUNCH
Nice giant hamster... verminion... thing...
HISSSSSSS
SNARL
Okay, so maybe I'll have you chase me into your pen.
I did it! Aaaaaand now hamsterzilla is blocking the only exit.

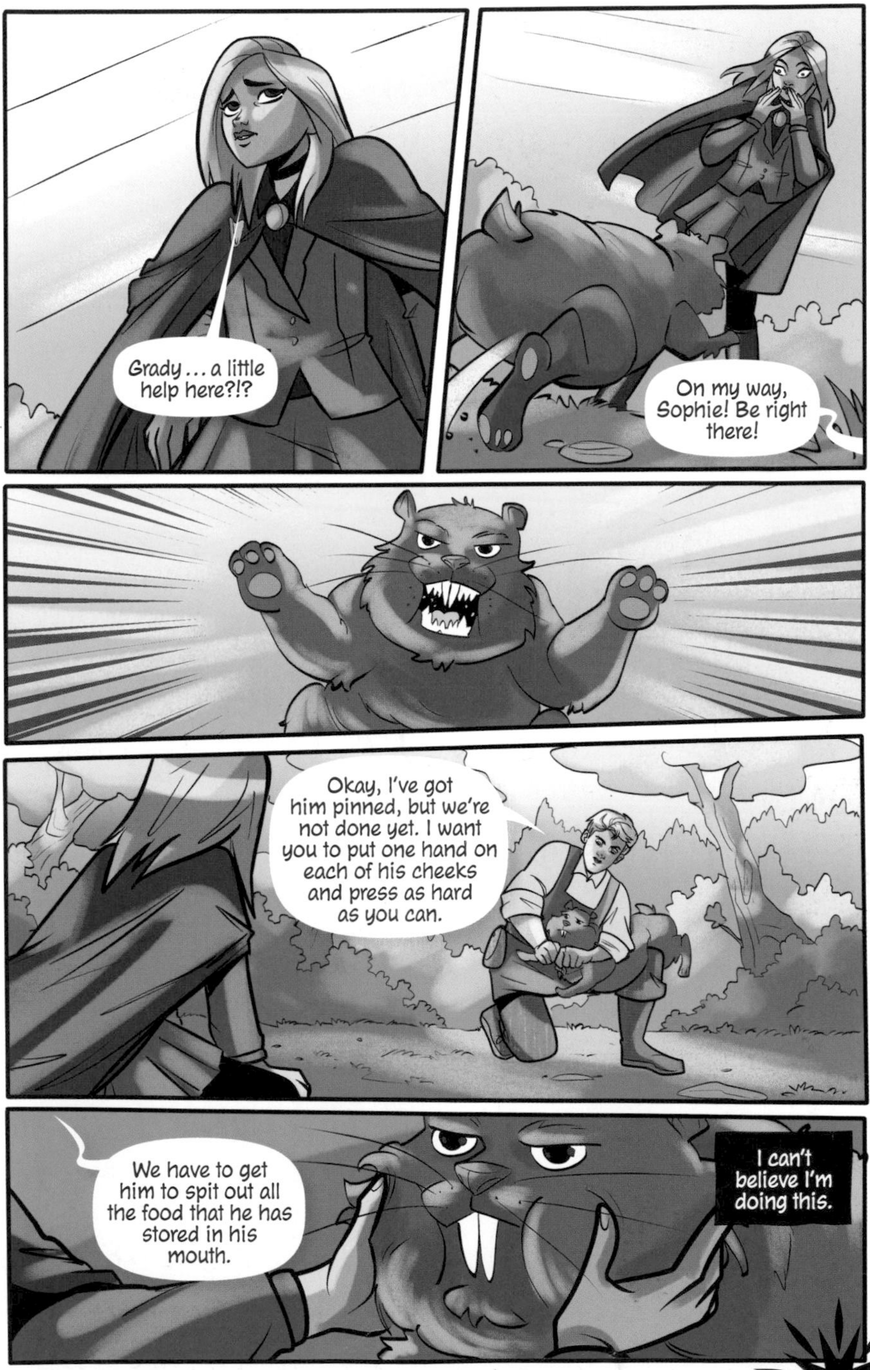
Grady . . . a little help here?!?
On my way, Sophie! Be right there!
Okay, I've got him pinned, but we're not done yet. I want you to put one hand on each of his cheeks and press as hard as you can.
We have to get him to spit out all the food that he has stored in his mouth.
I can't believe I'm doing this.

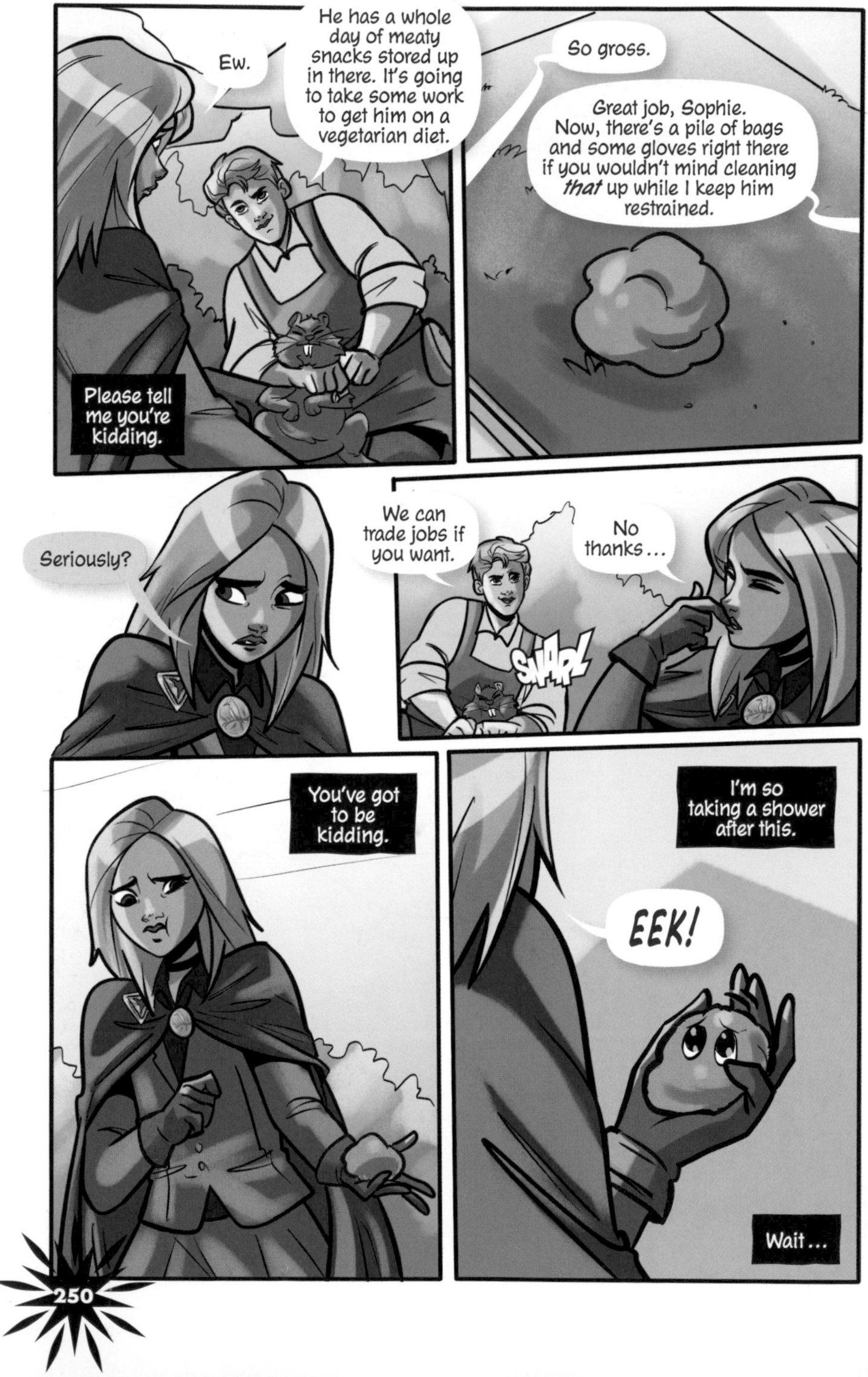
Ew.
He has a whole day of meaty snacks stored up in there. It's going to take some work to get him on a vegetarian diet.
Please tell me you're kidding.
So gross.
Great job, Sophie. Now, there's a pile of bags and some gloves right there if you wouldn't mind cleaning *that* up while I keep him restrained.
Seriously?
We can trade jobs if you want.
No thanks...
SNARL
You've got to be kidding.
I'm so taking a shower after this.
EEK!
Wait...

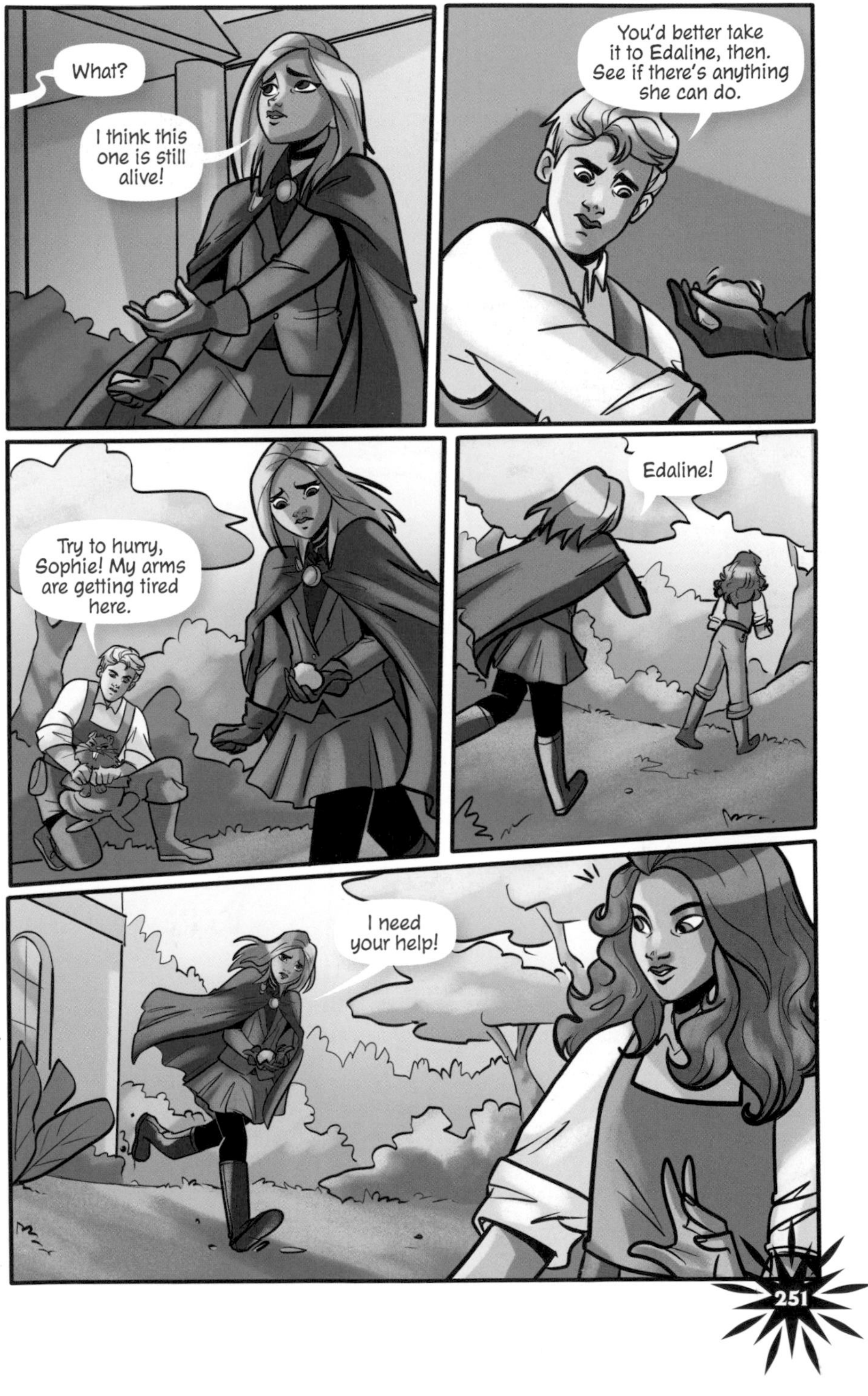
What?
I think this one is still alive!
You'd better take it to Edaline, then. See if there's anything she can do.
Try to hurry, Sophie! My arms are getting tired here.
Edaline!
I need your help!

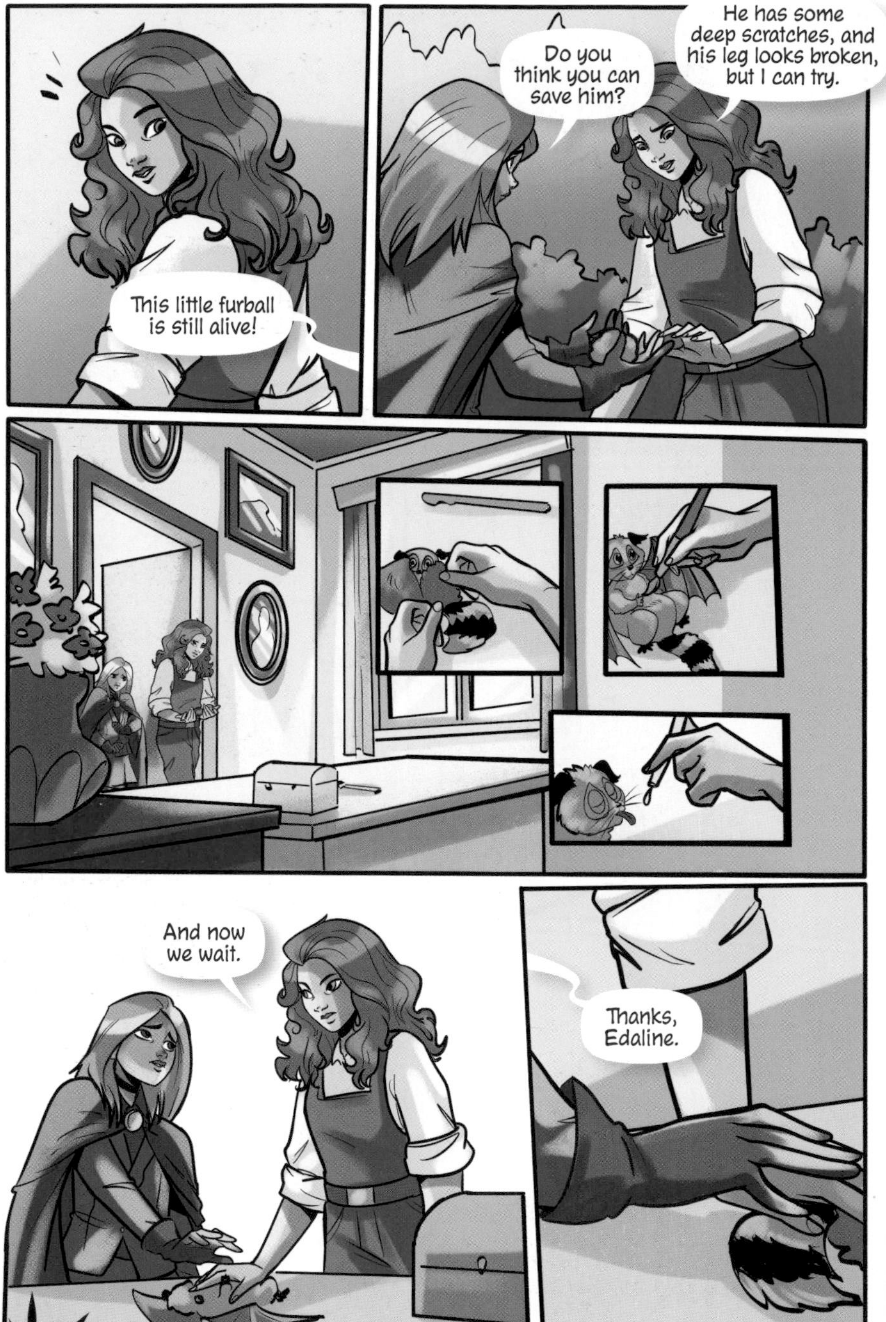
This little furball is still alive!
Do you think you can save him?
He has some deep scratches, and his leg looks broken, but I can try.
And now we wait.
Thanks, Edaline.

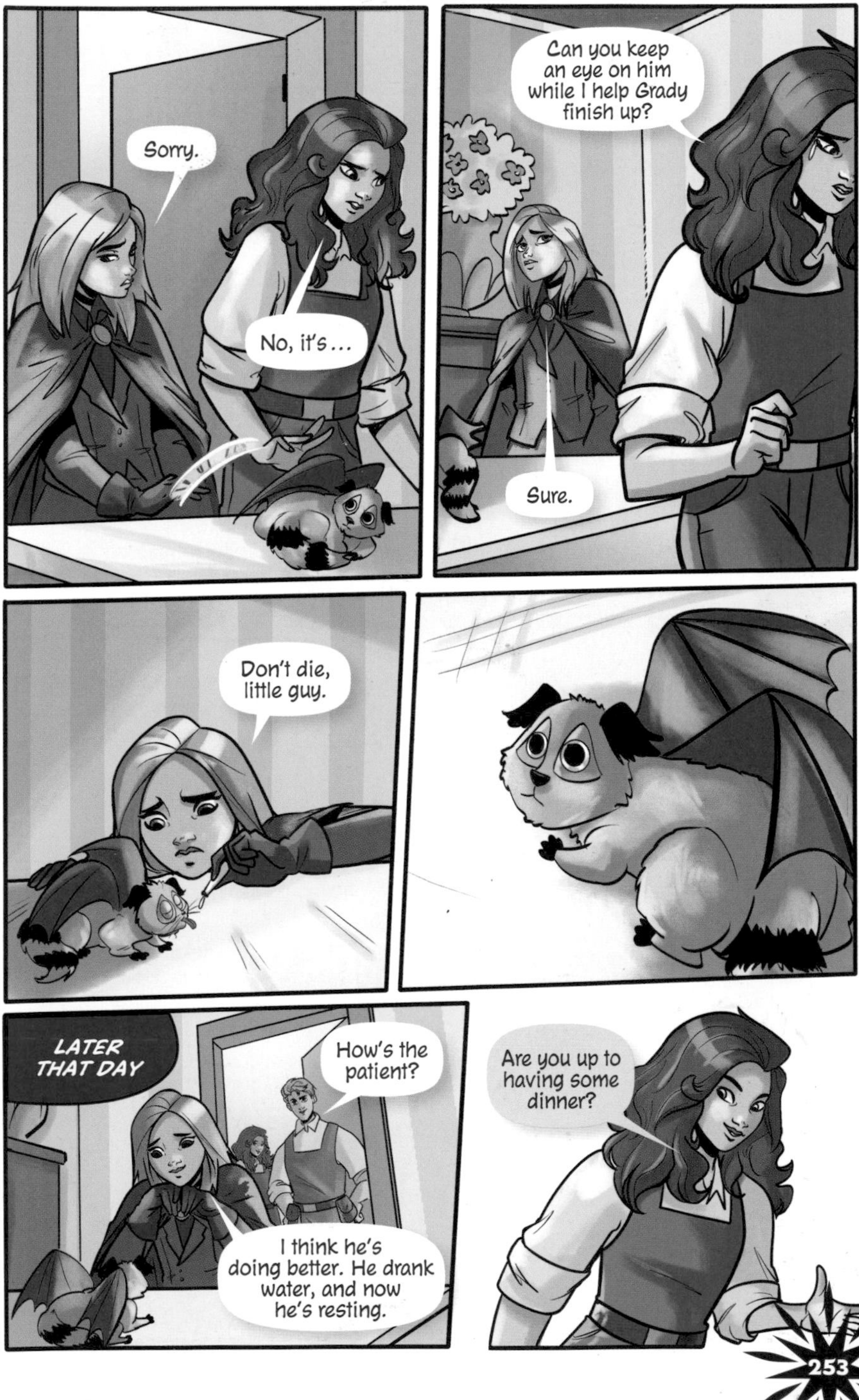
Sorry.
No, it's...
Can you keep an eye on him while I help Grady finish up?
Sure.
Don't die, little guy.
LATER THAT DAY
How's the patient?
I think he's doing better. He drank water, and now he's resting.
Are you up to having some dinner?

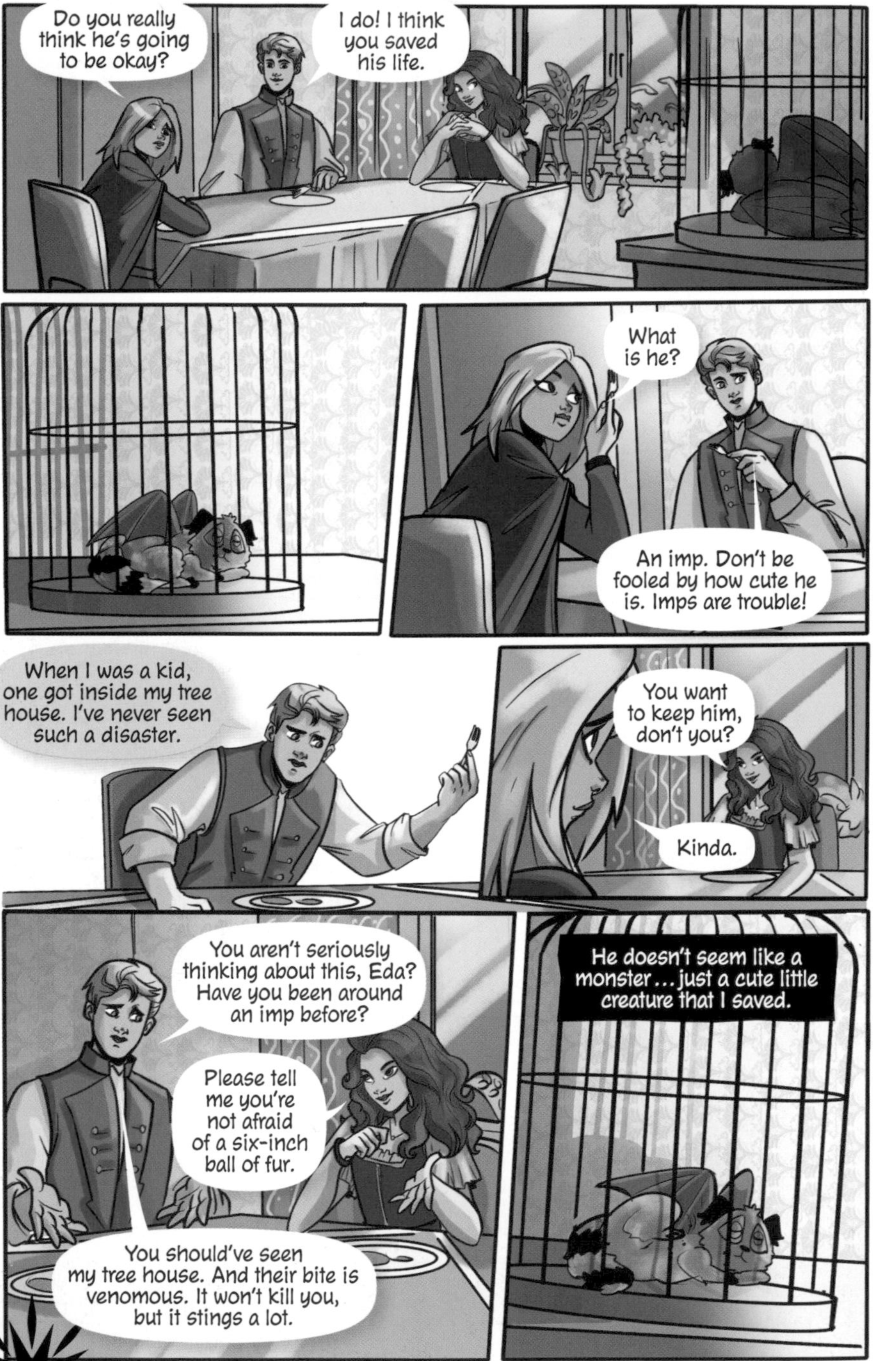
Do you really think he's going to be okay?
I do! I think you saved his life.
What is he?
An imp. Don't be fooled by how cute he is. Imps are trouble!
When I was a kid, one got inside my tree house. I've never seen such a disaster.
You want to keep him, don't you?
Kinda.
You aren't seriously thinking about this, Eda? Have you been around an imp before?
Please tell me you're not afraid of a six-inch ball of fur.
You should've seen my tree house. And their bite is venomous. It won't kill you, but it stings a lot.
He doesn't seem like a monster… just a cute little creature that I saved.

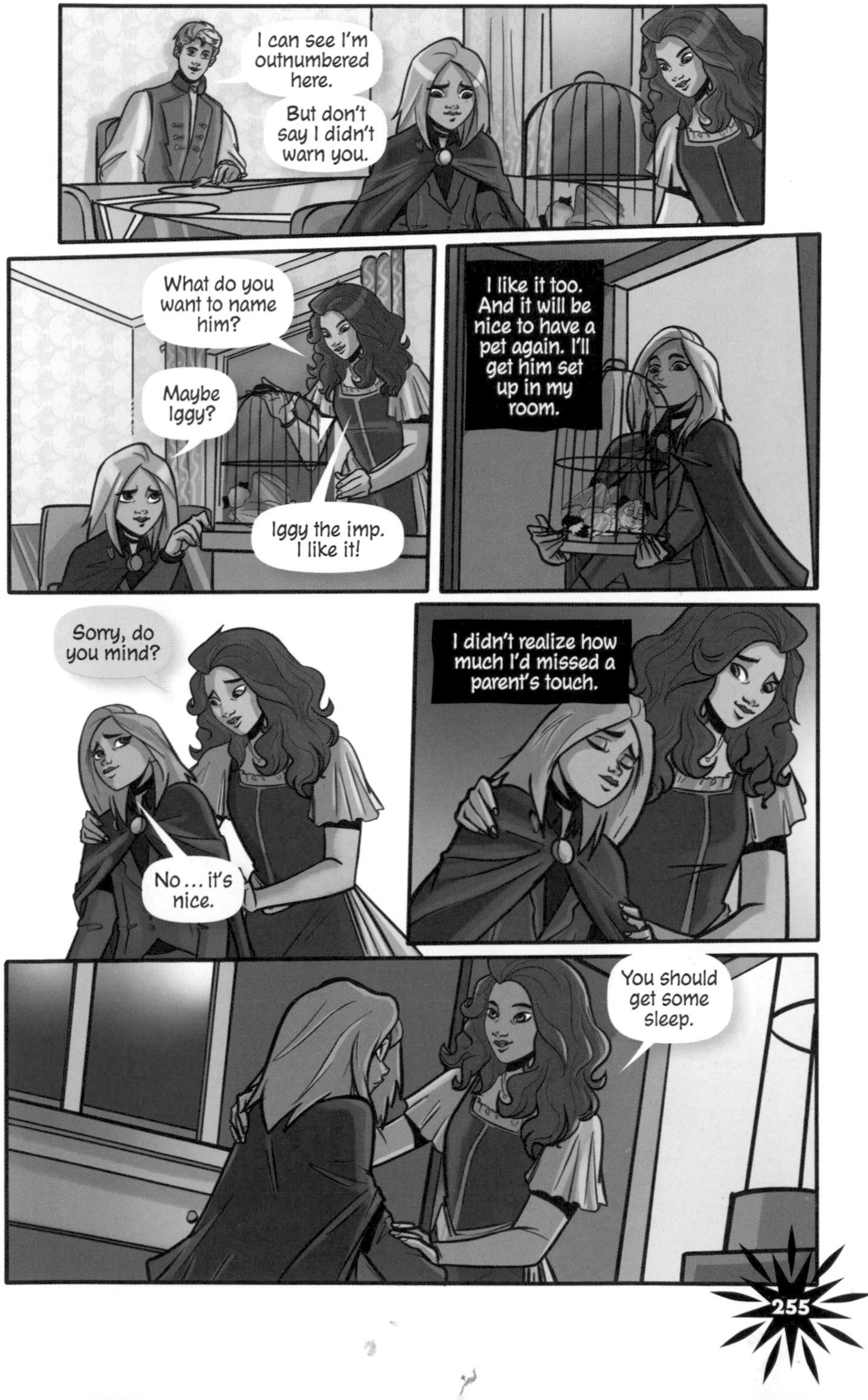
I can see I'm outnumbered here.
But don't say I didn't warn you.
What do you want to name him?
Maybe Iggy?
Iggy the imp. I like it!
I like it too. And it will be nice to have a pet again. I'll get him set up in my room.
Sorry, do you mind?
No... it's nice.
I didn't realize how much I'd missed a parent's touch.
You should get some sleep.

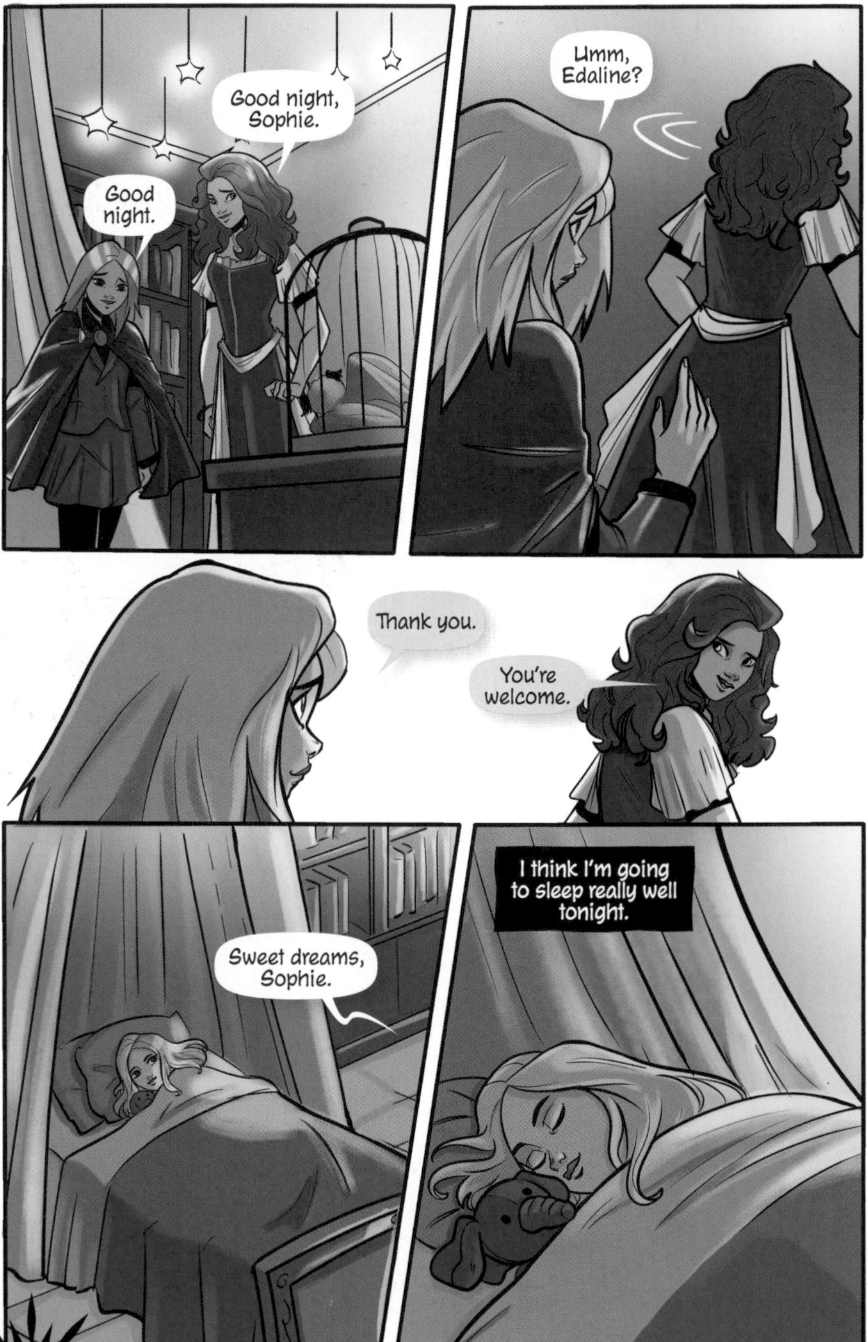
Good night, Sophie.
Good night.
Umm, Edaline?
Thank you.
You're welcome.
Sweet dreams, Sophie.
I think I'm going to sleep really well tonight.

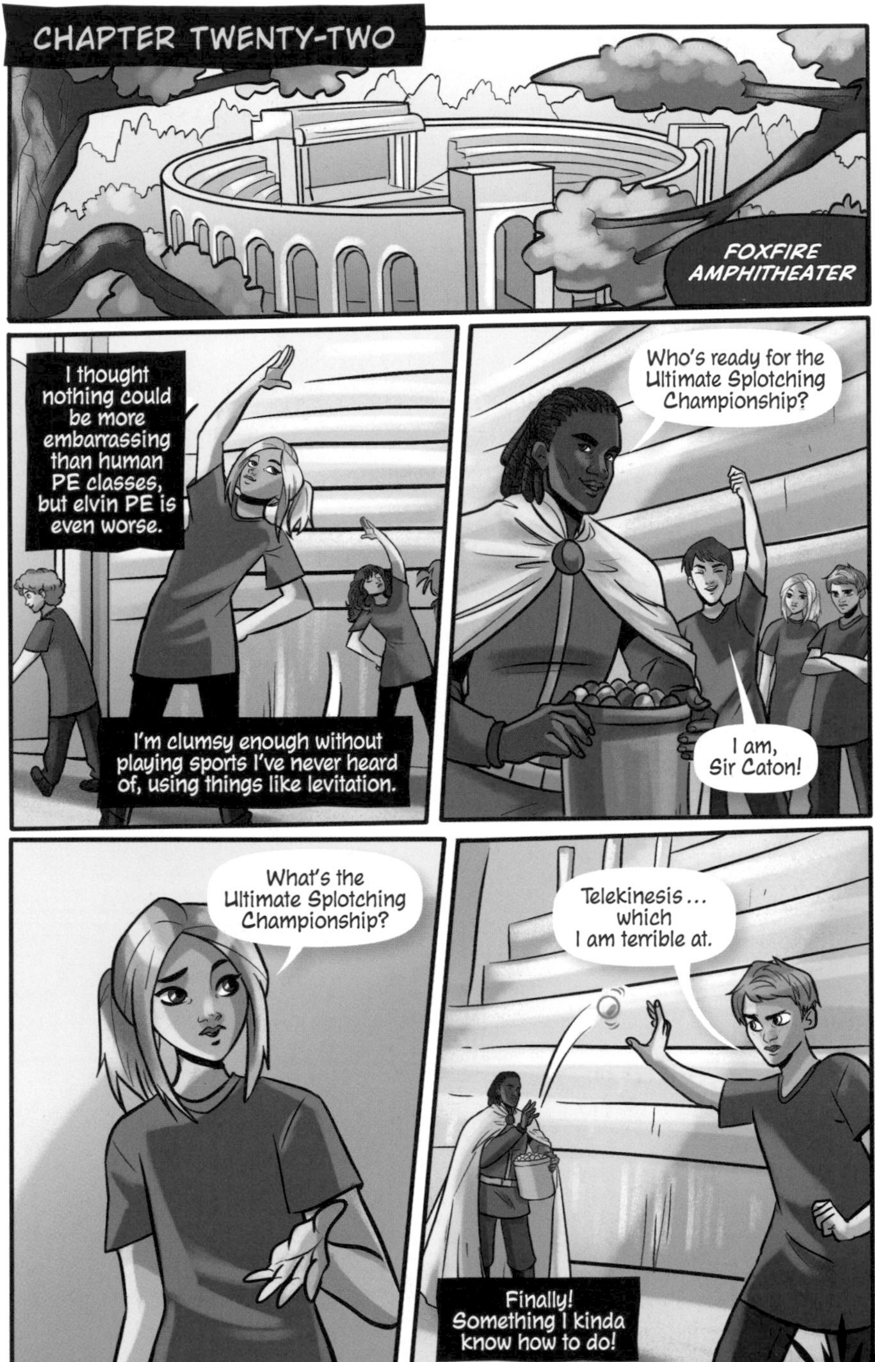
CHAPTER TWENTY-TWO
FOXFIRE AMPHITHEATER
I thought nothing could be more embarrassing than human PE classes, but elvin PE is even worse.
I'm clumsy enough without playing sports I've never heard of, using things like levitation.
Who's ready for the Ultimate Splotching Championship?
I am, Sir Caton!
What's the Ultimate Splotching Championship?
Telekinesis... which I am terrible at.
Finally! Something I kinda know how to do!

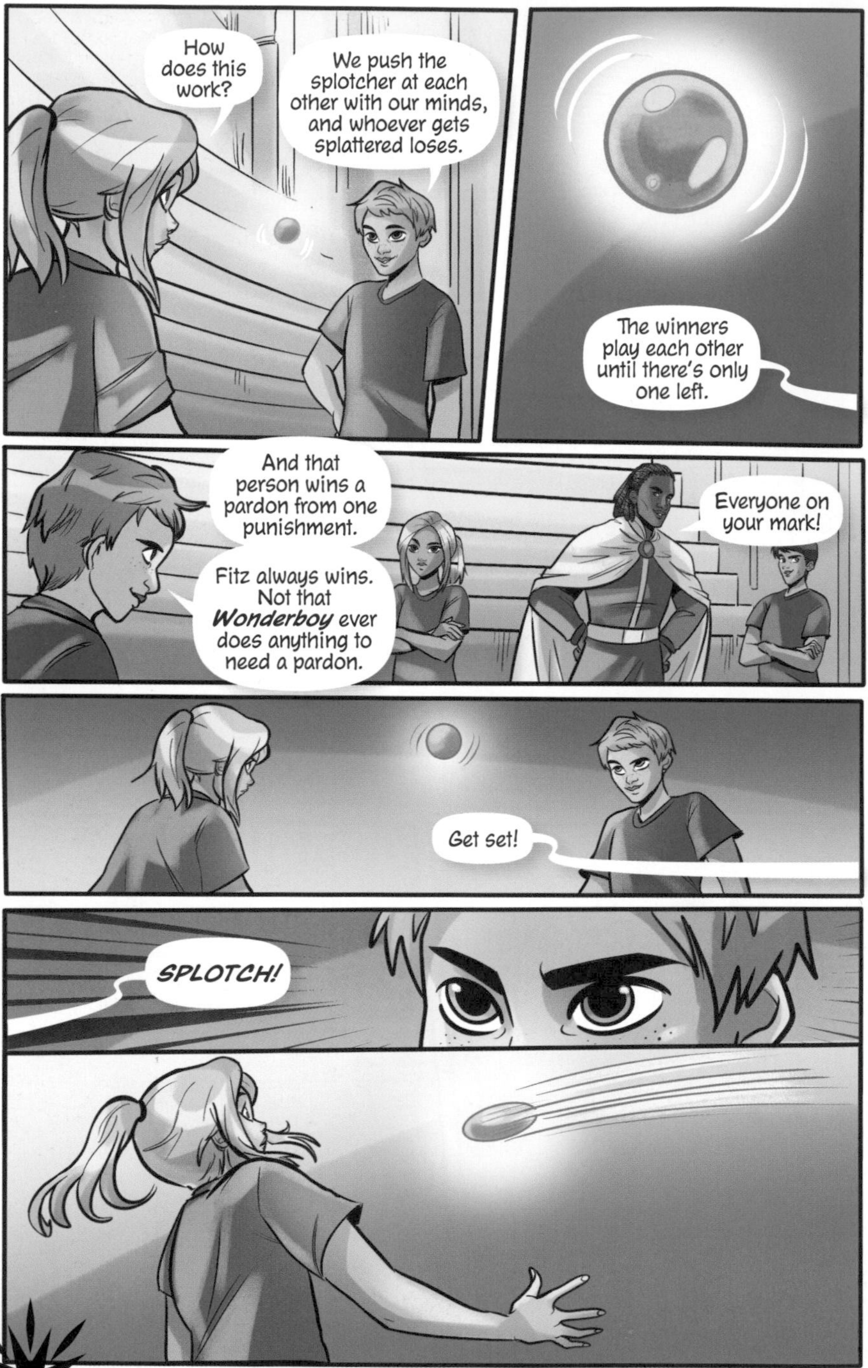
How does this work?
We push the splotcher at each other with our minds, and whoever gets splattered loses.
The winners play each other until there's only one left.
And that person wins a pardon from one punishment.
Fitz always wins. Not that *Wonderboy* ever does anything to need a pardon.
Everyone on your mark!
Get set!
SPLOTCH!

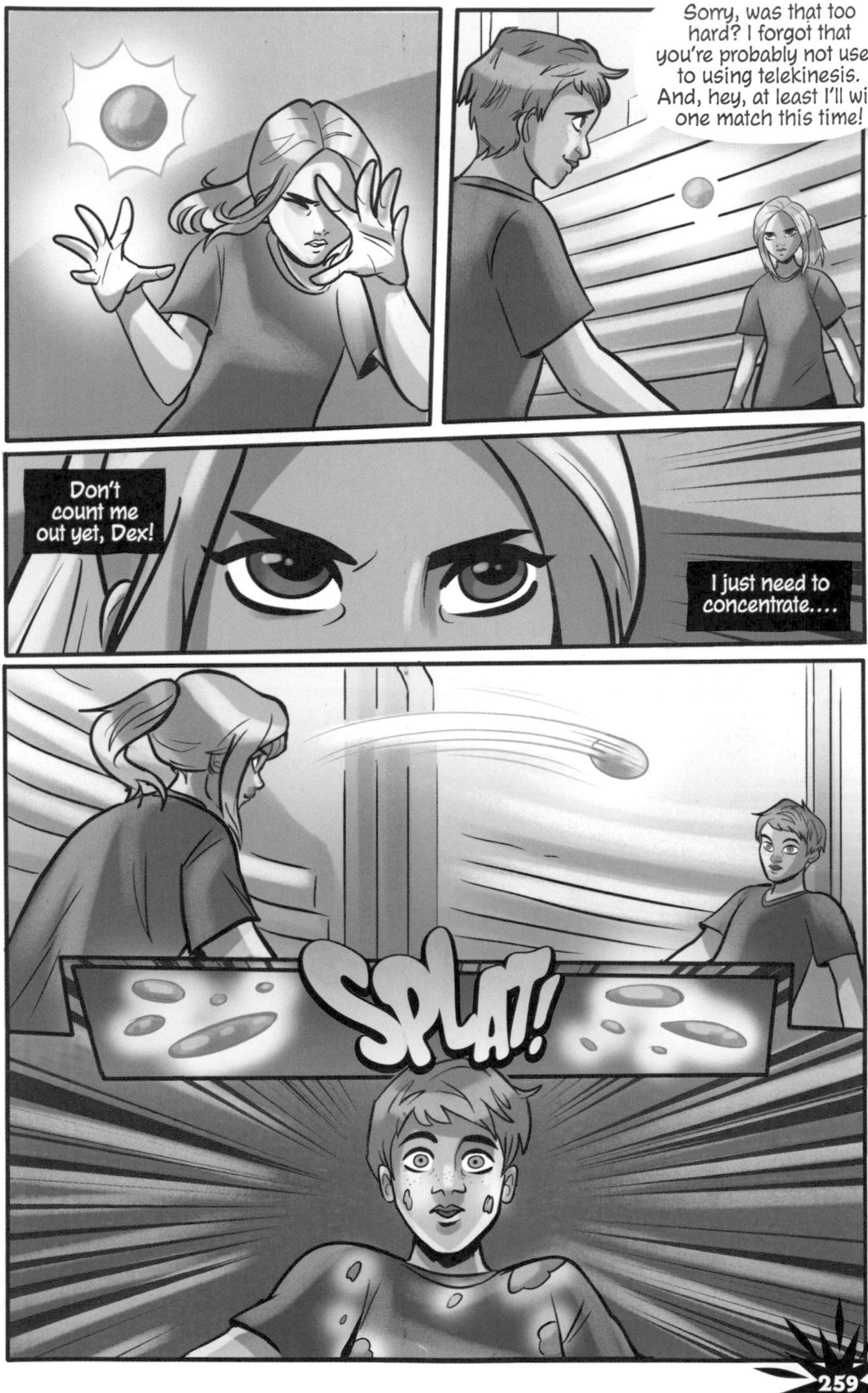
Sorry, was that too hard? I forgot that you're probably not used to using telekinesis. And, hey, at least I'll win one match this time!
Don't count me out yet, Dex!
I just need to concentrate....
SPLAT!

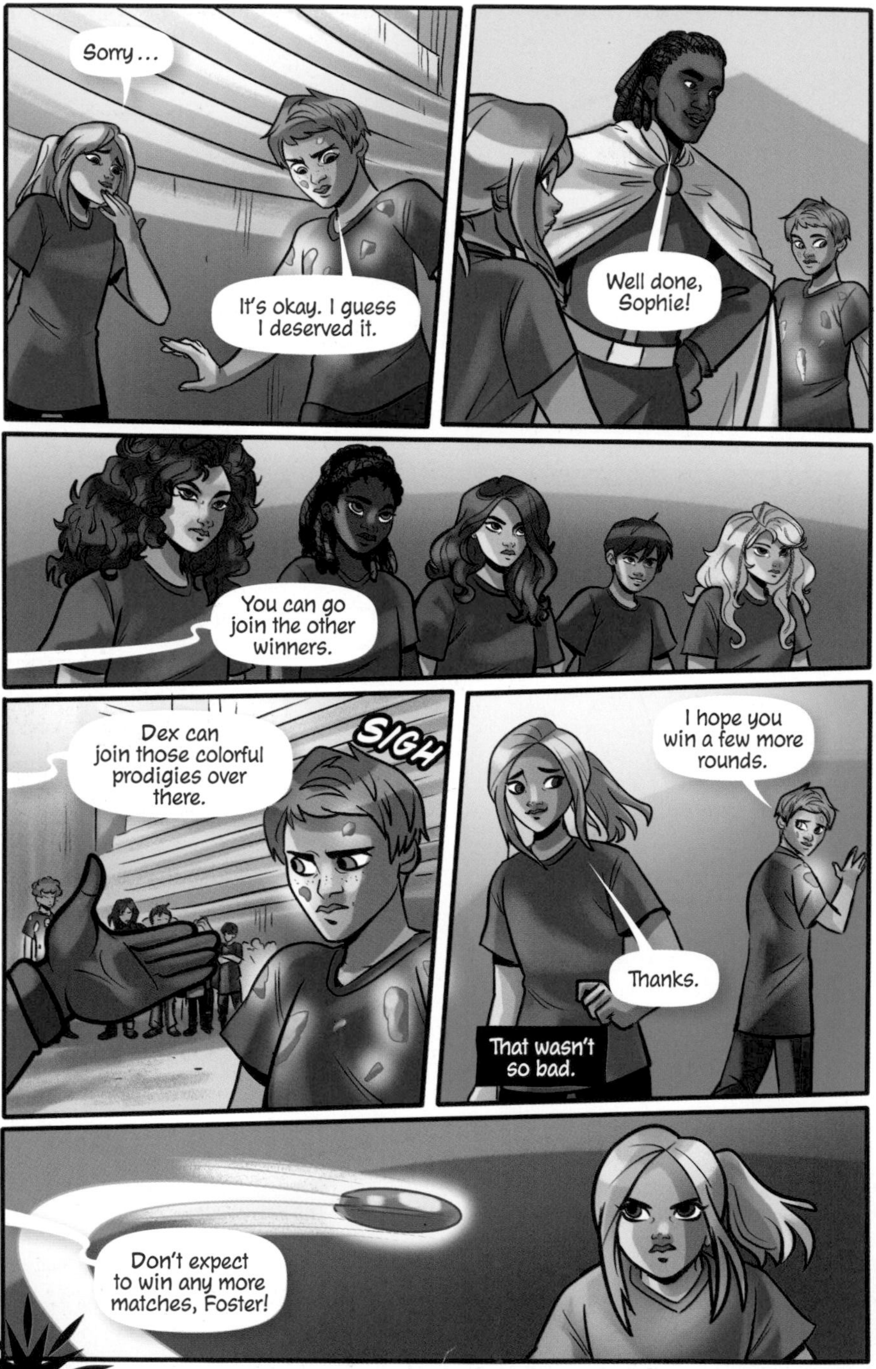
Sorry . . .
It's okay. I guess I deserved it.
Well done, Sophie!
You can go join the other winners.
Dex can join those colorful prodigies over there.
SIGH
I hope you win a few more rounds.
Thanks.
That wasn't so bad.
Don't expect to win any more matches, Foster!

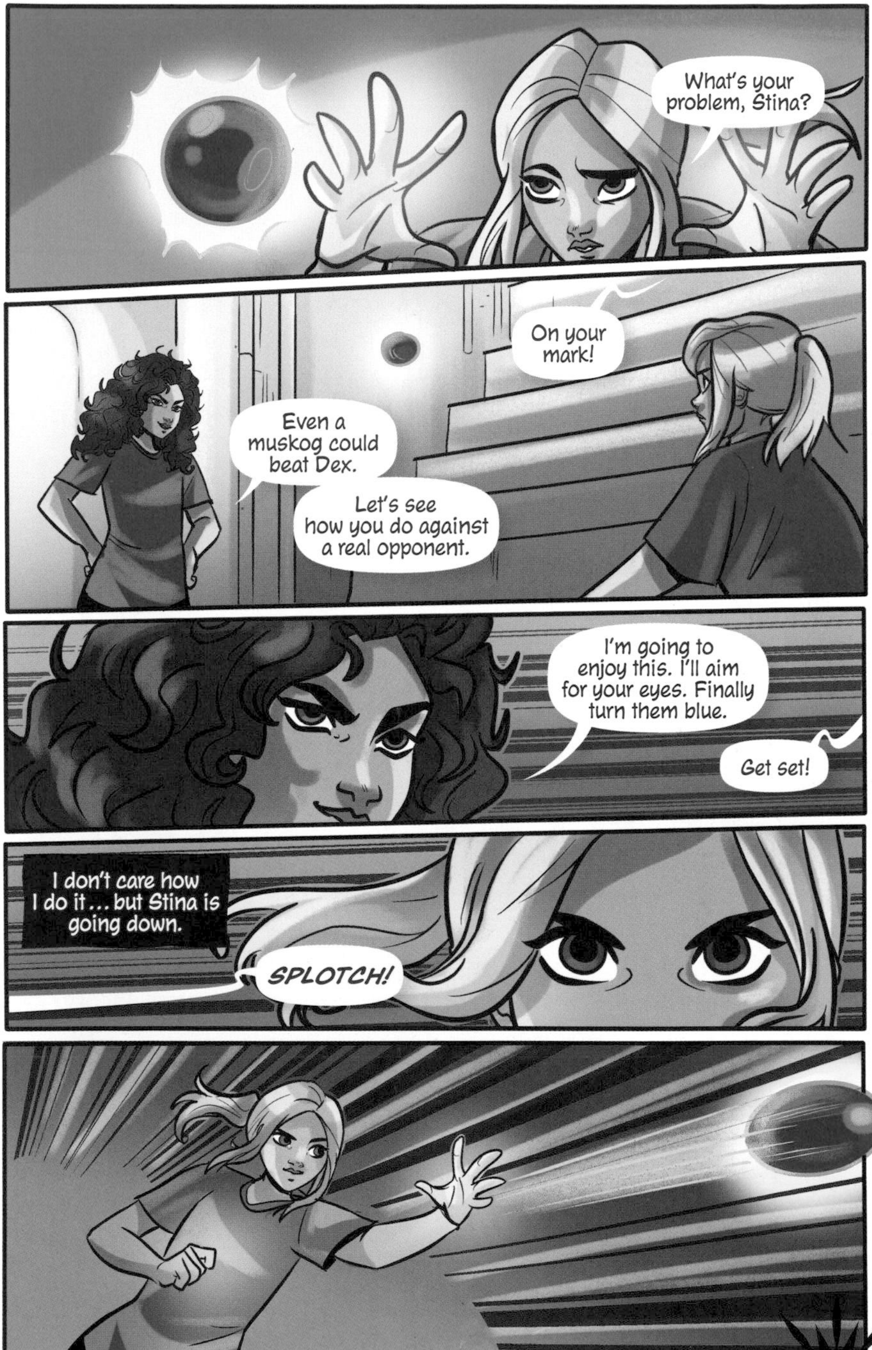
What's your problem, Stina?
On your mark!
Even a muskog could beat Dex.
Let's see how you do against a real opponent.
I'm going to enjoy this. I'll aim for your eyes. Finally turn them blue.
Get set!
I don't care how I do it... but Stina is going down.
SPLOTCH!

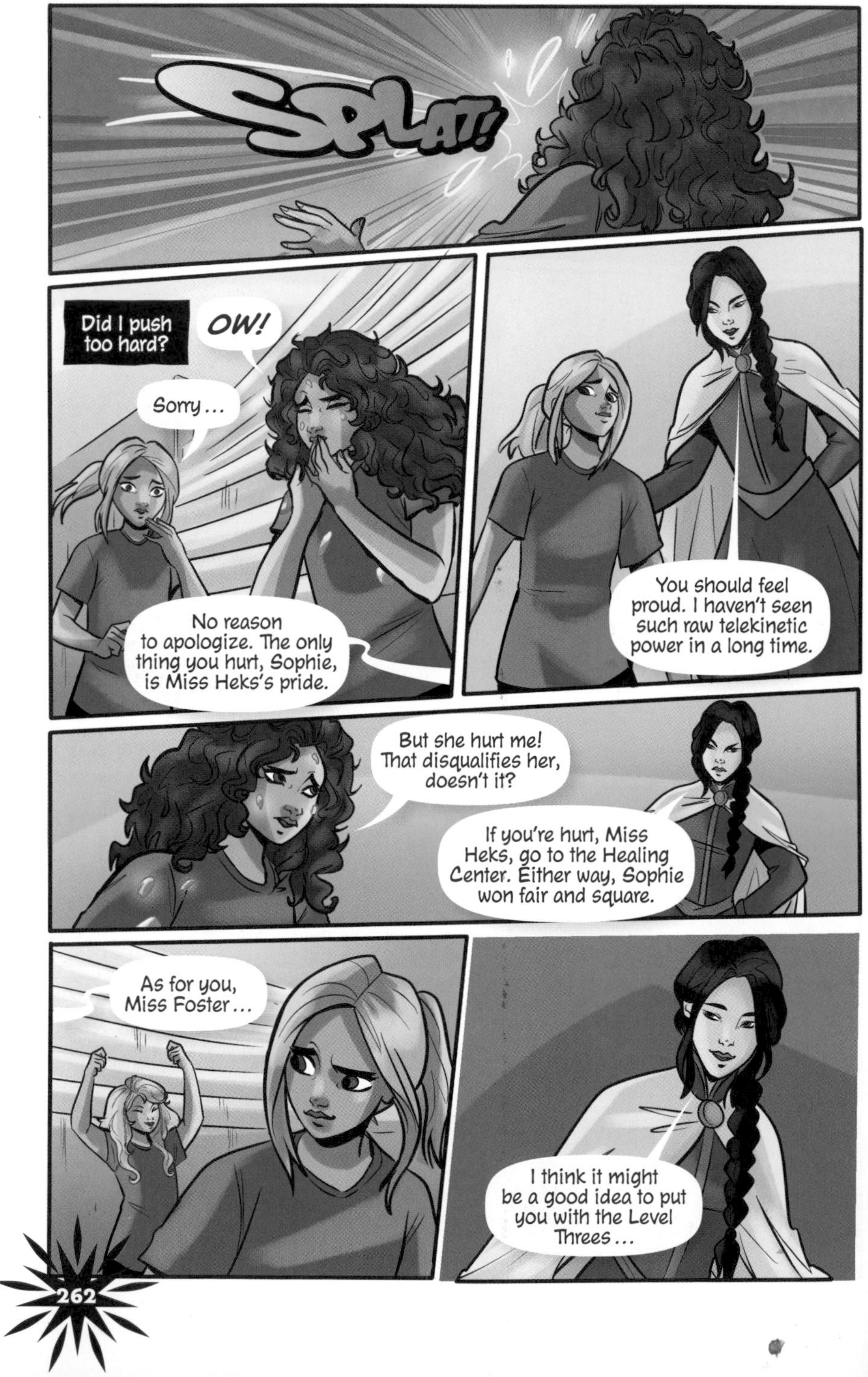
SPLAT!
Did I push too hard?
OW!
Sorry...
No reason to apologize. The only thing you hurt, Sophie, is Miss Heks's pride.
You should feel proud. I haven't seen such raw telekinetic power in a long time.
But she hurt me! That disqualifies her, doesn't it?
If you're hurt, Miss Heks, go to the Healing Center. Either way, Sophie won fair and square.
As for you, Miss Foster...
I think it might be a good idea to put you with the Level Threes...

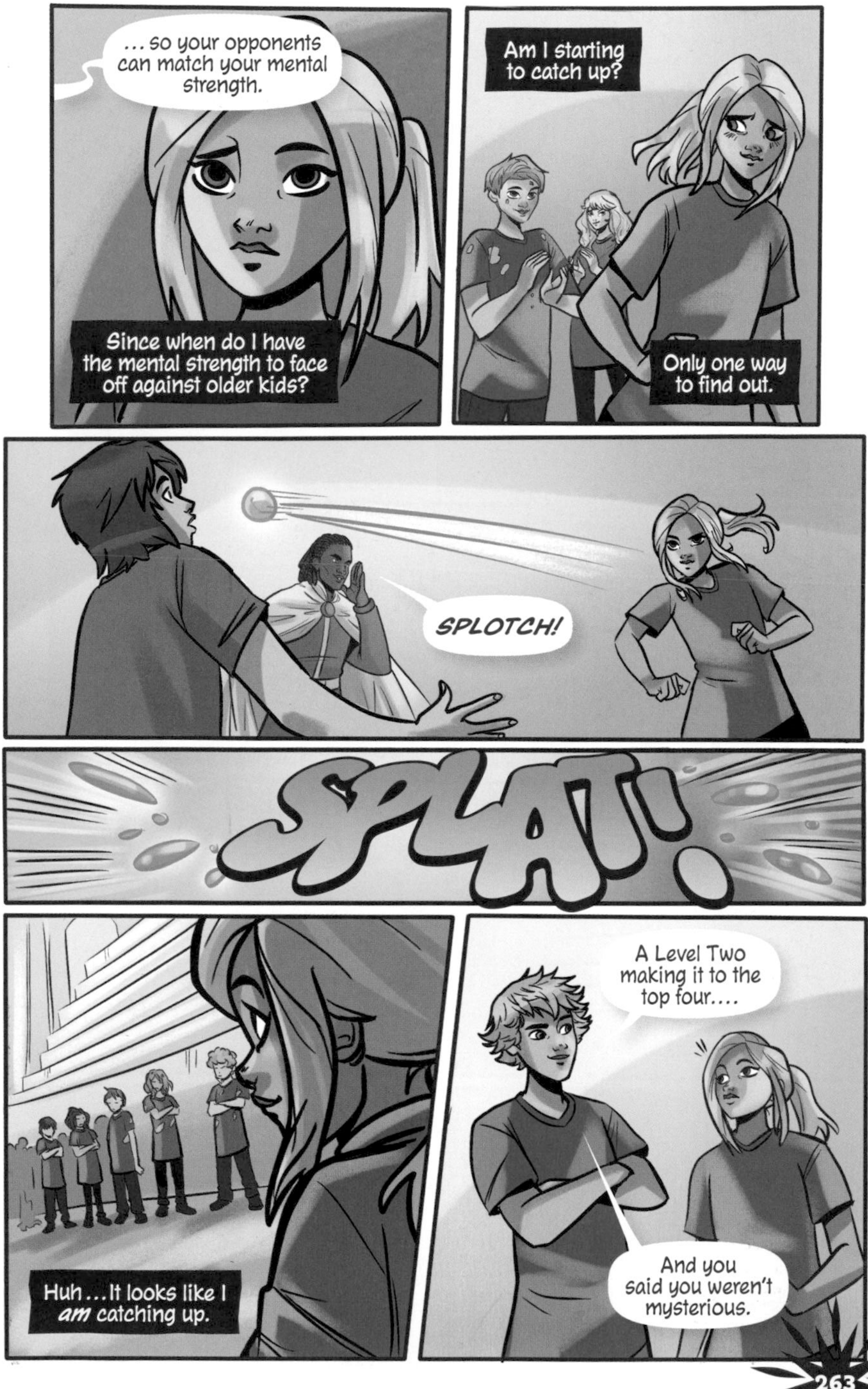
...so your opponents can match your mental strength.
Since when do I have the mental strength to face off against older kids?
Am I starting to catch up?
Only one way to find out.
SPLOTCH!
SPLAT!
Huh...It looks like I *am* catching up.
A Level Two making it to the top four....
And you said you weren't mysterious.

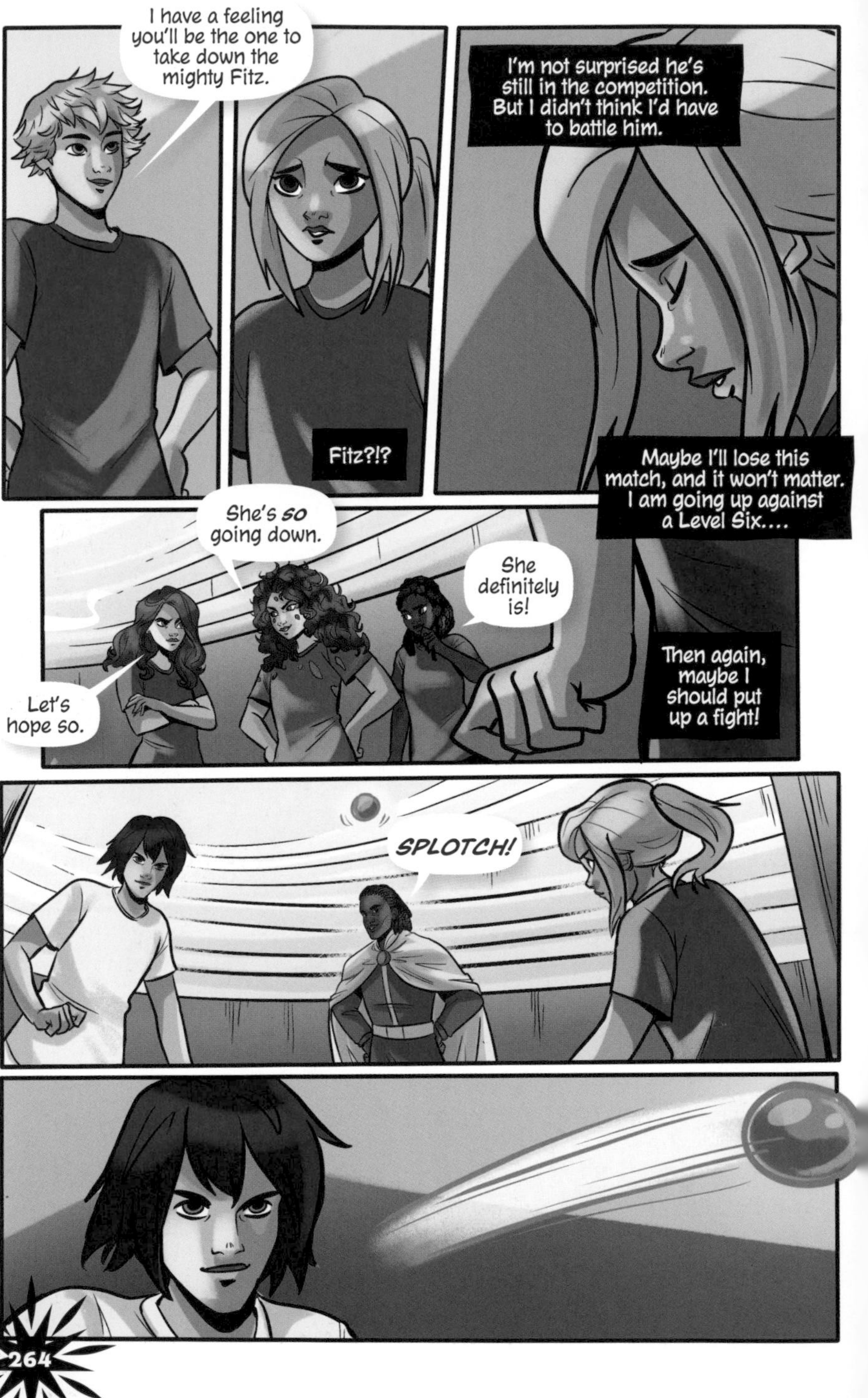
I have a feeling you'll be the one to take down the mighty Fitz.
Fitz?!?
I'm not surprised he's still in the competition. But I didn't think I'd have to battle him.
Maybe I'll lose this match, and it won't matter. I am going up against a Level Six....
She's *so* going down.
She definitely is!
Let's hope so.
Then again, maybe I should put up a fight!
SPLOTCH!

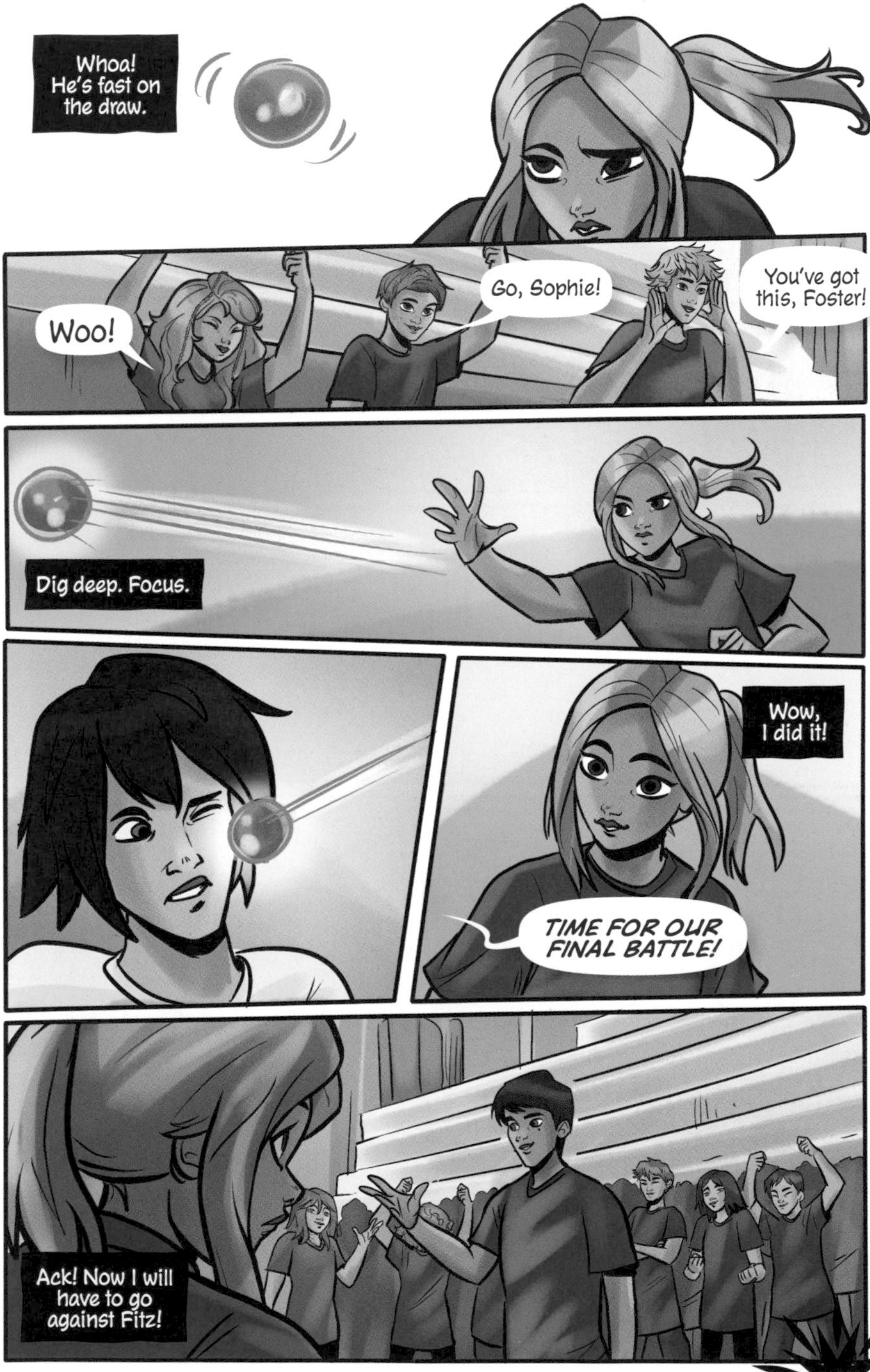

Whoa! He's fast on the draw.
Woo!
Go, Sophie!
You've got this, Foster!
Dig deep. Focus.
Wow, I did it!
TIME FOR OUR FINAL BATTLE!
Ack! Now I will have to go against Fitz!

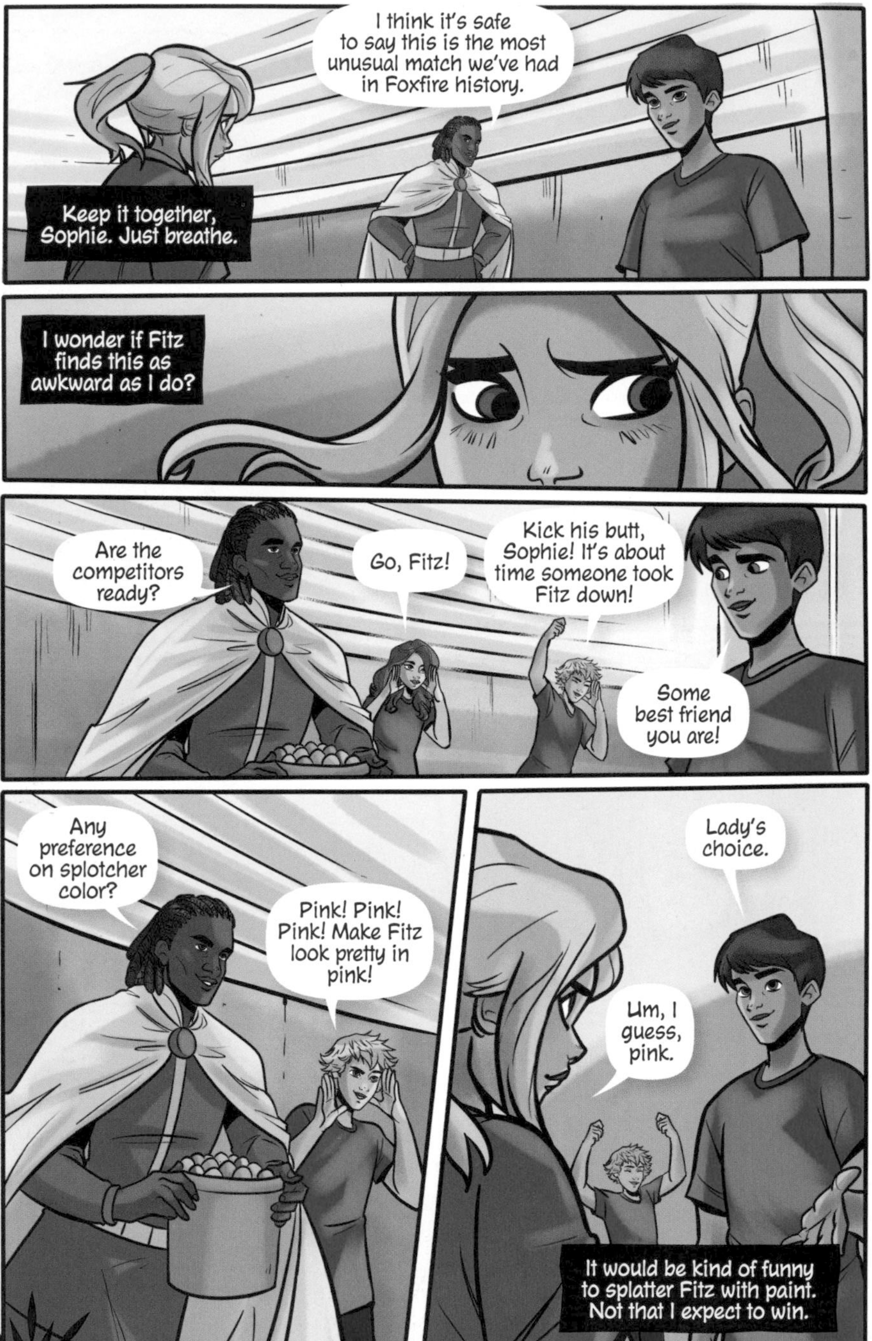
I think it's safe to say this is the most unusual match we've had in Foxfire history.
Keep it together, Sophie. Just breathe.
I wonder if Fitz finds this as awkward as I do?
Are the competitors ready?
Go, Fitz!
Kick his butt, Sophie! It's about time someone took Fitz down!
Some best friend you are!
Any preference on splotcher color?
Pink! Pink! Pink! Make Fitz look pretty in pink!
Lady's choice.
Um, I guess, pink.
It would be kind of funny to splatter Fitz with paint. Not that I expect to win.

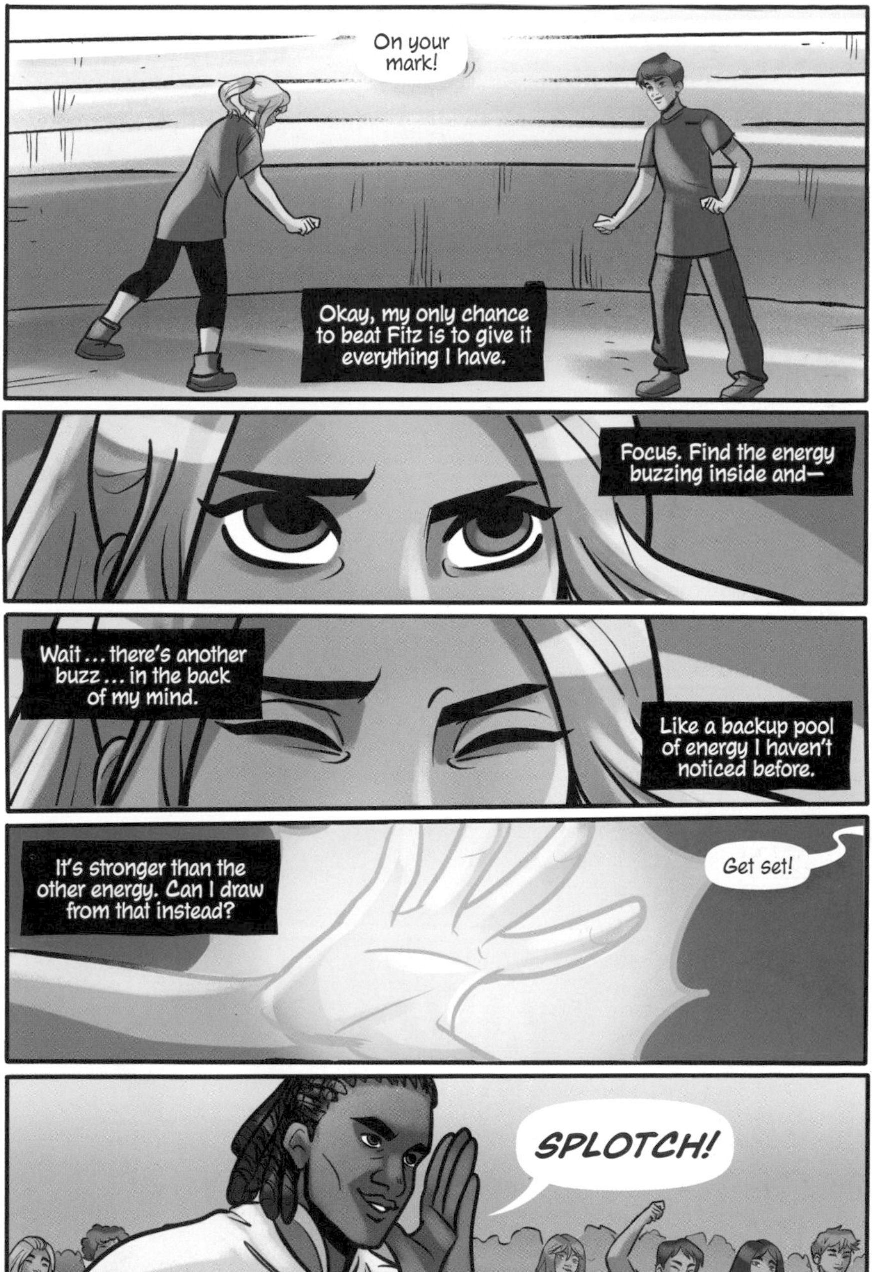
On your mark!
Okay, my only chance to beat Fitz is to give it everything I have.
Focus. Find the energy buzzing inside and—
Wait... there's another buzz... in the back of my mind.
Like a backup pool of energy I haven't noticed before.
It's stronger than the other energy. Can I draw from that instead?
Get set!
SPLOTCH!

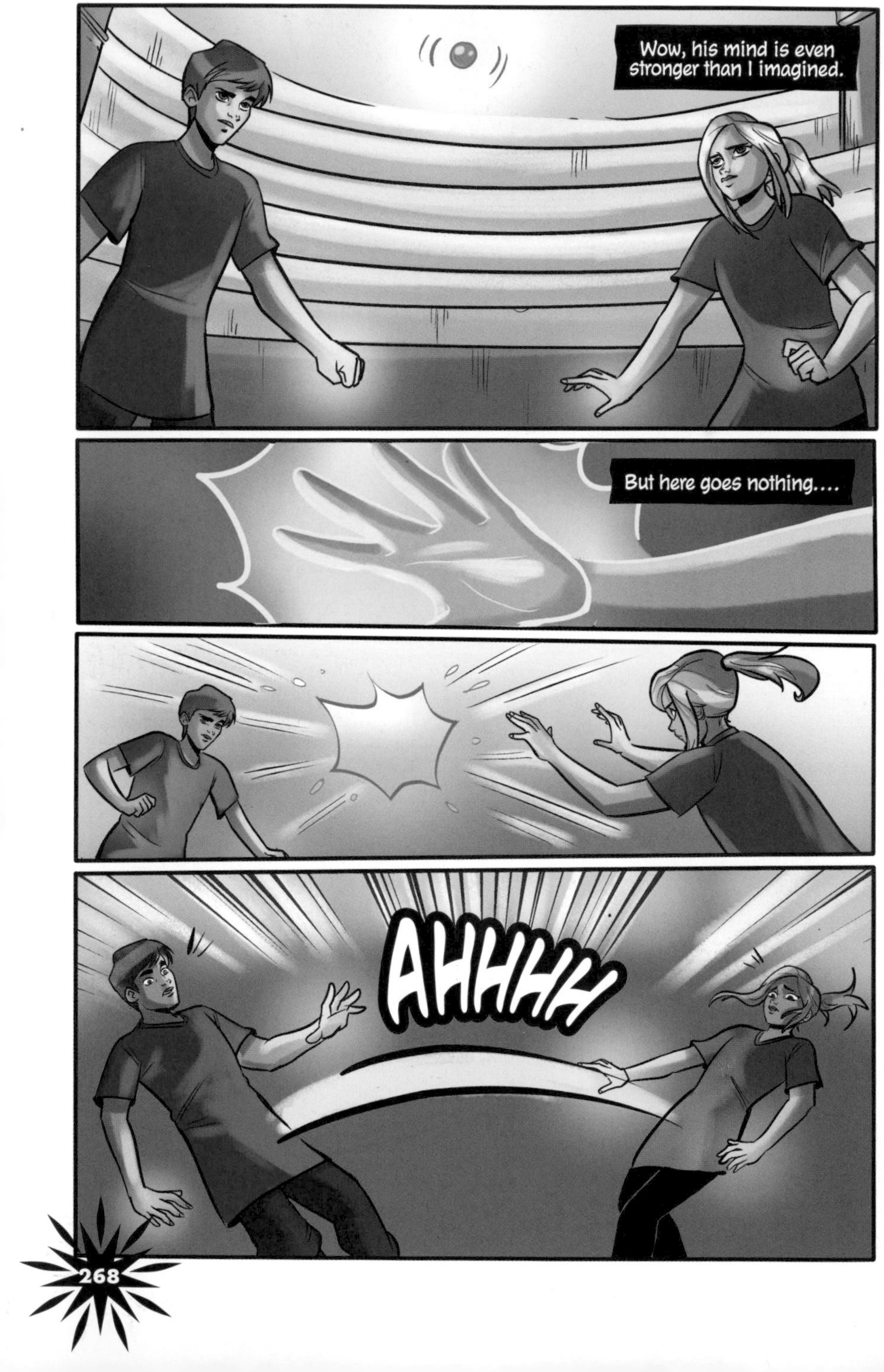
Wow, his mind is even stronger than I imagined.
But here goes nothing....
AHHHH

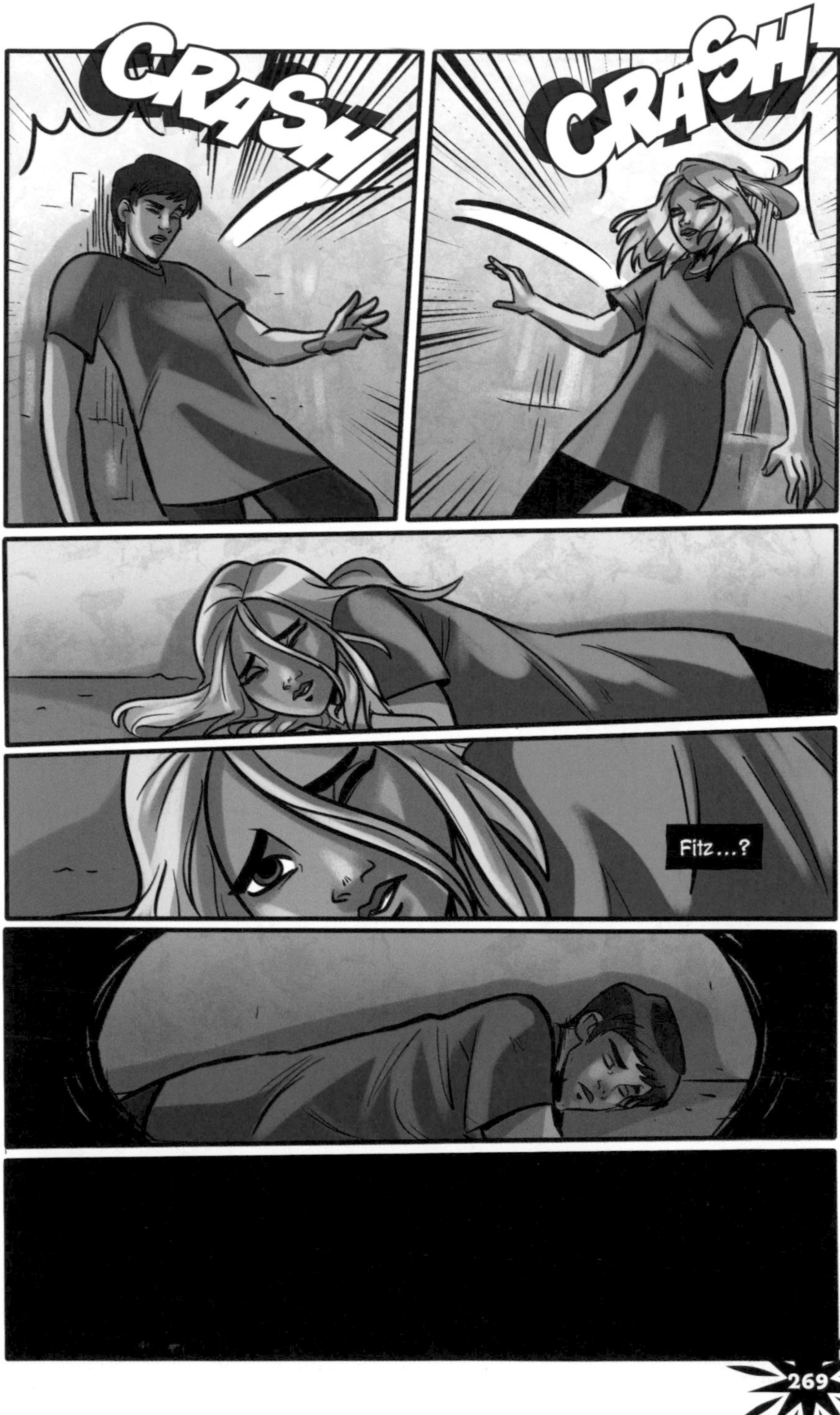
CRASH
CRASH
Fitz...?

CHAPTER TWENTY-THREE

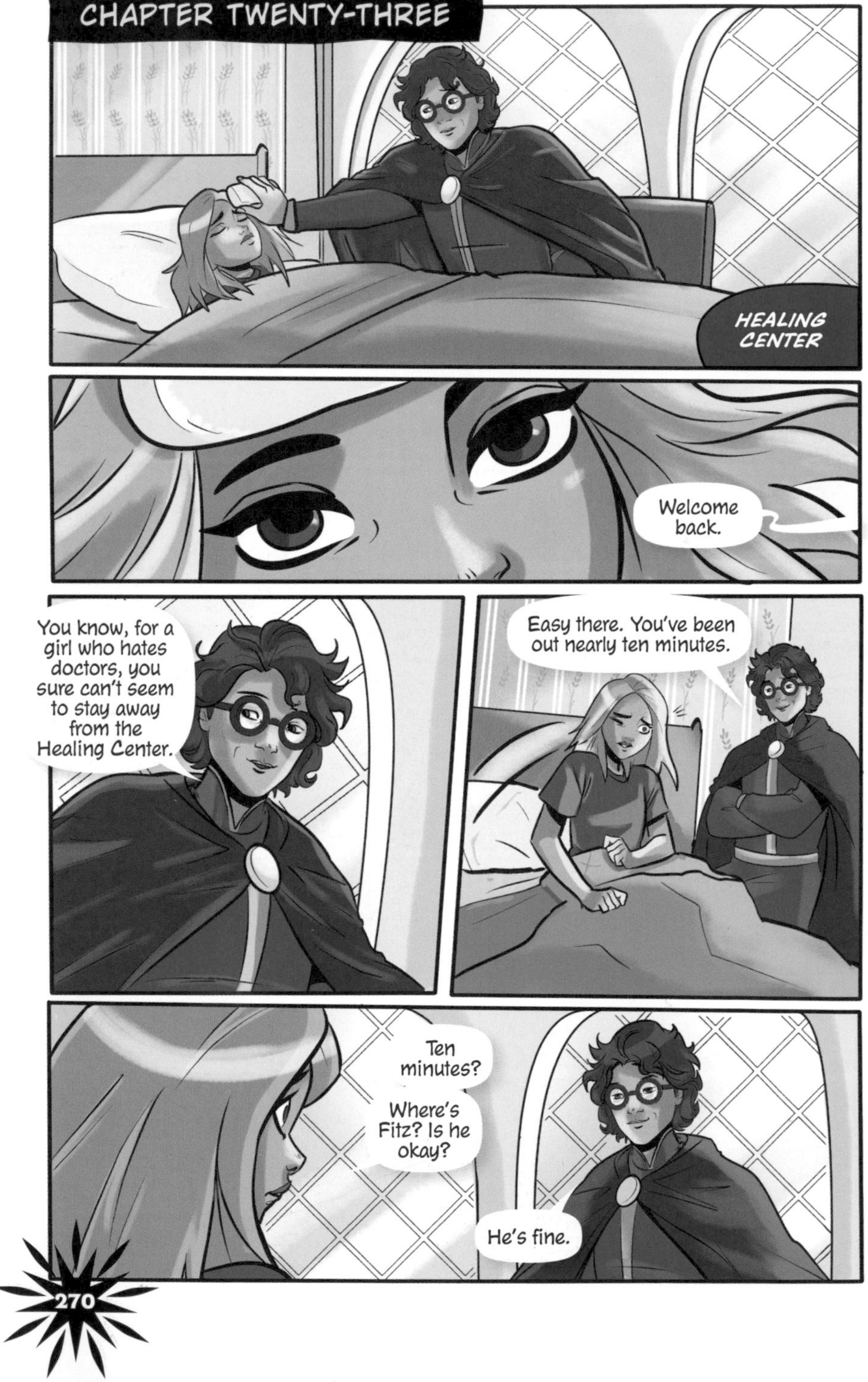

HEALING CENTER
Welcome back.
You know, for a girl who hates doctors, you sure can't seem to stay away from the Healing Center.
Easy there. You've been out nearly ten minutes.
Ten minutes?
Where's Fitz? Is he okay?
He's fine.

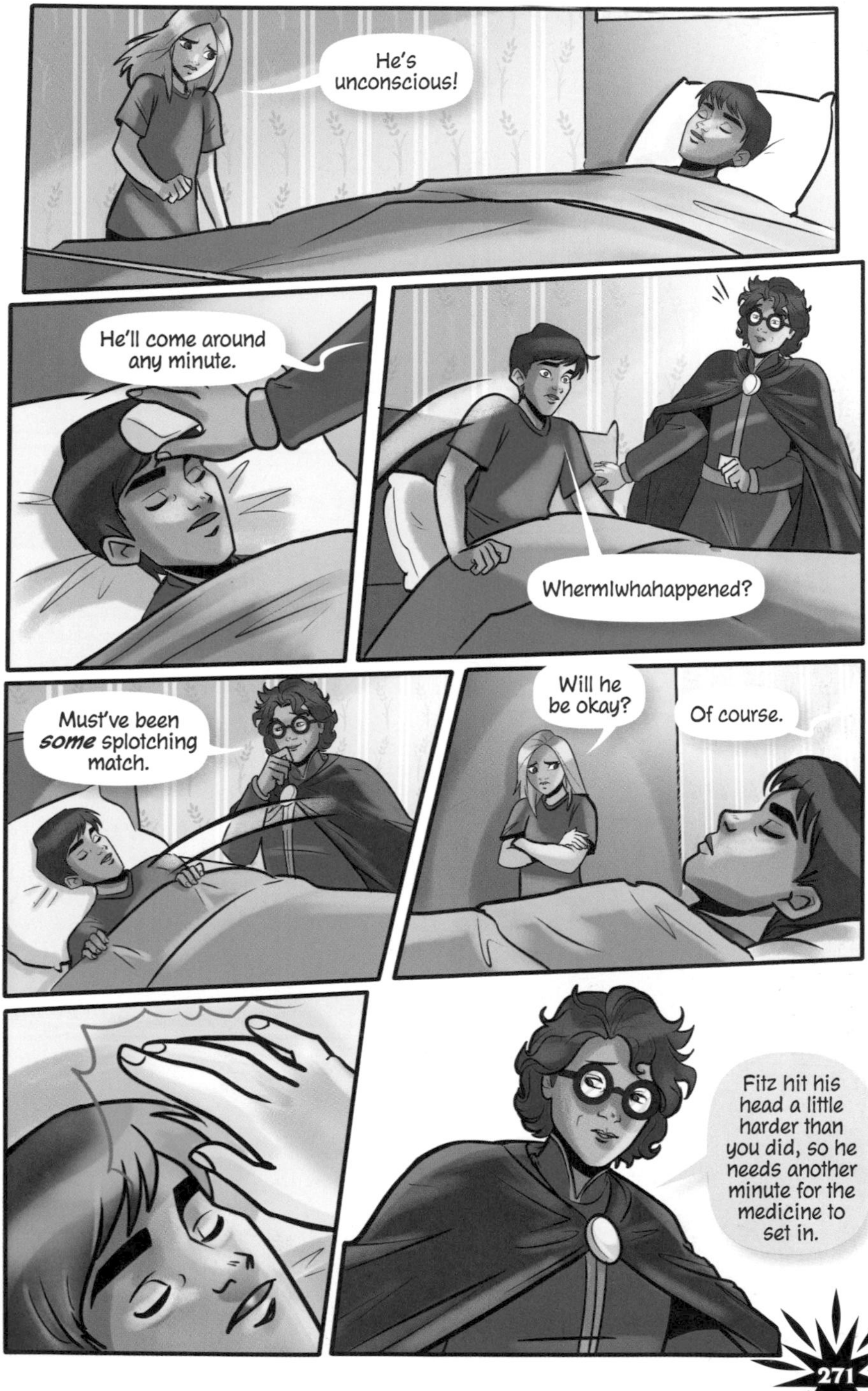
He's unconscious!
He'll come around any minute.
WhermIwhahappened?
Must've been *some* splotching match.
Will he be okay?
Of course.
Fitz hit his head a little harder than you did, so he needs another minute for the medicine to set in.

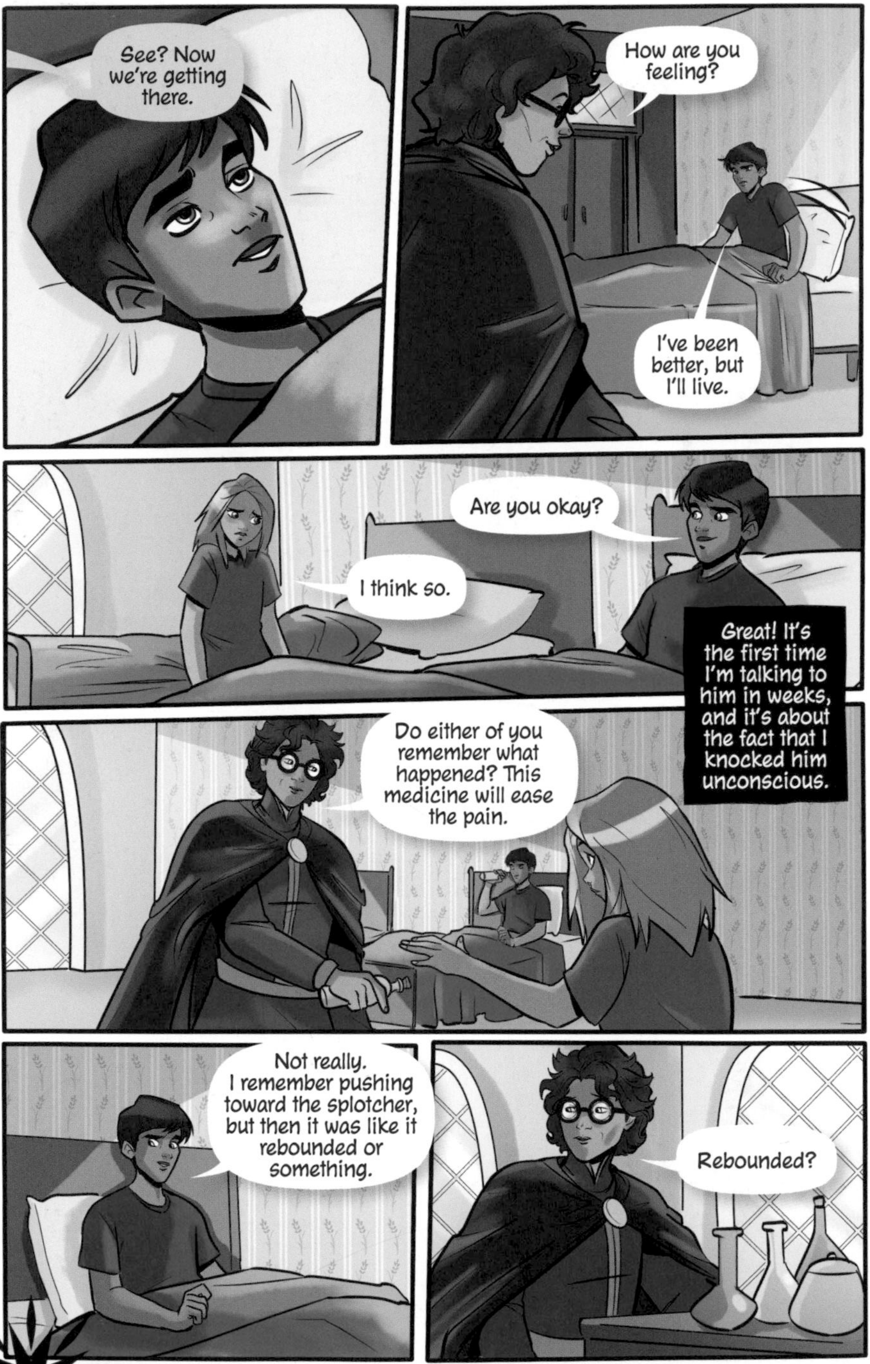
See? Now we're getting there.
How are you feeling?
I've been better, but I'll live.
Are you okay?
I think so.
Great! It's the first time I'm talking to him in weeks, and it's about the fact that I knocked him unconscious.
Do either of you remember what happened? This medicine will ease the pain.
Not really. I remember pushing toward the splotcher, but then it was like it rebounded or something.
Rebounded?

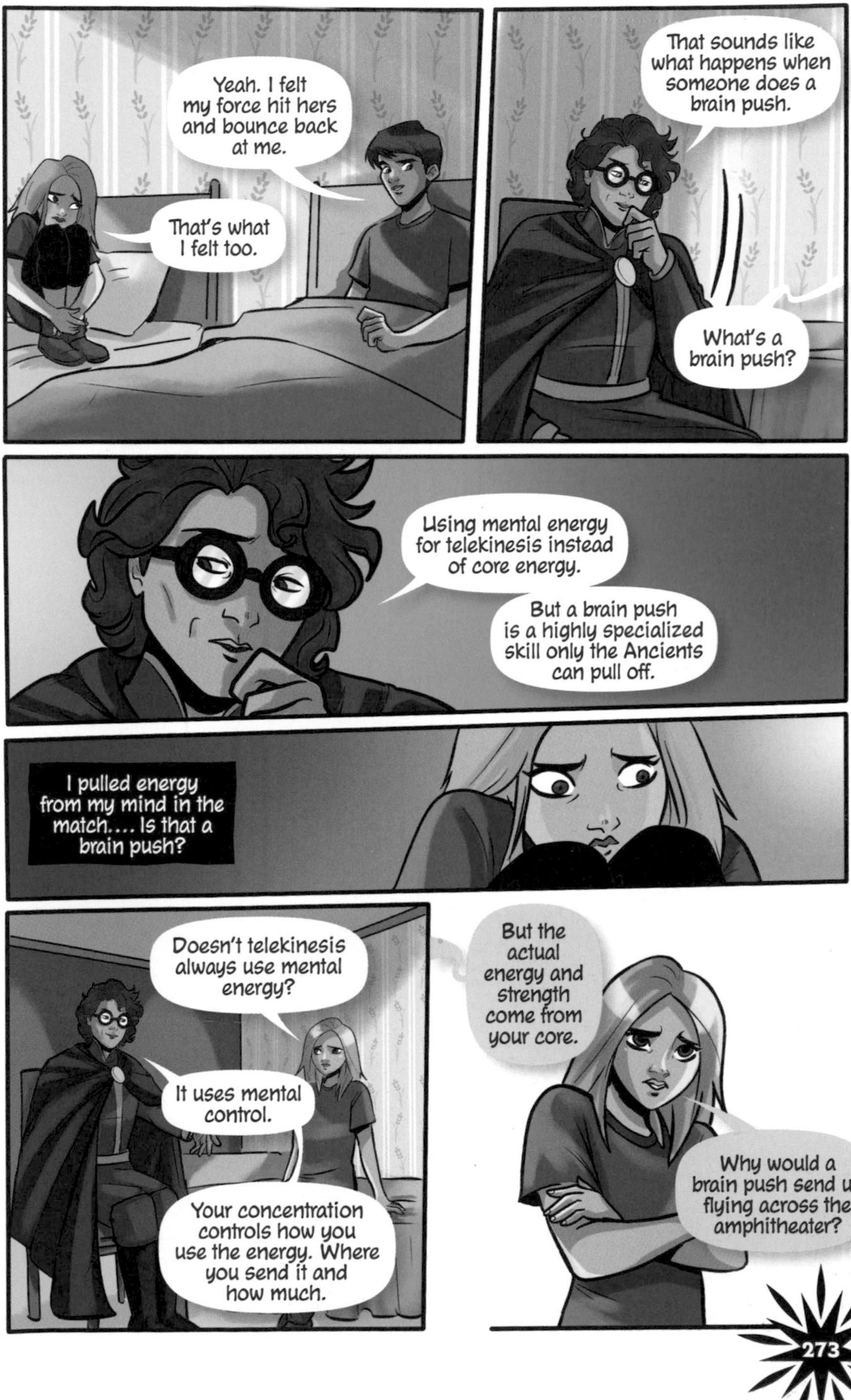
Yeah. I felt my force hit hers and bounce back at me.
That's what I felt too.
That sounds like what happens when someone does a brain push.
What's a brain push?
Using mental energy for telekinesis instead of core energy.
But a brain push is a highly specialized skill only the Ancients can pull off.
I pulled energy from my mind in the match.... Is that a brain push?
Doesn't telekinesis always use mental energy?
It uses mental control.
Your concentration controls how you use the energy. Where you send it and how much.
But the actual energy and strength come from your core.
Why would a brain push send us flying across the amphitheater?

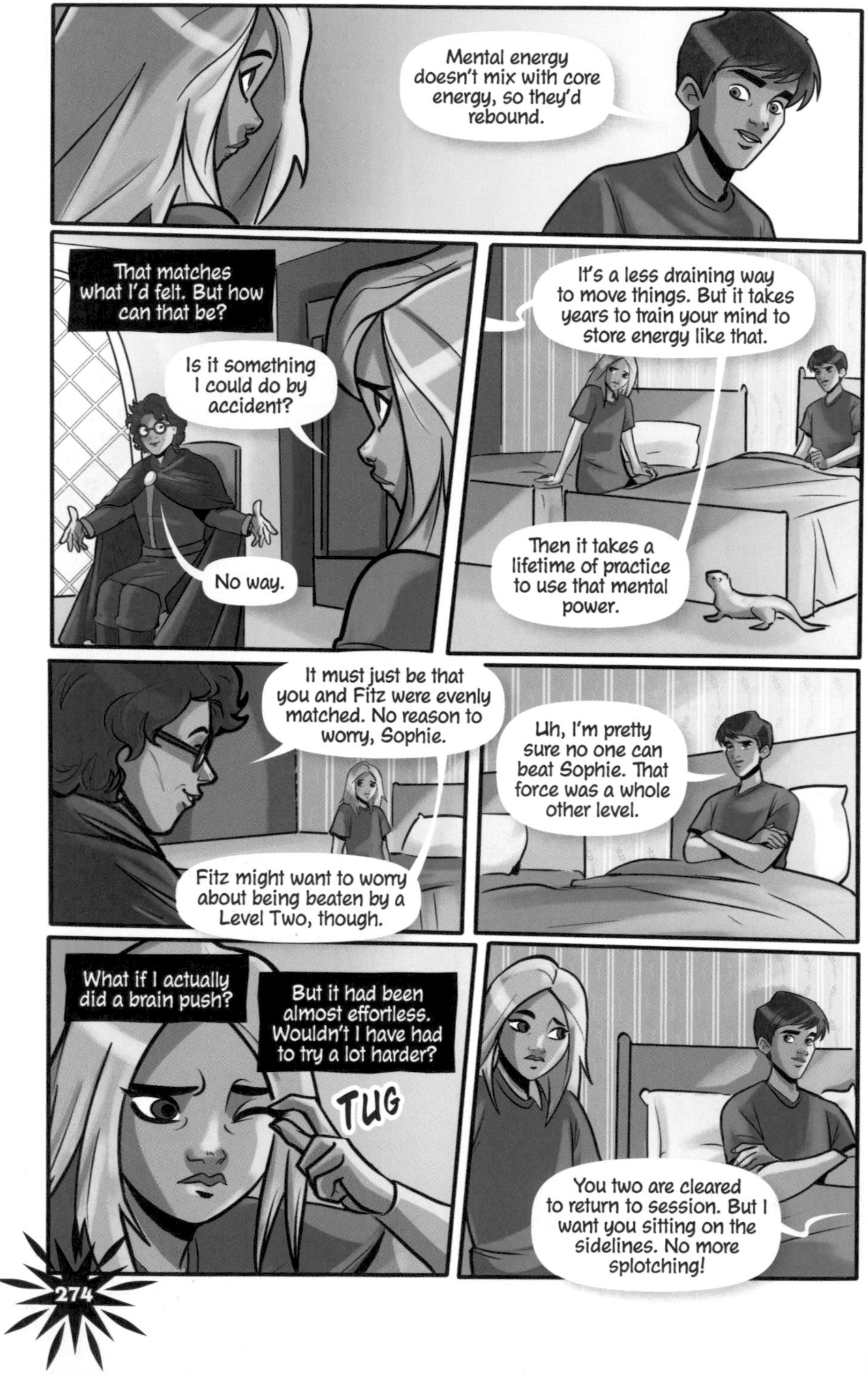
Mental energy doesn't mix with core energy, so they'd rebound.
That matches what I'd felt. But how can that be?
Is it something I could do by accident?
No way.
It's a less draining way to move things. But it takes years to train your mind to store energy like that.
Then it takes a lifetime of practice to use that mental power.
It must just be that you and Fitz were evenly matched. No reason to worry, Sophie.
Fitz might want to worry about being beaten by a Level Two, though.
Uh, I'm pretty sure no one can beat Sophie. That force was a whole other level.
What if I actually did a brain push?
But it had been almost effortless. Wouldn't I have had to try a lot harder?
TUG
You two are cleared to return to session. But I want you sitting on the sidelines. No more splotching!

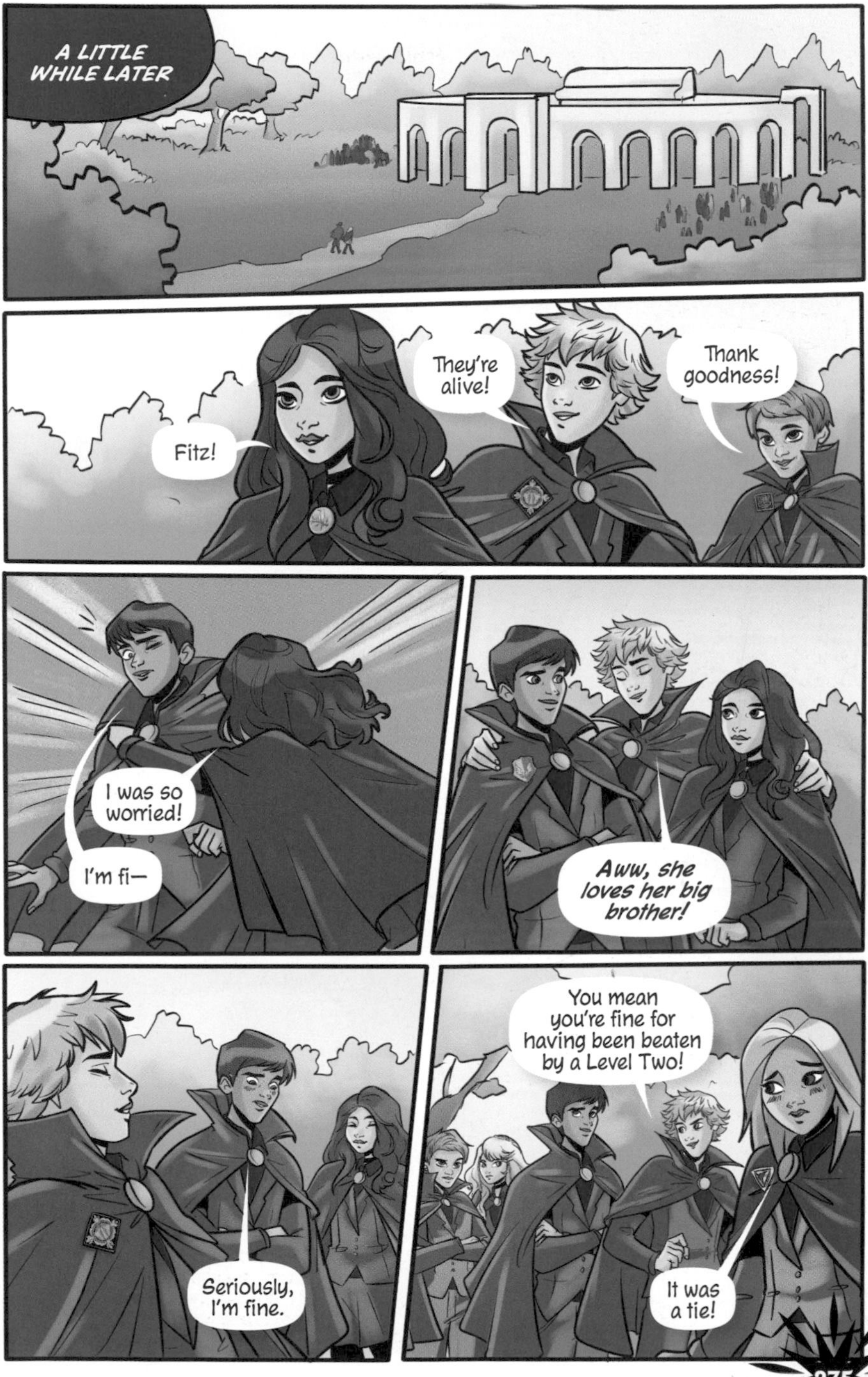
A LITTLE WHILE LATER
Fitz!
They're alive!
Thank goodness!
I was so worried!
I'm fi—
Aww, she loves her big brother!
Seriously, I'm fine.
You mean you're fine for having been beaten by a Level Two!
It was a tie!

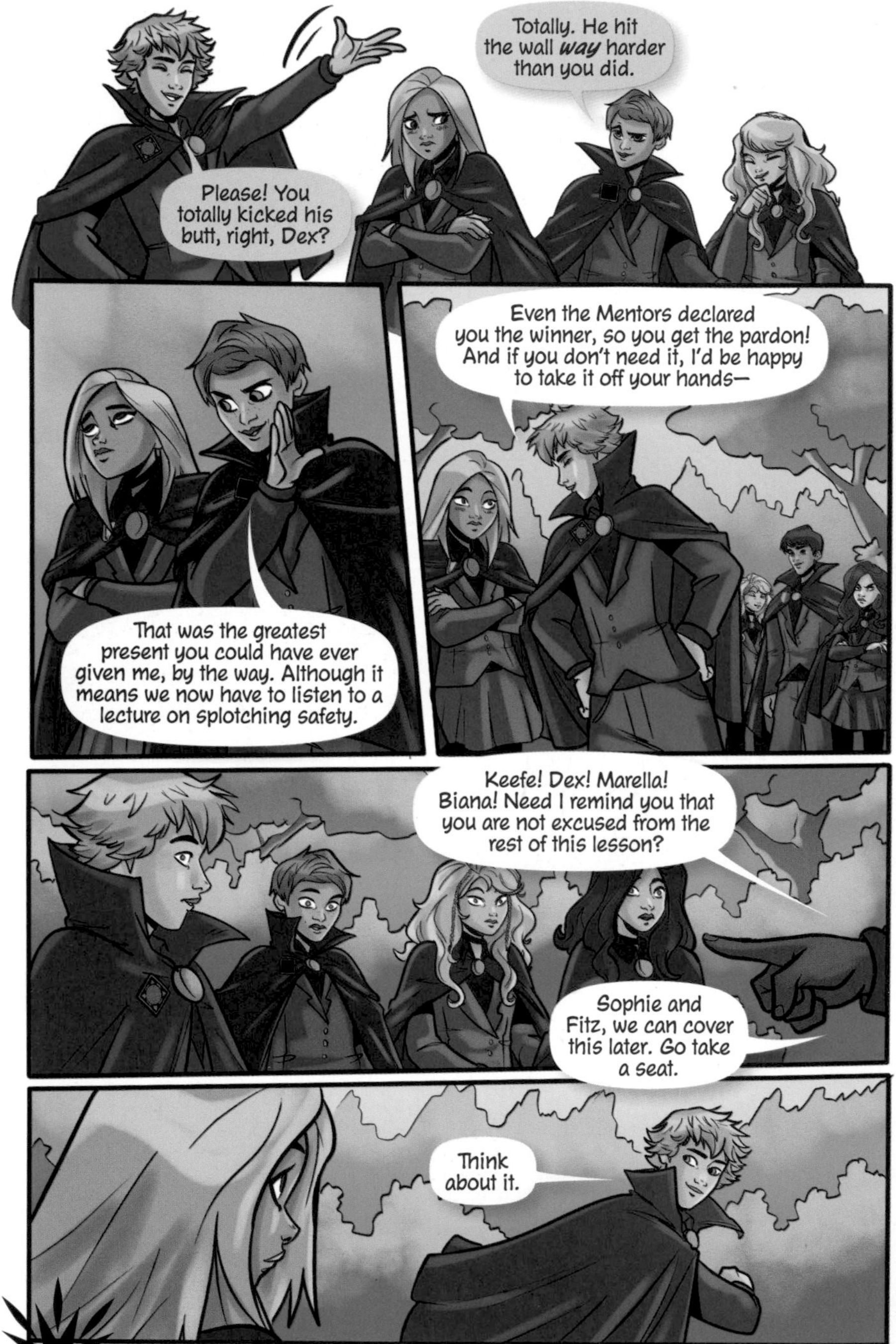
Please! You totally kicked his butt, right, Dex?
Totally. He hit the wall *way* harder than you did.
That was the greatest present you could have ever given me, by the way. Although it means we now have to listen to a lecture on splotching safety.
Even the Mentors declared you the winner, so you get the pardon! And if you don't need it, I'd be happy to take it off your hands—
Keefe! Dex! Marella! Biana! Need I remind you that you are not excused from the rest of this lesson?
Sophie and Fitz, we can cover this later. Go take a seat.
Think about it.

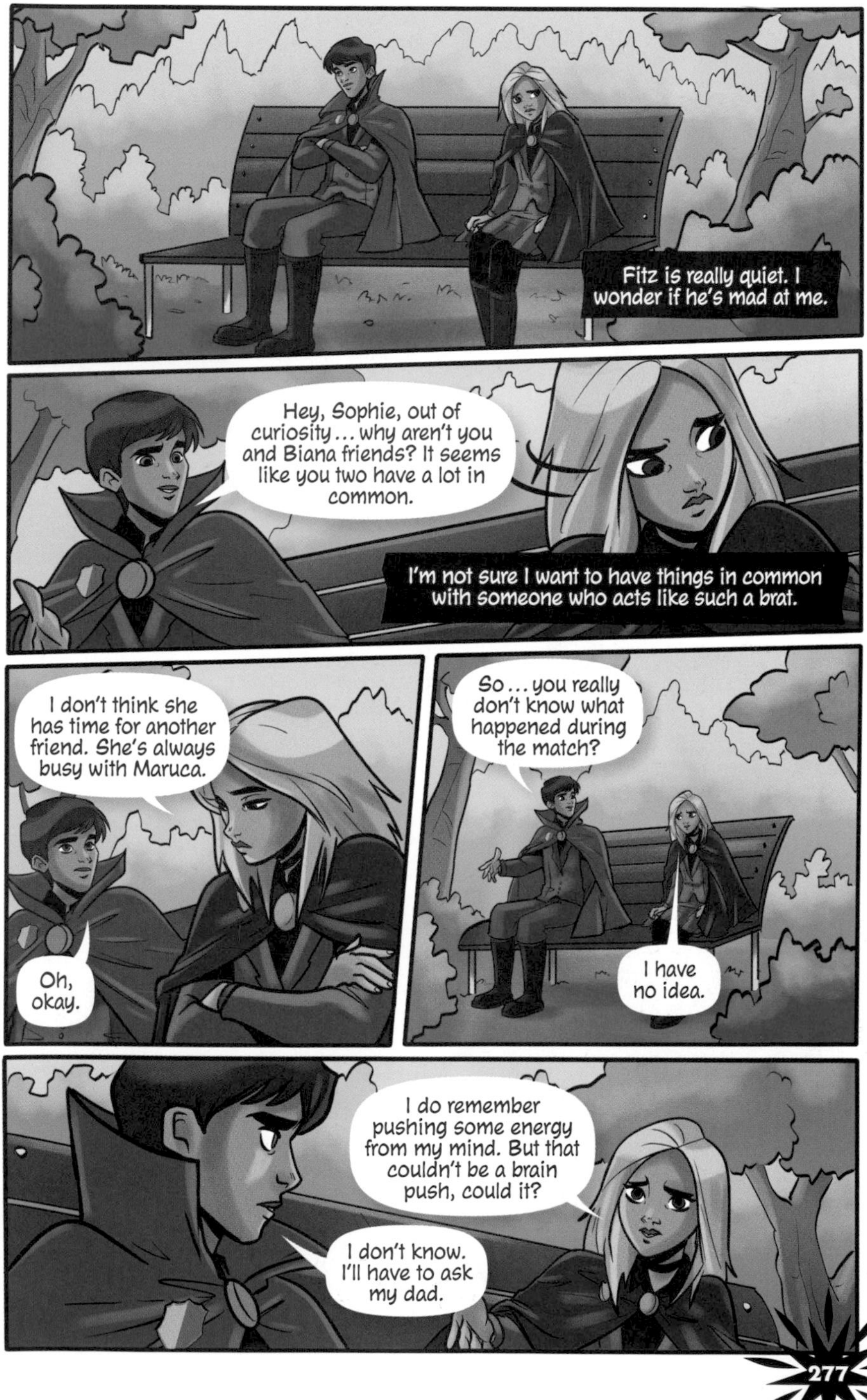
Fitz is really quiet. I wonder if he's mad at me.
Hey, Sophie, out of curiosity... why aren't you and Biana friends? It seems like you two have a lot in common.
I'm not sure I want to have things in common with someone who acts like such a brat.
I don't think she has time for another friend. She's always busy with Maruca.
Oh, okay.
So... you really don't know what happened during the match?
I have no idea.
I do remember pushing some energy from my mind. But that couldn't be a brain push, could it?
I don't know. I'll have to ask my dad.

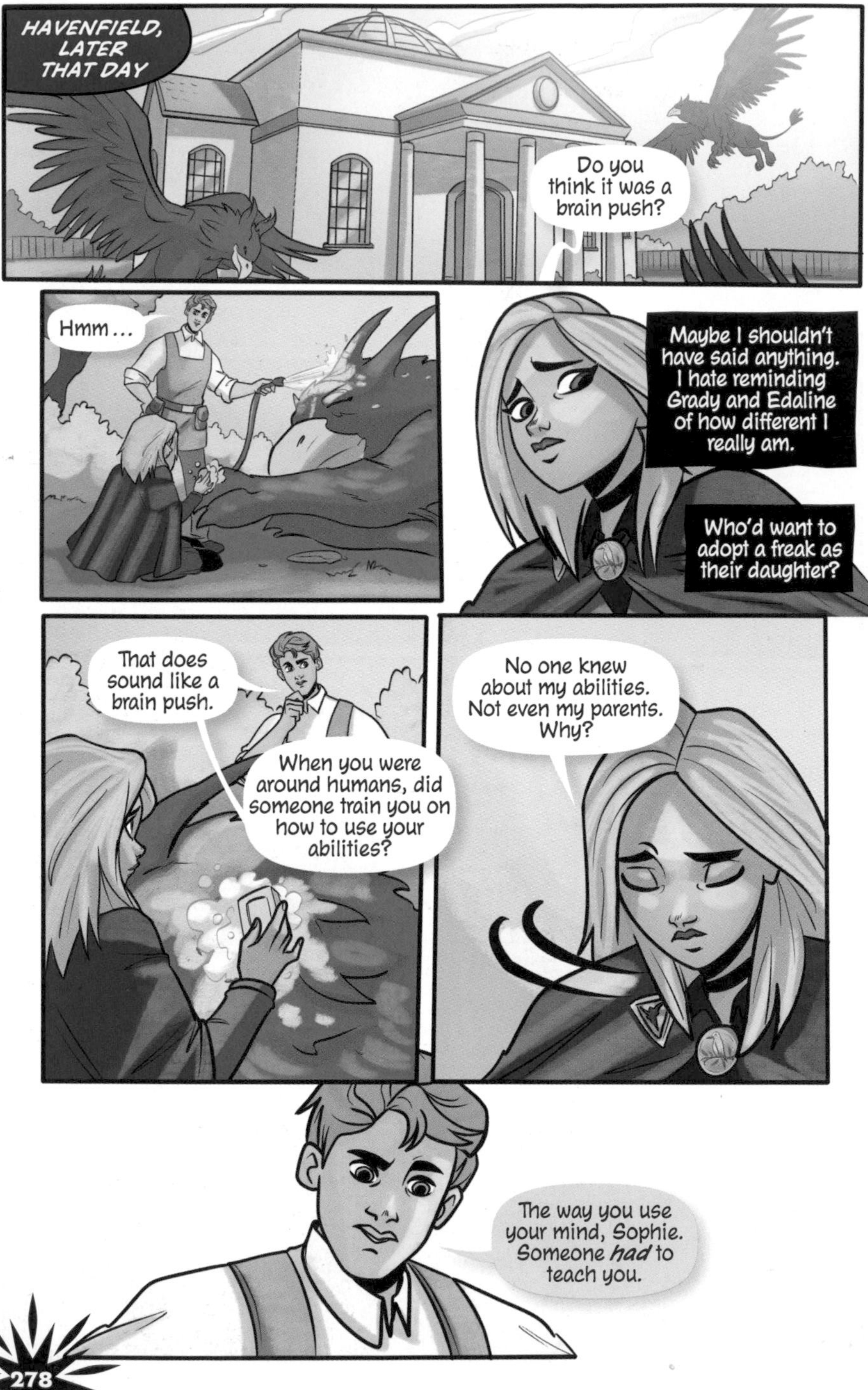
HAVENFIELD, LATER THAT DAY
Do you think it was a brain push?
Hmm...
Maybe I shouldn't have said anything. I hate reminding Grady and Edaline of how different I really am.
Who'd want to adopt a freak as their daughter?
That does sound like a brain push.
When you were around humans, did someone train you on how to use your abilities?
No one knew about my abilities. Not even my parents. Why?
The way you use your mind, Sophie. Someone *had* to teach you.

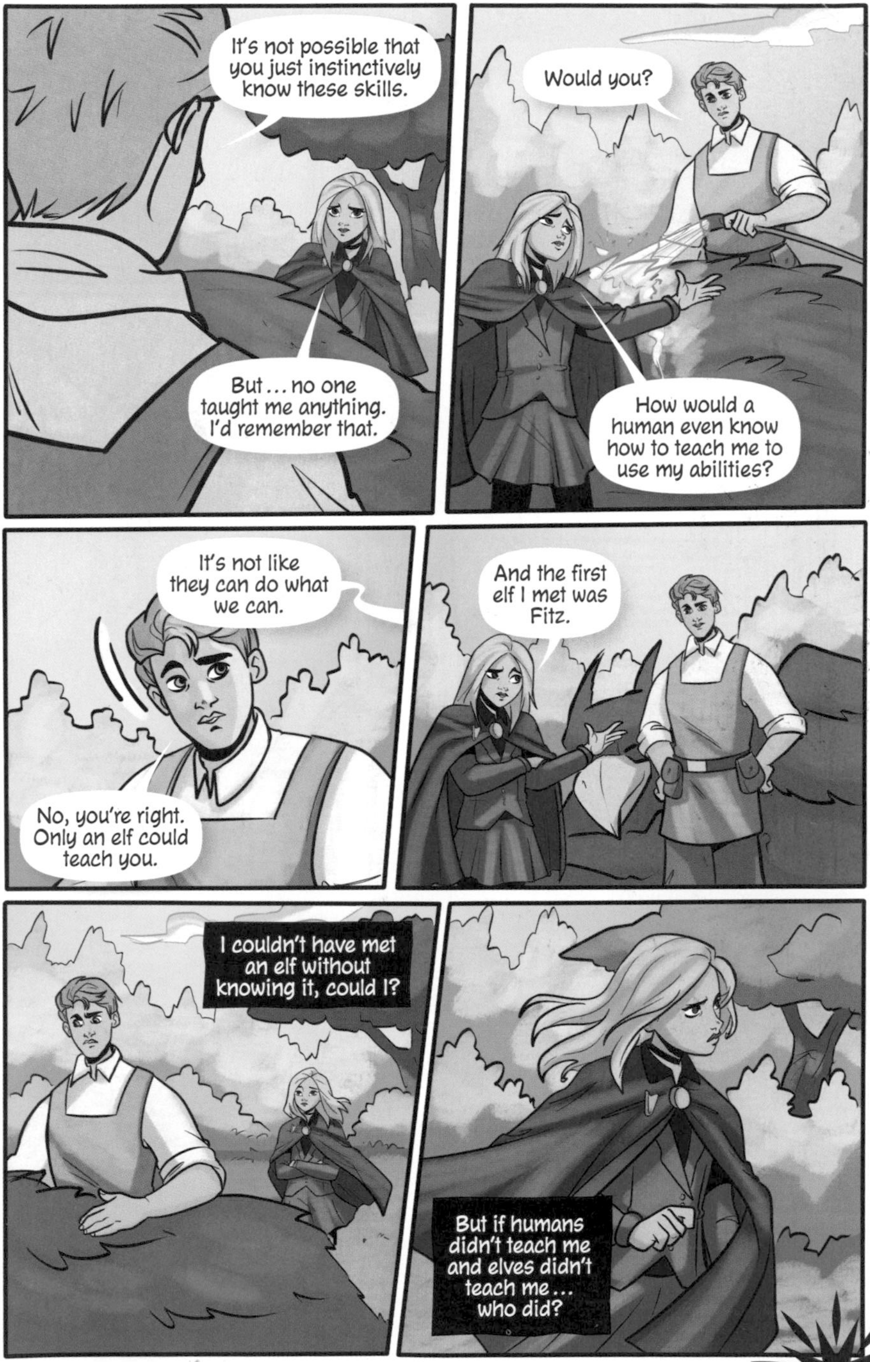
It's not possible that you just instinctively know these skills.
But... no one taught me anything. I'd remember that.
Would you?
How would a human even know how to teach me to use my abilities?
It's not like they can do what we can.
No, you're right. Only an elf could teach you.
And the first elf I met was Fitz.
I couldn't have met an elf without knowing it, could I?
But if humans didn't teach me and elves didn't teach me... who did?

CHAPTER TWENTY-FOUR

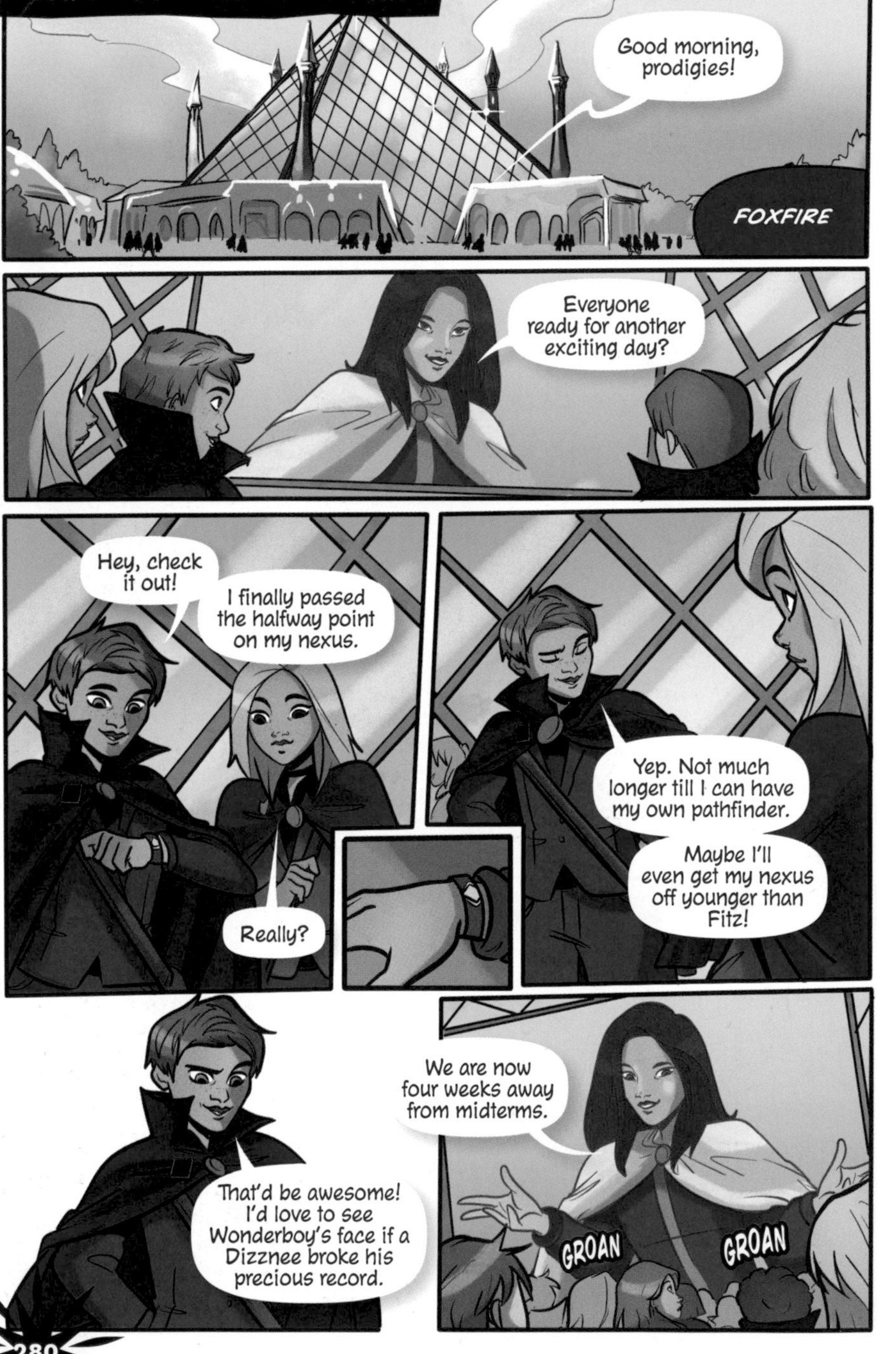
Good morning, prodigies!
FOXFIRE
Everyone ready for another exciting day?
Hey, check it out!
I finally passed the halfway point on my nexus.
Really?
Yep. Not much longer till I can have my own pathfinder.
Maybe I'll even get my nexus off younger than Fitz!
That'd be awesome! I'd love to see Wonderboy's face if a Dizznee broke his precious record.
We are now four weeks away from midterms.
GROAN
GROAN

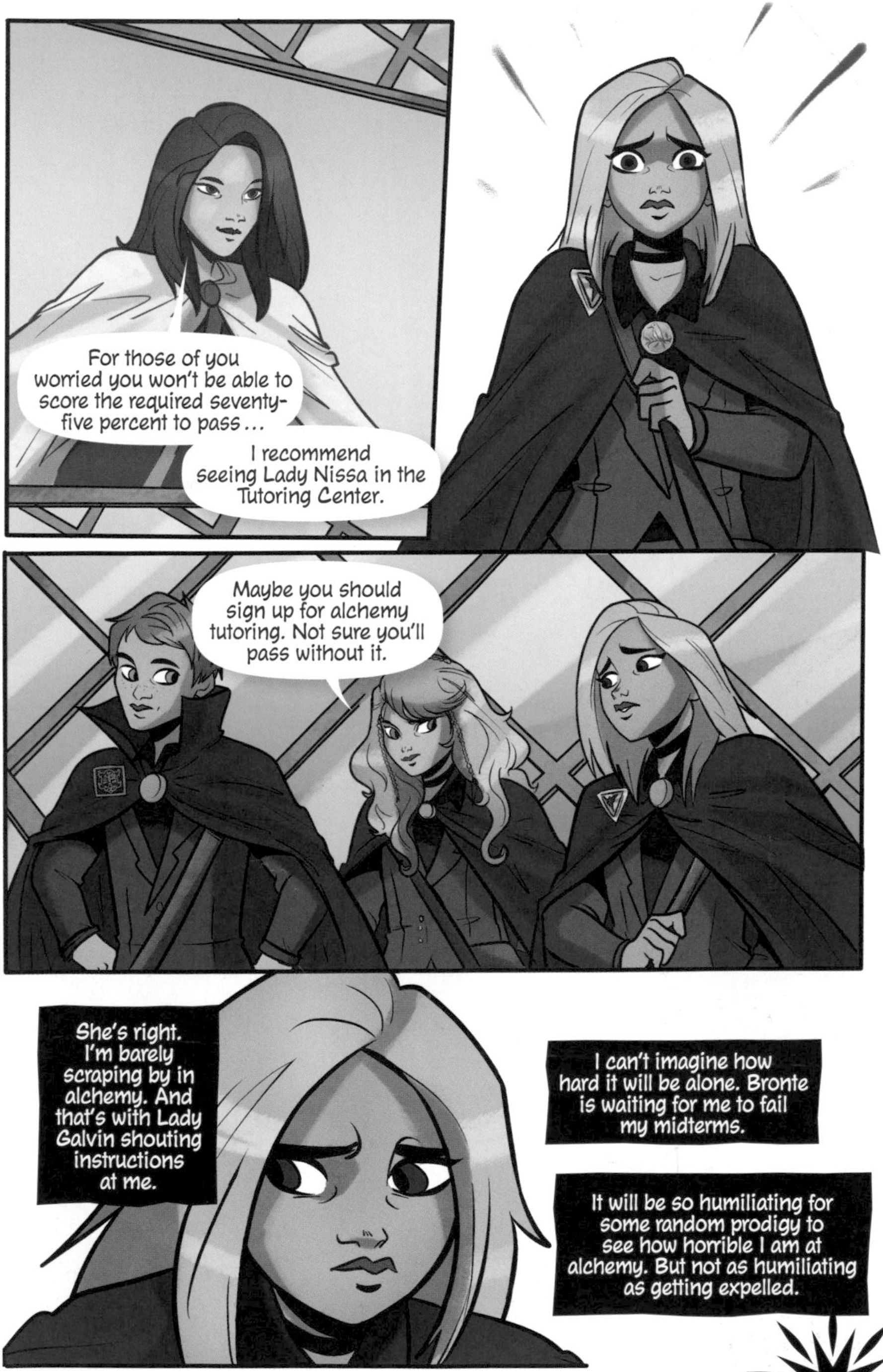
For those of you worried you won't be able to score the required seventy-five percent to pass...
I recommend seeing Lady Nissa in the Tutoring Center.
Maybe you should sign up for alchemy tutoring. Not sure you'll pass without it.
She's right. I'm barely scraping by in alchemy. And that's with Lady Galvin shouting instructions at me.
I can't imagine how hard it will be alone. Bronte is waiting for me to fail my midterms.
It will be so humiliating for some random prodigy to see how horrible I am at alchemy. But not as humiliating as getting expelled.

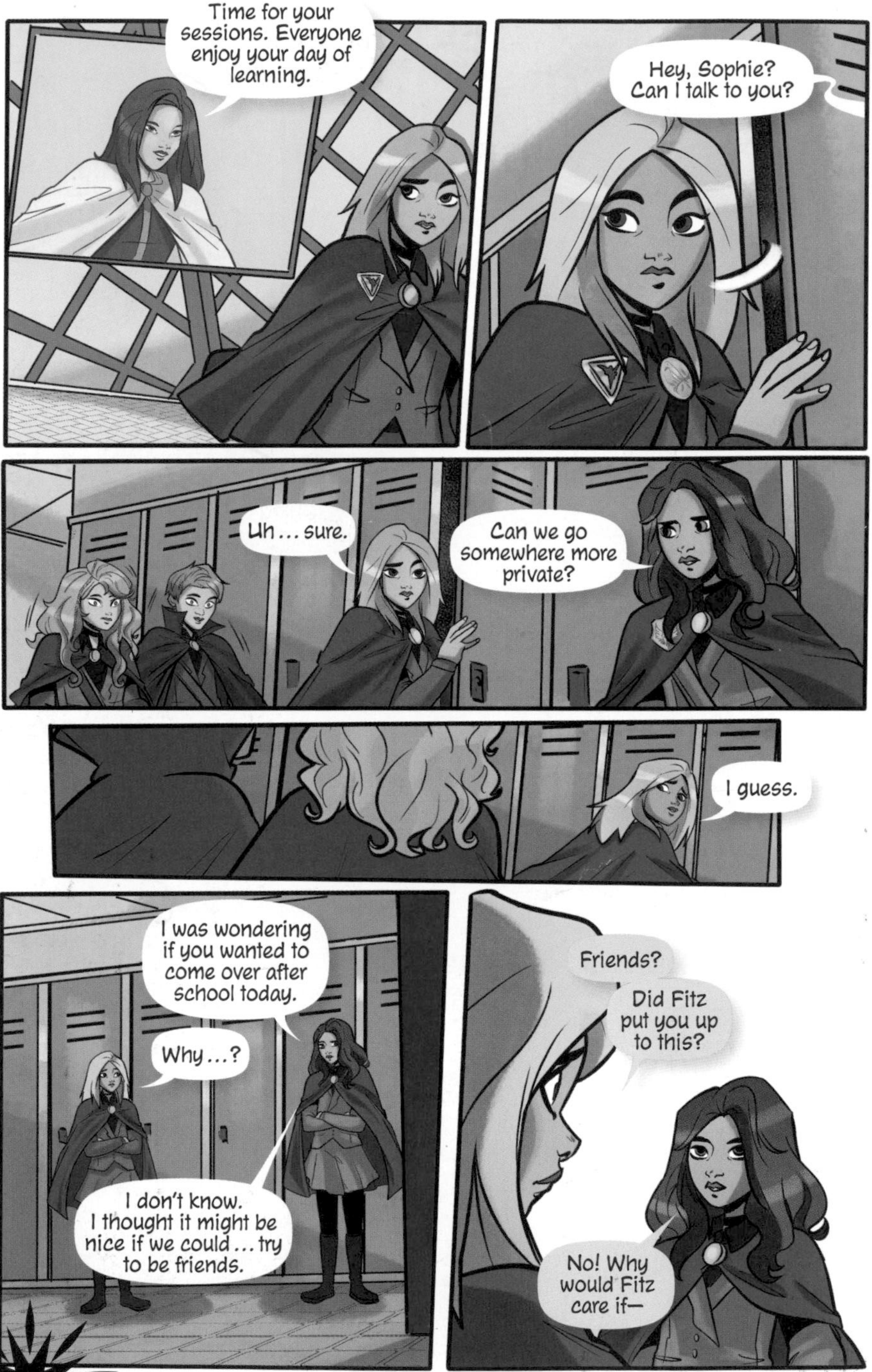
Time for your sessions. Everyone enjoy your day of learning.
Hey, Sophie? Can I talk to you?
Uh... sure.
Can we go somewhere more private?
I guess.
I was wondering if you wanted to come over after school today.
Why...?
I don't know. I thought it might be nice if we could... try to be friends.
Friends?
Did Fitz put you up to this?
No! Why would Fitz care if—

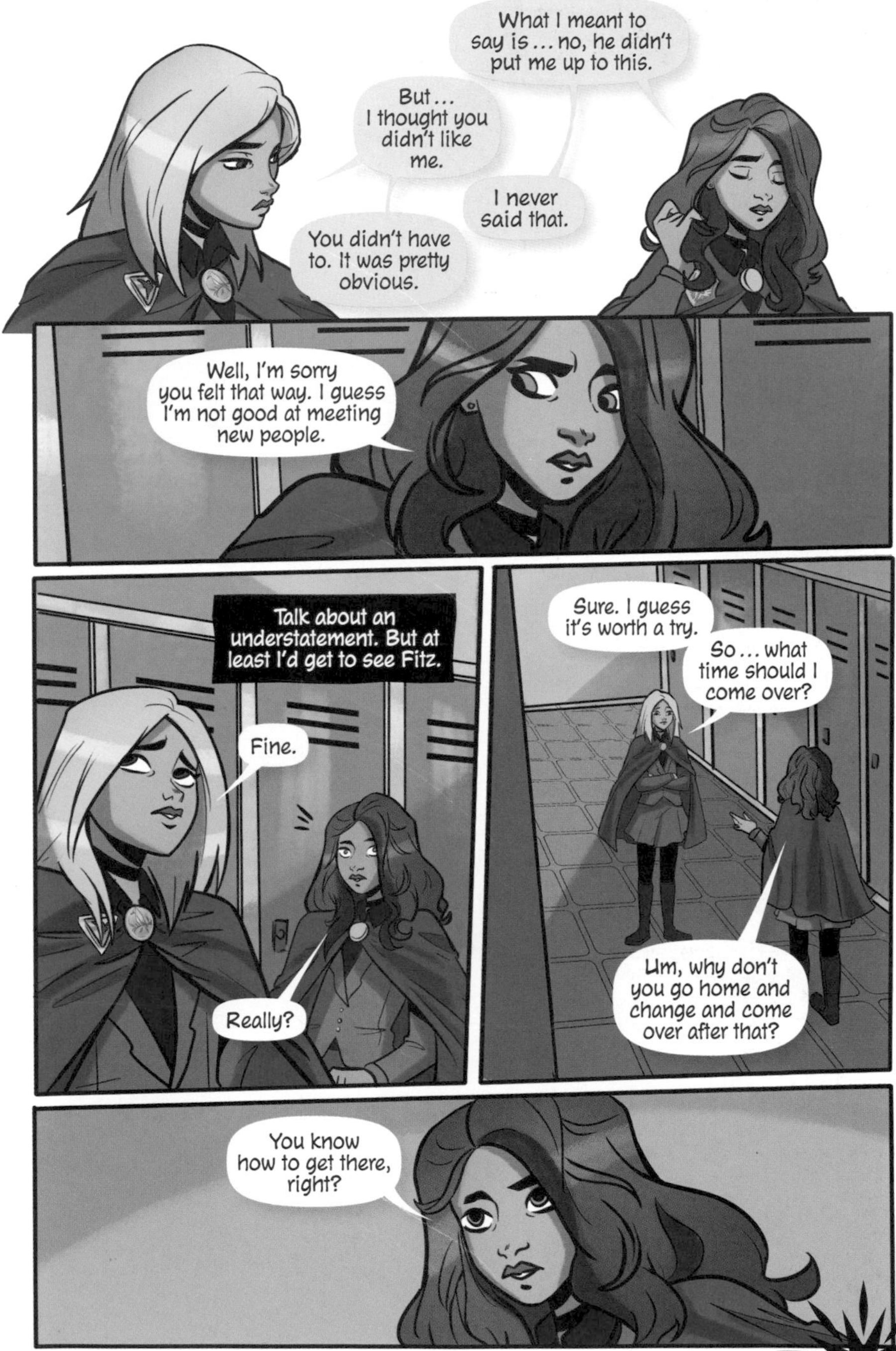
But… I thought you didn't like me.
What I meant to say is… no, he didn't put me up to this.
I never said that.
You didn't have to. It was pretty obvious.
Well, I'm sorry you felt that way. I guess I'm not good at meeting new people.
Talk about an understatement. But at least I'd get to see Fitz.
Fine.
Really?
Sure. I guess it's worth a try.
So… what time should I come over?
Um, why don't you go home and change and come over after that?
You know how to get there, right?

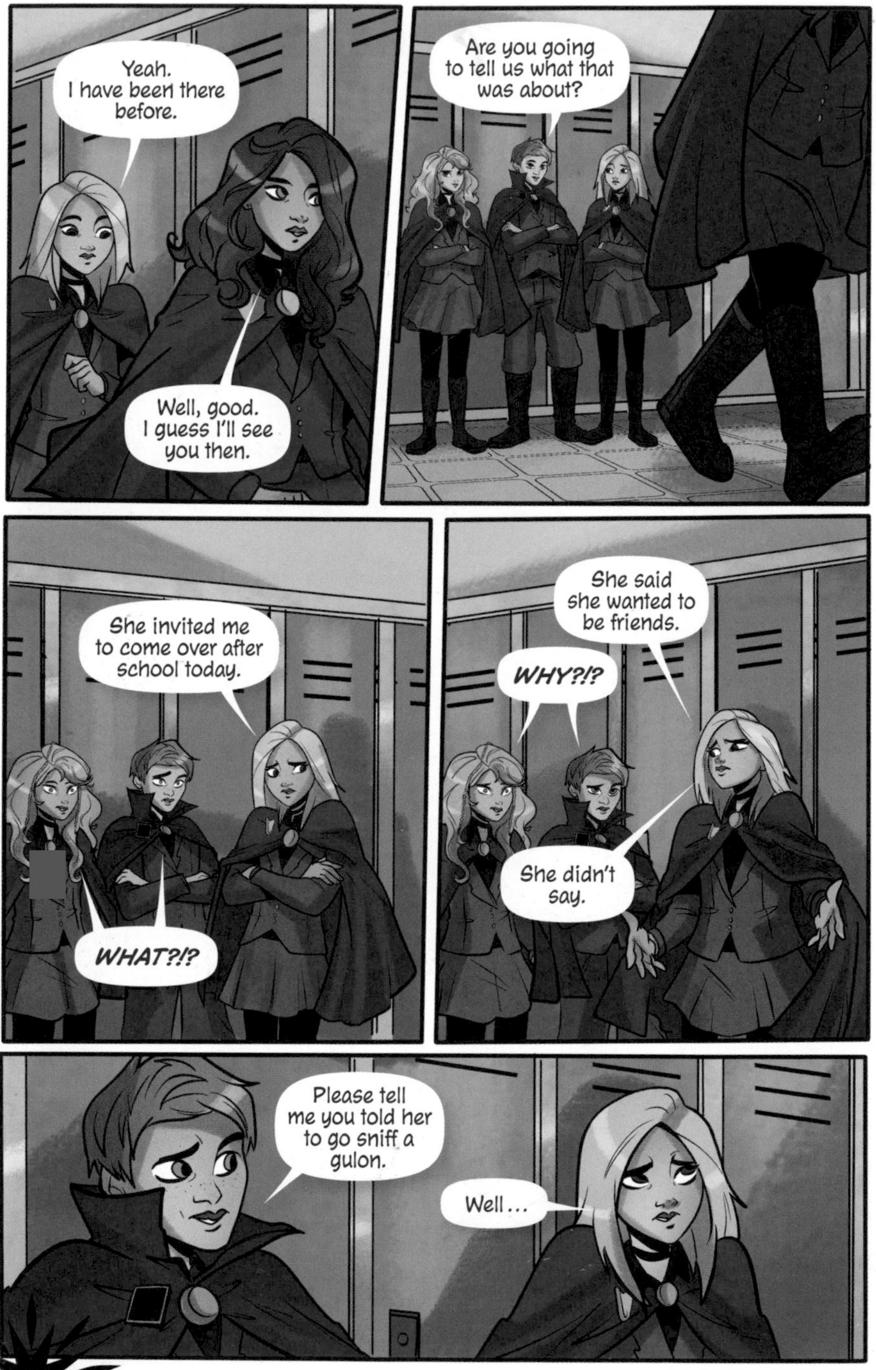
Yeah. I have been there before.
Well, good. I guess I'll see you then.
Are you going to tell us what that was about?
She invited me to come over after school today.
WHAT?!?
She said she wanted to be friends.
WHY?!?
She didn't say.
Please tell me you told her to go sniff a gulon.
Well...

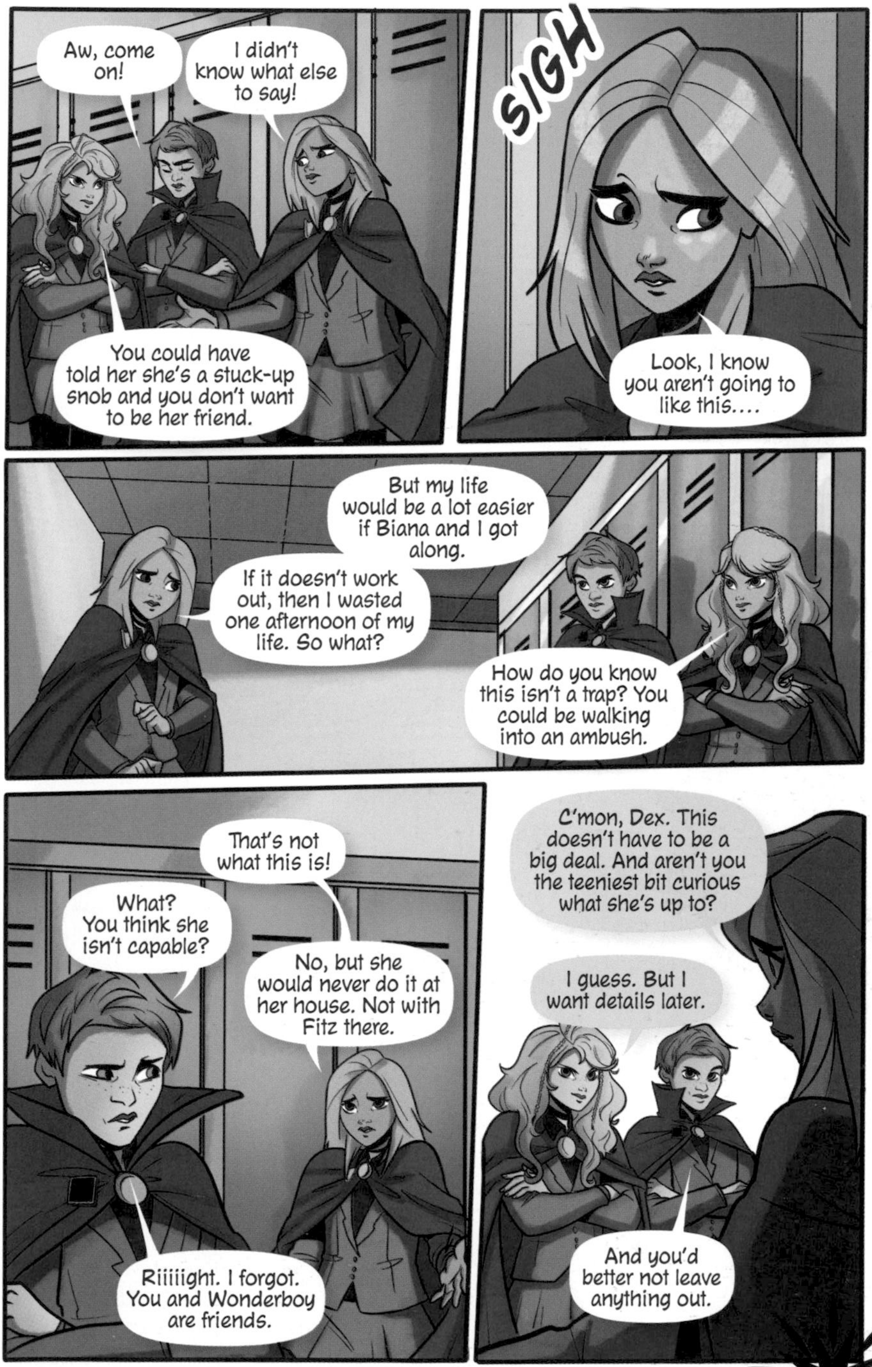
Aw, come on!
I didn't know what else to say!
You could have told her she's a stuck-up snob and you don't want to be her friend.
SIGH
Look, I know you aren't going to like this....
But my life would be a lot easier if Biana and I got along.
If it doesn't work out, then I wasted one afternoon of my life. So what?
How do you know this isn't a trap? You could be walking into an ambush.
What? You think she isn't capable?
That's not what this is!
No, but she would never do it at her house. Not with Fitz there.
Riiiiight. I forgot. You and Wonderboy are friends.
C'mon, Dex. This doesn't have to be a big deal. And aren't you the teeniest bit curious what she's up to?
I guess. But I want details later.
And you'd better not leave anything out.

CHAPTER TWENTY-FIVE

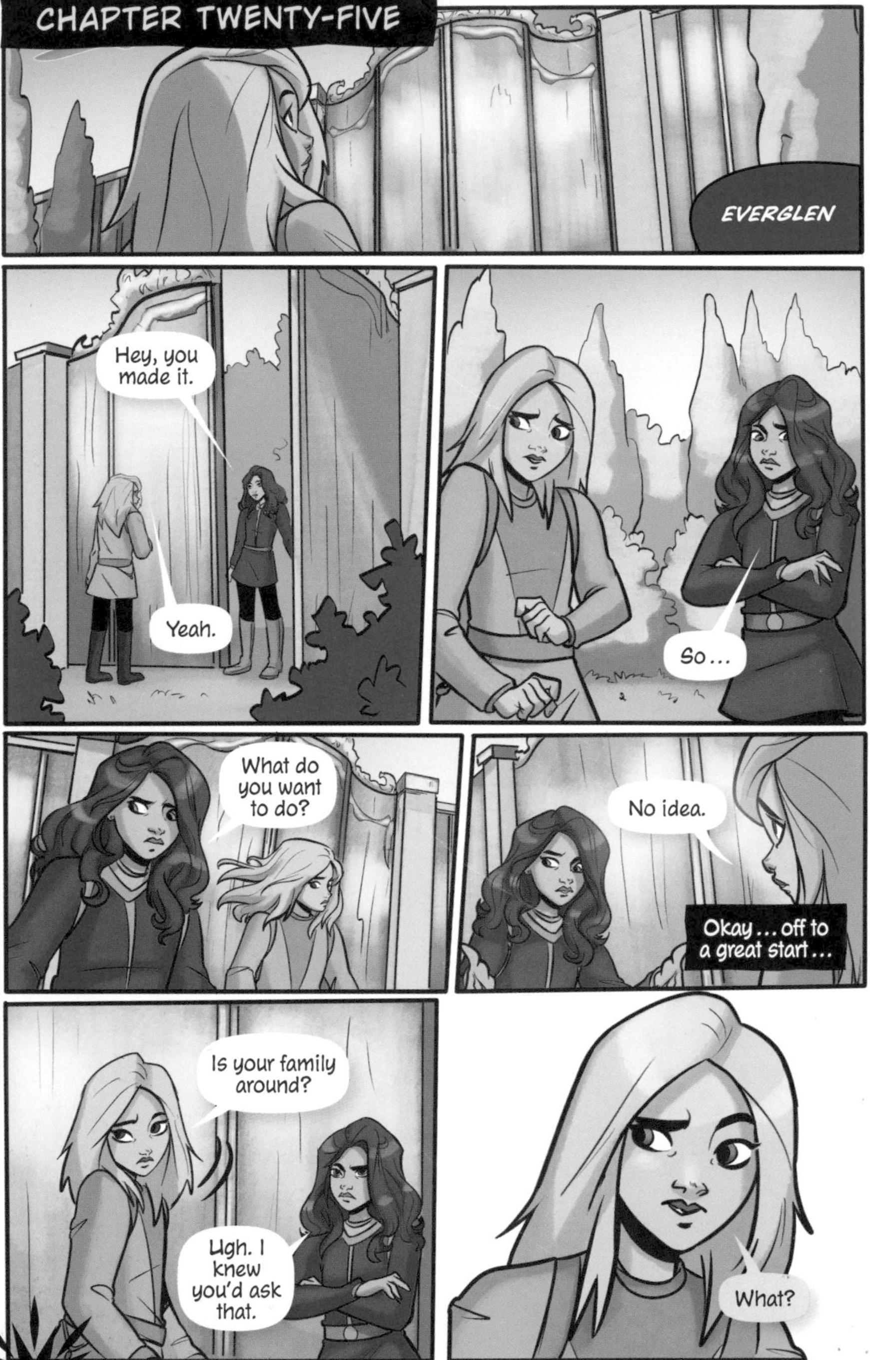

EVERGLEN
Hey, you made it.
Yeah.
So...
What do you want to do?
No idea.
Okay... off to a great start...
Is your family around?
Ugh. I knew you'd ask that.
What?

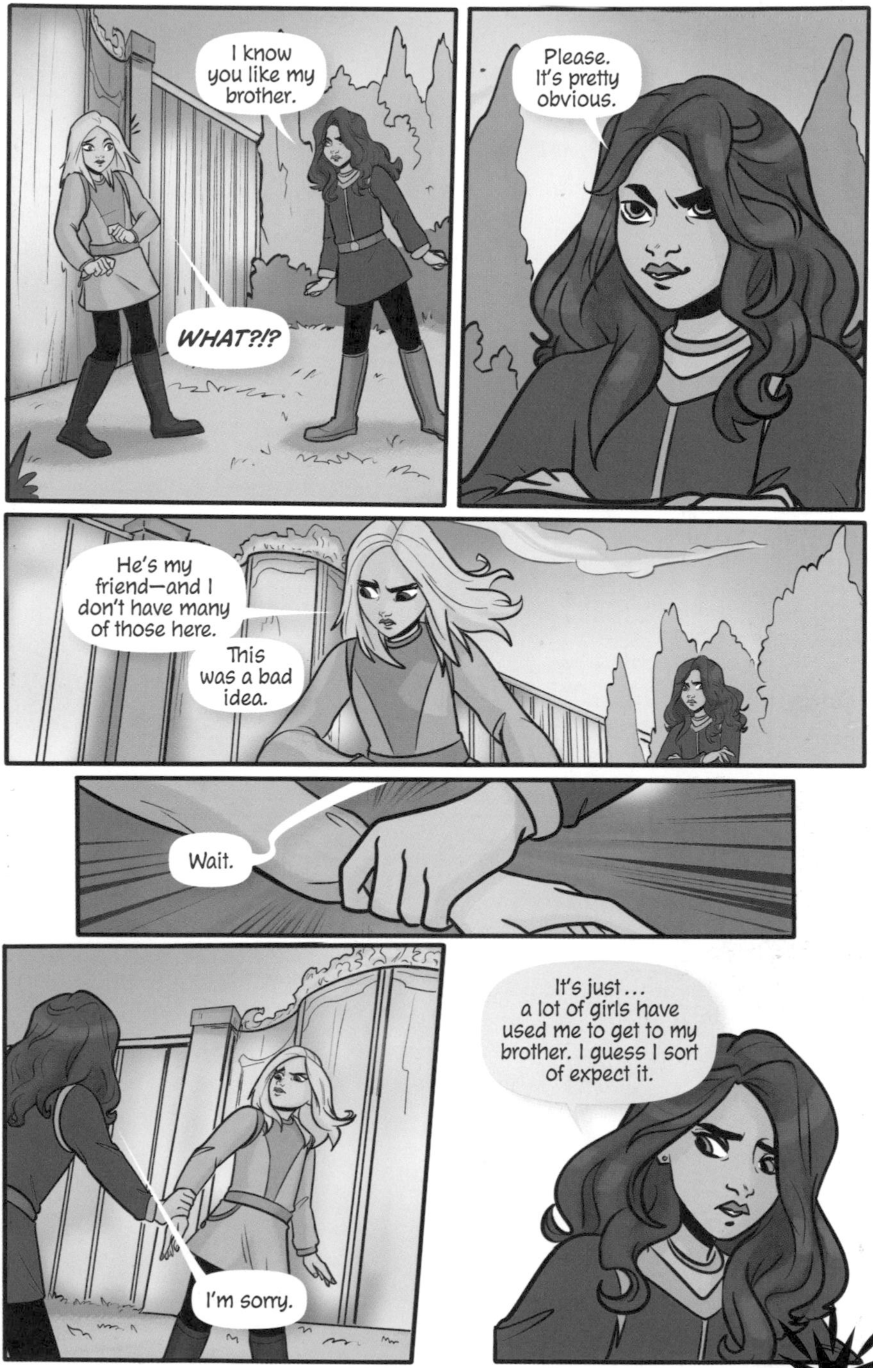
I know you like my brother.
WHAT?!?
Please. It's pretty obvious.
He's my friend—and I don't have many of those here.
This was a bad idea.
Wait.
I'm sorry.
It's just... a lot of girls have used me to get to my brother. I guess I sort of expect it.

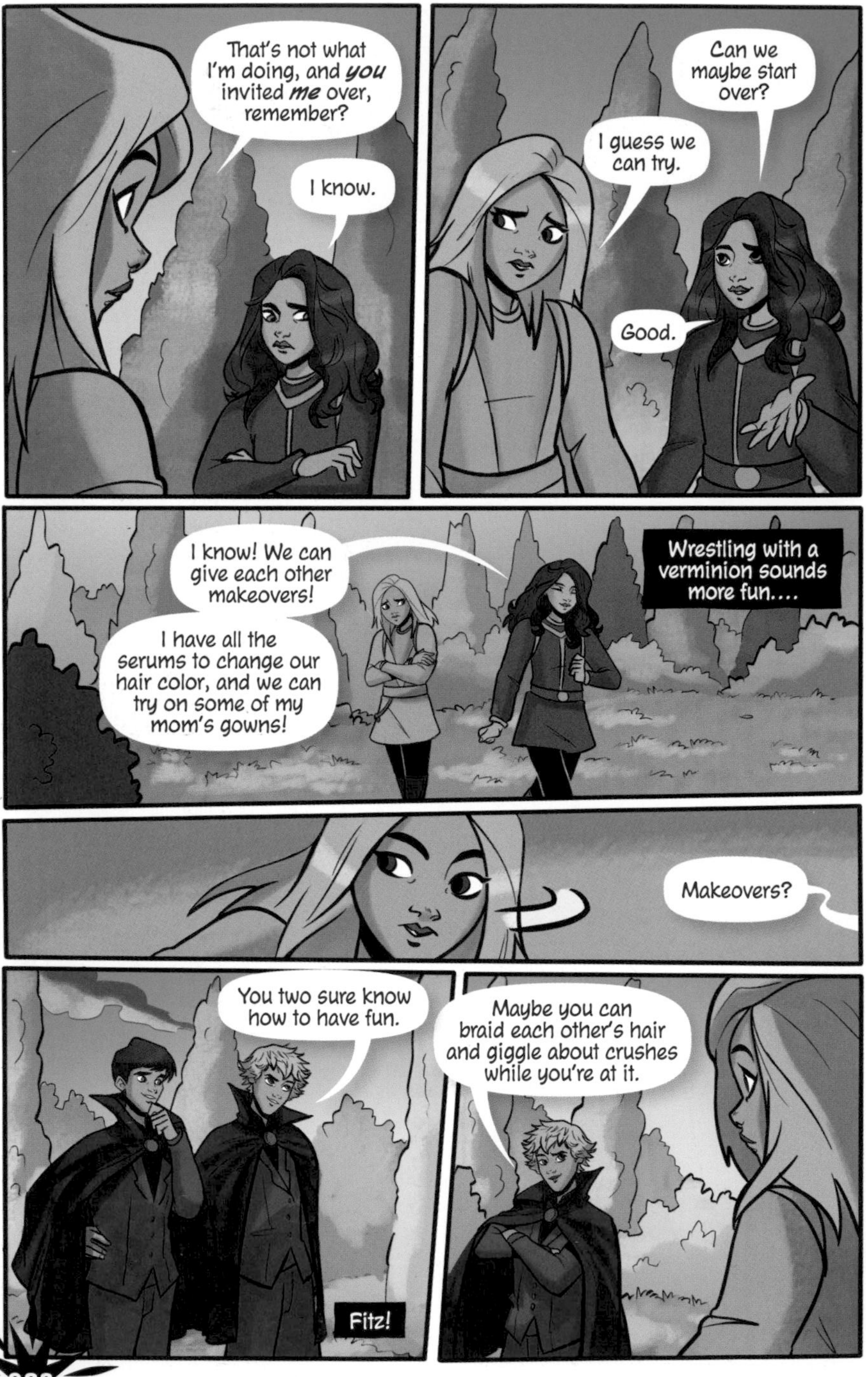

That's not what I'm doing, and *you* invited *me* over, remember?
I know.
Can we maybe start over?
I guess we can try.
Good.
I know! We can give each other makeovers!
I have all the serums to change our hair color, and we can try on some of my mom's gowns!
Wrestling with a verminion sounds more fun....
Makeovers?
You two sure know how to have fun.
Fitz!
Maybe you can braid each other's hair and giggle about crushes while you're at it.

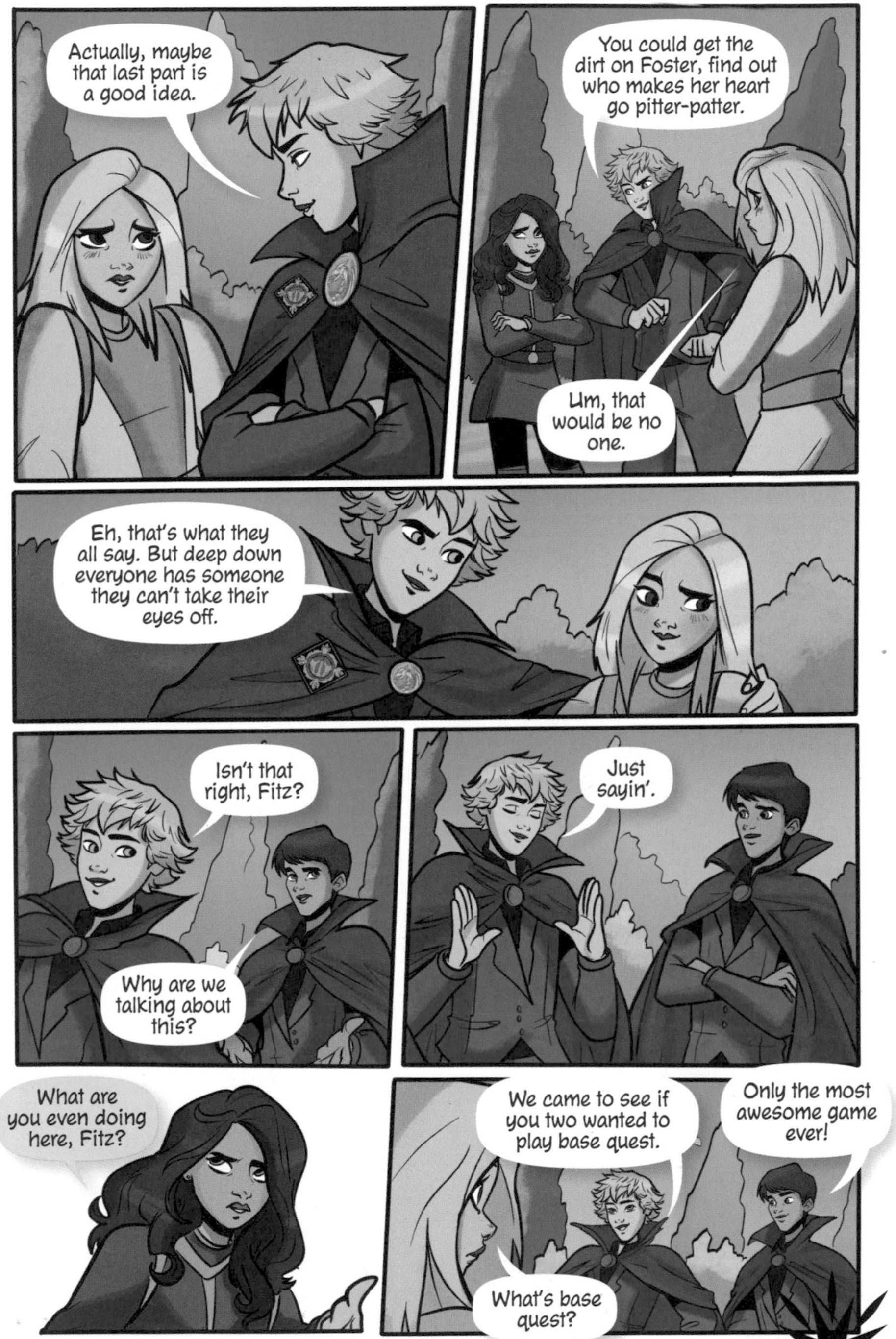
Actually, maybe that last part is a good idea.
You could get the dirt on Foster, find out who makes her heart go pitter-patter.
Um, that would be no one.
Eh, that's what they all say. But deep down everyone has someone they can't take their eyes off.
Isn't that right, Fitz?
Why are we talking about this?
Just sayin'.
What are you even doing here, Fitz?
We came to see if you two wanted to play base quest.
Only the most awesome game ever!
What's base quest?

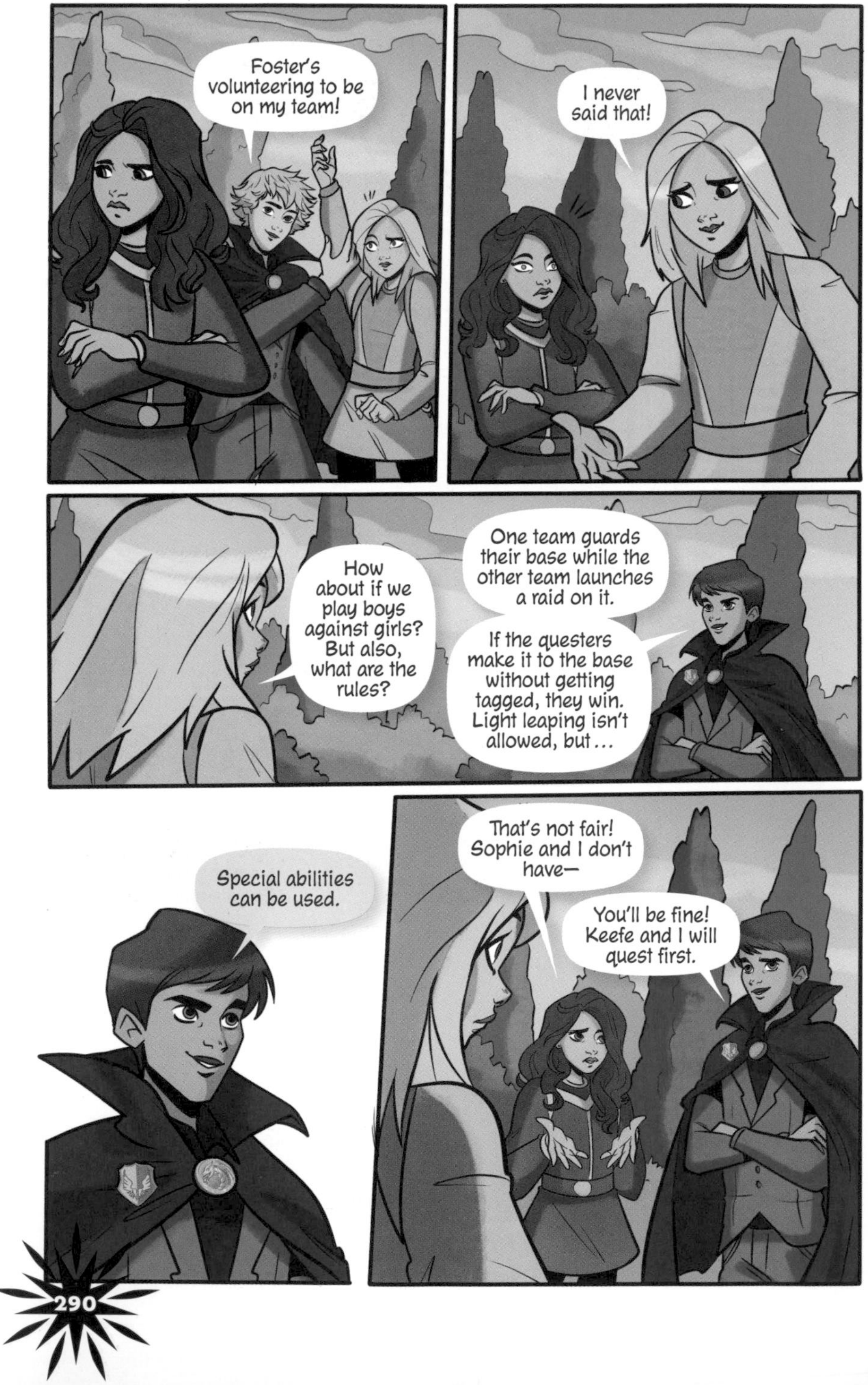
Foster's volunteering to be on my team!
I never said that!
How about if we play boys against girls? But also, what are the rules?
One team guards their base while the other team launches a raid on it.
If the questers make it to the base without getting tagged, they win. Light leaping isn't allowed, but…
Special abilities can be used.
That's not fair! Sophie and I don't have—
You'll be fine! Keefe and I will quest first.

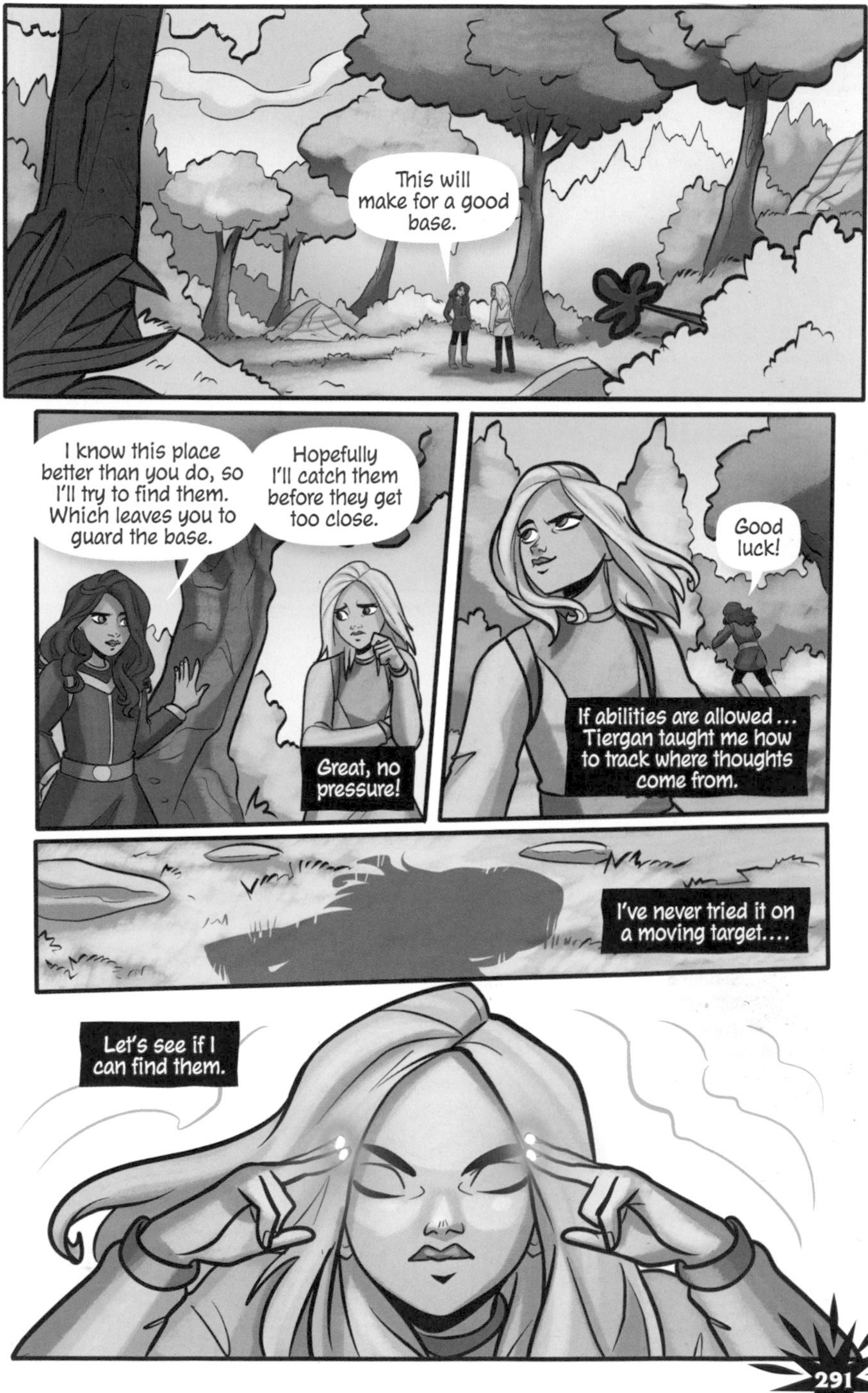
This will make for a good base.
I know this place better than you do, so I'll try to find them. Which leaves you to guard the base.
Hopefully I'll catch them before they get too close.
Great, no pressure!
Good luck!
If abilities are allowed... Tiergan taught me how to track where thoughts come from.
I've never tried it on a moving target....
Let's see if I can find them.

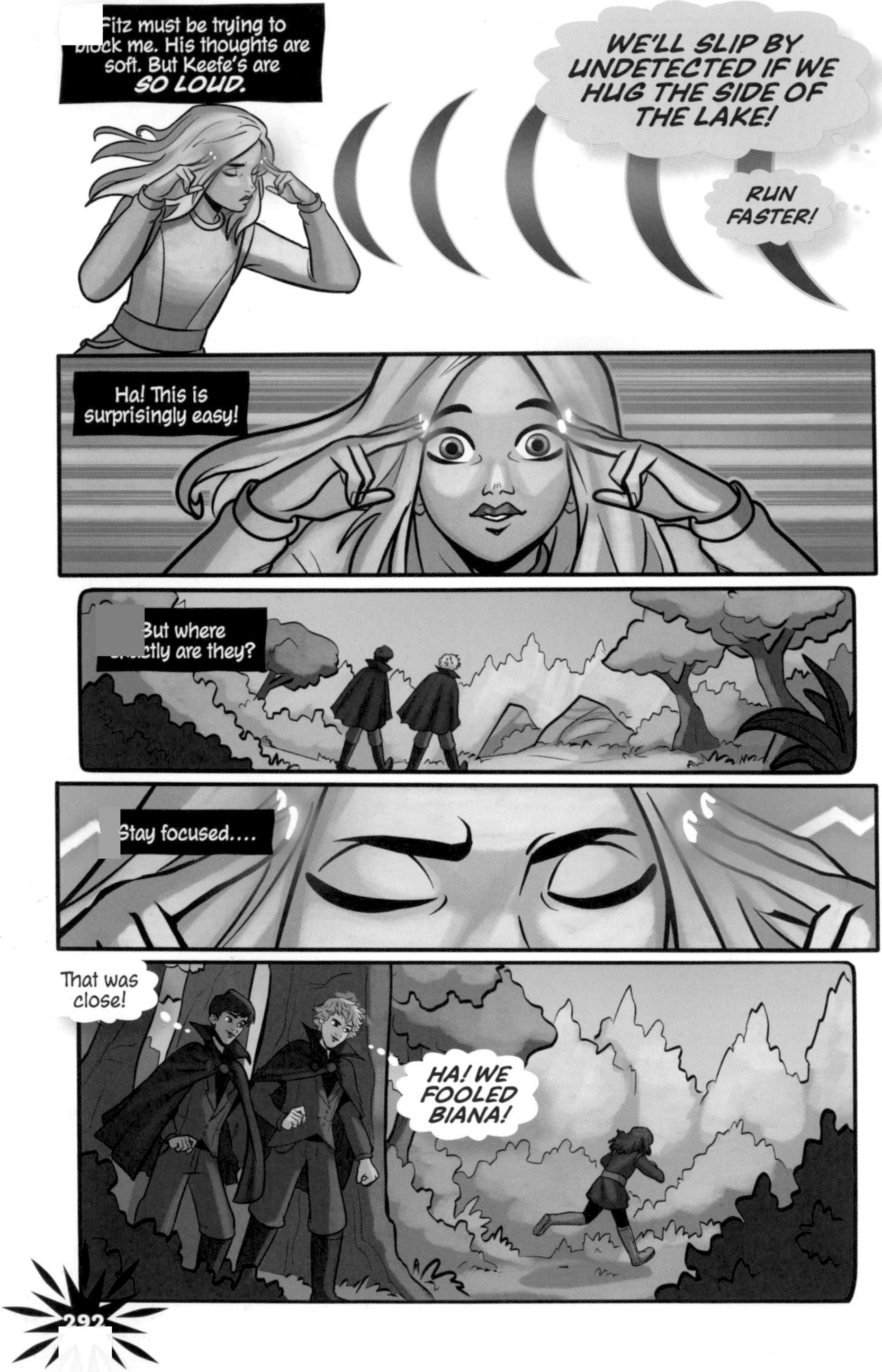

Fitz must be trying to block me. His thoughts are soft. But Keefe's are SO LOUD.
WE'LL SLIP BY UNDETECTED IF WE HUG THE SIDE OF THE LAKE!
RUN FASTER!
Ha! This is surprisingly easy!
But where exactly are they?
Stay focused....
That was close!
HA! WE FOOLED BIANA!

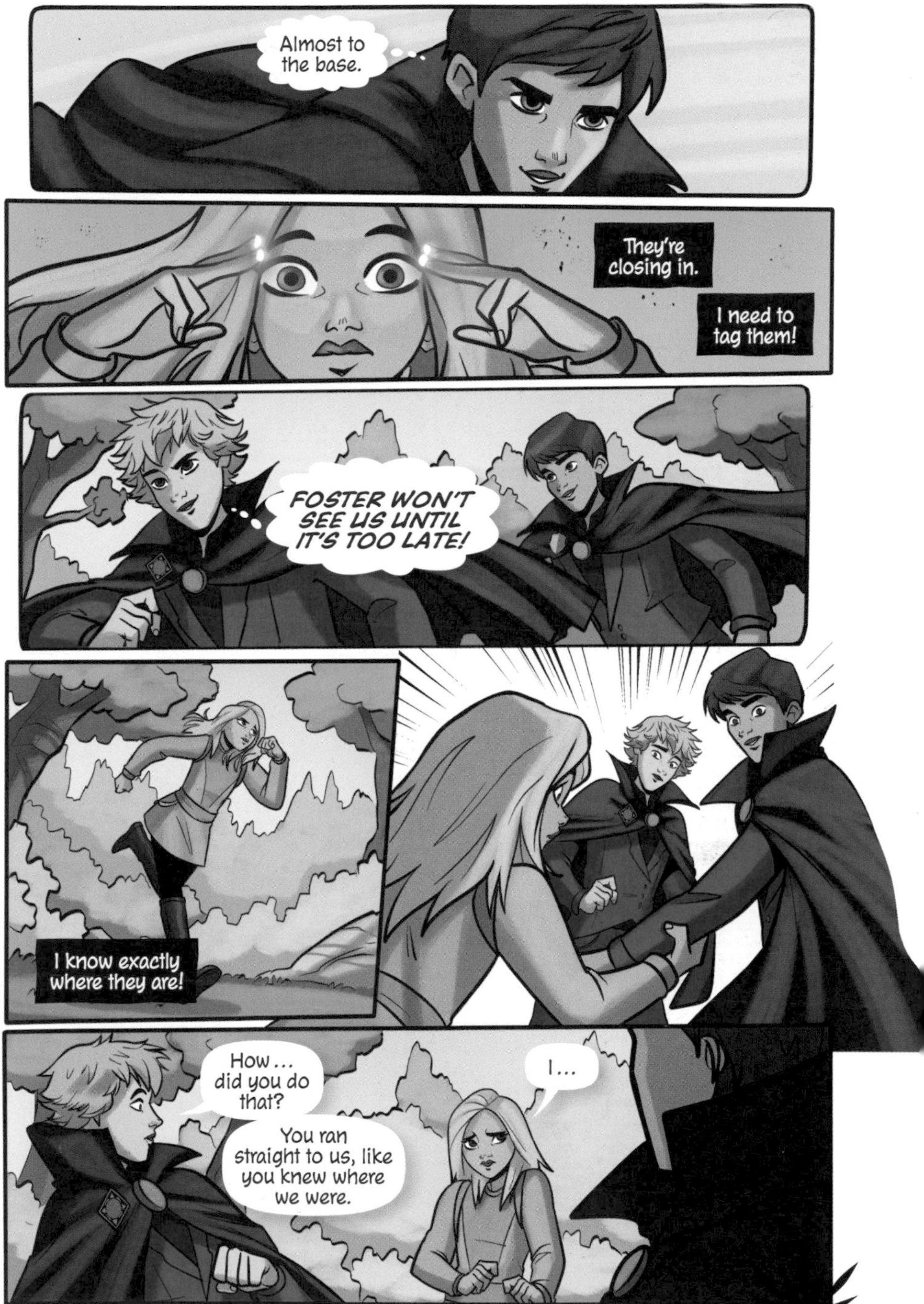
Almost to the base.
They're closing in.
I need to tag them!
FOSTER WON'T SEE US UNTIL IT'S TOO LATE!
I know exactly where they are!
How... did you do that?
You ran straight to us, like you knew where we were.
I...

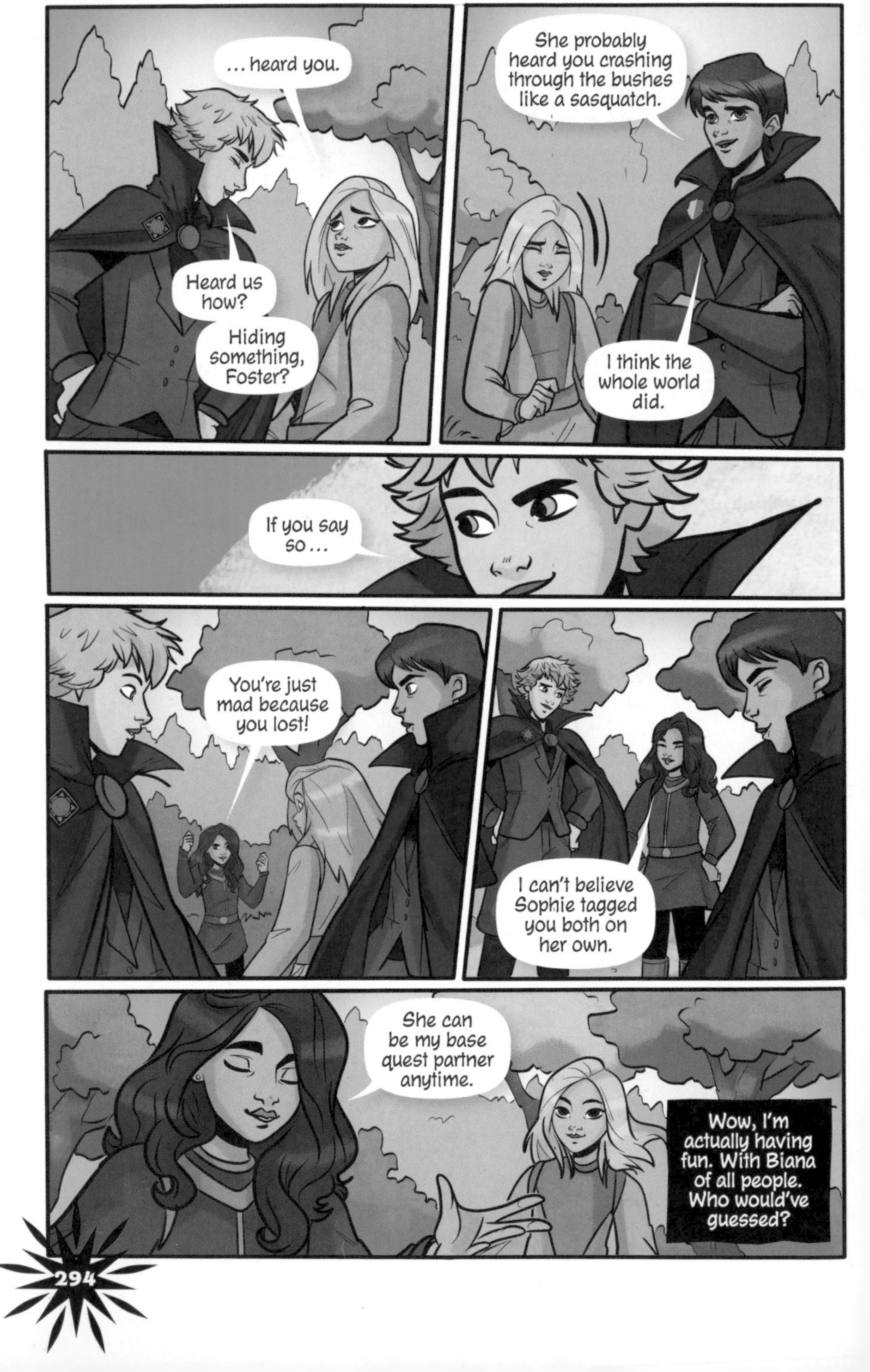

... heard you.
Heard us how?
Hiding something, Foster?
She probably heard you crashing through the bushes like a sasquatch.
I think the whole world did.
If you say so...
You're just mad because you lost!
I can't believe Sophie tagged you both on her own.
She can be my base quest partner anytime.
Wow, I'm actually having fun. With Biana of all people. Who would've guessed?

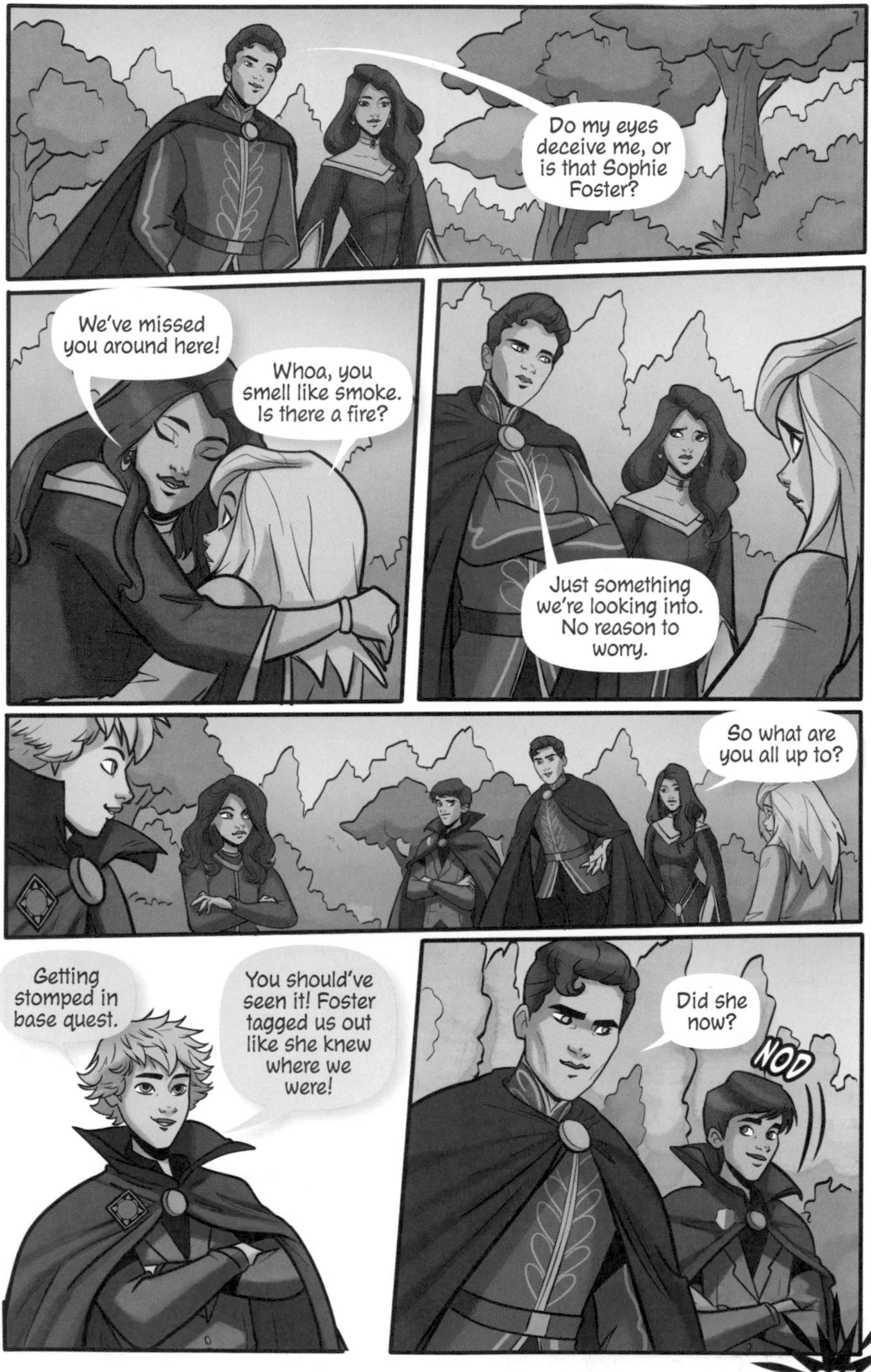
Do my eyes deceive me, or is that Sophie Foster?
We've missed you around here!
Whoa, you smell like smoke. Is there a fire?
Just something we're looking into. No reason to worry.
So what are you all up to?
Getting stomped in base quest.
You should've seen it! Foster tagged us out like she knew where we were!
Did she now?
NOD

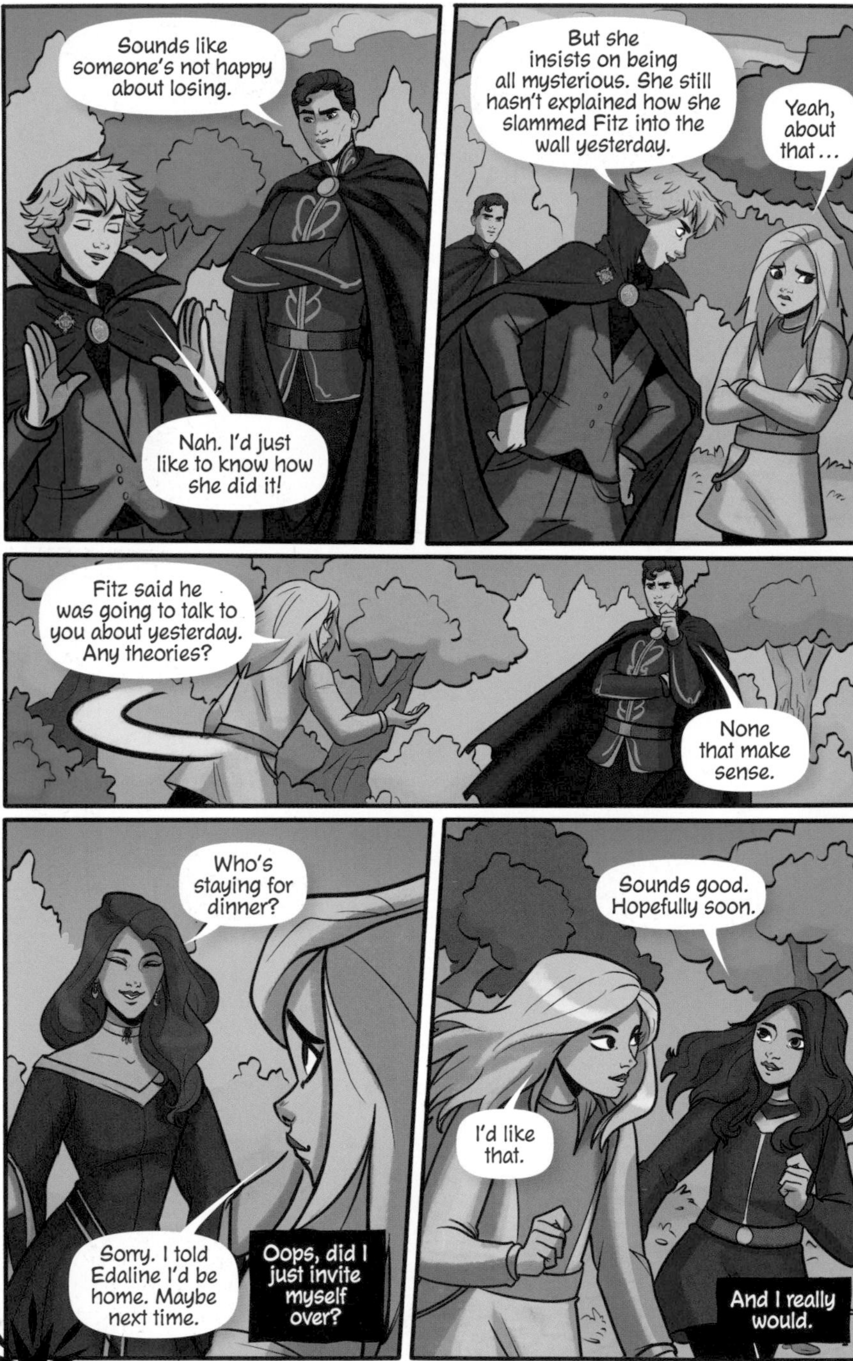
Sounds like someone's not happy about losing.
Nah. I'd just like to know how she did it!
But she insists on being all mysterious. She still hasn't explained how she slammed Fitz into the wall yesterday.
Yeah, about that...
Fitz said he was going to talk to you about yesterday. Any theories?
None that make sense.
Who's staying for dinner?
Sorry. I told Edaline I'd be home. Maybe next time.
Oops, did I just invite myself over?
Sounds good. Hopefully soon.
I'd like that.
And I really would.

CHAPTER TWENTY-SIX

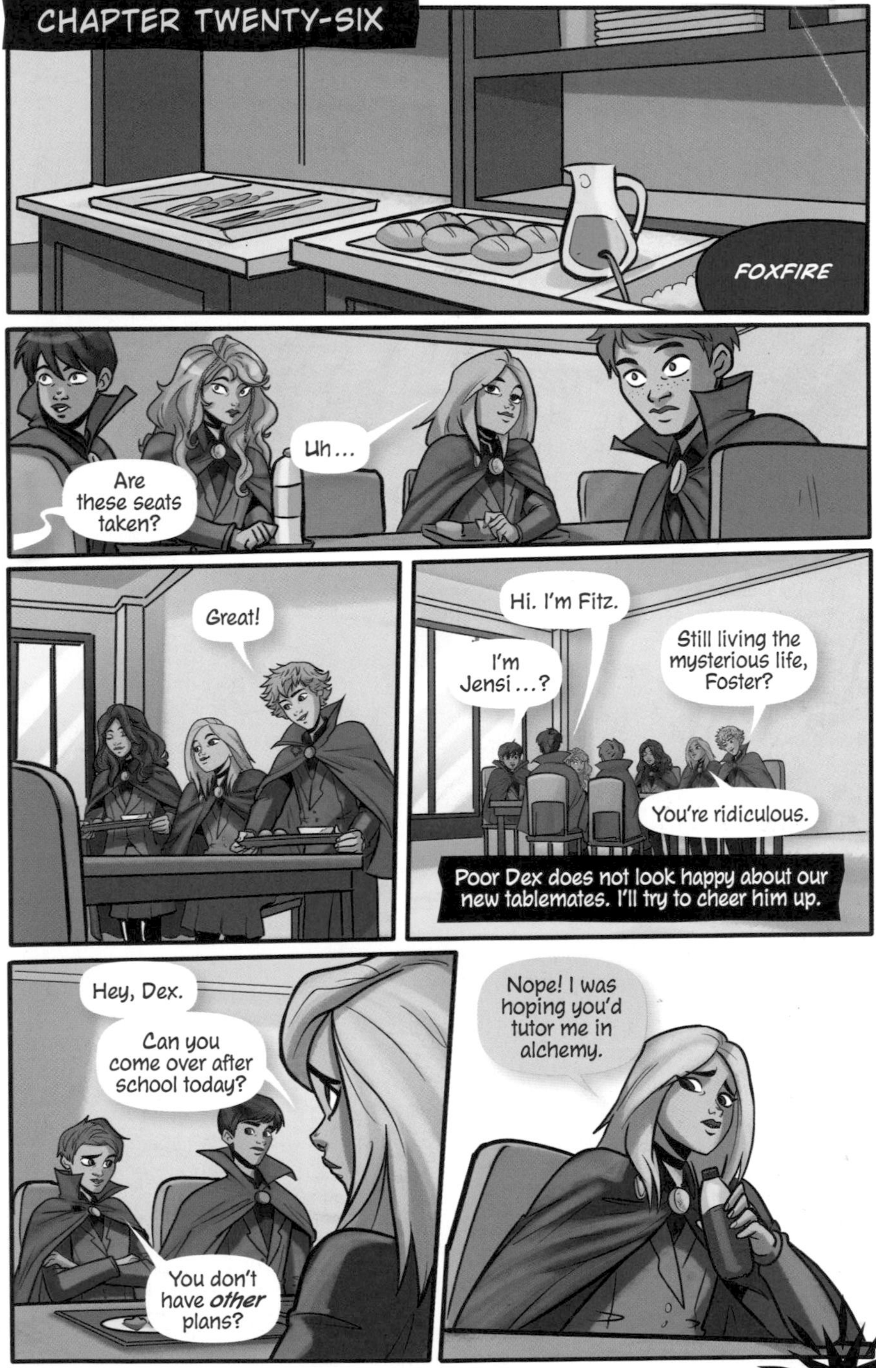
FOXFIRE
Are these seats taken?
Uh…
Great!
Hi. I'm Fitz.
I'm Jensi…?
Still living the mysterious life, Foster?
You're ridiculous.
Poor Dex does not look happy about our new tablemates. I'll try to cheer him up.
Hey, Dex.
Can you come over after school today?
You don't have *other* plans?
Nope! I was hoping you'd tutor me in alchemy.

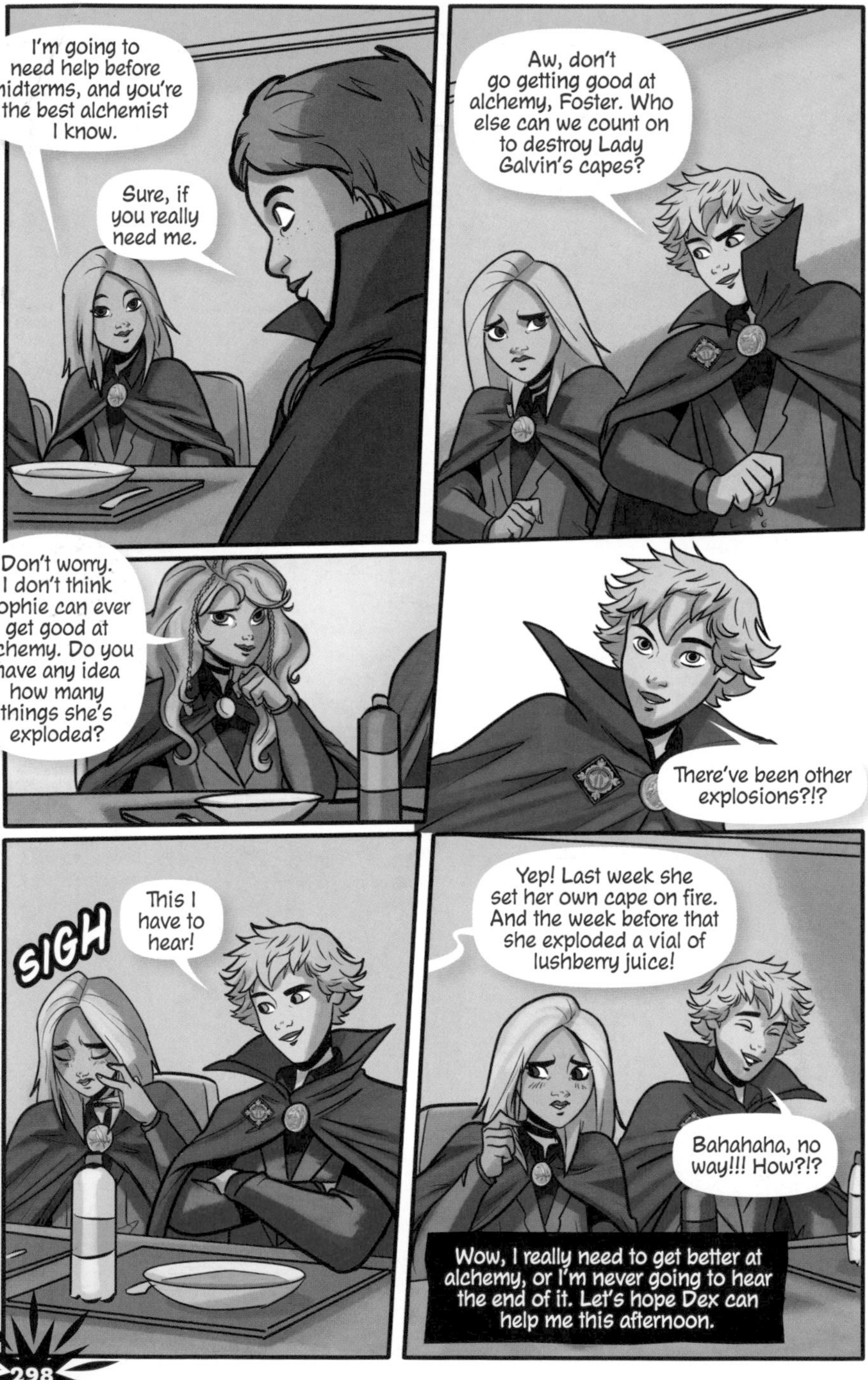
I'm going to need help before midterms, and you're the best alchemist I know.
Sure, if you really need me.
Aw, don't go getting good at alchemy, Foster. Who else can we count on to destroy Lady Galvin's capes?
Don't worry. I don't think Sophie can ever get good at alchemy. Do you have any idea how many things she's exploded?
There've been other explosions?!?
SIGH
This I have to hear!
Yep! Last week she set her own cape on fire. And the week before that she exploded a vial of lushberry juice!
Bahahaha, no way!!! How?!?
Wow, I really need to get better at alchemy, or I'm never going to hear the end of it. Let's hope Dex can help me this afternoon.

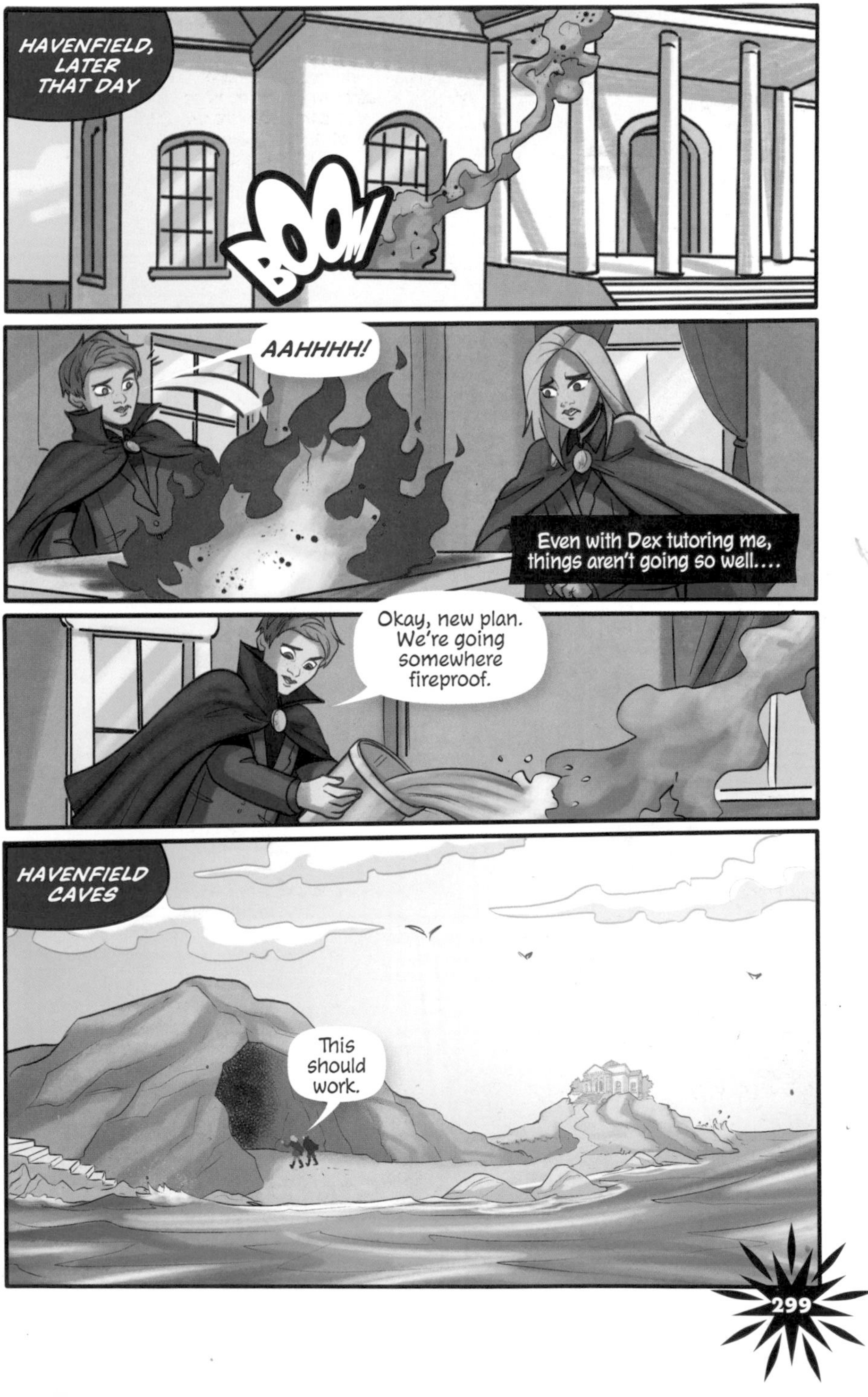
HAVENFIELD, LATER THAT DAY
BOOM
AAHHHH!
Even with Dex tutoring me, things aren't going so well....
Okay, new plan. We're going somewhere fireproof.
HAVENFIELD CAVES
This should work.

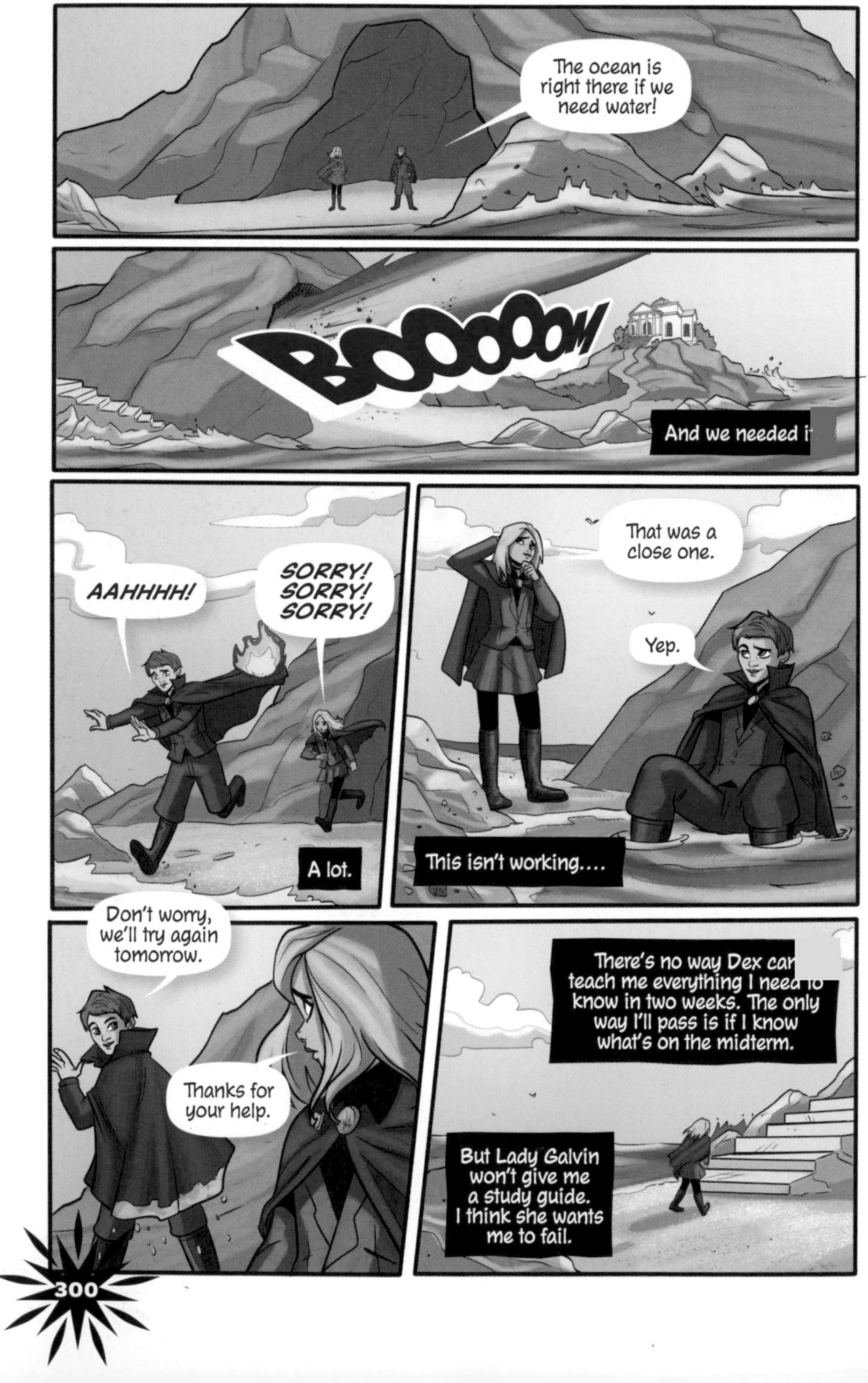
The ocean is right there if we need water!
BOOOOOM
And we needed i
AAHHHH!
SORRY! SORRY! SORRY!
A lot.
That was a close one.
Yep.
This isn't working....
Don't worry, we'll try again tomorrow.
Thanks for your help.
There's no way Dex ca
teach me everything I need
know in two weeks. The only way I'll pass is if I know what's on the midterm.
But Lady Galvin won't give me a study guide. I think she wants me to fail.

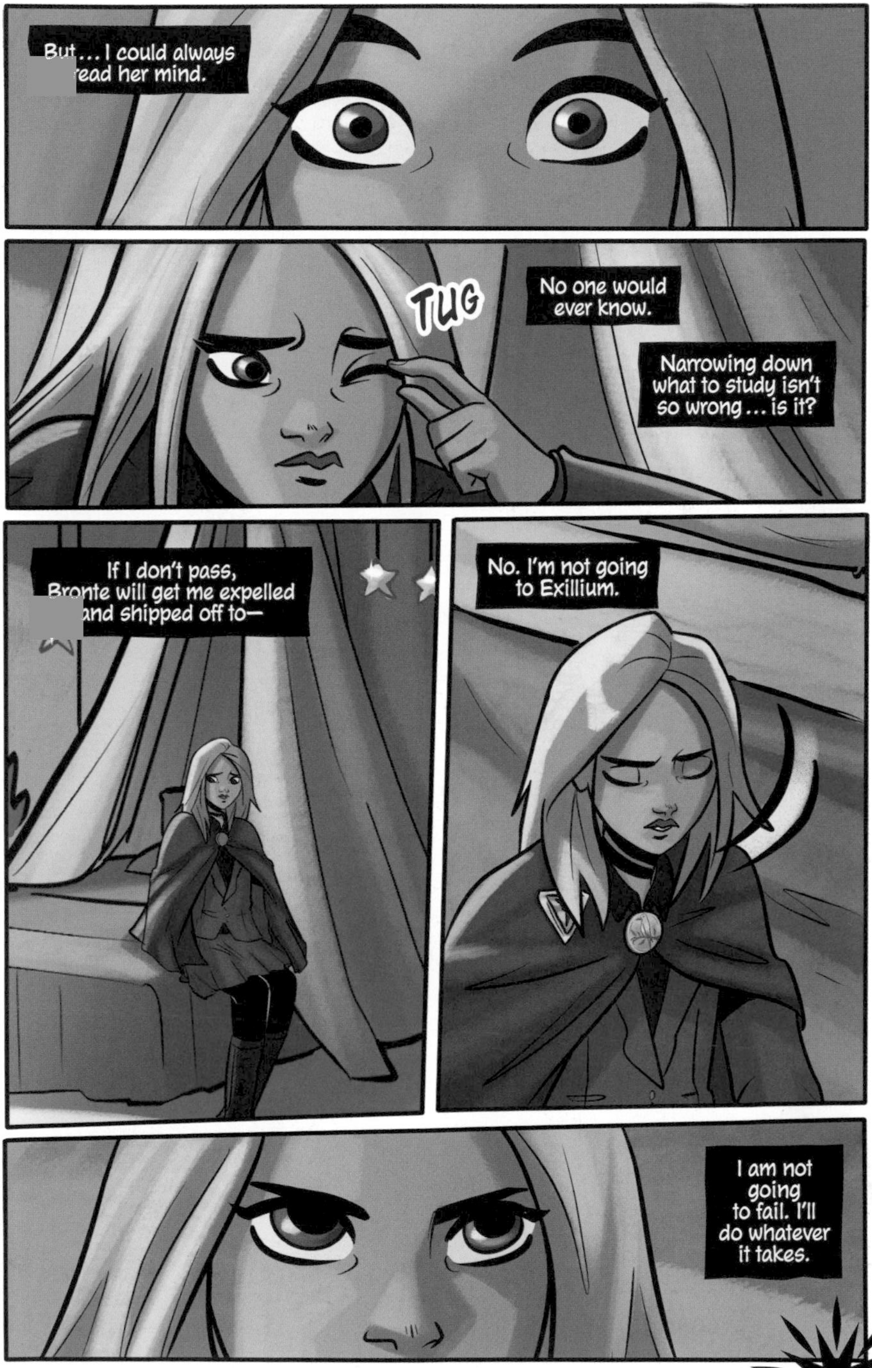
But… I could always read her mind.
TUG
No one would ever know.
Narrowing down what to study isn't so wrong… is it?
If I don't pass, Bronte will get me expelled and shipped off to—
No. I'm not going to Exillium.
I am not going to fail. I'll do whatever it takes.

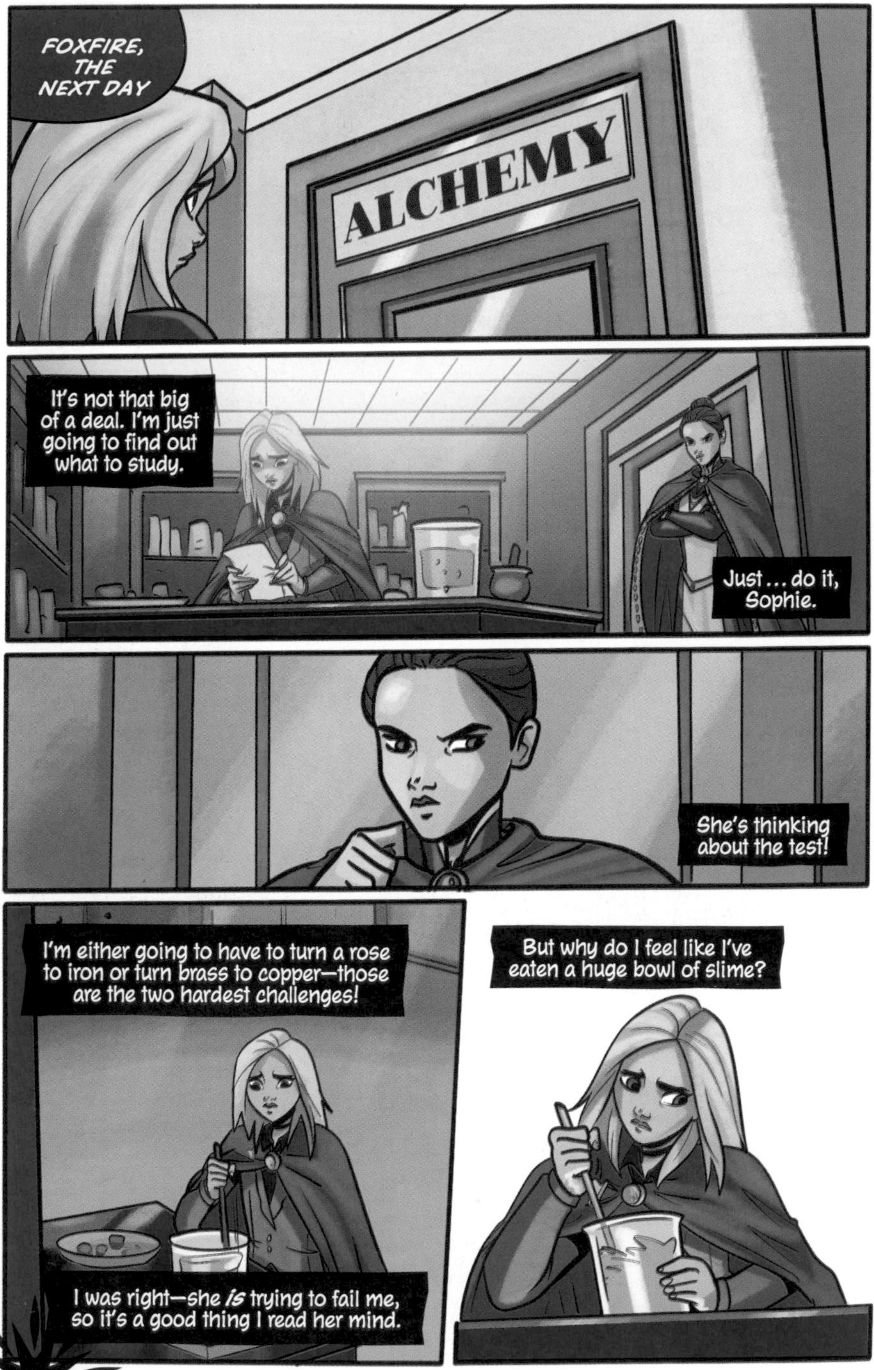
FOXFIRE, THE NEXT DAY
ALCHEMY
It's not that big of a deal. I'm just going to find out what to study.
Just... do it, Sophie.
She's thinking about the test!
I'm either going to have to turn a rose to iron or turn brass to copper—those are the two hardest challenges!
I was right—she *is* trying to fail me, so it's a good thing I read her mind.
But why do I feel like I've eaten a huge bowl of slime?

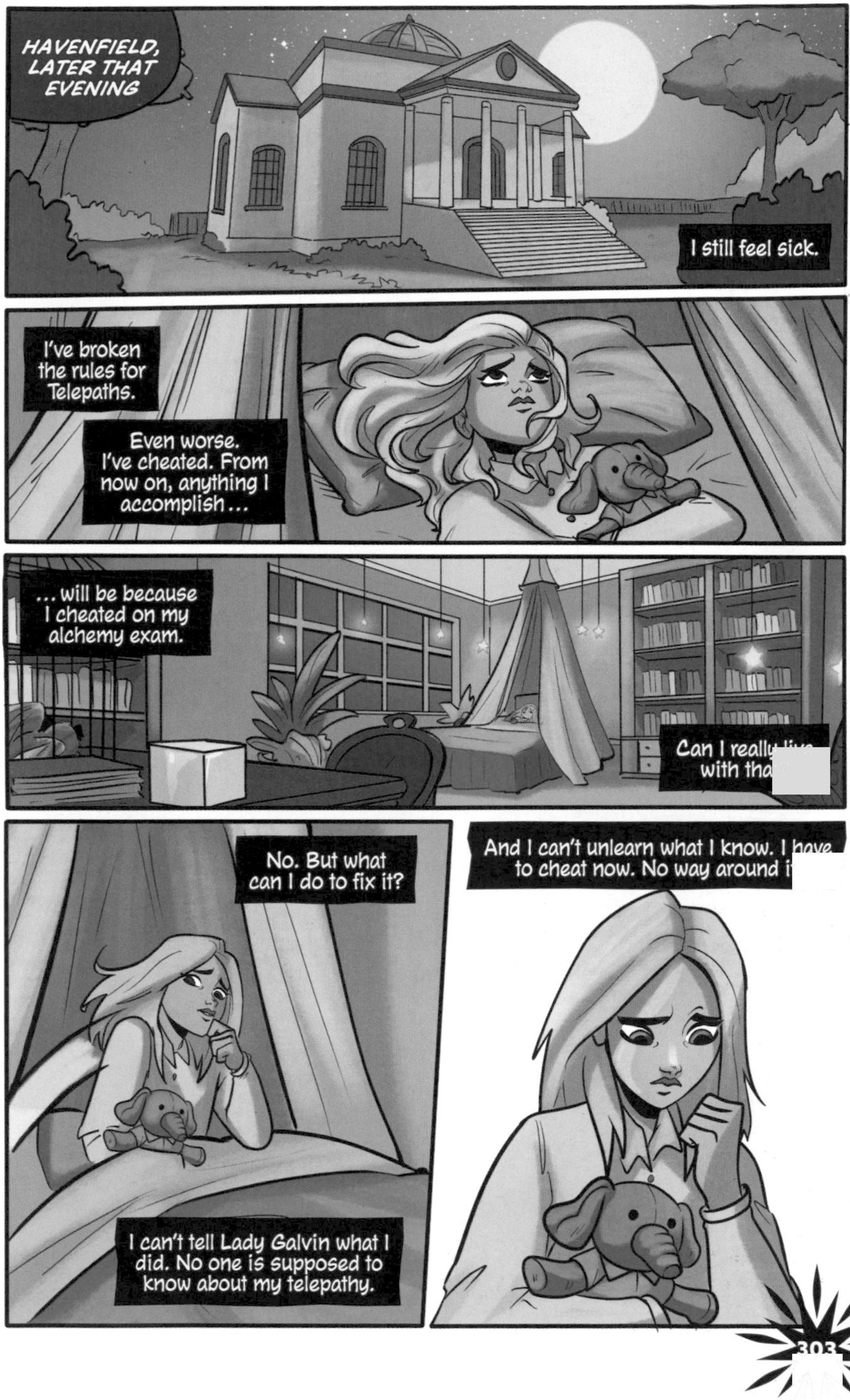
HAVENFIELD, LATER THAT EVENING
I still feel sick.
I've broken the rules for Telepaths.
Even worse. I've cheated. From now on, anything I accomplish...
...will be because I cheated on my alchemy exam.
Can I really
with tha
No. But what can I do to fix it?
I can't tell Lady Galvin what I did. No one is supposed to know about my telepathy.
And I can't unlearn what I know. I
to cheat now. No way around

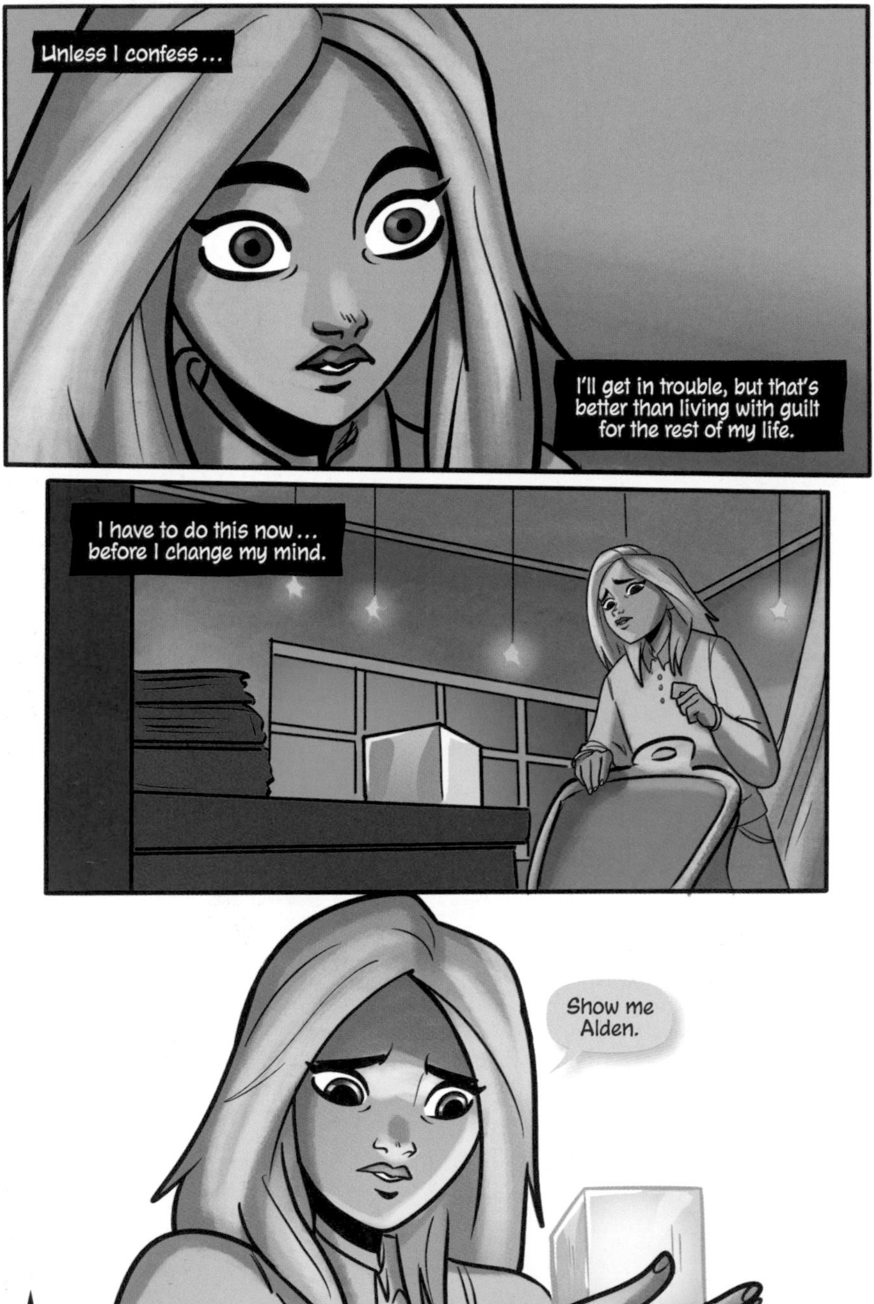
Unless I confess...
I'll get in trouble, but that's better than living with guilt for the rest of my life.
I have to do this now... before I change my mind.
Show me Alden.

CHAPTER TWENTY-SEVEN

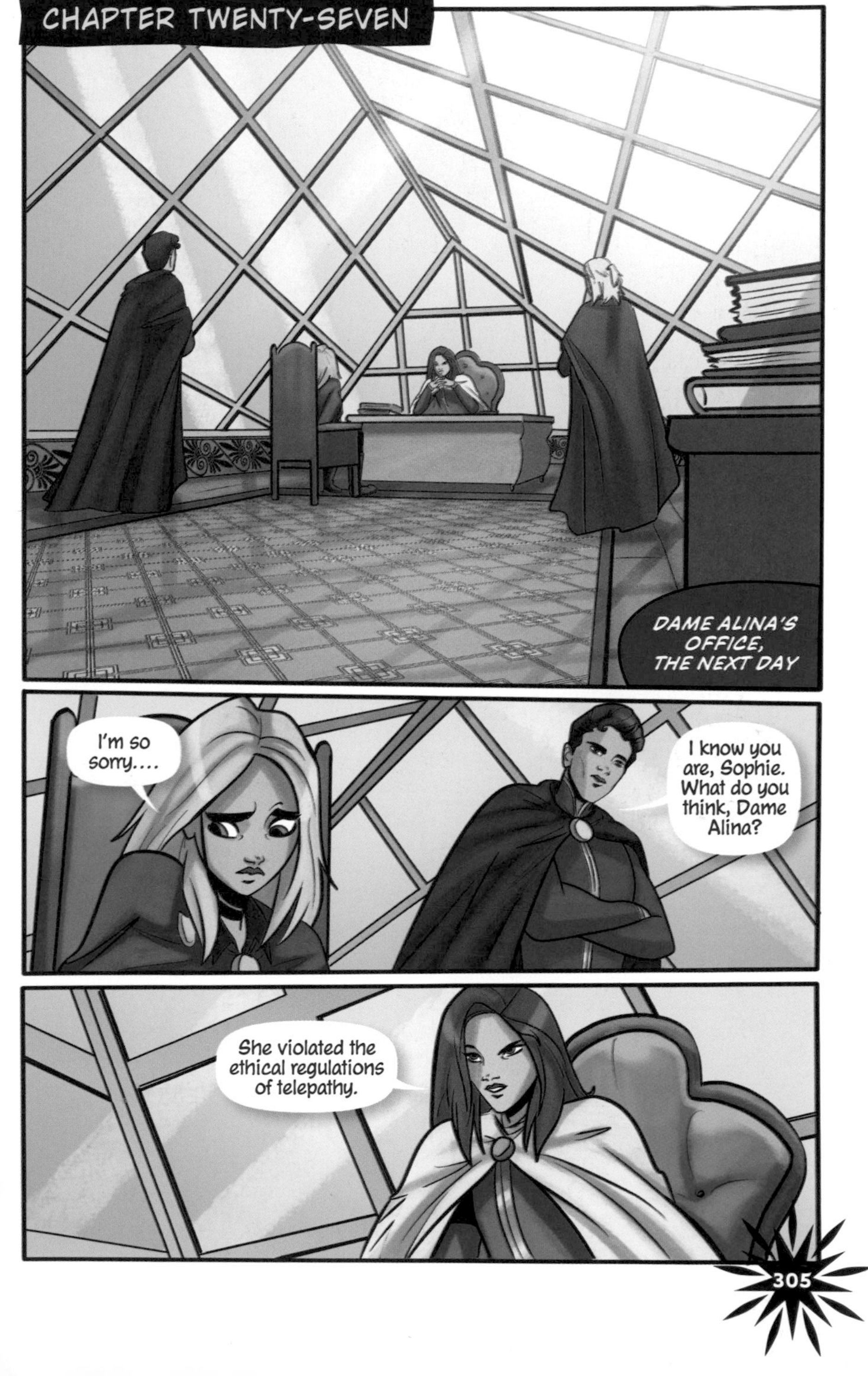
DAME ALINA'S OFFICE, THE NEXT DAY
I'm so sorry....
I know you are, Sophie. What do you think, Dame Alina?
She violated the ethical regulations of telepathy.

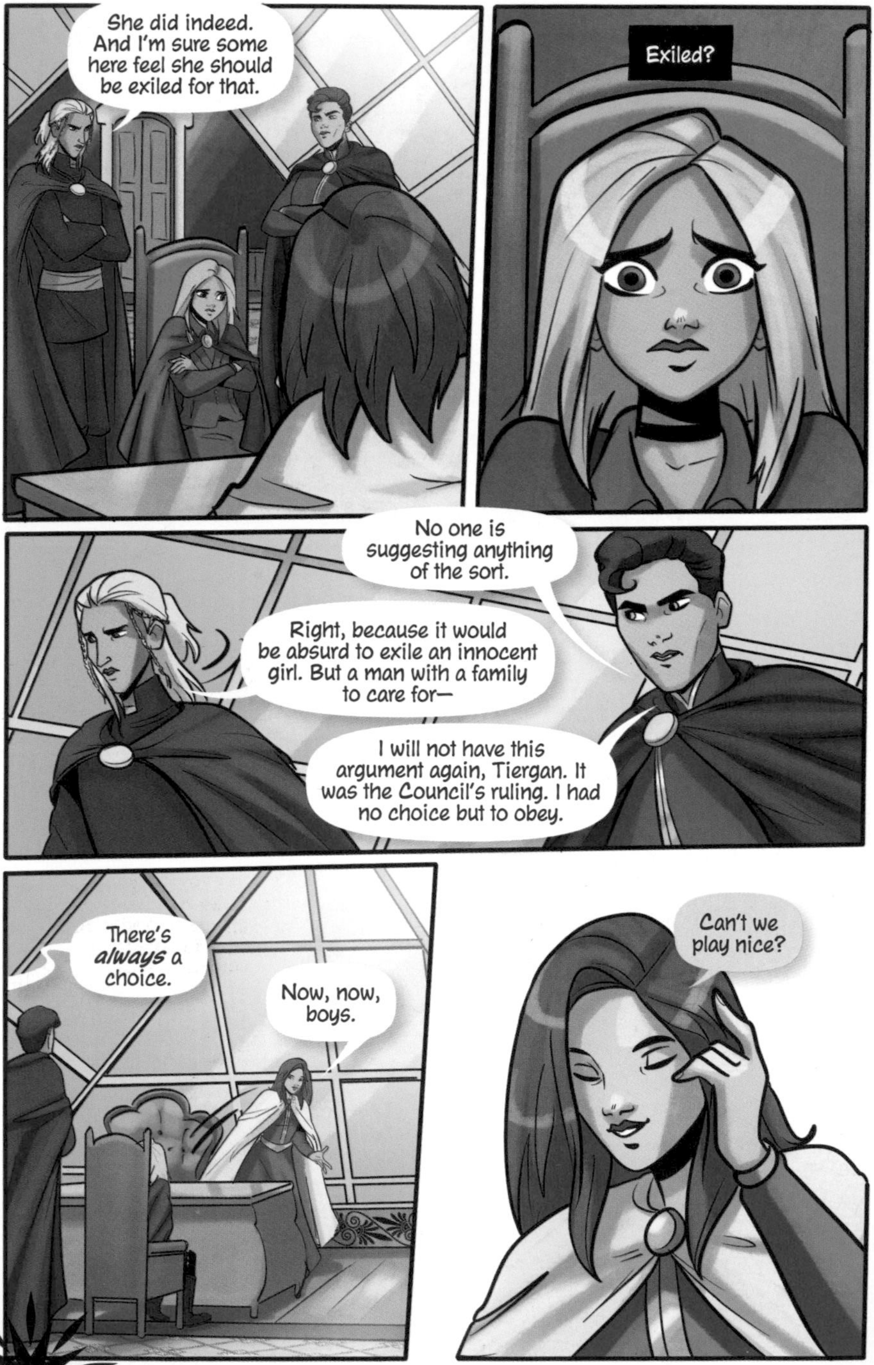
She did indeed. And I'm sure some here feel she should be exiled for that.
Exiled?
No one is suggesting anything of the sort.
Right, because it would be absurd to exile an innocent girl. But a man with a family to care for—
I will not have this argument again, Tiergan. It was the Council's ruling. I had no choice but to obey.
There's *always* a choice.
Now, now, boys.
Can't we play nice?

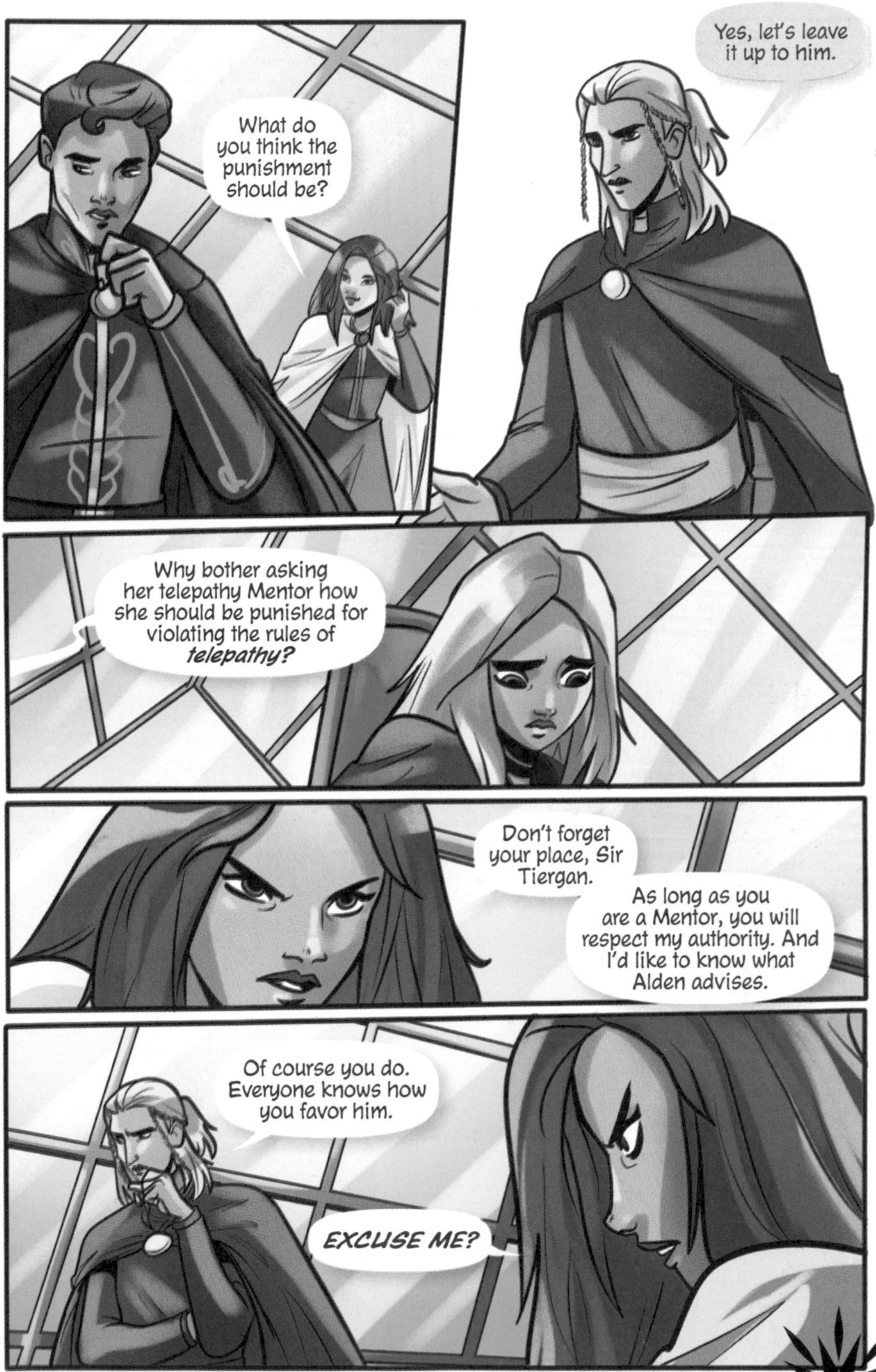
What do you think the punishment should be?
Yes, let's leave it up to him.
Why bother asking her telepathy Mentor how she should be punished for violating the rules of *telepathy?*
Don't forget your place, Sir Tiergan.
As long as you are a Mentor, you will respect my authority. And I'd like to know what Alden advises.
Of course you do. Everyone knows how you favor him.
EXCUSE ME?

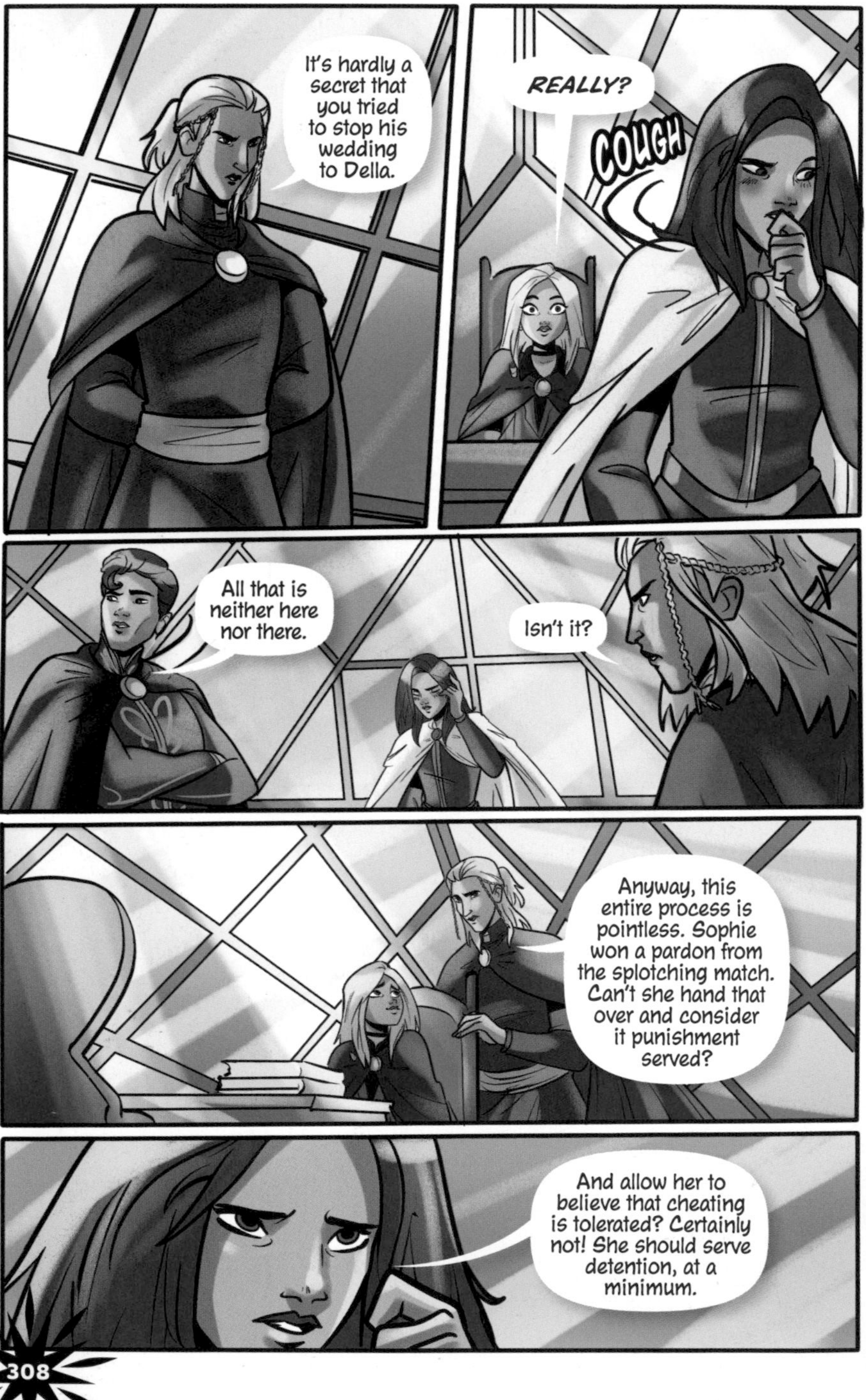
It's hardly a secret that you tried to stop his wedding to Della.
REALLY?
COUGH
All that is neither here nor there.
Isn't it?
Anyway, this entire process is pointless. Sophie won a pardon from the splotching match. Can't she hand that over and consider it punishment served?
And allow her to believe that cheating is tolerated? Certainly not! She should serve detention, at a minimum.

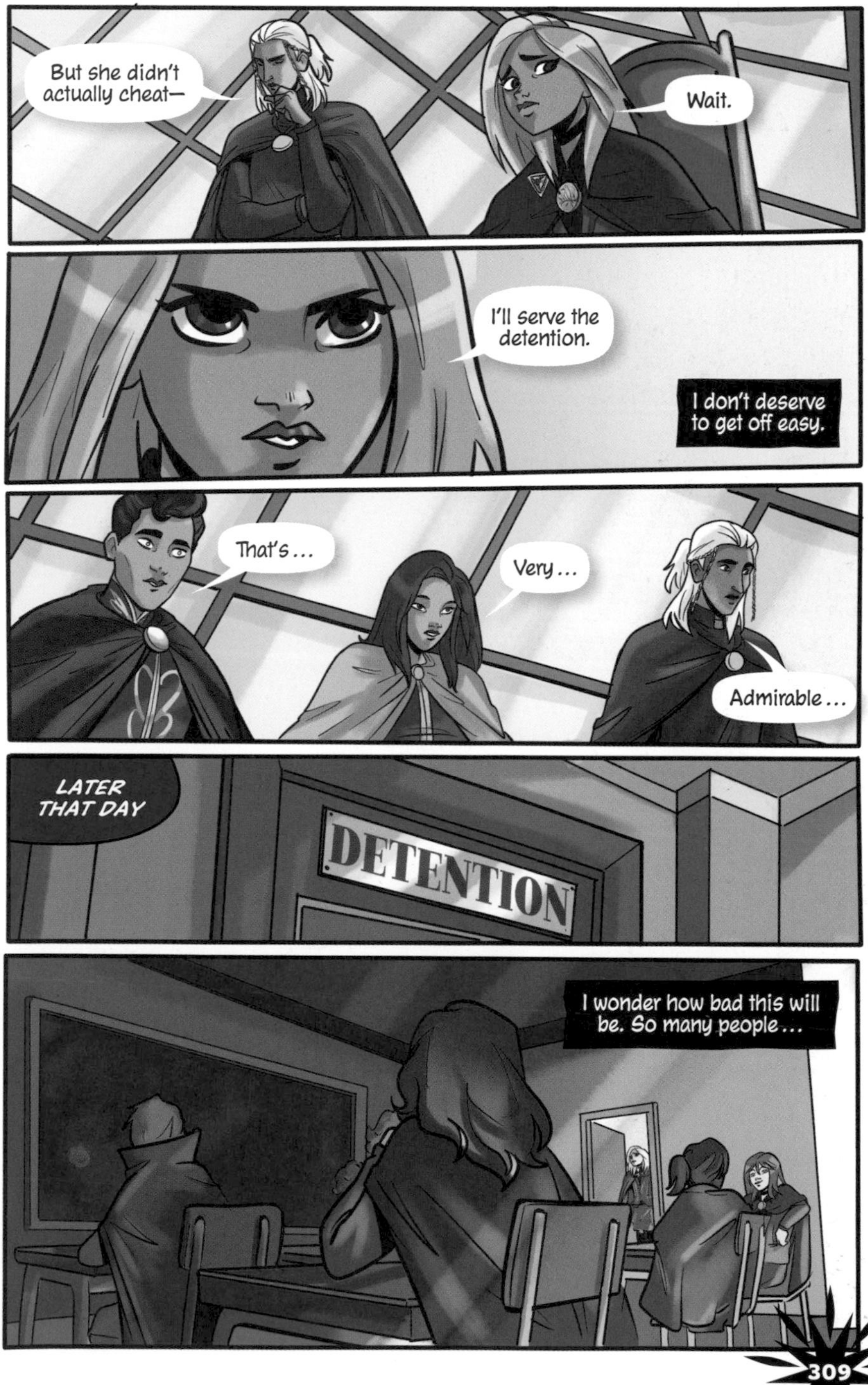
But she didn't actually cheat—
Wait.
I'll serve the detention.
I don't deserve to get off easy.
That's...
Very...
Admirable...
LATER THAT DAY
DETENTION
I wonder how bad this will be. So many people...

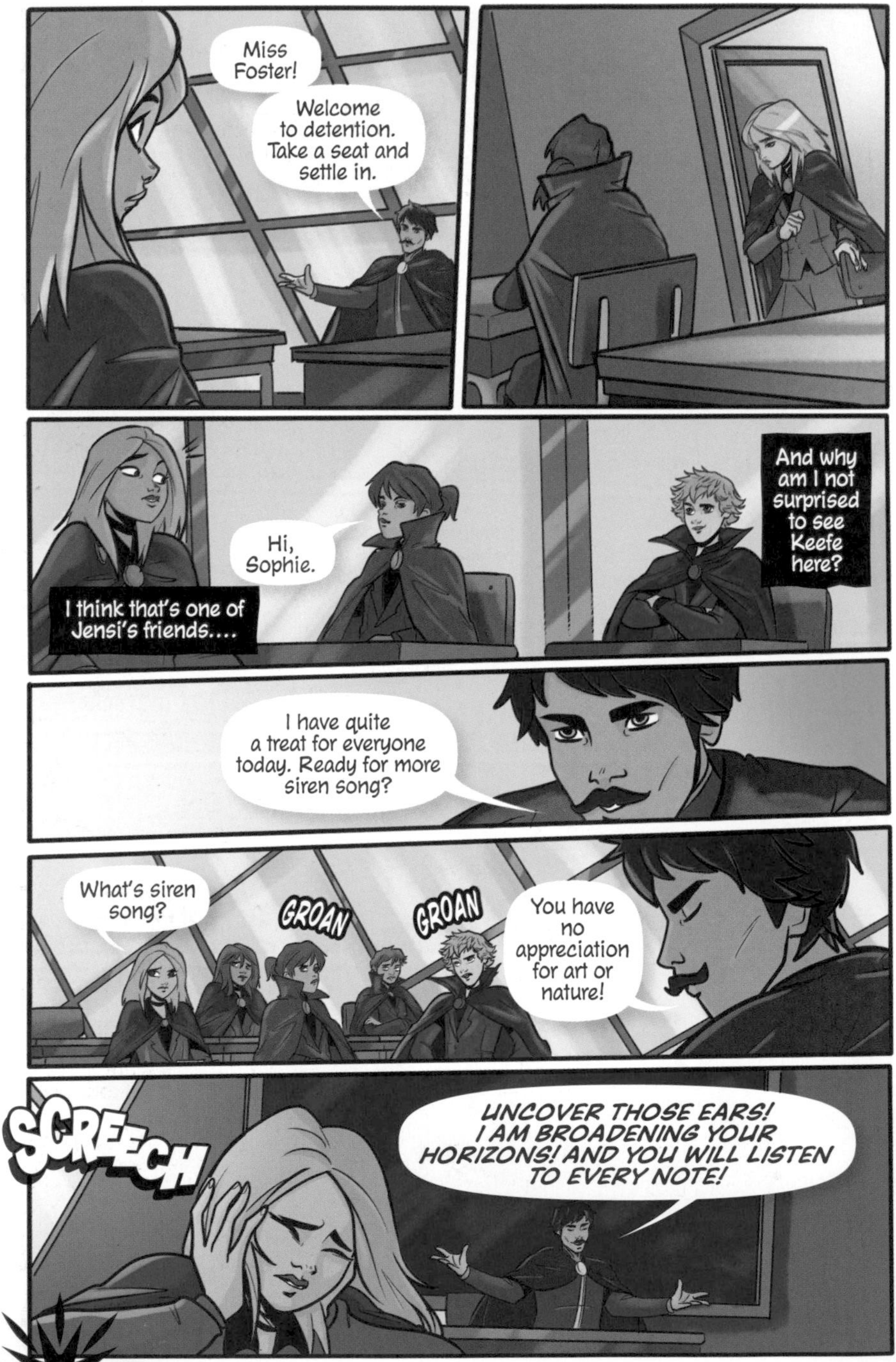
Miss Foster!
Welcome to detention. Take a seat and settle in.
I think that's one of Jensi's friends....
Hi, Sophie.
And why am I not surprised to see Keefe here?
I have quite a treat for everyone today. Ready for more siren song?
What's siren song?
GROAN
GROAN
You have no appreciation for art or nature!
SCREECH
UNCOVER THOSE EARS! I AM BROADENING YOUR HORIZONS! AND YOU WILL LISTEN TO EVERY NOTE!

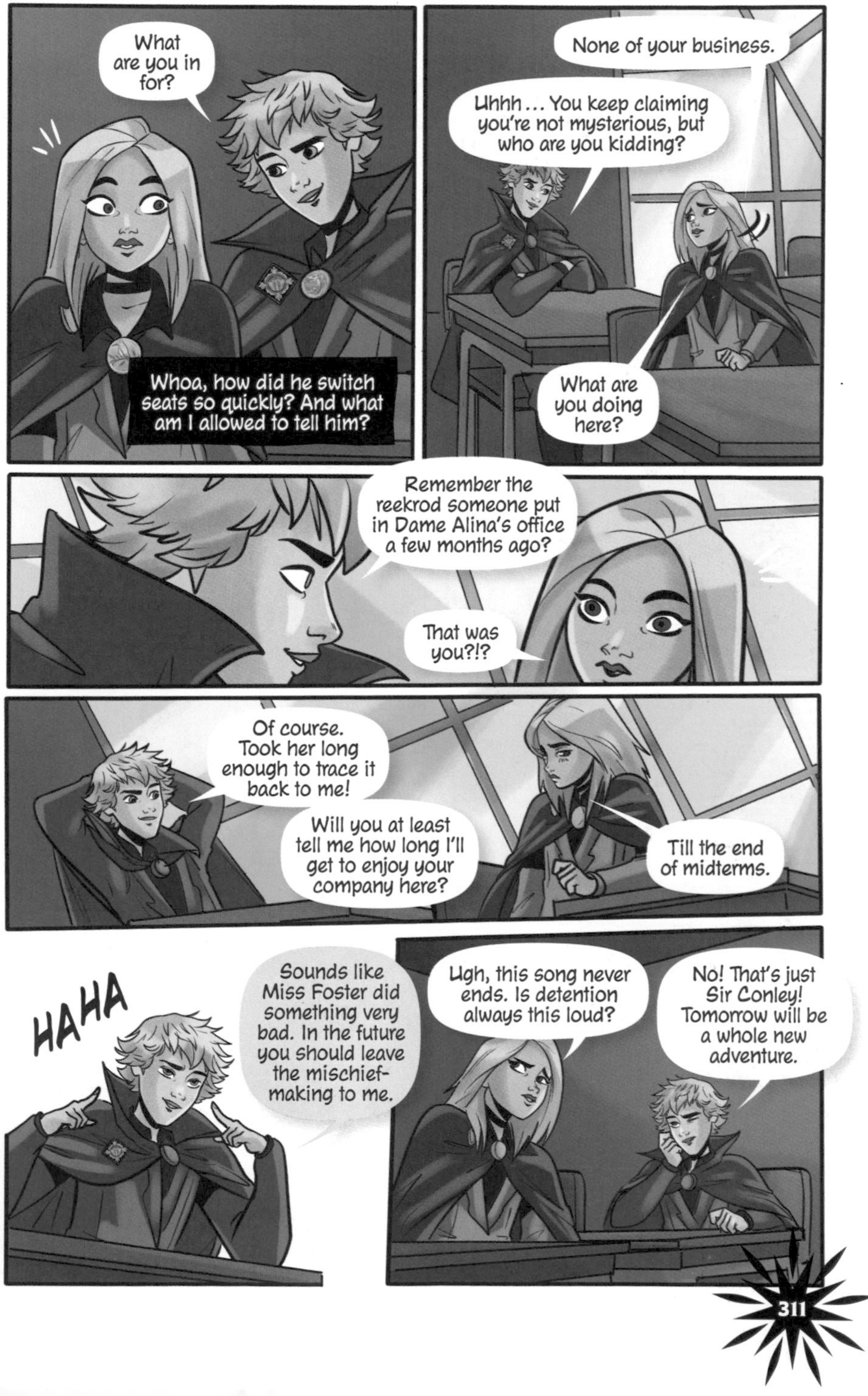
What are you in for?
Whoa, how did he switch seats so quickly? And what am I allowed to tell him?
None of your business.
Uhhh... You keep claiming you're not mysterious, but who are you kidding?
What are you doing here?
Remember the reekrod someone put in Dame Alina's office a few months ago?
That was you?!?
Of course. Took her long enough to trace it back to me!
Will you at least tell me how long I'll get to enjoy your company here?
Till the end of midterms.
HAHA
Sounds like Miss Foster did something very bad. In the future you should leave the mischief-making to me.
Ugh, this song never ends. Is detention always this loud?
No! That's just Sir Conley! Tomorrow will be a whole new adventure.

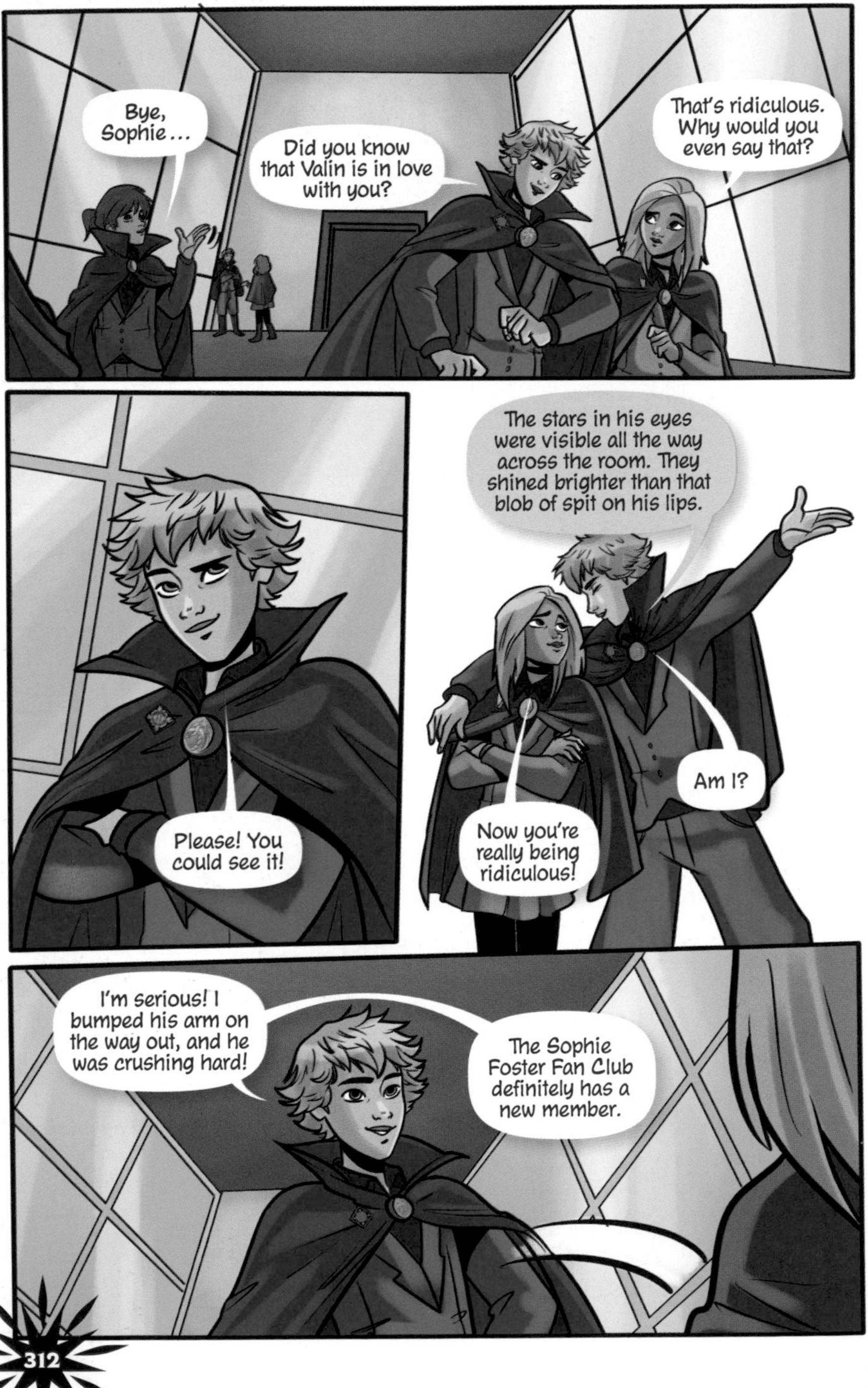
Bye, Sophie...
Did you know that Valin is in love with you?
That's ridiculous. Why would you even say that?
Please! You could see it!
The stars in his eyes were visible all the way across the room. They shined brighter than that blob of spit on his lips.
Am I?
Now you're really being ridiculous!
I'm serious! I bumped his arm on the way out, and he was crushing hard!
The Sophie Foster Fan Club definitely has a new member.

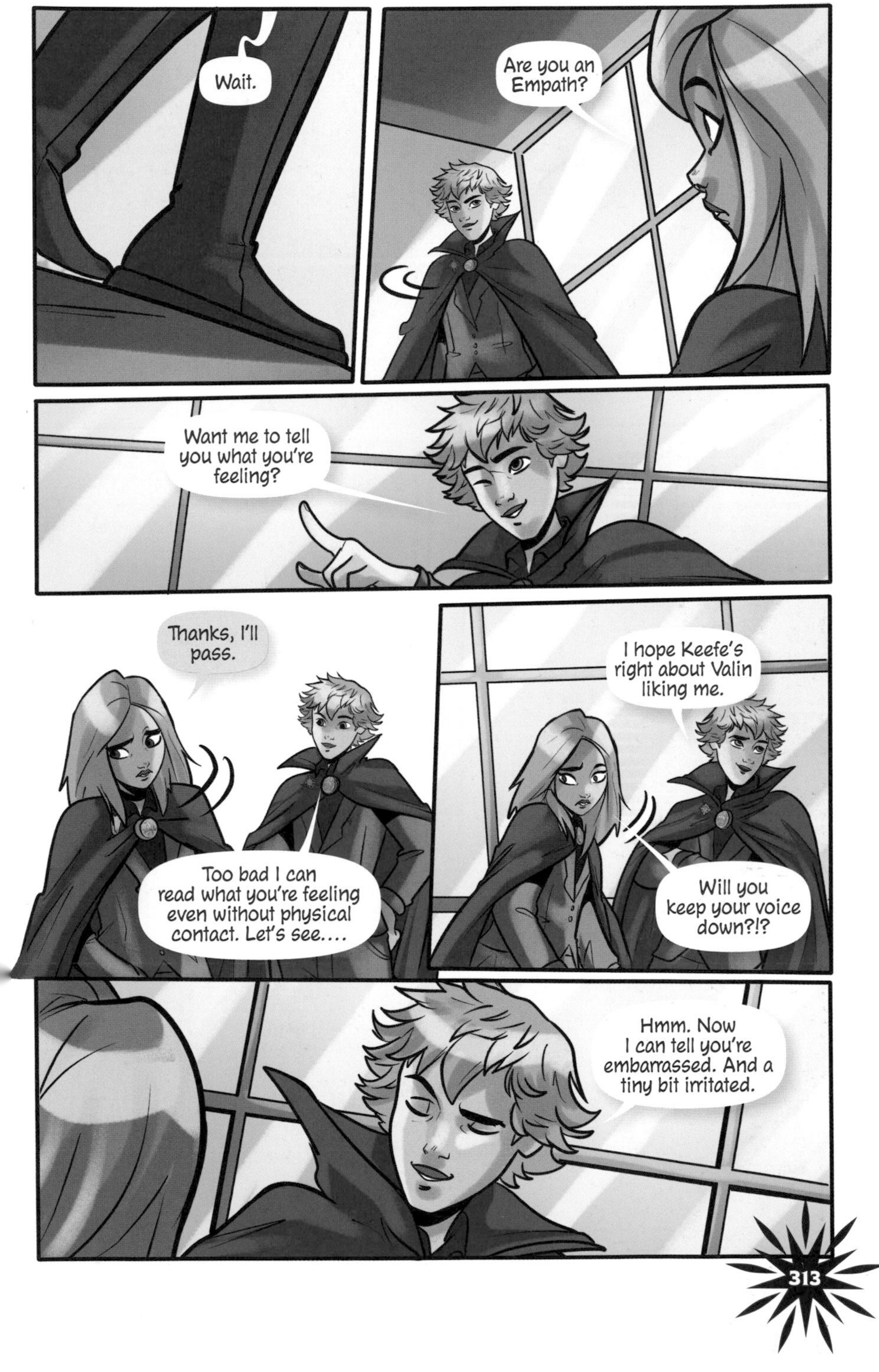
Wait.
Are you an Empath?
Want me to tell you what you're feeling?
Thanks, I'll pass.
Too bad I can read what you're feeling even without physical contact. Let's see....
I hope Keefe's right about Valin liking me.
Will you keep your voice down?!?
Hmm. Now I can tell you're embarrassed. And a tiny bit irritated.

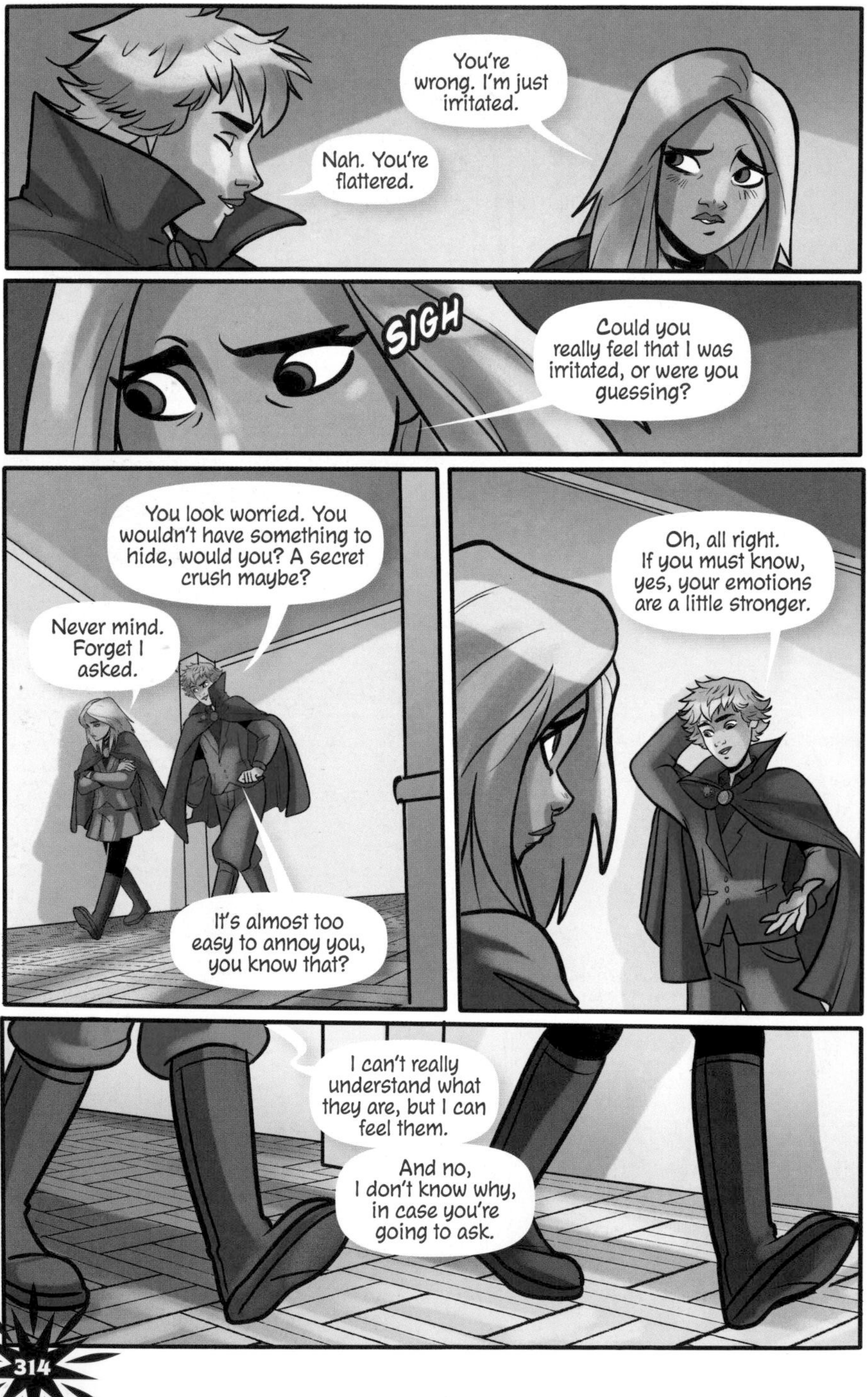
You're wrong. I'm just irritated.
Nah. You're flattered.
SIGH
Could you really feel that I was irritated, or were you guessing?
You look worried. You wouldn't have something to hide, would you? A secret crush maybe?
Never mind. Forget I asked.
It's almost too easy to annoy you, you know that?
Oh, all right. If you must know, yes, your emotions are a little stronger.
I can't really understand what they are, but I can feel them.
And no, I don't know why, in case you're going to ask.

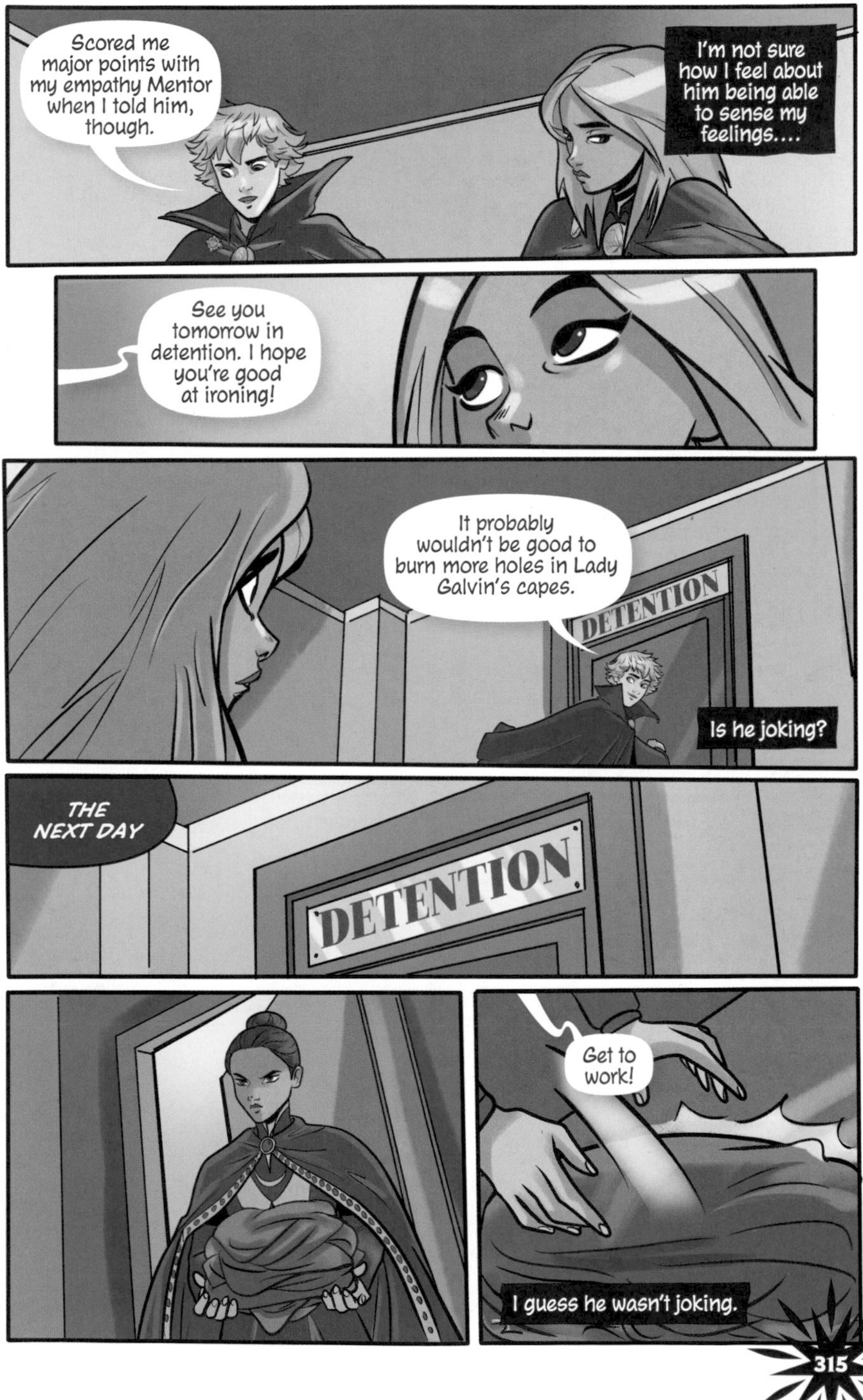
Scored me major points with my empathy Mentor when I told him, though.
I'm not sure how I feel about him being able to sense my feelings....
See you tomorrow in detention. I hope you're good at ironing!
It probably wouldn't be good to burn more holes in Lady Galvin's capes.
DETENTION
Is he joking?
THE NEXT DAY
DETENTION
Get to work!
I guess he wasn't joking.

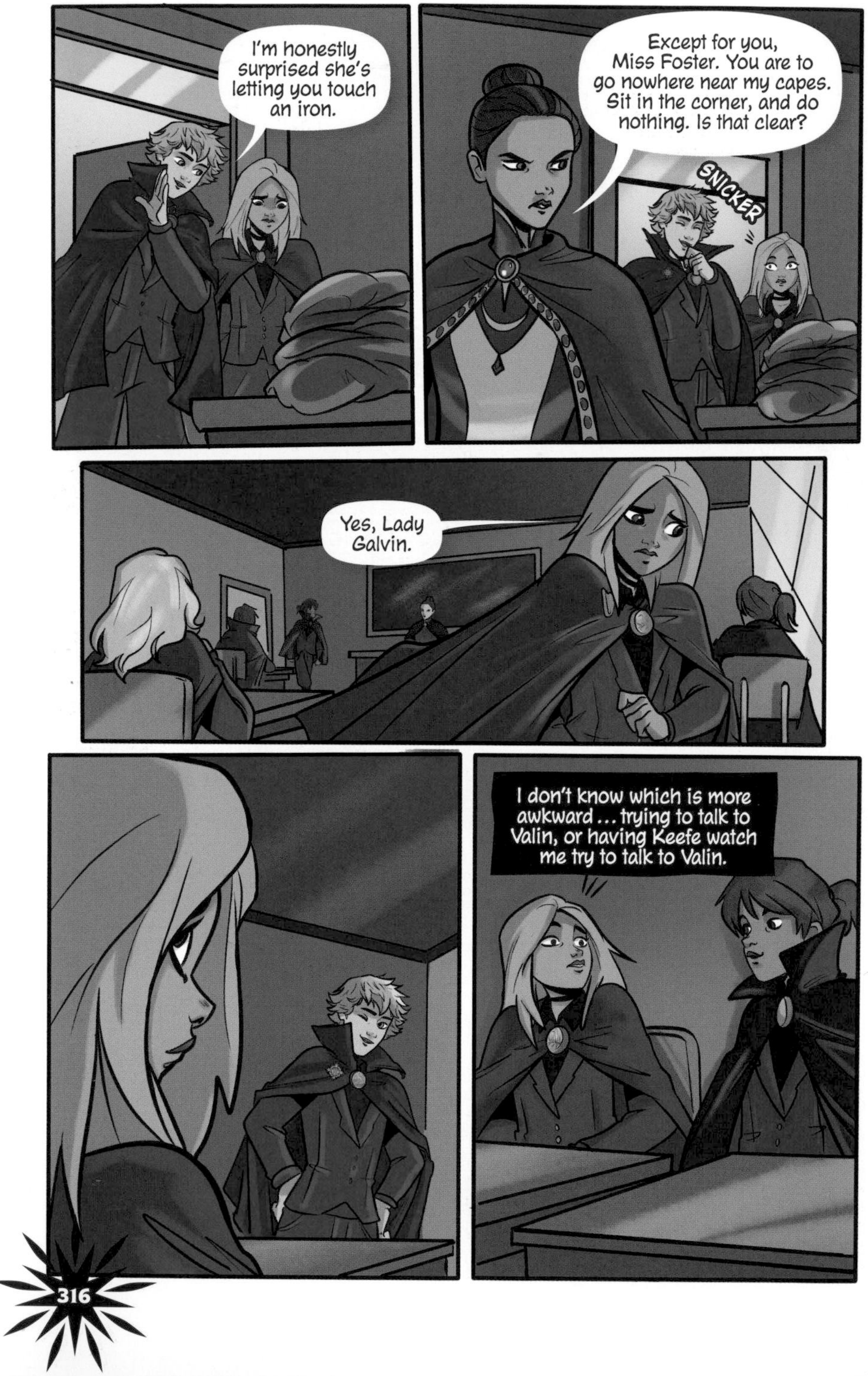
I'm honestly surprised she's letting you touch an iron.
Except for you, Miss Foster. You are to go nowhere near my capes. Sit in the corner, and do nothing. Is that clear?
SNICKER
Yes, Lady Galvin.
I don't know which is more awkward ... trying to talk to Valin, or having Keefe watch me try to talk to Valin.

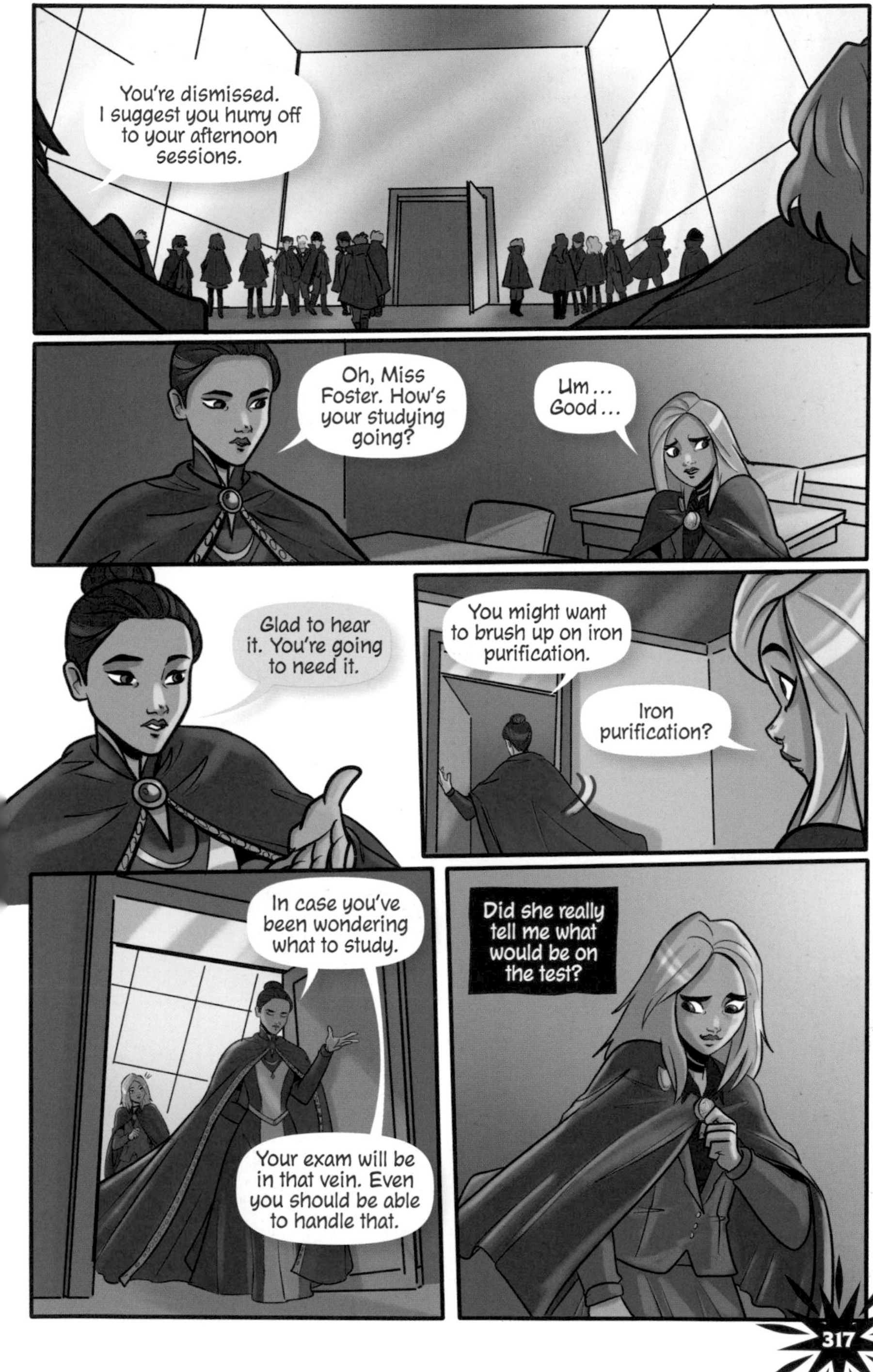
You're dismissed. I suggest you hurry off to your afternoon sessions.
Oh, Miss Foster. How's your studying going?
Um... Good...
Glad to hear it. You're going to need it.
You might want to brush up on iron purification.
Iron purification?
In case you've been wondering what to study.
Your exam will be in that vein. Even you should be able to handle that.
Did she really tell me what would be on the test?

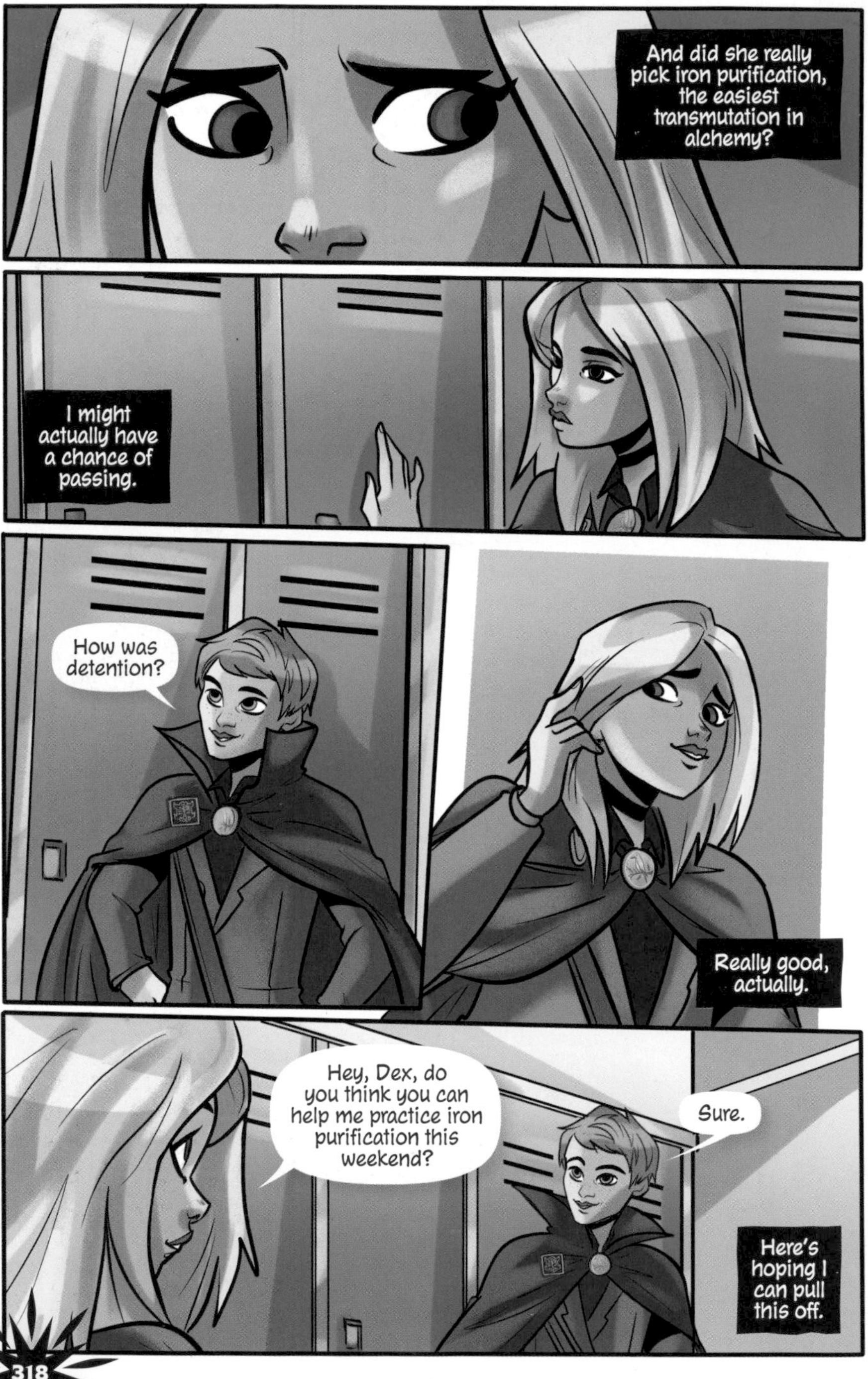
And did she really pick iron purification, the easiest transmutation in alchemy?
I might actually have a chance of passing.
How was detention?
Really good, actually.
Hey, Dex, do you think you can help me practice iron purification this weekend?
Sure.
Here's hoping I can pull this off.

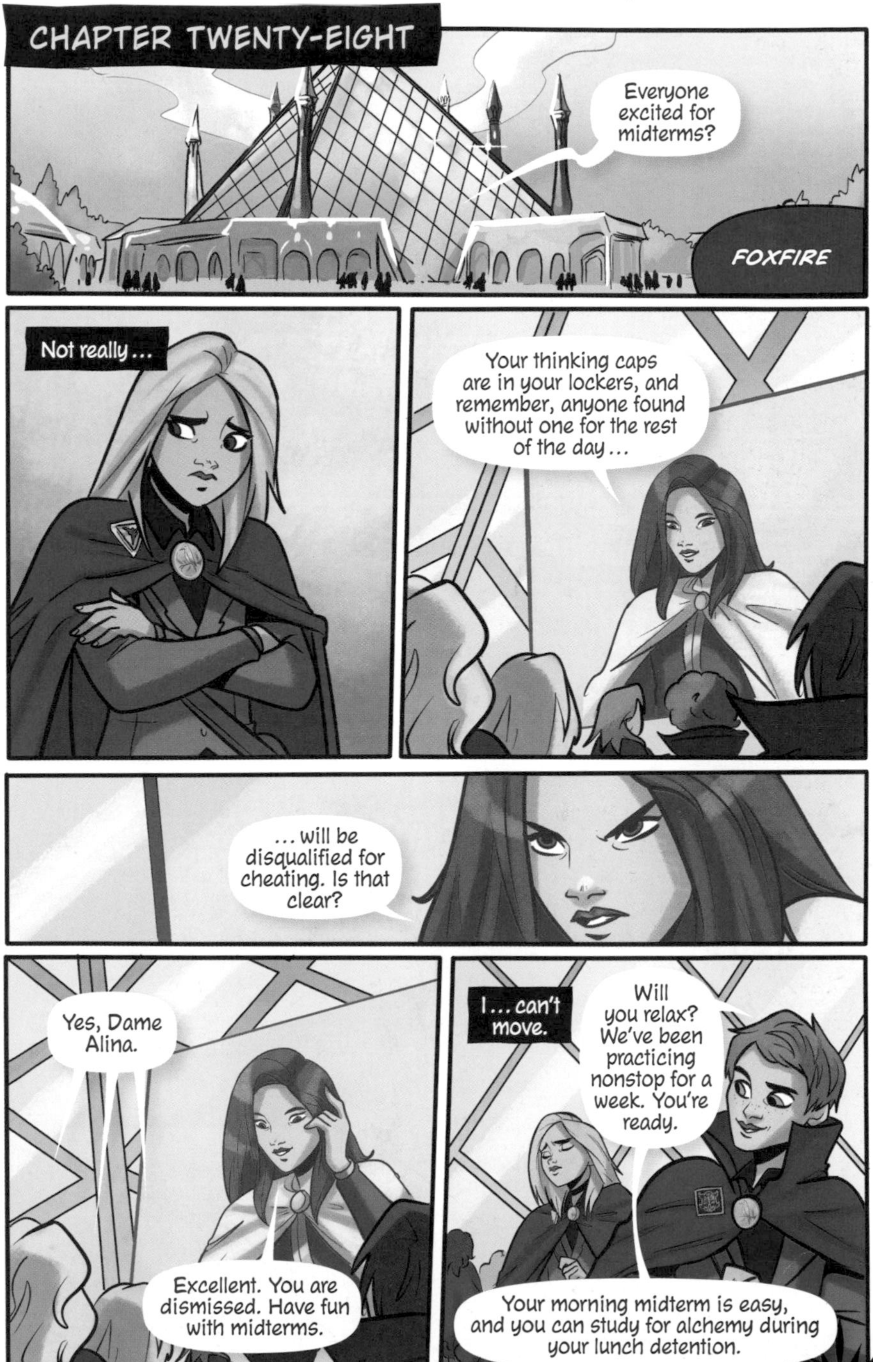
CHAPTER TWENTY-EIGHT
Everyone excited for midterms?
FOXFIRE
Not really . . .
Your thinking caps are in your lockers, and remember, anyone found without one for the rest of the day . . .
. . . will be disqualified for cheating. Is that clear?
Yes, Dame Alina.
Excellent. You are dismissed. Have fun with midterms.
I . . . can't move.
Will you relax? We've been practicing nonstop for a week. You're ready.
Your morning midterm is easy, and you can study for alchemy during your lunch detention.

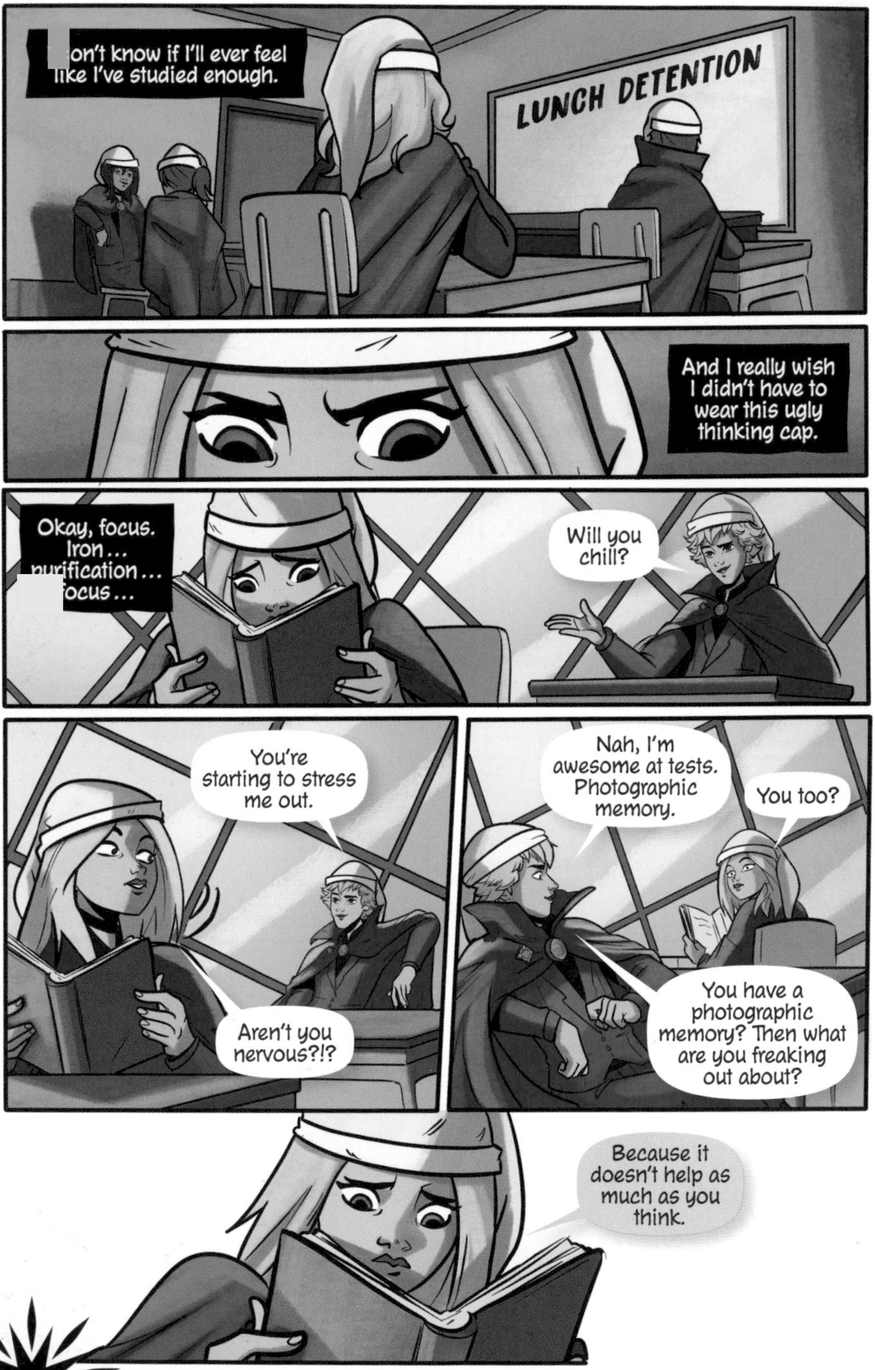
on't know if I'll ever feel like I've studied enough.
LUNCH DETENTION
And I really wish I didn't have to wear this ugly thinking cap.
Okay, focus. Iron... purification... focus...
Will you chill?
You're starting to stress me out.
Aren't you nervous?!?
Nah, I'm awesome at tests. Photographic memory.
You too?
You have a photographic memory? Then what are you freaking out about?
Because it doesn't help as much as you think.

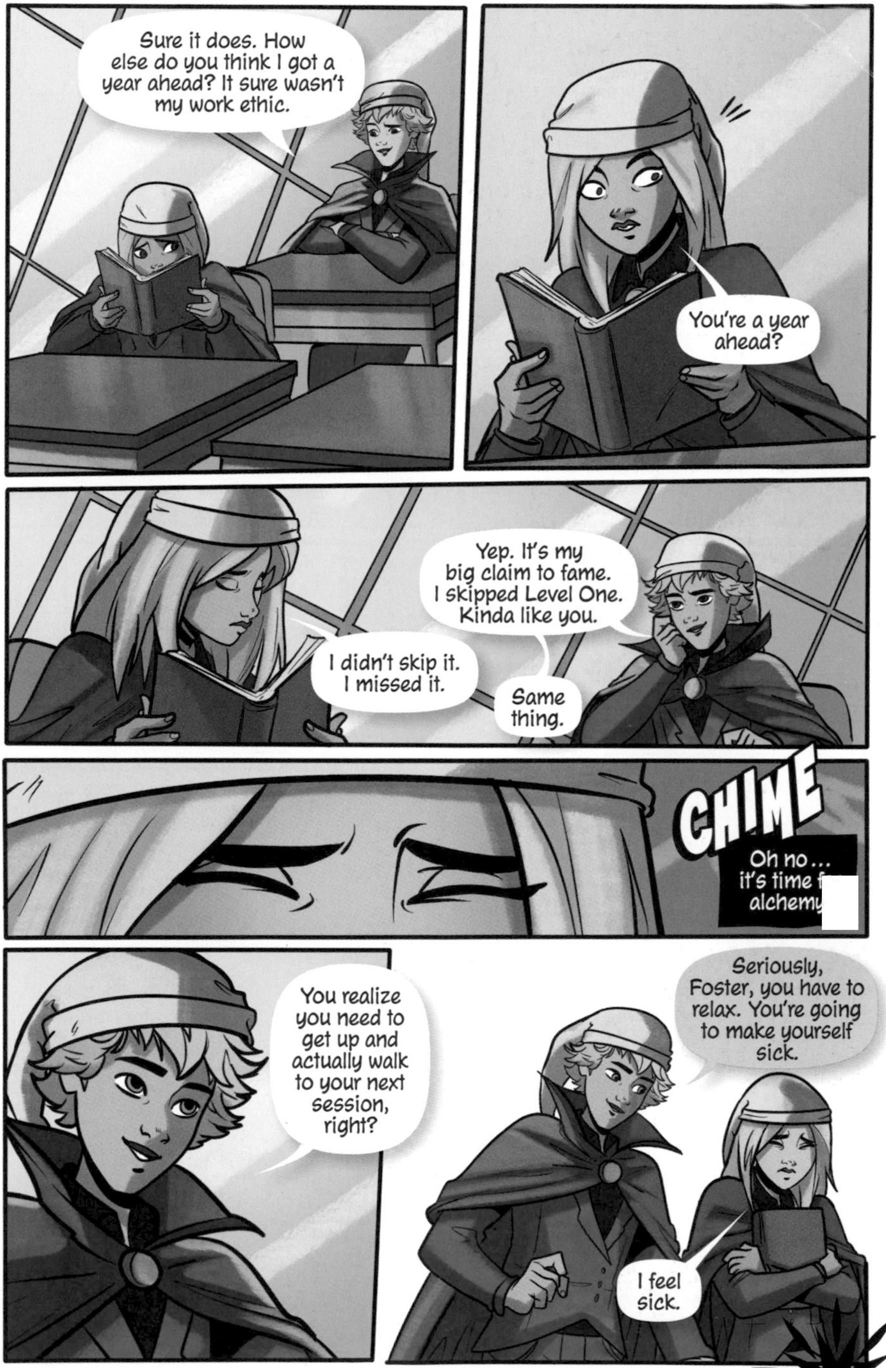
Sure it does. How else do you think I got a year ahead? It sure wasn't my work ethic.
You're a year ahead?
Yep. It's my big claim to fame. I skipped Level One. Kinda like you.
I didn't skip it. I missed it.
Same thing.
CHIME
Oh no… it's time f alchemy
You realize you need to get up and actually walk to your next session, right?
Seriously, Foster, you have to relax. You're going to make yourself sick.
I feel sick.

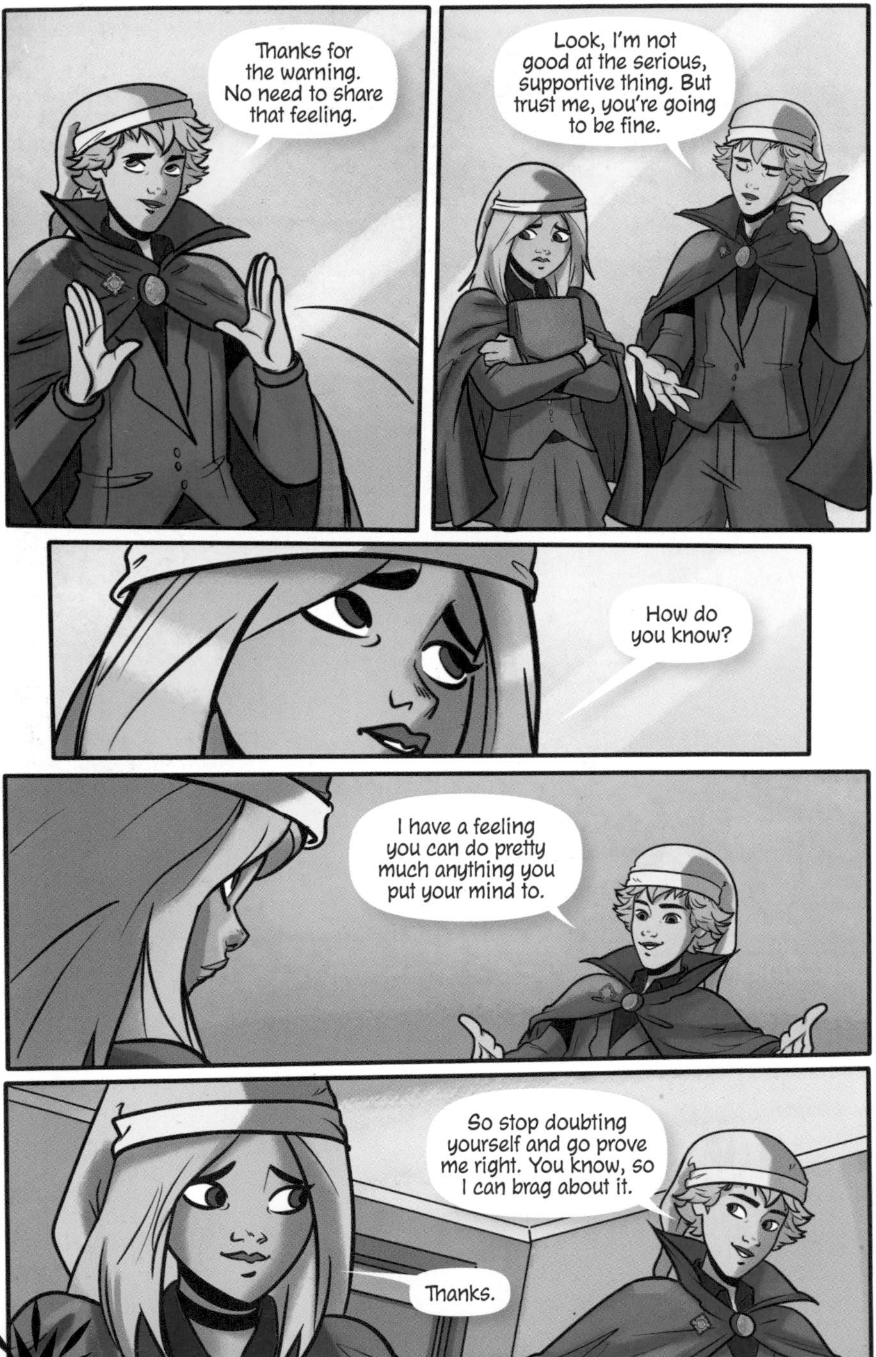
Thanks for the warning. No need to share that feeling.
Look, I'm not good at the serious, supportive thing. But trust me, you're going to be fine.
How do you know?
I have a feeling you can do pretty much anything you put your mind to.
So stop doubting yourself and go prove me right. You know, so I can brag about it.
Thanks.

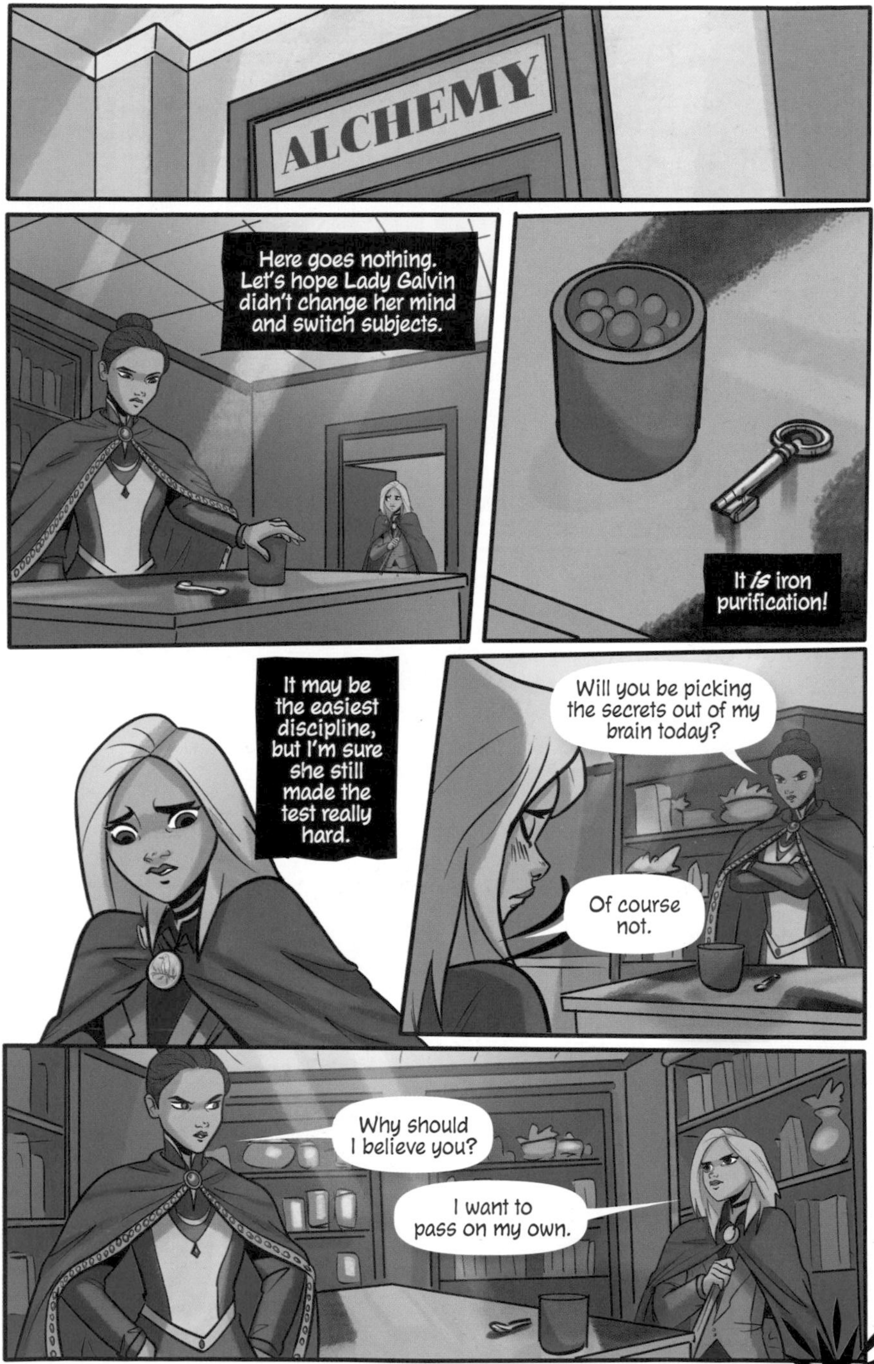
ALCHEMY
Here goes nothing. Let's hope Lady Galvin didn't change her mind and switch subjects.
It *is* iron purification!
It may be the easiest discipline, but I'm sure she still made the test really hard.
Will you be picking the secrets out of my brain today?
Of course not.
Why should I believe you?
I want to pass on my own.

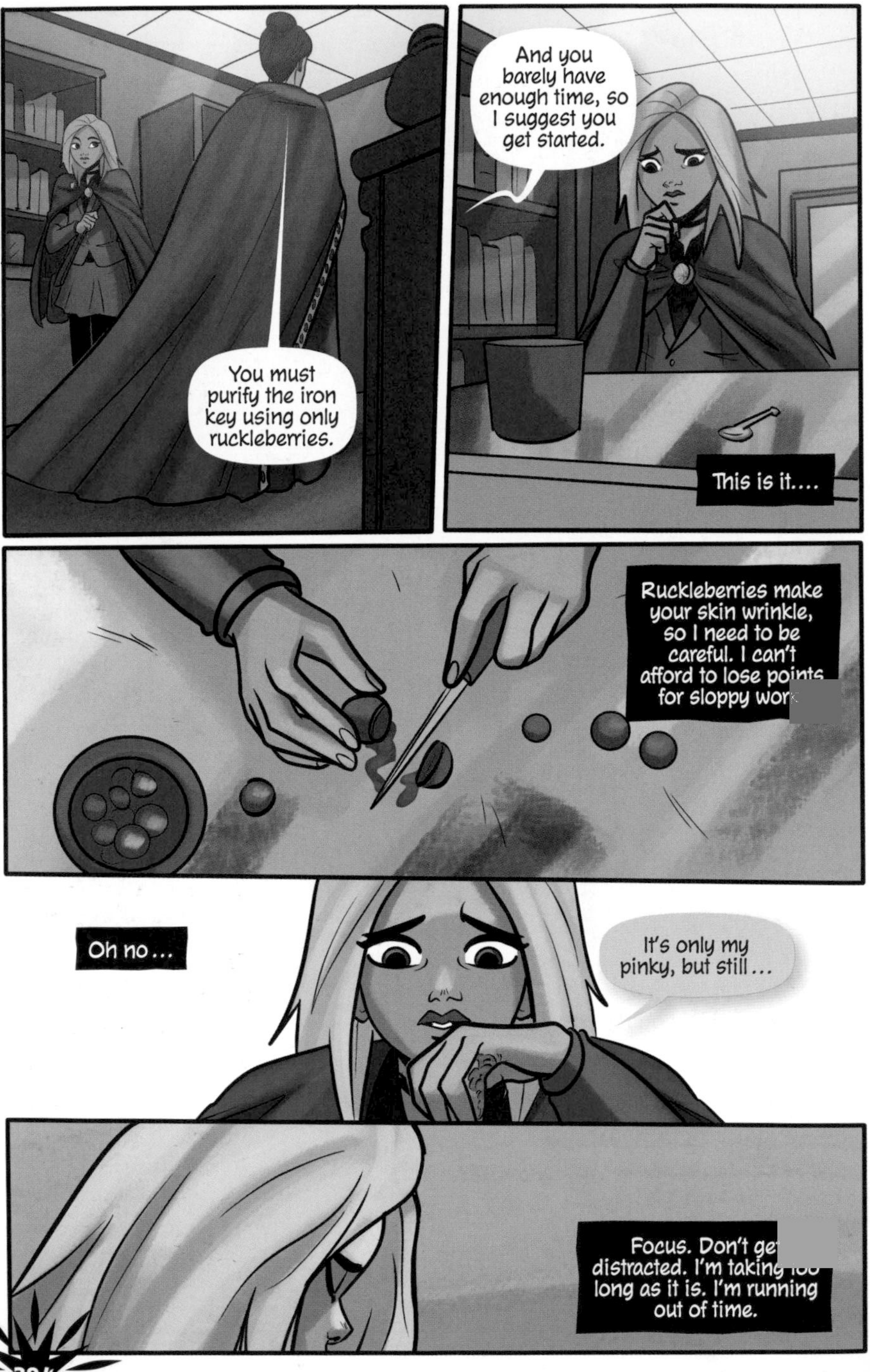

You must purify the iron key using only rruckleberries.
And you barely have enough time, so I suggest you get started.
This is it....
Ruckleberries make your skin wrinkle, so I need to be careful. I can't afford to lose points for sloppy wor
Oh no...
It's only my pinky, but still...
Focus. Don't ge distracted. I'm taking long as it is. I'm running out of time.

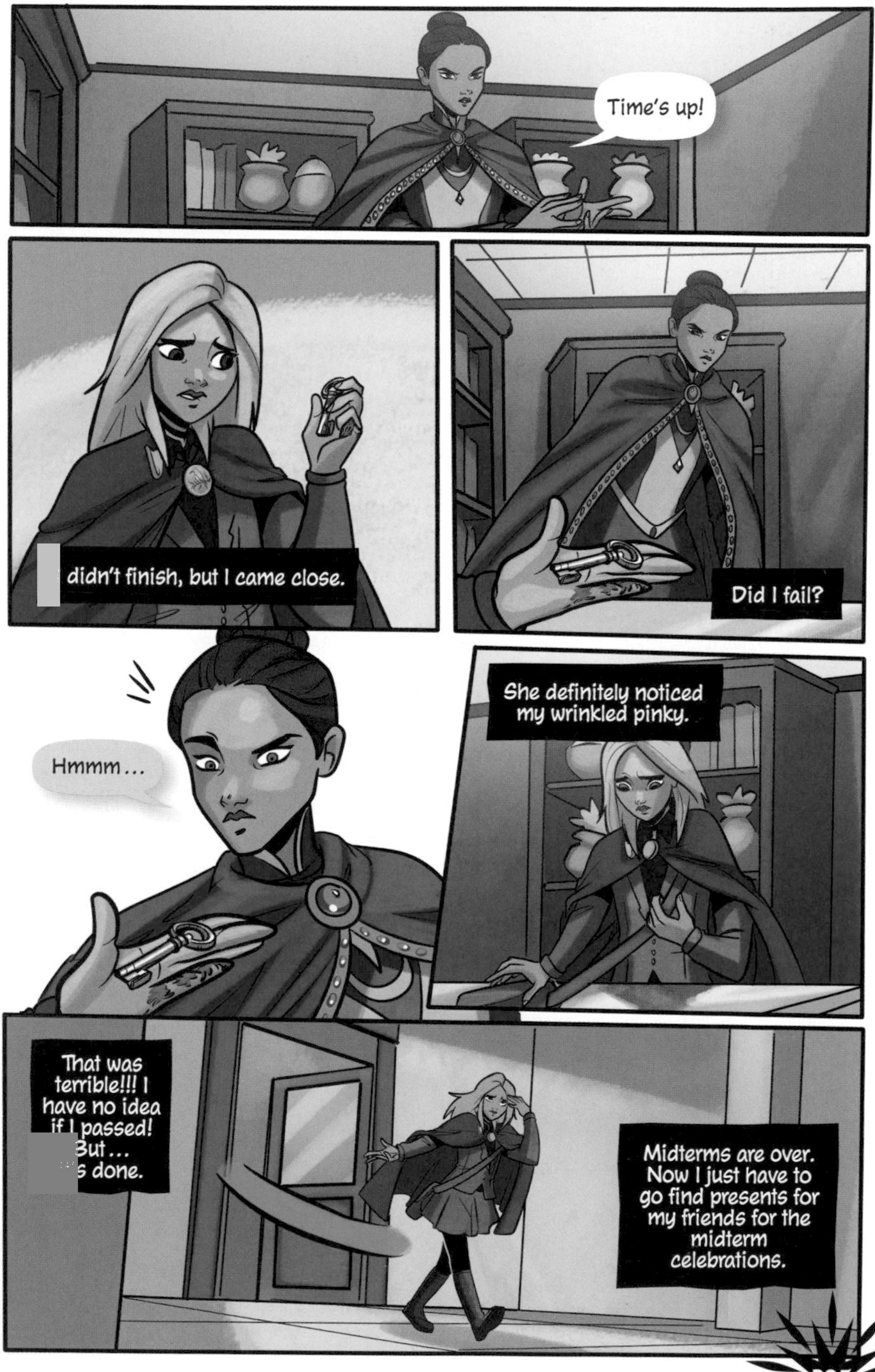
Time's up!
didn't finish, but I came close.
Did I fail?
Hmmm...
She definitely noticed my wrinkled pinky.
That was terrible!!! I have no idea if I passed! But... s done.
Midterms are over. Now I just have to go find presents for my friends for the midterm celebrations.

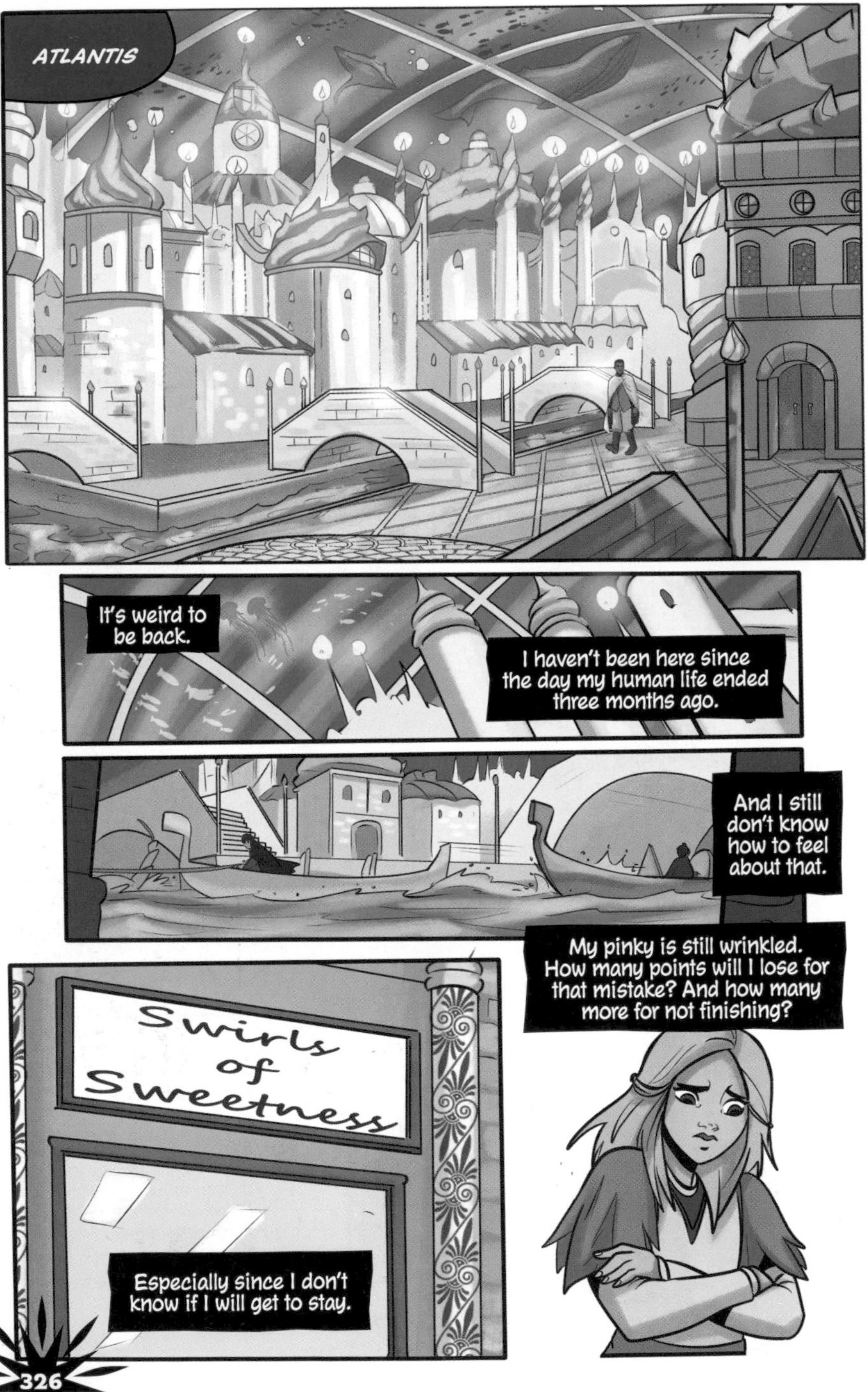
ATLANTIS
It's weird to be back.
I haven't been here since the day my human life ended three months ago.
And I still don't know how to feel about that.
Swirls of Sweetness
Especially since I don't know if I will get to stay.
My pinky is still wrinkled. How many points will I lose for that mistake? And how many more for not finishing?

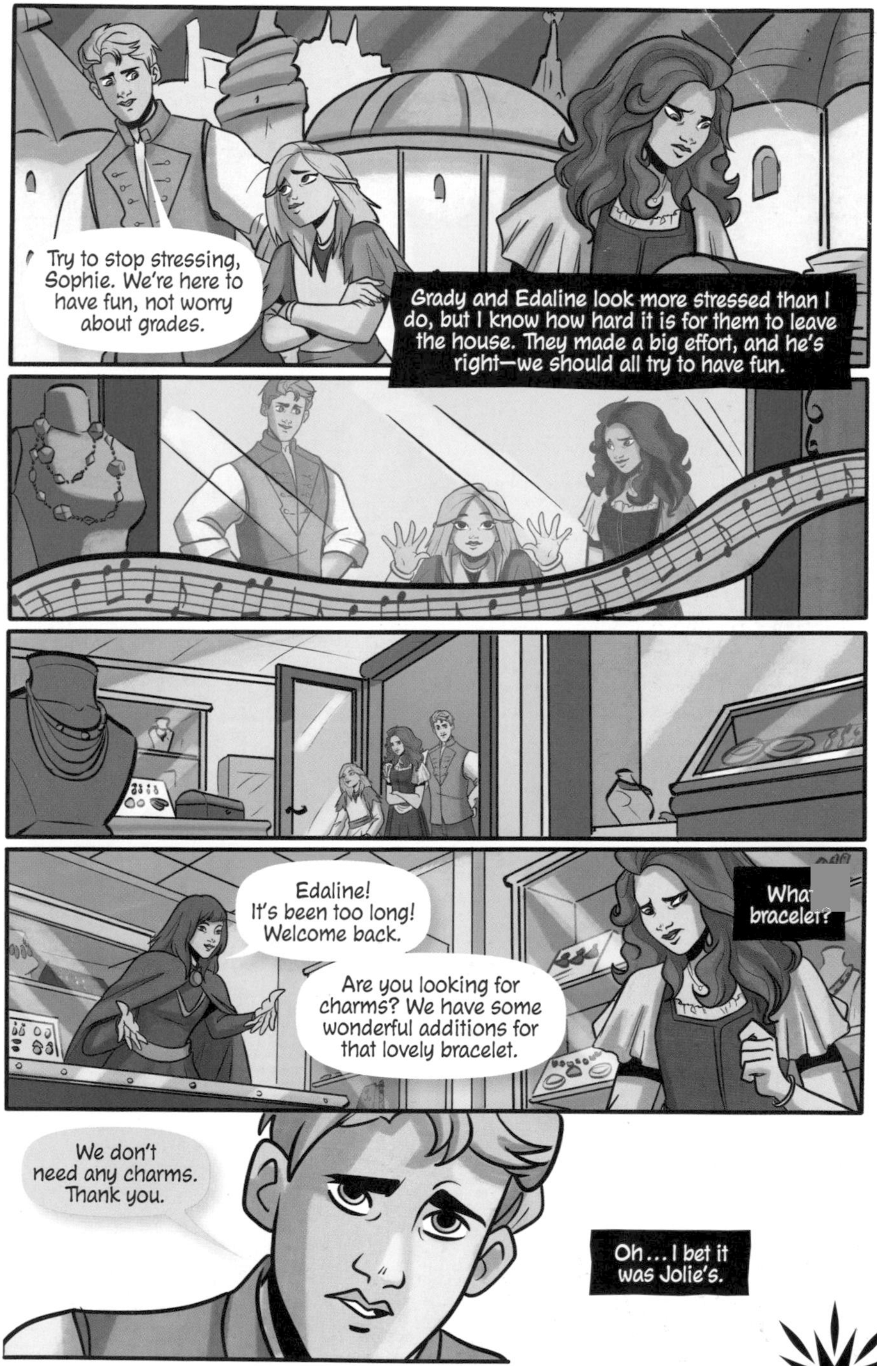
Try to stop stressing, Sophie. We're here to have fun, not worry about grades.
Grady and Edaline look more stressed than I do, but I know how hard it is for them to leave the house. They made a big effort, and he's right—we should all try to have fun.
Edaline! It's been too long! Welcome back.
Are you looking for charms? We have some wonderful additions for that lovely bracelet.
Wha bracelet?
We don't need any charms. Thank you.
Oh... I bet it was Jolie's.

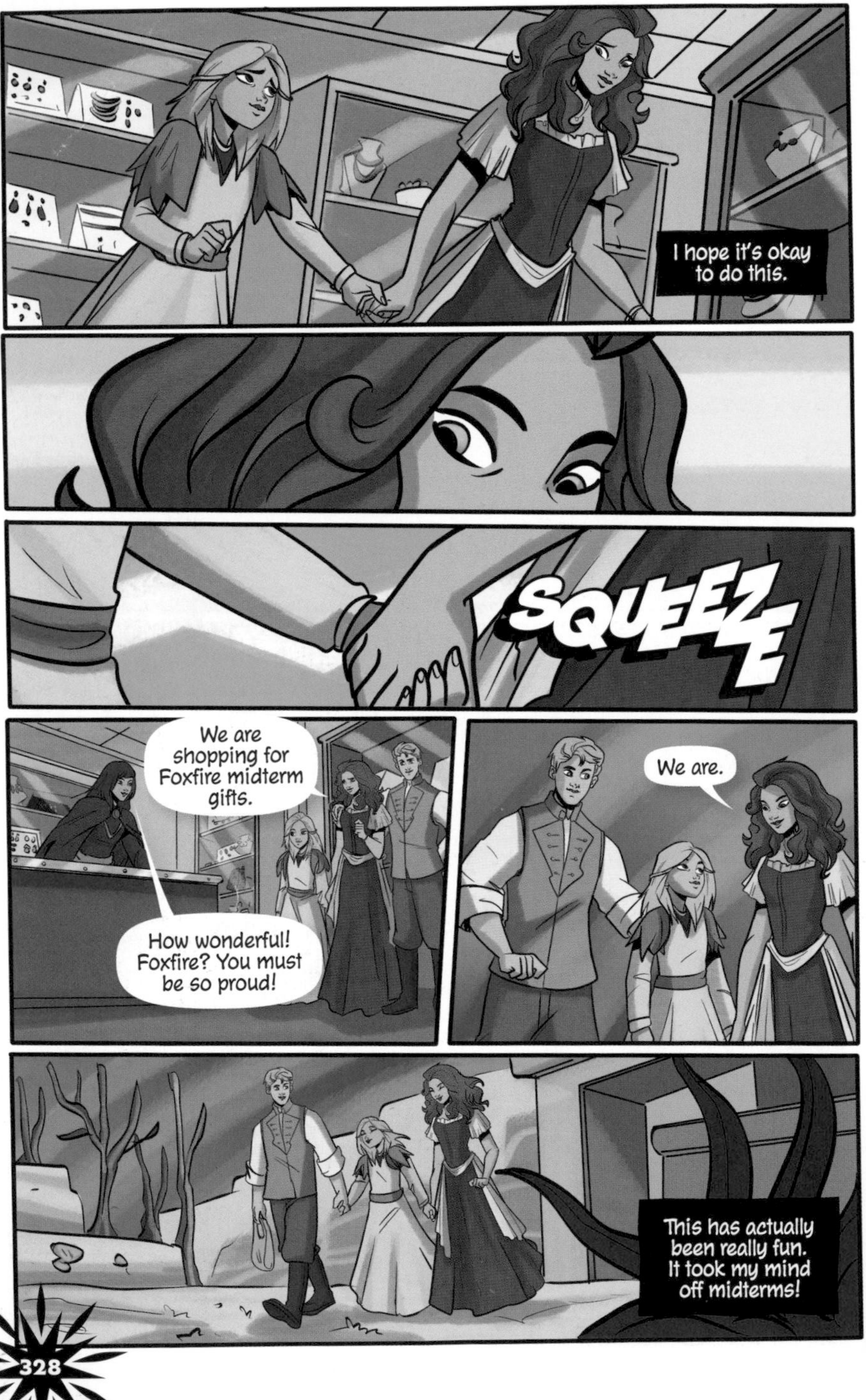
I hope it's okay to do this.
SQUEEZE
We are shopping for Foxfire midterm gifts.
How wonderful! Foxfire? You must be so proud!
We are.
This has actually been really fun. It took my mind off midterms!

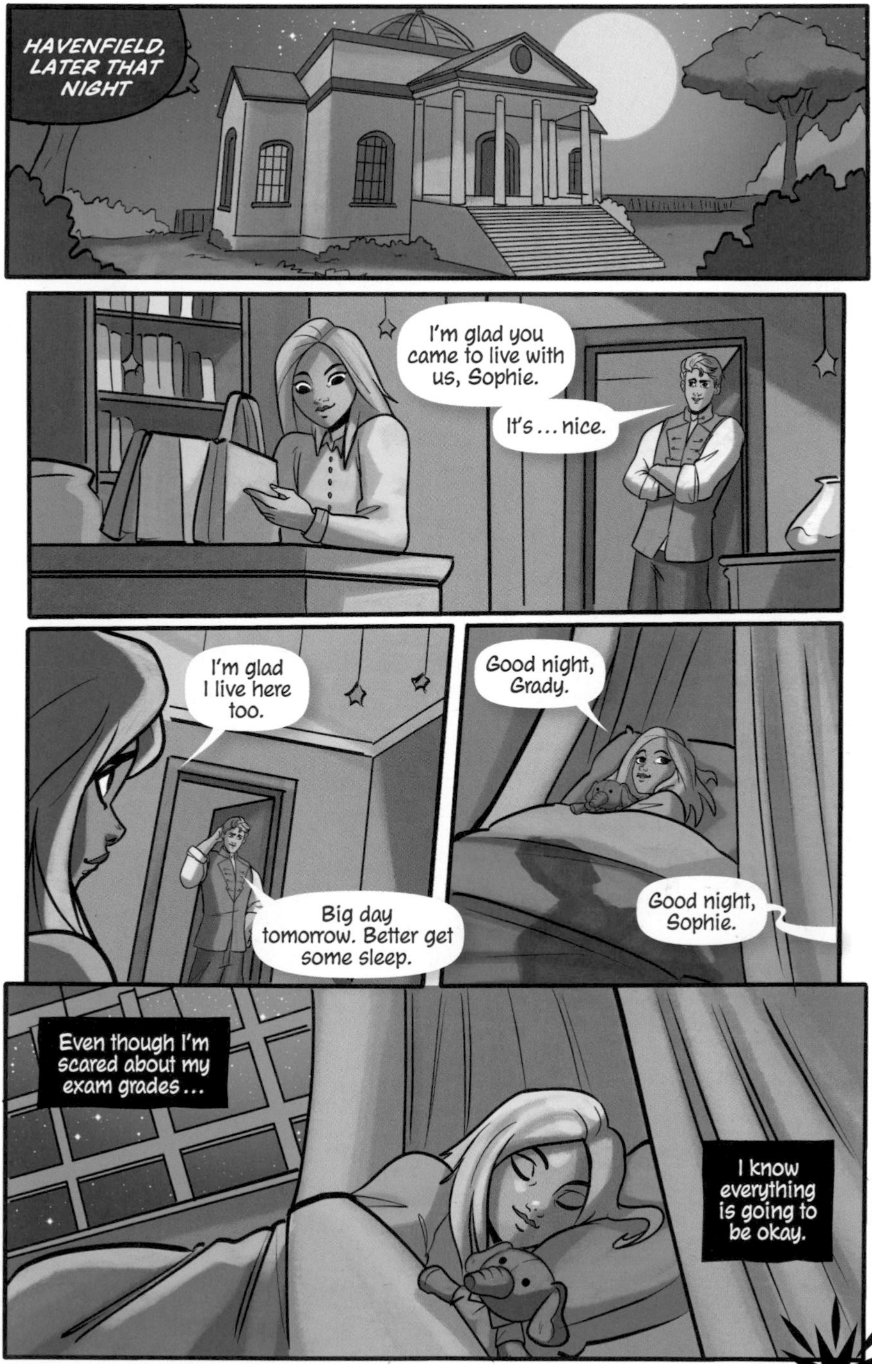
HAVENFIELD, LATER THAT NIGHT
I'm glad you came to live with us, Sophie.
It's... nice.
I'm glad I live here too.
Big day tomorrow. Better get some sleep.
Good night, Grady.
Good night, Sophie.
Even though I'm scared about my exam grades...
I know everything is going to be okay.

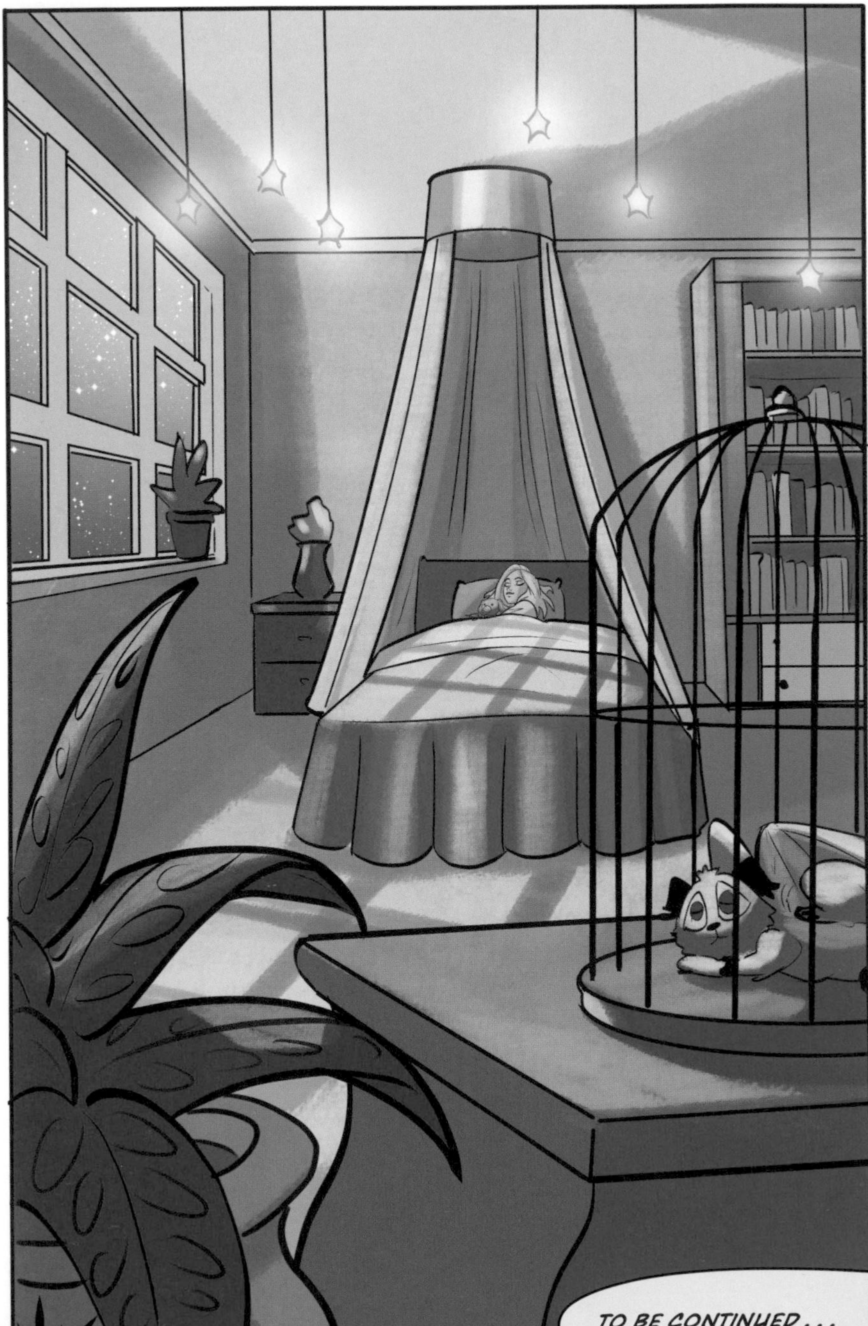
TO BE CONTINUED . . .

Part 2
coming soon!

Dear Keeper readers,

I know you're probably eager to get your hands on part 2 of this story. (Don't worry—we're working hard to get it ready for you ASAP!) But in the meantime, I thought it'd be fun to give you a special insider's peek into how this graphic novel came to be.

I was lucky enough to be involved in every single stage of the project, so I can assure you that everyone who worked on this book was committed to bringing the world of the Lost Cities—and the characters we love—to life in a way that would feel both familiar ***and*** fresh. And we knew finding the right artist was going to be key.

For those who've been fans of the Keeper of the Lost Cities series for a while, you've probably noticed that there isn't one single artist responsible for drawing all of the illustrations that have been used online or in the books, and that's been intentional. It's such a huge world with such a large cast that I didn't want it to be limited to one interpretation.

So I knew we'd be looking for someone with a style we haven't seen in the series before, but they still had to capture the right ***feel*** of the world and the characters. Over the next few pages, you'll get a glimpse of how I fell in love with Gabriella's art as well as how her sketches evolved throughout the creative process. I hope you'll be able to see how much time, thought, and love goes into every single detail in every single panel. Team Keeper truly is the best! And for added fun, at the end, you can even learn how to draw some of your favorite characters in Gabriella's style!

xo

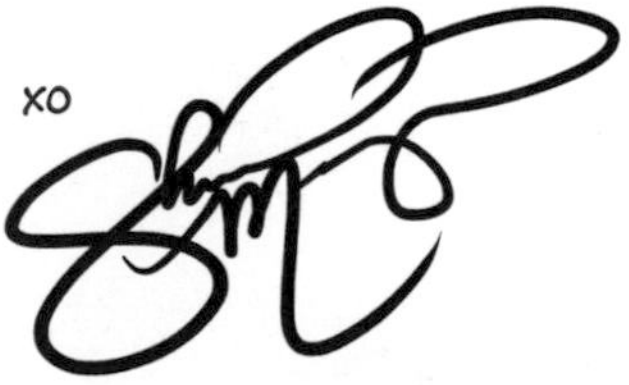

THERE WERE *SO MANY* AMAZING ARTISTS CONSIDERED for this book—sometimes I wondered how I would ever decide. But once I narrowed it down to a handful of favorites, the artists were asked to create audition pieces to show how they'd capture the world and the characters. And when I saw Gabriella's work, I knew she was "the one." You can see the rough version below—all the gorgeous details she worked in and the perfect expression on Sophie's face. It was a totally new style for the series, and yet it fit perfectly with all the other existing art. All I could say was "wow."

As part of her audition, Gabriella was also asked to create a cover sample, which you can see below. And while we ultimately went with a different cover scene (and there were some changes to Sophie as well!), I felt like she'd really captured the story. Keeper is about a brave, incredible girl discovering how truly amazing she is, and everything about this piece screams girl power!

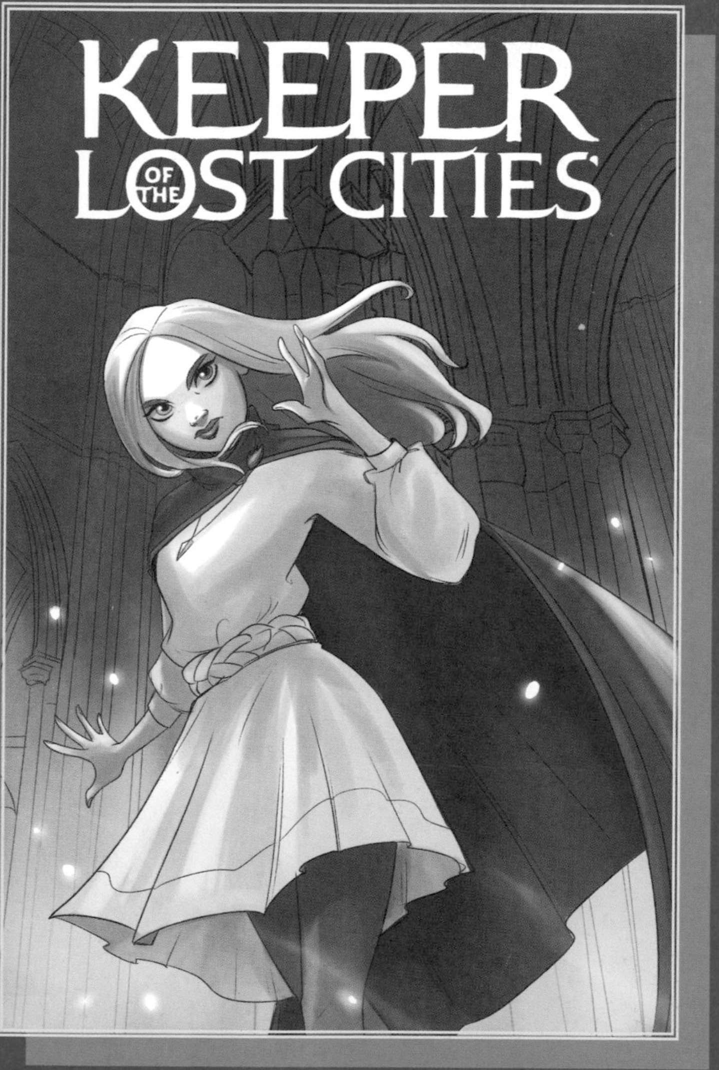
KEEPER OF THE LOST CITIES

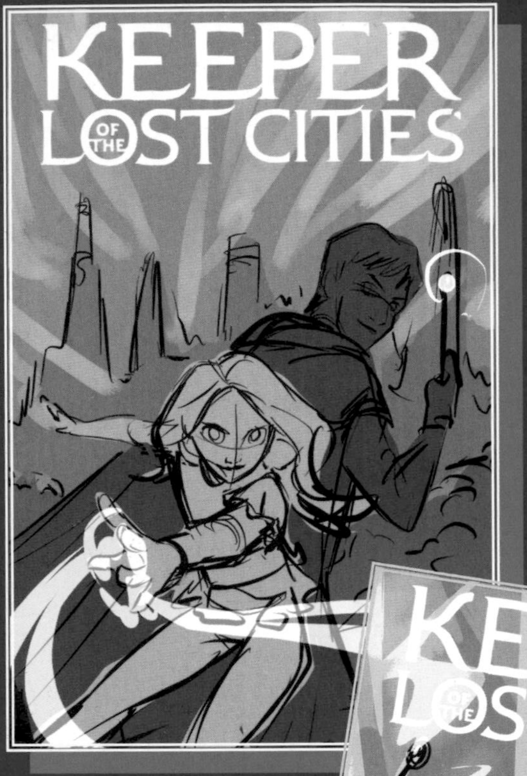
KEEPER
OF THE
LOST CITIES

And speaking of the cover, we went through ***quite*** a few variations before we found our perfect moment. Here are a few of the other sketches Gabriella sent us.

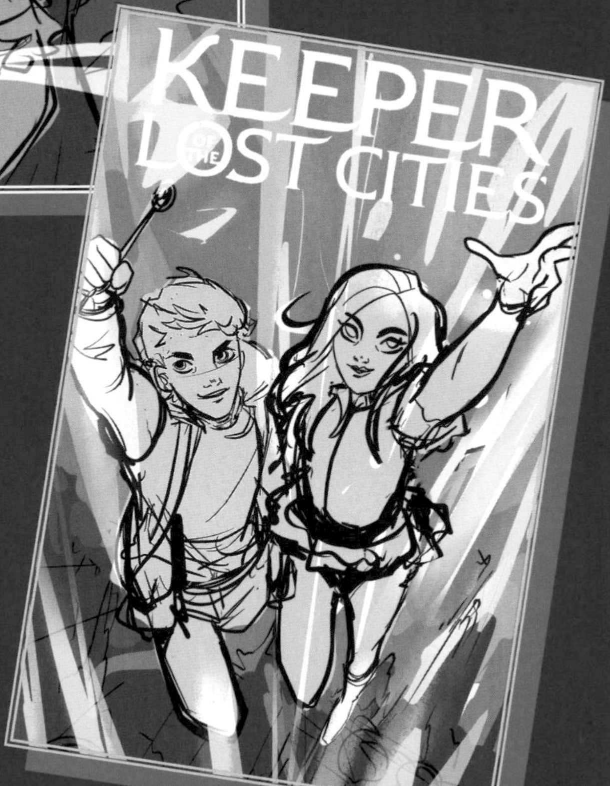
KEEPER
OF THE
LOST CITIES

And here, of course, is the final cover. I hope you love it as much as I do!

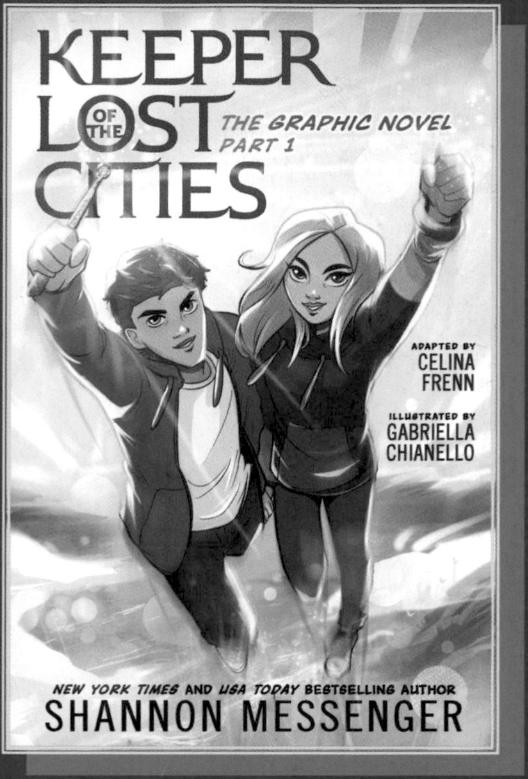
KEEPER OF THE LOST CITIES
THE GRAPHIC NOVEL PART 1
ADAPTED BY CELINA FRENN
ILLUSTRATED BY GABRIELLA CHIANELLO
NEW YORK TIMES AND USA TODAY BESTSELLING AUTHOR
SHANNON MESSENGER

I know some fans have wondered why we didn't go with the same scene we had on the first Keeper novel (since that's ***such*** an awesome cover), and there were a couple of reasons for that decision. For one thing, this book is just part 1, so the scene with Sophie and Dex isn't actually in this section. But more important: This portion of the story is about Sophie finding her place in her new world, so having Fitz bringing her to the Lost Cities for the very first time felt like the perfect cover moment.

Fun fact: An image of Sophie and Fitz light leaping was actually considered as a cover for the first Keeper novel, before everyone decided that having Sophie and Dex on the bridge was a better fit.

ATTENTION,
ASPIRING
ARTISTS!

· · HOW TO DRAW SOME OF YOUR FAVORITE KEEPER CHARACTERS! · ·

WE'VE INCLUDED HANDY INSTRUCTIONS TO HELP you draw the Keeper characters in Gabriella's style. (And there is some room on the pages after that for you to practice—though you're also welcome to use your own paper. Remember, any paper is drawing paper if you draw on it!)

It's best to start your sketch with pencil. That way, you can erase any guidelines. And when you have each character just the way you want them, feel free to ink in the outlines and color the sketch with colored pencils, crayons, or markers.

· · HOW TO DRAW ... SOPHIE! · ·

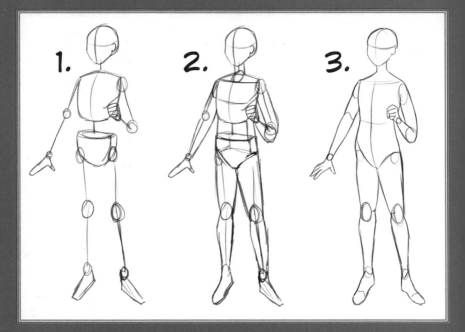

Step 1: Start with simple shapes to create the character's body, sketching the head, torso, pelvis, limbs, hands, and feet. This first step looks a little like drawing a stick figure skeleton with circles to show where each joint in the legs and arms would be.

Step 2: The next step is to refine the shapes of the torso, legs, arms, and pelvis to more accurately outline a human form. You can add dimension and connect the torso to the pelvis, outlining the shape of the arms and legs from joint to joint.

Step 3: From this point on, you will be doing some erasing along with the sketching! While keeping the outer dimension you created in step 2, erase the marks within the outline. Next refine the hands by drawing each finger. Then shape the feet. You'll add boots later.

Step 4: Now erase more and add hair and facial features. You can start adding the lines of the character's outfit, sketching details like a belt or the loose billow of a sleeve, following the character model as a guide.

Step 5: Then add the cape, the boots, and smaller details, like the cape pin, taking your drawing to the next level. Along the way, you can erase more of the sketch lines.

Step 6: By now, your character should really be coming to life before you! Sketch outfit-specific details, and add some lines to highlight dimension and complete the drawing. Erase any remaining lines that you had used to create the structure of the character's form. Now is the time to add color if you want to.

COLORING: A little bit of color can go a long way—especially if you add a little shading and texture. You're welcome to use a color scheme that matches the character descriptions in the book, or you can give each character your own twist. The key is to have fun and be creative!

Next you'll see how-to-draw guides
for Fitz, Dex, and Keefe. Use the same
steps to bring those characters to life with
your drawings!

• • HOW TO DRAW . . . *FITZ!* • •

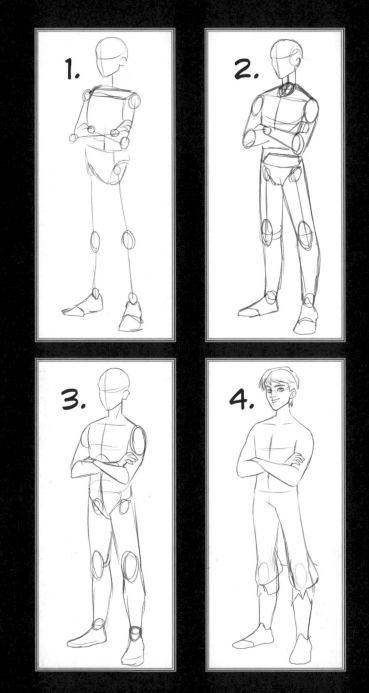

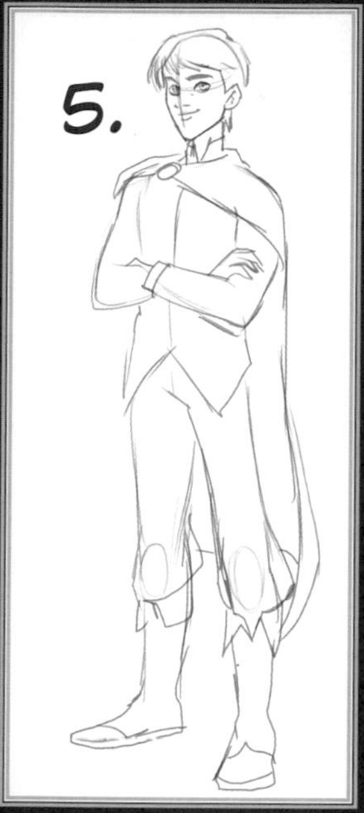
5.

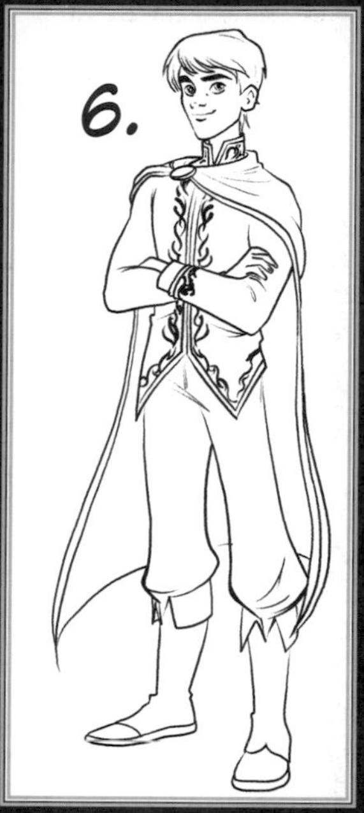
6.

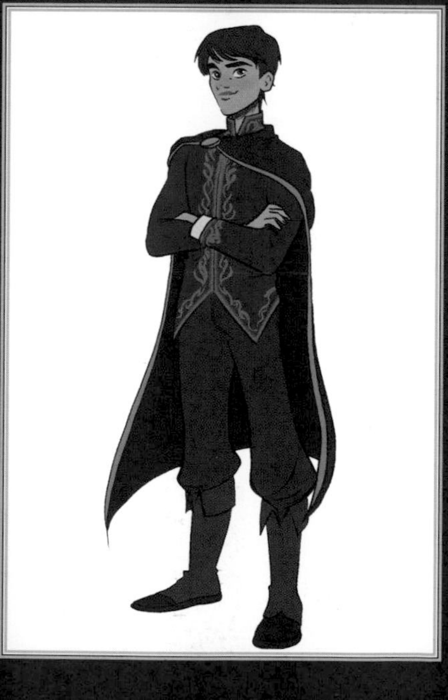

. . HOW TO DRAW . . . DEX! . .

1.
2.
3.
4.

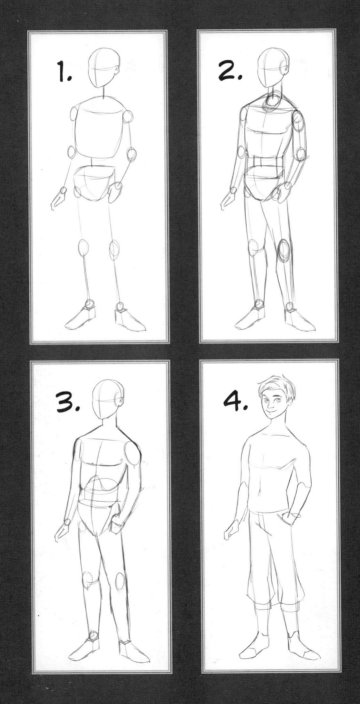

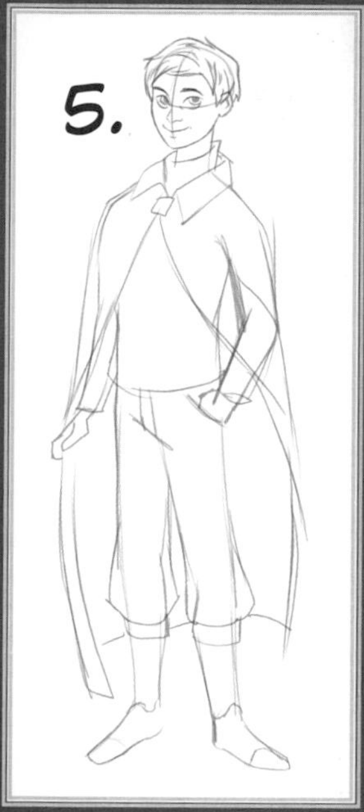
5.

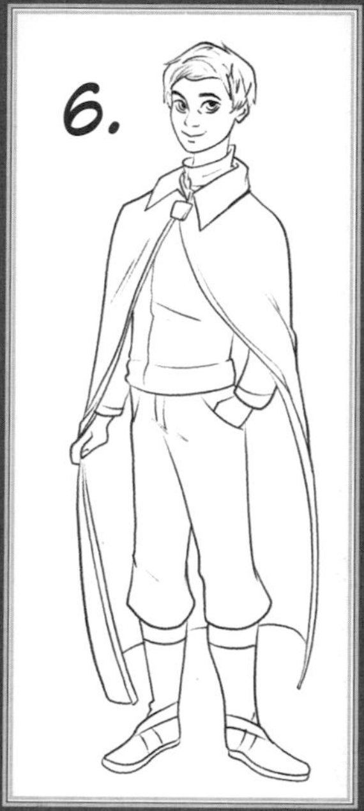
6.

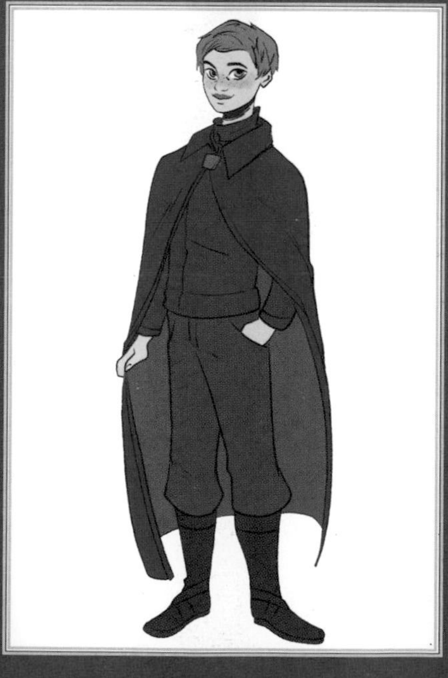

· · HOW TO DRAW ... KEEFE! · ·

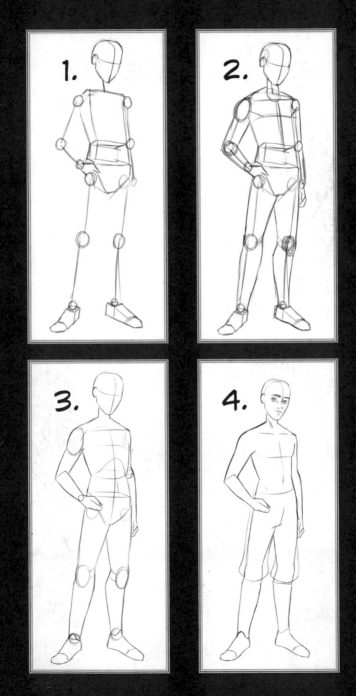

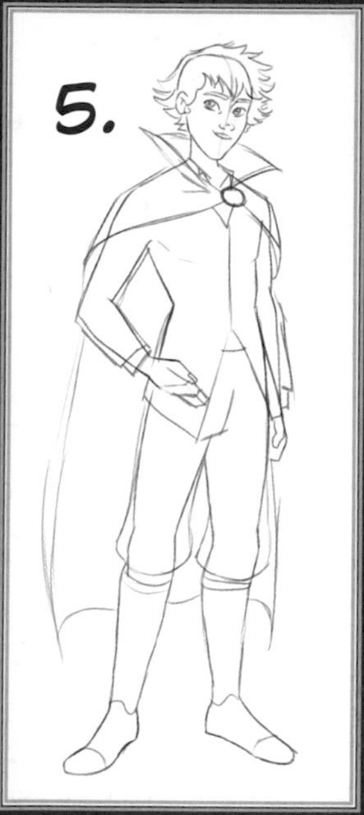
5.

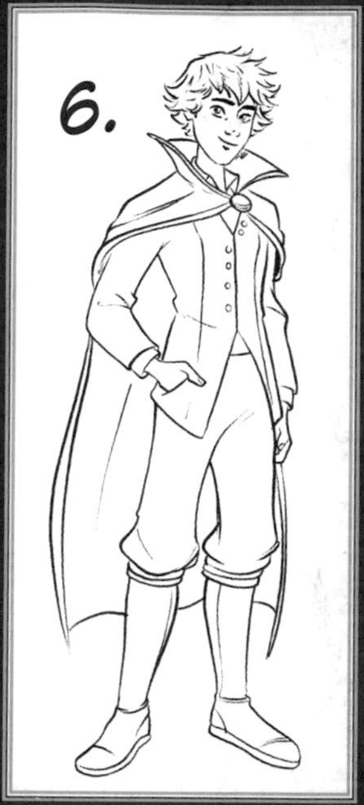
6.

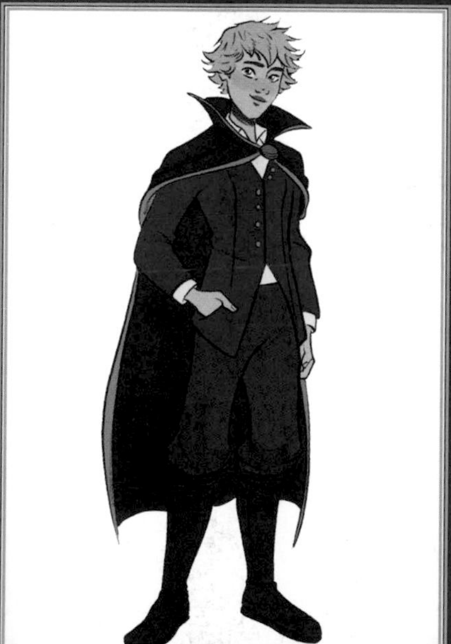